THE SECOND LAW OF DYING

THE SECOND LAW OF DYING

To my friend Tom

GEOFF LAUNDY

iUniverse, Inc.
New York Lincoln Shanghai

The Second Law of Dying

Copyright © 2005 by Geoff Laundy

All rights reserved. No part of this book may be used or reproduced by any means, graphic, electronic, or mechanical, including photocopying, recording, taping or by any information storage retrieval system without the written permission of the publisher except in the case of brief quotations embodied in critical articles and reviews.

iUniverse books may be ordered through booksellers or by contacting:

iUniverse
2021 Pine Lake Road, Suite 100
Lincoln, NE 68512
www.iuniverse.com
1-800-Authors (1-800-288-4677)

ISBN-13: 978-0-595-36333-9 (pbk)
ISBN-13: 978-0-595-80770-3 (ebk)
ISBN-10: 0-595-36333-4 (pbk)
ISBN-10: 0-595-80770-4 (ebk)

Printed in the United States of America

BOOK ONE

Chapter 1

Down by Hugo's Map

Equatorial Africa.

After completing his excavations for the hospital at Lambaréné, a young but depleted Hugo Haultain, uncertain about the days remaining until his death, was content to settle passage across the Congo-Brazzaville frontier for the price of fifty cigarettes to the customs man. He took care to skirt the army checkpoints strung along the south road and by nightfall was a hundred kilometers short of Mindouli. In the darkness of early morning, fatigue blurred his scrutiny of the narrow track. He steered the Land Rover into a clearing, spread a blanket on the ground, and collapsed onto it.

It was fully light when boots kicking his ribs woke him. He curled into a ball, waited for a few more annoying blows, then twisted upwards, took hold of a foot, and toppled its owner into the truck's fender. A rifle butt knocked him backwards. Groping for balance, he rolled to his knees and refocused on the ground. Between his hands a pool of blood expanded over the earth. In a few seconds it came to resemble the contours of a flower, with each successive drop deepening the luxuriance of the petals. He leaned closer to examine it. After a moment's indecision, he drew a broad stem in the dirt to balance the heaviness of the bloom. Provoked by this extravagant gesture, he raised his head and smiled. The officer who watched him grunted with disbelief, turned away and shouted to his sergeant, "Search the vehicle."

Soldiers began throwing tools and water containers from the rear of the truck. The officer gave a nod of satisfaction, switched his attention to the documents he had seized and walked away. Still on his knees, Hugo called after him, "My friend, I've got nothing in there that would interest you."

The man kept on towards a black sedan parked on the red clay of the track. The stricken man struggled to his feet and shouted, "Hey! I'm talking to you!"

The chief turned around. His voice was weary, like the manner of his walking. "Well, I won't be talking to you until later, monsieur," he replied.

The traveler wiped the blood from his eyes, weaved his way to the Land Rover and tossed an empty jerrican into the rear. A trooper shouted and aimed his rifle. He turned the barrel aside when Hugo waved a fresh cigarette in his face. The soldier behind also took one, lit it and blew the smoke out with a sigh. A few more gathered to receive the offerings, then more crowded in to sip from a bottle being passed around the arc of lounging men. Each took a full package of cigarettes to go with the drink. The officer walked back from his car and circled through his troops, turning his head to take them all in. With a tone of false sympathy Hugo said, "Don't be upset with them, Commandant. Who would refuse a free smoke and some decent liquor these days? Anyway, it's obvious that most of them are too young to know better."

He offered the chief a carton of cigarettes and a newly opened bottle. After three hurried swallows, the little man carried these to his vehicle and led the convoy south towards Mindouli. As the kilometers flashed by, Hugo amused his three guards with stories of the desert. The first set of tales made them grunt with approval; the next set made them laugh. With the merriment, they passed around more cigarettes. In time, fatigue and the oppressive heat imposed a weary silence. The men fell asleep. Hugo felt thankful for the solitude; yet he was aware that his gratitude would confer no lasting pleasure. Despite the morning's excitement, August 26 1965 was a common date. Like the majority of previous dates, it was not likely to yield a joy great enough to balance the weight of his past.

Late in the afternoon of this particular day, he stood on the open veranda of the customs post thinking how slippery the red earth of the town would be when it rained. In this aspect he was fortunate; it was the dry season and troopers milled about under a white sky. Some talked. A group of young ones threw their semi-automatic rifles on the ground and danced to a tune playing from a loudspeaker. Their ill-fitting uniforms flapped with the bird-like movements. Hugo tapped his foot in time to the music, stopped and swept back his thick hair, like an affectation or a pointless gesture of sorrow.

Scowling, the commandant marched up next to him. "As you can see, monsieur, there is no loyalty, now…no respect for the revolution. But what am I to do about it? Discipline? They would desert and take whatever weapons they could pack off. You're assessment is correct. I'm saddled with an army of children who fear nothing but the ju-ju priests of their village. A grasp of politics is beyond them."

He lit another cigarette and ambled away.

"So let them leave," Hugo called after him. "They'd be out of your hair and you could hire experienced men."

"Outsiders like you, monsieur? Would you consider such dirty work?"

Hugo shrugged his shoulders. "I'm only a tourist, Commandant."

The officer grunted and paced nervously back along the veranda. "I wonder about that," he said.

"You found nothing in my vehicle to prove otherwise."

"We found some luxuries."

"I have food to keep me alive, but nothing to wage war. Out of respect for the politics, you understand."

Hugo put his foot on the bottom pipe of the railing. The chief blew out a plume of smoke and continued pacing, with the occasional glance towards his dancing troops.

"That's a shame," he said. "I would have bought your guns at a fair price, you know."

"You would have killed me and got them for free."

The chief grinned and nodded his head. "My politics are flexible, monsieur. How about yours?"

Hugo looked at him with curiosity. The intensity of the sun highlighted the irregularities of the man's face and the pockmarks of disease. Coarse hairs grew like weeds from the depressions in his skin. Hearing no answer to his question, the officer continued. "As to your situation, you can't pass the frontier here—or anywhere. We are in a state of war with Congo-Leopoldville. Nothing moves now, not even across Stanley Pool. You may have to go through Kabinda, but that's a long way and leads only to the sea. Personally, I don't care where you go so long as you get out of here."

After demanding two more bottles and half the remaining cigarettes for a transit visa, the commandant handed back the documents. Reaching to take his passport, Hugo said, "Long way or not, Kabinda it must be. In the meantime, are you familiar with a trader named 'Birks'?"

"That way." The chief pointed west of the building to where the principal route across Mindouli moved upwards from the shade trees onto an exposed terrace some fifty meters higher in elevation than the town. "But he isn't home, monsieur, hasn't been for some time now."

As he drove away, Hugo waved to the young people and they shook the barrels of their guns back at him. In a few minutes he was idling along a dusty track where the vegetation was thin, almost transparent. South and east, the surrounding territory was visible for twenty kilometers. To the west was a compound fenced by brick walls and a wire gate leading to a crude warehouse. Inside were farm implements displayed in rows and hundreds of hand tools.

The sign indicated a Vietnamese name, but underneath was written neatly, "Birks." Hugo banged on a wooden door. He banged again with his good right arm. There was no shade; the sun was hot and the efforts of his beating made him sweat. A face appeared at the wire gate. He went over to it and the face disappeared. "I'm looking for Martin Birks!" he yelled at the small figure scurrying between the equipment. He went back to the wooden door and called in a loud voice, "Martin Birks, does he own this place? Is he here?"

From inside came a low, nervous chatter. The door opened and a small woman with sorrowful eyes peered out from the shade. "Are you a friend of his?" she said.

"I know of him. I would like to meet him."

The woman hesitated. "Why would you like to meet him?"

"Because I have just left Lambaréné and have a message."

Hugo handed her a letter. She glanced at it, then stood aside. They sat at a rough board table in the kitchen. A girl of ten, the child he had seen running away, stirred a ten-liter pot on the cook stove. A small boy clutched her leg. The woman handed Hugo a piece of gauze for his wound. As they drank the tea she had made, he told her a little of his background.

In reply she said, "Four months ago, Martin went to Congo-Leopoldville to look for a friend of his, a man named Louis Morrow, who might be in jail. I waited three weeks then made some inquiries across the frontier. The people here and all the way to the river are the Bakongo tribe. They asked on my behalf even in Luozi, where the ferry crosses the river. From what I understand, Martin is in Lufungula."

"And where is that?"

"Lufungula is a prison attached to the Leopoldville Police Barracks. In that place people starve. Many are beaten to death. That's what I'm told."

Her voice choked and tears filled her eyes.

"What is your association with Martin?" the stranger asked.

"I am his wife, but these are not his children. I was a widow, you understand. Their father was also a trader. He died of sickness a few years ago. Martin came along and now we are together."

She put her hands to her face and smoothed back her skin. "I miss him, monsieur. I need him here. But with war and fighting everywhere, what can I do? I have no hope." She got up and left the room. When she returned she had a small towel and used it to wipe her face. "Will you stay for dinner?" she asked. "And then of course be our guest until you leave for Kabinda, or wherever it is you're going. In the meantime I can dress the cut on your head."

The next morning Hugo walked the town to inspect the road that led to the barricaded frontier and the Bakongo village on the opposing side. He fed cigarettes to the few soldiers who loitered nearby and stayed one more night with Martin Birks' wife. She had supplied him a guest room, a kerosene lantern to complete his records, and a box of canned meats to supplement his food. With the needs of the moment duly met, it seemed secondary that the tales he told Madame Birks related honestly to his life. The important thing was that he made her laugh, then talk without regret about her loss.

When she said good-bye to him early the next morning, Hugo was thinking how little the sky had changed from the day before, and the day before that. If there had been such a thing as a radio station in Mindouli, it would have been easy for the weatherman to issue his predictions, because every day he would only have to say, "high temperatures and white-hot skies." Hugo determined quickly the logical sleight of hand necessary to equate the complexities of stable weather and human affairs—both produced the events of today as a verisimilitude of the events of yesterday. So he excused Madame Birks her pride of genius when she added her own forecast.

"I hope you are not going to Leopoldville, monsieur. What for—to add another corpse to the pile already inside Lufungula? You should go to Kabinda or back the way you came."

Hugo shrugged and took hold of her shoulders. "I should, madame. At best, detours are little more than wishful thinking."

He gave her a hug and a kiss on the cheek. She smiled, but only briefly, then waved sadly after him. "*Bonne chance* and take care of yourself," she called. There was no one in the rearview mirror when he rounded the first bend in the road.

At the frontier he removed the flimsy barricade blocking the track and crossed into Congo-Leopoldville. The chief of the border village said, "I have no stamp for your passport. Birks was going to make one for me. He said it would be official-looking and I could make some money collecting the tax. It's a duty for me to collect, since I have wives to feed and twenty children. Understand also, monsieur, that no one has crossed here for months."

With this comment the chief received his carton of cigarettes, Hugo's last bottle of scotch, and ten American dollars. This made him happy, or so it seemed, because he brought out his entire family to sing and wave good-bye. Hugo went alone from the village along a track that, according to the red line snaking downwards on his map, ran one hundred kilometers to Luozi and the Congo River. In two hours he was halfway across the plateau. The vehicle sped along at the limits of control. Dust poured from the wheels and lay behind him in a pall. On all sides was a dry land, but not too dry, with the vegetation insufficient to obstruct the views from either the hilltops or level grades. As he went slowly over a flat section of dried river silt, he could see the road ahead traversing upwards towards a high ridge and on it a flag of dust thrown up by another set of moving tires. In a few minutes an aged troop carrier swerved sideways and ground to a halt. Soldiers in ripped and dirty uniforms struggled down and circled the Land Rover. One pushed in beside him and gave directions. In fifteen minutes they were in a compound containing one small building and a metal lean-to for supplies.

While four soldiers ripped apart the contents of his vehicle, Hugo positioned himself to the side of a metal desk inside the building and pondered the chance of an easy escape to Luozi. He also considered the fact that the ferry might not be running, effectively trapping him on the north bank of the river. Deciding to keep the peace, he returned to his assessment of the young soldier of the Armée Nationale Congolaise across from him, who wore a forage cap in the American style, but dirty. The man held a pen over a document and asked questions, repeating himself often. At times he used the pen to scribble things or used it to twirl the handgun that lay next to the paper. When he did this, he smiled at Hugo, who had already inferred the general run of the man's thoughts: that the corpse of an enemy would be a feather, even in his neglected hat. But most importantly, encouraged by the fact that in the strategies of war, more than reputations perish if men are blind to detail, he inferred that the sergeant was showing himself oblivious to the things that would keep him alive. He rose from his chair and barked orders in a language Hugo didn't recognize. A soldier pointed a rifle at his head.

"Gunrunner," said the sergeant.

"You've found no guns."

"But you have canned food."

"I have the means to obtain luxuries, if I so decide."

"You have money?"

"A few francs."

"Give them to me and I won't kill you."

Hugo laughed. "You'd kill me later."

"No. I'm going to surrender you to the commander of the Orleanville garrison. He will take you to the capital to be held as a mercenary from Congo-Brazzaville. That's what I will tell him and they will give me credit. And more credit if you're alive. But only if I get all your money—now."

Hugo watched the sergeant's mannerisms and the focus of the soldier who paced up and down with the heat and the boredom. "Let's have a smoke and talk this over," he said, talking a cigarette and holding out the package. The sergeant took one and lit it from a soiled book of matches. Hugo put one between his lips, threw one to the guard, then lit both. He leaned back in his chair and breathed out the smoke with a sigh.

"Well that's good, Sergeant—all of us smoking away here like family, all willing to do the right thing. You appear to be a bright young soldier, who wouldn't deliberately choose to remain invisible for the rest of his career and banished to a place like this."

The man glowered, picked up the handgun and aimed it at the traveler's head. The gesture made him sweat. "I choose to be here," he said angrily. He shouted an order to his aide, who knocked the prisoner roughly to the floor. Hugo got up cautiously, holding the palms of his hands forward as a sign of peace, then sat gingerly back in the chair.

The sergeant lit another cigarette and sneered. He played with his handgun, cocking and re-cocking it. "I usually kill those who insult me," he said. "That shows them how important I am, why I've been chosen to guard the frontier. So go ahead, monsieur, tell me how important I am. If your story is a good one, maybe I won't kill you."

Hugo lit another cigarette and crossed his legs. "I think we should all try to remain calm, Sergeant, and talk this out," he said. "Perhaps you're the most important man in the Congo. You're certainly young, strong—ambitious even. But apart from that, I think it's time for the truth. In my opinion, there's a good reason you're here at this remote frontier, and the reason goes something like this. Far from seeing you as a soldier on his way up in the world, your superiors see you as a nobody. They've consigned you to oblivion to get you out of their hair. Now, why would they do that, my friend? The answer of course is that in reality you're a confused fraud, a man who impersonates an army commander but can't even read or write."

The sergeant stopped sneering. He squeezed the pistol into the belt holster, stood to attention and stared through the open door. The creased and stained uniform draped formlessly over his skinny limbs.

"I can," he said in a resentful, squeaky voice.

Hugo smiled at the guard. "Not true, Sergeant," he said. "The marks you've taken the trouble to put on that sheet couldn't be read by a chicken. And the document on the desk you've been reading from, with all the rules and regulations you've made up? Let me tell you that it's upside down."

The sergeant stared at the papers on his desk and made a threatening fist. "That's unimportant. Your money is going to buy me promotion."

Hugo rose from the wooden chair and walked to where the man stood in the corner of the hut. "Of course it is," he said. "Perhaps we can make a deal here. Your men seemed to have helped themselves to the few things they found in my vehicle, including the canned meats. But I have a few francs for you. We can negotiate on that. In the meantime, since all my documents are meaningless to you, my name is Hugo Haultain. What do you call yourself?"

The soldier looked at his prisoner with a seething rage twitching the muscles of his face; but he answered the question anyway. "Léon Mintou," he said. With a grimace of shame, he turned away. Hugo nodded and began pacing along the dirt floor of the shack. "I can't say it's a pleasure to meet you, Sergeant Mintou. But you, on the other hand, should be feeling grateful to have met the man whose money will ensure your promotion to the level of a real officer. Now, let me ask the next question. Have you ever been to the capital?"

"Once," Mintou replied.

"I'm sure you were impressed. For you and your men, the capital must be as the clean mountain water you see in your dreams. I'm a foreigner, but I know the story the Bakongo elders tell, the one where five drops of rain join on one leaf, on one branch, on one tree in the mysterious forest far to the east that not one of you has seen; and these five in turn join with the waters from other trees and forests to become streams, creeks, and finally the immense Congo River, which enhances the reputation of Leopoldville as a great, independent city."

The man stared at him. "I have not heard that story, monsieur."

"Of course you haven't, Sergeant, because I just made it up. I get pleasure from inventing stories. Life itself is a tale we make up to entertain ourselves and confuse our enemies. So in the next few days we'll see if you've got the wits to succeed at being more than you are now. Along the way, you'll get personal credit for delivering an alleged criminal to Lufungula."

The sergeant frowned and fingered the stock of his revolver. "You're a big talker, monsieur, a crazy man, wishing to go to a place like that," he scoffed. "In Lufungula people are tortured and die. It would be better to kill you now."

Hugo placed a finger to the side of his nose and shook his head. "Think about this, Mintou. Kill me now and you'll be stuck in Luozi forever. Keep me alive and you'll be helping yourself. My business in Lufungula has considerable ju-ju attached. And because of that, it gives me access to money."

He pulled a billfold from his pocket, removed some American currency, and handed it to him. The sergeant smiled slightly, picked through the notes, and moved to the door. When he was outside and the bills were in his pocket, he stood to attention. A few soldiers paced across the loose dirt with their weapons pointing this way and that, ready to shoot anything their commander ordered. The majority lounged sullenly in the shade, not prepared to move for anything but dinner. With his sloppy boots kicking up the dust and his head shaking, Léon Mintou slouched across the yard and ordered all of them to the vehicle. A few hours later, a minor occurrence woke the small contingent of Number Four Group, Bakongo Corps that remained on watch in Luozi. As a

Land Rover sped past into the compound well ahead of the troop carrier, they were curious to see the head of the driver wound with a bloody bandage. They were less curious that the man's left arm, reinforced by a thick strip of canvas, was draped comfortably along the back of the seat occupied by their sergeant. Since it was a full hour until the evening meal, they lost interest entirely and dispersed into the shade of the surrounding forest.

After a costly negotiation for two days of freedom, Hugo sought out the residence of a Portuguese man and paid him much less for a guarded room and his meals. With the cognac following dinner, he and the trader exchanged implausible stories of adventure in the tropics, leading to an impasse of thought and a silent smoking of cigars. Hugo had noted from the stories his father had read to him, that it was the habit of Europeans in Africa to blend tobacco, liquor, and a feeling for the casual lie. In the reality of experience he was not relieved by any such custom. The partial fiction he offered to the trader as a token for his past, for who his ancestors were and specifically his talented father, was not far off the mark. Conrad Muir was a musician of note, a friend of Albert Schweitzer, and a man who had given his son an exemplary education. In the environs of Luozi, however, smoking free cigars in the crude drawing room of Benoit Marse, Hugo considered how poorly his exaggerated story fit to the parting allusion Conrad had made to Christ's parable of honesty. That night, once the trader had ceased shouting abuse at his house girl and slumped unconscious to the floor, the traveler sat in the relative quiet of a tropical night and tried to recall what a unique sensation honesty was.

Before retiring, he wrote for an hour. When the journal was complete, he formed the word "truth" in his mouth, then exhaled it into the flame of the lantern. The room went dark. He moved under the netting, onto the soft bed, and lay face up. His thoughts, though burdened with many regrets, did not diminish the small residue of gratitude. Before sinking to sleep, he recalled the episodes surrounding the dissolution of his career. The change in life, while abrupt, was not a calamity. He had simply replaced the practice of medicine with the intent to write one amusing page for each day lived, using an old nibbed pen and an antique bottle of India ink.

May 6 1963, Seattle.

On a morning streaked with sunlight and blue, a doubtful and suspicious Dr. Haultain worked hard to stack his few pieces of furniture in the corner of a rented garage. Next, he went clockwise through the apartment methodically putting the smaller items into boxes. Before loading his car, he double-checked to be certain he had packed his spare nibs and inkwell. Carrying these out in the last container he was still troubled that something remained. A single glance resolved his anxiety. From the front door he could see that a veil of grime made the corridor window resemble a faded print he might have left tacked on the wall. He walked back. Out of habit he brushed his fingers across the dirty pane for a clearer view. A second time he wiped the glass with his fingers and smiled to see the pruned trees of the courtyard—and beyond that—the landscape of his childhood.

In the early years his mother had routinely cleaned the windows of the family home to invisibility. But he had been shut away nevertheless, a fading print of a boy, a creature as flat and boneless as the paper animals attached to the plaster. The effects of chronic disease had excluded him from the world outside—and the world inside, created from books piled high in the sickroom, provided small compensation for his expected death. Only the vast histories of human conflict were a consolation. He remembered now that his reading and rereading of them had fortified the anger that nourished his remaining strength. Or that was what he chose to remember as he looked at the cars moving on the quiet street below.

During the drive into the city, he turned off the radio to consider his predicament in silence. Discarding a medical career had required no more than a doff of his cap. The unavoidable corollary of uprooting himself had taken less than a morning. At a downtown stoplight, he glanced at the boxes full of books, documents, and art supplies. The leather case Conrad had given him sat on the floor full of much the same, except the one corner where he had put his shaving kit and medicine. With the satchel containing his personal papers on the seat, everything he needed to live in orderly fashion was there in his car. Conrad Muir waited for him in a wharf-side café. Hugo sat down and looked past his father to the boats on Puget Sound.

"Do you know where you're going?" asked the old man.

"East. I need a distraction. I think I'll pay Captain Korrolus a visit. I might stay the summer."

"Allan Korrolus?" Muir said. "Why him of all people? He won't be happy to see you."

Hugo shrugged his shoulders. "Why not? I recall he was fond of me. I still have the photos he gave me of military men."

Muir sipped twice at the lip of his cup. Except for the eyes, his face was a mottled panel of flesh.

"I don't remember any photo," he said.

"But I do, Conrad. It was an old snapshot I found stuffed into a book and showed to Corrine. Allan was in it—with his navy uniform, captain's hat, white gators. The few times he visited, I was thrilled to meet a hero of the war, and proud that he was your friend as well. I never understood why you brushed it off. Maybe it was the fear some men have of reliving unpleasant things from the past. You weren't a soldier, but you know what I mean. You've suffered. There are other terrors you've refuse to acknowledge."

"Yours are worse, Hugo, because they're self-inflicted."

"And yours aren't?"

"My fears are beyond any interest to you."

"All history is an interest, Conrad. Did you forget that there was a time when history was my only interest, my nourishment…my daily allotment of fun?"

Muir looked away and fidgeted. "All this talk of photos, the war, self-torture…this is not surprising to me," he said. "For months you've been twisting this way and that. You must get away from blaming yourself for the death of the child. It could have happened to anyone."

"But it didn't. It happened to me. But that's okay, because I don't blame myself, or anyone else for that matter. It's just that I should never have been there. It's something I could never make you understand. Medicine was a casual study for me, not a discipline or a career. It was more like reading a few books amongst thousands: *Gray's Anatomy*, the *Pharmacopoeia*, Da Vinci's drawings of the human body. Early in my studies there was a disconnect that remained permanent, a sense that a hundred successful outcomes could never overcome the outrage of one premature death. I should be doing other things now, Conrad. I need to retrench."

The old man sat back in his chair and made a fumbling reference to his apprenticeship in Alsace and his work at Coventry Cathedral, relating it as always to his meeting Hugo's mother, Corrine Haultain. Hugo became bored and drew lines on a cigarette package. In a few minutes they came to resemble the old man's face with the messy hair and slightly drooping eyes.

Muir hardly noticed and said, "One more thing, Hugo. Don't flaunt your knowledge. As if knowing the contents of a few books could be a cure for anything. If you want to make your point, take pains not to exaggerate. You were always one to embellish. Your long confinement caused that, but now it's not necessary. Remember that the Man with perfect knowledge told simple stories."

Hugo smoked his cigarette and watched his father squirm. Finally he said, "The fault is not in the knowledge, or God for that matter, but in the rules we live by. Your friend Schweitzer said as much. He wrote some things that appeared to be true. Personally, I believe his contribution misleading and overrated."

"I know only what I've read of him," said Conrad, sounding resentful for his son's persistence. At the café door they embraced. The younger man watched a tug towing wood chips cruise past the breakwater.

"As usual, your mind is elsewhere," Muir said, waiting for the moment of separation. Hugo held him firmly by the arms and said, "You shouldn't be worrying too much at this late stage, Conrad. As to making a living, I'll be fine. I have a job offer, starting in September. Whatever the outcome, I'll see you in a few months."

A small cloud blocked the sun and the chill of winter rushed back. The old man pulled his coat around him and looked out to sea. Hugo went to his car. After a few minutes on the highway, he glanced at his watch. Professor Mira Cormacks had said, "Come early, Hugo," and he wondered if she knew he wouldn't be staying long. Driving eastwards he heard the rattle and strum of a ukulele from the radio and turned up the volume: "Buffalo gals, won't you come out tonight and dance by the light of the moon." The reception faded. He turned the dial, first to silence, then a radioman's voice, "Hard to believe, folks, but so far it's been a great day. The forecast calls for nothing but solid sunshine for another week, with only a slight chance of showers along the mountains."

In contrast to a pleasant vacation, this prolonged dry spell had retarded the growth of spring flowers. As a result, the display of roses climbing the front wall of the Cormacks' mansion was a disappointment. Carrying a small bloom in his hand, Hugo mentioned this to the concierge, who nodded and had him sign the guest book before allowing him entrance.

The next morning he rose at first light. The birds sang repetitively. When he closed the bathroom door, the mirror on the back reflected his stream of urine. He thought of the physical things understood directly, the sound of his piss in the water, dressing himself in the same clothes everyday, the way he walked and shifted the gears of his car, contracting first the forearm next the upper arm, putting his hand back on the wheel and stretching his arms for relief. He imagined his muscles being leaf green and his bones wood brown, with these attached necessarily to the inner strengths of his torso, to the plexus and therefore his illustrious brain. He looked again in the mirror, at the distant blue of eyes examining themselves and realized his body was held together by surface tension and viscosity, being a particular type of gravity that directly constrained his actions. He stopped pissing, showered and dressed. Like an instinct for preparedness, he rolled the sleeves to his elbow, balanced on one arm, and leaned over the sleeping face of Mira Cormacks. Unable to contain his memory, he recalled the time a month previous when he had leaned over a smaller face. The surrounding corridors had flowed with nurses and physicians; but the antiseptic totality of the place had been powerless to constrain the fever that overwhelmed the child, and by noon had carried her away.

Long fingers rushed from the covers and clutched at the black hair of his forearm. "On your way, dear and glorious physician? Do call when you get back, if you get back," said the professor. Her arm crept back into the sterile warmth of the bedding. Hugo put on his shoes and left. He stopped to fuel the car and phoned Conrad, who was confused by sleep and said a terse good-bye.

That day he drove for eighteen straight hours, with only two delays to eat and put gas in the car. When he stopped, the proprietor of the only tavern in a rural town offered him one beer before closing the doors—maybe two if he drank fast. After he had finished both beers, the bartender put a nightcap on the table. Hugo smiled. "You know, when I first came in here, Leonard, I felt like a refugee. Now I feel like one of the family. I would say there's a particle of irony in that."

"What you say?" asked the man as he washed glasses in a deep basin. Water splashed noisily on the metal. His wife put some chairs upside down on the tables and began sweeping.

"I said, the look of your face doesn't matter, or if you're rich. Don't you feel there's an ugliness worse than a big nose or bad teeth?"

The bartender grunted, lit another cigarette and asked, "Like what."

"Well...failure is ugly, don't you think, especially if it results in death."

The man went back to washing. The doctor started on his third beer, took the paper sketch of Conrad Muir and examined it. For solace he thought of Allan Korrolus, tried to put a face to a pseudo-relative he knew nothing about and hadn't seen in years. He put the paper back in his pocket and began putting chairs up on the tables.

"It's okay," said the woman. "You go finish your beer."

"It's nothing, ma'am. I've been sitting in the car all day." Hugo continued to talk as he put the chairs up and the woman swept. "As I was saying about failure: take for instance the child who wasn't raised—as most people are—by the usual mother-father combination. The little wretch may not have known that his father was indeed his father or cared either way because the kid had extreme dislike for him. In that case his parents would have had trouble raising him to be anything."

"So what's being an orphan got to do with your face or your money?" the man said lazily, letting his ash fall into the sink water.

"Oh, no. Not an orphan, Lennie. The mum and the dad were there in full bloom helping to raise the little man. They didn't shirk the letter of the law concerning support of their child, even if they did pretend not to be married." Hugo sat back at the counter, lit a cigarette, and offered one to the bartender, who left his own burning on the counter and took a light from his guest.

"Ciggie, ma'am?"

The woman came over and took one. Hugo opened his fourth beer and drank half of it in a few swallows. "Well, that's good," he said, leaning back on the barstool. "All of us smoking away here like family. But it was good, as you say, Leonard. No bitterness at all on the part of the kid. Because he had the compensation in lieu of a decent upbringing of inheriting his father's big, rather deceitful mouth."

"What's that?" the bartender asked as he splashed more water in the sink.

"The big lie, Lennie. You know, the pressure that moves a kid away from a sure thing and into a bad choice."

"How did he know it was his father's big mouth and not his mother's?" asked the woman.

"The mom was quiet. A church mouse, although she had a spectacular singing voice."

"So, you know this kid?" asked the man as he went back to drying glasses.

"I knew him way back when. And believe me, he was no singer. Singing is of no real value in the cut and thrust of life, or the fact your mother raised you to be good looking."

"You can't raise someone to be good looking, Mr....what did you say your name was?"

"You know, I didn't mention that detail, Bernice. You see the real value in life is the willingness to say anything, anytime, to anybody as it pleases you. Wouldn't you say a big mouth is a greater asset than a pretty face?" Hugo looked at the woman, who frowned and held the door open for him. He thanked her for the four beers, went through it, and walked to his car.

When he had stopped in a field ten miles further on from the tavern, he took his case from the trunk and laid it out to see if he could use something for a pillow. He removed some of the books and a box, which he opened to put in the small caricature of Conrad Muir. Before closing the lid he removed a portrait of a young woman with long black hair and large eyes, and was convinced again that his mother had been exquisitely beautiful. So why had she allied herself to Muir? He didn't count for much—a fine musician perhaps, and a man who had some connection to the war. Nevertheless, he believed his father to be a man of dubious achievement and flawed judgment. He put the picture close to the photo of men in military clothes. The faded picture had been in a dozen scraps, which he had meticulously taped back together for an afternoon's entertainment. "Your father's friends," Corrine Haultain had said to him when she saw what he was doing. "Like Allan Korrolus, they were men who did their duty."

Hugo put the box back in the trunk. Then he cleared a place on the back seat and went to sleep until the heat of the following morning drove him back into the prairie wind. His legs were stiff, unsteady, so he leaned on the rear of the car and gazed across the flat, empty grasslands. He had a momentary confusion about where he was and with it the urge to reverse his direction and accommodate sensibly for wasted years. Instead, he found his way back to the highway and continued driving east. That afternoon, the glowing sky appeared to soak the land in a solution of aquamarine. It made his eyes ache. For relief he put on his sunglasses and slouched in the seat. As the miles went by, he imagined how it was to lay for years with his face to the window glass, with his mother shoving pills in his mouth. How futile it had all been, always lost in a sea of pity...paddling and paddling and no land under his feet except the sickbed—first his own it seemed, then all the sickbeds of the world. He turned on the radio and cruised past the fields of newly ploughed earth, realizing that the impossibility of retreat had become a tiresome cliché.

Chapter II

Ghost

On his way across the town to locate his estranged Uncle Korrolus, the former and determined Dr. Haultain appreciated the fact that trees along the boulevard had the intense green of leaves newly unfurled: fresh, young, and themselves feeling immortal, as does all life at the heart of the continent when spring comes and the thought of next winter is unbearable. He drove beneath these well-nourished trees until his own hunger was a grating discomfort; then, with a newspaper tucked under his arm he marched into the first restaurant on the block.

The place specialized in Salisbury steak. He ordered one and checked the "Rooms" section of the classifieds. Nothing appealed to him so he walked down the street to stretch his legs. The wind picked up—or more accurately, it resumed its usual pace over the flat land, and with this pressure retarding his progress he had the feeling that something else might give him a better sense of his own bearings. He passed a bookstore and glanced at a cover showing villages in Tuscany. A block down he looked into the window of a store that sold Bibles. On the door was a small bulletin board and on it a card that said, "Room to let. Good Christian gentleman. Non smoker." He stamped out his cigarette, bought a map of the city, and went to the listed address.

"I've studied some theology," he said. "Then you'll be suitable," replied the lady whose mottled skin closely matched the doilies on her velveteen furniture, and let him have the room for a reasonable price. When he went to take his leather case into the hallway, he noticed a portrait of Dr. Albert Schweitzer on the end wall.

"How do you know about this man?" he asked the landlady.

"I contribute to charity and do what I can for the hospital in Africa. One day I'll have read all his writings, you know. On your way out the front door you can read the quotation I've hung there."

When he left the house for the first time, Hugo stood in front of the plaque with his feet together, his hands stiffly by his side in the posture of military attention, and read the words engraved on the brass:

> Greco-Oriental piety, Plato, the mystery religions and the Gnostics, all alike say to man: "Free thyself from the world!" Jesus says: **Get free from the world in order to work in this world in the spirit and in the love of God, till God transplants you into another, more perfect world.**" [Christianity, p. 15]

"What does this mean, madame?" he said loudly down the hall to where Phyllis was baking in the kitchen.

"It means do your duty, Mr. Haultain."

The next day he looked in the phone book and found a gym close by. The young woman at the counter of Fulbright's Muscle Mecca offered him a free pass. "You look like you're in pretty good shape," she said. "You won't need much instruction to get started."

Hugo leaned on the counter. "I've been hard at for a little while. Haven't had much to drink in weeks. A healthy life improves appearances, don't you think?"

She pointed at his arms. "You've been at it for more than six months."

"A bit longer, perhaps…did you say your name was Mary?"

"I didn't say what my name was."

"That's right, you didn't. May I ask what it is?"

"Dido."

He took the enrollment card from her and completed it. "I was going to start today, Dido, but I have things to do. You're quite right by the way," he said after setting the pen down. "Like the brain, muscle grows slowly. The truth is, I've been at it since I was a baby in diapers and had tiny little weights in the crib." The young woman shook her head and giggled.

On the third day following this visit, Hugo went to Fulbright's gym and settled into the monotonous rhythms of lifting. The boredom of exercise was a thing he had always felt comfortable with because it provided him the longest uninterrupted time to think about his direction. On this occasion, he felt content with the altered journey. Books in the sickroom had taught him that excitement grew in unexpected places. He looked through the window, at the flatness of the land with only sky to see and a thin wedge of earth underneath, less in every way than his boyhood home on the terraced mountain that rose abruptly from the incomparable ocean. Yet he thought that the wisdom of books notwithstanding, it would be unlikely that this dull place offered him a diversion other than a sweep of dry, level ground.

Lowering the barbell gently onto the mat, he looked in the mirror, at his mouth, which was temporarily shut. It was a certainty to him that outspokenness was a trait inherited from his father. His mother, Corrine, although beautiful, had been a quiet person who seldom spoke out of turn or did much else to escape the heavy burden of Herr Muir's company. Hugo looked away from the mirror. Dido sat on a red vinyl bench and watched him. She held a clipboard, made marks on a sheet, and said, "You never finished telling me the reason you started to work out at such a young age, being a baby with dumbbells in the crib—a story I don't believe, by the way."

Hugo didn't answer, but picked up a towel from the bench and wiped his brow. He faced the row of mirrors and circled his arms up and over his head. The large blood vessels of his arms and shoulders pressed through the skin. "My apologies for the delay in answering your skeptical question, Dido. But the warm-up had to come first. Then the talk." He put his head up in an attitude of contemplation. "My tutor taught me that little snippet. 'When confronted with labor, with a challenge, or some grave danger,' he would often say, 'always prepare yourself first. This effort must include your brain as well…and all must be announced with a smile.' My tutor seldom had a pleasant look on his own mug but insisted that smiling was a potent weapon."

"Why did you have a tutor?" she asked.

"Because I didn't go to school."

"Why?"

Hugo looked at her with no impatience in his manner for her prying queries. "I was a wheezing runt, a sickly child. Nothing in my body worked. I couldn't leave the bed for years, and when I eventually did, I was so weak I'd groan just lifting the lid on the piano bench. That always gave Conrad an opportunity to laugh."

"Conrad was your tutor?"

"Yes. Conrad Muir was his name. I had, and still have, a grudging admiration for him. Only once did he claim to be my father. At first my mother frowned at that but later nodded her assent. I took that to mean he was at least a close relative, perhaps my father, because one never knows. There was never a discussion concerning the family tree."

With Dido watching, Hugo completed two more sets, put the dumbbells on the rack and wiped the sweat off his shoulders. "But I had no doubts about his person," he said, sitting next to her. "His teeth were crumbling and black with rot. It was bearable if he'd just had a puff outside before entering the sickroom. The smoke that reeked in his clothes would then cover up the stench. If he didn't I made sure to breathe through my mouth, which made things worse for my condition. Conrad said it was a miracle I was alive but would probably die soon." He took a drink of water from a bottle and looked at her.

She frowned back. "How could anyone say that to a little kid?"

"Oh, I wasn't little, really. More like a wizened old man. There's nothing to be pitied here. Even a cripple can accept death as a struggle with the devil."

Dido changed her frown to a half smile, shook her head, and said, "This is all bullshit, of course."

"Of course, but it's sincere."

"How can you have 'sincere' bullshit?"

Hugo removed a large bar from the upright rack, slid some plates onto it and shrugged his shoulders. "Good question. But never mind. Conrad taught me that the greatest asset one can have is the gift of entertaining people with a good story."

Dido hung her head down so that Hugo wouldn't see her laughing. He looked at her seriously and continued. "Did I say your name right? 'Dido.' Let me see, that has significance. The well-informed old Muir would say, 'North Africa. Dido, Queen of Carthage. Killed herself when jilted by a prince.' It's always the princes that get the action don't you think? Royalty are privileged in that respect. Anyway, Conrad Muir wasn't royalty but he seemed a well-connected man. But you were asking, 'Why did I work out?' You were skeptical just now of my claims concerning childhood."

Hugo did two more sets of presses in silence, then replaced the plates on the stand and the bar on the rack. He breathed deeply and shook his head. "I don't think I can say anymore today, Dido. It gives me a churning feeling in my stomach to contemplate the past. But tomorrow when I come back and register full time in your gym, we'll have to resume our conversation."

Outside the building, Hugo stood for a time watching the clouds scatter along the line of the horizon. He thought the flatness gave the illusion of freedom, or at least the absence of barriers. On the plains there were no rocks to buttress the seawater. There was no seawater. Conrad, if he were here, would be asking the question of why he was on the wrong side of the window, still pretending to be the aristocratic Prince Eugene from the second chapter of *War and Peace*...a difficult task with the sickroom door ajar, admitting the smell of turnips and corned beef cooked by his lonely, neglected mother. Hugo steadied himself on the fender of his old green car and thought that with the barren plains providing no restraints to anything, he better be getting on with his existence.

At the Catholic home he took out the phone book and turned to the "K's" but found no Allan Korrolus. He turned to "Chandlery" in the yellow pages, found

"Korrolus' Boat Yard" and wrote down the address. He dressed and had the meal prepared by Phyllis, who, he noticed, had a sour smell to her. But he admired her conciliatory attitude, as if she was comfortable with her limitations.

"Do you read much, Hugo?" she asked.

"Not much, Phyllis. But I have my favorites. One issue of *Sports Illustrated* I've read one hundred and ninety-four times now."

"Doesn't it get boring?"

"Not in the least. I'm just now beginning to appreciate the 1958 championship game, the sideline passes Johnny Unitas threw to Raymond Berry to stop the clock, then Alan Ameche sliding off tackle for the ten-yard run that won the game for the Colts. I never get bored reading that."

"I'd have thought being a Christian man you'd be reading your Bible."

"Once a year I read it all the way through. Only takes me a day or two."

"Really. You must be a fast reader."

"I took the sped reading course."

"You mean 'speed' reading?"

"Yes, but in the past tense, like 'I sped through the Bible last year, like I sped through it the year before and the year before that'." Phyllis hurriedly cleared away the dishes and went into the front room to vacuum. Hugo went to his car.

It was always a comfort for Hugo to slide into the front seat of his 1950 Pontiac and get it rolling down the road. On this afternoon, however, it was not a matter of silly, adolescent cruising through any of a dozen former neighborhoods, looking for women. He had to get on with locating Allan Korrolus. The river and the boatyards had just showed through the boulevard trees when a loud grinding caused him to pull over to the side of the road with a flat tire. He got out, opened the trunk, and stared in.

Next to a tire that resembled a swollen piece of intestine were four cases of beer, boxes full of books, and his leather case, items he believed were appropriate décor for a future home. He looked at the volume on the top of the first box: *Sayonara*. He liked the word. Loosely translated it meant "good-bye" or possibly "piss off", being sentiments that Dido would express to him soon enough. He dug underneath the first layer and pulled out *All Quiet on the Western Front.* Feeling in no hurry, he read again the first page and reconsidered the First Great War, the impossible scope of killing and enormous brutality. He thought what fun the planet must have been then, and most likely still was, when you take into account the red-rose color of blood and violent world events. Then he felt a troublesome prod that he should continue looking for the captain's chandlery shop. The numbers on the buildings suggested he might be close, but that in turn reminded him to look for a jack and a wheel wrench because his car was still only half off the road. He emptied the trunk and found neither.

The Pontiac was stopped behind a tall fence. On the other side he could see masts showing above the top rail and smell lead paint and epoxy. He walked down a short macadam drive. The dampness of the adjacent river cooled his skin. The water level was low and the shoreline had a dozen boats held up with cradles of beams and wedges. He took twenty minutes to walk to the south end of the yard and back. He saw no one. On the street side, one shop had no sign and windows grimy with dust. He wiped a clean patch, then put his face to the glass. Inside was nothing recognizable except a board printed with the words "Korrolus' Boat Yard", and on the wall opposite a framed portrait of a man with white hair and a bushy moustache.

The door was locked so he went back towards the river, weaving amongst the hulls that were being stripped and repainted, recalling as he went that Muir never tired of describing the boatyard in Magdala next to the Sea of Galilee and in it the young shipwright Jesus, who was so skilled with his hands that the boats he built never leaked a drop. He had never gotten the gist of the story beyond the obvious, and this time made no attempt to square the motives of Jesus, Prince of Honesty, with his own clear intentions of stealing what he needed if a human being didn't soon show his or her face.

After much pacing, he stopped to look at one particular boat. On its stern was the word *Penelope* and he thought that it was an idiot indeed who would give such a majestic-looking craft a mincing name like that. The boat appeared to be about forty feet in length, larger than most of the others. As he walked around it, he noted how the differences in perspective changed the contours of the hull. He could imagine the ribs like human ribs but bigger, providing shape for the flesh of planking and different profiles, some long and sleek like destroyers or short and squat like tugs pulling chip scows. He imagined how the frame seemed like a plot in *War and Peace* and the wood skin a tale of hopeless human affection, shrunk and shriveled out of water or splintered on reefs of ill-use, and there would be no shrimp boats to return and women left weeping. He smiled to think how fertile the brain was to invent such nonsense, the best of it being that each mind was quarantined from all the others so he could without qualm contemplate his seduction of Dido.

A pair of shoes moved slightly under the massive keel. Hugo walked around to the other side to see whose feet they were, and found they belonged to a man who appeared of the preceding generation, but not as old as Muir. He had curly gray hair and was lying on his back on a blanket with legs capped on the ends with scruffy boots. The legs were tanned and muscular but the right one had a sizeable chunk torn out of it. The flesh had sunk into the hole like a grotesque pucker. The worker looked up briefly at Hugo, who had a sudden thought that the man knew more than he appeared to know. He would have to be on his guard. When the boatman sat up, his smile of greeting was marred by a disfiguration of his upper lip giving the hint of a sneer.

"Good day, Allan. I'm sure you'll remember me, Hugo Haultain, who you've not seen since I was a child. Anyway, the first thing I need to do on this visit to your boatyard is to borrow a wheel wrench and a jack. I've got a flat tire...the car is just up there, on the side of the road."

The man nodded, lay back down, and continued to do something to the bottom of the boat. Some minutes went by. Hugo thought that he must not get impatient because the man was probably thinking about the request for a wheel wrench and where he might find his own. After a short time, he felt a tingle of irritation and thought that he might speed the car repairs along by alerting his pseudo-uncle to the risk of Hugo's pulling out one of the stays—not an impossible task, like Samson pulling down the pillars—which would cause the boat to fall over in a splat of mud with the captain underneath. But, of course, in the interests of harmony, he would be sure to take the edge off this threat with the qualifying remark that none of this would happen—if he got the required tools in a timely manner.

Pondering what else he might say, he paced up the long length of the vessel. On his return, he announced, "Don't be worrying yourself about my car being half on the road and a danger to others, Captain. I've learned to tolerate neglect. Conrad's favorite lesson related to the benefits of restraint. In fact, from early childhood he drilled into me the idea that, in the eyes of the priest, impatience is an evil."

The doctor took a step back, expecting his remarks might result in an invitation to quit the boatworks minus the required tools, because he knew he had not seen or heard from Allan Korrolus in many years. But nothing happened. The man still played with the bottom of the hull. Hugo watched the boat repairer, marveled at his equanimity, and continued his chatter.

"This talk of religion, Uncle Allan, has put me in mind of my tutor and your friend, Conrad Muir. Although you two were close, don't you think he's been a big disappointment? Throughout our long years of association, I waited in vain for him to write the formula for success on the blackboard. But all I got was a droning old bore roaming around the wasteland of my sickroom. I came to loathe his presence...and not because he was a slob. I could see that beneath the ravages of dissipation he was not a bad-looking man. No, I disliked him because he had no talent for translating the simple profundities of life, like how to go out and make a decent living at something you like to do."

Hugo continued to pace the length of the boat with the fleeting hope that this inflammatory history might rouse the captain. The man moved his body a few feet to the stern of the boat. Hugo shuffled in that direction with him, but felt no more annoyed than when he had arrived. Anticipating a response in due time, he began to wonder if Allan's voice still sounded musical. With a snake-like wiggle the man squeezed from beneath the keel, sat up, and spoke. His voice had a deep, rough edge to it.

"Can't say I'm glad to re-make your acquaintance, Hugo. I haven't seen you in a few years, but already have the displeasure of knowing too much, certainly more than Conrad has told me. But I'm sure that had he cared, he would have mentioned that you were likely to say anything that popped into your head."

He wiped his fingers on a rag soaked in solvent and they shook hands. Hugo had the impression that Allan Korrolus had shaken thousands of hands and asked, "One question, Uncle Allan: how did you know my name?"

"You told me."

Hugo frowned. "I did, come to think of it. You must have the effect of putting me on edge. I usually don't forget the smallest detail of life."

"You talk too much. That's why you don't remember what you've said. Too busy being the idiot. In fact that's probably how Muir would have announced your arrival here, 'Be forewarned, Allan. Now that he's a man with a degree or two, Hugo comes across as a bit of an asshole.'"

Hugo shrugged his shoulders and took one step back. "Others might take offense at that remark, Captain…be tempted to take their revenge."

"But not you, mate," said Korrolus. "Muir would have included the information that you're a bluffer—a tough bloke perhaps, but still a bluffer. Anyway, after we've had a cold beer, if you still feel cocky we can have a go. This will re-warm you for the hard labor I'll require as payment for using my tools."

Hugo nodded and squeezed out his lower lip. "The beer is a fair offer, Allan. Of course I meant to be offensive. I intentionally provoke people."

Korrolus smiled, his mouth curling into a sneer. "No offense taken," he said. "I only get provoked by people I take seriously."

The captain got to his feet and fetched his cane. As they walked towards the tool crib, Hugo said, "Don't get me wrong, Allan, in regards to Conrad and you being close friends. Despite my comments, he's not altogether as repulsive as I've said. He has taught me a few useful things."

"He's your father and deserves respect."

"He does indeed. You know him well, don't you?"

"Not really. I met him in North Africa during the war. My visits to your home were infrequent if you recall."

"I'm thinking that you were one of the military men in a photograph I once found stuffed in a book. Mother liked that picture but Conrad tried to destroy it."

Korrolus stopped by the door of the chandlery. "No doubt. If it's the photo I'm remembering, it wasn't a flattering shot of anyone. Your mother knew a couple of the people in that picture: Dring—the surgeon—and Lieutenant Birks. Your father would never have mentioned the others."

Hugo watched the crippled man stagger into the small shed. For a moment he could make no connection, even at twice removes, between this adventurer and his mother, who was so refined. Perhaps there was no connection at all, and his confusion was a product of the high fever that often distorted his memory. He could still hear an echo of Corrine's soprano-like voice saying, "Go practice your Greig, Hugo, but don't exert your little self. If you do, I won't allow you to sail with our hero, the captain." This recollection gave him the urge to go up to his car, dig out Tolstoy, and read the book to the British captain as a gesture of obsequiousness. But, whatever the nature of past connections, Allan Korrolus seemed no threat now, and came back with a small bottle jack and a star wrench.

"Like most you buy today, it's made from pot metal," he said. "If it breaks I've got machined sockets. And don't round off the nuts. When you've done your work we can have a drink."

Hugo ran to the Pontiac, changed the tire, and brought the tools back. Korrolus exchanged them for a cold bottle of beer. They sat quietly on a sawhorse at the edge of the docks, and Hugo felt no compulsion to say anything more. He felt tired in the growing afternoon heat. The sky was a deep blue, the breeze just right to cool him. The water was open like the open door of his boyhood home, which led to the rutted track, to the forest and the swamp hidden in the mountain canyon where he would have gathered weapons to use against the girls, had his health allowed. But with the doors now open and him free, there was no need to burrow like a mole to get away. Korrolus had made peace with the tools and the beer and put him under no obligation.

"One more thing, Allan. That picture of Albert Schweitzer in your shop—what significance does this man have for you?"

Korrolus sat without speaking and finished his beer. After fiddling with his cane, he said, "I should be asking the question of why you came here of all places. But I haven't the time really, or the interest. Other chores await."

He got up and walked towards the shop, being sure the tip of his cane didn't penetrate too deeply into the mud. He said nothing else to the visitor.

A few days later Hugo went to the gym in the morning, when there were fewer people. Dido looked surprised to see him. "I didn't think you'd come back."

"I wonder why?" Hugo said. "But I already know the answer. When I said, 'I will come back and register in your well-equipped gym,' you thought, 'This is bullshit, of course,' and assumed that was the last you'd see of me. Many people are led to the same conclusion. And I don't blame them. It's always a pleasant surprise to me when I keep a promise."

Instead of replying, Dido sold him a two-month membership. He was halfway through his workout when she wandered over to his area with a cleaning towel and a bottle of liquid soap. "Just keep going," she said. "I have to earn my money with chores." She started to wipe the benches and the mirrors. "You never finished your funny story. Is the churning gone from your stomach?"

"Entirely. I feel well up to conversation today, although it's a chore for me as well to plough through the necessary illusions. But where was I?"

"Your sickly youth. Or was it dumbbells in place of teddy bears?"

"Yes. What was the background of that tale?" Hugo squinted and scratched his chin. "The fact is that I passed many years with my runny nose pressed to the window of the sickroom—when the other kids were outside, passing the time as kids do: playing their childish games by running around and jumping over things. It was not approved that I be allowed to run around, ever. So I was tutored instead and put to sleep with mother tinkling lullabies on the piano—'little sonatas,' Muir called them. To compensate for the lack of friends I had a make-believe visitor. Most children invent playmates, but this was different. I modeled my companion after a character my mother once described, whose name was Albert. But I never asked or cared who the real Albert was. He was my friend and always thoughtful to drop in when I was running a high fever or otherwise on my last legs."

Dido smiled and made notations on the cleaning log. Hugo did another set of curls, watching himself in the mirror. "Tell me, how come when you have pictures of your childhood floating in your mind the sky is always blue, especially when the kids are outdoors and you're in the sickroom? And the other side of the coin is that when the street is bare of the little devils, it's always raining. Why is that?"

"Because kids don't like to play in the rain, stupid."

"Is that it, Dido, fear of the ocean rain, aversion to the cold and dank with the forest dripping and uncomfortable, a fear of getting sick or being washed away? You don't have a clue in this flat place…to have water streaming down the open ditches and the moms keeping their little buggers safe inside. I always thought it was God torturing me, you know, the bright sunny weather adequate for an invalid to convalesce and me confined to barracks. And only on the foul days was I like everyone else, inside with a cup of hot choc against the inclement weather and being tortured by the learning and the books.

"At any rate, one day the medical men say, 'The little nipper is well enough for some activity.' I thought they meant out in the fresh air and I put on my pants, gearing up for life. But that was a hideous dream. At the insistence of my tutor, mother plunked me down on the piano bench so that only my extremities would get the exercise. She was shocked when my fingers couldn't reach the keys, so she gets Conrad to place some of his precious books on the bench and sits me up on them. And *voila*, I'm right up there. The top one I remember was *War and Peace.* Then underneath, *Gray's Anatomy* and underneath that, *All Quiet on the Western Front,* followed by *Robinson Crusoe* and books on the Second Great War, all owned by my alleged father and placed ceremoniously with his varicosed hands. I could see all of this quite clearly. My brain wasn't wizened and useless like my arms and legs."

Hugo sniffed, exhaled some air, and continued with curling the dumbbells. Halfway through the set he let the weights fall to the mat. "The kicker was this, Dido. My mother could see I was still an inch or two short of the mark and quietly put a small book at the bottom. As she placed it there, I could see a picture of an old goat on it with a moustache and white hair, looking more like my imaginary friend than the god my mother had described him to be. I asked Muir about it later, because it was one of few books I had never set eyes on. He dismissed it as being of no importance."

Hugo lay on the bench and began doing flys with fifty-pound dumbbells. Between breaths he continued, "And so it was that the slim volume at the bottom—a compendium of Albert Schweitzer—got me high enough to perform. Now who was Tolstoy? Remarque? Dafoe and the others? Muir knew them all. But I suspect from Mother's winks that despite his protest, he also knew who Schweitzer was—and that he was more than just a preacher."

Dido said, "It sounds like your old man was nasty to you. Did he beat you or anything?"

Hugo put the weights down and sat up. "No, he pushed me to perform. But he was gentle. Mother was timid but she would have ferociously opposed abuse. But never mind that, the problem being for me was this: now that I was tall enough to spread my fingers over the keyboard, I also had a clear view of my friends playing outside on the street and in the field under the blue sky and the mountain all from a new perspective, which became a double dose of torture."

The young woman stared blankly at him. He picked up the weights for his last set and closed his eyes. He could feel the center of his spine running from skull to tailbone and the contraction of all the individual muscles extending out from it. He was aware of how they held his wide shoulders securely, uniformly, exactly even and balanced on both sides. It was a sensation so relaxing that he imagined his body was like smoke spreading in still air from Muir's cigarettes, or his own smokes now that he had the same habit. He didn't notice that Dido had gone back to the front desk.

Luozi, Congo-Leopoldville, August 30, 1965.

The duration of recall for these events was irrelevant and therefore not calculated in the scheme of Hugo's present life. Responsibility for time, for the welfare of anyone or anything seemed a triviality. Only Mintou's threats put demands on him. While he waited for the completion of repairs to the ferry that would take them across the Congo River, he saw less of the Portuguese trader and more of the sergeant, who displayed a knack for listening, for gathering and remembering evidence in the fashion of a man who is deprived the security of records. Mintou walked from the direction of the ferry and sat beside him a few feet above the level of the river.

"You're thinking that you could escape by swimming across, aren't you?"

Hugo glanced at him. "Not likely, Sergeant. Even twenty feet of water is too much for my ability. Anyway, if I wanted to escape I'd just walk into the bush."

Hugo took an offered cigarette. The sergeant pointed with the shaft of his own smoke to the far bank of the river. "That's the way you would go," he said. "Because the bush leads only to starvation and more bush, with animals and many hazards. Across the water is not too far for a desperate man and leads to towns, to the capital. But then I don't believe anything you say, monsieur, because I can never tell what you're thinking or what you might do. You read and mumble to yourself. You're a prisoner and happy to be one, like a drunken man who pretends that he needs a wife to prepare food and dress him. I know you for a few days only. Already I feel like your house girl."

They both turned their eyes to the river. A piece of driftwood floated past and around the ferry's steel hull. When it had disappeared, Hugo said, "Since I can't give you more money just yet, what is it that I can do for you, Mintou?"

The soldier smirked. "Very little happens in the Luozi territory, no fights, no battles. And since you have nothing else I can take, I want you to entertain me. You have books, monsieur, for that purpose. I've heard you talking to the trader."

Hugo shrugged his shoulders. "I can tell you any story you'd like to hear. The problem is—they may or may not be true, like the parables mission priests tell your children."

"I don't have children or a wife to bear them. So I don't care about that. Make up your stories as you go along. If they're about yourself and not true, how will I know?"

So in the quiet murmuring of the river's presence, Hugo told the soldier a story he thought appropriate. "I'm telling you this tale to put your mind at ease, Sergeant. It relates both to water and your fears that you might lose your excuse to see the capital. So here it is...There was a time recently when I was inspired to become a boat-builder like Christ himself so I could be near and on the blessed water. With this in mind I went to the boatyard of a relative with the hope of receiving the position of apprentice. It was late afternoon when I arrived hoping my uncle, whose name was Allan, might still be there in his desire to escape the heat of midday. I found him underneath a boat.

'What exactly are you doing there, Allan?' I asked.

'Caulking.'

'I take it that caulking is necessary to the proper maintenance of a boat.'

'You assume correctly, mate,' he answered.

'Hugo is the name.... in case you were confused as to my identity.'

'Not confused at all,' he said in an unfriendly manner. 'Few people in life confuse me less, at least as to their identity. And few people cause me such acute desire to be rid of them.'

Mintou frowned. "Your uncle didn't like you?"

"At first not much. But as you'll find out, things changed. My uncle wriggled out from under the keel and I said to him, 'I'm here for a reason, Allan, trying to make the connection between you and Conrad Muir.'

'We met in North Africa,' he replied.

'Yes, you said that before.'

'I did, mate. So let's cut the chitchat and let me get back to work,' he answered. His rudeness wasn't a bother and I was just interested in helping, so I replied that I should be repaying him for the use of the tools to fix my car, nothing permanent, just an hour or two of skilled labor. And he answered that the lending of the tools was a favor not requiring repayment, but that my presence there was a nuisance and a waste of his time. As I said before, Mintou, I'm never bothered by insults so I sat and happily watched my uncle until he had finished caulking a seam halfway up the port side. Then I said to him, 'If you're thirsty after all this work, Allan, I can offer to buy you a drink, as a favor to an esteemed uncle that likewise doesn't require repayment.'

'You must be at loose ends,' he sneered. 'Not much to do, eh, now that you've thrown in the towel?'

Mintou frowned.

"A figure of speech, Sergeant, which means to give up, to surrender. You see I had just quit my job because I disliked it, something you can't do. But I didn't give up my thirst for liquor. Nor had my uncle, who continued his talk. 'If you insist on buying, I'll oblige,' he said. 'It's hot and I'm dry.'

"When we arrived at the hotel bar for our drink, he insisted we sit well off the main aisle with our backs to the wall. 'In respect of the entertainment,' he explained. It was not a nice place. The room stank of smoke. The carpets had gone musty with the spilt beer and the walls were coated with a slurry of dust and cigarette tar. After we had consumed much liquor, events turned nasty. For some reason a small man near the bar hit the man next to him. Out of revenge, the waiter and other men hit the small man very hard. His head was cut to the bone and soon blood ran from his nose. People cheered. I told my uncle that as a military man he should order the men to stop. But he said he had no intention of soiling himself with brawlers and asked me to do it. I was already drunk, you see, and could only stagger over to the group and plead to the waiter that he show mercy. But he shoved me into the bar and said rude things as a challenge."

Mintou frowned and ran his fingers over his head. "Did that make you angry, monsieur?"

"Oh, I was prepared, my friend, as you are prepared to see that justice is done, which might result in violence and many deaths. Another man lunged at me, so I hit him with a right jab and he collapsed to the floor. An arm went round my neck but soon let go when my uncle stabbed his cane into the owner's ear. Then life became the fun it was meant to be. The room erupted in all corners with fighting patrons and drunks eager for revenge, for fun, or vanity, until a smiling *moi*, with my clothes torn and stained with blood, threw a table through the front window.

"Like trumpets blowing down the walls of Jericho,' I explained to the gloomy man who was trying to avoid the glass, most of which shattered outwards onto the empty sidewalk. As the police came in the door, I crouched out of sight. Across the street I could see my uncle straightening his shirt, oblivious to the officers who were about to trap him against the river. So I went around to the other side of the forest to lure them away. Taking the bait they shouted and gave chase. In a few moments they were on me. I threw the stick at them, leaped in, and struggled through the water with my lungs aching. Even as a youth I was never a swimmer, but had no idea how bad. As I drifted downstream, the far bank appeared no closer. Each time I got my head above the water I could see no lights, hear no voices, no sound of traffic. I could do nothing but imitate the paddling of a goat until I felt the ground on the opposite shore. A pair of hands helped me out followed by a whisper in my ear, 'You ain't much of a swimmer, mate. I had no trouble following you along, what with the thrashing around and your gasping for air. I didn't mean for you to drown on my behalf."

Mintou smiled and threw his smoke into the water. Hugo nodded his head.

"He spoke the truth, Sergeant. Sacrifice for mom and the kids is one thing, but to die for an insolent uncle would be a waste in my opinion, although the pleasure of mocking God is always appealing." Hugo threw the stone he had been juggling into the river's current, then looked at the soldier. "The truth of it is this, Mintou: I learned to fear water as a thing I would have to avoid like the plague. On the other hand, men like you are merely a nuisance."

The sergeant giggled and threw another stone into the water. "You were right to help your uncle, monsieur, even if he is bad. Relatives are your duty, water or no water. And me, well, I will become more than a nuisance, you'll see." With a slurred remark concerning other responsibilities, the ranking soldier of Four Group, Bakongo Corps marched in the direction of the barracks.

The next evening, after his meal with Benoit Marse, Hugo resumed his vigil by the river. A short time later Mintou marched towards him at the head of a half-dozen soldiers. They boarded the ferry and Hugo was pleased to hear bitter protests from the mechanics. He had not moved when Mintou appeared and with a grunt seated himself on the riverbank. "The ferry will cross tomorrow morning," he said. Hugo chuckled. "Then tomorrow will be a good day, Mintou, even better than yesterday."

The sergeant sneered and lit a cigarette. "You laugh now. But soon those under my command will take their duty to me seriously."

"Of course they will, so be patient. They'll learn. It's a bad habit they've gotten into. They think they have responsibility only to relatives, less to the others in their village, and none to those outside. You, on the other hand, should know that we're obliged to consider a wider world, have a duty that flows outwards like ripples in a pond. Because sooner or later, when time stops, we have to deal with spirits greater than our ancestors, some with good ju-ju and others with an evil intent."

Mintou nodded then began softly hitting his swagger stick into the palm of his hand. "Say what is on your mind, monsieur. I'm prepared for stories of evil. I would be happy to know you have as much to fear as I do."

Hugo lit two more smokes, threw one to the sergeant, and began talking. "Pay close attention, Mintou, and you will find out that sometimes fear brings rewards. On a memorable Sunday morning, at my uncle's request, I found my way back to the boatyard. The summer sun had not yet moderated the general dampness of the riverside. The mud was still soft with the night rain when I walked over to the *Penelope*. Uncle Korrolus was underneath but gestured to me. 'Over there is another canvas for you to lie on,' he said. 'Next to it is a bucket of oakum for the seams and you can put your mind at complete ease for the day or the week by helping me re-caulk this vessel.'

"I walked over to the container and looked at the hairy coils of stuffing, at the *Penelope*, then lay on the canvas and began to imitate my uncle in his winding and stuffing movement. After an hour had gone, I reached into my satchel and brought out two bottles of beer. Korrolus took immediate notice and eased himself out to sit on a sawhorse and drink. The alcohol focused my mind on the altered circumstances, giving me the notion that re-caulking a large vessel was the thing I should be doing in life, having a duty to make it shipshape so Allan wouldn't have my fear of drowning. We were both silent for a time and I became aware of the shifting of the shadows and the utter perfection of the changing angles, the multiple shades of color, the evolution of smell, and the various quantities of matter that touched my skin. It's good to notice things, Mintou. In fact it's your duty if you wish to survive. Sitting with my uncle, I sensed the presence of deep water but also the sacred sky above it. I also sensed that it was my duty to get over my dislike for him, although he didn't seem to be my father's close friend or a relative at all, merely a distant comrade from the wars.

"We've almost exhausted the supply of oakum,' he said and asked that I walk over and get some more. Being a little tipsy from the beer I sauntered along the flats and up to the old shop. I hadn't been in it, or near it, since first peering in and seeing the framed picture on the far wall, of a man you would know if you could read books and through them know more of the world's history. The room was hot and smelt musty, greasy. Sweat ran into my eyes. The portrait of Albert Schweitzer hung impassively. His eyes were dots of charcoal on the paper. I breathed slowly and stuffed oakum into a sack. When I turned to leave, I saw the white hair of a man sitting behind paint barrels, his head bowed as if in prayer.

I stopped, and with no attempt to mask my amazement, said to him, 'It's been a few easy years, Albert. Once I attained the status of adulthood, I'd given up ever seeing you around, and never so near a place that has your picture hanging on the wall. So forgive my surprise at seeing you worshipping in such disrespectful circumstances.'

"No place is disrespectful on a Sunday,' he replied. 'The believer prays where he must. It's only important that he give thanks.'

'In the generally bad scheme of things, what have any of us to be thankful for?'

'For yourself,' he answered, 'for your rather luxurious life. Show gratitude that God saw you taken care of to a point where you have the option of being a fool.'

'That's a bit cheeky for a man of your stature.'

'No stature at all, Hugo. I do what I must. It's sufficient for me to know the world requires my services, and for you to know that I oblige.'

'Well, my stature depends at the moment on delivering this important shipbuilding material to my new employer, who is waiting patiently for it. Can't stay and chat, although at this point in history we could have a fruitful chin wag on issues, I'm sure. We've been denied that opportunity far too long.'

"The old man hummed softly to himself and shuffled pages of sheet music I could see was titled with the name, JS Bach. I stopped filling the sack and said, 'You must miss your time as the savant, Albert, a life filled with music, philosophy, the memories of Mulhausen and Strasbourg, the privilege of occupying number 36, the Old Fish Market, once home to the inimitable Goethe. Imagine the privilege of hearing Wagner at Bayreuth in the last century and being a friend to his widow. I mean, you've been around the block, old man, and even to Paris. I was envious that you learned piano theory from Marie Jaell-Trautman, who taught that to create an organic unity the finger touching the key must be conscious of itself. Muir could never quite grasp the concept.'

"You treat history as if you were a schoolboy reciting his verse,' he answered. 'It can be no surprise to anybody that I miss episodes from my past no more or less than you appreciate your origins. In the meantime, I've had other employment, other enterprises greater than these.'

"He slipped away from the grimy barrel and came over to me. 'Forget the past, Hugo. You have other considerations now. Since you seem willing to do some work, I have a job for you.'

'As I said before, my services are engaged at the moment.'

'This job can wait until you've finished repairing your friend's boat.'

'The thing is, I'm not looking for work, not now or in the future,' I answered.

'Work, however, is looking for you,' Albert pressed. 'In this case a skillful job, with prestige attached. In this respect you are indispensable.'

'I can have fame, money, power, and perks in the world of business.'

'Mine is a better offer.'

'The indispensable details of which are…?'

'Humility and sweat. Your return on investment is a chance at a treasure that at present you could not imagine.'

'I can imagine most things.'

'You cannot conceive of love.'

"I scoffed at him, Sergeant Mintou. I put the greatest ridicule into my tone, because he was offering me what? The great treasure of love?

"You're really quite adept, Albert,' I replied, 'offering me the elusive, weepy feeling a dad has for the kiddies or a mother for her dying child as he fades away under the watchful eye of the family doc. Or do you refer to the scent of romance that spices up an otherwise dull day? Best you don't offer me anything. You've already given me a few laughs, a few good quotes via my father. Let me see if he quoted you correctly: "Men must learn by the book of example, or they'll not learn anything."

The white head nodded, then Albert grinned at me. 'It's funny how men glow with pride when others repeat what they've said. I'm no different. I can puff myself up like a peacock. However, I thought that particular epigram a bit overwrought.'

"I completed filling the bag with oakum and slung it over my shoulder. At the door I said, 'You know, Conrad said nothing of you directly. He was a poor example for me to follow, as I would be an even worse example for others. But don't fret; a few educated men will remember your written works, because Albert Schweitzer is an icon men revere. The problem is, who besides God could rise to the level of your example?'

'You, for one,' he answered. 'Instead of glorifying yourself with self-pity, you could cultivate a consistent sympathy for those who despair of their pain. And as for love? We can only guess what the love of a woman would do for you, especially if you were moved to reciprocate.'

'Perhaps a woman I know already? Just tell me her name and I'll give her a ring.'

'You've had affairs with too many women.'

'There can never be enough,' I said.

"The old man looked out the window to the boats and the river. Without turning he said, 'Remember this one trite but appalling little saying, Hugo, from the least of mouths: In each life there is time only for one true love, and one adventure.'

"He got back onto his knees with his hands clenched together, elbows resting on the grease barrel. The portrait on the wall shrank behind the glass, the air packed close around me, and the smell was sour. I grasped the heavy sack of oakum, opened the door, and ran into the clean air. When I was back underneath the *Penelope* I said to my uncle, 'There's a man in your shop.'

"He finished caulking a seam to the end, taking him some minutes before replying, 'You said that when you first arrived. But I suppose it's not every sod who notices Albert hanging there.'

'I thought only dead spirits had the right to haunt.'

'Not haunting at all, mate, just a good likeness. Anyway, his picture is of no concern to us. Our job is with the caulking and, before we get too thirsty, to enjoy our beer."

When Hugo had said nothing for a full minute, Sergeant Mintou hit the swagger stick into his hand with a final thump.

"You have an advantage over me, monsieur. I understand very little of what you say, not being able to read books. And I don't understand why you say all these things except to show that you're better than me. But I like you anyway. I might keep you alive for a while, even feed you some of your own food and cigarettes. You seem to respect your uncle, or whoever he is, and that is good. And you seem to fear the spirit of the ju-ju doctor like you fear water. If you have any more to say on him, I'll listen. As I said before, it gives me pleasure to hear of things that scare you." The sergeant grunted and smiled. "And when we reach Lufungula," he concluded, "you'll see things that will do more than scare you."

His eyes were large when he marched from the riverbank and Hugo could hear the grinding of boots on the pathway. He woke the soldier who was his constant escort and took him closer to the ferry slip and listened to the mechanics' increasing activity echo from the trees. It was going dark. In the kerosene lights, the glistening mud of the river appeared like the mud of all rivers he'd seen and, therefore, was a reminder of similarities, conjunctions, comparisons, and the false value that comparisons have in illustrating a man's connection to the world. Because even Hugo's finely cut detail of personal history could change none of it. Later that night, lying under the netting in Benoit Marse' house, he recounted his mastering the art of twisting the oakum strips into the seams of the *Penelope*. He recalled that the enormous effort of the job took his mind off Albert's exhortations. It was also a relief from the tedious, futile penance he did each morning at the plaque in the Christian house, with the small, white face of the dead girl overwhelming the fancy brass letters.

Chapter III

Music and Memoir

Two days later the trader said, "Have another beer."

The sentry who accompanied the prisoner wherever he went accepted with a bow and a smile. In an hour he was drunk and lying in the dirt. After a squad of the Bakongo Corps removed the man to the barracks, Hugo used the trader's supplies to clean the soldier's rifle and surround himself with a sense of security by shooting fifty rounds at an effigy of Sergeant Mintou formed by the crumbling bark of a dead tree.

The next morning, as the huts of Luozi receded to the north, Hugo tried to further pacify his misgivings by ignoring the sergeant and noting instead the counterclockwise direction of the whorls of water that spun down the side of the ferry, putting that turbulence into a category with other rivers and man-made pools in which he imagined himself drowning. In contrast, the leader of Number Four Group watched his captive with unwavering attention. From the manner of this scrutiny, Hugo was confirmed in his suspicions that Léon Mintou was a murderous double-dealer and as big a liar as he had once been. With the south shore of the Congo River drifting closer, he contemplated the security that might result from striking a preemptive blow. Setting aside speculation on the resulting pleasure, he would have to decide if Mintou's death would give him less or greater opportunity to hear from Martin Birks. He glanced at the shrunken face of Benoit Marse, who looked dead already, a self-made corpse on its ill-tempered way to the capital to secure an obedient virgin to replace the willful and aging house girl. The thought crept into Hugo's mind that he had much less reason than the trader for his journey to Leopoldville. As the men of the army had already told him, to risk death for the advice of a condemned man was an act of madness.

The road leading from the ferry landing at Matadi towards the prison followed the arc of sun that rose in the east and dropped perpendicular in the west. It was going dark, therefore, when the men of Four Group, Bakongo

Corps, accompanied by the trader, the sergeant and his prisoner, stopped in Mbanza and climbed the stairs to a vulgar second-floor dancehall. After a few drinks, all the men removed their boots and began a two-step shuffle with an earnest rhythm. For hours they went up, down, and across the rough wood floor in circular repeating patterns, bearing the weight of their soiled uniforms with grace, clutching voluptuous women wearing bright skirts and silver earrings.

Servants lit the lanterns. Hugo drank his beer next to a sweating Sergeant Mintou and removed the bandage from his left hand, massaged the numbness in his fingers, and decided that he would not join the dancers. Instead, he looked through the spaced openings in the wall that served as windows and recalled specific items from his memoirs. The most trivial was the image he recorded of a waltzing Irishman who had wept openly to say how sorry he'd been at the news that his countryman Brendan Behan had died. Hugo thought it fitting that the man's only recollection of Irish culture was the playwright's warning that a man should drink no more than twice a day—when he was thirsty and when he was not. But Hugo also knew that Behan was an old man when he expired at forty-one and looked more at death like the Portuguese trader squirming rat-like on the dance floor in contrast to the army of bush people glad to have escaped captivity, their bare feet making a thunderous drumming on the floor. As the prisoner watched, they all twirled around together until the moon had followed the sun below the horizon, and eventually set their shoulders towards darkness and the first clearing next to the road where they fell onto the ground. Hugo put a blanket over his guard, then fed the campfire with twigs gathered by crawling over the ground using his hands to feel for the wood.

The last sticks blazed up. Their light gave give him a welcome hour to read from one of his spiral scribblers the story of how heartened he had been by the hard work he did for Allan Korrolus at the shipyard. He turned the pages forward in the story. The words grew fewer and increasingly obscure. There appeared to be no space on any of the sheets large enough to draw the face of the woman he would never see again. When the fire died and he couldn't recall where he had left his vehicle, he stretched out on the earth, staring at the stars, less clear than the stars he had seen above the Sahara, with the night hotter than nights cooled by the slow passing of years.

June 1963, Korrolus' Chandlery.

All day the heat in the boatyard had been within the range of forecast temperatures for that time of year, and that place. It was much less hot by the time he went home to the Christian house with the idea of going back later to help Uncle Allan with the task of caulking the *Penelope*, if just to keep some activity in his hands and brain other than mindless lifting at the gym. Nevertheless, he relished his strenuous sessions with Dido, each time telling her it was a purge to remove the toxins and not indicative of a change in habit.

She would say, "You don't look like an alcoholic."

And Hugo would reply that he had full knowledge of his shortcomings, and that the drinking and gym time had always gone together since he was little. One afternoon he came out of the locker room to begin his stretching and warm up. When he looked up, Dido was standing to one side.

"Did I tell you I have someone to meet?"

"No, you haven't said anything to me today."

Hugo smiled and began a set of dumbbell presses. "But I don't as yet know who that person is for sure," he went on, "besides one man who has concocted a job for me, something associated with Muir. This is associated, in turn, with something I have to do generally, not today but in a week or a year maybe."

Dido waved back at him as if she had not heard, and went about her duties. Hugo continued silently with his workout. He was almost finished when she came back to find him sitting on a bench wiping away the sweat with a white towel.

"About your youth, I have a feeling you haven't told me everything."

He got up and walked towards the shower room. Then he walked back. "As a matter of fact I've been saying more, but you were occupied elsewhere. But I will risk repeating myself...As a decrepit youth, I got tired of banging out the chords, you see. Playing the piano is not like making love to a woman, I might add."

Dido had leaned over to stare at the floor, sitting with her arms on her knees, the perfect valley between her breasts running visible to her navel. Hugo stopped.

"You know you should always cover up when you're with me," he said.

A red flush came to her face. "Why? Don't you like what you see?"

Hugo moved his gaze to her eyes before continuing. "At the time, because I was still a boy, I wasn't sexually involved with women, you understand. As a mere runt I couldn't have known such things occurred. I would have been embarrassed by it. Instead, I was playing the chords to Grieg's *A Minor Concerto*, while outside, the other children were smashing balls, riding bikes, vanishing into the swamp and bringing back pea shooters cut from stalks of swamp reed—the bore just right for mountain ash berries. Thus, they had their Napoleonic wars to terrorize the girls as if in preparation for the real horror to come in a few short years—inside and outside the bedroom.

"One day I worked up this ploy. When my mother didn't hear the expected chords of Chopin's *Etudes*, she came rushing in, and there I was squatting down. 'Just reading a paragraph of Tolstoy, Mother, and the occasional dissection of the thorax.' She consulted with Muir and he agreed to the substitution of one classic for another, as long as the musical work got done. When the kids were playing out and about, to relieve my negative feelings I'd be down on my bony knees right into the story of Russian blue bloods, with their palaces, their wars, and their loves; the much-decorated captains banging away at will with the young princesses in the gold-plated drawing rooms on velvet divans. Then I'd bang out a bar or two of Mozart to end the session. In this way I read the whole book, and then the whole stack, and eventually the whole library. And the copy of *Gray's Anatomy* that added a bit of height? I was fascinated by the pictures and this swayed me to try my hand at medicine."

"You're going to be a doctor?"

Hugo turned down his lip. "Doesn't seem likely, does it, to succeed at something that complicated?"

Dido shook her head. "Not likely," she said. "But you could make your living as a clown. Generally speaking, you talk too much, but sometimes when you get wound up you amuse me."

"Being wound up is a neurological complaint, like a tic. Most of the time I'm silent like winter. Except when we go out tonight and I tell you more. In the meantime, here's another small story: Late one night, when the street lamp shone through the curtains of my room, I saw a man sitting at the bedside stroking the yellow-tainted hair on his lip. And I said to him, 'Albert, is it true that you keep deer under your house and that these spindly creatures help you plant vegetables in the garden?' He put his large hands on my chest and even with the incomplete light I could see the dirt under his fingernails and his strong brown hands.

'True it is, Hugo,' he said. 'Because no one helps me plant the food required. You have to rely on the life that is around you, including your own.'

"I knew then that this was indirectly the hand of God on my chest as if I were Lazarus; but I couldn't explain to my wizened mind why He had not sent a real saint like Thomas à Beckett or Jeanne d'Arc."

The young woman did not look up from her sheet, and eventually wandered back to the counter. After showering, Hugo approached the glass doors to leave. He stopped to look through them, to examine the blue sky and say to Dido, "I'll pick you up at seven for our date."

She laughed and shook her head. "You must be mistaken, Sir Clown. I don't recall us having a date. Believe what you like about miracles, but this time there won't be one."

"Miracles happen at the most unexpected times," he answered, and for a moment they stood watching the breeze moving the leaves of the bushes. Dido sighed.

"I'll go out with you tonight," she said, "but only for a quick drink and nothing else; because you should know I'm engaged to be married."

With a sweep of arm, she held up her left hand. Hugo took it. "That's a very nice ring your sweetheart has given you," he said. "It puts me in mind of little story relating to jewelry. Do you mind?"

Dido shook her head.

"Very well," he said. "There was a man named Solly, you see, a jeweler by trade, who used to attend the social night my tutor would host for his friends once a month. Conrad would get up and play the piano. The guests joined in with their assorted instruments. The man I mentioned, Solly Pelham, played violin; but what I liked most about him was that he would always arrive with a case filled with trays of gemstones and gold settings. He would let me look through the jeweler's glass and taught me about the stones: how to determine the value of a diamond and a sapphire from a piece of glass. I could tell he wanted me to take up the trade. When I was older, he would bring rings and brooches and taught me how to design settings that would be secure but original. The whole thing was like an elaborate toy set. It never occurred to me that the stuff he brought was worth thousands."

He rubbed Dido's fingernails with his shirt as if to buff them to a gem-like finish. Then he swiveled the ring so it shone directly at him.

"What I'm saying to you, Dido, is that if I had a jeweler's glass I could tell you exactly how much your future husband loves you."

"Does the amount you spend show how much you care?" she asked with a frown, and Hugo replied, "It's as good a gauge as any."

*   *   *   *

The next time Hugo arranged to meet his quasi-uncle at the boatyard, Korrolus was sitting in the front seat of a new, white convertible.

"We're going for a ride."

"Which means?"

"I require the brute strength of your back to help me move something."

They said nothing more until they got back to Korrolus' attic suite in a district of the city known as "Tuxedo." Following the climb up a narrow staircase, Hugo could see from the open door that it had sparse furniture and down one wall, a large case full of books. An army handgun rested on the coffee table.

Hugo reached to pick it up, changed his mind, and went instead to the adjacent wall and its row of diplomas.

"The Latin's a come-on," Korrolus called from his small kitchen. "But it's in keeping with the basic flavor of scholarship, pretending to be ancient and venerable. Mavis accused me of buying them from a pawn shop."

The old man emerged with glasses of beer, and as he drank, paced across a spot where the floor squeaked. Hugo took his glass and moved along the wall to a large print showing a bizarre, vertical landscape of rock and shadows set off by a full moon. Korrolus explained, "Heinrich Barth was a German explorer of the Sahara in the last century, the first through Timbuktu, known to us as the furthest place on earth." After putting his face close to the picture he picked up the sidearm, sat on a small wooden chair and crossed his legs so the red pucker stood out. Hugo sat across from him and nodded his head with surprise. The barrel of the pistol pointed at his face.

"Conrad suggested you might be bothered by my presence," he said, "He implied that there might be a risk for me to come here. Why would that be, Captain?"

Korrolus moved the barrel towards the window. "Only the inconvenience of dredging up a smell from the past. No more risk than that. One bullet wouldn't do a thing against a bad memory, although it might remove a nuisance." He placed the weapon on the table and pointed the neck of his bottle at the ceiling.

"But the risky thing is this, Hugo. War, violence, treachery and murder—all of these require a judgment. How do you perceive the outcome? Most people believe the afterlife is in the clear blue of the sky, which seems to their advantage. But there are some who argue heaven and hell are two sides of the same coin and, therefore, can be here on the land, perhaps immersed in mud at the bottom of the river. It's a confusion of immortality that's been around for longer than this era."

He leaned his head completely back, aimed the neck of the bottle down, and poured the beer directly into his throat. A few drops spilled down the front of his shirt. "What a mess," he said and rubbed them in. "A famous person once said that he had never met anyone worse than himself. For me, name-droppers are the most tedious we have to endure. Cocksure people who parade themselves up and down the high street are merely noisome. The truly heinous are beyond comparison. Morrice Crasson was one, god dam him, and George Blenkinthorpe another…both of them greedy and vicious, people you should avoid."

Hugo nodded and said, "We must all pay a price for living."

Korrolus laughed. "Let me bounce a little more glib pretension your way. What has been the price I've paid for living? Let me see. I've done a penance. I've begged forgiveness for the killing."

"What would be the penance for killing, Allan?" Hugo asked, "And who did you kill?"

"I was in the war, mate, at sea with the Royal Navy. And the penance? Let me see. On occasion, I've interfered in the lives of others, even memories of the dead. I've browbeaten many an asshole, kicked the legs out from underneath a few bullies. And in my dealings with the swaggerer? I handle them by planting the seed of doubt. Remember this, Hugo, there's nothing finer than doubt for the nagging erosion of character that gives the best revenge. It's the price Morrice and George have paid in lieu of dying young."

Korrolus fetched a second round of beers and with the tipping of the glasses, continued to pace nervously along the floor. Hugo stood next to the larger of the two windows. From that angle he could see a photo of military men propped against the window frame. He took it into his hands, and after he had verified its familiarity, turned it over. On the back was a list of names. Korrolus was third from the left, leaning on the same cane. "How old were you, Allan?" he asked.

"Oh, I don't know. Early thirties."

"Who are these guys?"

"Of course Muir would never have told you. But just in case your own personal price for living comes down to pursuing a history lesson, I'll start you off with an important tale."

Hugo shook his head. Korrolus sat down next to him and looked at the picture. "During my travels around Algiers before the war ended, I found myself at the Mission to Seamen on Rue Santeria. It was a summer night on that exciting sweep of harbor and the arc of terraced city, and below it at waterside, me playing darts with a Spaniard. A bloke I knew sits at a piano next to the dartboard and starts playing a tune. He's the fourth from the left in the photo…Martin Birks, standing next to George. Birks was a soldier who landed with the Allies in western North Africa, then fought at the Kasserine Pass. But that summer night he was a pianist playing for his own peace of mind, while I, on the other hand, was a beaten sailor, adrift on a sea of booze and forced by the music to contemplate his misery."

He paused, took a drink and leaned forward onto his elbows. "The others in the photo are British soldiers, except one, the villainous Frenchman I mentioned previously. George was a Londoner like me, but a cold fish and a sapper. The one on the left is Major Dring, now a surgeon practicing in the English Midlands. I believe Birks has spent his years somewhere in equatorial Africa.

God knows what Wallace Fraser got into, besides the ladies' beds. We should have had Von Raynor, the kraut, in that picture as well, but he was to enter the drama later. Unlike myself, he returned to the sea with the merchant navy."

Korrolus went to stand at the row of diplomas hung on the wall, and made no effort to continue. In turn, Hugo examined the poster of Africa and felt hot, thirsty. The captain's story made his throat drier than it ought to be; and he thought that he should be drinking more, because beer always has a good taste on a hot day. He imagined how it would have tasted to Barth, and all the other foreigners in Africa who had voluntarily exposed themselves to hot weather and other adventures. He recalled from his years of sickness, that when there were no interruptions from the kitchen, he would sneak comic books under the bedclothes. The bright drawings would transport him into the steaming jungle, much like the dripping forest he could see through the glass, except it would be warmer, no sweaters and mitts ordered by moms, but maybe loincloths, and no snobbish behavior or rules of etiquette or dress or which fork to use. He imagined how hot it would have been playing under a tropical sun, pretending to swing on vines to visit the animals, with no glass or thick walls to cage them.

"You know, Allan," he said. "When I was a boy, the biggest crime I could imagine was not murder or thievery or false pride. It was being caged. I had a horror of imprisonment," he said. "To make things bearable, I watched the birds flying around and the insects that crawled along the sill. This gave me a respect for life. It would give Albert a reason to hope."

Korrolus looked away from his diplomas and raised his eyebrow. "I've seen you in action, Hugo," he said. "And I would say there's not much respect for anything in your behavior, not least in imitation of your father's friend. Personally, I know only what I've read of him. It was the last tenant who put his picture in my shop. But given your father's history, perhaps you should have the opportunity to know more. That said, if you wish your moral code improved from that quarter, you'd best be getting on with it. At close to ninety, Albert Schweitzer won't wait long for you to come knocking."

Near Leopoldville, Equatorial Africa.

Hugo roused himself, sat upright, and threw the last of the brushwood into the fire. He lit a cigarette, then removed a notebook from his satchel. In the dim light of the approaching dawn, without thought to style he sketched onto a blank page his rendering of a summer afternoon, with a hot wind baking the ground and high above the glazed, pastel cloud. With his weak left hand clamping tightly to the notebook, he took an hour to draw a likeness of himself lying motionless on the canvas and the smoke from a cigarette curling upwards around the curvature of the *Penelope's* hull. Before he had finished the sketch, a throbbing in his left arm became as acute as the pain he had suffered from the endless twirling of the oakum between the planks. He massaged the tightness from his muscles, and while doing so, had a few vague thoughts on the contradictory nature of suffering. He wished Mintou were there so he could explain to him that pain, as he had read, could be therapeutic and enhance power. It might also cause acute distress and thereby diminish strength. In fact, Muir had told him that the contradictory problem of suffering had induced men to use it as the most confusing metaphor of the age. On the shelves of his library sat a dozens of divinely constructed books testifying to the fact that taking infinite pains was the mark of genius. He had concluded, nevertheless, that an equal number of books say that genius guarantees nothing. Ships built with painful attention to detail might not leak a drop in oceans greater than Galilee; but a mutinous boson might sabotage the lifeboats anyway, and all hands perish. Being long past any prime of genius, Captain Korrolus was a spent individual. What useful facts did he remember of tide and weather? What therapies could he apply now to neutralize his remorse? Hugo watched the embers of the fire wax and wane in the breeze and pondered the questions he should have asked the absent sergeant. He looked at the books in his open case, at the boat he had just drawn in a notebook next to several renderings of a woman's face. Other facts, more useful therapies escaped him, and the only thing he could vouch for in the way of suffering were the pains he had failed to take.

    Getting up stiffly from the African dirt, he recalled rising with less effort from the shoreline mud of his uncle's boatyard to stretch his legs. He recalled wandering to the edge of the river next to the boatyard, with hardly a storm wave on it and deciding it was time to confront his fear of water, to consider the canoe drawn up on the bank with its bow treading down the foreshore grass. He ran to a shed and brought back a paddle and a float. To counter his weight he loaded river rock in the front, then pushed the boat into the current. Out of concern for the dangers of deep water, he kept tight to the shoreline and exploited the slow churning of the back-eddies.

    A few weeks later he replaced the cold rocks with Dido's warm body, made warmer he hoped by the sight of his bare torso, now that he had less fear and used the life jacket as a cushion for his feet. When they got to a place on the river miles upstream from the boatyard, he put the canoe close to the bank and felt easy enough to lounge in the stern with his legs stretched. The boat drifted along the bank, now and then catching a sweeper and turning end for end. After sipping the wine she had brought, he set his face to the huge dome of sky and away from Dido, who lay on the seat, legs spread on the gunnels and back eased comfortably into the wedge of the bow. Her lips were burgundy red. She had pulled her blouse open to expose her breasts to the sunlight.

"Will you be having children?" he asked.

"Thinking of sex?"

"Only as an impulse any man would have at seeing a perfect example of twentieth century woman."

"And who is she?"

"Let me describe...I see you breast-feeding openly in the front seat of your new Buick, quite into loving and caring for the little fatso. As he sucks contentedly, you're planning all the details of his education, his career, his future prospects. In the olden days the princesses, after screwing the valiant knights in a corner of the jousting tent, couldn't afford to love their grubby offspring because, just as soon as not, the wheezing runts would die off. So it was pointless affection—the romance, the loving, and then soon to follow, the inevitable, wasted grieving."

"So how is that different from today? If I were to lie in the grass with you, it would be wasted affection—no romance, perhaps no babies, and I would be left in tears."

"Only if you had expectations."

"Isn't expectation the point of it all?"

Hugo had no answer to her question, so turned the canoe in where the shore was sandy and the grass smelled sweet. With the expectation that a meadow furnished with singing birds would be their only experience of love, he helped her go further onto the solid ground away from the river. When they were well hidden, Dido asked him, "Am I your princess? Is this mud the velvet divan?"

"The dirt will wash off," was the only remark he could think to reply and led her back to the boat, onto the exposed river so they could consume the last of the wine in peace. Dido had her head back and her hat over her face. "Are you ever happy in your moronic state?" she asked.

"I'm in heaven. Despair comes from having no access to conflict."

"I'm listening to you, crazy man, who makes women grieve. I'm hearing the sound of your voice before I go to sleep and forget." And she did forget. Hugo took pains to post this detail to accounts and thereby assure she never went out with him onto the river past this one time, although she said how addicted she might become to the routine of an evening's paddle, as he had become accustomed to wandering through the boatyard saying hello to the shipwrights and chandlers.

Nevertheless, the hull was completed none too soon for his liking. During this time, Korrolus gave hints of an indenture, as if to say his slave would never break free. Hugo, on the other hand, decided that Korrolus had no more to say on this than did the man whose portrait hung on the chandlery wall; that he would be gone when the work was done. And the work was done in a week. They completed the caulking and in a few days applied paint to the entire hull above its waterline, giving careful consideration to the red plumb line. Hugo watched Korrolus sweep the last few strokes of the brush across the hull, put the tools away, and join him on the small, high porch of the shop. Below them, the small figures of boatmen moved through the yard. The low horizon showed sky, a few clouds, and a pale crescent moon. Dry tussocks of grass sprouted from the wedged timbers that held the waterless boats from falling over. Hugo became aware that the end of summer was near, with fall and winter round the corner. He worried about listless games of chance, the pain of drifting, and put his hands at shoulder height with the palms facing the old captain.

"You know, Allan," he said. "If I was to look at you through the wrong end of a telescope, I'd see you as a navy man fighting his battles far out at sea. And if you did the same, you'd see me stuffed into a comic book. What I'm saying here is that you have a glorious past to sustain you. My history amounts to a few books read and a pitiful stab in the dark. I need something else, a new direction."

Korrolus took the bottle away from his lips, squinted, and replied, "I'm just a fucking sailor, mate. It wouldn't be good to have me sort out the puzzle of your life."

    *   *   *   *

The summer light shining on the boulevard trees in Tuxedo contributed less to brazen colors and more to obscuring shadow. The dormer of Korrolus' attic room protruded like a cluster of dark, brittle leaves. Hugo went up the stairs. The top door was open. He could see a woman with bare legs and slender arms sitting by the window. Korrolus lurched from the galley kitchen when he saw his guest come in.

"Mavis, meet the nuisance who thinks I should know what he ought to be doing with his life." The woman rose to her feet and introduced herself as Mavis André. Hugo replied with a compliment to her character, which was sufficiently stalwart he said to endure Allan's surliness. He added that she should consider making him over; and she answered that correcting the captain's faults would be impossible. In the meantime, Korrolus paced the room. His body shook intermittently from the drink. The crater in his leg gaped with a reddish, unhealthy fringe, like a mark against him.

Without looking at them he said, "Forget my character. The beer's on ice and I'll put on the music. Hugo, sit over by the window next to Mavis so you can look out on the green leaves of summer that will soon turn red and fall off." He stepped up to the carved oak lectern that Hugo had helped carry from the bedroom. On its cradle was a large, open book. "I told you about this, my friend, the institutional edition of the unabridged *Oxford English Dictionary*. A backbreaker. I have to call in the movers for this one." He thumbed through it, raised a foot to the rail, and began talking in a slurred, heavy voice. "Until we die, none of us are left to stand still. We are always on the wheel, attempting to satisfy demands."

"Demands of what?" asked Hugo.

"Demands of the law."

"Shouldn't we be satisfying the demands of conscience?"

"Conscience is not the issue, my friend. The issue is survival. Every transaction in life tends away from the particular towards the general. Energy saved but no advantage to us. We start with completeness and end with a disordered, random uniformity...objects reduced to their constituent elements, i.e., the broken glass on the floor. We've all learned the lesson—the more you exercise, the more you have to work to maintain your gain. The more knowledge you acquire, the more hours you spend in study to beat back forgetfulness. This is the notorious second law, Hugo, plagued also by the law of diminishing returns."

"Didn't we agree that this is the price we pay for being alive, Allan?"

Korrolus raised his hand. "How adroit. How insightful. Indeed, you did say it before: everyone and everything pays the price. In human terms, it's a relentless attack on our integrity. Loss of individuality is the price of healing, the bill you refused to pay." As he talked, the captain moved silently back and forth along the aisle except in the spot where the floor squeaked, twice wiping the foam off his misshapen lip. Hugo went to sit on the window bench with the evening sun warming his back.

"To ensure you keep up the pace, I have a job for you," Korrolus continued.

"No job. No more work," Hugo said.

"It relates to myself but more directly to you. Look at these pictures." On the lectern Hugo saw a second book, identical to the volumes of war books in Muir's library. It was open to a page illustrating submarines, merchantmen, destroyers laying down smoke screens, and depth charges spewing geysers of seawater.

"Next week you're leaving for the South," said the captain. "You have several weeks to putter around but a destination that is preset and one task to perform. Along a particular river you will find hundreds of ships beached on the mud. You are to find one ship amongst the others, assuming it still exists, and take pictures. But you must ensure that in one photo you have recorded the name and number painted on its upperworks."

"That's it? Take a few snapshots?"

"And bring them back to me, along with a folder of papers you'll find according to instructions I've written here."

"Should I ask why?"

Korrolus laughed. "The boy wants to know why, Mavis. Do we tell him or no? I say no." Korrolus smiled at him. "When you get back I will explain."

"This can be of no benefit to me."

"Then be on your way to wherever it is that obstinacy leads you."

The old captain stepped away from the lectern and sat heavily on a bench. The long shadow of the slanted ceiling hid his face. Hugo went to the war book and flipped through its pages, noting the machinery of death, the weapons of killing and illustrations of perverse beauty; he felt irritated with a petty regret that he had been born too late for the fun. He took another beer from the fridge and had the urge to smash the insolent old sailor with his fist, but held out his hand instead. "I'll go," he said. "And I will assume this has something to do with the attack life has made on your integrity, that seeing a photograph of an old ship and a bundle of papers is an effective way of beating back the forgetfulness you just mentioned."

Mavis helped Korrolus to his feet and supported him as he gave Hugo a piece of paper and ten twenty-dollar bills.

"You can assume what you will. But your only certainty in this enterprise is that when you come back, I'll have your wages ready for the work you did on the *Penelope*." He paused then added, "What was your mother's name again?"

"Corrine Haultain."

"Yes, of course. She would never have known George Blenkinthorpe, the man who lives out west, whom you would not be happy to meet. He was a Londoner and a cold fish. But Owen Dring was from the Midlands…and the other one. You would like him. It was Birks who taught me to play the piano as I said before. I play only one piece well."

He sat down at the rosewood upright wedged under the ceiling and played a few scales. Mavis fetched two bottles of beer from the kitchen then sat down next to him on the bench, watching as Korrolus took a drink then resumed by setting his fingers lightly on the keys. "I'm going to play for myself now," he said, "the first movement of a sonata I learned from Birks. I render this with a sugary air. I know you don't wish to be tortured so I will say *au revoir.*"

Mavis leaned over and kissed him on the forehead. Hugo went through the open door and started down the stairs, not wanting to be embarrassed for the old man, anticipating instead the evening breeze and pure air to help him in his search. But before he could reach the first landing, music drifted down the stairwell and made him creep back to the top. From this hidden place he could frame the defunct, soul-less sailor in the edge of the doorway and hear him play, head bowed, hands not appearing to move until he had completed the end of the first movement. When his fingers left the keyboard, he reached for the beer. He took a drink then turned half around to face the kitchenette while Mavis ran her fingers along his neck. Hugo bowed his own head and cupped it with both hands. He recalled that on the worst nights of his illness, it was invariably the rising notes of this music that drifted into the sickroom. Later, he asked his mother what tune he had heard. She denied any knowledge of the piece, saying instead, "Perhaps it's something you've invented in your mind, Hugo. Fever will do that to someone who is nearly dead."

Chapter IV

Kyle Mission

Democratic Republic of Congo-Leopoldville, September 3, 1965.

Dawn showed as a regrettable sensation to Hugo's eyes. When he had rubbed them clean of aggravation, he could see Sergeant Léon Mintou squatting before the ashes of the fire. The soldier nodded with no indication of friendship. Hugo watched him light his first cigarette, then put the pack down without offering one. With no anger Hugo lit the burner, made coffee from his dwindling store of grounds, and offered the sergeant a full cup, who took it and said nothing in return.

"Mornings must be a joy to you, Mintou," he said, breaking the silence. "In the daylight, all ju-ju spirits—both the evil and the good—hide in the shadows. Daytime is best for those who lack self-reliance."

Sergeant Mintou reached over and offered a cigarette from one of the packages he had taken from the Land Rover. He stood up, lit another one himself and smoked it while making rounds of the camp. When he returned, Hugo said, "Your men still belong to the dreamers, so what do we do?"

"Cook us some of your canned meats. I want your money, but the food will have to do for now."

"There is no more money, not until I get to Lufungula. Make do with what I've given you." Hugo opened the tin of cooked sausages the sergeant had brought with him, put some on his plate, and passed the can to the soldier. After they had eaten and Hugo had filled their cups with more coffee, he sat with his back against a small tree. The sergeant fidgeted then paced around the ashes of the fire.

"This journey to the capital is boring. Did you forget that you are supposed to entertain me with stories of good and bad ju-ju? It's too early to pass down the road. Even the army is forced to pay the thieves who work at night."

"I didn't forget, Mintou. Be patient. We have lots of time as you suggest, because no one should ever give a *sou* to bandits."

The sergeant sat down and listened with eyes squinting. Hugo relit his cigarette. "At one happenstance," he said, "my Uncle Korrolus instructed me to visit a graveyard—not the resting place of people, but of ships. During each night or day or morning of my trip into the South, wherever I stopped I routinely wandered through the locality to see what there was to see. As I said at the outset, Mintou, it's a good thing to be curious. The point my uncle had marked on the map caused me to take pains with my curiosity. From the bridge crossing the James River estuary I beheld a long line of dead ships and knew as fact from the books in my library that these rotting hulks were a remnant of the civil fleet that supplied Europe throughout the Second Great War. The cordon of high fencing around it was torn with holes. The surrounding territory appeared abandoned. I climbed through a gap in the metal and went between the hulls of two vessels so I could look up and down the river. I saw no activity, no movement of watercraft, just hundreds of ships beached in the river mud. Each was secured to some object above the high water mark and each was the same as the last, a species once immortalized to the public as 'Liberty ships' but now a million tons of decaying scrap metal.

"I began walking the grassy slope above the mudflats to see if I could locate one vessel with the name my uncle had written on the piece of paper. Having no luck in the first sector I made my way back through the hole in the fence and went in elsewhere. After hours of searching on both sides of the river, I saw the desired name. The ship looked no different than most of the hulks. Some were in bad condition but this one was average. I took pictures from the angles Korrolus had suggested. His note also requested I locate a folder of paper hidden in a ship's locker. This seemed impossible. There appeared to be no way to get onto the ship except to climb up the frayed hawser. I concluded that this was risky, foolish business with the reward only of a few moldy souvenirs. I was about to leave but instead, fought my way through the soft mud to stand underneath the bow.

"Looking up to where the anchor chains came through, I had an urge to catch a sense of what men felt on the sea. Never wishing to go there myself, it seemed a safe bet that I might catch some lingering bravery, perhaps a residue of cowardice on the deck of this merchantman. I began to climb hand over hand up one of the hawsers. Towards the top, my forearms lost strength—but with a last swing I hooked my legs over the railing and stepped onto the metal deck.

"I made my way around the circumference of the ship, then went up the stairs to the bridge. It was musty, wooden, ulcerous with the pungent smell of rust. I ran my fingers along the brass helm and had the urge to hoot instructions down the voice tubes. But thinking of no meaningful commands except what is in the books, I yelled a stream of gibberish instead. Far below, the corrosion of iron dulled the echo of my voice. On the wall at the back of the bridge was a locker. I opened it and took a step back. Hung on the door was a portrait of Doctor Schweitzer framed in glass. Out of respect I dusted it off then whispered to his ju-ju spirit, 'I'm relieved you're here to meet me. Korrolus, Muir, whoever you serve can do without you for an hour. We must all learn to share.'

"Using a screwdriver I had brought along for this purpose, I pried up the metal bottom of the cabinet and took from it a leather dispatch case and in it some meaningless lists spread over sheets of mildewed paper. I replaced the metal floor, closed the locker, and went to stare through the fog port at the sycamores along the riverbank. It was like sailing through a forest, a futile cruise up the mountain of my home, so I left the ghost of the pilot sitting in his chair, stepped through a door leading to the interior of the ship, and walked two decks down. In the darkness of the corridor I saw a faint glow coming from the galley.

"The light from the porthole illuminated stoves, sinks, and utensil racks. I sat on a bench to observe the imaginary clutter of cooks going about their sea-bound duties, balancing themselves against the heaving floor, preparing the evening meal, always the last meal before the shudder and blast of the expected torpedo. But there was no danger to me. The ship was dead still and silent. I was forced to contemplate the leather case and imagine what value a few pages of ship's manifest would have to Captain Korrolus. Then I thought of my growling, hungry stomach and the shelves empty of hardtack and rum. There was one voice tube, and out of mischief or fantasy, I took the cover off and asked the ship's master what he would like for dinner. To my amazement, a muffled voice sounded from the flared horn, 'All I want is braided rolls, still hot with a little butter.'

"I was annoyed and confused, Sergeant Mintou. The gospels teach us that men cannot live by bread alone. When I repeated this glorious idea into the horn, two feet began making their way from the bottom of the ship. This frightened me. I scampered back up to the bridge so that I would not be caught by ghosts in such a gloomy space. From the companionway came the reassuring sound of gulls and a sliver of blue sky showing through the hatch door. A gentle breeze blew against my skin like the breath of the voice that said, 'Who wakes me?' A moment later, feet scuffed along a passage and paced up a metal stair, another set of stairs, and along the deck. A gaunt man with white hair and a stained moustache moved into the bridge. He squinted towards the bright light of the open door and wiped the sweat away with a rag. You would have recognized the ju-ju doctor, Mintou, and died of fright.

'Not dead yet, Hugo,' he said. 'Phew. It's hot, even for me. I was beginning to doze off. I tend to get fatigued in stressful places. Who sent you? Korrolus? Of the crew, you've only met him so far, I take it? Muir would have never suggested it, out of loathing. But out of a perverted kindness Allan would have moved you along to past glories.'

'Does this ship represent glory?'

'You don't know the half of it.'

'I'd rather not know any of it,' I replied.

'You will know and have no choice in the matter, the same as one day you'll work for me.'

'There's always a choice.'

'Only when you're aware of the options. I'm sure you noticed the name on the side of this ship and photographed her as Korrolus instructed. But he was not clear at all on the significance of the *Kyle Mission*, so I will tell you. The Liberty ships were all named after dead men, with one exception. The authorities named one vessel after a man they thought was dead, but showed up alive after the war. The ship we stand on was an exception never noted or recognized. Some speculated that it took the name of the mission-house, which stands on the eastern fringe of the Serengeti, duly described on page 512 of *Encyclopedia Britannica*. Others think that it was named out of respect for the man who bore responsibility for that effort.'

'Why should we care?' I asked.

"The old man mopped his brow with a thread-worn sleeve. 'It's hot today. But I said that already. How quirky things are in the southern lands, with the heat and the border of unknown stars and the poet with his correct and unforgettable phrase: "the sun's rim dips, the stars rush out, at one stride comes the dark." It's the truth—and I should know. How merciful Captain Von Raynor was for his hesitation, or his cowardice; so sparing of lives and the cargo that would have seen us well looked after in the material poverty of the tropics—the cargo, I might add, listed on the manifests inside that leather case. Von Raynor was aware of his options. It was a moment's decision—as it will be yours, once you know what is on one hand, and what the other.'

"He went out on deck. I went to the door but did not step across the high sill. 'In my opinion you're in for rough seas, Hugo,' he said. 'Now, I've got to get back to my nap. The dinner bell will be going soon and keeping to the custom, I'll be wanted to say the grace.'

"The ju-ju doctor turned to go. I held out my hand as a gesture for him to stop and asked, 'Explain to me why a meal blessed by God tastes better than one eaten *sans* prayer.'

'It doesn't. Prayer is an attitude of mind...done more for yourself than for God, though some would say that to exist at all, God requires that we acknowledge his contribution. Since we eat to live, perhaps a good appetite is a miracle. Anyway, I'll see you around and not often approving of your conduct. And we'll talk some, although you should be aware that I'm not capable of absolving your sins.'

"I watched him struggle along the companionway and called after him. 'I'm beginning to enjoy playing tourist. It takes my mind off things.'

"The old man stopped and held to the railing. 'That's good because I'll be with you elsewhere, Hugo—as a fellow traveler.'

"When he stepped through a door and the door shut behind him with a clang, I clung to a stanchion, miles above the murky river and reminded myself that in the sickroom I had once seen a picture of a Viking ship beaching in high surf and a Dhow on the Nile with sail pushed out by the desert wind. What other things should I be aware of to justify the journey? I stepped over the high sill going forward to the circular gun turret on the Liberty ship hull 920 laid down in Boston in 1940, the *SS Kyle Mission*, then turned and went to the stern. I looked eastwards towards the Atlantic just beyond a downstream bend. I could smell the salt, but the flagpole showed no fluttering colors. On a threadbare tablecloth in some farmhouse might sit a photograph of men saluting this pole, with flag flying. In place of mud would be the clean, rolling ocean. Instead of an arbitrary line of hulks would be the circular horizon and small black silhouettes of other ships. It would all be more real than the Dhows or Viking ships I'd seen in books."

Sergeant Mintou took another cigarette, reached over and offered one to Hugo, who lit both with his Zippo. "What are your violent sins, monsieur, that require a ju-ju man to remind you of them?"

Hugo shrugged. "A little of this, a bit of that. You know how life takes us astray."

The soldier rose and shouted for his men to get up, but engine malfunctions set their departure back to noontime. Because of this, the journey to Leopoldville was exceedingly hot and the delays chronic. Only kilometers from the capital, no traffic moved through a junction. Someone wanted special passes; some expected money. Mintou told his prisoner that he had learned not to ask why. Hugo slouched in the seat with a slight breeze fanning his hair. He looked at his captor, the myopic, illiterate Léon Mintou with his eyes dulled already with childhood disease, far worse and debilitating than Hugo's meager pain. The sergeant stared blankly at the stationary vehicle in front. Hugo smoked one cigarette after another, thought of Korrolus' manifold complaints and what might have become of the old sailor given the details of their parting.

Late summer, 1963, Tuxedo.

When Hugo next wandered down the tree-lined avenue, his stomach felt tight. Three weeks had passed since he asked Allan Korrolus if he could borrow Albert Schweitzer's book to read during his circular tour. Korrolus had cut him off by saying that he would not take payment as long as it was returned. Hugo had the book in his hand as he approached the old house, looking up at the attic window and thinking he would keep it anyway. His knock went unanswered so he sat in the darkened stairwell by the small window over the landing, through which he could see a patch of sky with clouds scudding below. An hour had passed when the street door opened and Korrolus climbed up the three flights with his cane thumping the worn tread rubbers. Half way up he called in a flat voice, "Welcome back, Hugo. Go in. The door is open."

Hugo did as instructed and was reading the book when Allan stumbled through the doorway holding two bags. "Yes, there you are. Sporting a good tan? Not quite. Then let's have a beer and a look at what you brought back."

He came out of the galley with two beers, sat on the bench by the window, and melted into a silhouette with his hand drifting against the backlight, sorting through the snapshots then the brittle pages of the ship's manifest. Hugo said nothing but turned the pages of the dictionary, staring at the print and letting his eyes blur with fatigue. Finally he said, "Let's do this later, Allan. Right now, how about a walk by the river? Tomorrow we can tell stories."

Korrolus leaned away from the window. His hair was shaggy and his skin gray. "Let's do that. Let's drive around, drink some beer, make music, and tell stories."

"I've heard most of your stories already," said Hugo. "But you can tell me what you know of Albert. This much you've kept to yourself, like Muir did."

The aging leaves of beech trees scratched across the window; occasional traffic sounded in the street. The air became stale, broken. Allan held the photos of the *Kyle Mission* in his hand, going from one to the other then clutching at the leather case. After a few minutes he shut his eyes. When they opened a few seconds later, he said, "The episode with Albert has not been through my mind for years now, only a faint echo of him."

The next day they didn't go driving but went to the boatyard. As they sat close to the river, he told Korrolus all that had happened with the *Kyle Mission*. The old captain sorted through the pictures a second time as Hugo talked.

"I'm going back to the West Coast soon for a short stay to tie up loose ends," he said. "Then who knows? I got a letter from Conrad saying his health is failing and he has family matters to attend to. I doubt it on both counts. Nevertheless, sometime next fall he's planning to go back to Alsace." He pulled a letter from his pocket and read the last few lines:

> *I'm doing this now because I don't think there's much left for me to do here. It has been my life to help Corrine raise you. I tried to contribute to your finding an appropriate place in society. We've not seen much of each other the last few years, yet I've not been able to pass a day without wondering where you are and how you are doing...*

"It was a surprise to me that Conrad has the energy to travel. But he's going light. His parting gift to me is the library, all nicely packed in boxes. What am I going to do with two thousand books?"

"Read them."

"I've done that, twice already."

*   *   *   *

Early on the morning of September 2nd, Hugo was surprised when Korrolus had him drive to the airport. "Where are you going?" he asked.

"The Caribbean," Mavis answered.

"What about the *Penelope*?"

"I never owned it," said Allan. "I like to restore old boats. I haven't commanded a vessel or sailed in one since I stepped off the *Kyle Mission*. Because of the wound, I saw no more action. After the war I did a desk job for a few years, then took an early retirement. When I came out here, I flew."

"What are you going to do?"

Korrolus sipped at his coffee. Mavis answered, "Allan owns a boat in the Turks and Caicos. For years I've been trying to get him to go down there permanently and sail it himself."

The old captain toasted Mavis and touched Hugo's glass. "Our work this summer has convinced me to move on. In the meantime it would be wise for me to tell you something of the *Kyle Mission* to arm you against possible outcomes."

Korrolus watched the planes land and take off. After a few minutes he lit a cigarette, blew out the smoke with a sigh, and said, "It was November 1942. I was the first officer of the destroyer *HMS Mowbry*, a few hundred miles west of the Azores, doing convoy duty, part of the armada involved in Operation Torch—the Allied landings in North Africa to counter Rommel. At 1400 hours we were informed that one vessel, the *SS Kyle Mission* had suffered an outbreak of disease. The captain and two officers were incapacitated, perhaps dead amongst many. We went alongside and I was ordered, with our chief petty officer, to swing over to assess the situation and take command if needed until we could transfer merchant officers from another ship. This proved impractical so we resigned ourselves to being on her for a few days at least.

"It was a beautiful morning with a gentle rolling swell, a placid scene. I felt relaxed standing on the merchantman's bridge, watching the ships steaming over a blue sea. The war seemed distant. On our flanks I could see our own ship pacing the fringes of the convoy. Suddenly, like a fright from hell, the freighter a quarter mile to starboard exploded amidships with a shower of metal and seawater. Smoke and fire belched out of her. Bodies thrashed in the burning water. She broke in two and sank in five minutes. The *Mowbry*, which was still close, began the hunt, dropping a series of depth charges; inside ten minutes she too was hit by a torpedo. In the confusion and the chaos of explosions, with the other escorts making smoke, the *Kyle Mission* was separated from the convoy. It seemed that in short space of time we were alone on the Atlantic. It was a large convoy but we could see nothing but the black screen laid down by the escorts. The sea itself was a mess of flotsam and the occasional dead body.

"Then with an ominous gush of air, a German U-boat surfaced next to us, so close I could count the rivets on her upperworks. I ordered men to the forward gun and took evasive action. The gunners swiveled to fire on her, hitting the sub above the waterline, with the second shot taking out her deck cannon. At the same time I ordered the mate to swing the ship to port with the intent of ramming the enemy. I remember leaning against the railing, almost giddy with the scene, certain of winning the battle. But the sub was so close she could easily evade us. So we danced around each other with no real effect. But we at least prevented her from backing off to a safe distance and launching a torpedo. From curiosity I focused my glasses on the conning tower and the man who wore the skipper's cap. I could see him using his own field glasses, watching me, perhaps knowing that he had blundered by taking us on in a surface battle. We had damaged her to the extent that retreat was his only option. With a salute he disappeared off the tower and with a barely audible sound of air, the sub dove and I felt we were safe, at least for the moment. We reestablished contact with the convoy, going first to the aid of the *Mowbry*, which was still afloat."

Hugo wriggled around in his seat before saying, "That was an entertaining tale, Allan, but I'm confused. You paid me to go a thousand miles and take photos of a derelict ship. If these pictures were to be your survival mementos, a tribute to your prowess in sea battle, and something to show the grandkids, you could have done this yourself years ago."

Korrolus watched another plane rise into the air before answering. "Here's the epilogue to my 'prowess in sea battle' as you call it, a little reward for a job well done. After a few days, during a routine scrutiny of the cargo manifests, I came to a few curious pages, pages you retrieved from the *Kyle Mission* and I have here in my hand. Aboard the ship was a small shipment, ten tons of miscellaneous goods consigned to Dr. Albert Schweitzer, Lambaréné, Gabon, French Equatorial Africa. It was to be transferred in Oran to a coastal packet bound for Libreville. So besides the war materials that we were able to deliver into the hands of Allied forces, we did our bit for charity and thus offset our multiple sins, albeit not intentionally."

Hugo sat back, smoked, and watched the aircraft on the runway. Finally Korrolus said, "There is a larger conclusion to this, Hugo, that concerns your father and this cargo. But it won't come from me, even if we were in no danger of missing our flight." He took out of his case an enlargement of the *Kyle Mission*, which showed her name and number. In white letters across the bottom was stenciled "Albert Schweitzer." He put it unfolded in a brown envelope, sealed it, and handed it to Hugo.

"What do I do with this?"

"Think of it as the whim of an old man. I had word a few years back that the *Kyle Mission* was adrift on the banks of the James River and planned to go there myself for the justice of seeing her one last time. But it was never at the top of my priorities. Don't concern yourself further, because the outcome of it is beyond any benefit for either you or me. When you next get together with Conrad, the picture would give him a chuckle. In the meantime, think of him as having endured. Some of the others would tell you lies. Now, we must be going."

Hugo put the photo in his satchel. "Did you say that George Blenkinthorpe lives on the West Coast?"

"He does, but I wouldn't contact him. He knows little of this ship except the disposition of the cargo that came off her. He might do more than just tell you to piss off—as I should have done. George is a cold fish, a sapper, a crack shot if memory serves, and now a semi-recluse. He was a partner with Crasson. He would not be pleased to see this photo or be reminded." Korrolus held out his hand. "We're not likely to cross paths again, Hugo, but it's been an adventure." They shook; Hugo embraced Mavis and gave her a kiss. Allan took her by the arm and together they receded down the ramp until they were two heads disappearing in the crowd.

From the airport Hugo drove to the gym. He felt in need of a purge, a workout, a steam-room rub down. For two hours he worked hard until there was no more ache in his head or queasiness in his stomach. The sweat poured. Eventually Dido came over. "You haven't been in for a while. It shows. You're lathered like a horse."

"I'm dissipating." He stood up and took her hand. With the other he wiped off his brow and neck. "Got a minute?"

"One minute. Sixty seconds. Because, Hugo, I really can't see you anymore."

"It's okay because I just want your quick opinion. I remember an episode involving a young lady that caused me to view sex as having an element of destruction. Is it true that mutual pleasure relies on the annihilation of self within the self of another?" Dido nodded, replied that he was correct, and walked away. Hugo looked at his image, standing alone in front of the mirror, seeing his reflection from an impossible number of angles.

Later that day he left to go home; but first he put money in an envelope and stopped by the manager's office at the McDonald Hotel. "Payment of an outstanding bill," he said to the small man behind the desk. "Sorry, but I can't cross-reference it to the invoice involved. But here's a hint. Imagine what a delight it was a few weeks back to have the dusty wind blowing through your smashed front window."

After he got to the highway, he drove eighteen hours before stopping to rest.

Leopoldville, September 4, 1965.

With Sergeant Mintou watching from the passenger seat, Hugo steered the Land Rover into the city of Leopoldville. On the Boulevard du Quinze Juillet they could see by the light of cooking fires the neglect of five years since independence. Hugo noted the crumbling statuary, the broken pavement, lawns grown over with weeds or gouged with wheel tracks, and commented to Mintou that with independence, the civic goals apparently had become less rather than more. The soldier replied that this was the policy of Colonel Joseph

Mobutu, head of the army, who had had little trouble disposing of Patrice Lumumba by cutting off his head and announcing the same treatment for all who opposed him—and that no one should be concerned because soon the city would reflect his own magnificence.

As they drove in, the lights of the Lufungula compound swirled around. Hugo leaned over the steering wheel and forced himself into a state of close observation. He watched the soldier in the back squirm and pick at the stock of his rifle in a peculiar way. Sergeant Mintou walked into the jailer's office, then returned and ordered, "Get out of the vehicle."

Hugo put his satchel around his shoulders, opened the door, and put his leather case on the ground. Then he reached for the small orange radio he had purchased in Lagos and hid under the seat. Inside the jailer's room, a guard pushed him to the side. Another smiled and pointed at the radio. Before he could reach out to grab it, Hugo stepped to the jailer.

"For you, monsieur, so you will always think of my needs."

The guard lunged forward and the jailer moved nimbly behind his desk. "For me? *Merci*," he said and nodded his head as a gesture of appreciation.

Hugo touched his case. "And this always goes with me, *n'est-ce pas*?"

The jailer frowned and touched his mouth with a finger. He unlocked the steel door that led to the cell wing and motioned for them to follow. Jangling a heavy set of keys in one hand, he walked ahead down a corridor that stank of urine, feces, of neglected, diseased bodies. The man stopped to slide open the observation slit on a cell door, then slid a pry bar under the jammed outer corner. With a grinding shiver, the door swung on its hinges to show a space eight foot square with a single grate high up for ventilation and light.

The cell was full of black bodies, all with their ribs protruding like the bars covering the grate. Many were naked. In unison they drew back from the door, fearful, confused, writhing together like snakes. One of the guards said, "*Allez, allez*," and they scurried out. Driven by swinging sticks, they ran down the corridor past the latrine, which consisted of ten holes in the floor, half-plugged with rotting waste. Hugo entered the cell carrying his satchel, case and the carved walking stick the leper, Basile, had given him at the hospital in Lambaréné. He sat down, carefully avoiding a pool of urine in one corner. Sergeant Mintou looked around the cell and breathed out a sigh.

"I would die in here," he said, then walked out. The last guard pushed the door shut with the stuttering of metal on concrete.

Hugo opened his leather case, spread the blanket on the driest part of the stained floor, and sat down. Through the grate he could hear a woman's voice, strident with her annoyance at a dog's barking. A car engine passed by and blended with the chattering of birds. Through the interior walls came a low perpetual moaning, like sea waves breaking on rocks, a sound not much different from his own breathing or the brush of fidgeting hands. With a flourish he unhooked his satchel and took out a spiral notebook and a pencil. He placed these on the top of the books together with the flute he had purchased in Nigeria, then stood against the opposite wall for the widest possible view of his confinement.

His first thought was to avoid the yellow puddles of urine and scatterings of shit. His second was a formulation of the means by which he would compensate for the lack of electric light. He paced the cell for a few minutes, smiled, and pulled from his case a candle he had taken from the dancehall on their way to Leopoldville. From outside came a strumming of strings, the tuneful blending of voices, and occasional laughter. He felt comforted, surrounded after all with a few benevolent things. The day wore into evening. Darkness hid the sordid space of his new home but did nothing to mask the cries of night torture that echoed down the passageway. When the final agony died away, he sought one last vestige of comfort. He lit the inch-long butt of cigarette he had in his pocket. After a few puffs, with the tiny glow guiding his hands, he removed an inner corner of leather from his case and pulled from the lining two thick wads of paper money.

During the first week, Hugo was let out only three times a day to use the latrine. Otherwise, he saw Antoine each morning and night when the jailer brought rice and plantain, at times garnished with a strip of rancid flesh. When Hugo gave him a few francs and asked for bread and mangoes, he became suspicious. "You have money, monsieur?"

"Yes."

"How much?" the jailer enquired.

"More than you can imagine. It comes to me at night, delivered by an evil ju-ju man."

The jailer grinned with disbelief, but squirmed uneasily and looked hard at the barred grate.

"I like you, Antoine," Hugo went on. "You're a hard-working man. Big responsibility. How many wives do you have?"

"Too many, monsieur. I've lost count."

"Then be content to know that this ju-ju man can cause you grief...or he can ease your burdens. But he will help only if the money goes to the support of you and me. Mention this arrangement to anyone and, shwoosh, he will spread it over the camp like dust and nothing left for either of us."

When he left the cell, Antoine looked fearful. But that night he secreted in a bottle of red wine to seal the agreement. And during the months to come, in return for a regular stipend, the jailer kept his prisoner alive on a sparse but varied diet, with the red wine a weekly treat. But to the request a few days later that any excess of food be fed secretly to a prisoner named Birks, the jailer refused, saying an incursion to the north wing would mean trouble for him. That evening Hugo screamed "Birks!" through the observation port. He waited and heard the shuffling of the guards behind the wall. One came to his cell door. Unable to force it open from the bottom, he locked the slider. Towards midnight, after Antoine had reopened the port to let in the general sounds of agony, Hugo thought he heard an English voice calling to him. Throughout the night he continued to shout the name "Birks!" down the corridor. He heard nothing more in return, and in the morning, Sergeant Mintou came into his cell, warned of disturbances and threatened him with severe punishment for any further breach of the peace.

Hugo slept that night in the shallow, groping confusion of two minds. He felt it his duty to breach the peace, to make mischief for his tormentors, principally Léon Mintou, but he would do nothing to jeopardize Birks' welfare. So other issues, greater torments sunk him into a stupor of visions, or "vision" was the term he used the next day when the sergeant slipped into the cell and Hugo felt obliged to reprimand him for his shortcomings.

"Sit down, my friend. Since you're reluctant to tell me how long my world will remain the size of this cell, let me relate a few facts that surpass the birth and death of your entire universe." The young soldier squatted sullenly in a dry spot, with only his boots touching the concrete.

"On many occasions now I've said that if you could read a few words and understand them, you would know who it is that lives not far from your village."

In front of the soldier's eyes Hugo held a small book illustrated with a portrait of a man with a stern face and a bushy moustache. Mintou hissed and waved his hand as a sign of dismissal. "It seems you can't talk of anyone but the ju-ju man who haunts and insults you," he scoffed.

"I talk of him because he's a man of greater worth than both of us put together." Hugo answered with disdain. "By comparison, you and I are little more than rats creeping along the dirt. Here, look at him. What you see here is the photograph that hung in my uncle's shop and also on the derelict boat, a likeness of Albert Schweitzer, author of this compendium of thought, which is a record of what he saw in the world."

The sergeant looked at the cover and grunted. He opened the book and looked with less comprehension at the pages of print. Hugo took it back with a shake of his head. "It is forever a pity," he said in a quiet voice, "that you'll never know such magnificent things as this or any transmitted knowledge except what you hear and, at the same time are unable to verify a thing except the hodgepodge of superstition that follows you like a shadow."

He sat down on the leather case and breathed deeply. The soldier frowned, lit two cigarettes, and threw one to his prisoner. They remained silent for several minutes before Hugo said, "You should know, Sergeant, that I had a visitation last night from the ju-ju doctor who insults me."

Mintou scoffed again and replied, "Too bad he was not here to save you, monsieur."

"I have no clear idea why he was here, except to say that he was trying to warn me about death, perhaps his own. I also had the sense that the time was significant. So I did my calculations. The date today is September 5th, and the moment of his visit was about 4 am. Remember that. There was a hint of light, and the morning birds had begun to sing."

Hugo ceased speaking and looked away. Mintou rose from his haunches. "You should not be bothered by this insignificance," he said. "You had a bad dream, not a visitation from a ju-ju man."

"You can tell such things, Mintou?"

"It's clear to me that the ju-ju doctor has not deserted you, monsieur. A magical man would not speak of his own death."

Hugo took a deep puff of his cigarette, exhaled into the air. "It would be good for me to believe it's only the smell of this place that confuses my thoughts," he answered. "But I doubt it. Whatever the truth is, Sergeant, be aware of what is around you. Evil, like this cloud of smoke, can spread in every direction. It can mask the stench; but it can destroy all your other senses as well."

The soldier took a step to the door. As he opened it, Hugo added, "If you have the courage, Mintou, I can tell you about other ghosts and things that have a great risk for you, but also the possibility of reward." The sergeant shook his head and closed the cell door with a swift grinding of metal.

Over repeating, similar days of incarceration Hugo paid cash for the food Antoine brought him. And to each complaint that it was not enough to cover expenses, he repeated his request that Antoine go into the north wing to find a prisoner named Birks. Antoine's answer was the same. "I don't go there. Guards from the barracks have jurisdiction. As I said before, I will never go to the north wing."

Sometime later Hugo discovered the observation port had been left open again, so he cleared his throat and yelled, "Allan Korrolus!" When the guard came to look in, he lay as if asleep on the floor and heard the closing of the sliding port. It took another week of such opportune openings for him to shout the next name down the corridor. Following this second triumph, he was surprised that it took much less time to complete the list. But it was the rapidity of his success that heartened him the most—because the interference from the guards had ceased from the moment he overheard Sergeant Mintou's voice restraining them.

One evening Hugo had the sense to say, "This man Birks is from my family. I have not seen him in many years."

"That is a different thing," the jailer replied. "Why didn't you say so earlier? Now I will do something for you." Later that same evening, when Hugo was paying him for bread, Antoine said, "The one you asked for, Birks—he is down the passage, around the corner, quite far. I slipped in a piece of bread and told him that a relative waits for him in cell six."

That night Hugo stretched out on the concrete to relieve his aching back. Above the general moaning he could hear one voice. The tone of accusation rose and fell and he wondered if this voice was perhaps Birks, or whether he was by this time reduced to silence or beaten flat with disease and despair. But on one occasion, in the silence of an evening, he heard a voice shout out, "Schweitzer!" That one name caused him to light the candle and set out the first line of a history that would take him a month of daylight to complete. After outlining the first paragraph, he recited the words he had written. The sound of it compelled him to speak other lines recalled from his small library and afterwards relevant passages from Muir's magnificent collection. Later, he climbed to the grate and waited until a fragrance of flowers made its way to him through the stench of human waste.

Driven by habit to connect these sensations to recorded history, he lay on his blanket and began the process of creating faces, noses, lips, and ears from past events real or imagined, from portraits and yesterday's memories of portraits and past events, until third and fourth-hand, fourteen and twenty times removed he was creating people he hadn't met. The next morning, after a night of fervent dreams, he woke with the idea that it was better to accept the blocks of his cell. Because, to his chagrin and regret, the path of his own mind had taken him to a woman on some far away green, and not to any ideal of freedom.

Chapter V

Living Next to George

September 1963, Seattle.

Motor traffic rushed past to the side of Hugo's table. Boats glided by on the other. Ignoring both, he scrutinized the photo Korrolus had given him, noting especially the printed words in his notebook, "George Blenkinthorpe, the Bazaar." He had taken this from the phone book listing for Booth, Blenkinthorpe Associates, Civil Engineers, but could make no sense of it. After drinking more coffee to go with his smoke, he swung his eyes around to watch the waitress with her tight dress and jerky, hip-swinging lope. She winked at him and hurried by for a fourth time. Her agitated walk suggested a friendly conversation before intercourse: a vigil of crazy words in a smallish apartment with tiny candles and stringed instruments playing on her vibrating Seabreeze record player. His eyes drifted away from her hips and legs. If the thing were to happen, he would talk in long sentences before taking off her clothes. It wasn't just a matter of seeking permission. He had concluded long ago that harm invariably results from too hasty a traffic in pleasure not sanctioned by prior discussion—which should include a disclosure of expectations as suggested by Dido. Yet he didn't feel any moral uplift from this decision. Regardless of dreams or hopes, he was homeless and would appreciate the temporary use of the waitress' bed, kitchen, and television.

He thought then about the arrangement he had made in the spring with his old friend, Cyril Ibecks, and the necessity of his reneging on the tentative employment deal with Ibecks Senior. This would lead inevitably to a difficult debate with Ibecks Junior, who no doubt deflect Hugo's concerns in his usual flippant manner, "You just jump in with any waitress you like, Hugo. In fact, the more the better. It'll put you in the mood. Like everything else, sex sells real estate. The two fit naturally. People can't screw on the street. They require bedrooms, and you'll get top price. You'll be the best god dam salesman Ibecks Inc. ever had, with huge commissions and intriguing complexities of finance to sort out; architecture and landscaping to consider over martinis and talk of Hawaiian vacations. In fact, don't worry about leisure. Between brief bouts of work, there'll always be a carload of broads to bang. Welcome home, Dr. Haultain. The old man will be delighted. We'll be like family, since you don't have one yourself.'

Hugo knew, however, that Cyril Ibecks would not long be saying complimentary things. His gaze swung out to watch the tugboats steaming to assist the freighters and for a moment he had doubts. Doing the right thing had costs. As he drank a second cup of coffee and took more frequent glances at the waitress, he was burdened by other curiosities. On the return trip from his summer away he had wondered why George Blenkinthorpe would not be glad to see him, beyond the fact that they were strangers and perhaps the old sapper was as the captain described—greedy and vicious. He went to a pay phone and called the private number listed for the engineer and listened to it ring twenty-two times.

The next afternoon the St. Regis Hotel was crowded with drinkers. For the safest view of the action Hugo sat at his usual place with his back to a central pillar. For an hour he scanned the classifieds for suites or houses to rent. When Cyril Ibecks walked in, he was reminded of the remark Muir had made to him years ago that it was a person to avoid who kept his shoes shined to an obsessive degree.

"Don't start," Ibecks said when he saw the expression on his friend's face.

"Cyril, I notice only the important things. For example, I've observed that you never use a mirror to comb your hair. You just look down at the reflection in your shoe tops. No harm in that, you might say. But in my opinion, it's an investment in image that points to something profoundly disturbing."

Cyril sat into a chair by the pillar, crossed his legs and swept a finger across the gleaming black of one shoe. After lighting a cigarette he said, "The St. Regis really is a shit hole. You should be more choosy about where you drink."

The waiter put four glasses on the table and said, "Seen Cyril's new Corvette, Hugo?"

Ibecks smiled. "He hasn't, Rosco, and a whole lot of other things either. He's falling behind in life. Take note of his shabby, mismatched clothes. But he shouldn't worry, because now he can think about this. The apartment my old man promised is ready for him. It has two bedrooms, a view of the mountains and the sea. It's his on lease. Tomorrow at nine sharp, all he has to do is sign the contract indenturing him to Ibecks Inc. The old man wants his commitment."

Cyril took a full glass, wiping it carefully across the terry cloth. Hugo smiled. "Rosco, would you inform Cyril that I'll be finding other accommodation."

The waiter smirked, cleared the empty glasses, and walked away. Ibecks stopped drinking. "Other accommodation? The apartment I described, with cheap, subsidized rent not enough? You're not even good with the jokes."

"It's no joke. I'm not moving in, because I'm not signing the lease, because I'm not signing the contract. The altered fact of life is that I'm not working for you or anybody else."

Cyril leaned back in his chair and breathed out with a loud whistling in his throat. "I thought we had a deal, Doctor, but apparently not. So let's go over to the Sportsman, have a steak, and talk about this. You're beginning to upset me."

He said nothing further but pushed out of the chair, put a foot on it, and used a cloth from his pocket to buff one shoe. Hugo put on his coat. When they were out the door he said, "You're a property man, Cyril, so tell me all you know about a place called the Bazaar."

"The only Bazaar I know is on the north side, adjacent to the Cedar Galleries. Used to be called Pacific Imports Bazaar, but the stevedores shortened the name. It's derelict now. Most of the warehouses have fallen down. There was talk of other dangers and threat of investigation so the city condemned it."

"Before we eat let's go out there. We'll use your new car."

"Why?"

"Humor me, please. At the very least, you owe me a ride in your new car." With that, they climbed into Cyril's Corvette and pulled onto the main road leading north from downtown. In a few miles, they had driven to the edge of a residential area where run-down homes blended with the warehouses and offices of industry. Cyril parked the Corvette on one side of a quadrangle paved with crumbling, broken macadam. It was bordered on the ocean side by tattered frame buildings. The light was fading. The finer points of detail slipped from Hugo's view. With difficulty he could see a structure larger than the rest, jutting into the water and supported by piers. On the east side of the common stood a row of tall, skinny houses. In front of one was a "For Rent" sign tacked on a wooden post. Cyril got out and spun around.

"I suppose this is your other accommodation, Hugo. And I tell you what—this shack is no Versailles. I get the creeps just looking at it. What the hell would Conrad say if you moved in here? In my opinion, you're taking one more step from the sublime to the ridiculous."

"Actually, I have an interest in the building over there." He pointed to the shambling disarray of sheds.

Ibecks frowned. "You can't live in there. It's uninhabitable."

"It certainly looks that way. But now that we're here, I'll take your suggestion and inspect this rental house."

Hugo strode around in circles through the dust and made semaphore movements with his hands. "There are positive details to filth, Cyril. The rent would be cheap. Conrad would like that part." He turned and gestured to the ruins of the Bazaar. "Furthermore, on any day of the week I could load up the .22 and wander over there for sport. The rat population in that ruin would exceed the latest count of your shoe collection."

They drove to the Sportsman Café without further conversation. Cyril ordered a steak and Hugo a sandwich. Ibecks chewed his meat vigorously and pointed to the untouched meal on his friend's plate.

"I can't eat when I'm worried," Hugo explained. "Now that you're a grown man and your mother no longer tolerates your whining, I suspect you'll focus your complaints on me."

Cyril wiped his mouth. "You're right. I haven't said anything yet. But believe me I will. I don't care how cheap that shack is. You're taking another very wrong turn in life." He stopped eating his french fries to watch the gray ash from his friend's cigarette drop into the beer. Hugo took another long drag. "The only impossibility here, Cyril, is concocting a lie that justifies my reversal. As you just suggested, a change is not as good as a rest, nor is settling."

When Hugo looked up from the table he expected the usual fidgeting awkwardness from his friend, but Ibecks was already saying, "You got one hell of lucrative contract already, Hugo. I don't know if I can wangle anything better from the old man."

"I don't want another deal."

"So what should I say to him?"

Hugo sipped his beer and lit another cigarette. With his first words the smoke poured out of his mouth. "Extend my apologies, of course. But if he were here right now I would say to him that he and I are the same in some respects but different in others. I've been satisfied with a bit of this, a modicum of that. Yet the things he has are seldom enough. It seems he can never run enough miles in a day, never laugh enough, eat enough or own enough. It's a gruesome death in my view. Half the world is in slavery to the annoying dogs who flit down the corridors of power with gaudy clothes and hats that serve no purpose. And only a meager few of us see the sow's ear and not the silk purse. But you're probably thinking that I'm playing the hypocrite—and there's truth in that. I would admit to your old man that we've both been pigs at the same trough. Monday mornings we each did our penance in the church of commerce, bowing to the ritual of buy and have, hoard and flaunt as a willful blessing for the future. The lesson is: There are those who share and those who don't."

Hugo paused and played with his pack of cigarettes. Cyril looked bored as he chewed the last of his steak and washed it down with a sip of wine. "Here's a shared blessing, Hugo, the one I like to flaunt. My Corvette is one bitch of a machine. It's got a 327 quadra jet, positraction, four speed, the works. The broads love it and me too."

Hugo smiled and then let the sound of a ukulele on the radio move him away from the café and into the plush interior of his own car... "Buffalo gals, won't you come out tonight and dance by the light of the moon." The song faded, faded more, then silence and a radioman's voice saying, "The weather today, clear, except a slight chance of showers along the main ranges."

For a moment Hugo was confused about which radio was playing and what room he was in. When they left the restaurant he let Cyril pay the bill and suggested leaving a large tip.

The next morning Hugo was chatting to the waitress at the Carousel when Cyril drove up. They went together to a realtor's office where a thin, neat man droned out the details of the rental house. Hugo made calculations.

"Factoring a small margin for administration, there'll have to be four tenants. So I need two more people."

Cyril wheezed. "There's you. Who's the second one?"

"Our old friend, Ralph Mel-Phesance."

"He lives at home."

"Used to live at home. Last week his dad found some organ specimens in a jar. By mistake he cooked them for breakfast, then gave Ralph the boot."

"You can't live with that misfit. There's something wrong with him. What is it...thirteen years in medical school now? He should quit and become an orderly."

"I had two fat guys in here earlier this morning," the realtor remarked. "One of them asked about the place up there. Didn't say anything about renting, though. Said he knew someone who lived close by."

"I don't want fat men," said Hugo. "I'll get some women to move in. Cyril, write the gent a check."

"What, a few hundred going to wipe you out? Maybe you should consider the fat guys." Cyril rubbed the top of one shoe against the back of his pant leg.

"If you do need them they should be there now," said the realtor. "One of them said he was trying to locate a resident of the Bazaar. I told him not even squatters could live there."

"True," Cyril answered, "But my friend says that rats love the place."

*   *   *   *

Carrying the semiautomatic rifle Hugo had lent him, Cyril Ibecks walked across the large dusty patch in front of the derelict warehouses, then continued on to the grass strip fronting the shoreline. Hugo veered right towards the dwellings on the east side of the square. Halfway down the first row, he stopped at a gate with the numbers "836" cut into the wood and examined the exterior of the house. All trace of paint had vanished from the siding. The grass in front grew eighteen inches up the gray picket fence. Before he could go through it, footsteps sounded behind him. When he turned, instead of Ibecks, he saw two men walking towards him, both in their middle twenties and large. One advanced with the sideways lurch of a fat man whose thighs got in the way. The second was a misshapen giant who shuffled over the rough surface with tiny, delicate steps. He wore a chest harness tethered to the first man by a dog leash; attached to the giant by a string was a small wooden horse that bumped over the stones on one-inch wheels. Hugo took a few steps closer to them and said, "Were you asking about this place down at Carens Real Estate?"

The lead man stopped and the man on the leash stumbled into him. "Milton, watch me, watch me," he said impatiently to the hulk that followed close on his heels. Then he turned to Hugo and answered, "Sort of, why?"

"Just to let you know that I rented it. Bought and paid for with the lease signed."

Without prejudice the fat man said, "Congratulations. We're looking for a home too, but not necessarily this one. It's a bit pricey, don't you think?"

"There are cheaper houses," Hugo replied. "But I can see you have other considerations."

"We do. Milton does anyway, so we're more interested in the place over there." He pointed to the row of decayed warehouses.

"It's against the law to live there," Hugo said. "If you look closely on that pillar, you'll see a sign that clearly reads, 'Condemned.'"

"Too bad. We need something big. Milton would be able to have an arena in there and a stable. As you can see, he has special needs."

"A stable for a little wooden horse?"

"Milton is particular."

"Milton looks demented."

"Actually, he's a certified moron."

The smaller of the fat men patted his companion with a wary touch as if he were patting a pig. The noise of gunshots echoed through the space. The moronic man cowered. "It's okay Milton," whispered his companion.

"That would be my friend shooting rats," said Hugo.

"We best not let Milton know about that." The man reached up again to pat the moron on the head.

"So what do you do in life," Hugo continued, "besides looking after your retarded friend?"

"Not much; last year I graduated from a seminary. The name is Billy Bartholomew." He held out his hand.

"Glad to make your acquaintance, Billy. And Milton?"

"A cousin, Milton Muxlow."

Hugo took the flaccid hand of the moron and shook it. A perplexed frown showed on the man's face. He looked intently at Hugo's hand, muttered, and made stuttering noises in his throat. Hugo noted the look in his eye, not quite vacant.

"I expect no one's ever shaken his hand before," said Billy.

"Where is he a student?"

"He's a student of life generally. He's a bit behind but learns quickly. It's been only two years since I taught him to walk."

"Must be a hell of a job. Why isn't he in the nut house?"

Bartholomew shook his head and his shoulders sagged. He fingered the lapel of his creased, black suit. "It's a long story, but it'll be over soon. I've looked after Milton for a while now. Provided I can find somewhere to dump him, I'm taking a position at the Cathedral in Canterbury, England." The fat man wiped his brow and went to untangle the lead rope.

"What's with the horse?" asked Hugo.

"It keeps him quiet. He thinks it's real, of course. Without the horse, the bugger's inconsolable. He cries, howls, goes berserk, and we have to commit him. They pump him full of dope and he's manageable for a while…as long as he has his horse."

Ibecks came back.

"How did it go?" Hugo asked.

Ibecks shook his head. "I'm not going inside that ruin until you decide to come along too," he answered. "On the far side I took a couple of shots at one rat the size of a dog."

Hugo introduced the two fat men. "Billy here is a card carrying member of the clergy."

Ibecks squinted. "I can see that from his clothes. Once we had a new priest come into the neighborhood. Remember that Hugo? It only took him a few days before he was acting like God."

Billy swiveled his head and his jowls shook. He adjusted his glasses. "I'm God only to Milton. But for him, anyone could be the Almighty. It makes me wonder if the real God thinks we're all morons."

"Make you a deal, Billy," Hugo continued. "If you need somewhere to live, you can have the third and fourth rooms in my house…and a place for Milton's pony. Because you don't want to go into those sheds, ever—especially with a moron in tow." Milton smiled slightly. Hugo watched his eyes rotate back and forth. "Does he understand anything?"

"Just coincidence. He's an infant really. And mute. Never said an intelligible thing in his life. Anyway, I appreciate the offer. How much do we pay?"

"Half the rent, which is cheap. And for a bonus, if you teach me about your religious training, I'll cure Milton of his complaint."

Billy Bartholomew sniggered. "Not much of a deal," he said. "But we'll have a look tomorrow and if Milton likes it, we'll move in next week and pay you a month's rent in advance." With that comment, Billy led the huge man towards the thoroughfare.

"Do you need a ride somewhere?" called Hugo. Neither of the walkers turned back. In a few minutes they were out of sight in the maze of the Cedar Galleries. After they were back in the Corvette, Ibecks said, "How the hell would I have fit them into this?"

"Beats me, Cyril. It's your car." They continued onto the freeway. When they were back amongst the tall buildings and Ibecks had parked, he said, "I thought you wouldn't live with fat men."

"I liked the horse," Hugo replied and walked back into the hotel.

*   *   *   *

The first thing Hugo did when they moved in was to assign rooms. He took the master bedroom on the main floor and gave the three upstairs rooms to the others. Ralph Mel-Phesance was happy with his ocean view. But when Billy saw the arrangement, he complained. "Milton can't be on the top floor. He's too unsteady to go up and down stairs."

Hugo hung his chin for a moment, then walked down the hall to a door and opened it. A single interior light showed a large room full of junk. "He can stay in here."

"A storage room?"

"It's the only option. Clear it out and there's space for his horse as well."

That afternoon Billy went to get his things. He was reluctant to take Milton so left instructions for him to pack boxes from the storage room to the top of the cellar stairs. Hugo sat alone in the kitchen. The photo of the *Kyle Mission* was taped to the fridge door. He looked at it for some minutes then dialed the office number for Booth, Blenkinthorpe, Civil Engineers. A woman said that Mr. Blenkinthorpe was not there. Hugo could think of nothing to say except, "Tell him Allan Korrolus sends his best."

After hanging up, he listened to hear if Milton was still carrying boxes. The silence in the house made him feel uneasy. Before he could get to the kitchen door, a musical note sounded mutely, as if it had drifted in from outside. Seconds later the same note came again, modulated this time by walls and ceilings, then louder at intervals until it shook the house. Hugo ran into the storage room. Milton was bent over a piano. He had his enormous finger on middle C and struck it for a sixth time. The sight of it gave Hugo an apprehension about future events that made him shudder. By the time Billy had returned with a vanload of goods, the doctor's furniture occupied the storage room and Milton was roaming witlessly around the master bedroom. Hugo explained, "I want the piano," then set up his desk, putting the framed portrait of his mother next to photo of the soldiers. As an afterthought, he put the caricature of Conrad Muir between them, noting for the first time that it could have been a likeness of himself. As he looked to see if that were true, he had the strange impression that he had known Milton Muxlow from the beginning.

A week later Hugo found the office building he was looking for in the core of the city. Booth, Blenkinthorpe was listed in the directory as being on the eighteenth floor of an ornate, refurbished building. The main door to the suite was high, with a stained glass transom. The door was half-open and he stepped in without having to swing it wider. The woman at the reception desk said, "Yes." Hugo announced his name and told her whom he wanted to see. The woman glanced through a second door to a man with a balding head, an otherwise tough looking face behind a large desk. Hugo could see a clutter of papers, teetering piles of blueprints, books in no order lining shelves not parallel or plumb; he could smell the dust and see diplomas on the wall much like the ones in Korrolus' suite, medieval in appearance with heavy Latin script. The man wore horned-rim glasses and a pressed suit of clothes. Seated to one side was a young man, who may have been a student.

"What would they be chatting about?" Hugo said to the receptionist and began to pace. "Do you think they're discussing philosophy or music?" He smiled at the deadpan face of the woman as she typed and continued. "I don't think so. George would be saying, 'Of course you want to graduate with a Ph.D., Elmer, and get a good job here at the firm, with enough money to raise the kids, and make the wife happy with a vacation to Rome and diamonds for the mistress. Civil Engineering is a solid career. The work has to be solid as well—precise, unimpeachable, and not shoddy—and by that I mean we can't be changing plans in mid-stream, because our clients hope dearly their buildings will stand the test of time and tide, not to mention earthquakes.' That's what George is most likely saying."

"He's with a client, sir, not a student," the woman replied, her voice hinting at annoyance. George Blenkinthorpe did look busy with his guest, so Hugo concluded he would wait another day.

"Does Mr. Blenkinthorpe have a home address?" he asked.

"He does," the receptionist replied. Without saying more, she went through another door and closed it behind her. Hugo took the elevator down and drove the ten miles to the Student Union building to see if the social worker in Ralph's carpool, Lee-Anne Hobbes, would like to screw him that evening. "At your place," he explained. "It's unsatisfactory at my house, you understand, with a mute madman roaming room to room."

Before the young woman could come calling, however, Hugo had an unexpected visitor. He was outside repairing the picket fence when a car drove into the square. An old man in a brown coat struggled onto the pavement.

"How did you find me, Conrad?"

"Your friend, Cyril, gave me directions."

Muir walked along the line of the fence, hands in his pockets, the sea breeze moving his gray hair around. Hugo followed along behind and asked, "Why are you here?"

"Does a father require an invitation to see his son?"

"I phoned you last week. We talked."

"Yes. I appreciate that. But I was curious to know when you're going to arrange for the books. From the appearance of this place, I should have some concern about how they're to be housed."

"Come in and see for yourself."

In the front room, Muir sat in a battered chair. After locking Milton in his room, Hugo served coffee. "Is this what you had in mind when you said, 'retrenching', Hugo?"

"It's only temporary."

"It seems your life has taken on a flavor of impermanence."

"That's not a bad way to be. Allan Korrolus reinforced the idea."

"What idea?"

"It was his opinion that the only experience that traps a man is the regret he has for the bad things he's done. It follows that we should move on, before the future becomes as big a prison as the past."

Muir laughed. "How trite, Hugo. Sometimes I marvel at how you've elevated self-serving nonsense into an art form. But there you are. Now, perhaps you could give me the details of your summer with the captain. Describe to me the prison cell he lives in."

Hugo related an abbreviated account of his time with Allan Korrolus, the work on the *Penelope* and his trip to the James River. He put the photo of the *Kyle Mission* on the arm of Conrad's chair next to the snapshot of the soldiers. Muir picked them both up and looked from one to the other. After a moment of silence, Hugo added, "As an addendum to my attempt at photojournalism, rumor has it that George Blenkinthorpe lives across the way."

"No one could live over there," the old man replied.

"At least we agree on that."

Muir straightened in his chair. "Go back to the hospital, Hugo," he said in a quite voice.

"I'm not ready."

"When, then?"

"When I'm prepared."

"And what would bothering George Blenkinthorpe prepare you for?"

"He could add something colorful to my collection of thoughts. He might suggest some answers."

"Answers to what?"

Hugo shrugged, saying, "I don't know. George is an engineer, and that would make him a problem solver. Maybe he could make my doubts vanish."

"Your doubts will cease the moment you go back to work."

"It seems the topic of my work is much in vogue these days, and not very helpful. So let's discuss your work instead."

"With the exception of one small adventure, my work is finished. My only labor now will see me abroad to visit relatives."

"You have living relatives?"

Conrad stared up at the dented fridge, down at the peeling lino on the floor and replied, "Don't concern yourself with family, Hugo. Forget Korrolus, and George Blenkinthorpe as well. Your task now is to continue the journey you began when I first let you out of the house."

"I let myself out."

"Only when it was safe to go."

"It wasn't safe until Corrine died."

Muir nodded and exhaled slowly through his nose. "You know, she would have wept with joy to see you out and about," he said. "But she would have been shocked by this, by you living like this, with guns in your house; and such a house, rotted and falling down, inhabited by a madman, across the road from a garbage heap haunted by a demented ruffian, and you quite gone yourself."

"I have nothing to say on that, Conrad. It's enough for me to know that tomorrow you're leaving. And it's best for you to know that before too long I'll be sniffing along behind, tracking your footsteps like a dog. That's the journey I'm comfortable with because it allows me to pass the days in peace."

After a prolonged silence, Conrad completed his monologue with a disjointed apology for his war years and a curious reference to jewelry. When he phoned the next morning, it was Hugo's time to be confused by sleep and choked out the words, "*bon voyage.*" They were never to meet again.

*   *   *   *

After he had settled in to 836 and everyone else had accepted their status, the doctor took to assessing firsthand the Pacific Imports Bazaar, keen to establish the nature and whereabouts of the engineer, the ruffian and marksman his father and Alan Korrolus had described. The complex of sheds, however, appeared beyond habitation, as he and Conrad had agreed. From outside, the outer cladding appeared rotten and falling off, revealing a skeleton of timbers. Sea worms had bored through the pillars supporting the entrance monument. At dusk he took a flashlight and one of his rifles, entered through a crack in a sliding door, and advanced only far enough for the scurrying sound of vermin to quiet. Away from the opening, the gloom was insufficient to gauge the full extent of the rubble, but he could smell the overwhelming decay. A hundred years of rain had driven water into every exposed crevice; percolation had taken it to the core. The fascia, roof boards, and shingles were crumbling to dust. The remaining paint clung like scum to the soffits. When the wind blew from the east, it fetched dust from the square and bore particles of dry humus to mix with the pervasive damp. There was slime and mold on every surface he could see. It seemed no element of the building was able to perform its assigned task as calculated by the deceased builder, perhaps an antecedent of Blenkinthorpe, who had used simple instruments to determine load factors and spans. It was a place only for rats, and, perhaps, the old man he would not be happy to meet. He backed out carefully with the thought that next time he should bring Ibecks along and teach him the finer points of hunting, specifically the necessity of good planning. The skill of shooting a rat dead would come with practice.

After lunch the next day, Hugo put a box of shells in his pocket and slid through the door with his rifle held vertically. In the happy light of an afternoon he could see clearly and to a considerable distance the details of the colossal wreck. In the years since the roof had collapsed, a mask of vegetation had grown up. The great central shed had blossomed into a forest, with some trees already twenty feet high. Birds flew amongst them. He walked warily along the surface. Underfoot the floorboards were soft with rot. Caverns whose purpose he could only guess at in the profession of stevedoring gaped like open mouths. He held his weapon lightly and sensed that rats were noting his movements from places just out of his view.

Using a tree in the center shed as a landmark, he set off deeper into the ruin. After a few paces he stumbled and fell onto a heap of rusted spikes. He rose to his feet and confirmed that the taut wire snagging his foot was a recent addition. The common nails securing each end to fallen timbers showed no evidence of rust. He returned to the sliding door and found Billy Bartholomew loitering in front. The priest's eyebrows arched with surprise. "Did you find anything, see anybody?" he asked.

"Who would I see?"

"I was hoping," Billy said.

"Hoping for what?"

"That you might have seen a man I believe lives in there."

Hugo paused. "This is interesting speculation, Billy, because I have the same hope. But as you can see, it's not only illegal to live here but impossible." Billy turned away and massaged his fat neck. "I guess I was being too optimistic. It was only a rumor that this man lives here."

"What would you want with a man who lives in a wreck?" Hugo asked.

"I was hoping he would give me his opinion."

"An opinion on what?"

"On Albert Schweitzer."

"Why him, of all people?"

"Apparently this man met Schweitzer and I want to know more about that, for my studies as a priest, you understand." Hugo sat on an upturned pail and stared at the silver of the weathered wood. "Does this man have a name and a history?" he asked.

"George Blenkinthorpe, a civil engineer. That's what I was told."

Hugo put his hand on Billy's shoulder and said, "There are two possible solutions to your curiosity. The first is easy. This George character's number is probably in the phone book. The other solution is easier. I know a thing or two about Schweitzer, and in my opinion you're wasting your time studying him."

"Why would you say that?" said Billy with a raised voice. "I know only what I've read of him, but it's clear enough the good he's done...the many things he's accomplished. He's unique."

Hugo nodded his head, took the priest by the arm and said, "Watch this, Billy." They went to the opening in the door and Hugo threw a piece of scrap metal into the growth between piles of rotted wood. A rat twelve inches long darted from beneath a bush. Hugo brought the rifle barrel around and squeezed the trigger. The rat's head exploded, the corpse fell into the dirt, twitched and lay still. Billy's fat body quivered with disgust. "I'm afraid of rats, Hugo. Tomorrow I should borrow one of your rifles, lock Milton up, and help you exterminate them."

Hugo smiled and waved his arms out in front of him. "Think about killing generally, Billy. Killing is at the core of Albert's ethical dilemma. I'm sure you've considered the problem of hideous parasites and disease-spreading insects that we have to eliminate or face death ourselves."

"Schweitzer wouldn't hesitate to treat disease, the good outweighing the evil. But he says that if you deliberately flatten a beetle under your foot, you've a disregard for life, and a disregard for the God who created all life."

"Aren't rats life?"

"True. They are. But rats are also a menace to public health. As such they are a pestilence, a scourge, and serve no godly purpose. I've heard that one day they might take over. Killing them is like removing sin from the world." The priest dabbed at the sweat on his brow.

"Would God have a problem if we turned Milton's wooden horse into kindling?" asked Hugo.

"Milton's horse is not alive."

"Milton thinks it is."

Billy shook his head. "You're a tricky bastard," he muttered. "Smart enough to be a doctor and pretend you're not, I would say."

"Gossip's as good as a laugh, Billy."

"More than gossip, Dr. Haultain, although how you wish to be known in society is really none of my business. So, since you're the expert on choices, I would appreciate your honest opinion on a man who chose a philosophy that favors life over death."

Hugo sat down again on the upturned pail and lit a cigarette. "My expert, and non-medical opinion would be this, padre. In these trying times, with war and inhumanity filling the history books, do we trust anyone who advocates an inflexible attitude of mercy? I would suggest not. What's more, I've had direct illumination of the character of Albert Schweitzer, and believe me, he's as disregarding of life as the next man."

    *   *   *   *

 Like his friend, Cyril Ibecks also had an interest in exploring the Bazaar. When Hugo warned him of the dangers, Cyril replied that he had found a survey of engineering reports and draft blueprints in the city archives. This data apparently buoyed his courage; a dozen times over the first few weeks he drove out from the city, shined his boots in the upstairs hallway and set off carrying one of Hugo's rifles. But he never got further than the exterior of the sheds where he could take potshots without any risk. One morning at breakfast Mel-Phesance laughed and accused him of being in love with the concept of killing, that thinking about it took less courage than actually doing it.

 "It's not just the killing, Ralph," Cyril replied with no irritation in his voice. "I intend to buy this land and build a big motherfucking resort on it. First, I have to convince the old man to see the potential in person. But he's terrified of rats and won't come out here until they're gone. I'll get better at hunting. In the meantime, I'll just keep shooting for practice."

 Hugo continued to make breakfast. Milton shuffled in and stood beside him. Ibecks made a gagging sound and his eyes rolled around. "I'm going to practice now," he said directly to Billy and grabbed a rifle from the corner. Milton cringed. Ibecks made another gagging sound. "Make sure this misfit doesn't come along."

 "What do you mean by that?" asked Billy. Ibecks sighed. "He follows me. I told him to stay away; but what does he understand? One day he might go inside and stumble into a hole. If he hangs around me, he might even get a bullet in the face. Yesterday I had to slap him around to teach him a lesson. I didn't want to hurt him…it's for his own good." Billy's eyes narrowed. "You hit Milton?"

 "How else do I let him know it's dangerous? He's got to learn."

 Hugo lit a cigarette. "How can Milton follow Cyril over there, Billy?" he said, "He has trouble finding his way down the hall."

 "I don't know," Billy replied and went over to examine Milton. "Christ, I hope you didn't hurt him."

 "Just a tap," said Cyril. "Like a slap you'd give a dog."

Chapter VI

Moron Milton Muxlow

On a cold bitter day early in November, as Hugo made soup and sandwiches, Billy Bartholomew came to lunch towing Milton by a leash tied around his neck. He eased the moron into a chair. "You know I used to think there was no life worth considering over there," he said, "just the stink and gloom, the waves underneath singing like voices of the damned. But yesterday I smelt something unusual—like fresh rolls with butter."

Cyril's eyes kept to the page he was reading. "The other day I smoked a big rat over there, Billy. It was his carcass you smelled. But then again, maybe you smelled the reek of your own stupidity for going there in the first place. We've warned you against that."

"You think you're a witty bastard," Billy replied. "I know what I smelled and it wasn't a dead rat. And I had to be over there…to find Milton. He wasn't in the house so I wasted a whole hour looking for him. When I came back he was sitting on the porch. Today was the same. I looked all over for him. Nothing. And when I went over to the Bazaar, all I found was a radio."

"A radio? I think you've lost your mind."

Billy fidgeted with a carved piece of soapstone. "I didn't actually find a radio—I just heard one. It was playing strange music and scared me worse than the rats."

"And Milton?"

"Don't be jumping to conclusions, Hugo. I can't watch him all the time or chain him up. I don't know why he wants to go over there but I can't punish him for wishing to get out of the house, if that's what he chooses to do. Anyway, I caught up to him by the sliding door. He hadn't actually gone in."

"You'll pay a price for your poor attitude," said Cyril and thumbed noisily through the documents he was reading. "I'm more worried about you than the moron. First you imagine hot rolls, then you hear the top forty. Maybe that's why Milton goes over there…to eat and have a sing-along."

Billy took another piece of soapstone from his pocket and juggled the two in his hands. "Maybe he went over there to play with the dog."

"What dog?" asked Hugo.

"A shiny, big dog. It was standing inside the sliding door. Milton reached in and patted its nose. I think it belongs to Blenkinthorpe."

"By what perversion of fact did you reach that conclusion?" asked Cyril. Billy shrugged and continued to clutch the soapstone in his hands. Without answering, he wandered into the front room, every few seconds giving a twitch of his shoulders. Cyril walked after him. "Look Billy, nothing can be done about your delusions. As for the rats, I want you to know that today I bought us some guns—one for you and one for me, both .22 pump actions. We need protection."

Billy laughed, held his head gleefully in his hands, and ran to catch Cyril, who was on his way to the Corvette. Through the window Hugo could see them examining the rifles, Billy with his soft hands rubbing the stock and Cyril pointing at the breech and a box of bullets. Hugo had a sudden nervousness about death…not just the death of rats but the demise of every living thing in the vicinity, including the animals that moved across the uplands beyond the windswept rows of hemlock he could see to the north.

The next day when Billy had classes, Hugo volunteered to look after Milton. Near to lunchtime he hid in the front room and watched the moron ease himself down the stairs, take small, staccato steps across the common and disappear through the sliding door. Hugo ran to the opening. From there he could see the moron shuffling away from him along a trail. Over the course of an hour he followed from shed to shed, up and down stairs, along mezzanines, with the giant man stopping to expose a hidden wire or make his way deftly around rotting floorboards and patches slippery with oil. In the expanse of the largest warehouse and well ahead of his pursuer, he let out a whooping cry. A noise resembling a woman's voice answered. The sound repeated twice more. The moron accelerated his lope, leaving Hugo to catch infrequent glimpses of him through the debris. Where the trees were tall, he disappeared altogether. With a regret for his recklessness, Hugo sprinted to catch up. But he became confused in the dense bush, tripped and fell into the moron, who shook him like a toy then set him next to a parti-colored dog. The animal made a playful gesture and ran off in the direction of the fading voice. Hugo took hold of the large man's arm for support, but he was uncertain of the way back to the sliding door and allowed Milton to lead.

"It was a peculiar noise that called the dog away," Hugo said that night to Lee-Anne Hobbes, the social worker. He turned off the motor to hear the surf pounding the beach. "It was like the groan of a dead person."

"It sounds too horrible for words," she answered. "The sea wind can make uncanny noises and fool us all." She made no effort to stop his rhythmic caressing of her breast.

"This wasn't the storm," Hugo continued. "And for certain it was none of my enemies. It was more like someone determined to argue trifles or vanity." Lee-Anne answered that conflicts were defined by pride and that she didn't believe in ghosts or evil spirits; but she feigned a child's fright anyway by pulling her shoulders down and her knees up, pressing Hugo's hand tighter against her chest.

"The right and wrong of past wars is a problem; but the present is clear," Hugo continued. "With his new rifle, Billy will exterminate life with no regard for Milton and less pity than the prophet he mentioned last week. Like Cyril, he considers provoking mischief a birthright."

"What mischief are you suggesting?" she asked. He took away his hand and stared off into the headliner. "According to present custom, the Bazaar is a space on the earth reserved for the use of one man. Apparently he doesn't live there, but by the letter of the law he can place a taboo on people who cannot, or will not, recognize private property. And feeling threatened by my presence, George Blenkinthorpe has already invoked that taboo."

Lee-Anne opened her eyes and looked out the window, past rainwater pushed in all directions by the rushing air. "I know nothing about that. But the right to private property is a battle we all fight," she said, "about who has the protection of a home and who does not."

Hugo kept his gaze level on her face. "Those who have no home, refuse to belong. But that kind of stubbornness doesn't matter. Outside a few meaningless decorations, none of us belong. My friend Cyril is a good example. He might dress himself in the clothes of a millionaire and sermonize in the church of commerce as Billy does. His moral home, however—the place where his peers dwell, is the common space of alleys, streets, and buildings, but only when the doors are open and the curfew hasn't tolled."

The young woman frowned at him. "But that isn't mischief, for Cyril or Billy. People have no choice but to shelter themselves wherever they can."

Again Hugo looked at her with sympathy. "Listen to this, Lee-Anne. One night I took a flashlight, and led by the moron's sensitive nose, I searched the corners of the ruined warehouses, peering under debris, hoping to confront the cold fish, George Blenkinthorpe. But apart from the traps he's set, I've found only the residue of burned-out campfires, rusty tin cans, enamel cookware, old shoes. In friendlier places I've discovered musical instruments, tambourines, children's toys. But when I listened that night to hear the singing of prior generations, I heard only the scrapping of rats' feet. Rats endure. They genuinely belong. Like all animals, they embrace their fate. With our fantasies of heaven, human society thinks it's above life. In this sense, the curfew has tolled permanently for us. I feel even now like a child with its runny nose pressed to the cracks in the fence hoping to comprehend my ancestors, but each time my experience was only of boards shaking as the wind howled in from the sea. Outside was no street, no children playing, or the accomplishment of electric light, only white-capped waves and the comfortable soaring of gulls."

"Please take me home," said Lee-Anne. "I feel like a hot bath and my own bed."

Hugo stared back at her and had the desire to move his fingers further around to the front of her breast but instead took them away.

"You've scared me tonight," she said with a slight curl of her lip. "So let me remind you. Contrary to expectations, we will never belong to each other, not even for the time it takes to turn out the light." She looked away. Hugo noticed the trap of her dead face and the twinge of fear that tightened his muscles.

* * * *

The following Thursday, the wind rolled in waves from the deep south bringing unseasonable warmth and clear skies. After an early lunch, the residents of the house sat outside on the strip of grass bordering the square. Billy Bartholomew struggled to convince Mel-Phesance that God was Jesus Christ and the other way around, either way being an adequate description. Hugo asked Ralph why he had not yet dated the girl of his dreams and his reply was that he had no interest in dating anyone.

With this revelation going round his head, Hugo closed his eyes and stretched out on the grass. The warmth tingled in his hair and gave him a sudden fear. The previous summer, Dido had laid on coarser grass, in keener heat, more amused and determined than Ralph to seek pleasure, knowing common, boring things were lurking around the next corner. It was for this reason she had shrank away from Hugo, as smart people like Lee-Anne reject the idea of ghosts. What Ralph was avoiding, Hugo was not prepared to admit.

Meanwhile, Milton Muxlow sat on the dirt of the square with his stomach still bulging but covering less of his knees than when he arrived. He smiled vacantly and with a spasm of comprehension moved his pudgy fingers over the grass. At a distance, Hugo could see a figure emerging from the Bazaar.

The object at the man's side streaked towards them, bounding rhythmically like fast-moving waves. Before he could rise to meet it, the dog had run the one hundred yards of macadam and stood licking the face of the moron, who caressed the feathered hair on the animal's legs. Billy Bartholomew looked at him and the man who walked over the square cradling a shotgun in his arm. "Do we know who this is?" he asked.

"I do," answered Hugo.

Alarmed, Cyril and Billy sat up. The man came to stand in front of them. The dog sat at Milton's side and their noses touched. "What kind of a dog is he?" asked Ralph with a nervous voice.

"Do you have a genuine interest, or are you just being polite?" the man answered. Ralph went red, shrugged his shoulders and said, "Just curious."

"Then I'll reward your curiosity with some useful history. This dog is a Saluki, an Egyptian breed older than the pyramids and considered a deity. I'm told that only the cheetah is faster. Let him out the door to open space and he's gone. Across the lone and level sands, centuries before Ozymandias and Christ, it raced, all loins and chest, a miracle of shape and utility. Observe those wisps of hair and how they curve like the scroll of a violin. All energy with little mass." The man pointed at Billy. "You look just the opposite, chappie, all mass with little energy, like a blob of surveyor's lead."

Billy's mouth fell open. Hugo said, "Billy, meet George Blenkinthorpe, your man of interest." The old man appeared to ignore the introduction. He stroked his fingers over the dog's long snout and continued his monologue. "Doesn't he have an intelligent eye? I once heard it said that Moses had one for a companion, and I, being ignorant, disputed it. The ancestors of this dog represent the transition phase of an extinct breed that once hunted hippos east of the Tanezrouft Desert. I saw my first Saluki when I went to Palestine after Montgomery defeated Rommel. I want to tell you something else. An ancestor of this dog followed close on the heels of the Carpenter of Nazareth on his travels from Galilee to Calvary. An old deity following the new God, Christ."

He paused and Hugo heard someone mutter, "Sam Ting," and thought that the words had come from the direction of the fat, moronic Milton who patted the dog's wet nose. No one spoke. Dust picked up a scrap of paper and blew it at them. A voice as distant and soft as the south wind whispered, "Christ and God, Sam Ting."

Billy turned his head. His mouth fell open again, with a stupefied limpness to his lips. He looked from the moron to the lounging crowd. Ibecks said, "He really sounds like a moron now, eh, Billy. Do us a favor and keep him quiet."

"No. I mean it's impossible that Milton said that. He can't speak. Hugo, did you hear him say something? How would he know about the risen God, let alone speak His name?"

The engineer laughed with disdain. "I didn't come out here to be involved in your squabbles or discuss history. I came here to make it clear that you're not welcome on my property. None of you, including the 'moron', as you call him. So take this as a clear warning. If you persist in your trespassing, you'll be risking the same fate as happened to the few notables who, until today, were fellow residents of our brave new world. In fact, the author of that remarkable book is himself one of the dead. Take heed of the operative word—'dead'."

"Aldous Huxley, dead?" asked Hugo.

"Sam Ting," Muxlow grunted with a gloomy look on his face. Billy inched away from him. Ibecks raised his hand to shut him up and the moron recoiled in fear. Blenkinthorpe took no notice. "Passed over in the early hours," he replied. "In New Mexico, the reports say."

"You mentioned 'notables'," said Hugo.

Blenkinthorpe ran his fingers along the barrel of the gun. "Oh yes. With a wonderful sense of precision, the renowned scholar Clive Staples Lewis crossed into the western lands only a few hours after Huxley."

Ibecks shrugged and lit a cigarette. "A good obituary for the day, sir. But I suspect your intent was to divert us from the threats you've made."

He blew smoke defiantly in the clear air. Blenkinthorpe ignored him and continued to slide his fingers along the barrel of the gun. His tone changed. "I must sadly reiterate that Huxley and Lewis are gone, today, both dead on November 22nd in this year, 1963."

"Are we supposed to weep and lower the flag?" Cyril replied. "You're repeating yourself."

Blenkinthorpe turned away, and putting the gun to his eye, took careful aim towards the Bazaar. Ibecks sprang to his feet and backed to the fence. The old man turned and took a pace forward. In a loud, declamatory voice, he said, "Before you begin your insincere mourning, hear this: Less than an hour ago, a madman assassinated the thirty-fifth president of the United States by shooting him in the head. John Fitzgerald Kennedy therefore joins Lewis and Huxley as a trio of guests entering together into the place where Christ and God are the same thing, where no one is distinguished and all are praised."

The little patch of grass was silent with the horror. The occupants seemed fixed in their positions like statues, even the dog, which sat next to Milton. With astonishment they all watched Blenkinthorpe as he said in a growling voice, "Death and glory," before commencing his march back to the Bazaar. Milton Muxlow sat up straight and turned his head to watch the old man's departure, dog at his side. His face shone and for a moment the vacant look was replaced with a profound good humor. He nodded his head and said, "Sam Ting."

    *   *   *   *

 Dawn was a hint to Hugo of his collapsing dreams. The pale glow pulled him back from the voices dripping into his ear like rain in the forest with him running through trees to evade the shapes of taunting children. Soon the expanding light broke through the gap in the shelf, between *War and Peace* and the other books of the piano bench collection. He rolled over and saw on the table an illustration of a square-faced man with a large moustache; he remembered that his mother had told him early on that the man on the book cover was Albert Schweitzer.

 The chatter of memory went away. Hugo sat up and put his legs over the edge of the bed. He was impressed by the quiet. The house was silent on its foundation. No boards chaffed; the rigging of doors and windows lay still with no wind to move them. At that point he had thoughts concerning the person he was about meet, of things to do, the death of a close relative to deal with. He searched for his address book and was disturbed not to find it on the dresser. In Milton's room he found only a carefully made bed. He dressed hurriedly, walked across the dusty square to the dark slit of the partially open door, and called in. The word "Milton" went no further than the first open space. Yelled from the second or third space, his call echoed all the way to the ocean and the farthest pier. Seconds of silence followed, then a returning flow of songbird music to blend with the cooing of pigeons.

 With deliberate haste he searched his way through the debris, through shed after shed on a succession of paths worn through the vegetation like a trail winding through woods. Using keen eyes he strained to detect the slender wires or holes disguised with boards brittle with dry rot, until he was in the central coliseum and around one corner had to jump aside to avoid Milton Muxlow loping carelessly after the dog. Seeing Hugo, the animal veered into a forest of shrubs with the moron close behind. Hugo followed through other spaces until he found them lying together on a blanket next to a packing crate stenciled on one side with the marks, "*Yildun—Deutschland*". Next to it was a flight of stairs leading to a wooden door like those in old, well-tended buildings. The landing was tiled and swept. From inside came the muffled noise of a radio and the smell of fresh baking. He gently shoved on the handle. The thumb latch was secure and the door locked. He rapped his knuckles on the shiny wood. No one answered. As he turned to go, he saw the shape of a woman moving into the shadows. Hugo held Milton's arm and letting the moron lead the way, went back to the house and locked him in his room.

Although he had not repeated any attempt to make intelligible sounds, Milton learned from Hugo how to retrieve the mail from the box. In early December he laid a bundle on the kitchen table. Hugo opened one letter and glanced at the essentials, which informed him that the storage of Conrad Muir's library was past due. With Milton's help, he made three trips in a rented van to haul the boxes from a warehouse in the city. The other residents complained about the blockage in the hall, so he built crude bookshelves extending from the floor to the ceiling along the walls of the piano room and sorted the volumes as he remembered Muir had kept them.

Lying in bed one night, comforted by the insulating quality of the books, he again searched the bedside table for his address book. Outside he could hear the gulls crying and imagined the grass bent with the storm winds. He roused Lee-Anne and said to her, "I often wonder how it is with Billy. It seems his faith leaves him little to go on, less even than these books. I wear him down but he smiles through his misery and often has a pleasant word."

Frowning, she rubbed her eyes. "You should watch out for him," she replied. "He's the type who will want revenge. He is more of a threat to you than your engineer acquaintance."

Hugo shook his head. "He hasn't the strength for revenge. Recently I taught Milton to cook some basic food. Sometimes he and Billy eat porridge three times a day. Billy's big complaint in life is that about mid-morning, faith and oatmeal let him down. I said to him yesterday that it was a good thing the Last Supper is a symbolic event and not the literal end of eating; he replied to me that soon enough I would see a miracle. Are miracles merely a way of settling old scores, Lee-Anne?"

Hugo looked at her profile against the glow of the window and knew that the imperial brow, straight nose, and perfect lips were the visible aspects of an impossible ecstasy and, therefore, had no capacity to answer. He sorted through papers in the drawer but still couldn't remember where he left his address book or why it mattered.

*   *   *   *

During a pre-Christmas toast to himself Hugo dozed off in the St. Regis Hotel. He dreamed of a formless shape, which asserted that Jesus was a Jew after all by chanting, "Sam Ting, Sam Ting." In his dream the voice came from many directions, perhaps no direction at all. When he opened his eyes all the seats around him were empty. In fact every seat in the room was unoccupied. Rosco and the other waiters stood frozen to attention. Only the bartender moved with a slow, disinterested dance. It was late afternoon in the heart of the city, but life had stalled. Hugo felt annoyed with this dizzy confusion and lit a cigarette. The sweet smell turned his annoyance to apprehension. With the fear that it was already too late to postpone someone's death, he hurried into the street with a sudden urge to apprehend George Blenkinthorpe at the place where necessity forced him to intersect with common life.

Walking through the semi-darkness of the downtown streets, he observed how the Christmas lights highlighted the solid, and common, objects of the city. The primary purpose of buildings, squares and parks—their size, design, motif, and appearance—he believed, was to give momentum to the doctrines of the day, none of which apparently addressed the problem of killing. For a confirmation of his opinion, he detoured past a building festooned with red and green decorations and remembered that a recent search of the public records had uncovered this contribution to solid things: "Schweitzer, Albert, physician, humanitarian, philosopher, musician. Born January 14, 1875 (a few months after Winston Churchill) in the village of Kaysersberg, Alsatia...won the Nobel Peace Prize, 1952."

Comforted by these facts, he continued his journey beyond the sharp end of the library and into the anonymous space of the Grand Boulevard. Light drizzle fell. Cold water flowed across the contours of his nose and lips. This sensation filled him with anticipation of rigorous debate, possibly a good fight with an accomplished creator of bridges and buildings, who, inspired by the season, might expand the topic of religion and its benefits for society. George Blenkinthorpe may or may not have universal savvy, but Hugo had observed that he wore Harris tweeds, a London Fog, brown Daks on his feet, and it was highly improbable that the old soldier had not used his shotgun repeatedly, perhaps in the service of public health.

Following his entry to the main block of the office tower, Hugo went up the elevator and down a hall of thick wooden doors, over which flourished a gallery of rainbow colored transoms. He stopped at a closed door bearing the name Booth, Blenkinthorpe. He knocked, and knocked again. Just as he put his ear to the door, it opened with a jerk, leaving his head askew.

"You have a bad neck?" the old man asked.

"I thought you weren't in, sir. I was listening to hear if your heart was beating wildly in anticipation of firing your shotgun point-blank and having an instant rush of pleasure at seeing the blood. You may remember threatening me and my friends a few weeks ago, outside the Bazaar."

The man sneered and said, "You almost make me smile, chappie. Except you appear to be as big a moron as your friend. But enough babble—what do you want?" The engineer backed into the office and walked to a coat-rack.

"I left a phone message some time ago," Hugo said. "In it I mentioned the name 'Allan Korrolus.' Since you two knew each other, perhaps you could tell me about him."

"To be moderately polite, I'll say that I met him during the war in North Africa."

"He led me to believe he was in the Royal Navy."

"He was. But we had mutual interests besides the Germans and Vichy."

"You didn't like him?"

Blenkinthorpe fidgeted with things in his coat pocket. "I'm afraid I'm tied up for the moment. I have a dinner date with Juliana, my wife. So the best I can do is make an appointment for later, although I don't feel obliged to recall things from the past, let alone discuss them with you."

"Korrolus said much the same thing."

"I daresay he did."

Hugo looked around at the clutter, the mess accumulated through the years to guide a troubled mind through the silences of thought and endless interruptions. The engineer began to pace, then sat in his chair. Hugo stared at his face, at his ordinary bridge-building hands and saw how perfectly the old man blended with the empty, anonymous space inside his own memories. Then he said to him, "To approach this from another angle, Mr. Blenkinthorpe, if you have a few moments. We might in that time discuss the nature of the freedom you just mentioned."

"I mentioned only that I must be going to my dinner."

"One moment and all will be clear."

The engineer sighed and leaned back. Hugo sat in a chair opposite before he resumed talking. "Before us are the rules God sets out in the hopes that we will obey Him...these rules being for our own good. We are told by the prophets that our will is free—free to either obey the rules, or not. To obey, or not to obey is our choice, because if we don't have the choice, we are slaves and life is no test of loyalty. Am I making myself clear on this?"

George Blenkinthorpe raised his head with impatience. Hugo continued. "We are free, as I said, to stumble hither and yon, to test the waters wherever it pleases us. At every setting of the jib we are faced with a decision. And here's where the argument gets sticky. If you follow the rule—that is, let your free will set the course of outright obedience, you retain your freedom. Shun the rule, decide for yourself that you're going to sail off to the island of your own choice and, *voila*, freedom vanishes in the chains of some other slavery.

Of course, you retain the freedom of setting the proper course the next time the wind and current of experience require a decision—for example, the decision to shoot either rats, or people. This is a cunning argument, is it not? The illusion of freedom, the sham of a just morality. To me it implies cosmic slavery. The question is: Do we really have a choice or do we let circumstance choose for us?"

"If you'll excuse me, my circumstance at the moment demands that I leave."

"Yes, of course. Because it cuts both ways, don't you think, sir? If you obey, you're free but a slave. If you disobey, you're a slave but free. Or does it cut deeper? There's a hitch here somewhere, a formula I haven't anticipated. Put another way, in regards the circumstance of the *Kyle Mission*, of Allan Korrolus and Albert Schweitzer, considering these in the light of your present willingness to choose the welfare of rats over people. What exactly are your personal choices?" Hugo took from his shirt the photo of the Liberty ship, together with the reassembled portrait of the soldiers and put them both on the desk.

Blenkinthorpe examined them briefly then looked at Hugo. He sat immobile in his chair. The vague color in his fleshy, lined face disappeared. The light in the room dispersed. The shelves and all the clutter of years showed no inclination to impart anything of value and like the old man, faded to a uniform gray. "I really must go," he said. "You are groping around for things that can mean little to you and are none of your business, regardless of what Korrolus insinuated. The conversation is hereby ended."

He handed the photos back to Hugo, who said, "Of course you must leave. Talk of morality is hard on an empty stomach. Nourishment is the one rule we must obey. I told that to Billy. Feed the body first and hopefully the rest will follow. But we have so little time. Someone recently said to me, 'It would be desirable to spend a whole year studying the dialogues of Plato,' and I replied, 'It would be a bloody miracle.'"

The engineer made no answer. He put on his topcoat and in an instant they were going together down the corridor past the rows of thick wooden doors, all locked. Even the transoms were closed. No light colored their glass, with only the janitor inside keeping company with the shelves full of Tolstoy and Beethoven, or more likely, compendiums of engineering tables. Then suddenly they were in the cool air, seeing the lights wrapping the branches of evergreens. Near to the park stairs, they stopped and the old man pace downwards. He said, "There are differing ways to look at the world, young man. Water runs where it does because the ground is sloped. And the ground we assume is sloped because water runs where it does." He shivered under the layers of clothing and at the bottom of the stairs looked back. "Sam Ting, your moron would say."

"Sam Ting indeed," Hugo replied. "But know also, Herr Blenkinthorpe, that both Korrolus and you knew my father from Algiers."

The engineer's face twitched, but he straightened the crook n his back and said, "And you should be aware that my wife was also a resident of Algiers." Then he turned on his heel and hurried in the direction of his club.

After Hugo had made his Christmas gift list, he looked at the balance in his bankbook and suggested to Ibecks that they cut back on holiday giving. Cyril suggested he relent and accept work. The next day Hugo introduced himself to the person at the other end of the phone.

The voice said, "I heard you'd quit."

"I never quit."

"What's up, then?"

"I've got no more money to lend you, Puj."

"I don't need money. You phoned me, asshole."

"Then I assume you're overwhelmed with cash?"

"Christ, the Doctor needs money? Go stitch someone up."

"I need other employment."

"You are confused."

Hugo went to hang up the phone but before he could put down the receiver, he heard a voice shouting, "I'm not slaggin' on you, Doc. You need a job, you got it!"

"You pay as well as you did?"

"Who would do it for less?"

"I assume things are okay."

"Business is booming, but generally speaking the scene is quiet, like a fucking morgue." The next day Hugo made his first visit to the San Francisco Club. The impresario, Puj Banno, said to him, "This is a gay club now."

"What do you mean 'gay'? 'Gay' as in fruit?"

"Gay, queer, homo, fruit—a natural for me and the only club like it in town. I've got a corner on the market because these people have no place else to go." He removed the steel pipe from the door and they climbed two flights of carpeted stairs. The small landing at the top was faced with a double door leading to the right. Directly in front was a cashier's window. He pressed a button next to it and Hugo could hear a ring from within. A minute later a guttural voice spat through the steel grill. Then the door opened and Hugo began an instant survey of familiar features: plain café-style booths, a jukebox, dim lights, washrooms, a counter with shelves behind. Puj disappeared into the washroom. When he came back he said, "This is what I want. The situation is different from when you worked here before—because of the changed nature of the business. You don't throw people out..."

"You throw them in?"

"You throw them down the stairs is what you do. The thing is, I can't afford to let undesirables in. Straight people like you I can spot a mile away because they're all troublemakers. You understand? This is a gay establishment, a haven for queers in a world that don't like queers. Your job, for which I will reward you royally, is to keep it safe for my people. But when you're out on the street and you see one of my customers, you ignore them. No eye contact, no recognition." The owner walked to the door and opened it. He nodded then called after Hugo, "A word of caution, Haultain. The trash who try to get in are usually violent and they're looking for action."

Hugo stopped and looked up at the figure in the stained white shirt. "Another thing, Puj, word of my employment goes no further."

"Who would I tell?" Banno replied and shut the door.

Chapter VII

San Francisco Blood

Christmas, 1963. The Bazaar.

Armed with his favorite semiautomatic rifle, Hugo went looking for Milton and found him in one of the sheds digging a tree out from the dirt floor. It was a symmetrical conifer so he put it into a discarded container, then packed it with compost taken from a place where timbers had rotted into the earth. Together with the dirt it was a sizeable burden, but Milton carried it to the house as if it had the weight of dried flowers. On Christmas Eve he set the brass pot in the front room and helped Mel-Phesance decorate the tree.

In the morning, after the exchange of a few gifts, Ralph and Billy left the house. Hugo declined a dinner invitation with the Ibecks family in order to tend Milton. All day the moron went from room to room, agitated. He often stood for long stretches of time in front of the Christmas tree, and on each of these occasions Hugo noted expressions on his face resembling sadness, compassion, forgiveness, and hope. Given the day and the promise of miracles, he imagined the deranged man trying to involve himself directly with the birth of God. His pain, therefore, was not much different from the sad disappointment of the faithful millions, who were praying for the light of sacred joy but receiving toaster ovens instead.

After a lunch of canned soup, Hugo announced to him that this Christmas day, God's consolation was permission to lug heavy boxes from the cellar door and unpack them. Milton gave a grunt of delight. He loved to handle the books and all the items that came out of the gift from Conrad. As the moron labored, Hugo was pleased to see the volumes he might never read again: Lock and Hobbes, Sartre, Aristotle, Plato and Socrates. He had his helper place them on the shelves spine out, titles readable, much the same as Hugo had done as a boy, with his father guiding his hands. Milton finally carried in the last crate of the day. The volume on top was a common edition, still in print and available in lending libraries, the difference being that this particular book had a photo of Albert Schweitzer on the cover and his signature inside.

Underneath were books that were uniformly large. Hugo let Milton line them along the bottom shelf, then looked to find the one volume of *Encyclopedia Britannica* he desired. He consulted the notes in his satchel and turned to page 512. He ran his finger down to an entry that said, "Kyle, Dr. James Mortimer, Episcopalian minister and missionary from Baltimore, founded a mission hospital on the edge of the Serengeti in Kenya, East Africa. In 1890 he published his memoir, which for reasons never made clear was titled the *Manifesto of Despair...*"

When the books were done, Hugo turned to the folders containing loose papers. Amongst invoices, bills, receipts, and memos, he found documents neatly secured with an elastic band. The first was the birth certificate he had never seen. It indicated he had been born in Manchester, England, February 14, 1936. The mother was shown as Corrine Haultain. The section for the father was blank. Under the birth certificate was a bundle of letters. Next was a piece of sheet music. Hugo set it on the piano cradle, then paced around the room. The light had diminished as the day wore into late afternoon. Out the darkening window, the grim wreckage of stark and empty houses ceased to be a feature of the landscape; radio carols gave way to Bach's *Saint Matthew Passion*. Hugo threw the empty boxes down the cellar stairs, sat at the piano but kept his fingers off the keys.

"Milton, how would you like to make Christmas tea?" he asked. After the moron put the tea tray on the dresser, he stood obediently by the side of the piano. His eyes were better focused than the first time Hugo he had seen him, less the eyes of a half-wit, although what Milton was, he couldn't say. His eyes were narrower than usual, and Hugo understood that it was this mechanical focus that conveyed the impression that his brain was more comprehending of the world than it ought to be. Hugo had an urge to embrace him, but knew the impossibility of getting his arms around the huge body. Instead, he grasped the shoulder, which prompted a deformation of Milton's mouth into the shape of sorrow.

Once the darkness outside had consumed the remaining light, Hugo went into the front room, turned up the volume on Muir's radio and stood by the window. Christmas music spread through the house. Images floated in his mind of a boy kneeling on his cot, watching flakes of snow drift onto the forest and the hill, down which the sleds filled with children plummeted. Some of them waved as they sped by. One Christmas morning he had shivered to see the delicate wave of the neighbor girl, thirteen or so, who came to the door, and with no introduction pressed her red cheek to his, brought her mouth around and kissed him. Remembering this gift, he went to the kitchen, poured two ounces of liquor into a glass then sifted through the gift of old letters, considering which ones had the greatest appeal. One at the bottom of the pile seemed different from the others. It was just a half-page and was signed, "Martin Birks." Hugo read the short, stiff sentences, then folded the paper and placed it with the others. When he went back into the room to see what Milton was doing, he had to brace himself against the desk. The moron held the piece of sheet music in his hand. He looked at it with his huge head shaking and his mouth whispering, "Sam Ting". In his eyes was a curious dedication, but worse were the tears that ran down the fat cheeks and speckled the whiteness of his bulging face. When he saw Hugo watching him, he moved his hands in some unknown expression of complicity and turned to go out and down the hall to his own room.

*   *   *   *

    The first collective hunt did not happen until early February. Led by the doctor, the group marched in a military manner through the winter rain, which made a slurry of mud from the patches of dirt in the square. The interior of the Bazaar was sodden, the wooden floor slippery. Hugo allowed Milton to go in first together with the dog. He went next himself, then Billy, with Cyril far in the rear. Within a few minutes of their presence, the rats scurried for cover and the shooting began. The dog busied itself with sniffing out the dead ones, which Milton collected, then buried in holes he dug with a camp spade.
    When they moved to the main shed, the Saluki uncovered an aggressive colony. After a volley of shots, the big rats disappeared. Hugo moved to prevent their escape. As he ducked under the mezzanine, he heard a scream from Cyril followed by loud noise above him. On the crumbling overhang crouched a bald man aiming a revolver at Billy, who stood frozen by the blast.
    "If any of you move, I'll shoot," the man said. "Your loud-mouthed friend was fortunate he tripped, or he would have a larger hole in his head than the one providence supplied him at birth."
    Hugo put his rifle down and walked into view. "I would say that we're doing you a favor by eliminating an infestation of vermin from your property."
    "You're doing no such thing. You're trespassing on private property against my warnings. Worse, you are disturbing the peace and upsetting my wife." The man on the balcony yelled to one side, "Not so, Juliana? The rats, the sea, the wind never made a fraction of this noise."

"Are you threatening us?" asked Cyril, wiping the sweat from his nose with a hanky.

"You're the smart lad and all, and quite correct—if you take my nearly killing you as a threat." The man swung the gun towards the undergrowth. Milton lurched into the clear space with a handful of rats swinging by their tails. The man aimed the gun at him and Billy cried out with his arms waving frantically, "No—wait! He doesn't understand. He's a moron." Milton took no notice, but dug a hole with his spade and laid the carcasses neatly, with the tails all in one direction.

"What the hell is he doing?" asked the man.

"He's burying the remains."

"A moron has a concern for public health?"

"It's nothing to do with health," said Billy. "He has a concern for animals. He's burying them out of respect. It's a ritual for him."

Muxlow was on his knees, patting the earth over each small grave.

"If he's a moron, like you say, he can know nothing about respect for the dead."

"Didn't our early ancestors bury their dead, sir, with ritual? And they weren't even human."

Hugo walked further into the open space. "Our ancestors not human, Billy?…with the world a mere six thousand years old."

"You know what I mean. After Eden there was Piltdown Man."

"That was a hoax," said the man. "You don't even know what you're talking about. Apparently you're the moron, not him."

Billy went into to a spasm of shoulder twitching. Smiling vacantly, Milton continued with his burials.

"Get on with it," continued the man on the mezzanine, gesturing with the pistol. "Ask your friend what he's doing,"

Billy shook his head. "He can't know and can't say. He's mute and crazy."

The man hesitated. "I can only assume that crazy or not, one of you has got him believing life transcends death." He laughed with derision. "Now, get the hell out of here and don't come back, or I guarantee that death will certainly transcend life. And take the cretin with you."

"Moron," corrected Billy. The man spat on the railing and walked away. With a careful focus Hugo followed George Blenkinthorpe's path along the mezzanine, with the old man feeling his way along the rotting boards through many twists and bends until abruptly, he disappeared.

Late September 1965, Lufungula Prison.

Each day Hugo recorded the best he could the flow of prisoners passing his cell, the ones squatting on the latrines, or being led in shackles in and out of Lufungula Prison. Nowhere did he see Martin Birks, his alleged friend, Louis Morrow, or hear any shouted words from down the corridor at night. When he asked Mintou for news of the other men, the soldier dismissed him. "I say nothing about this to prisoners," he said. "Including you."

Hugo smiled. "I'm glad to see that at least I'm a 'prisoner' now. That's an upgrade to my status."

Mintou smiled back. "You have no status, monsieur. Only your friend, the juju doctor, has status in here."

"As I said before, he has more than both of us combined. But don't worry, sergeant, eventually you'll have status—when you become educated, that is. You'll have so much status that you'll attract ten adoring wives…"

The sergeant angrily held up his hand to stop the talking. Hugo laughed. "Don't blame me for your ignorance, Mintou, or yourself for that matter. Because that's the way it is and no one can change it but you. So stay put for the duration of a smoke and I'll give you new information towards the time, years from now, when you'll be smart enough to read, and smarter yet to understand what you're reading."

The sergeant threw down a cigarette and went to squat miserably in the corner. Hugo wrote another half-page in his spiral notebook, then began. "In my former place of residence, I obtained a job similar to yours, with little status but the occasional chance of a good fight. The San Francisco Club matched perfectly to its neighborhood, being a place where life was dulled by elements of weather, of weakness, of misfortune—or the shape I imagined misfortune might appear. The concrete in all directions was stained with spit and half-digested food. In other words, it was a prison much like Lufungula, home to a redundancy of faces each scarred by anxiety and cut across with a sputtering mouth.

On one particular night, since it was too early for the ten o'clock start to my job, I went next door to a squalid little diner. The neon lights flickered inside, the seats spewed stuffing where they were slashed open, and the air reeked of grease. I was consoled only by the high rate of pay I would receive for the inconvenience of a bad smell. All the booths were full. I slipped into one whose occupant frequently smoothed back his white hair. He was reading, so I pulled out of my pocket a notebook with the pages marked by scraps of paper. Perhaps to highlight my insignificance, he kept his eyes fixed on his own book when he spoke.

'This is my first memoir, Hugo,' he said. 'Perhaps you never knew it, although it was a volume tucked into a far corner of Muir's library that he refused to show you. You read it much later. But with the possibility that you've forgotten or worse still, misunderstood my meaning, I'll refresh your memory. I said in this book that the world is inexplicably mysterious and full of suffering, sentiments apropos to this place. I also said that if our thinking is to be fruitful it must renounce our determination to explain the mystery or rationalize the misery.'

Hugo stopped the recitation of his story. "Excuse me for a moment, Sergeant. I'll leave the ju-ju doctor's statement for a minute while I create a little more smoke to mask the stink in this cell." He re-lit a half-burnt cigarette and with a fragrant cloud filling the space, he continued. "With a quick look at our surroundings here, Mintou, we can see why the ju-ju doctor was concerned with misery. But the apparent misery seemed to intensify his preaching...'We can never fully understand what happens in the universe,' he went on, seemingly unperturbed by sorrow. 'What is glorious in it is united with what is full of horror. What is full of meaning is united with what is senseless. The spirit of the universe is at once creative and destructive, as you know. It creates while it destroys and destroys while it creates, and therefore it remains to us a riddle.'

"Now, in the booth opposite us, Mintou, sat two men who shouted obscenities at each other, then began fighting. Noticing this, I said to the man at my table that it was no mystery that the world suffered. Violence had infected all periods of history and was everywhere. And the only available antidote to this anarchy was a multitude of cocked fists and loaded guns. Further consideration on the matter was wasted effort.

'Oh, I'm familiar with violence and resigned to it,' the ju-ju man answered. 'But this resignation led me in the other direction, to the ethical position that many years ago I called "a reverence for life." In that principle my life found a firm footing and a clear path to follow. My goal aimed at rendering men less shallow and morally better by making them think.'

'Thinking?' I protested. 'The people in here think mostly of the next swig on the bottle or a needle full of dope. And the general mass of us tend to think very little beyond the color and smell of our waking nightmares.'

"I glanced across the scratched arborite towards my friend, who wiped his moustache clean of the coffee. 'Quite true,' he continued. 'We do what we must to survive. I take an occasional nip myself to deal with contradictions and clear away the depression of the night. But I've never had the willingness to proceed further into the collective amnesia. The things I've done were best faced alone, unarmed, with a resignation to accept my terror in a sober, rational manner.

But you're quite right, Hugo, we're all frightened, because the moral contradictions, even of this eatery, reside in an abyss of darkness that thought cannot easily penetrate. We decide in a fraction of a second what it is we must do to help or hinder. But if we haven't thought deeply about the consequences, we risk everything.'

"He stopped his lecture to watch the two men who had just entered the café. They walked to the opposite booth. One slammed the occupant's head back against the wall, while the other leaned across the table to fish out of his slavering mouth a plastic bag of white powder. Then, with the victim choking and going blue, they dragged the carcass out, while one cop smiled and tipped his hat at the other patrons, who seemed concerned only that they be given time to spoon their swill from chipped crockery. I finished my coffee, then went with the ju-ju man to walk up the block. On the way he sensed the shallowness of my comprehension and simplified his narrative.

'To eat slop from a plate, Hugo, or guide yourself towards love, you must have thoughts of something. So be careful what you allow into your head and know where it came from. The carny-barkers of the modern world entice us with cures for every ill; in effect they demand our surrender. Every turn of the eye or a casual listening exerts a pressure on us to purchase their version of nourishment and luxuries. Ultimately, they would have us buy a tyrant's view of the world. And crushed by this pressure, we voluntarily relinquish any confidence we had in our own thinking. The summary is this: In spite of his great capacity in material matters, the person of today is an altogether stunted being who makes no use of his mental capacities. Resist. Take my offer of employment. It will allow you your integrity, will encourage your own precious thought.'

"I turned aside when we came to the door barred with the iron pipe. The club owner, Puj Banno, waited in the twilight. He didn't notice when I waved briefly to a white head that went with the irresistible flow of bodies along the street. The two of us stood for a time on the pavement, smoking, watching, smelling the sorrowful odor of need as it passed by."

A clear noise of other conversation issuing through the grate interrupted Hugo's narrative. Mintou looked up towards it, then asked, "Is that what you smell in here...the stench of misery?"

"Outside I smell the cooking fires at night; in the daytime, flowers," Hugo answered. "In here I smell something resembling myself."

"Is living here beating you down into a stunted being, monsieur?"

"On the contrary. The pain is making me stronger, Sergeant, and my ju-ju more confident. Very soon I will murder my enemies because I know what they're thinking. Perhaps you should tell them this."

October 30, 1965, Lufungula.

For the first time since Hugo's incarceration, Sergeant Mintou entered his cell early in the morning. He squatted next to the prisoner, who sat motionless on the leather case.

"I want to ask your forgiveness."

"For what, Sergeant? The missionaries taught you that your sins are already forgiven." Hugo leaned back against the cinder block and closed his eyes. The soldier smiled and said, "That's funny, monsieur. I laugh at that. We had no priests in my village. What I'm saying is that I am forced to treat you badly, to show my qualities so that you will remain under my charge. This way I can keep them from killing you."

Hugo opened his eyes. "No one is trying to kill me, Mintou, besides you."

"Not true, no. It's only them who want to see you die. I have my heart set on other things, master."

"Don't refer to me as 'master'."

"I will, because you are...my master, or I hope you agree to it."

"You are a confused man, Mintou."

"Please call me 'Léon'."

"You are confused either way."

"I make you a deal, monsieur. My side of the bargain is that I will do everything I can to see you survive and leave this place sometime."

"And my side?"

"Teach me how to read and write."

"I'm to be the master of your reading and writing?"

"Yes. And I'm the master of what you eat, who you see, if you live, and how long you live here. And I've decided that you will stay here just long enough to see that I can read a book and write a letter to my brother, who is in France."

"And you think I may not survive that long?"

"Perhaps yes, perhaps no. But we can start. I will do my best to see we finish."

Hugo opened his case. "I have only one book written in French. But it will do." He shuffled through his library and pulled out a volume that had on the cover a man with a bushy moustache. "This is the book you will study, Mintou, only for language, you understand. For the other, there's no hope. The ideas the writing represents are larger than your brain."

The young man smiled when he recognized the photo. "I will learn, monsieur...and understand. Because part of the bargain is that you teach me to read and also that I know who this ju-ju man is and what he thinks." With his eyes fixed in contemplation, Mintou added, "What would you like for your dinner?"

"I eat rice and goat meat three times a week and some fruit on the others."

"Then you shall have at least as much as that. And one other thing, my name to you now is 'Léon'."

Over the course of months going into the year 1966, Hugo had the challenge of each day crafting a lesson the young soldier could master. And the challenge grew with his rapid success. Mintou had a stubbornness that took him over the difficulties, often goading him into taking assignments away with him, the required paper supplied from Hugo's stock of spiral scribblers. In return the sergeant assisted Antoine in the procurement of food for his teacher and in the later months did his best to keep the general abuse from killing him.

After one particular lesson, which wore away only a small portion of the day, Hugo paced in circles to keep his knees supple and compose the next night's theme. Then, as dark came, he completed his meditations sitting cross-legged on his leather case. Images of things in his life he had done incorrectly straggled over the surface of his mind. He decided then that he needed to salvage a span of time long enough to remedy the errors, or at least give him the few additional months that might save him.

Seattle, March 1963.

Because of approaching spring there had been fewer days of misery for the tramps outside the San Francisco Club, fewer trips to the morgue with bodies topped up with chemicals and removed from alleys on chastened mornings. Hugo drank three cups of coffee at the diner with the purpose of amplifying his presence of mind. He knew that war was approaching and wished to be warm, prepared, and alert. The woman on his arm was assured that silence meant security for Banno; when they reached the door still barred with the pipe stem, she spoke first.

"You're a nasty prick, Hugo. Listen to me. I come from a place where...Never mind. Take me upstairs where we can talk. No one's here yet, but it'll be hell later on with all the foreigners in town."

At 1:50 am the bell rang. Hugo walked towards the counter, through smoke, perfume, and a plume of prohibited alcohol. "It's the worst, Hugo—you having to face down men who still believe the Royal Navy is worth a pinch of dog shit. Good luck."

Banno faded into the twilight of jittering bodies. Hugo glanced down at his invisible watch. Holding it to the faint light he could see the hands indicating it was past closing time for the three cabarets in the next block. Men of the visiting navy would be on the move. Waiting for his presence outside the door was not a peaceful mustering of the ranks. Likewise, what he heard coming up the stairs was not a wail of the boson's pipe in salute of the Union Jack, itself moving aristocratically in the sea wind, with officers marching up the gangway while sailors stood stiff to jingo, confident attention. It was the moment for these same ratings to gather on the threshold of the San Francisco Club and wail in dog-like voices. As Banno had said, there was no gang worse than this one, no navy in the world more bitter. They hadn't come for tail, booze, glory, or any satisfaction beyond the pride of pissing on open wounds and the taste of cheap tobacco when breathing subsides. Hugo had read many times that these were historical British pleasures.

He went first to look out the cage window and counted ten sailors with the rank no higher than seaman. They were all drunk, their faces the color of newsprint. Puj forewarned him that the police would not come to his rescue. He went into the storeroom to prepare. Looking at his image in the mirror, he wondered how it was to take a vicious boot to the head and face a lifetime of drooling into a nurse's hanky. "Never you mind, Doctor," he thought, "Pain is life and encourages good planning." He warmed himself up with a few stretches and twenty pushups.

"Hugo, Hugo, come along, I need you."

Puj smoked furiously and waved his hands. "Remember how much I pay you," he said, then urged him to win, for the queens inside, for the land of queer people, and underdogs. Walking out, Hugo felt no emotion besides a general happiness and a vague sense that he should have the moron with him, who, if he had a mind, could sweep away the scum without a moment's concern. Instead, he balanced himself, opened the door, and moved towards the livid sneer on a face that tried to barge past him. But with one blow it came instantly to form a curious aggregate of blood, snot, and fragments of gristle, some of it flying backwards to stain the blue uniforms of his brethren, who shouted and cursed with the language of the distressed. They all fell backwards in witless unison down the steep stairs, all soaked in the vomit of the biggest sailor, which streamed down the railing and the wall. The repulsive mixture flowed like the Styx onto the carpeted stairs to join the blood running from noses and eye sockets, through lips split open by hammering fists and the toes of well-prepared shoes.

Hugo went only half way down to clear the last of the ten, a young sailor, who tried a word or two of diplomacy as a ruse but had no chance to finish his three-word speech before hitting the wall near the door, already the scene of confusion and cries for revenge. Hugo walked up the stairs and on the way whispered words to the effect that his efforts vis-à-vis the Royal Navy would sadly provide his friends at the hospital with enough work for an hour. And he thought he heard someone in the pile at the bottom of the stairs call his name, and it reminded him of the voice calling him as he left the hospital for the last time, a call to forgive himself if he couldn't do that for others. But he sensed that he would not be forgiven this time or the statistical implications, which on this occasion guaranteed his loss. Of the five British warships in harbor, HMS Newcastle alone carried a thousand men.

"Of that number," he told Puj as he changed his shirt, "a few more ought to come our way tonight, and perhaps the police. I turned a little mean at the end."

Hugo went into the washroom and began cleaning himself off. When he looked in the mirror, at the bruises and the nasty cut just under his scalp, he wondered about Cyril Ibecks, who had money in the place and should have been around to defend it. After finishing the repairs, he looked in the mirror to see that his hair covered the gash nicely and there was nothing else to mar his features. All was well. He was satisfied, happy with the shallowness of present life. He walked proudly from the room and came face-to-face with Solly Pelham, who was holding another man's hand. The jeweler stiffened. But before he could turn away, Hugo put his hand on the little man's shoulder, smiled, and said in a friendly voice, "Mr. Smith, I beg your pardon, but my name is John. I represent the security here. Did you know that my tutor, a man named Muir, once taught me that no matter how great it is in heaven, the people there can never pass that good news outside. Consider this a bit of heaven for you and your friend. And what happens here can never go beyond that door. When I walk out of here, I become whoever I am out there and this place disappears. It should be that way for you too."

Hugo walked away with a soft drink in his hand, adjusting his collar as he went. The young prostitute sitting in the reserved booth seemed annoyed and took a tissue from her purse. She insisted Hugo move closer to her while she gave his face the dressing up he thought unnecessary, even as she complained to him that there was blood on her shoes from the stair carpet, which might be a problem to remove. Hugo's thoughts were on her age and the assortment of men who had, and would in the future, stroke her flesh. In the diminished light she could have been the girl standing at the door of the sickroom, marking Christmas day with a kiss. She was probably the age at which his mother had taken a room with a view of the Kings Cross Station, and fallen into the small cot next to a debonair man, who at that time brushed his teeth and bathed frequently. But no sense to moralize, he thought, to bring the least humiliation to the young woman who dressed his wounds like Mary of the cross. Because who knew when he would be pure enough for that.

Following the extermination of the navy and a further three hours' work, Hugo closed the alley door leading to the back of the San Francisco Club. He hunched himself against the cold wind of early morning and walked straight to the Turkish bath, thankful that the military police had cleared the street of sailors. Nevertheless, he was satisfied with the night's work, happy to be on the path that was best. Being in the spa hot room opened him up to good influences and was better at relaxing his attitudes than a dozen beers.

When Billy saw Hugo enter, he said, "Tobacco, booze, bad food, etcetera are best removed through sweat in the hot room. I don't know very much about sweat produced by other means, Hugo—about calisthenics, laps around the track, heavy weights pushed all the Sabbath long."

Hugo sat still. He had brought with him the book he couldn't finish. He felt comforted by Billy's remarks and thought that the Turkish bath is indeed best when you wish to purge images of bickering queens as described inwardly to himself and never his friend, who would consider it a duty to find his way into the club to perform his missionary work.

"Must have been a battle royal at the St. Regis for you to get marked like that," the priest said in a drooling, hoarse voice. Hugo intended to nod his agreement, but saw that Billy's eyes were closed. Instead he talked. "It's the small hours of the morning, my friend. But speculate on this, anyway. Goodness is only a theory, but nastiness and mayhem is real. Does justice change with how you feel about it? I would say that the answer is yes."

Billy nodded and squirmed in his large towel. "The heat makes me feel like a vegetable and rooted to the bench," he croaked. "Were you talking?"

Hugo lay back with his eyes closed. His skin shone. His large muscles rounded themselves and his thick, dark hair fell back on itself—"hair as black as anthracite coal" was how Lee-Anne Hobbes had described it.

*   *   *   *

After a weeklong session sketching the likenesses of everyone he knew except Milton, Hugo took from his briefcase the sheet music for Beethoven's *Sonata in C Major* and locked himself in his room. He came out an hour later to listen to the wind and refill his wine glass from a small decanter stored on the back porch. When he sat on the piano bench to begin the second movement, he tried to recall the many unique subtleties his mother had devised for it. As he explored a dozen such variations he became aware that Milton was in the room and turned to see what he was doing. The moron was standing in one spot on the floor, arms dangling at his side. He had about him an attitude of dumb, persistent curiosity that gave him look of partial normality. His grunts were timed to pauses in the music, like someone posing a string of questions designed to interfere. Suddenly, Hugo resented his presence, felt less tolerant of his affliction. It was a feeling Conrad must have had, of being trapped by duty, burdened by the futility of tending to a body condemned to languish and die. Looking again, he concluded that Milton would probably live, but never achieve sanity. The pungent odor of his body was not the result of slothful or even normal neglect, no more than the swiveling, contrary motion of his head and eyes was the product of ordinary ignorance. Just as well that he remain in the safe zone of hibernation, mind in abeyance and sheltered by the opaque glass of stupefaction, which absorbed the pressures of life without shattering.

Hugo got up and sat the moron firmly on the piano bench. Taking first one and the other of his two hands and putting their fingers on the keys, he painstakingly sounded out in slow but perfect time the rising notes of his mother's sonata. Afterwards Milton went down the hall to lie down on his makeshift bed with eyes closed. Hugo had an inspiration and went early the next day to the outer edge of the north beach to sketch Milton playing at the Steinway.

*   *   *   *

Through the days of winter when there was nothing to do, Hugo often went alone to the St. Regis Hotel. One day, after a drink or two he imagined the polished door in the Bazaar opening and seeing the man with the pistol, the dog's master, Billy's person of interest and his too, because Blenkinthorpe was the man standing fifth from the left next to Allan Korrolus in the reassembled photo on his dresser. That night, after the moron's piano lesson, Hugo was alone and had no interest in going to the gym. Since the weather had been dry and the Bazaar not fouled with rainwater, he dressed a second time in good clothes, took his flashlight, and found his way back past the snares to the polished door. At the foot of the stairs he heard music and a singing voice. He smiled because they were the same words that had issued from the radio next to where his beautiful mother, Corrine, prepared the food. The lyrics and the tune were clear in his head, as was the memory of his father strutting into the kitchen to turn the radio off before he commenced the broadcast of Beethoven from his own superior machine.

The music continued and became louder. When he had marched to the top step, he was not surprised to see the door already open. A woman blocked the entrance and asked him a question. Her voice was stern and gave Hugo a shiver of fear, because it was not the pleasant soprano of his mother and was tainted by a foreign accent. "Are you one of the armed men who have been wandering through the sheds?" she asked.

"I am, Madame. The purpose for my visits is to kill rats—as a precaution, you understand."

"There are many in the world who would protest such a slaughter."

"Yes," Hugo replied, "but I would not be one of them."

"Apparently not. Anyway, George told you not to come back."

"Most of the time I come to retrieve the moron. He has no idea of wrongs or rights, not a clue about his own shoes, far less private property."

"As his friend, are you not responsible to see he doesn't come in here?"

"No, because he's not a friend."

"And the others?"

"Adversaries. Acquaintances. People of interest. Billy, the priest, calls your Mr. Blenkinthorpe 'a person of interest' because it's rumored he once met Albert."

"Albert?"

"Schweitzer."

The woman turned away as if she were going back through the polished door. "He never did, you know."

"Did what?" asked Hugo.

"Meet Albert Schweitzer. If he said so don't believe him. He'll have you believing that's how you know the name."

"Whose name?"

"Blenkinthorpe, your person of interest. My, my, you are thick."

Hugo nodded and felt the brow of his head going clammy. The woman backed into the arch of the doorway. "You will have a bad episode sooner or later. What do I call you?"

"Hugo Haultain."

The woman gestured for him to come in then said, "I don't recall George mentioning a priest named Billy…even as a person of interest."

When Hugo was at the door she stood aside. Hugo took a step forward and partially into the suite. The woman put up her hand. "I am George's wife, Juliana. Please wait here."

As she left the room, Hugo shuffled his feet and began to account for the sensations in front of him. He could not hear the usual sounds of the Bazaar: The creaking wood, the wind, the water slapping on the piles and rocks, suggesting that the apartment was built on a firm foundation and of sound material. The furnishings gave the appearance of high quality. The art on the wall matched the room's general appearance, yet was aggressive and stopped casual thought. When Juliana returned and gestured for him to follow, he could see that the main salon had high walls rising into darkness as if capped by a night sky. The walls were light gray, made lighter by the dark sheen of wainscoting Hugo guessed had been milled from tropical hardwood. Overall, the room had an aristocratic charm and put him in mind of the grand salons in which the lords of *War and Peace* seduced their mistresses during the all-too-few moments of privacy Tolstoy allowed them.

The man from the engineering firm sat rigid in an armchair, paying attention only to his dog. Hugo anticipated that in the ensuing conversation, his host would purvey well-conceived ideals backed by solid syllogisms after the habit of his profession. Yet even in the security of home, George Blenkinthorpe had a coarse, peculiar face, with much the same moronic look that disfigured Milton Muxlow. A polished revolver rested on a side table, beside which lay the velvet-haired dog. At first the old man said nothing to Hugo but stared at him with narrow eyes.

"I won't pretend to offer a serious introduction, sir," Hugo said after awkward moments. "That would be a bit phony given the circumstances. My purpose for the visit is that last summer I met a man who said he knew you from the war. I found the association appealing because I have an academic interest in armed conflict and a particular fascination with the concept of one man mutilating another, up close or from a distance. It's an art form, I think, to multiply this behavior ten thousand fold into the mass murder of pitched battle. Apparently my father was involved in this picturesque madness, in North Africa I believe, though he refused say much about it."

Blenkinthorpe frowned, stroked the dog's head, then said, "The formality of your speech makes you sound as big a weasel as I remember you. I take it that you're also one of the boneheads who still come to shoot rats in the sheds and otherwise disturbs Juliana with your incursions."

"Actually, I prefer killing things with my fists," Hugo replied.

"Who said anything about killing?" said Blenkinthorpe. "I only mentioned shooting. Shooting can also mean missing what you aim for. It can mean the failure of one form of mutilation and consideration of the other, more personal kind you alluded to, like bayoneting your enemy in the throat or snapping the heads off animals with your bare hands, if that's what you prefer...although some would argue against the resulting inefficiency."

The man's coarse voice clashed with the sound of crystal touched against crystal as the woman at the sideboard poured the cocktails from decanter to glass in a flawless stream, then offered them on a tray. Blenkinthorpe took one and sipped at it. Hugo did the same. After wiping his mouth, he said, "I'm a bit fuzzy myself on the ethics of killing, or of laying traps such as those in the sheds—traps I suspect you put there. But murder is a thought that passes frequently through my mind when I think of what some people have done. Death and annihilation."

"I would argue that you know little about either. You would be one of those people who spoil Armistice Day with fake poppies and platitudes. A true memory of death comes only to those who were at Ypres, Gallipoli, Dieppe, or Kasserine."

He put his hand down to pat the dog. "Now, about our alleged acquaintance."

Hugo handed him the envelope. Blenkinthorpe laid its contents on the tabletop and for some time stared at the photo of the *Kyle Mission*. Then he turned it over and examined the name printed on the back. To Hugo it seemed the engineer had the face of a man teetering on emotional fences—disturbed by an unwelcome remorse or bothered by a nuisance. After a time had passed he put the photo back in the envelope and asked, "Who sent you along with this?"

"No one. I came myself."

Blenkinthorpe shook his head vigorously. "Where did you meet him?"

"Meet who?"

Blenkinthorpe tapped the words printed on the photo. "Schweitzer, certainly not the pestilential Korrolus, whose ship this was and whose name you mentioned on the telephone, and again at my office. I believe he died years ago, or that is my hope."

The wind moaned outside. Hugo let the drink go slowly down his throat, then said, "You seem to have a dislike for Allan Korrolus."

Blenkinthorpe said nothing and sipped at his drink. After a few minutes he went to the window and said, "I want to keep this photo. I promise you I won't destroy it and in time you can have it back."

"In time, yes," replied Hugo. They talked little more than this. When Juliana showed him to the door, Hugo felt a reluctance to set forth into the stinking decay of the sheds. Before he had gone ten feet on the mezzanine, Blenkinthorpe was at the door calling after him, "You should have some concern that the moron has been in the sheds many times—alone."

The door closed and Hugo was quickly down the stairs. The interior of the Bazaar shook once more with the resumption of gales; water dripped from the wood as the winter rain streamed in through a multitude of holes. He was soaking wet before reaching the sliding door.

Lufungula, October 29, 1965.

According to Hugo's entries in the spiral notebook, after fifty-five days had passed in Lufungula, a man in civilian clothes came to his cell. He put his prisoner in arm shackles and escorted him outside to a black Fiat. They drove for fifteen minutes and parked outside a large bungalow near Stanley Pool. There were no signs or markings to indicate its official identity. Men in civilian clothes put him in a windowless room and asked who he was and why he had crossed into the Congo without papers. The same man took him back to the prison. On the journey out and back, soldiers rode with him in the back seat and laughed at his jokes. In the days to follow, on random mornings, the same man came to Lufungula and with the escort of two guards, rode with him to the building next to the river. Hugo learned from one of the guards that the place was referred to on the street as the "house of interrogation". On each successive visit Hugo was asked questions that increased in number, became longer, specifically oriented to his habits, but less rational. One day just before Christmas, when his answers displeased the interrogator, he was beaten with fists to the head, and kicked in the knees.

After a month had passed, this journey and the abuse became a daily routine. About the sessions of interrogation, Hugo concerned himself with two specific details. The first was that the content of the questions seemed to be entirely peripheral to the circumstances of his capture. The second was that each session saw an increase in violence. When he left the ministry late each afternoon he was barely able to walk. His knees were swollen from the kicks, his face cut and bleeding.

At first he was certain the charade had no value beyond the fact that the results of the abuse might be a graphic warning to others. If that were the case, it seemed more reasonable to put in a good hour's torture and go home. As he lay awake in the dungeon of his cell he wondered if any part of this situation had a lesson greater than mere suffering. He rubbed his knees and used the few bandages he had to stop the seepage of fluids from numerous breaks in his skin. Each time he did this, he let the annoyance of the discomfort rouse him to reexamine the events in the hope of seeing a clear purpose.

The conclusion he reached was not puzzling or difficult. He chastised himself for being slow, for being too much concerned with trivialities. Long before now Conrad would have parsed out the essential and well documented elements—it was a known fact that those who mutilate and murder must justify it with logic, must make their inhumanity appear normal, inevitable, desirable. Hugo's tormentors, probably not realizing the brilliance of their technique, took it one step further. By gradual steps they decreased the value of each line of questioning with the aim of reaching the zero point. To a question of absolute triviality, and therefore of zero value, there could be no proper answer. And a man who, day in and day out, over weeks and months was hostile to the point where he would not protect his life with a proper answer, was an enemy who deserved consequences.

With the possibility of self-debate also reduced to nil, on his return to the cell each afternoon he had to do nothing but collapse inward from the door, sometimes assisted by Antoine. He would sit on the leather case with the cool of the wall relieving the soreness in his back and continue his reconstruction of history. This chore required none of his sorrow, only that his memories flow into the solitudes separating day from night, between the pain of torture and its absence. Time wore on. As each day faded from the grate and the dark became entire, he would ignite the candle and imagine the flame being the San Juan Beacon visible from the window of his childhood home, blinking out to sea as a caution to ships. As he tried to sleep, he would let the light and the growling horn prepare him for the woman's recurring incantation that caused him more grief than his wounds. Each night with no exceptions the voice from the stones said, "Hugo, let me help you." Realizing no help could reach him, he stretched out, hoping the cool floor might reduce his fever.

Seattle, early spring 1964.

The decrepit facade of the Bazaar seemed frozen in winter shadow. As Hugo went across the square he felt the cold sting of this and other incongruities. The wharfs in front of him had no ships. Strange to have a boatyard in the dry middle of the continent, ringed with the stubble of wheat fields and only a shallow river to float the *Penelope*, but deep water here, just beyond the sheds and no boats, not even a scow for hauling away rubble. Juliana stood next to the rotting pillars.

"George is inside somewhere. It's cold today, don't you think? We all feel the cold these days. It lingers well past the season. But it's worse for me. I can still see the masonry of the seawall where I played as a child next to the mosque in Algiers, the day the Legion shelled the villa and my relatives were killed. Only occasionally do I remember the eyes of my mother and her tears reflecting the arc of the ridge. Most times I see only the city dwindling to uplands with everything obscured by mist and the rheum of tears. I will be dead soon. Perhaps tonight."

Hugo looked into her eyes and said, "It'll come to death soon enough, Juliana. Have you been home recently?"

"No. We had planned to go a few years ago but were put off by the nuisance of the revolution."

"It would be better now?"

"Independence was a mixed blessing, perhaps no blessing at all. Rulers are a passing fancy. The streets will always be poor. Heat rules in a sinister way. It disintegrates the land. You should travel to Africa, Hugo, just to feel the sun bake your flesh. In the country south of the High Atlas, people are stooped like figurines and live in a bowl of dust. In the Sahara, the greatest of all deserts, water is a balm."

They went through the little gap in the sliding door. Hugo shivered in the damp air. "My dear George," Juliana called, trying to project her voice into the replication of woods. There was no echo to her call. The tree trunks, branches, and undergrowth absorbed the disturbance and replied with a bird's song and the distinct rustling of bushes. Hugo expected the old sapper to emerge panting and sweating from laying his traps. Instead, the moron lurched along a grease-covered trail, dragging a timber behind him like dry kindling, followed closely by the Saluki.

"We've been looking for you, Milton," said Juliana and took his arm. Together they made their way further into the sheds to an opening where the roof was still intact and the dampness underfoot less. Hugo could see solid boards. On this space were wooden chairs and a folding table over which cards were spread. The engineer was warmly dressed in a wool sweater over his tweeds. An insulated bottle sat next to his elbow.

"The dog stays in the sheds these days," he said, seeming to address his wife and not Hugo. "But I don't recall giving you an invitation. But now that you're here you should consider this. It seems like a hundred years that Milton has been wandering around this forest and evading the traps as if they didn't exist. And it is much longer since I bought this museum and set them out as a protection. Let me give you one fact before you leave, a fact that is rife with irony and the self-evident. The Morse brothers were the last useful occupants before me. After the war they had a shop in one small shed on the north side where they restored a series of Mercedes Benz limousines. Prior to the shed collapsing, their final effort was to refurbish an armored staff car, allegedly used by the Nazis. So what is my point?

"The Third Reich rotted away in ten years but was meant to last a thousand, or simply put, ten times the age of the shed that the brothers let turn to dust and thereby put an end to their livelihood. Some structures in England are already that old and still producing products of value. That's a bit like saying the obvious—that rock maintains its integrity longer than wood, or pride. There are those who succeed at postponing the inevitable. This universal struggle gives the human perspective a quaint depth, don't you think? As a child I was oblivious to the age of stone walls I climbed over, whose Saxon masons, I read later, had given a perfunctory salute to William the Conqueror as he rode by."

Blenkinthorpe filled a demitasse with coffee from the insulated bottle. He took a drink, cleared his throat, and for the first time spoke directly to Hugo. "The moron is useful. That's why I tolerate him and not you—or the fat priest and his tiresome questions. The other day, Milton was sitting next to Juliana on an upturned keg watching me trying to get my Royal Enfield to start. Occasionally, he would shoot out a finger and grunt. I almost know what he's trying to tell me, that it must be the fuel or the carburetor."

"Sam Ting," said the moron and hung his large head.

"Quite right," said the engineer. "But where is the defect?"

Chapter VIII

Middle March

Through the rest of the winter, Hugo used the mornings to hunt the subspecies of rats that emerged to rule the north end of the Bazaar. He did this out of boredom, not from any desire to assist Morley Ibecks and his son in their land speculations, or Billy in his quest to rid the world of sin. On one such morning, he lay awake, quite warm under a single sheet, thinking of the alteration he was making to the process of evolution. He was uneasy with it and stared at the dark rectangle of open window to deflect his thoughts elsewhere.

After brewing coffee at seven thirty, Billy informed him that the breeze blowing early from the south was real spring air, not the death wind of the previous November. And to this regeneration of weather, he said, the animals of the forest would respond by running, flitting, and prancing through the undergrowth already thickening in the rising sun. Hugo replied that he was not much concerned with spring and warmth. Temperature was only a matter of a touch on the skin, whether ice cold or pleasant for lounging. Why would anyone wish for hot sunshine when the poison of human life can be purged faster in the spa? As for the animals of the forest, they were concerned with none of this, even if spring would be death to some, regardless of their prancing or flitting. Billy and Cyril would see to that.

He turned to Mel-Phesance. "Is it because I'm losing touch, Ralph? Am I lacking in Cyril's simplicity—who never misses a wink over the misery of others?"

Ralph shrugged his shoulders and remained silent. Hugo was worried by this condition so added, "Are you going out with the girl of your dreams yet? No? The season is changing to spring."

The next morning, an unusually warm March day, just as the faint crimson of dawn made walking safe, Hugo slipped through the doors and into the Bazaar. The greenery dripped with the night dew. The tops of trees poking through the ruined roof caught the first light coming over the clouds. He climbed the stairs to the mezzanine and surveyed the wreckage of the largest warehouse. The disintegrating spars fed the new life of undergrowth, through which baby rats would have pranced and flitted in a springtime dance if their moms and dads (together with all the parent rats of this territory) had not been dropped head first into their tiny graves by the moron. Hugo sat down on a barrel to consider the impossibility that burial of dead things could be a ritual of equilibrium for a man with no more sense of his mortality than the animals he laid to rest. Likewise, Milton would have no comprehension of the violence, misery and impoverishment that spawned the conditions necessary for such rituals to exist. He would never cherish Saturday night at the club as Hugo did, with the prancing and flitting of the queens on one side, and on the other, the awe-inspiring howl of pain. Just thinking it made him feel giddy. He tapped his feet on the floor. With no thought to words, he crooned:

"A glass of wine in Lichtenstein,
A red rose for a rover."

More phrases came to him so he sang out loudly, like one reciting from the hymnal:

"Oh nonsense is the word we like, nonsense is the thing.
We get away with murder and flagellate Lord Byng.
Oh screwing is the word we like,
Screwing is the thing.
Ramping all the wild ones,
While the straight ones get the ring.
Oh prudent is the thing we're not, and tsk, tsking leads to beer,
We fight and fuck..."

A board cracked under his foot, so he grabbed for the railing with the hope that the noise would wake George Blenkinthorpe, cause the sapper to appear out of the wet air with his revolver and either shoot him dead or make an offer of coffee and fresh baking. But Hugo saw no one at the end of the catwalk. Instead, he had the sense that he had been prancing around to string music and not a coarse sound in his head. He could hear the flow of notes pulsing in time with his feet, like a jig played on a violin. He stopped and went to the railing. Below, in the tangle of growth that led to the stairs of Blenkinthorpe's suite stood a fresh-faced, girlish woman wearing a cotton dress and light sweater warming her shoulders. She had a violin at her chin, but had stopped playing to watch him closely. When Hugo stared back, she averted her gaze to ground level as if trying to see a way she could dash out. But he looked ahead on the trail and shook his head. "Don't run, Miss," he said. "You won't get fifty feet before I'll be onto you like Milton onto a dead rat.'

She let the violin drop to her side and said, "What are those things on the beams?"

Hugo had no answer to such a question. "What things?" he asked.

"Over there. They look like masks." She pointed to a stained wooden beam above and to the side of Hugo's head. He could make out in the grain of the wood what looked like masks of bearded men with curls in their hair, like green men he'd seen in books. He smiled at the girl's attempt to divert him. She smiled back, then stooped to put her violin and bow back into the case.

"Those are evil spirits that guard this place," he answered. "But they haven't succeeded in keeping you out, have they? What are you doing here?"

"I was looking for the Milton you just mentioned."

"Did you say, 'Milton'?"

"Are you hard of hearing?"

"I'm confused. Because, of all the people in the world you might wish to see, Milton is not one of them."

"I'm not interested in all people. I'm interested in him."

"You're a friend?"

"That's my business."

"Not here and not this morning."

"Well, I happen to know this is not your place and the time of day doesn't matter. I'm a night person. I like to stay up late and listen to the radio while I practice. I'm learning to compose music. Actually, Milton Muxlow is going to show me some things."

"Muxlow couldn't show you the time of day."

"That's not what George told me."

"What does George tell you?"

"Every week I come here so he can give me a lesson."

"What, lessons in bridge construction?"

"Music composition."

"Blenkinthorpe composes?"

"You ask a lot of questions that aren't your business."

"So I'll ask another one. Have I ever seen you before?"

"Yes."

"Here?"

"I must be going now."

"Would you like coffee, tea, breakfast?"

"No. Tell Milton I was looking for him."

"I'll be sure to tell him."

The girl swiveled her head around, making a point of looking again at the water stains on the beam. As she ran towards the forest and the door hidden behind, Hugo called, "What's your name?"

"Middle March," she replied and disappeared in the trees. Hugo leaned against the railing for a several minutes. He could smell her, every inch of her, and wondered what she would be wanting with the moron. He thought also of the insignificant things Milton could show her besides his technique for burying rats. He went to the polished wood door and sought admittance from Juliana on the basis of seeking information about the woman he had just encountered.

George Blenkinthorpe and his guest had their impromptu morning coffee served with the fresh rolls. The morning sun rose to their backs and the roiling water in the bay seemed warmer than winter, with the whitecaps less like a blistering frost. Hugo detailed his morning experience. The engineer explained. "I don't know what business this is of yours, but here it is anyway. I play the violin and compose some. The girl's father, surname March, is the editor of several magazines. When he was at school, he had a passion for George Eliot. With a shameful sense of his own cleverness he saddled his only daughter with the name 'Candace Middle March'. From an early age he addressed her by the name of the novel and it stuck into adulthood."

"What would she want with Milton?"

"Like me, she's taken a shine to him. They wander around the Bazaar together, which is good thing since you lot on the other side seem to have lost all interest in keeping track of his whereabouts. At any rate, Milton knows all the trails and their dangers. And she names things for him—the trees, the birds—and plays her violin down by the beach. Sometimes they both come into the shop and watch me tinker with the motorbike."

Blenkinthorpe lit his pipe and began pacing the floor. Juliana came in and offered more coffee. As she poured, the engineer handed Hugo the envelope containing the photo of the *Kyle Mission*. He sat down with the pipe loosely between his teeth and said nothing more. Juliana came to sit next to him. Hugo stood, looked at the photo of the rusting hulk of the ship, and then out the window. With the silence of the others, he felt the need to justify his presence.

"Isn't it strange how history goes, sir?" he said. "Strange that we are diminished by the past—how, as the song says, the days dwindle down to a precious few, and the memories fewer than that and more precious because of it? One night recently I had a dream. In it, I saw ahead what seemed to be forty years, but into a place where the houses were familiar. All around me was a regretful dimness of light, so I pressed my nose to a glowing window.

Rainwater dripped off my hat and ran down my neck. I was standing together with you and the feeble Korrolus. We were all soaked to the skin, trapped by advancing years on the wrong side of the glass. It was the wrong side I concluded, because on the other side lounged dry, clichéd people preserved by artificial light. Amongst them sat the women of abused romances, all with perfect limbs and frozen, bone-white smiles. But it was ever more poignant than that, Juliana, because the pain they suffered as a result was cruelly sharp, and the remorse deep.

"Do you ever imagine something like that, George? Perhaps you've had the dream of stepping back empty-handed from the window of past life into the crowded street of the present, hearing the laughter of children just out of your view—and you peering into other rooms to see furniture, ceilings, and paintings tacked on the plaster. And amid the pantomime of circling residents, you see one dear, familiar face. You look back furtively and see other houses and stranger neighborhoods. Still further away, you're confronted by a landscape of distorted memories and friends who see at other windows, your own grief-filled face. And me, I watch myself kneeling at the piano bench, too exhausted to bang out the chords to Grieg's *Concerto*. I hear through the walls and above the sea wind the poet's recitation: 'What a gift to gae us, to see ourselves as others see us...' and of course the lines are a requiem because by definition we're already dead. And downstairs, today, the girl played a dirge on her violin, with the words going something like this:

'A glass of wine in Lichtenstein,
A red rose for a rover.
A drop of blood to join the flood and get me down to Dover.'

When he left the suite an hour later, and maneuvered himself across the infirm boards of the mezzanine, Hugo's rolling, painful thought was of Milton Muxlow. What could a certified moron possibly say to a young woman who allows herself to be called by the name "Middle March"?

At Blenkinthorpe's unexpected invitation, Hugo returned the following week for dinner. In the main gallery of the engineer's suite of rooms, he stood by the tall windows with his legs apart and stretched the muscles down his back. In the kitchen, Juliana sang a song in Arabic while she baked. As a counterpoint to her sharp voice, string music from a cabinet radio spread over the blanched walls like strokes of paint. "I like to sing each morning," she said, "a passage dedicated to Allah, to the infinite. To me, music is about loss and death. George likes me to sing to his dead comrades, but only patriotic marching songs they would appreciate in heaven. How quaint. Has he mentioned his comrades?"

Hugo shook his head. They had more coffee. The old man sat close to the window. "After I returned from Palestine," he said, "I got into the export business, first in Algiers with Crasson, and then here. This place was for sale so I bought it. It was still an operating company but new facilities had sprung up closer to the city. The business didn't warrant pouring in new capital. When I helped found the engineering firm, I made a suite for myself over the pier and the rest of the structure...well, it just slowly collapsed into what you see today."

Blenkinthorpe opened the envelope, which had been sitting in the same place Hugo had left it on his last visit. He took out the photo, looked again at the *Kyle Mission,* then said, "First Officer Allan Korrolus, master by misfortune of a merchantman transporting goods bound for enemy territory. Did he mention this?"

Hugo nodded. Juliana served a plate of buttered rolls and poured coffee from a silver carafe. Hugo ate the bread and looked at the framed prints on the walls. Blenkinthorpe wiped the butter off his mouth. "Juliana is from Algiers, but I told you that already. Did she tell you that she once worked for Crasson?" Hugo shook his head.

"He had a large operation, and still does for all I know. I was overseas with the Tenth Field Squadron, Royal Engineers with the rank of major. In November forty-two, we landed with the Yanks between Oran and Algiers. Later, I fought the Germans southeast of Algiers at the Kasserine Pass. It was a vicious battle. Birks was with me. I still have medals. I could parade around here like Montgomery himself if I wanted to."

"How old were you?"

"I was a lad, much younger than you are, marching onto the battle like you once wandered into the high street to find your mates. Major Dring had been with Birks at Dunkirk and escaped just in time, with the Bosch staring up their backsides. The British had compensation for that at El Alamein. What a famous name! Dead middle of the night, February forty-one, and each minute the artillery pouring tons of high explosives into the heart of the German line, then the armor smashing through. Must have been a big shock for Rommel."

Blenkinthorpe got to his feet and marched around the room at a brisk pace. When he got to the window he stopped. "Albert Schweitzer is the greatest humanitarian of the century, perhaps of all time," he said. "But he is still a German. Actually, he was a resident of Alsace, a territory bounced between France and Germany. He speaks both languages and many African dialects. In the First Great War he was interned as an enemy, and in the last one closely watched once the free French had defeated the forces of Vichy. Of course it was unjust. He was the enemy of no one—only disease, starvation, and hopelessness. Did Korrolus mention Von Raynor or his brother?"

Hugo shook his head again. Blenkinthorpe took a sip from his drink and went to the counter. "I could name the men in the tattered photo you have. But I have little knowledge of where they are now, whether alive or not. During the campaign to wipe out elements of Vichy resistance, we found Crasson to be of use because of his trade contacts. Korrolus, who had been wounded at sea, was transferred to Algiers for treatment. A quirk of the planning put him back on the *Kyle Mission* supervising the disposition of the cargo, making it natural that he have official business with Crasson."

He went to look out the window. "So how is Korrolus?" he asked, still looking at the sea. "I recall that his leg was shredded."

"Didn't you say he was dead?"

"Still enjoying his drink?" Blenkinthorpe asked.

"A glass of beer now and again."

"And again many times, I'm sure."

Hugo walked to the window and stood next to the engineer, who said, "It was only my belief that he had died, Dr. Haultain, and my wish. In a sense it has also been my wish that some others had died."

When Hugo got back to 836 that evening, Milton was sitting on the piano bench stroking middle C with an even tempo. Hugo put him to bed, then lay awake for hours before sliding into the piano bench himself to play the first few chords to Grieg's *Concerto*. Then in the darkness he thought about Conrad and Corrine and why it was they had failed.

*   *   *   *

Upstairs in the empty space of the San Francisco Club, the jukebox played the music of violins and minor keys, giving a sense of foreboding. Martine knew where Puj kept the sandwiches and chewed them like she sometimes chewed her own vomit. It was 9 pm and her eyes glowed with drugs. Hugo sat in a booth where he was not visible from the counter or the door. Above him was a single light, barely sufficient to illuminate the printing. The book with Dr. Schweitzer's signature on the inside cover lay open in front of him. Besides that one item, the table held a glass filled with ice water and an ashtray with a lighted cigarette.

Hugo heard the bell and moved out of the booth to watch. A young hooker slipped in. Puj peered down the stairs, then closed the door. The young woman sat with Martine in a booth marked "Reserved". The owner brought her a sandwich. The bell rang again. Cyril Ibecks walked through the door followed by Billy Bartholomew. Cyril took off his coat, walked smiling to the reserved table, and sat down next to the younger woman. Billy looked uncomfortable and wandered around. When he saw Hugo at the end of the room, he drew back with a fright. "I won't ask!" he blurted.

Hugo responded by saying, "I'm here on Friday nights, Billy, because I work here and the weekends are as big for the queers as it is for us—even preachers absorbed by their mission work."

"I think its good for me to learn about manifestations of sin," he said after clearing his throat.

"Of course it is, and you'll see a variety of it in here."

"It's part of my education, Hugo. I'm not going to cause trouble."

"Of course you won't. If you do I'll heave you into the alley."

"Heave me where? Thank you, no. I'll be discreet."

Hugo got up and went over to the reserved table.

Cyril smiled at his approach. "Sit down, Hugo. Have you met Martine and little Andrea?"

"Why would you call her 'little', Cyril? To be cute?"

"To be friendly."

"Cyril's more than friendly, Hugo," said the older woman. "He's good at business."

"I'm sure he is, Martine. Billy's not, though. He's terrible at keeping accounts. For example, he knows nothing about pimping, which is an unnecessary greed, wouldn't you agree, Andrea?"

She shrugged her shoulders. Cyril smiled and squinted through the smoke. "Billy and I are just here for a look-see."

"Then look-see," said Hugo. "But be aware that who you see is none of your business." Billy looked frightened and shook his head. An hour later the San Francisco Club opened. Cyril and Billy had departed and both women had gone with them. Through the rest of the evening, Hugo did his duty. When it was slow, he read. When required, he fought. He sliced his knuckle to the bone on a chain necklace and talked a jealous patron out of slitting his throat with a razor.

At two in the morning he went to the fire escape for a smoke. A large woman with short hair and a pressed business suit stood at the railing. She had the ankles of another woman in her hands and was shouting obscenities at her. The woman who dangled head down gave out an intermittent sob. Hugo lit a cigarette, and with no apparent concern leaned against the opposite railing. "Isn't this kind of behavior a bit self-serving, Emily?" he said.

The large woman pulled the victim up, spat in her face and said to Hugo, "You're a piece of shit too." She didn't resist when he led her into the alley. For several seconds they stood facing each other. "Is this high noon, jerk boy? Should I draw first?" the woman said.

"Aren't nurses supposed to take the oath? Something like—do no harm."

"What could you tell me about harm, with the grotesque war you've waged here over the last few months?"

Hugo shrugged and said, "It's past your bedtime. Want me to call you a cab?"

When she saw Hugo's posture sink from aggression to fatigue, she relaxed and straightened her suit coat. A sigh drifted between her thin lips. "I got a car and I'm not too hammered to drive," she said, and raised her arm towards him. "No hard feelings."

When he held out his hand, the motion opened the cut on his knuckle. Blood dripped onto the stones. The woman laughed. "Come with me, I'm parked around the corner." She removed a first aid kit from her car and bandaged his hand. "How did you know who I was?" she asked. Hugo shrugged his shoulders again and turned to go down the alley. She walked after him staring with amazement. "Now I see. I always thought I knew who you were. Jesus, and I thought I was confused. It got around that you had quit and left the country."

"Correct on one count."

"Why? I know death is hard to take, Dr. Haultain, especially the death of a child. But a certain amount is inevitable, isn't it? Goes with the job. No one blames you for that failure, except apparently yourself. My God, a career gone in an hour and you working in a place like this."

"It's a living. Anyway, I enjoy it."

"Hurting people?"

Hugo moved to walk away, but stopped and said, "I kept you from doing that just now. Take care on the drive home, Emily, and thanks for the assistance." Leaving her by the curb, he held his breath and went past the overflowing garbage cans. At the top of the stairs he paused to throw his cigarette into the darkness. Inside the club door he stopped again. A face he knew glowed in the light of the jukebox; he couldn't decide if he should go up to Ralph Mel-Phesance and say, "Ralph, it's okay—we can still be friends," or just leave and wash his hands of the place. He lit another smoke and slipped into the storeroom to get his coat. With the cigarette between his lips, and without looking back, he walked down the cobblestones of the alley.

Leopoldville, November 28, 1965.

The guards from the north wing were stern in their laughter and taunts. When Hugo returned from the cottage near Stanley Pool, it became their habit to greet the Fiat with a salute and open the doors with mock subservience. Often they would gesture with a sweep of an arm, playing footmen or butlers. At best they would point to his new disfigurations, screw their eyes up with dry tears before slapping each other and stomping the ground with merriment. Sergeant Mintou was always impressed that he was still alive. He came into the cell the day Hugo returned with a slash over his eyebrow that leaked blood down his face.

"You don't have proper answers, monsieur. You should answer them what they want to hear. It will be a long time until I'm ready for my test. The teacher must survive."

"Don't be afraid, Mintou. My childhood was unending torture, with questions that had no reasonable answers. But I'm still here."

The soldier began to examine the cut, but stopped when blood got on his hands. Hugo opened his case and handed him a roll of gauze. Mintou went to the door but came back when Hugo said, "I'm going to give you something to divert your fear, Sergeant. Another story would put me at ease too. I've found that talking does that and relieves the pain."

He heaved himself over to his case and sat on it with shoulders tight against the bricks. Mintou dabbed reluctantly with a gauze pad. Hugo began with a hoarse voice. "In an alley that was as dismal as this cell, my journey down it was interrupted by the rattle of a garbage can. It was on a night when I was on my way home from my job, which I had just quit. Above me I could see a man sitting on the step of a freight door. He appeared not much older than I was, but in that part of the city, ten or a hundred years old sometimes looks the same. I stopped and said to him, or more exactly to his shadow on the wall, 'I was thinking just now of an epigram attributed to Oscar Wilde about the blight on his life for having a different attitude towards pleasure. Conrad would know it, although unlike you, he was never happy discussing the more troubling moral questions.'

"The man moved into the glow of the one bulb hanging high up above the ramp, glowing like the sun might appear from Saturn. I continued, 'There you are, Albert. I thought it was you. I feel uncomfortable with anonymity. I was nervous to the core when nameless bodies skittered under the yellow glow of the streetlight next to my family home. Uncanny for me they were and awful, as if they'd drifted in from a distant world I could know nothing about. I get a similar feeling in your presence, a sense that you've flown in here god-like from somewhere long out of touch with this alley. Or perhaps this last stretch of life's been too damn long.'

'It has, and not easy for me, either,' he replied. 'I don't get out much anymore so I like to wander, especially to the seedier parts of town. More to see here, more potential with you around, eh—you who delights in telling the world that I'm as disregarding of life as you are.'

'I see you wandering around here, more like Morley's ghost, wishing to intervene for good, but having lost the power.' I replied.

'Not dead yet, Hugo, and it's a good thing too, with you to keep track of. Here is yet one more place beyond your curfew. You should realize that no one here requires your neglect. Young Emily had her own conflicts, but took the time to figure you out.'

'Her impulse bears false witness,' I replied. 'She pretends to have compassion for people, but like all bleeding hearts, she does it to either beat down conscience or pander to glory. It's the thing Muir did for me, and you did for him. You were so much a false god that he pretended to deny you.'

'This is more your concern than mine, since you talk of it in the past tense when we all live yet. But have hope. You seem apt to think things through and a bit further I might add than Descartes' infamous dictum—I think therefore I am—which I put on the record as being one of the stupidest comments in all philosophy. It leads people to believe that the content of their thought doesn't matter much. As I told you a few weeks back, we have no choice but to think—but you can think well or think poorly. Thinking well includes the accomplishment of playing the piano or a humble gesture like teaching Milton to bake bread, like your father taught you to read and write.'

'I don't do things for his benefit. I do them to make life easier for myself.'

'Easier and better. We all do that, and sometimes to extremes. Muir had too little a moderating effect on you. But you've had some recent rehabilitation. Milton's ghastly presence has made you suffer through the rough edges of your thought and resigned you to weakness. Only the man who has gone through suffering and resignation is capable of accepting the world. I've done it for many a year, trying to work things to my advantage without lashing out in despair with the whip hand and the rifle; me stuck in the jungle with all the primitives who need help and who knows if I'm meeting their needs beyond the alleviation of suffering, going beyond into fancy words and the delineation of ethics. I've longed many a dark evening for a glass of lager and a bit of money for a nice house. Many times if I had my druthers, I'd rather be playing the organ for a living, receiving the bows and curtsies. Do you know I had a friend once who described my life as "saving old niggers in Africa and old organs in Europe"?

"I snuffed out my cigarette and replied, 'Why didn't Conrad tell me where he was going?'

'He didn't know himself. Or perhaps it wasn't for him to say.'

"A car entered the alley and forced me back into the reeking bins of a loading dock. When the pavement was clear, I called into the dark, 'Tell me Albert, when I was confined to barracks as a child, you would march in like a staff officer and cheer me up with orders. I did as I was told, read this or that, and talked to the crows as instructed. I was happy and sang in my chains.'

'Go home, Hugo,' ordered the ju-ju man, 'and by that I mean to the only place on earth your presence is missed.'

"The figure in the alley stepped back into the shadows, then dissolved into a pastiche of slatted crates. I stood with hands by my side for some minutes, listening to the groan of city noise beyond a ridge of tenement blocks. Then I went straight home, Sergeant Mintou, and in the dark began to play Beethoven's music."

When he had finished talking, Hugo stared at the block wall of the cell and recalled the ride home, the act of sitting deliberately at the piano and being moved to play the sonata twice, then a third time as dawn showed over the sparse reaches of the city. He recalled being exhausted, bent over at the waist with the whole of existence motionless except for the sweat, which dripped steadily onto the keys. A large hand came around from the side of Hugo's head, and with the delicacy of a mother, the moron dried his face with a towel.

Mintou, on the other hand, squatted in the corner without expression and asked, "Did the ju-ju man save us niggers out of duty, or was he paid money?"

"He was paid the same coin as anyone who does something out of compassion," Hugo replied. "Which is to say, Sergeant, that he was paid in kind."

The City, 1963.

His time at the San Francisco club—the stupidity of the disputes, the episodes with Ralph, Emily, Solly, and the others—all these combined to put Hugo on edge and skew his thoughts. The ensuing journal entries began to focus on end times. His sketches depicted varying degrees of sunset. He had difficulty finishing chores. Any commute into town became a trip of silence. Easter Friday came. The owlish foghorn hooted all night and grew louder. Dampness squeezed through the cracks and into the bedclothes. It was not spring after all. Hugo put his feet over the side and waited for the nagging light. He tried to think what day it was. Good Friday? Good for him. Good for everybody including Cyril Ibecks, who had taken Billy Bartholomew the previous week on their first hunting trip to the uplands in search of the spring birds.

He sat on the edge of the bed, stared at the piano, and called to see if Milton was awake. A noise from the kitchen indicated he was, which was not alarming because the moron had recently taken to getting up on his own and busying himself around the house. He wondered if it was Milton's connection to a girl with a moronic name that turned his life towards something better than a nightmare. As a consequence of these efforts, Middle March would often lie on Hugo's bed, as she was at that moment, clothed only in sheer underwear, her naked hip curved up and then down to the leg and knee, with the texture of the books behind lending softness to her flesh. When she smelled coffee and the sweetness of baking, she ran into the kitchen to hug the madman, who was standing in front of the stove. On the table was a plate of fresh rolls beside a dish of butter.

"Well done," said the girl. "Good Friday and hot cross buns."

"Sam Ting," said the cook.

When the fog lifted and it was fully light, Hugo pulled on his oily pants and for no particular reason went out. The sun warmed the air as he walked along the meadow trail, circling west to the sea then north towards the headlands. The towers of the city bubbled up through the mist. He chanted some gibberish to the seabirds that hopped along the mounds. At a gap in the dunes he sat and watched wave segments break on the shore, waiting for the one that would curl to a perfect lens and magnify the interior of the ocean. He made a face to imitate the gape-mouthed fish that peered back at him and tried to reverse the image into a compressed and distant space. "Sam Ting," he said loudly and wondered if Milton Muxlow's brain was amphibious and capable of two realities: a wet one and a dry one, with his mental transactions going back and forth like oxygen through membranes, like wind in the grass, like wind moving, always moving, then inevitably fading, like the vibrations of a plucked string.

"Tomorrow, class, the second law of thermodynamics as it pertains to music," he recalled Professor Mira Cormacks announcing. The next day she feigned illness and didn't show at the lecture. Hugo thought it a nice touch and quite effective. Given the ensuing chaos of the class, he reasoned that her absence itself presupposed the second law, excusing her from having to be there at all. Later that same night, as Hugo played the piano and watched the wily educator expose her breasts in the bedroom of her manor house, he had an instant joy that by some miracle of association he too could make some therapeutic use of entropy. The recollection of Allan Korrolus' words cured him of that fantasy. The ecstasy of sex was indeed nihilistic, but the second law was immutable, unavoidable and contrary; in effect, it was the law of dying. On his way back he plucked a sheet of paper from the hedge. It was a circular of political propaganda trying to stir up the resentment of ratepayers to incursions by the City board of Variance. He crumpled it up, then wove through the evaporating puddles. At a fork in the trail he turned south again, past the windbreaks of wooden buildings most of which were falling down despite the published codes of city planners.

Overwhelmed by a feeling that he was approaching a finality, Hugo packed up some books and walked over to the Bazaar. It was warm. The sun still had a finger's width to sink level with the straight line of ocean. He slid through the gap in the warehouse door and ambled down the path, which was now free of traps. He found Blenkinthorpe, Juliana, Middle March, and Milton in the center of the arena wreckage, one bright light suspended from a rafter giving illumination to the card table set on firm boards. On a fallen beam was an assortment of baked items and drinks on a tray. Standing behind at attention hands at his side was the moron.

"We require a fourth at bridge," said Juliana. "The young lady suggested that you would be here shortly. That way we wouldn't have the job of teaching the game to Milton, who, after learning, might be inclined to beat us all."

Hugo sat down. Blenkinthorpe dealt. "Just a few rubbers," he said.

They played and talked. Milton passed around the tray. Hugo complimented Juliana on her treats and she replied that Milton had done the cooking.

"Jesus liked food," said Middle March. "Take a close read of scripture—there's a lot of food there. Without the eating, the Last Supper would have no meaning."

"I've had a lot of hunger and many suppers," said the old soldier. "There are times I wish I could get to the last one." The young woman nodded, went to stand beside the moron and took his arm. "Milton has a good grasp of the hunger issue," she said. "The primary hungers are the real ones."

Blenkinthorpe disagreed. "It would be unwholesome to live by bread alone," he said. "All that kneading, fondling, shaping the dough into the forms of animal, then baking and eating it like flesh."

"Whatever are you talking about?" asked Juliana.

"Nothing," he replied. "I'm trying to decide what to bid. I have to know what will work in these circumstances."

"Well, bid something."

Milton picked up an empty plate and turned to go back to the suite. Middle March followed. Hugo sat back in his chair and stared past her, through the skeleton of timber, past the branches of new trees to the purple hills and the saffron sea. After they had gone he said, "Does she really believe Milton is going to help her with the music?"

"She has an imagination," said Juliana. Blenkinthorpe added that it was more than make believe.

*   *   *   *

Early Sunday morning a week later, Hugo received the last installment of cash from Puj Banno. After breakfast at the diner, he went downstairs to the gym. The workout was not intense, as he felt tired. When he arrived home, the front room was a circle of bodies. Ralph sat in the armchair and picked at the fraying material. The door rattled with a heavy knock.

"Who the hell could that be on a Sunday?" said Cyril. "Billy assured me the Lord does not make house calls."

Ralph walked to the door and to a man dressed in a dark suit, said, "We don't need religion."

"Apparently not," the man replied. "However, Billy Bartholomew needs me." He shoved past into the front room. At the sight of the assembly he shivered visibly and announced that his name was Robert MacPherson. Heads nodded. The man looked at Milton and made no move to shake anyone's hand.

"Do you wish to talk to me in private, Billy?"

"Not unless you do, Bob. But let's not, okay, because I don't want to move. Whatever you've got to say, say it right here. Milton, get him some coffee. Would that be with cream and sugar?"

"Black," replied a frowning Robert MacPherson as he watched Milton shuffle to the kitchen. Then the visitor said to Billy, "As Milton's cousin you are paid to look after him. But I understand that at some point you desire to travel abroad to pursue a career in the church. To assist you, Milton's family wish to secure other care for him."

"Hallelujah," said Billy.

With a suspicious look, MacPherson took the coffee from Milton and continued, "As you all know, Milton Muxlow has disabilities."

"He's a moron," said Cyril.

MacPherson lit a cigarette and blew the smoke in Cyril's face. "In point of fact, sir, he is mute and entirely incapable of doing anything for himself."

"I disagree," said Hugo. "Just now he brought you coffee. He can look after himself—dress, cook, go to the toilet. He knows the inside of the Bazaar like his own bed. He is learning to talk and in a month will play the piano."

"Milton should not be going out or doing anything else that might injure himself or others. The family would not be pleased. It appears that Billy, in keeping with his usual overstuffed idleness, hasn't been up to the job."

"Given the circumstances, I've done well."

MacPherson glared at him then turned to Hugo. "And begging your pardon, sir...."

"Hugo."

"Hugo...I find it an exaggeration that he talks, plays the piano, or does any of those things. At any rate Milton can't go home, as Billy knows. In the company of his family he goes berserk and has to be locked away. That, of course, is why he's here. Until now the family has resisted putting him permanently in an institution. But if you wish to have your career, Billy, an institution is precisely where Milton will have to go."

"Lock him up?" said Mel-Phesance.

"Not quite. Milton's family is well-off. His father owns the largest packinghouse in the country. He also owns many of the ranches that produce livestock and, to complete the circle, wholesalers and a chain of restaurants. Truly, he is the king of meat, wouldn't you say, Billy?"

MacPherson turned to the others and grinned. "Mr. Bartholomew may have been shorted on the cash side, but otherwise, as a favored nephew he was spoiled to excess. So much so that he developed a resistance to satisfaction. I remember him as a little boy and the many helpings it would take to fill him up. It became the law of the table. His mother never tired of saying that Billy could always be counted on to lick the plates clean."

MacPherson seemed pleased with the humiliation on Billy's face and lowered his voice. "The Muxlow family have arranged suitable accommodation for Milton. It's well managed place and quite humane. The cells are substantially larger than a dog kennel and some would accommodate a horse. Next May we'll finalize the arrangements. Thanks for the coffee." MacPherson walked a wide berth around Milton and let himself out. No one spoke. Hugo looked at Billy, whose face was white as flour, his mouth a hole in the dough.

"Milton's dad the biggest producer of meat in the land....King of the T-bone," said Ibecks. "We should be impressed. It sounds like Milton's going to the slaughterhouse."

"He won't be going anywhere," said Billy. "If I have to, I'll take him to England."

"Was it really the law, Billy?" asked Cyril.

"The law?"

"The law of licking up the gravy, finishing the pea dung, scrapping out the burned bottom of the scalloped potatoes. I've always been impressed by anything that rises to the level of law."

Billy appeared morose. "Right now I'm not into law," he said. "I'm into fear."

"Sam Ting," said Muxlow, who stood passively in the corner.

"Shaddup," shouted Billy and held his head between his hands.

As spring progressed into early summer Hugo no longer felt comfortable at the house. Ibecks had taken to hosting weekend parties. He would stock them with an inventory of girls from the club and bring in live bands. The fridge was always full of beer. Each weekend all the crockery in the house was broken and replaced, then broken again. Ralph's aquarium stunk with stale liquor and dead fish. Cyril always provided compensation, had everything replaced with better than the original and the cleaning done professionally. Neighbors never complained, because there were none. The police had no interest to intervene. In the spring of 1964 the Cedar Galleries was beyond any zone of interest.

At the St. Regis Hotel early on a Saturday night, Hugo drank off another glass. The place seemed old to him and the roof paper-thin, a twin to the roof over the Bazaar with the stars shining through. He sat in his usual chair with its back to the elegant pillar. The table in front of him had only one full beer glass and a few empties. Sam Ting, he thought and felt secure, unable to drift towards any idea of adventure. Ibecks walked in. When he sat down he took a napkin off the table and polished his shoes. "No party tonight, Hugo. Billy is hung over—and what's a party without him?"

"You buying?"

"Broke again? In case you didn't notice, I've been hosting the weekly party at Versailles so you can join in at no cost."

Hugo shook his head. "The actual reason is that parties in the city were costing you too much."

"True."

"And don't forget the hunting." Ibecks shrugged as Billy walked in and began talking half way from the door. "Three rabbits and a grouse. Cyril has become such a crack shot he tore the heads off two of them and got a bunny right up the ass. We'll have the rabbit for dinner tomorrow, no sense in hanging it." He raised his glass and continued. "Let's drink to the souls of the dead. What we are about to receive…"

Hugo raised an eyebrow. "You've got problems you should see to before you eat, Billy. And I'm not referring here to your child hooker or your gluttony, your lying, your neglect of the moron's needs. What I'm talking about is your poor choice of profession. Just who are you trying to please?"

Billy lurched to his feet but Mel-Phesance rushed in the door and cut him off. He had blood running down his shirtfront. "It was a bunch of goons and a guy called Horseface. Called me a queer—Jesus, Hugo."

Billy sniggered and slopped beer over the table. Ralph followed Hugo out the door into the glare of the neon. They found the assailants boarding a bus several blocks away. Without waiting for the others, Hugo boarded at the next stop and shoved past the driver. He feigned one way then smashed the first man with a left hook. Horseface tripped back onto a seat and said something about a man up the street who catered to queers. With one blow Hugo cut him off in mid-sentence. He left the bus and half-walked half-ran up a familiar alley. The San Francisco Club was barred shut. Outside the diner, a Chinese porter confirmed they had just taken Puj Banno away with a sheet over his head.

*   *   *   *

Hugo met Ralph often in the library of the Department of Medicine to encourage him past his sexual problem in a way that wouldn't seem contrived. On this occasion he let his gaze slide around the perimeter of the hall, which seemed overly pungent with formalin. He began to name each of the organ specimens on display in glass cabinets…bits and pieces that, if assembled might make half a man. It was an aspect of medicine that put some people off, the physicality of blood, bone, soft tissue you could cut, remove, and examine. He turned to sift through the book he had pilfered from Korrolus' attic room: Bertrand Russell's *ABC's of Relativity*. He read again about the necessity of having a fixed speed of light so that matter could keep to itself to form objects—among them cells, organs, bodies, and possibly souls. He thought about the insanity of the moron's soul keeping rigidly to itself, about the girl who sat for hours with him on the bed asking questions about tunes she played on her violin, and the pity it was that there were never any answers. After getting coffee from a vending machine he peeled back the pages of *Gray's Anatomy*.

"Waitin' for the Doc, waitin' for the quack," he said in a loud whisper, and out of boredom watched the rain blown along the pavement by gusts of wind. Ralph showed his face at the door and they left for lunch at the Carousel. As Hugo watched the hip-swinging lope of the waitress and invented in his head the conversation they might have to sanction intercourse, his companion said,

"I'm going hunting with Billy and Cyril this weekend, for ducks and geese, I think."

On the way back, Hugo was meaning to reply that the occupants of the house were grateful to have wild foul for a change. But once in the building, the smell of the hospital was a shock to him, so he said nothing.

Lunchtime of the day the boys went hunting, Hugo sat on the porch and noted a darkness forming on the coastal mountaintops. But it was far away and the damp was no concern to the hunters, nor a risk for him. Storms and rain were an inconvenience at worst and required no further judgment. He recalled the prairie sky of the previous summer, a sky of land as opposed to sea, with the regular outline of charcoal cloud flattened on the bottom and meshed to the earth. A girl he knew might have judged it a benefit to have the shelter of clouds, perhaps even rain to cool things down so that she wouldn't have to lounge naked to get relief from the heat. Perhaps the summer rain should fall closer to the sea, he thought, and so ease the general striving for comfort and him no different, sitting at the tomato-red table not yielding an ounce to opportunity until the hunters came home from the hill with a few fool hens or something just as forlorn and dead. Out of continuing boredom he described to himself details of the lost boy standing at the edge of kitchen and framed by the door casing. His eyes seemed like two dots of charcoal on the paper, his face drawn tight and paler than usual.

"Ralph, you look dumbfounded. Are all the birds extinct?"

"It's Milton."

"Did he scare away the game with his yelling and arm-waving?"

Hugo laughed as Ralph walked back into the house, down the corridor, and into the front room.

"Do you have a cold beer for me?" he asked.

Hugo went into the kitchen and brought back two bottles. Ralph took one and sank into a chair.

"Milton did better than you thought?"

Ralph took a sip. "Your teaching him to do things didn't cure him, Hugo. He was retarded, deficient. He was born that way."

"But you must admit he does more things now than when he showed up here. Things are unfolding for him. But what concerns me, Ralph, is the change in tense—from present to past."

Mel-Phesance took another drink from his bottle and wiped off his mouth with an elegant gesture. "Stumbling around the ruins of the Bazaar," he said, "retrieving mangled rat carcasses. That's not an unfolding of life. Being accustomed to gunfire is not a step towards sanity. He became a grave digger, who put vermin in a particular order before burial, performing his perverted little rituals over the grave, with a repetitive 'Sam Ting, Sam Ting.'"

Hugo nodded his head.

"You tried to make him better, I'll give you that," Ralph went on. "But you have no power to cure the insane—those who drag their wooden horses on tiny little wheels, being led themselves by a rope and a harness."

"He gave up the horse."

"Oh, a great leap forward." Ralph drank some more beer and wiped off his lips with the same flip of his fingers.

"You haven't told me what happened today, Ralph. Did Milton put the bloody little carcasses into a grave instead of bringing them home for food?"

"What is your assessment, Hugo? Did you develop your cynicism in the sick-room, putting up with Conrad Muir all those years, and his continual talk of how you were going to die—and the sooner the better. When I was playing in the street I remember seeing your face pressed to the window, nose out of shape."

"I'm here, Ralph. Not dead yet. Don't forget what glass Milton looks through."

"Not any longer."

Hugo went to the window and looked at the Bazaar, which gave off its reek of creosote to mask the smell of rotting wood. "Go on, Ralph. Tell me what happened to Milton today that didn't happen to him yesterday, last week, or all through the blighted years of his life. Let's get this over with. Did someone shoot him?"

Ralph smoothed back his hair and rubbed his eyes, which Hugo thought were filled with tears. "We were hunting birds—in the uplands, just beyond the meadow. I was walking behind the others, trying to keep Milton from barging ahead and getting in the line of fire. Billy saw what he thought was a blue grouse. He aimed into the bush and pulled the trigger. After the noise of the blast died away I could hear a pathetic whimpering from the trees. It wasn't a bird Billy had shot but a small fox. The bullet had taken away part of the animal's back, just by the hip. It was trying to hop away but was too injured. Christ, it was awful. After a few feet of dragging its one leg, with the blood seeping down the fur, it collapsed. Milton was watching and looked very disturbed. Before I could stop him, he ran up to the fox and got on his knees. He touched its wound with one hand and stroked the head with the other. Billy told him to stand away and he would finish the animal. In a panic I pulled him roughly to one side, but not far enough. When Billy shot, I thought he had hit Milton. He stumbled back and fell on his side.

"The second blast didn't hit him, but it blew the leg right off the fox. Shit, there was blood everywhere. Milton took one look at the state of the poor animal and crawled away screaming with a look of terror on his face. He had only gone twenty feet into a low bush when he stopped crawling and got deliberately to his knees. Then he stood on his feet. He looked around him, walked past me, and over to the animal. He went back down to his knees, not with the usual halting, fumbling way he had of bending. It was slow and graceful. I could see on his face a mixture of horror and compassion I never want to see again to remind me of my own disregard for life. He bent over the animal for some seconds and we all looked at each other, not knowing what to do. I could see something dripping from Milton onto the open wound—it was his tears. I've never seen him cry before. He cradled the dying fox in his hands and cried; his lips moved and the tongue in his mouth made crude noises like sounds of dismay and I expected him to start repeating 'Sam Ting, Sam Ting' like he usually did. Soon his arms and hands were dripping in the animal's blood and into it poured his big moronic tears. As he cradled the dying animal, he looked at Billy and spoke. It was a firm voice, without bitterness. 'You ought not to have done this, Billy—a man in your position.'

"Then he held the fox and caressed its sides. Suddenly it stopped breathing and died. When Milton lifted him up, Cyril gasped, 'For the love of Christ', stumbled backwards, and fell from sight. Milton took the dead fox over to the stream and put it on a rock. He dipped his huge hands into the water and began washing the face and head and body of the animal until it was clean of blood. He washed his own hands and arms then got up lightly, like he was half his own size and began to walk. As he passed where Cyril lay stupefied, he looked down at him and shook his head with contempt. I had to help Cyril stand up. I thought he had lost his mind. Billy suggested we take both of them to the hospital—that something must be wrong with the pair of them, a knock on the head or a terrible shock."

Ralph remained silent for a time. Hugo went to the window, looked across to the Bazaar and had the obvious thought that sanity is what happens when you let someone out on his own for the first time. "Where are they now?" he asked.

"Cyril got into his car and left. He wasn't fit to drive but no one cared. Billy is wandering around outside. Middle March was waiting for Milton by the door of the Bazaar. They went in together with Milton saying to me that he would be over for dinner, but first wanted to tell George how to fix his motorcycle."

For the rest of the summer, while Hugo made plywood panels at a nearby mill, Cyril rarely came out to the Cedar Galleries. His father confined him to headquarters doing estimate work, which required no initiative. Since the episode with Milton, he had become aloof, slovenly. Hugo saw him briefly at the St. Regis Hotel and noted that his shoes were scuffed and dirty. Ralph had passed his medical exams and drifted south for the summer with his new friends. Middle March moved into 836 and stayed with Milton, who helped her compose the first of her many works for violin and string orchestra.

Billy prepared himself for his career abroad with fasting and prayer. But he accomplished only two things. The first was to inform Andrea that he could no longer pay for sex. The second was to stand in front of the mirror and marvel at the fat that had slipped away from his body since he had met Hugo Haultain. This fact had escaped his attention, until his pants fell down to his knees the morning Milton came to his senses. And all the while he worked to convince Hugo that he must go with him to England for support, "to smooth the way" was the phrase he used. With the settlement he received from Milton's grateful father, he offered to pay all expenses, including his friend's onward flight to wherever he wished to go. Hugo accepted and booked their passage for Europe. When his passport came, he put it with the birth certificate and reminded himself that it was not important that the line reserved for his father's name remained blank.

*   *   *   *

George Blenkinthorpe sat on the divan with the Saluki at his left knee. Juliana put some tea and baked items on the side table next to the revolver.

"Did Billy make your travel arrangements?" asked the old engineer.

"Billy has only arranged for his trip to heaven."

"Of course. Churchmen have a way of using people. And he will use you."

"It's of no concern to me."

"What is your concern? You have other skills; why you don't use them is none of my business. You seem to have interests that interfere with the obvious, so one last question—how are you traveling?"

Hugo sipped his tea and took a bite of muffin. "I've booked our passage through an agency in Montreal, to Rotterdam by boat. It was one that I particularly wished to sail on, the *MV Yildun*, registered in Hamburg."

Blenkinthorpe frowned and went slowly to the desk overlooking the bay and the mountains beyond. He stood for a moment and said, "In a sense you owe me a goodly sum for the inconvenience of a bitter memory. But you gave me Milton, who saw to it that my Royal Enfield runs like new. And now he will be of further use, I'm sure. That's a small miracle. Are you a miracle worker, Doctor?"

Juliana came into the room and cut off Hugo's answer. She sat next to Blenkinthorpe and for the first time Hugo had seen, he reached out and took her hand.

Billy left first by train. He had stops to make and some church business in the east. They arranged to meet in Montreal the third week of September. At the station Billy said, "The King of the T-bone thinks I was responsible for Milton's recovery."

"You were."

Billy shrugged his shoulders. "I shot a fox, that's all."

"Apparently that was enough."

"Milton's father thinks that it was the Lord working through me."

"It was. All things come by way of the Lord."

"You say that with your tongue choking you, Hugo. The truth is the gun scared the shit out of him."

"And the suffering of the fox?"

"Suffering usually drives people insane."

"You'll never know, Billy."

"The thing is, must I believe in miracles or not?"

Hugo patted the priest on the back and shoved him towards the train. When he was sure that Billy was safely aboard, he went to assemble the things required for months on the road. He laid out his wardrobe on the bed to select the most practical items. His mood improved when he noticed how worn and unfashionable his clothes were. And as he stacked up the books he might like to read, he found that he had no difficulty fitting them in because the case was mostly empty. Over a year had passed since vacating the apartment in the city, and he had done well. With the exception of Muir's library, he had accumulated nothing. As he packed each volume carefully he had a momentary urge to find Conrad, to show him that he was happy. He went outside to do a final check of the car. A small man was standing by the gate.

"Hello, Hugo," he said. Hugo went quickly forward and took his hand.

"Did you know I was leaving, Solly?"

"I heard it from Ralph. Where are you going?"

"I'm going to catch up to Conrad. But that might take me some time, so come in and have a beer."

"Just a quick one." The little jeweler sat in a chair at the red table. "I guess Conrad must have known he was going his separate way. Last year he had me start a piece for you, a ring. It took me a while because I wanted to make the design special. But I'm glad it's finished so I can give it to you before you go. It's a 'thank you' from me for what you did."

"I did nothing, Solly."

"You've got a way with words, Hugo. But most of the time you only fool yourself." He opened a briefcase, pulled out a box, and put it on the table. Inside was a gold ring with intricate designs across the inner surface. "It's mainly scroll work with a little filigree. I didn't put any gems in it because in parts of the world they'll cut off your finger for them. From a distance this looks plain and shouldn't attract attention. I figured you might be doing physical work, you know, and fine gold doesn't wear well. I put my best work in the art. If you put it under the glass you can see a passage from *Leviticus*, that Conrad picked out." He smiled briefly and his splotchy skin went red. When Solly drove away Hugo read the passage on the inside of the ring and feared for an instant that he would be away much longer than he intended.

Dusk was falling on the square when Milton carried Hugo's case and satchel down the wooden steps of the house as if they had no weight. Hugo was aware how he had changed. His body conformed to his altered state; it was still large but proportioned. Middle March stood on the porch. She wore a floral dress and a sweater pulled over her shoulders. Her eyes shone. Milton went up the stairs and put his arm around her narrow shoulders. They had agreed that he would stay on at the house with the girl as his companion where they could see to it that Ralph was settled. Hugo was surprised when Blenkinthorpe and Juliana came through the gap in the sliding door. They walked the distance over the square holding hands. For the first time, Hugo saw a trace of dignity and pride in the old soldier.

"You have the photo of the *Kyle Mission*?"

Hugo didn't answer.

"There will be some surprises for you, possibly some excitement. But I can see nothing good coming from your pursuit, if pursuit of the facts is your aim. Otherwise, take care. Sometimes people are left with complaints about the way things went for them."

Juliana hugged Hugo. She whispered, "Write and tell us your experience."

Hugo made no promises to them. Instead, he promised inwardly to remember only those few things that were common to them all. For a moment he looked to the derelict wreckage of the Bazaar, a place transforming itself according to the laws of death and life and death again, with new growth nourished by rotting spars and the suffering of people. Only the brilliance of sunset made a concordance of the crumbling shapes, which faded, grew less intense, less intrusive as he watched.

There was nothing left to load, but he checked his room a final time anyway. He went to the piano in the corner and put his finger on the keyboard. The sound of middle C gave a resurrection to his thought, and his thought concluded that whatever power woke Milton from his disease, the role of music had been a coincidence. Art was a human creation with no power apart from a diversion in the face of despair. And he believed more than ever that the force endowing humanity's quirks and foibles was obscure sorcery. He ran his fingers across the volumes of books belonging to Conrad the Shaman, the Mandrake of comic books, the Merlin of Hugo's fantasies, with his sickbed the island of Shallot and Corrine the lady who never quite got her arm above the level of the lake. He felt that he owed them little, had no penance to perform for the man who would tiptoe from the room when his mother entered, herself as quiet and undeserving as a mouse. Her portrait was the last thing he put in his case, next to the crude drawing of his father.

He went back onto the porch and faced the people that would disappear in this next alteration of his life, including Milton Muxlow, himself traveling into a new, more demanding day. Hugo could only speculate with sadness on the things the former moron would do or become as a memorial to his years of mute observation. Perhaps his only consolation was the woman standing beside him, the violinist, whose real name he had already forgotten. She came over to him and said, "It's none of your business how we are getting on without you, but if you write and ask, I won't tell you anything you don't want to hear."

Hugo hugged her and then the large man as best he could. Then he walked away. The young woman took up her instrument and played the first rising notes of a familiar sonata. Hugo got into his car. Driving down the road, he glanced once in the rearview mirror to see the four figures standing arm in arm like statues. His only thought was that it was a great comfort to be sliding away from the edge of the world, with familiar music providing him the necessary diversion.

BOOK TWO

Chapter IX

MV Yildun

Montreal, September 23, 1964.

The former and diminished Dr. Hugo Haultain strode up and down the narrow room at the Hotel Bonaventure. His coat was buttoned up and his leather case sat by the door. In his hand was the envelope containing his passage to Rotterdam. After ten minutes of pacing, he pulled from his satchel the photo of the *Kyle Mission* beached in the lineup of hulks. He turned it over, and seeing the name on the back recalled Korrolus' description of ships that never made the safe haven of land. He imagined the vast ocean that waited at the outfall of the river, and knew his options to avoid it were dwindling. This put him more on edge. Images throbbed in his mind of hurricane winds pushing enormous waves. In the adventure books he had read, oceans were invariably angry and swollen, giving writers an excuse to invent men with nautical skills. Hugo would have to trust that Juri Von Raynor had not lost his touch.

He would also have to trust that the new day would arrive soon, that futile situations were behind him. In his ears he could hear the parting oration from the stairway of the Ibecks' mansion—with Morley Ibecks standing stiffly to attention, swollen with his own dignity as he told Hugo with his sarcastic, executive voice how little he thought of him. Hugo stared from the window of the hotel and recited to the street below the thoughts he had then: that being a shill for anyone's ego was bad business. God alone adjudicates issues of good or bad character and accordingly sends good weather or foul. He paced for few minutes more then stopped again to peer out the window. In the late afternoon sun the St. Lawrence River sparkled white and gold between the buildings. He felt a spike of goodwill and concluded that the recent cloudless, sunny skies could be none other than a favorable judgment on him.

He circled the room twice more and with every noise in the hall glanced up to see if Billy Bartholomew were coming. Fearing they might miss the boat, he went down to the lobby. The desk clerk called him to the counter saying, "This is for you, monsieur," and handed him a cable. Hugo sat in an armchair and read the night letter addressed from Boston:

> Regret unable to join you in Montreal stop Will meet the Yildun Quebec City stop Looking forward to the passage stop Have great news from Milton stop Regards Billy

Hugo took his bags into the café to wait for the cab. He sipped coffee and wondered about the alleged good news of Milton. He smiled. Perhaps the King of the T-bone had written his only son back into the family fortune. He lit a cigarette and let no other thoughts interrupt his observations of two men eating dinner and his assessment of prints on the wall illustrating winter scenes. The sight of snow made him shiver, so he scanned the room once more hoping to see warm, red-cheeked women. But the waitress looked to be a grandmother, and the crowd passing the window moved as a genderless mass. Beyond was the vehicle that would take him to the docks. On the way, it wound in and out of traffic before entering the street that led close to the river. Through one window Hugo watched the harbor lights, and rushing past the other, a row of bleak, degraded warehouses much like the Bazaar but with a faint murmur of common life within.

The cab stopped at a gangway leading up the side of a freighter. On the railing of the main deck was a brass plaque engraved, *Yildun, Hamburg*. The ship appeared a mess of rust, with the decks awash in filth. Cargo swung from cables under oppressive mercury lamps. Hugo's excitement turned to dismay, and he cursed himself. The *Yildun* looked more a wreck than any of the ships beached in the mud of the James River and hardly able to withstand the rigors of the open ocean. A mean, tough looking man stood by the gangway smoking a poisonous-smelling cigarette. Hugo could not determine if he was an employee of the steamship company or a stevedore. His clothes were dirty and his cloth cap was stained with grease. The man made no reply to his greeting or any indication of hearing, so Hugo decided he could say what he liked. In few loud words he announced his own fear of the sea and questioned the poor state of the ship.

"Actually that's not quite the case," said a young man with narrow, rounded shoulders, who was inching cautiously up the gangway.

"Then, what is the case?" asked Hugo.

"This boat is not very old—five years to be exact. I expect that before we're a week at sea, the crew will have it newly painted for inspection by the owners when it gets to Hamburg."

The young man struggled further up the gangway then stopped again to catch his breath. "By the way, my name is Frank Ormes. This is my first time on a boat. I'm going to school in England."

He stopped talking as if to get more air into his lungs, then continued. "Actually, all of what I said—about the boat and stuff? I got it from the old man standing on the deck up there next to the girl. He seems to know everything."

Hugo nodded and said, "Well, let's hope he's right about the ship. This is also my first time at sea, and I'll admit I'm nervous, Frank. Nervous." He helped Ormes carry his heavy luggage into the ship, then found the purser's office and put his things in cabin eight. When he came back on deck the elderly man was still at the railing watching a silver-gray Mercedes swing into the hold.

"Car's going all the way to Tenerife," he said. "Its third trip. That's more times on the Atlantic than most men have in a lifetime. I was telling the young lady who was here a moment ago that my wife and I are retiring to the Canaries and need transportation." After a pause he continued. "When I saw the car swing into the hold, I was moved to speculate on the math—all that mass swinging about under the effects of gravity. I'm a physicist by training and have an eye for such things. Einstein saw an aspect of matter others couldn't fathom, at least an outline of truth made slightly weird by the quantum principle. Nonetheless, there's brilliance in the uncertainty of it and a risk for God. My wife always reminds me of this, how uncertain things are, how risky. But I remind her that's not really the point, not meaning to be rude…But I'm being rude already. My name is Richard Appleton. My wife and I like to play bridge. Do you play bridge, sir?"

Hugo held out his hand and replied that he was an expert player. They shook and Appleton said, "Good. I can see that you and I will get along. Perhaps we could play a few rubbers on the voyage. Well, must be off to inspect the unpacking. Estelle likes my taking special interest in her activities."

As Richard Appleton limped along the deck, Hugo started down the passageway after him but remembered the girl who had been at the railing. He sauntered back. As he expected, she was nowhere in sight.

Cabin eight had two bunks. Hugo lay down on the one next to the porthole. After shutting his eyes for a few minutes, he sat up and looked through the heavy glass. He could only see an outline of dock, the gloomy shapes of the warehouse and stacks of pallet boards. He contemplated the coincidence of meeting Richard Appelton and his wife, Estelle, both bridge players and him a man of science much like Allan and George. With the lighting of a cigarette, his thoughts turned to the riddle of how events fly randomly in all directions but somehow mesh tightly together. He would talk to Appleton about the inherent risk in that. Stowing the things he would need for the voyage in the footlocker, he left the rest in his leather case. His satchel containing his personal notes he placed gently on the desk next to the folder in which Blenkinthorpe had put the two photographs. He opened it and was surprised to see that the engineer had included a page from a book carefully cut away from the binding, which had on it a passage marked with asterisks. Hugo took it to the bunk, sat down, and read:

> ...I remember my youth and the feeling that will never come back anymore—the feeling that I could last for ever, outlast the sea, the earth and all men; the deceitful feeling that lures us on to joys, to perils, to love, to vain effort—to death; the triumphant conviction of strength, the heat of life in the handful of dust, the glow in the heart that with every year grows dim, grows cold, grows small and expires—and expires too soon, too soon—before life itself...

The top of the page bore the title, "*Youth.*" At the bottom, "Joseph Conrad" was written in pen. The blue color of the ink had faded. Hugo paced the cabin and looked at the sheet. He read the words over once, twice, a half-dozen times, and memorized them easily; because he knew the passage, even the location of the book—bottom shelf close to the piano—and Muir's comment to him on a day when he could see no one playing in the street.

"Joseph Conrad was not an Englishman but a Pole. The remarkable thing is, Hugo—here we have an immigrant who mastered a language foreign to him, and in a manner so thorough he was able to produce this masterpiece and many more."

Hugo recalled the affection that built in him for the fictitious youth of the title, himself at sea for the first time, watching his ship burn apart and sink, then in his escape seeing the east greet him with the stares of curious people. Still pacing the tiny cabin, Hugo speculated about his own place in the world. He had had few meaningful victories and one substantial loss. Less effort had gone into his affairs than the struggles of an immigrant Pole. Deceit had led him to vain effort; he knew that because of his reckless disregard, most men would outlive him. Already he felt cold, dim, unable to muster any conviction of strength that might go beyond the glow in his heart when he first saw Milton Muxlow coming up the front stairs with his outstretched hand stained with fox blood. It had trembled with joy as Hugo shook it, with the smiling ex-moron saying, "Hello, Hugo," as if he were challenging him to accept the fact that two common words could carry the weight of a miracle.

Hugo lit another cigarette, read in artfully crafted words the record of this event, then went back on deck. Longshoremen continued to hoist cargo into the hold under the glare of the lamps. At the back of the promenade, the woman of interest leaned against the railing.

"Evening," Hugo said.

She hesitated for a moment, looking surprised, then held out a hand that was small, with long fingers. "Good evening. You're a passenger are you?" She looked briefly at his clothes. "I'm sorry. At first I thought you were one of the crew. I heard you talking to the boson at the bottom of the gangway an hour ago. He's Bulgarian but speaks many languages, and you were talking as if he didn't understand. Well, perhaps he didn't, which would be good for you. I'm Violet Lewellyn by the way."

In the sharp metallic light the young woman's skin was clear and uniform. Her frog-like fingers slid the red beads on her long necklace; the light flashed and sparkled off her hands in a way Hugo thought peculiar. Stepping back to frame her body, he concluded that she was perhaps twenty-five, had well-shaped legs and her neck and face resembled the profile of Nefertiti he had seen in books. He couldn't make any further judgment, except to infer that the fingering of the necklace suggested an inherent, exclusive religiosity. Although her voice was polite, Hugo felt her manner to be sarcastic and unfriendly. Intimacy with Violet Lewellyn seemed out of the question. To his inane comments on the weather, she replied with a glance that opposed him on principle. It made him feel the night cold more completely so he turned aside and went along the deck without saying goodnight. He felt relieved to step into the warmth of the hatchway and lean against the bulkhead. Voices murmured inside the purser's office. A trembling vibrated through the steel floor and into his shoes. He walked to his cabin and locked the door.

Late that night, the *Yildun* dropped lines and swung eastwards into the sour flow of the river. Hugo lay on his bunk with his eyes open, relaxed and listening to the throb of engines. He felt happy in his expectation of the time to come—not with anticipation of the voyage, with the young woman's presence, or with time generally—but with the sharp edge of the present moment. He stretched, then allowed himself a shallow, intermittent sleep. During the times when he was awake, he noted the occasional light flashing through the porthole. At four in the morning he groped for his cigarettes, lit one, and sat on the edge of his bunk. Nothing rational came into his head until a problem he had long forgotten formed itself concisely: *In each life there is only one love and only one adventure.*

He repeated the phrase slowly to see if he could detect more substance now than when he had first heard Albert pronounce it in Korrolus' shop. He concluded that analysis of the puzzle was not complex; but it had an element of disappointment. As life succeeds from one episode to the next, it's obvious we can never know the hierarchy of quality in advance. From the beginning of our experience, we must be at least one step further on to judge better from worse. We may be two or ten episodes removed from a grand opportunity or an irreplaceable ecstasy. Hugo's one love might have been Dido, or Middle March, or Mira Cormacks. His one adventure might have been his victory over the sailors at the San Francisco Club, or the imagined voyage of the *Kyle Mission* up the banks of the river. He felt apprehensive and sat up sweating. He shouted, "Albert." No one answered. The cabin was gray and the other bed lay flat, unoccupied. He felt the need for a glass of rum but fell asleep thirsty.

The next morning was bright. He opened the porthole and stuck his head out. The river frothed below. On the north shore of the river he could see the outskirts of Quebec City. At breakfast he was disappointed that the dining room lacked one essential element. Before they docked in the harbor, he asked the steward, "I expected Captain Von Raynor to be at breakfast."

"Tomorrow he will be here, sir. Until we have left our last port of call, he is too busy."

*   *   *   *

Billy Bartholomew sat on his bunk in cabin eight.

"Milton and Middle March are getting married."

Hugo smiled.

"I'm not smiling," said Billy. "Personally, I think they should have done it when I was there. It could have been my first official duty."

"They didn't have time, Billy."

"They could have said something....told me what their intentions were."

"Sam Ting," Hugo said.

"Sam Ting, my ass."

Hugo sat on his bunk and lit a cigarette. "You've turned into a selfish man," he said. "You should be happy for them, especially for Milton."

"Good riddance, I say."

"No. It's neither good nor riddance. You'll be back there sooner or later, getting your tithe out of them, praying on the family connection."

They both smoked in silence.

"Let's forget this, okay, doc."

Hugo stiffened. "Don't call me that, Billy. We made a deal. You were to never refer to me as 'doctor' in public. Start calling me that now and I'll be pestered with advice for every little complaint."

Billy backed into the corner. "It slipped out, Hugo. You know I would never break my word. Anyway, let's not argue. We should try to have a good time." He went to the sink to put his shaving gear in the cabinet.

Hugo walked over and put his hand on Billy's shoulder. "Thanks, Billy," he said. "I know you're the type of person who always does the right thing. And you're correct, by the way—this voyage should be a memorable occasion. And here's a tip towards making that happen. There's a specific passenger on this ship you should make contact with."

"What contact would you be suggesting, and with whom?"

"She's superior to any woman you've met so far in your rather sheltered life. But you should advance your interests anyway. Have a brief chat with her. Talk about spiritual deliverance, profane pleasure, whatever comes to mind."

"Superior woman?"

"I know what you've become used to, Billy—teenagers like Andy, who really knew not what she did, or what you did to her, for that matter."

"It was an experiment, Hugo. Nothing more. I regret it now. It's over and won't happen again."

Hugo stood, touched his toes and flexed his torso in the mirror. "You don't say. Well best I say to you, Reverend, that should you treat Miss Lewellyn poorly, you might get your fingers burned."

Billy frowned and unpacked his case.

The *Yildun* got underway early in the morning. No further stops slowed the inevitable rolling of the Atlantic. The north shore receded. Hugo could see a remote village and the launch coming to take off the pilot. He felt nervous, vulnerable, about to drown, and went in from the cold deck to the warmth of the dining room. When he was seated, he glanced towards the empty captain's chair. The steward stood over him smelling of cardboard.

"This morning we have oatmeal, or if you are hungry, sausage with eggs, sir."

"Sausages and eggs sound great, Hans."

"Sausages, sir? How many would that be?"

"At least four. The sea makes me hungry."

The man turned away nodding his head and saying as he went, "As yet we are still in the St. Lawrence River, sir, and not at sea."

Hugo made mental note to complain about the steward's attitude but changed his mind when he saw Von Raynor walk in. The master of the *Yildun* was tall but stooped and overweight. His chin disappeared into a neckpiece of puffy flesh that shook when he spoke. He smiled at the room of faces and within five minutes was saying ingratiating things to the women at the table.

"Yes, the crew is away a good deal of the time. The North Atlantic is our real home," he said and nodded regularly at the polite comments offered by the chief engineer. Appelton leaned over to Hugo's table. "Here's some new about Von Raynor: the war is not yet finished for this man. It will be a long voyage—good for a few rounds of whatever he stocks in the bar."

They drank coffee and talked; Billy examined the conditions of his passport. When the steward stepped from the galley with their meal tray, the cabin went silent. Hugo gasped and his face flushed. Von Raynor raised his head and gawked at the three pounds of sausage that lay in a pool of grease. Guenther, the steward, moved solemnly across the carpet and set the platter ceremoniously in front of Hugo.

Billy put his hands behind his head and smirked. "You must really like meat. King of the T-bone would be proud of you."

Hugo noted the circumference of each piece, its length, the half-inch of liquid fat washing over them. Captain Von Raynor half stood to get a better look. "Herr Lutz, did we load sufficiently from the packing house to feed this passenger?"

Guenther shrugged. Hugo put his hand on his stomach. Next to the captain sat Violet Lewellyn, who smiled at Hugo and gave a little wave of her fingers. He smiled back at her, cut through one of the pieces, and chewed with a satisfied nodding of his head. After finishing one complete sausage, he stopped for a swallow of coffee. When the master of the *Yildun* looked his way again, Hugo said in a loud voice, "It's a pleasure to travel on a ship that is generously provisioned, Captain."

The man hesitated at the comment, then went back to chatting with the ladies. When the steward came with more coffee, the three remaining sausages had cooled. On their flanks, grease settled into contoured patterns like old candle wax. Billy finished his porridge and leaned back. Guenther sidled over to the table to clear away the bowl.

"I hope you have enough room for these. The Captain hates wastage.... the habit of rationing left over from the war. Do enjoy them, *bitte*."

The steward began clearing dishes. Heartened by the frequent hand clapping of the women, the captain continued his comments on wartime service. Appelton winked at Hugo, pushed back his chair and stood up.

"We congratulate you, Herr Von Raynor. I mean that sincerely. It's an honorable thing to serve one's country, no matter what the outcome. And no one can tell of the sea like a man who has fought on, and beneath it."

The guests nodded. Violet smiled and ran the beads through her fingers. The women stood and clapped again, all except Señora Manguel, who was eighty-three and claimed to be the aunt of the exiled King Juan Carlos of Spain. Appleton continued with his platitudes. Guenther turned around to see Hugo toss the last bite of sausage into his mouth. He stared at the empty plate and then at the open porthole. Hugo smiled and wiped the napkin across his lips.

"What's your name, Franz?"

"Norbert."

"No it's not, it's Guenther. Well, Guenther, I'd like some more of these but I see you're busy. Let's not skimp with the portions next time. Tomorrow I want at least as much." Appleton grinned at him, and Hugo nodded back. With his face expressionless and arms swinging, he marched out of the dinning room.

Later that day, as he watched Richard Appleton in the lounge, Hugo began to have an appreciation for the scientist's abilities. Besides his professional talents, Appleton was fluent in six languages. He ordered beer from the steward in High German. He debated in Spanish with the old ladies from Barcelona. He spoke Dutch to the radio operator, English to his own wife, and French to customs officials in Quebec City. When drunk, he sang Italian arias to the guests, and on his infrequent sorties to the fo'castle, ranted to the crew in Low German. Hugo, however, given the consequences of his own bookish upbringing, felt uneasy with such grossly augmented levels of education. Conrad had made it clear to him early on that language was the foundation of experience, and alone makes possible the categories you can think and argue about. As he drank more wine, Hugo reasoned to himself that if you have more languages, you have more categories to think and argue about, which makes for even more expertise, more languages, more categories. Linguists would have a lower impulse for spontaneous action; multilingualism generally would curtail violence and interfere with sex. Hugo laughed inwardly at this ridiculous logic. He knew that his own experience with women and brawling tended towards the opposite. His sympathies for the old scientist faded. As the *Yildun* glided through the Straits of Belle Isle, Appleton seemed content enough to be shuffling the cards and chatting mindlessly to his shipmates.

"As I was saying before, Hugo, I don't think our captain has surrendered," he said. "It's a dangerous thing. With a few beers in him he's not even running on the surface. You are aware that he was a submarine commander during the battle of the Atlantic—led an entire wolf pack, or so he says. He still thinks of himself as being in the navy, still fighting the war. He's a tyrant and might provoke the crew. You must watch him."

Hugo finished another glass, and added paranoia to Appleton's list of characteristics. But he was also aware that the captain did have his quirks. During the day, Von Raynor was a polite and competent commander. In the evenings when he was in a mood and slouched in his bar chair together with the chief engineer, no one would go near him. Hugo noted the way he moved around, agitated, as if he were trying to pull his fat body into the past, into the war, down into the hideous depths of the sea. His round face glowed in the bar lights. Hugo imagined him in the conning tower with his instruments and maps, his cap on backwards as if he was prepared at any moment to stick his eye into the periscope to advance his predatory impulses. He spoke in short guttural bursts as if he were itching to launch an attack.

"They're a perfect pair of losers," said Appleton who was usually drunk himself by eight in the evening. "I understand that Von Raynor had his precious U-boat blown from under his feet. And the little weasel next to him shares his outrage. As well he should. Mueller served as a stoker on the *Admiral Graf Spee*…was humiliated right up to his square Bosch ears by its infamous scuttling." The scientist drank the last of his scotch, nodding and grunting with certainty, and mentioning as an afterthought that Violet Lewellyn had just come into the lounge together with the two Spanish passengers. Hugo noticed that she never once looked in his direction.

*   *   *   *

A day out from Newfoundland the numerous icebergs rocked sideways in heavy, building seas. As the ship plunged higher and lower, the arc of its swinging increased. Passengers hung listlessly around the lounge or went to their cabins. Appleton and Billy organized a bridge tournament. Throughout the day, as the ship's motion grew more violent, the games themselves dissolved until only the Appletons, Billy, and Hugo remained. The old couple sat contently sipping their cocktails, each immersed in total concentration. Hugo developed a vague, uneasy vertigo exaggerated by the efforts of the game. The cards seem to shine back at him; the jack danced lewdly in his hand. The king took on a resemblance to Morley Ibecks. Hugo had the urge to ask him what to bid, three clubs or three no trump? Cyril would not have had to ask, because his parents were obsessive players and he had attained top status in the commerce building. The bid would have been automatic: "Three hearts is all you'll get out of this." The words flew from Hugo's brain to his mouth and into the face of Estelle Appleton.

"Oh, a cautious bid, Mr. Haultain," she said with a coy wink, apparently unfazed by the worsening conditions. The ship heaved again and glasses slid to the stoppers. To complete the next game, the players were forced to wrap their legs around the furniture, which was bolted to the floor by turnbuckles and hooks. And with each game, the ocean swells seemed to grow larger still. Billy Bartholomew retched into his glass as he was completing a trick and left the cabin. Off the port side, a huge iceberg disappeared in the five o'clock dusk.

"I suppose we ought to have a nap," said Estelle Appleton, and left with her husband. Hugo slipped to the floor. An ashtray smashed next to his head. The weighted light of the North Atlantic settled with it, and gloom shrouded the lounge.

Violet Lewellyn walked into the darkened room and reached out a thin hand to him. "Let me help you up," she said. "Some fresh air will make you feel better."

They walked out onto the deck. The wind ripped from the northwest, pushing twenty-foot swells under the *Yildun*. Hugo felt giddy and began to talk. "I should tell you sometime the experience of being on a heaving bed instead of a ship, the sea only a figment—and the people..."

"A heaving bed?"

"It's not as lustful as you might think. The movement was all in my head. A fantasy, a sick boy's adventure."

"You are strange," she said laughing, and held firmly to the rail. The ship descended to the pit of a trough. Hugo grabbed for her arm, but slipped and came down chin first on the metal. He sank to his knees and blood dripped on the deck. She kneeled to him, and with a handkerchief tried to close the cut on his chin. Her hair drooped with the salt spray. When her eyes rose level to his, Hugo knew he was on shaky ground, in fact no ground at all for mistaking her chronic sadness for anger. As she attempted to pull him up, he could only get to a bent position. "I'll help you inside," she said.

On the way back to the lounge, he sniffed the rough air to settle his stomach then turned to thank her. But she was grabbing for the door handle, allowing him to slip his arm to her waist, to her thin hips, and stagger with her into the passageway. The lounge was deserted. Violet took off her coat and sat down. Hugo sat across the table and watched her fingers moving the beads rhythmically up and down along the silver string that hung between her breasts. For a long time the only sound was the wind through the door, and glasses sliding from edge to edge, tinkling musically amidst the groaning of wood and steel.

Finally he spoke. "Can I be frank?"

"Yes."

"At first I thought you were angry at the world."

"Why would you think that?"

"Because I suffer with the idea that women have no choice but to be angry at the way they're treated by men. Some hide it better than others."

"I'm not angry with anyone, at least at the moment. And I agree that women suffer, Hugo, but so do all people. Some understand and get beyond their bitterness quicker than others. But I am saddened that you are sick and now injured…even if slightly."

Hugo held his abdomen and gulped back his retching. "Then I offer my apologies and would do more to make it up. But as you can see, I'm having difficulty."

"I understand," she said. "Your apology is accepted."

She came around and daubed his swollen chin. "We should find that useless Guenther. Apparently he's the medic on this ship. But by now he's probably drunk and no help to anyone."

"Maybe he's with Ormes," said Hugo. "I hear he's the worst of us all."

"Who knows what poor Frank needs—medicine, or just someone to tend him."

"He needs more in the way of a miracle; and to tend him in his condition would require a martyr."

Violet smiled. She leaned across the table to wipe the continuing stream of blood from his chin with her long white fingers and a napkin. Hugo stared at her eyes.

"A martyr?" she replied. "Simple kindness isn't martyrdom, Hugo. I will do my best for him."

"Let me tell you, Violet, that Ormes was queasy when the flag fluttered and isn't likely to recover until we reach the other side."

"That will be a safe haven for him then. Anyway, isn't that what we all seek? A refuge? Trust in the Lord and we shall have it. Frank Ormes trusts and will survive. In the meantime he has no choice but to suffer."

A door opened and Captain Von Raynor made his way into the lounge. He stopped when he saw the occupied table. "Not feeling well, Mr. Haultain? Hurt yourself already, I see. You have the young lady for a nurse now, but I'll have the first officer come down anyway. Guenther is occupied with another passenger." He left the room without nodding good-bye.

In four days the North Atlantic reduced Frank Ormes to a shriveled sack. His cabin stank, and the steward had to swab it out with disinfectant. Fearing the worst, he threatened a boycott. The dried biscuits grew mold by the door where Norton had shoved them. He was certain Ormes had died, but apparently no one had gone near the cabin. At dinner one evening, Estelle Appleton said, "Apparently he was last heard to cry out on Sunday."

"All this ship's movement has put his body out of synch and his heart has stopped," said Richard, "I heard of a man dying that way on the Tasman Sea, in the fifties."

"Norbert's soup has the same odor as Ormes cabin," added Señora Manguel with a suspicious look on her face. The other passengers sniffed their bowls.

"Don't be so morbid," Violet said. "Mr. Ormes is in the hands of the Lord. He is working out his destiny."

"The poor bastard's working out his guts," said Appleton.

Next morning, when the seas were rolling mightily and black clouds scudded to the southeast, Hugo snuck into Ormes' room for a second time. Violet Lewellyn was sitting next to the stricken student. The erstwhile doctor gave her more pills to reduce his nausea and this time a written recipe for liquid and nourishment. It came with the promise that she say nothing about it to anyone on the ship. That night he dreamt sadly of the shore medics in Rotterdam carrying Ormes out on a stretcher and Mrs. Appleton peeking under the sheet and confirming that he was, like the biscuits, dead and moldy.

The first officer remarked some days later that it was a shame that the young man was unable to see the source of his misery. Hugo thought on that. It was an unfortunate void in Ormes' life he concluded, that given the extent of his sacrifice he would never get to contemplate the vast ocean at night or during the violent day, with green spray and seas as high at their crest as the open bridge, with a strong nor'wester pushing them higher. In the early afternoon of that day, Hugo read and did his exercises. Things flew round the cabin and Billy crawled in the door.

"What a godforsaken place. Will this storm ever end? And in spite of it, Guenther's going ahead with the dinner." He shinnied over to the bunk. "However, it will be a sporting night, Hugo. Good weather to be drunk and more good reasons to throw up. I heard the boson suggest we join Ormes in his cabin for a chorus."

"Friends with the boson?"

"Oh no, no. He's a vicious little bastard. You stay away from him, Hugo. He would make short work of a tiger. When he's near, the captain backs off.

Rumor has it that contrary to ship's rules, he sold a case of Slivovitz to the Señora for tonight's celebration."

Hugo finished his exercises. He flexed his shoulders, spreading his back out like an angry snake. He felt strong, determined. His fight with panic seemed bearable now that he had his sea legs and the nausea was gone. When he came out of the shower Billy had already slid a box from the bunk drawer and was half finished drinking a liter of beer.

"Aren't you starting a bit early?"

"Not in earnest. Only one beer, which is nothing."

"It's your duty to stay competent, Billy. Administering the last rites for Frank Ormes will be your first function of office. This storm might be his final adventure."

"No, no, he'll be fine. I overheard Violet Lewellyn say that he's getting better. I'm a little suspicious that you had something to do with that."

Hugo grunted. "Only God saves," he said, "and by way of you, Billy. As you know, it's cannon law that the Lord works through His clergy."

*   *   *   *

Oscar the boson lay in his grimy bunk stroking a Siamese kitten. As a matter of habit, he ignored Hugo's entry into the cabin and instead drew a leather sleeve across his moustache. The cabin reeked of sauerkraut and beer. The doctor had to fight down a lingering vertigo.

"What are you doing in here?" asked the boson. "Passengers only come when invited."

"Am I invited?"

"No."

"But I'm here now."

"So get out, before someone throws you out."

Hugo sat down on a stained deck chair and smiled. "I like that kind of talk, Oscar. It shows what you're made of. Man stuff. I mean I came here because Billy told me that it's the only place on this ship with real life—gritty, dirty, filthy, squalid life, and I can see with a quick look that he was right. But before you try to throw me out, I think you should offer me a drink. In fact, I'll buy it, and one for you as well."

"I don't sell liquor. Anyway, no one should be drunk tonight," he warned.

"It's a bit late for that," Hugo replied, "now that you've gouged a fortune from the Señora for a dozen bottles."

Oscar sneered. "I know your kind. You think I'm thief, eh, a dirty bastard. You call me bad names that first day in Montreal. But I know how to survive. I'll do more than throw you out of here."

He fixed his pitted eyes on the intruder, then reached under the shelf by his bunk and tossed Hugo a knife. "You a tough guy, a real smart-ass guy," he said. "Every time we load hides in Chicago, I fight someone like you. I always win. You, mister strong-guy, the ship pitch a little, you fall on your head and cut your chin. The cute nurse put a band-aid on it. You gonna have trouble coming in here, getting smart. You think you can use that to beat me?"

Hugo stopped smiling. "I tell you what, Oscar. The Reverend Billy has confessed to me that he's forgotten the words to the last rites—and you of all people would have a horror of death without the blessing. So why don't we have small test of strength. The wager is my twenty bucks against your kitten."

The boson spat in a dish. "What would you do with a cat?"

"I don't like cats so I'd toss it out that porthole over there."

The boson nodded his head and moved stiffly to get off his bunk. But when his feet touched the floor, he brought his fist around with a smooth gliding motion and caught Hugo squarely in the face. He fell backwards over empty boxes and landed on the deck. When he staggered to his feet, Oscar took him by the hand like a child and sat him on a stool. "Now let's see what we will see. You got ten years on me, mister wise guy. That tap on the chin was to even things out. Now, get your hand up where we can start."

Oscar grinned through stained, irregular teeth and brought his right arm onto the table. Hugo had a moment of elation as he contemplated the corded muscles, like a section of rope with tendons pressing through rigid brown skin. He breathed four or five times to clear his head, and took his position. After a minute of stalemate, he brought Oscar's hand backwards into the flame of the candle; when he saw that the boson would let his flesh cook to the bone before relenting, he released his grip, got a cold beer from the box, and poured it slowly over the blistering spot near the knuckle. The man took a deep breath and sat back on his bunk. Hugo handed him the half empty bottle. Wind whistled through a gap in the door and the storm gyrated the ship. Hugo took the kitten to a porthole and opened it. Oscar lunged off his bed. His shriek of despair blended with the wind. Hugo closed the hatch and walked back. With the ship's lurching, he threw the small animal at the boson.

"I don't think she can swim as far as Ireland, so I'll make you another deal. You keep the cat in exchange for a little unpleasant labor."

Oscar lay back down on the bunk, smiled and stroked the kitten's back. "No honest labor is unpleasant for me."

"Good, because for the rest of the voyage, I want you to go into Frank Ormes cabin everyday and clean it out. The stewards won't do it. Their stomachs are too weak."

"Why you ask me this? You think you're a good guy all of sudden? A wise guy and now a do-gooder. Are you trying to impress the Virgin Mary?"

"We got a deal Oscar. You got your cat back so don't let me down."

The boson waved and spat again into the dish. "I won't. Oscar is a man of his word and always speak the truth. So listen. The storm gets worse. Señora Manguel should cancel her party. Believe me, in this weather, the *Yildun* a crumb on the bed when Oscar humps, eh." He laughed with a coarse rattle in his throat. Hugo walked away. When he was at the door, Oscar yelled after him, "You're right when you say the little one can't swim. I pull her from the lake when we load hides in Chicago. She was half frozen, but I towel her off and put her between the tits of a whore. That warms, yeah? And only cost me an extra twenty."

Chapter X

Storm

On his way back from the fo'castle, Hugo noticed with growing apprehension that the light had gone early. Sunset flickered through a tear in the weather, and a yellow glow sullied the *Yildun*. The deck heaved up and down. Richard Appleton turned on the cabin lights and carefully stitched his way to his chair. He arranged things on the table, cleared his throat, then talked straight to Morton Schoolhouse from Indianapolis.

"Let's just imagine for the moment that where a thing is at any moment determines what it is," he droned. "Remember that Morton: where, determines what! This observation expands the laws of elementary particles to a general principle. Art, for example, is location. Living is location. Religion is location."

Hugo nodded and said, "My friend Cyril keeps telling me that real estate is location. Is that the same thing?"

"Your friend is probably quite ignorant."

"Actually, he's quite rich."

"Suggesting what, I wonder?"

"Suggesting that you're right. Certainly Ormes is reliant on this ship for his misery and so is Violet, at least for the opportunity of bringing him back from the dead."

"Exactly," said Appleton. "And she has been effective, I must admit. But I still maintain that her spirituality, and its results, are as reliant on the circumstances as an electron is for its existence."

Hugo sipped a glass of schnapps and wiped his chin delicately. Then he said, "There is an expert here who can offer a counter-argument."

Billy looked surprised when Hugo gestured towards him. "The priest is being modest so I'll substitute for him in giving the relevant quote:

> A mind not to be changed by place or time,
> The mind is its own place and in itself
> Can make a heaven of hell, a hell of heaven.

"That's from Milton," said Schoolhouse.

"Correct." Hugo replied. "John Milton says location doesn't matter; the mind doesn't change wherever it happens to be. To say otherwise is heresy. Is that not the teaching of the church, Billy?"

Appleton took the bottle from Hugo and poured himself another two inches. "Please hear me out. I will also answer for the priest, because we are talking different things here. The effective piety of the clergy is not portable. It's not a thing within him, a characteristic he can carry along like a bad temper. It flows to him through the baptism of colored glass and Gregorian chant. The Cathedral around him—the color, smell, shape, the great windows, the icons and relics in the corner—all of these redeem him from worldliness. Even his savage costume transforms him."

"I think the clothes are nice," said Billy.

"Exactly," Appleton replied. "Avant-garde to the last fold. It's a stage dress designed to create an illusion. Together with the plain chant and all the trappings of the building, it absorbs and rebroadcasts the divine atmosphere. The priest's voice exudes the essence of mystery and the worshippers—now in trance, of course—bow to the altar, to the unspeakable reverence of the Holy Father. Guenther, another beer, and one for my friend Billy also, and let's not forget Hugo. *Danke schoen*. Schoolhouse, are you okay? Now where was I? Yes. Remove the cleric from his Cathedral—stick him with the riff-raff in the bar with their aimless, silly chat and our man of the cloth will soon be jabbering nonsense."

Appleton swayed side to side and drank some more. Morton's head was on his chest. His eyes were glassy, unfocused. The steward filled his glass again.

"Come on, Richard," he pleaded. "Must be time for a game. Why don't you call your wife over?"

"I'll get her," said Billy, getting to his feet and steadying himself against the pitching of the floor. Schoolhouse shuffled the cards. Guenther set down another bottle of scotch and Appleton continued.

"I've lifted most of this from the *Bioscope Verité*, memoirs of the Bishop Elias Morrow written on Jersey, the Channel Islands in 1906."

He turned to Hugo, saying, "We go quite often to the Channel Islands as well…oh, and did you know that Violet is going to Guernsey? Yes, apparently she has a position of some sort there, and relatives in the church. Anyway, I think we should have a change in the music. You must have something besides polkas, Guenther. Some Wagner or Tommy Dorsey. That's it. Big band music. We're in the mood. Thank you."

He laughed while Estelle Appleton made her way up the lounge. Schoolhouse excused himself to go to the washroom, followed by Billy, who staggered and had to hold onto the furniture. Appleton called after him, "Yes, Yes. It's all true, Reverend. Thank you. My, what a nice tune. What do you think, dear?"

"The last one was a big wave, Richard. But you probably didn't notice when you were talking. It must have been the seventh wave," answered Mrs. Appleton in a singing voice.

"Now, are we going to play one more rubber before it gets so rough we can't keep the cards on the table?"

As she predicted, the weather worsened. Hugo excused himself and walked the corridors before going to cabin eight. He found Billy struggling to get off the cabin floor, stunned and holding his head. Hugo sat him on the edge of the bunk.

"I told you to layoff, Billy. It's not even dinner and you're piss-drunk already."

Billy nodded. "I agree. No more for me. I've had far too much, believe me. On my way here, I bumped into Violet. The moment she walked around the corner I remembered what Appleton just said. You know me. I'm a poor theologian and only know what I've read. And I've never read stuff like that. It can't be true that 'where' you are determines 'what' you are. But when I saw Violet it all came into my head. I couldn't help noticing how she looked."

"How did she look?"

Reverend Bartholomew wiped his face with a small towel. "Have you ever examined Violet—up close, I mean? Did you see how her skin sometimes appears perfect, but at times you can look right through her, as if she were transparent. I saw her in the hall just now and can't describe it. She looked like an angel."

"I don't know what you mean, Billy. First she has perfect skin. Then she's an angel. Does that mean she has no skin at all? She hasn't changed. How could she change?"

The priest lay back on the covers and shook his head. "Open me another beer. I'm going crazy with this ship rolling around, nothing stationary or permanent." His voice trailed off to a whisper.

Hugo brought over two bottles. Billy poured beer into his hand and rubbed it on his face. "Maybe Appleton's right," he said. "Something awful has happened on this ship. Look outside. Where the fuck are we? We're going down like Ormes."

Hugo lay in his own bunk and smiling, stared at the ceiling. He drained the last of the beer and let the bottle rest on his chest. "We're in the middle of a storm somewhere on the Atlantic Ocean, Billy. That presents no problem. We all die after all. You will drink yourself to death very soon, perhaps tonight. But Violet is a spirit who will live on. Ormes will live as well. Doesn't that give you hope?"

Billy lay frowning on his bunk. His eyes bulged outwards when he said, "I don't see why Muxlow didn't have me perform the marriage rites for him. I think it was an unforgivable slight. For years I had to tow him around with that harness on and that shitty little horse behind. I think I'll write the bastard and demand he put into his will that I be allowed to bury him. Dust to dust. That would be good."

He got to his feet and staggered to the mirror. After touching his face lightly with his fingertips, he put his nose close to the glass. "Just the same, Hugo, I'm going to take your advice and get myself real close to Violet Lewellyn—tonight, tomorrow, or next month if need be."

Two weeks before Christmas, 1965. Lufungula Prison.

Sergeant Mintou used the excuse of Hugo's interrogation to enter cell six late each afternoon for his lessons. During the slow process of reading from the designated text and a slower journey towards understanding what the words meant, he showed no letup in his determination. After twelve lessons, Hugo said, "You frighten me, Mintou. You have an aptitude that's grimly mechanical, like a man preparing for war."

"Thank you," he replied. "That is exactly what I'm doing. When you were learning, monsieur, what were you preparing for?"

"For entrance to heaven. I was not expected to live."

"Then you weren't much different than many of my brothers and sisters who died as children."

Hugo nodded. "I had doctors and priests to save me."

"And Africa has your friend, the ju-ju man who saves old niggers. As I said at the beginning of my lessons, I want to understand more of what he thinks. What would he do about me?"

"You're not old, Mintou. But had you been like your brothers, the doctor would try to save you anyway. That much is recorded history and a lesson you would have learned if your village had had a better school. But school is in session now and I have the job of teaching you."

A week later, Hugo had the sergeant squat in the corner and give him a cigarette. He sat himself wearily on his case with his weakening shoulders supported by the cell wall and talked directly into the drooping lids of Léon Mintou's eyes.

"The following events happened on the ship that transported me across the same ocean your ancestors traversed in the opposite direction. This ship, however, was better equipped than theirs and the niceties of shipboard life more refreshing. On the *Yildun* there was always time for a quick drink in the bar before the evening meal. One night, when a huge storm raged across the Atlantic, Captain Von Raynor sat at the tiny counter on a stool next to Mueller, the engineer. As usual, he wore his hat on backwards. The lights of the bar splayed over his puffy face, over the crust-like skin of the chief stoker. I sat in a chair next to the bar's only table and asked, 'Does the name Korrolus mean anything to you, Captain.'

'Should it?' he replied.

'It might if you had a good memory, which I suspect you do. You seem to recall every aspect of your defeat in the war.'

"Mueller muttered something that sounded like 'Fuck Americans,' then proceeded to speak to the captain in German. I tipped my glass to the old man who had come to sit in a second chair at my table."

"Was this the ju-ju doctor?" Mintou blurted with a grin.

"Don't jump to conclusions," Hugo replied. "This white-haired old man reached over to take a sip of my drink, then said to me, 'Sounds like the chief might have had his comeuppance.'

"I didn't know so I whispered across the table, 'What can you add to this, Albert? You who knows all of history.'

'An anecdote, no more,' he replied and stroked his stained moustache. He looked thirsty, so I went to the bar to bring him a tall glass of beer.

'Thanks. Most kind of you,' he said, taking the glass from me and draining half of it with one motion. 'Now let me tell you the rest of his history. After the war, the chief's initial employment at sea was aboard the ship transporting me back to Europe for the first time since the armistice. He was in the habit of telling war stories in the ship's bar to the usual collection of war-weary travelers who should have been spared his bragging. According to him, his first and only love was the *Admiral Graf Spee*, the most feared of the so-called pocket battleships of the German Navy. At that time he was a mere stoker, and according to him on watch in early 1940 off the tip of France, when his unsinkable man-o-war blasted apart a ship named the *General Brazza*. Not a great loss, a few score merchant seamen and four thousand tons of cargo. Except some of it was for me. My cargo. Stuff to see my hospital through the misery of French interference and the general hardship of war. I still carry the grudge.'

'There were hostilities, Herr Doctor. They would have sunk what they saw,' I said. 'Who would have done otherwise?'

'Not him, to be sure, not the Nazis. Later on they would have not done other than engage the British Navy as well. But their ships were armed and wouldn't be sunk so easily. In a glorious turnabout the German navy ended up sinking itself instead.'

"I couldn't resist turning to the chief. 'Is that true, Herr Mueller?'

'Is what true?'

'That you sank yourself. The history books I've read say it was an unnecessary betrayal. After the first action, the *Graf Spee* steamed into Montevideo for a quick refit leaving behind a destroyer full of holes, a light cruiser with only one gun firing, and a cruiser reduced to scrap metal. Three crippled wrecks barely afloat and Captain Langendorf panics and blows up his own vastly superior ship.'

'Big mistake,' said the engineer. 'We were tricked by British Intelligence.'

'I understand. We must always forgive ourselves for being the victim of subterfuge. Allan Korrolus once told me that Captain Von Raynor was tricked as well. He let six thousand tons of ordinance get through to Algiers aboard the *Kyle Mission*, which he allowed to sail away unharmed. It's fully documented in the history books that most of those shells exploded under German armor. But he has a dozen times forgiven himself because it was really a trick of conscience and not the skewed judgment of pride or poor seamanship.'

"Von Raynor winced and said, 'Contrary to Korrolus' recollections, his ship survived because I had no choice in the matter. It wasn't luck, incompetence or a bleeding heart. I make no apologies for my actions. If he told you otherwise he is lying.'

"The chief engineer patted Von Raynor on the back, saying, 'Don't listen to those who would revise history, Juri. We know the truth on this.'

'The history is correct on the *Graf Spee*, Chief Mueller—and about my experience, I have a clear conscience. Now it's time for dinner.'

"I sipped the last of my beer alone. Had Albert stayed longer, we could have discussed the revision of history in its various nuances, its benefits and liabilities, because as we all know, a revision that nudges mass murder towards the two-step oom-pah of marching bands must include the regrettable drift into self-annihilation. But never mind. Both bad and good things benefit from an association with evil. Charity work is the shining example of that. Outright goodness is just too bland to be effective. Albert Schweitzer notwithstanding, in time of peace, mission work lacks the cruelties of war to excite people to dig deeply into their pockets. But Von Raynor? He was well past bothering with thoughts of charity as he wove his way down the far passage on his way to dinner. The ju-ju doctor, as I said before, had already excused himself for the chore of doing rounds in the leper colony, saying to me before he went, 'I guess that much is settled, Hugo. History has no choice but record me as being the quintessential bleeding heart.'"

Mintou grunted and wiped his forehead. He remained squatting in the far corner.

"As I said before, I understand very little of this, monsieur. But I will learn it all and speak of it as you do. And the thing is, even if the ju-ju doctor is not here to save me, of the two of us, I will be the last to die."

He smirked again as he came to stand by Hugo's leather case, reaching down to pick up the book. "I'm taking this with me," he said. "The closer I am to it, the easier it will be for me to learn."

Hugo made no attempt to stop him. Mintou opened the cell door with its customary grinding of stone. Before leaving he asked, "How can a heart bleed, monsieur, and still remain a heart?"

Hugo shrugged his shoulders and sat back on the case. The cell door closed. Nothing came through the grate to him but a slight breeze with no smell of salt. The weather that night was the same as the night before, hot and dead still.

On board the *Yildun*, October 25, 1964, 5:30 pm.

The swells came obliquely from the northwest. Each wave rolled underneath, tottered the ship from port to starboard, and the scuppers foamed like small rivers. In the dining room, sky and water seemed to slosh back and forth. The rattle of dishes blended with the voice in Hugo's head telling nautical stories. At the captain's table Estelle Appleton sat next to Violet and Señora Manguel.

"Here comes the seventh wave," they sang as an ensemble and locked arms.

"Dinner will be served soon," said Richard. "Be patient. A good meal gives one strength."

With each stupendous rolling, the captain winked at the ladies. He sat rigid in his chair and told more of his stories concerning past storms and other wonders. Norbert staggered in with a massive tureen brimming with thick soup and set it at one end of the sideboard. Mrs. Appleton looked at the bowl with horror.

She tugged at her husband's sleeve. "Richard, here comes the seventh wave." She tried to interrupt Von Raynor with a flutter of her hand.

"Of course, on a submarine, Frau Appleton," said the captain, "we had only to dive to escape the turmoil of the open water and have our meal in peace—and on a level table. But here, of course, we have to be brave. Don't worry, on the *Yildun* we are all safe and secure."

Hugo wasn't listening. He was thinking about Violet going to Guernsey over calm seas on a little ferryboat. When he looked at her, she stared back and slid her beads. Then as the ship rolled onto another, larger wave she nodded towards the old master and frowned. Hugo knew he had been warned. He backed his chair off and braced his legs. Estelle Appleton looked aghast at her husband. She whispered again in a voice vibrating with anticipation. "Richard, the seventh wave!"

The ship rose like a cloud. Behind them, the soup tureen inched along the sideboard, its increasing velocity greased by the broth foaming over the edge. Hugo saw a lesson in elementary physics that Appleton was going to appreciate. On one hand, was a container of borsht to be neatly ladled by Norbert into smaller bowls, with a care for equilibrium so as not to spill a drop. On the other, a simple application of excess energy would soon replace this tidy connection with an alternate conclusion. Hugo's mind swelled with sympathy for the expected casualties.

The tureen struck the sideboard ledge, flew like a bomb across the salon, and exploded against the wall a few feet to the port side of the table. Broth, cabbage, carrots and chunks of meat rained down on the diners. In the aftermath, the scream of the nor'wester distorted the random plop of vegetables dropping from the ceiling. Shocked, Hugo stared at the captain. An agony of humiliation wrinkled the old man's skin. His eyes were shut to the sting of salt and herbs, his faith collapsed. Like the defeated generals in the Potsdammerplatz, this was an end of history. The war was finally over, forever lost. Hugo felt a privileged humility at being a witness to Von Raynor's capitulation. Over his sodden head, crowned with a toupee of cabbage leaves, he draped his large monogrammed napkin. Breathing apologies through the cloth, he rose and walked towards the door—smack into his steward. They danced briefly in a grotesque mime of the confused, then the captain disappeared and was not seen publicly until the pilot boarded at the Hook of Holland.

Billy guffawed, "Silly old bastard. Serves him right."

Richard Appleton picked the vegetables from his wife's shoulders. "Every seventh one is huge, Richard," she announced sadly. "He's a sailor and should have known that."

Hugo cleaned himself up and looked around at the other guests who were doing the same. In the corner armchair sat Violet Lewellyn, clean, undisturbed, and smiling graciously. She got to her feet, balancing against the storm. Hugo went over to her. "I think I'll put on my coat and go for a walk," she said brushing past him. "It's a bit stuffy in here. I love being out with the storm, almost in the water, you know. It's like being close to God."

With that comment she went through the cabin door, leaving the other passengers to grope their way through the mess on the floor. Señora Manguel thanked Hugo for wiping off her back. "What do I care for appearances at my age?" she said. "This voyage will bring a conclusion. I've had nothing to drink and already I'm having difficulty. Do you know that I'm a great aunt of King Juan Carlos? I take these old ships to elude the agents of Franco. Go to Spain, young fellow, and experience for yourself the land of the Generalissimo and his infamous Guardia Civil; meet a real tyrant—not a man with cabbage on his head."

In cabin eight, Billy Bartholomew was showering off the remains of his dinner. His body pounded off the tile and he sang incoherently. Hugo put on his jacket and put the photo of the *Kyle Mission* next to his chest. He roamed the corridors and found the Señora's cabin empty. Crude decorations hung from the lamps. Norton had already set out the party food. Then he went onto the lee-side deck concerned to find Violet Lewellyn. Outside, the air had no rain in it. Light from the cabins showed waves that boiled away from the ship in huge hydraulic bursts. He moved towards the stern, stuck his face round the corner and walked at a radical angle to reach the windward rail. The sea wall was vertical and water swirled in at the scuppers. Crawling and groping for handholds, he moved forward to the bridge stairwell and listened. The wires screamed. Wind blew pleading voices down the passage. It was like hearing his own perplexities beating against the sickroom glass or the distress of recent time: Ormes pleading for his bowels to dry up, the Chicago whore with legs pried open by the boson, humping away like the sea. But from where he stood, all up and down the length of the *Yildun*, he could see nothing alive but the phosphorescent sea foaming over the decks.

He held tight to the stair rail and let a rush of optimism push out his fears. What was the sea after all? What was it for either him or Violet or anybody to drown in the depth of a storm? It would be over in one numbing moment. The piddling energy of the lectures and books that for years had washed him side to side in the shallow turbulence of the sickroom had been a greater terror. Muir had been in command of his ship then, and Albert the pilot of his conscience, hoping to make his life less shallow, less turbulent by making him think. But the insipid blandness of both faith and logic had failed to subdue the turbulence or deepen his humanity. Hugo looked out on the swollen, angry waves and feared that part of him would always have an appetite for conflict. Like the storm force of ocean wind, anger has a bite to it, a flavor that lasts.

When the salt spray began to sting his mouth, he slipped inside the passageway and climbed to the top of the stairs. The deserted bridge was lit by a green fluorescence bleeding from the instruments, the autopilot, the compass, and radar. One door led into a passage. Hugo yelled down it and heard back the muffled pounding of the engines. A door banged with the rolling of the ship. No one came. A phantom crew, he thought—pie-faced mutinous ghosts, right under the nose of the ancient submariner himself and him the largest fake of all, supposed to be on watch but dead asleep in his cabin.

The door was open but he knocked anyway. The old man snored. Looking at him Hugo felt his fear and ecstasy subside—had the sense that the opportunity for experience aboard the *Yildun* was dwindling to a pantomime or a one-week farce. He picked the captain's cap off the chair, went back onto the bridge, and put it on. The autopilot clicked steadily. In the map room he saw the blueprint of their journey through the night: a precise arc traced across empty space on the white chart of great circle routes. He pulled a small flask of schnapps from his pocket and sucked at it hard and long. He took a second pull to ensure the alcohol went straight to his head, bettering the odds of his being as good a proxy captain as Allan Korrolus had been on the *Kyle Mission*.

He stepped up and let the wheel slide through his hands. It had the smooth, soft give of woman's flesh. With his fingers pointing east towards perilous seas and fairylands forlorn, he felt himself becoming as irrelevant as the slumbering old man, both unable to attract peril or an adventure more forlorn and hapless than the *Yildun*. It was only required of Hugo that he locate the insubstantial Violet Lewellyn, and just short of rape, lay her on the main hatch, white frock pulled over her pointy breasts, legs summarily pried open…

"As you were, sausage pirate, on my bridge."

Hugo jumped straight up in fright. Captain Von Raynor stood at his side peering through the fog port. He took the cap from Hugo's head and placed it on his own. He put his hand on Hugo's shoulder to steady himself, wiped stains from his uniform and talked in soft guttural phrases that made his jowls flap. When he squinted, his eyes seemed to weep. He gestured towards the rear of the bridge. "Come and help me, young fish feeder," he ordered, then sat on a raised chair at the rear. "What is the reading on the compass?"

"98 degrees 31 minutes," Hugo answered.

"Heading?"

"East by south east."

"What is your name or should I just call you Bratwurst?"

"Hugo Haultain, sir."

"Through that door is my cabin. And on the wall is a picture of my wife and young son. Come and see."

They went into the small neat room. Next to the bunk on a night table was a black pistol sitting on dog-eared stained papers. On the walls were several portraits. The most prominent was of a ship's company standing to attention along the deck of a submarine. Next to it in a gilt frame were a posed couple: a woman with her hair pulled straight back and a surly-faced youth.

"What do you think? He is the image of his father, ya, the glorious master of the high seas but really a ghost who haunts his family four times a year when he gets to Hamburg—a walking war medal tarnished by years of denial and absence. It's too late now for reconciliation. Pass the water. Thank you. These two as they hang on the walls, are the crew of this ship. You see there is no one else here. Deserted. A mutiny of the drunk, who have contempt for a master who wears a hat of borsht. To me the world's quite gone. So let's have a look."

He stood on his feet and straightened his master's cap. With care he surveyed the instruments, adjusted the autopilot, made entries into the ship's log, then paced back and forth with Hugo on the careening bridge. A jabbering of messages came from the Morse key.

"A Mayday," he said. "Two hundred miles from here. There are other ships close on in the area. Godspeed to anyone foundering tonight."

Von Raynor went back into his cabin. "Have a small drink with me, sausage boy." He broke off speaking and looked at Hugo. "Pardon my rudeness, Mr. Haultain. I don't deliberately demean my passengers, but sometimes the temptation is irresistible."

As he poured two small glasses full of Slivovitz, Hugo removed the envelope from under his jacket and placed it on the small table.

"What is this?"

Hugo ran his fingers through his hair. Von Raynor put on a pair of reading glasses, removed the contents and put the photo on his lap.

"Perhaps you can tell me what it is, Captain."

"From your comments earlier this evening, Korrolus must have given this to you."

"I took the picture and he gave me this print."

Von Raynor shook his head in disbelief. "The *Kyle Mission* beached among other ships," he said and turned the photograph over and looked at the stenciled name on the back.

"I was curious that you showed such little interest in how I came to know your history," said Hugo.

"Oh I was interested...and waiting for you, lad, biding my time until you showed up. Now you are here, tell me what you know."

Hugo recited an abridged account of his talks with Korrolus, Blenkinthorpe, and his interest in knowing more of their adventures. Von Raynor took a swallow of the clear drink, leaned forward with his elbows on his knees with his head hanging. For some time he stayed in this position with his eyes closed, making low noises in his throat as he listened. Then he sat up and started speaking.

"Here is what I can tell you of my own adventures as they relate to your uncle, and to the others. To make them clear I'll start with a little history. My brother was an energetic man who took to assisting his fellows. For much of the thirties he worked in Africa. At the start of the war he used his connections throughout the Swiss apparatus to secure goods for his charity work. One day before we set sail from Brest with a squadron for mid-Atlantic duty, being the shipping lanes from Africa to the east coast of North America, I received a personal letter from my brother. It said that with the onset of war, the hospital was in great need and that a load of supplies destined for Lambaréné was aboard a cargo ship sailing with a convoy leaving North America in November. He begged me that, as squadron commander, I do what I could to spare this ship. Apart from the name of the vessel, there were no details other than this."

Von Raynor took a drink and adjusted himself on the side of his cot. He looked straight at Hugo.

"You see, the war and much else divided my brother and me in our assessment of benefits for mankind. I loved him, could appreciate his work, his sacrifice. But I had no intentions of letting even one ship through. My duty was to the Reich and the Fuehrer. I went so far as to issue a directive to my commanders that should the *Kyle Mission* be spotted, they notify me. It was my intention to personally give the order to sink her. I thought my brother colossally naïve in this regard. As we set ourselves for duty I was determined to find this vessel, knowing that the odds of finding one of a thousand such ships was small.

"One day late in the month we engaged with a convoy and the escorts guarding it. We sunk many ships in a few hours including an escort, and my vessel was in pursuit of a ship that had been separated from the pack. I was at the periscope setting up for firing, but something about it made me hesitate. I went quickly to my cabin and checked the letter from my brother. The ship a few hundred meters from my vessel was clearly marked the *Kyle Mission*. It was like destiny. So smug I was that I allowed for a moment of indecision. We surfaced and before they could fire on us, the gunners quickly disabled their cannon. It was at this point I recovered my senses and was about to give the order to fire a torpedo, when through my glasses I could see a man pulling himself across the deck away from the smoking wreckage of the gun.

"He reached the portside railings and pulled himself upright. I had him framed in my glasses, and found it strange that he wore the uniform of a British naval officer. I moved our vessel so close that I could see his face—even make out the detail of a scar on his lip. It appeared that he had small part of his leg blown away by the blast. He stood there motionless, at attention, as if knowing the final blow would come at any moment. I dared not let it show on own my face, this dereliction of duty, but I thought briefly of my brother's work and of Schweitzer, a countryman engaged in different kind of conflict. On that date I suffered a moment of weakness, which of course was a good thing for your uncle. I gave an order to signal with the lamp, sending him a message that at the time I thought he would never understand, but later knew that he came to the truth.

"The war ended and I can't describe, nor could you conceive, the ignominy of defeat. I was not only shipless but rudderless, casting around for some solid piece of life to grab hold of. Through some good luck, I received from Algiers a note concerning the fate of my brother, and I made it a personal objective to discover what had happened to him. This quest was a welcome diversion from my bitterness concerning the outcome of the war."

Von Raynor stopped and got to his feet trying to smooth out his uniform. He went to a mirror and ran his fingers through his gray, messy hair.

"Once there I went to the Mission to Seamen on Rue Santeria. Being with other men of the sea helps. There is bond. I was well into my second drink when a man who had being playing darts sat down at an old upright piano next to the board. I watched his hands as he warmed them up playing little ditties. I recall staring at my own hands, the scars, the veins running along their backs thinking of the things they had done, when out of that decrepit instrument I heard the precious Beethoven filling that stinking place with light, not the bright sun of the Ninth, but the simple Moonlight. I had to fight back tears—me, a man who would not blink an eye to kill—because I heard a few notes of music that reminded me of my youth and the things we turn our backs on in wartime. When he had finished, the player went into a back corner and I was drawn to follow him there and talk.

"We discussed Beethoven and music generally as strangers would do. I was aware that another man had walked in and when I turned to face him, a matter only of politeness, I was confronted with a face I could never have forgotten, the face of the British officer who had stood at the railing of the merchantman, this ship that you photographed rusting away on the riverbank. I could see he still had the scarred lip, but, although he walked with a cane, he at least had the use of both legs. The man who played the piano said, 'My name is Martin Birks and this is Allan Korrolus.' I stood and said, 'Good evening, my name is Juri Von Raynor.' We shook hands, then I said, to their amazement, 'It is a privilege to meet you, Lieutenant Birks, British First Army and you Captain Korrolus late of the *SS Kyle Mission*. I believe you both knew my brother."

The captain lay along his bunk. He looked exhausted and shut his eyes. After some minutes of silence, he said, "Now, Mr. Haultain, get along to the Señora's party, and thank you. One other thing, a warning: keep inside tonight. And keep an eye on your friend, Miss Lewellyn. I've seen her on the decks when she shouldn't be. Tonight she would not survive such recklessness."

Hugo waited for five minutes before covering the sleeping man with a blanket. Leaving the photo of the *Kyle Mission*, he went back to the alcove below the bridge and considered what he had just heard. His cigarette glowed brightly in the gusts of wind whipping around the baffles; he admitted to a grand confusion. Given the chaos of altered history, it was important to emphasize Von Raynor's recollection of a simple piece of piano music, the same music that Hugo's father insisted to the point of threats that he never learn to play.

After showering and putting on dry clothes for the party Hugo went along the passageway to Señora Manguel's door. Inside, the dance partners swirled and shifted like flotsam on the sea, adapting to the pitching steel floor like the beer that ran this way and that. He looked for the woman he hoped might give him another version of truth, but she wasn't there. The Señora said she had been in briefly, then left. No one else had seen her. After a few dances, a drink or two, a hug and a kiss with the other women, Hugo went back down the passageway to open a second door. The stateroom was empty. He felt another surge of apprehension.

Billy staggered after him and grabbed his arm. "Listen, just leave her be. Who cares anyway? She rudely ignored my attentions. Tonight Violet Lewellyn is having her baptism in the ugly world as we all must do."

"What happened to your consuming love, Reverend?"

The priest stopped and tried to scrape off the spittle crusted on his lips. Hugo backed slowly down the passageway with Billy stalking forward, leaning on the wall for support. "Listen to me, Hugo. Violet is a sinner and must do a penance. But if you must know, she was last seen going forward to the crews quarters."

Hugo turned away silently. Billy yelled after him, "Better hurry, El Cid. No more virgin!" His attempt to laugh caught in his throat.

In the fo'castle, the crew was drunk and surly. The boson could no longer stand up. He lay naked, covered only by a scrap of sheet, all the while stroking his cat and swigging from a bottle. "Is who here, mister asshole guy?"

"The young woman called Violet."

"Violet? Is that the one I call Virgin Mary?" He laughed and wiped his mouth. "If so, she is not here." Hugo grabbed his throat. Oscar grinned, spat out a stream of black juice into a bucket, and said, "Because if they show their face in here, *bitte*, in five seconds not even the cockroaches are virgins."

Hugo went back to her cabin. It was still empty. The lounge was also deserted so he ran up to the bridge. The first officer was slumped carelessly in the pilot's chair. Hugo turned and went down to the main deck. The wind was ceaseless. The night sounds howling from the ship were like gestures of remorse. He heard a pleading voice roil with the air across the curvature of a ventilator saying, "Please!"

"Who's there?" he shouted and ran forward. As the *Yildun* broke low in the huge swell, an intermittent current of seawater flowed a foot deep to the main hatch. Hugo turned to go back and stumbled on a piece of metal. The incoming tide washed him headfirst into the main hatch cover, splitting open the gash on his chin. He got to his knees and fought for breath. A hurricane blast of wind pinned him into the canvas and again a voice shouted, "Please!"

"Please what?" he answered. An irritation rose in his chest. As a boy he had concluded that the word "please" sat atop the pinnacle of dishonesty. Countless storybooks were filled to the back cover with nauseating tales of misery and the attendant pleas for mercy, for wealth, for deliverance, all prefaced with that groveling insincerity, as if to suggest that God would deliver on any request to which the word was attached. Wiping the cold water from his eyes he shouted, "For Christ's sake, Violet, just tell me where you are."

The wind screamed through the bow gear. The ship broke under the next wave and a flood of oily water swept the decks to the level of the hatch cover. He struggled knee-deep through it, trying to keep from falling over. Ahead, long white fingers reached out from behind the winch housing.

"Here it comes!" a voice screamed. "Give me your hand or you'll be swept into the sea."

Hugo ran forward, leaped towards a gap in the steel and caught hold of the fingers. Four arms desperately intertwined themselves through the links of the anchor chain, then the bow of the *Yildun* disappeared beneath the seventh wave of the seventh storm on the seventh night out from the new world. And in the solitary black of the ocean, the thin, transparent skin of Violet Lewellyn withstood the enormous dissolving brine that tore at their hair and clothing. Hugo faltered, and she felt it necessary to draw him tight against her. In the lull between waves, she led him down the lee side of the main hatch to the shelter of the companionway and up the stairs to the bridge. The first officer was gone and Captain Juri Von Raynor paced the watch. He wore a clean and pressed uniform. His master's cap was set firmly on his head and his shoes were shined. When he saw them, he narrowed his eyes.

"Good evening, Master Hugo, Fraulein Lewellyn. May I remind you that this is not a night for wandering the decks, or is this the folly of romance? Whatever your pleasure, it's time to tend yourselves properly. We have no competent medical staff at the moment. Fraulein, the first aid kit is by the door. Please take the young man to your cabin and see to his chin...again."

A half hour later, when Hugo rose to leave with his wound bandaged, Violet put her hands on his shoulders and pushed him backwards onto the bunk, saying, "The captain said it's no time to be wandering around."

When she took off her clothes, he could see nothing transparent as Billy had suggested. She was normal, with goose bumps on her flesh from the chill and delicate veins in her breasts. The ship moved so violently that she had to hold on to his pants as he struggled to get them off. And with the coming of the seventh wave, they were flung together onto the blankets.

The next afternoon as Hugo sat in the still air of a calm day, he could not stop smiling and shrugging his shoulders. The sun shone on the deck and the few passengers lounging outside. Sliding by the horizon of a placid sea moved the upper parts and massive funnels of the *Isle de France* bound for New York. When he saw Billy wandering along the deck he said, "There are no antidotes to chaos and storms, Billy. There can be no penance for a sin as large as yours."

The Reverend Bartholomew paid no attention but walked on, past Richard Appleton who was sitting in a deck chair. He leaned forward and said, "Do you know how filthy the galley is? Filthy, Hugo. Do you know how I found out? Last night I went to find some dry bread for Estelle, who was sick with the storm and irritated with the awful noise from the Señora's party. Everyone was roaring drunk. Fortunately, I was too. But there you are. I didn't let Estelle know I was enjoying the tinny music with the crew and officers and passengers, all rowdy except Ormes who is quite alive and well, I'm happy to report, and that bag lady from Barcelona unaffected by the din, floating above it with her aristocratic airiness when everyone else was down on their hands and knees. Except your friend who was in the passageway on his belly, doing God knows what, sniveling about his burdens and doing push-ups, I think, which I must agree would be an awful penance for him, as soft as he is and him counting 9 - 10 - 11. A strange fellow. Can't believe he will someday be leading someone's flock. Do you know just now he hadn't a clue why we could only see the top of the *Isle de France*. I said facetiously, 'Do you think it's sinking?' And he couldn't say. 'Maybe it's in a hole,' he answered, and quite serious he was. Anyway, when I went to find something for my wife's upset stomach, I found the breadbox full of cockroaches. God, these long voyages get on my nerves. Estelle gets on my nerves too. The first mate says that tonight we'll see the Scilly Isles beacon. We have that to be thankful for. Tell your saintly friend to pray for the light because land can't be far behind."

Hugo stood on the portside deck at seven-thirty that night. For an hour he leaned against the railing watching the rolling sea to the northeast. He knew he was not alone when he smelt a fragrance other than salt and rust. Violet stood next to him at the railing saying nothing. Another hour drifted past with the dolphins dancing through and over the swells made visible in the dusk by light from the ship's portholes. A voice cried out. Someone said, "There it is," and Hugo could see just off the port bow a flash on the horizon. In a few minutes the flash came at regular intervals. For another two hours it drifted low in the northern sky. Then it disappeared.

"The outpost of home," Violet said and caressed his chin.

"It is indeed," Hugo said. Appleton wandered up the deck. "What a sight, eh Hugo? It's not much, but after twelve full days on the *Yildun* chained to Estelle, any outcropping of rocks above high tide is a view of heaven to me."

The next morning Hugo went outside early. As the Somerset coast moved slowly past the ship, there was an increasing uneasiness in his mind that the soil of his birth presented a peculiar obstacle for him. Yet, notwithstanding the depth and wide expanse of his education, he could not reason why that would be true. The drawings of Beaker people, Druids, Romans, Angles, Saxons, Vikings, and Normans recalled vividly from books in Muir's library amounted to a boy's fantasy. Likewise, his knowledge of Arthurian legend, the storied line of Plantagenet kings, of tales told by the immigrant Joseph Conrad, and all the history of the surrounding sea were merely an academic chore of his childhood and not an attempt to indoctrinate.

In the lounge at teatime, he and Appleton agreed, to their mutual relief, that jingoism and politics had distorted English culture into a vulgar trademark of commerce. To talk of it was to invoke parodies of Empire, of dance hall songs, cartoons in *Punch* showing men in Beefeater costumes and cheap souvenirs sold in London shops. In the dusk of his final afternoon, however, when he saw the chalk cliffs of Dover, he sensed a common threat. He kept them in view until their whiteness faded into dark and the winds of the North Sea forced him into the lounge. On that last of evenings, he felt it comforting to turn his focus to a stunning finesse halfway towards a three no-trump victory in the final game of bridge with the Appletons. At the end, Guenther weaved into the lounge and said, "Expect some rough seas tonight. We won't be able to approach the harbor until daylight."

That night the *Yildun* held position, twitching and banging in the North Sea chop. Flashes from the revolving Rhine Beacon lit the cabin. Billy complained and pulled his shirt over his head. At the first light of dawn, Hugo could see through the porthole a dreary rain washing the mist from the air to expose Europe in the waning fall season. In all directions it was colorless, bleak with the forms of weary labor, and lines of ships that formed in the river. Its banks showed steel constructions, rows of fractured ironworks, gantries, cranes, tall brick chimneys.

"The new industrial Europe," said Appleton from the top deck. "Post-war Holland built from the ashes of destruction. New and ugly."

Morton Schoolhouse was ecstatic. "Rotterdam, bombed to ruins by the Luftwaffe but now the busiest port in Europe. I saw it eighteen year ago and it was a flat desolation. Now it handles 25,000 ships a year. This is the Rhine, main street Europe and gateway to the heartland."

"Was this worth the price of your passage, this and the exhilarating company of Von Raynor?" asked the physicist.

Hugo's answer was cut off by Norbert, who hurried over to him. "The Captain wants a word with you in his cabin." Hugo's knock was succeeded by a tired, rasping voice ordering him to step in. Von Raynor held the photo of the ship in his hands. He glanced up at Hugo and nodded. On the envelope he wrote a few words, put the photo inside, and handed it back. "If you are at a loss, this might be of use as an introduction. But for anything of value, you are much too late for that."

"It's of no real concern, Captain. In a week I'll be elsewhere."

"Whatever happens, think about settling, Herr Haultain. It's good to be a traveler, but don't wander too long as I have done." He went to a cabinet and poured two small tumblers of liquor. One of them he handed to Hugo. "A last toast to the lady, Violet."

They touched glasses and downed the drink. Von Raynor re-seated himself and said, "About the few words I have written there, a small explanation. On the night of November fourteen, nineteen forty-one, the Luftwaffe raided the aircraft factories of Wolverhampton and Birmingham. Apparently they mistook the city of Coventry for their target and dropped a thousand bombs on the center of the town. One of the losses was the Cathedral. I believe in some capacity Major Dring has something to do with that place. He once told me how sad it was to find no trace of the organ pipes in the wreckage."

Hugo got up to go. He turned when he had reached the door. "After Algiers did you ever see the others?"

Von Raynor's form merged with the nut-brown of the woodwork, which blended itself with the gray iron of walls and pipes. A single porthole showing the autumn day was insufficient to light the cabin. The captain switched on the desk lamp. "My trip to Algiers did not go well," he said. "There was too much war left behind. I came away disappointed and bitter with the word from Korrolus that my brother was dead. With the exception of Dring, I have no idea of the others. Martin Birks stayed in Africa as a trader. And as you say, Blenkinthorpe and Korrolus went to the New World. That's my understanding of it."

"Why did you mention Coventry in such detail? After the bombing of Dresden you could have no conscience on this."

Juri Von Raynor shrugged his shoulders and took a sip of his drink. The glass rattled when he put it down. "My brother also had something to do with the place. Dring knew him from before the war. In Algiers, they all knew him, to their advantage, certainly not his." He rose awkwardly from his chair, steadying himself with the table. "Nine years ago we had cargo for the West Coast. It was my first time through the Panama Canal. I was excited with the hopes that I might locate others of my family. But having no information, that was not to be. Ironically, we had some cargo, a lift of Java hardwood milled in Düsseldorf and consigned to George Blenkinthorpe. I watched the pallet swing onto the dock and was glad he was not there to fetch it." Juri Von Raynor donned his master's cap and put his foot on the iron stairs leading to the bridge.

Hugo turned as if to walk towards the door, stopped and said, "By the way, what did you say your dead brother's name was?"

"I didn't," answered Von Raynor. "But for the record, his name was Conrad Muir." The captain took one step and held the railing. "I see your confusion so let me explain. It was a long time ago that Conrad ceased using the name Von Raynor. He changed it with the hopes that he would escape the stigma of his ancestry. As I said, my brother and I had little in the way of similarities. Even in appearance we seemed to be of different races. Good-bye, Herr Haultain, and good luck."

He took a tighter grip on the rail and struggled up the stairs. Hugo listened to the old man's shoes grinding the metal treads and thought it was indeed a confusion to mistake one sea captain for your uncle when it was really another. But he felt no compunction to inform the old man that it was his own brother, still alive and wandering God-knows-where, who had raised the man who had been his passenger.

Two orderlies carried Frank Ormes from the hatchway on a stretcher. They paused on the deck for the launch to come alongside. The student smiled at Hugo with a look of gratitude, took his hand, then struggled to sit up and peer through the railing. He looked exhausted but well short of death. Boatmen took him and Violet off first. The launch bumped the stone pier one level lower than the embankment. Ormes rose from the stretcher and, supported by the young woman, staggered onto the cobblestones. When he was clear of the boat, he stomped his feet lightly on them and wept. Violet put her arms around him. Together they left the area of the pier and vanished into the door of the customs building. The launch returned for the rest of the passengers. Estelle Appleton stumbled into the arms of a puffing boatman. Richard greeted him with smiles and spoke proudly in a guttural torrent. Halfway to shore, he leaned over to say that Dutch was not so much a language as a disease of the throat, prompting the doctor to add this as a final complaint to Appleton's burden of accomplishments.

The next day, Hugo took a long walk down a boulevard lined with bare trees, then rode a cab with Billy to Rotterdam Centraal Station. The cab reeked of Galoise. The driver was a large man wearing a stained raincoat and unconcerned in his perpetual cloud of smoke that the tiny conveyance lurched through the streets at the outer limits of control. Still sweating with fear, Billy went into the restaurant. Hugo bought tickets for them both, then went alone to a lunch counter. He thought briefly of Violet Lewellyn, who had already left with no good-bye. This bothered him. It was discourteous for them both to have neglected a final parting. Picking up his case he turned on his heel and nearly knocked Miss Lewellyn off her feet. He prevented her from falling to the floor by grabbing her around the thin middle of her body, padded one inch thicker by a winter coat. She straightened the gray hat she was wearing and wiped the hair from her eyes.

"Where are you going?" asked Hugo.

"I have a train to catch for France. Once there I can take the boat for the Channel Islands where I will be picked up by my uncle, the Reverend Arthur Morrow, rector of the parish of St. Peters Port. But then you know this already, while I have no idea where you're going."

"Billy and I will catch the night boat to Harwich, train to London. Billy will go to Canterbury to serve the Church. I will be met at the station by my future wife, a person I don't know yet, but whose presence is assured."

She put down her small bag. "You will be met by no such person. The thing is, will we ever meet again?"

Hugo shook his head and answered, "No."

"You sound sure of that."

"Life hangs by a thread, Violet. It's usually a very strong thread. But in our case the thread joining your life to mine is so insubstantial that a minute wasted over a cup of coffee, a glance in the wrong direction can alter destiny."

"So the thread for us is too thin?"

"Almost invisible."

"What will you do—ultimately?"

"I'll be in England for a short time, then who knows? If I stay, I'll get right down to stealing the money required to live."

"Steal? Why not earn?"

Hugo stared down the terminal for a few moments and then took both her hands.

"Why do you have to steal, Hugo?" Violet insisted.

"Did I say 'steal'?"

"Yes."

"I did, didn't I? You must have the effect of putting me on edge. Usually I don't forget the slightest detail of life."

"You're too busy talking. That's why you forget."

Hugo put his arms around her. "Then the long and short of our future is this, Violet. You are not a person who needs a mouthpiece in her life."

After a brief hug, Violet stepped back, took Hugo's hand, and kissed it. But the curve of her lips, the movement in her face and eyes were devoid of any future. She picked up her bags. Without smiling or looking back, she walked away. Hugo watched, until her thin body dispersed into pieces and became part of the general body of travelers going for their trains. When he turned, he saw Billy watching her, with a look on his face as if he were crying. They said nothing as they walked down a parallel platform. When they were seated in a compartment, Hugo looked at the words Von Raynor had written on the envelope, which said, "Major Owen Dring, Coventry and Warwickshire Hospital."

Chapter XI

Foleshill Baths

Through the train window, dawn showed wet fields, rock fences, bleak buildings huddled together, with the train running fast overtop narrow roads. Hugo's chain-smoked cigarettes increased the musty smell of the compartment. The dreariness of it caused him to consider the bright presence of Violet Lewellyn. He was troubled again with the minor regret that he had sent her away heedlessly. In the beginning she seemed a person of dubious nature. But he knew that when they parted in Rotterdam, it was Miss Lewellyn who was divesting herself of a nuisance. He brushed back his hair and felt content with this lapse of judgment and forgiving also of present company. The hawk-nose man across from him struggled to make intelligent comments. He was saying proudly that the book in his lap contained strange stuff; but he had been a student at Cambridge and gave notice that he was well acquainted with the classics. He asked Hugo what he thought.

"Yes, sir," the doctor replied, "I was a student once, but I don't remember much about Gurdjieef."

He settled back into the seat, justifying his disinterest on the grounds of a well-earned solitude. If some greater necessity intervened, he would confess to knowing on which shelf Milton had placed *Meeting's with Remarkable Men*. This book of Gurdjieef's he had studied at age eleven and discussed with Muir, along with an accompanying volume by Ouspensky in case anyone might ask. If pressed further by the man opposite, Hugo would be forced to answer that his tutor had given books written by the demented Russian a place of honor next to his elbow, almost on top of the ashtray. The study of them, he would say, had given him no idea of what miraculous events might call people to account for the abuse of their fellows, including him; because in all the land under the street light no one seemed more remarkable than himself. He concluded with the thought that it wouldn't have mattered a jot to

Gurdjieef if the whole world, including the Cambridge man, were readers of classics or readers of smut.

Instead, Hugo asked, "Could I borrow one of your cigars, sir? Thanks. Very kind of you. Anyway, in regards your question—I've never been in search of the miraculous as I recall the book suggests. Existence to me settles into ordinary patterns: travel, novelties, getting bread to eat, etcetera. Yes, I see it, Cambridge Station. The trains do go fast. As I was saying, I fear even more that I won't see the light of true being, with my life becoming an example of art tacked on the plaster. I create the odd thing myself in the attempt to dress up my thoughts, which lately have become more barren than the winter earth throughout East Anglia. I've read that the earth in Britain is everything, the foundation and core of history; and built on it, the gorgeous castles, fine churches, abbeys, manor houses, pubs, and other museum pieces. I'm deeply impressed. One day the call will come for me, and when it does—still being a British subject—I'll march for England. None of this can be allowed to fade away—not fade away." He tapped his feet in time to his voice. The hawk-nosed man slid back into his book, leaving Hugo alone to watch the land outside rush past, overlaid with the memory of the thin, receding figure of Violet Lewellyn.

In an hour they reached the boundaries of London. A thick drizzle washed over the city. Hugo's unease grew and he sensed the threat of obstacles. The light struggling through the rain seemed not to come from the quarries of brick, the monuments of chimney pots and occasional silvering streets showing little traffic, but from a source beyond the horizon like an ancient light reaching earth after centuries. Hugo had never seen this place but had a false sense he had never left it either. It was false, and irritating as well, because he knew that all things are seen as if they are not new to us, when they really are. The trucks clicked across a switch and the sound was familiar. He had the foreboding that when he married, it would be in the remains of the old Cathedral in Coventry—or never blessed by God. The coach slowed and rocked sideways towards its predetermined stop. St. Pancras Station drew the long series of cars inside with a sucking sound. He woke Billy; and when they stepped from the train, the splendor of the high arching girders was a baptism, a christening, a communion at the rail of past sorrows. With his feet at last on old ground, he tried desperately to feel invigorated and renewed. Clutching his case he strode along the shining gray of the platform, through a new and freshly riveted creation. Or that's what he wished to believe.

In Russell Square they walked into the hallway of a shabby bed and breakfast, not so much run down but worn out, as if the bricks themselves suffered erosion by being arrayed close to the rubble next door.

"Eighteen shillings a night for your bed and your breakfast," said the proprietor, a perfumed lady with blotchy skin. Hugo suspected that breakfast would be all the drippings they could mop from the plate, but, like the room, it was the most Billy would pay for. She gave them the key and they started up. The sunlight failed to penetrate the grime on the stair window. The beds inside were hollow and covered with chintz spreads. Hugo took off a pillowcase and cleaned the mirror. The reflection of his clothes appeared no different, with a shirt that didn't match his pants and ugly socks.

The breakfast room in the basement stunk with the smoke of Woodbines. Thin fag ends burned holes in oilcloths covering wood tables, themselves wiped over with a greasy rag. The bread set next to the tea mugs was a blotter for the bacon lard. Old men wiped their faces with colored hankies. The young men sucked in the fumes and ate the fat, knowing it was a way of life, a culture they enjoyed but would not survive. Billy went up to wash his socks in the basin. Hugo stopped at the stair window and cleaned a hole to look through. He could discern with difficulty a vacant lot filled with loose bricks submerged in a slurry of rainwater, all this being the waste not cleared in the two decades since the blitz. He calculated that he had been just five years old when these bricks tumbled down. For him the war was no worse than summer heat, sweating under a thin sheet and hearing the tramp of marching boots, the intermittent breeze carrying the music of pipes and drums. He had no déjà vu of the bomb flash, no fear of the imploding walls, the fire creeping down the walls, melting child's flesh, and no sense even now of the scores of un-recovered war dead on the other side of the wall. When he went down for dinner that night, he neglected to look through the window.

On the street he bought papers. The *Mirror* and the *Telegraph* had pieces on Africa. The fat man in the bar said the dissolution of empire was a ghastly mistake but offered no data to justify his opinion except a tenth pint of beer drunk like a clockwork soldier, arm up, arm down in perfect time to the tune blaring from the jukebox. Hugo excused himself and asked the publican where Coventry was.

"In the Midlands, mate," he replied. "Warwickshire, eighteen mile from Birmingham."

They found a gym close to Leicester Square and Hugo made Billy work out until he fell down. "A bit more of this and you'll look like me," he told the priest, who lay on the floor exhausted.

"Do you think Violet finds me unattractive?" Billy asked.

"She finds you repulsive in the extreme."

"I thought so."

"But then she never has to look at you again, does she?"

Billy looked blankly at Hugo, then tried to lift more weights before mopping his head. That evening, he came back from the bar with two young girls. "Meet Maggie and Eileen, milkmaids from County Down," he said. "Show the man your biceps, Mag. Unbelievable."

The girl with auburn hair sat proudly on the edge of the bed and flexed her arm.

"Sturdy," said Hugo.

"Sturdy? More than sturdy," said Maggie, and her clear-skinned friend agreed with a nod. In the evening they swung along together through the chill night air. Eileen talked without pause of her home in Ireland. When they were back in the room, Hugo sank under the weight of the beer. He turned over and put his hand on Eileen's arm. As he drifted downwards, the confusion of sleep gave him the notion that the buildings in Russell Square had collapsed. Bricks in the empty lot swirled around and pelted the window. The frightened child squirmed under his smoking chintz spread. Debris like grimy fingers dug in and out, smothering him with pain, screaming with pain and shouting oaths of fury, beating, smacking flesh and the light coming on and someone furiously shouting, "Haultain, help me, you idiot! Wake up! The bitches…"

Hugo opened his eyes and saw Billy holding his suitcase in one hand and trying to hit Maggie with the other. For every slap she took, the girl struck the priest with three blows to his face from her closed fist. She was pulling the case and him towards the door. The bed next to Hugo was empty.

"The other one's got your stuff out the door," Billy shouted. "Get with it and quick. You're getting rolled by a farm girl."

Hugo could hear Eileen laughing, panting, and gleefully dragging his heavy case along the corridor, her voice trailing away as she went down the stairs. "Catch me if you can!" was the last he heard, which didn't make sense because Hugo was aware that his case, full of books and old clothing, weighed eighty pounds. Naked and trying to hurry, he bounced off the two beds, sprinted warily into the dark hall, and fell headfirst down the first flight of stairs. He caught Eileen at the bottom of the second flight. She aimed a kick at his crotch and then struck with her fists. Doors opened. A young man ran down the hall pulling on his pants and yelling that he would help. When he punched for Hugo's head, Eileen caught the man with a right jab, then a combination to the side of his head. He fell back with a yelp of pain and dismay.

"Mind your own fuckin' business, toff!" she shouted, winked at Hugo, then lugged his heavy case back up the stairs. Hugo helped the young man to his feet, shrugging. When he got back to the room Eileen was saying, "Give over, Mag."

The other young woman lay on the bed with her blouse torn off and a large bruise over an eye. "I already have," she said.

Billy paced up and down, panting. "Oh my, oh my, oh my," was all he could say while he wiped the blood from the cuts to his nose. When the landlady came knocking, Eileen said in a soft voice, "Oh, Missus, please be pardonin' us. It was a tiff, nothin' more. We've made up and will be quiet as mice now. Yes, we'll be out shortly. Thanks, love." Before dawn the milkmaids had crept away as invisible as fairies; the suitcases lay untouched at the foot of the bed.

The next day Hugo bought three papers, sat on a park bench in Russell Square, and waited for the Apple Orchard to open. They had a beer, then he saw Billy off at the Russell Square underground station.

"What are you going to do?" asked the priest.

"I'm just going to hang around here for a couple of days. I've always wanted to visit the reading room at the British Museum."

"What for?"

"A general interest."

"You have my address. It's close to the Cathedral. You can stay for a few days. Your flight doesn't leave for a week."

"The issue, Billy, is my allowance. My pockets are fast approaching empty."

Billy gave him a ten-pound note. "I'll give you a bit more if I can when you get to Canterbury, to see you through until you go."

Worried, Hugo wandered back to the bed and breakfast. The frown on Billy's face did not reflect a concern for Hugo's condition. And when they had shaken hands, his friend looked regretful, ashamed.

Lufungula, Christmas Day, 1965.

On the afternoon Mintou returned with the stolen book, he appeared exhausted, ill at ease, refusing to look at his special prisoner. Instead of squatting in the corner, he paced between the door and grate, incensed at the barking of a dog and a woman's angry shouts.

"Calm down, Sergeant. It's not easy to learn," said Hugo. "Neither you nor the ju-ju priests of your village can translate these symbols directly into your brain by magic. Your lessons have been going on only for a few weeks. Given months and years, you will learn. Don't get frustrated and beat your wife. Of course, you don't have a wife yet, do you? So sit down. I'm ready to expand on an idea quite novel to your idea of the human race."

The soldier put on his cap. When he was sitting comfortably on his haunches he replied, "The ju-ju man who saved old niggers would have noticed that today is what you call Christmas, I don't know about that because I can't read yet. The missionaries told me that God was born on this day so he could save us. Will God save you, monsieur?"

Hugo squirmed on the leather case to get comfortable, lit two cigarettes, and threw one on to the ground in front of Mintou, who snatched it up from the floor.

"He doesn't need to do anything for me, Sergeant. Christmas or not, the only kind of work that needs to be done here is for me to save you from the worst kind of boredom. You've probably asked the question of why I would be bothering to help you. But this impulse to see you along to a better life was no revelation to me, was it? Not a reform in my moral point of view. I mean, you asked me to do it, which is not the same as the time God coerced Paul into writing his letters and by so doing launch yet another option for the religious. It's well documented that the man was trying to cadge a ride to Damascus when he twigged. But I never twigged, Mintou, had no light flash on in my brain to announce my arrival at the shrine of truth. When I first arrived in London I didn't have a clue about my general direction but had a strategy to deal with minor uncertainties. You've probably noticed yourself that when you're temporarily undecided about which way to go or who to follow, you simply follow the crowd. There's no harm in that and for me it was no different on that day. The gate leading to the British Museum showed me a steady flow of people. Unthinking, I went with them. Once inside I was moved by some inclination to go directly to the reading room and locate a book on African travel that would mark my way forward—and eventually here to you.

I found a table under the dull glow of the neon lights and started to read. The late afternoon sun slanting through the windows illuminated dark corners of the room. Between two stacks, the bright light fell on a man holding an open book. I pushed my chair back and walked over to him, going close to him so my mouth nearly pressed against his ear.

'Do your worthy ideas give you a lifetime pass to this institution?' I asked.

'The strength of my published works, available in the next row but one, gives me immediate access,' he replied.

'The sad truth, Albert, is that anyone wearing clothes is allowed in. The important thing is: Do we have anything to say to each other or are we merely disturbing the peace?'

'Tell me your plans.'

'Most likely I'm going elsewhere.'

'Elsewhere? Hasn't your investigations proved that you ought to be doing important things like figuring out how to become self-supporting? I would say that nowhere is the destination of your travels, or *Erehwon* as another misled optimist described in his book, available by the way in the next room but one.'

'Such a famous place the British Museum reading room,' I replied. 'Full of famous people. I believe Marx wrote his epic over there under the bust of Newton—"From each according to his ability, to each according to his need." That's the kind of thinking I would call important, a great plan for humanity and men willing to sacrifice a day's pay to achieve it.'

'Humanity as such does not exist, nor has never existed except in the mind of the egoist,' he countered. 'Only the joy and the suffering of the individual exist. Marx and all the other ideologues make that error. Systems and broad categories for progress never apply. There is no utopia, no such thing as the accumulated pain or pleasure of mankind. Moral reality is the man in front of you, whom you decide to help, or not.'

'You once attacked Schopenhauer's negation of the self.'

'I attacked his inconsistencies. Time and again he was forced to make concessions. He may have turned the individual into a figment. But he is a figment for whom we should have compassion. At every opportunity we should turn away from ourselves and towards him, risking if need be our own survival. Even in his pessimism Schopenhauer couldn't destroy ethics without throwing all of this in the trash. Don't be quick to judge. Find out from Major Dring, the futility of that.'

'Was he a friend of yours?'

'He came to hear me play the organ at Coventry Cathedral many years ago, before that magnificent building became a casualty of war. Your duty is to put the past to rest, a courtesy to an aging man.'

'That courtesy would lead to still more aged men, most of whom I don't wish to meet. I have no such obligation.'

'You have to me.'

'I owe you nothing.'

'You've benefited from my thought.'

'The bookseller was paid. You received your pennies.'

'I wrote for the ages. In the public domain are no royalties only the benefit to succeeding generations of helping them cope with sorrow. And sorrow we shall have in abundance. Years before the degradations of the present, I wrote that as a race we have lost the ability to foresee and forestall. With the likes of you leading the way, mankind will end by destroying the earth.'

'Is browbeating me with your pessimism an example of your ethical worldview?' I asked him.

'That's part of it and needling you with my clear if not happy opinion. It seems that your first impulse, Hugo, with its twists and turning of words, is to confuse and confound. Your life—not mine—has become an abyss of pessimism. Now, to relieve my tiny concern for your problems, I'm going straightaway to the public house across Great Russell Street for a pint; thence home to say the grace. The staff is hungry. Then, in the sullen night of the tropics, I'll begin the final stanza of my thought. Time runs short for me. It runs short for you as well.'

"Albert Schweitzer stopped talking. He also stopped squinting because the sun had moved behind a pillar. With no thought to that coincidence, I replaced the book on trans-equatorial routes and was relieved that when next I looked, no one stood in the corridor."

When Hugo had finished speaking Mintou asked, "What is this thing 'pessimism' that the ju-ju doctor beat you with?"

Hugo made no reply. He could have explained to his student that pessimism had its place; indeed, it could not be avoided. For years he had willingly beaten his own head against a closed, negative youth and beat it now against the grate of his self-styled adult cage. But he beat it silently and without complaint. The sergeant stood, then waited for the answer that never came. After some minutes he exhaled loudly and left the cell.

London, November 3, 1964.

That evening Hugo carried his case into the alley off Bedford Place so that the Irish girls could store it for him. A glow of sharp light from a door high up on the fire escape made lines on the cobblestones.

"Shh. There he is," said a voice. The ironwork of the stairs thrummed with Eileen's running feet. "We'll have to be quick," she said. Hugo sighed. He felt empty, hungry. "For a big bloke you're quite a toff with this heavy case, aren't you?" she said, laughing. "Never mind, you can't come up anyway. We'd get the sack. The pay's not much. Only four pound a week and our digs…you understand? But it's very tiny. I'll take this up, and come right down."

She started up the six flights of stairs at a jog, stopping at each landing to change hands. When she returned, Hugo gave a half-crown to the newsstand vendor then handed her the package.

"Thanks for the fags, Hugo," she said and took the smoke deep into her lungs.

"How old are you?"

"Sixteen," she replied.

After they had groped their way around Russell Square to eat and drink, Hugo kissed her on the cheek. He went back to his room fearing that in a world infested by men who could neither foresee or forestall, no child could safely find its way in any city. He went to bed that night with the sense that things were turning against him as well, although there was no concern for his possessions. The books in his case would fetch only a few bob for them at the pawnshop and otherwise had little value. There would be no sense in either Eileen or Maggie delving into books of arcane metaphysics or the descriptions of war. They would be burdened by it. At the newsstand he had seen Eileen turn away from photos in the *Times* showing bloated corpses stacked along the road leading from Leopoldville.

With a few things stuffed into his satchel, Hugo took the express train from Kings Cross Station to Rugby. He transferred to a self-powered unit for the short trip to Coventry. When he arrived, he rode a bus through the rebuilt heart of the new town, ringed by the old town, with the embalmed remains of the Cathedral adjacent to the body of its replacement. He had just enough money to take a room at the Craven Arms Hotel. He thought it a unique blessing that from his window he could see on the eastern wall of the new building, a fifteen-foot metal sculpture of the Archangel Michael treading down the sneering face of Lucifer. That afternoon he walked through pouring rain to the Coventry and Warwickshire Hospital. The information clerk looked him over, then frowned at the puddle of rainwater at his feet. When he asked directions to the office of Major Dring, she pointed reluctantly down the hallway. On the way he tried to shake more water from his sodden clothes. Further down was another nurse.

"Good day. I'm trying to locate the office of Major Dring."

She took a step forward and looked at his chin. Her voice was bland, neutral when she said, "The outpatient surgery is through that door and down to the south wing."

"I don't need surgery," Hugo replied, "just a pointer towards Major Dring."

"The doctors here see no one without a referral. And for your information, there are no majors working here, Dring or otherwise."

Hugo thought she sounded unfriendly, but knew he had made that mistake before.

"Let's try for Dr. Dring," he continued. "As a matter of fact, the Dring I'm trying to locate is a medical doctor and probably hasn't been called 'major' for years."

The nurse looked closer at his clothes and the muddy water dripping onto the shiny tile floor. "I could take you to the door of Mr. Dring, sir. That's the best I could do."

She had unwavering, unblinking eyes that matched the disinterest in her voice. They made Hugo feel concerned for having some gap in his intelligence or at least in his circumstances. He gently stroked the bandage. "Actually, Miss, to avoid further argument on the matter, Dring is a man of medicine I would say, and that would make me want to call him 'doctor' rather than 'major,' which he was by the way, now probably retired. But in my opinion, it would be quite demeaning to refer to him as 'mister', don't you think?"

"This is your definite opinion, is it?" the nurse said folding her arms over her chest, with her lips pouted and her large eyes unblinking. "Let me complete your education as I can tell from your accent that you're a foreigner. In this country if a doctor is a specialist, we refer to him by the common term, 'mister', or 'missus' if she is a female."

"I see," said Hugo, smiling. "I am a foreigner as you say and don't understand that. But maybe you could explain—just for fun—why things here go in the reverse direction than what one would expect. If Dring were President of the Royal College, would we refer to him as something more common, like 'dosser', as you say here?"

The young nurse frowned. She stepped closer to him and cocked her head in disbelief. "Are you taking the mickey?"

"Beg your pardon?"

"Are you being facetious, if you want it in language you can understand."

"Not in the least. I'm quite serious."

"So if I referred to you as a common, cheeky sod, you'd be pleased as well."

"Actually, you could just refer to me as 'Hugo', and I could refer to you as…?"

"As nothing, chappie, so leave it. And to set you straight, Mister Dring is in surgery until much later, and even then I believe he will be leaving for other appointments. In other words you won't be able to see him until, say, next summer—if at all."

Hugo smiled again. Behind her he could see a sallow-faced man standing in a doorway looking at him. He nodded and walked away. Outside the hospital entrance he stopped and looked at the pale sky from which the rain had ceased to fall. He sat on edge of the stairs for a few minutes to consider his direction. The blond nurse walked down the stairs, turned for a moment when she saw him, then walked on. An ambulance backed in to a ground level dock. The nurse stopped until it had cleared the entrance. As Hugo went towards the bus stop a block away, he found himself walking beside her, turning his head to observe how gracefully her legs moved.

"Does being around death bother you?" he asked.

She laughed. "Am I a nurse?"

Hugo brushed back his hair. His left arm was crooked against his satchel. "Of course we're all familiar with death. But to me, the most fascinating variety is soul death—being the journey of epic literature as it describes the western lands. Could I say something on that? If you get bored you can shut your ears or walk the other way."

"I will," she said and quickened her pace.

"The great philosopher and humanitarian, Albert Schweitzer, talks to us…in a fictitious way, of course. This is what he says, and I quote…'We live in the constant expectation of an enlightenment that will explain death. This is a consequence of our obsession with the desire for predictability, which is the legacy of science. But the knowledge of facts gives a false sense of security. And we sense that it is false. We don't fear direct intervention by evil spirits or spells or the uncanny but we have a horror of disease or starvation or mutilation.'"

Hugo stopped talking for a moment. The nurse walked faster.

"It's a bit like the man coming from the ambulance back there, who looked like he had fallen from a great height, very similar to the fate of the storied Mr. Bons, who injudiciously tried to return from heaven. We can predict only so far, Miss…?"

"I didn't say."

"No you didn't."

"And now I'm at my car. Ta da." The nurse got in, and without a wave drove into the high street.

To save money, Hugo walked the four miles back to the Craven Arms. The clerk said it was against policy to refund his room charge so he wandered over to the new Cathedral to listen to the organist practice. He wondered how his mother would have reacted to singing in the new building now that the sonorous architecture of the old was reduced to a few stumps of rock. That evening he sat in the bar and thought about the blond nurse. He debated with himself the justification she had of thwarting him, apart from the dispute over a quirk of language he was vaguely aware of. But he didn't believe a word she said about the doctor not being available. He suspected from his recollection of the shattered photo, that the tall man in the hallway was Dring himself. Before giving it up as unimportant he would try one more time. The next morning he walked back to the hospital. The information clerk said, "Mister Dring is not in the office today, sir. Nor tomorrow. But the outpatient surgery is…"

"Thank you," he said, and thinking his chin wound sufficiently bandaged, he retraced his steps out of the hospital to the station, then by local train to Rugby and express to Kings Cross. He decided against lugging his suitcase all the way into Kent just to bring it back. So he took the tube to London Bridge and caught a train directly to Canterbury. The uniformed officer in the compartment looked content with the seating arrangement. He asked questions, and Hugo explained where he was going.

"Have you ever been inside the Cathedral?" the man asked.

"No, sir. I've never been anywhere in Kent."

"I once had a friend in the church, posted to Canterbury for many years," the military man continued. "I used to enjoy nobbing it with the Deacon…getting tours of the fixtures, very old it is, followed by a pint of County Kent's best ale brewed especially for the clergy. Could a chap get used to that sort of stuff—regularly scheduled garden parties, sermons, marriages and funerals, dressed in ecclesiastical purple, confessing the lapses and trying to imitate Christian as he makes his way through the temptations of Vanity Fair? Did you ever read the *Pilgrim's Progress*? As a lad, I was into things like allegories. No harm in it, my father used to say."

The image of a pious John Bunyan interrupted Hugo's answer. He wondered how it had been for the rebel priest to rot in prison, scribbling his best-selling book on sheets of moldy paper, if he could get any. Bunyan's incarceration, however, had been a voluntary act of rebellion, a manufactured opportunity to record and subsequently foist on believers his fantasy of heaven, and how to attain it. In other words, it was not a punishment. He had a moment of envy and replied to the officer that Bunyan had been correct to illuminate the path of righteousness for doubters and apostates because it made him feel better about his own miserable life. The man smiled.

When they arrived Hugo found the administration office in a new building some distance from the medieval, sinking remains of the Cathedral that housed the bones of the saint. He sat in the anteroom, waiting and waiting with no magazines or any reading material except old copies of the *Church Times*.

Finally a man in a black suit ushered him into an office. "Reverend Bartholomew is not here, I'm afraid. He was yesterday but only long enough for a talk with the Deacon. He seemed a bit battered, and we did have some concerns. He left this for you." The man gave Hugo an envelope. He returned to the outer office and opened it.

> Dear Hugo,
> I've decided against my position here at Canterbury and instead am going to Dover to catch the boat to Guernsey. I will attempt to get whatever position I can in the Anglican parish of St Peters Port. Why I am doing this needs no explanation except to say that Violet Lewellyn plays the largest role. The only thing that needs explanation for you is the fact that to live I was forced to cash in your airfare. I am sorry about that, as it leaves you in a bind. However, I'm told

that work is plentiful in England. I also suggest you wire Milton to see if he would be willing to advance you some money.

Hugo, you taught me a lot since we first met. Some of it was not good. I see the world differently now. I hope I survive. I am in love with Miss Lewellyn and wish to become something in life, to be worthy of her.

Take the utmost care and God bless.

Your friend,

Billy Bartholomew.

Hugo took the letter and wandered into the street. It began to rain heavily. The woman behind the counter said, "It's not my concern what the weather's like, sir. You must be a member of the Youth Hostel Federation to stay here; otherwise, there's a bed and breakfast in the next block."

Hugo felt like whining in the obnoxious way he had seen Billy do. He could see the last of his few pounds slip away, a turn of events would not have happened if he had had more commitment and alternate plans. He was becoming flotsam at the hands of other people, a refugee as he had described to the bartender, Leonard, in the country tavern he had visited at the outset to his long journey. He realized that his life so far had not accommodated sensibly for wasted years. Inside, it seemed he was capable only of inventing stories that illustrated other stories and realized that a progression of tales that receded to infinity was also a tiresome cliché.

Next morning the mist was already burnt from the oaks trees when the exquisite maidens whom Hugo suddenly had no desire to meet came out of the hostel. He had no impulse left to say appropriate, articulate things to them on this sunny morning. This he considered a shame. The conversation would be free of the slurs, spittle, and nose blowing that usually went with a night of booze because there was no money now for luxuries. On the walk back to the station he amused himself by kicking the acorns that had fallen from trees he had been forced to sleep under and get soaked through from the downpour.

In London the gaffer at the Apple Orchard said, "There's work here. But the wages aren't high. Cost of living is, though. You should try the Midlands. Good wages in the factories. Try your luck in Wolverhampton, Birmingham, even Coventry."

Hugo retrieved his case from the tiny room of the Irish girls. They offered to let him sleep under the bunk and would keep him alive, they said, by smuggling sandwiches from the kitchen. But he declined and took the case from Eileen at the foot of the fire escape. He took her face in his hands, "Don't let anyone ever say you are not a good person, Eileen. If I were religious, like my friend Billy, I would say to you, God bless." He kissed her forehead, put a full pack of Woodbines in her hand, and walked away.

A half-mile south of Warwick, a solitary, ill-dressed man stood on the shoulder of the A429 with a leather case set next to him. He seemed agitated and kicked at the gravel. A luxury sedan stopped. Surprised, he got into the back seat and thanked the driver, a woman in early middle age. After a polite introduction of names she said nothing further. The silence put him at ease; but to cut short any annoying questions, he thought to assail her with a few stories that would have her responding with polite comments such as "frightful, splendid, well done." But he couldn't get his tongue to say much of anything. As the miles went by, he thought instead about the opportunity a job might give him to glimpse the circular path that lead further round into Muir's history, and at the end of the spiral allow him to track Conrad's steps to a place where they were both free of past sorrows. The trail was a thin thread, as he had recently described, but he had a sense that it was made of bright gold in a dull, hungry world.

Miles went by before he said, "Picturesque country around here."

The woman glanced into the mirror with blue eyes and a puzzled smile. "You've probably had a few adventures yourself in nice places, Hugo. Do I have the name right?"

"You do, Miranda."

The Rover sped down the hill into Leek Wootten with Hugo silent in the back seat staring at the rich color and texture of the driver's hair. In five minutes they were beyond the remnants of Kenilworth Castle. In fifteen minutes she had dropped him off on the Coventry ring road. For an hour he wandered around the newly rebuilt shop district until he had come to a small pub called the Rose across from the Courtaulds Chemical Works. He ate a bun with ham in the middle, watched an inebriated man play darts with amazing accuracy, and wrote some thoughts comparing the nurse he might face tomorrow and the kindness shown to him by Eileen. He sketched the Irish child as he remembered her, but could not recall any distinct features of the nurse's face, except her stylish, bleached blond hair.

Halfway through a night thick and dreary with fog. Hugo felt his muscles cramping in the cold, although he was curled as warmly as he could get with his knees drawn up to his chest. A light shone in his eyes. "Hello. What's this? Up with you, then. This is a church memorial, chappie, not a kip house."

The constable's torch was blinding. For a few seconds he looked away then rubbed his eyes saying, "My apologies, Officer. Not enough money for the inn. So had to sleep in the manger, so to speak."

"Very funny, mate. Where would you be from?"

Hugo told him.

"Then stay put for tonight. Tomorrow you might try the newspaper for cheap digs."

"That's more help than I expected, sir. I'll take your directions. Thank you."

The constable smiled and backed away from the offered handshake. Next morning, the fog remained thick on the streets. Hugo found a café, and for an hour, re-warmed himself with several cups of tea, as there was no money left for food. After making some entries in the notebook he set off for the hospital. Inside the entrance vestibule, he stood his leather case against the wall with no fear that anyone would move it. The information clerk rolled her eyes when she saw him and gestured down the hall. On his way, he checked each door. A plaque on one said, "Owen Dring, MD FRCS." The door was ajar so he pushed it open. The same blond nurse stood by a filing cabinet. She grimaced and came around the side of the desk.

"You again! Has anyone recently described what you look like?"

"No."

"This is a hospital. You're lucky someone hasn't dragged you to the RSPCA and fed you a bone."

Hugo sat down in a chair. He leaned forward as if to rest his back. "I'm certainly not as well turned out as you are," he replied. "However a comparison of wardrobes is not the issue."

"What is the issue, then?"

"I suppose it would be my need to speculate on the details of the moment. For example, I distinctly smell the fragrance of roses. That leads me to wonder why it is that even clear skin and jewelry don't have the same intoxicating effect as quality perfume."

She came a little closer and looked down at his hand, which rested on the arm of the chair. "I won't comment on your smell, sir, but I see that you're wearing a nice ring yourself. Did you steal it?"

"Off the finger of the archbishop."

She smiled. "I suppose you're back to see Mister Dring?"

"He is away in the Canaries on vacation and not available for a month?"

"You are as perceptive as you are filthy."

She took a tissue from the table and handed it to Hugo. "You've got a dirty big smudge on your cheek and the bandage on your chin is bleeding through. Obviously you never went to outpatients last week."

"Afraid not. You must excuse the soiled clothes as well. The facilities in the alley were less than five star." Hugo wiped his face and dabbed at his chin, then he let his head fall slightly. "Look, Miss X. Please excuse the rudeness of my barging in here, but I want to occupy Mister Dring for a few moments only, no more. I have something to give him from a few friends of his, from the war. Once done, I will leave and you will never have to see the smudge or the chin again. I'm not here to bother you."

"Mister Dring is away in London."

"And I've just come up from London…again."

"What a pity. If you had stayed in London, Mister Dring could have visited you at…what, the Savoy?"

Hugo struggled up from the chair. "Normally I relish a bit of repartee. But not today."

"You slept in an alley last night?"

"Do I look like a hobo?"

"Yes."

"Actually, I slept in the remains of the old Cathedral," he said, moving towards the door, then stopping. He noticed that her manner had changed slightly, becoming more professional and with it a visible sense of compassion. "You know, you ought to have someone in outpatients examine that chin," she said. "And if you want to clean up, there are public facilities. Do you know the Foleshill Swimming Bath?"

"No. I know nothing about Coventry. But the swim is a good idea, two laps of the pool with the chlorine to sterilize the chin and water up the nose to clear the sinuses…"

She moved away. "You really are a sarcastic bugger. I should call the constable and get rid of you. But I'll do you this one favor. Foleshill has slipper baths for rent, the ones where you can jump in and wash the dirt off with hot water and soap. I could give you directions, if it would get you out of here."

Hugo slung the satchel around his shoulders. For a moment he watched the reflection in a glass door. The bottoms of his jeans were frayed. The coat was formless. He regretted his flippancy. "The truth of the matter is this," he said in a quiet voice. "I'm going to make my own way to the baths, get cleaned up then I'll be back for Mister Dring. And tomorrow I'll do my best to ensure there'll be no more nastiness." The nurse said nothing in reply, and when Hugo looked back from the entrance, she was still watching him.

Near winter in the synthetic Midlands of England—specifically Coventry, the county of Warwickshire, whose oily terrain was forested with the spewing smokestacks of Courtaulds, General Electric, the Rootes Group,

Standard-Triumph, and Jaguar. Dogged by the hastening cold, Hugo anticipated only one good thing from his slow journey. Beyond the far rise of land he would come to the baths at Foleshill where he could warm his feet and clean his body. On the main door to the building was a notice: *Wanted— qualified swimming bath attendant. Certification on demand. Fourteen pound six per week. See Mr. Tolly, Foleshill Swimming Bath, Foleshill Road, Coventry.*

Hugo went in and paid a shilling, six pence for a hot bath. The old tubs were scrubbed to a gleaming white. The room was humid and smelt of strong soap. The Bath ladies had set out clean, soft towels and the warm water to his neck soothed his anxieties and gave him hope. After drying off, he combed his hair and tried to make his clothes seem as pressed as possible. Leaving his case by the door, he went into the office. "Yes, sir," he said, "I can swim—not well, mind you, but I get by. I also have some medical training, which I can prove when I receive my papers from back home."

"Any other training, qualifications, diplomas, schooling beyond the regular?" asked Mr. Tolly.

"No."

"Not much, my man, in fact nothing at all. But you look a husky bloke who might learn. So we'll give it a go. At the bare minimum I want the first aid papers here within a fortnight, or at least prior to the annual lifesaving test next month."

Hugo went next into the cafeteria, which was next to the children's pool. He ordered tea from the red-haired woman behind the counter and stared into the whirlpool of brown in his cup. A large man with a pipe stuck into his round, ruddy face sauntered in. "You're the new man. Here are the rules." As the supervisor droned on, Hugo watched the children playing in the pool and the ladies serving tea from behind the counter. At critical times, he nodded agreement. With each rule, Gordon Moffat puffed with greater satisfaction until a cloud of smoke obscured his head. "And lad, no one likes a pint more than I do," he said, "assuming you can find a decent drink this far south of Yorkshire. But no attendant is to be intoxicated on the job. No exceptions…"

A cheery youth came through the door and smiled at them. He sat a few stools away and shook his head in sympathy. Moffat continued, "Miss Sutton, the other supervisor, enforces the rules more strictly than I do." He lowered his voice and let the spittle drip from the pipe stem. "But she packs a real wallop behind that flapping mouth of hers. Never you mind about that because a big man like m'self has no problem asserting authority. I toss offenders out by the seat of their pants. You're a robust bloke, Hugo. Just assert yourself with the rabble that comes down from Bedworth. And one more thing, I know you're after digs, and where I stop—the Stokehill Guildhouse—may be just the place for you. Five pound twelve a week for a room and two meals a day. Big bloody barracks really, built during the war to house munitions workers. It's on a bus route, not far from downtown, and it's got a telly and billiards. Of course you'll have to contend with old men coughing up their lungs first thing in the morning. The great fall of soot I call it...Ah, Miss Sutton."

"What misinformation have you been passing out here, Mr. Moffat? Never mind. For the time being Hugo you will be under me in the small bath." Hugo did a quick tour with the pie-faced woman. At the end of the pool she yelled into the men's change room door. Two men appeared.

"This is the lockerman, Tom Mahoney, and young Nigel, Mr. Tolly's son and a trainee," she said. "Tom calls himself a student, but is good for nowt unless he's had six pints."

The lockerman sneered at her and returned down the passage. Hugo went back into the office. "A request, Mr. Tolly—a possible advance on the wage packet? Against policy? Very well. Thanks anyway."

The young man, Nigel, stopped Hugo in the hallway. "The name's Toby, from the large bath. Come back this afternoon and I'll have some money for you. I'm broke meself. But I'll touch up me mom for a fiver then you can pay up at the Guildhouse, get bed and a meal. Fucking Tolly's a cheap bugger and all. Trouble is, others around here get paid end of the week and come Monday, after a weekend at the boozer, they're after an advance to see them through till Friday."

Hugo came back at four o'clock, got his five pounds, and set off for Stokehill and the Guildhouse. That evening he drank tea after the first good meal he'd had in a week.

"Only two more years till me retirement," said Jimmy Smythe, the man next to him. "But I'll stay here. I moved to this place when me wife died. I used to have a garden, grow flowers and Swiss chard. This is my retirement—but could be worse. There's companionship, it's cheap and someone else does the cooking. Did you get to do something social on the weekend?"

Hugo nodded his head. "I was in London."

"Must have had a good time there."

"A few pints."

The millwright winked at him. "Speaking of the booze—did you know that they threw out Tom Mahoney last night? You know him, the lad from the Foleshill Bath where you're working. Pissed the mattress once too often. Lost control of his bladder, he has—and him a young man and all. Only twenty-seven."

The Stokehill Guildhouse was an efficient, military place, as Gordon Moffat had described. The center block housed the kitchens and dining hall. The four wings radiating out from that area contained the sleeping rooms. Each wing had a lavatory with cold showers. In Hugo's unit a sign read, "Spitting spreads disease." The eight-by-ten room had one cot, a sink with a coldwater tap, a locker, and a light bulb hanging in the center. He stowed his things in the locker, except the books, which he put along the very back edge of a metal desk because the top was concave. After setting the bottle of India ink next to the nibbed pen, he stood the framed photos upright on the desk. The small caricature of Muir he slid into the frame next to his mother.

In his spiral notebook he began calculating how much money he would need to go elsewhere. He tore out a blank sheet and wrote, "Dear Milton," then threw the paper in the trash. The room was cold. The light radiated no warmth and the heating pipe along the wall was cold to the touch. He lay in the cot, pulled the coarse blanket well up to his face, and tried to sleep. As he drifted away, he was aware only of the quiet and occasional murmuring through the walls. It was still dark when he heard the residents getting up on a Tuesday morning. The buildings echoed with grating, gasping coughs from the first cigarettes of the day. The narrow corridors filled with shuffling feet, the clink of cutlery and enamel tea mugs.

"Morning, mate," was the full conversation from drooling mouths under weeping eyes. Hugo went into the dinning hall, through the lineup at the counter to receive his breakfast of bacon, eggs, and beans. After eating, he took one of the five Woodbines left in the packet, then handed around the rest. In a week he felt comfortable. He wore a cloth cap given to him by Jimmy Smythe, the millwright. Evenings he played billiards with the drunks returning from the local. He soon lost his taste for youth or remembered faces and felt it sweeter surrounded by the stubbled cheeks of old men. At the bath he learned to imitate the dialect and could identify the dark-skinned schoolboys from Bedworth by the way they talked.

The first Friday was pay-back day. Hugo looked at the four bank notes and small change left him. He calculated the things he should buy after paying rent: shoes, a new razor, but knew he was far short of the needed cash. In front of him wet heads bobbed in the pool. Eyes glimmered from water level. He was dead tired and poured into his teacup the rest of the ale from a bottle hidden in a boot. The door opened and Mrs. Green from the ticket office walked in. She knew the habits of the bath at a glance. He edged the boot further under the chair, closed his eyes and drifted off. A sky appeared, a lighter shade of blue than the artificial sea in which Captain Korrolus floated. The old man's finger pointed to a cloud in the rafters with its brilliant dazzle and whiteness around the edge, suggesting a treasured land for them both—a rolling around heaven on a newly re-caulked and re-painted fantasy boat.

"Blimey, less than a week here, and he's already asleep on the job." The old woman rolled her eyes, then went back from her rounds to the outer hall.

"Just resting my eyes from the glare, missus," Hugo called after her. Miss Sutton came in to relieve him. In the café he pulled a five-pound note from his pay packet and gave it to Toby. As he took it, the boy looked with alarm to the door. Walking through it was a young woman with large blue eyes, blond hair, and wearing a nurse's dress, cap, and stockings. She glanced suspiciously to where he was sitting, then walked over to the table.

Toby turned to her. "There's your fiver back, Beth. Thank you from me."

Hugo scrutinized the nurse's features to verify her identity. Her square shoulders and body seemed more firm and contoured than he remembered. "And thank you also," he said. "The money was for me and kept me from another night in the ruins." The nurse stared at him with her lips parted. Hugo got up. "Tea break's over. If you don't mind, I'll stop by the hospital in a couple of weeks. Mister Dring might be back by then."

From the pool, Hugo could see Toby Marshall arguing with his sister, before he came out afterwards and said to him, "She can be such a bitch. But you better get used to her if you stop here. She was Empire and Commonwealth free style champion at the last games and instructs the racers four times a week."

At the Rose a day later Hugo said, "It's none of my business, Tom, but do you know that your eyeballs—rather than being the usual white—are an identical color to your hair, an unhealthy orange color."

"What do you mean by that?"

"No offense," said Hugo. "But I know for a fact that liquor acts like a solvent. The quantity you drink has made the color run from your hair into your eyes. You could save your health and improve your appearance by purchasing less for you and more for me."

The Irishman looked stunned and dropped his ham sandwich on the dirty floor. "You drink as much yourself," he said. Hugo shook his head and pointed to the cup of tea on the table. Then he bought a replacement sandwich and put it in front of the lockerman's pint glass. After a quick chew and a swallow he said, "Another thing, Hugo, forget the blondie…Toby's sister. She goes with an executive from Courtaulds—a bloke who'd put the boot in quick enough."

Back at the bath, Hugo went to the common room to get a pail and a mop. The pools were empty, the building closed. He heard a familiar voice, walked in to see a woman sitting lengthwise on a bench beside Toby. She was wearing a swimsuit. Next to her was a man in smart, pressed clothes. When Beth looked up, her smile faded. She stared, drew her knees tight, and pointed all her fingers at him. Hugo went to leave but Toby saw him. "You okay, mate. No one head-butt you down at the Rose?" he said, smiling.

The man with the smart clothes frowned at them. Beth looked embarrassed and said, "I don't like your friend very much, Toby. He acts strangely." She got up.

"Don't go on account of me," said Hugo.

"We were leaving anyway, mate," said the man. "If you'd like to step out of the way."

After swabbing the decks Hugo walked the long road back to Stokehill. Along the varied streets, rows of lights glowed in the thick fog. People moved vaguely in shop windows. The watery gloom refreshed him, sharpened the nerves in his skin. The length and tempo of his stride increased with each block and he soon forgot the episode at the bath. Inside the Guildhouse, he went to the small gym instead of the dining hall. Dust covered the floor, the weights, and benches. The charwoman gave him some cleaning cloths and he dusted the equipment. After a workout of stretches and dumbbells he took a cold shower, drank a cup of tea, and wrote in his notebook for two hours. With light from the single bulb, he sketched a woman whose hair color he had not determined.

On his daily journey to work Hugo often detoured past the Craven Arms for the savory smells of good cooking. Because of this habit he was often forced to contemplate the Cathedral ruins across the street for purposes other than a night's sleep. On his first daylight examination, a thin mist had formed with the rain making it uncomfortable to be outside. The door to the new Cathedral was open so he slipped in. The quiet was uniform. Beyond the rows of pews and the altar, a row of golden pipes cascaded from tall to short. Since the building was new, he concluded that the organ would also be of a modern design. Electric switches would operate the stops; automatic pumps would keep a steady flow of air moving to the main chest. He became curious to know more and crept along to the organist's compartment. The keyboard, pedals, and bench looked no different than any he had previously seen in older churches. He sat down and placed his hands on the keys. He had to fight down the temptation to bang out the opening bars of Grieg's concerto. If he played just the first seven chords he would get to hear the sounds reverberate through the vast interior without disturbing anyone. But he restrained himself, slid off the bench, and looked instead at the collage of photos on the wall. He recognized the one closest to the organ. The finely detailed photograph gave him the sudden urge to shout into the church that the beautiful woman portrayed there, his mother, Corrine Haultain had abandoned him by dying seventeen years ago.

The organist arrived to find a solitary man sitting in a pew, staring silently at the organ pipes. Without delay, the man commenced his practice. The music turned Hugo's thoughts away from his mother and towards the celebrated characters represented on the stained glass. At his break the organist went into the church and Hugo told him that his own mother and her ancestors were less famous than the group depicted in the windows, but were bred to the English Midlands and for generations had attended services here. The man escorted him to the door.

"They would have seen the old Cathedral in its intended glory," he said. "It was a large building, began in 1410 and annihilated by the Nazis in 1940. The church council wanted it preserved as a reminder. If the rain's no inconvenience, you should wander through it and have a look. While you're there, note the cross built from ruined timbers. I'll be inside practicing when you're finished."

Hugo stepped through an opening, past truncated stumps and jagged barriers that were once walls, pilasters, pillars, and buttresses not made of timbers, but the stone of Blenkinthorpe's description. He went respectfully to the remains of the altar and stared past it to the new Cathedral and the Archangel stepping on Lucifer's head. He took special notice of the one hard corner near the street where he had slept his first night in Coventry. Through the open door he could hear the organist practicing the fugues of Bach. Even at that distance and in open space, the music resonated in his chest and vibrated through the burnt spars of the remanufactured cross. The downpour had increased; water dripped from the wood.

For a moment the sight of it and the feel of cold rain put him on edge. He felt close to weeping just a few of the tears he should have cried for the death of his mother. He sat on a dry spot below the rubble of the altar and recalled the funeral day, the small gathering of mourners at the verge of the forest that ringed the cemetery. The tall trees dripped with the excessive rain. But rain is what it is, he thought, and by definition cannot be excessive. So it must be people and their beliefs that are excessive, in this instance friends and relatives deliberately placing themselves in weather that was cruel and unwelcoming to say good-bye to a dead person. If his mother had been alive she would have had him inside like the other children, with their moms slipping mugs of hot chocolate to them. He remembered the coffin descending into the mildewed hole and the desperate look on Conrad's face. It was this recollection that put him in mind of the tears his father had shed that day because there would be no more hot chocolate for either of them. He took a deep breath, smoothed his old clothes, and left the ruins. It was still raining so he caught the #44 bus to Foleshill without further delay.

At the bath Hugo changed into his swimming trunks and jumped in the pool to scour off the scum line. After finishing, he swam two lengths in a clumsy, varied stroke. When he looked up Beth was sitting in his seat.

"Is Toby not in yet?"

"Not yet," said Hugo. He resisted an urge to be nasty, to retaliate for her rudeness. But he remembered his promise, and her eyes showed only a superficial contempt overridden with a curious goodwill.

"How did you get this job?" she said. "You can barely swim."

Hugo pulled himself onto the deck and dried off with a towel.

"The alleged qualifications?" she went on. "That was a lie, wasn't it? If you went to someone's rescue right now, I'd have to jump in and save you." She straightened up in the chair as if she were going to dive into the pool. Instead, she smoothed down her sweater.

"Not here," he replied. "The secret is knowing I can stand up everywhere in this pool."

"That excuses the deception? What if you were in the large bath?"

"Then I'd drown as well."

"After the test next month you won't have a job."

Hugo shrugged his shoulders.

"Toby told me you claimed to have a first aid certificate. Is that also a lie?"

Hugo gave another shrug.

"What training do you have, Boy Scouts?"

Hugo took a deep breath and couldn't keep himself from smiling. "Let me complete the information," he said. "Before I decided on a real career, I took a degree in big books from a prestigious university, with a minor in small books. Afterwards I obtained a certification in specific books. Then I quit books altogether because I couldn't stomach the excess knowledge."

"You have been dreaming."

Hugo gave a turn down of his mouth and went to the change room. When he returned she was still sitting in his chair. He long legs were crossed and she flipped her foot nervously.

"I just want you to tell you that if I had known the money I lent my brother was for you, I wouldn't have given it to him."

Hugo smiled again and put his hands in his lap. "I wouldn't have either. It's a fine act of charity to fund the poor, but you're not doing them any favors. I read in one of those books I just mentioned, the part where Ebenezer Scrooge says, 'Are there no poor laws? Are there no work houses?'"

She got up to leave. "It's no wonder your chin's a mess. Did someone do that to you in the alley or right in the pub?"

"Seasick."

"Seasick?"

"On a ship. I was dizzy and fell into a railing."

"I have the feeling that everything you say is horseshit."

Hugo cocked his head. "But it's sincere," he said.

"Well here's another bit of sincerity. I would examine your chin myself but I'm off duty." She went out the door and Hugo watched it close with a sigh of the hydraulic arm.

After work he took the bus to the Coventry and Warwickshire Hospital, went to the Outpatients ward and an hour later walked into the office wing with a new bandage on his chin.

"I'm sorry, Mister Dring sees no one without a referral," said the receptionist.

A tall, sallow-faced man Hugo recognized strode the corridor past them. The receptionist called after him, "Mister Dring, I have a package for you."

Hugo stepped in front of him and said, "Sir, my name is Hugo Haultain. Could I have a moment of your time? It's personal, something I think would interest you."

"There is a sign on the door, chappie, which says 'No solicitations.'"

"This is something from your past."

Dring stopped and looked at him closely. "I'm quite certain you could have nothing from the past that would interest me."

He waved the package at the woman, said, "Thank you Gladys," and walked on. When Hugo got back to Foleshill, Tolly warned him again about the need to confirm his qualifications.

Lufungula, January 1, 1966.

After a vicious debate with Antoine concerning the cleanliness of his cell, Hugo ate his New Year's Day rice while preparing Mintou's lesson. That afternoon he requested that the young soldier, as an offering to the new year, recite a passage from the book he had stolen. Hugo relied on his recall of the book's contents to choose paragraphs or sentences appropriate to the student's abilities. He felt comfortable with the guesswork involved and the verification of his knowledge in Mintou's presence. The many weeks of his torture in the bungalow beside Stanley Pool had given him many opportunities to test theory against reality. And in the case of his interrogation, the theory proved correct.

The repeating circular patterns and differing themes of the questioning—what he had been told to eat for dinner a year before, the forms of written permission to use the bathroom when he was at school—all were designed to persuade him to confess acts of habitual rebellion. He went into each session with forecasts of absurdities more accurate than his prediction of the weather, which because of the dry season, was almost perfect. Fortunately, his analysis of the torture also supplied him with the endgame. He knew with certainty that as soon as the headman was satisfied that Hugo had willfully not sought, received or deserved permission to breath, he would reward him with death. Until then, the severity of the abuse advanced a punch or a kick each day. Antoine became alarmed at his prisoner's condition. He requested more money, went to the market, and brought back bandages. Hugo directed him to find some antiseptic ointment and the jailer returned one evening with a large tube and some adhesive tape.

The next night, the door grated open and a black figure limped in. Hugo hissed, "Who the hell is this? Get him out of here."

Antoine's voice whispered into the cell with a heartfelt pleading, "He has sores too, master. He is from my village."

"He could be Christ himself, Antoine. Just get him out of here."

The door ground closed. Hugo heard whimpering from the corner of the cell and lit a candle. He was surprised to see a boy no more than ten years old. His eyes showed fear and he squatted tight into the corner. When Hugo put the candle to his face, the boy turned his head to the wall. Tears ran down his cheek. Hugo thought for a moment, then knew the night would never end if he refused to act. He examined and cleaned the parts of the boy's body he could see, then spread ointment on the infected lesions and applied bandages. The boy wiped his eyes with the back of his hand and smiled.

"*Merci, merci,*" he said and grasped Hugo's arm tightly before limping out when the jailer re-opened the door. Hugo sat back on his case, hung his head on his chest, and tried to sleep.

For two weeks, while Hugo endured the pointless torture, the boy crept in each night to have his bandages changed and the comfort of a friendly hand. On one of these nights, because Antoine had become obsessed with his procurement of medical supplies to the neglect of other things, the candles ran out. After his nightly doctoring, Hugo sat in the uninterrupted darkness thinking of his predicament and deciding the time had come to consider an alteration to his captivity. He drank the half-cup of expensive wine Antoine had purchased and recited for the jailer a tale of daring heroes in a far away place where snow fell. Buoyed by the drink and the story, he traced across his mind a course of future history tailored to his own plight. Step by step, over many hours he planned the necessary showdown with his tormentors that might put an end to the gruesome sores on his face. He slept when the details of the plan were complete. His night fever spawned the usual dreams of death. But shortly before dawn, squirming half-awake across the floor, he felt a dream-spirit shower a fragrance of roses over his wounds. When he woke and touched his face, expecting a miracle, he was disappointed to discover that his fingertips still slid along the same oozing fluids.

Chapter XII

The Second Law of Dying

Foleshill, Coventry, November 27, 1964.

Toby called his new friend into the café.

"It's Friday, pay packet day, and I've got some spare cash. Take this and go buy yourself some clothes. You can pay me back when you get ahead."

"You didn't borrow this from your sister?"

"I would never get it, would I? She's got a thing against you."

Hugo went to the shops in the Precinct and bought some new pants, shoes, shirts, and a tailored gray jacket. The next time Toby saw him, he smiled and Nigel said, "You should have bought some leather, Hugo. Then you could have ridden my bike."

"A bike?"

"A big one, almost new. It's all fixed up and shines, mate."

"You're too young to get a permit."

"Never mind that. Come 'round the weekend and take it for a spin."

One morning Hugo went with Nigel to the rented garage near the cycle shop where over the course of two years the boy had assembled a multitude of used parts to manufacture his sky blue Triumph Bonneville. The stoop of the garage was littered with bike parts.

"I was twelve years old the morning I took out my first BSA and toured the streets. Can't wait for the day I get a bird on the back and set out weekends for trips to Blackpool and London. Get on the M1 and do the ton-up start to finish."

"The what?"

"It's the test, to go above a hundred mile an hour, London to Coventry. Ever been on a bike, Hugo?"

"I've done everything," he replied with a smile.

Over the week it took Hugo to master operation of the motorcycle, he toured the pubs around Nuneaton. For solitude he found corners of Kenilworth forest to sit and draw. He developed a theme based on empty places, sandy plains with the incandescent sun setting to the southwest over remote valleys. It was an escape from his increasing thoughts about Beth Marshall and a forgiveness of himself for thinking about her at all.

He was thinking about other things the day he glanced into the large bath to see someone doing a slow, rhythmic crawl up and down the pool. With a turning of her head at precisely timed intervals, the swimmer sucked air from the perpetual curve of dry space behind the wave pushed forward by her body. Bare shoulders glistened in the rivulets of water that washed over them and the perfect curve of her buttocks. Hugo stopped watching and went into the cafeteria to write about what he had seen. After three paragraphs he became thirsty. It was an hour before start of the afternoon shift, time enough to slip down to the Rose. Half way along the block he heard footsteps catching up. It was Beth.

"Hardly recognized you," she said. "I hope you burned your old clothes."

"Actually, Miss Marshall, the question is this—was it the chin that first set off your dislike or the dispute over your boss?"

"It's your lack of genuine wit that puts me off."

"I was going in here for a drink. Would you like a pint?"

Beth's head moved.

"I'll take that as being affirmative."

"Think what you like. I don't want a drink. But I'm hungry and have to eat somewhere."

They went into the Rose sat in a corner and ate. Hugo took the darts and without hesitating, threw one into the double twenty ring.

"This may not mean much, but I apologize for my flippancy," he said.

"No, it doesn't mean much. I get the impression that when life's hard on you, you're hard on everyone around you. That's an excuse, not an apology." She lit a cigarette.

Hugo sat down. "I was watching you swim just now. I'm impressed, of course. Who wouldn't be? As you know I'm rather clumsy in the water and in a few weeks have to take the test. I want you to give me some tips about the breathing. If I could copy your form I might keep my job."

"Copy my form? I'd hate to think what your real interest was in looking at my form." She let out a plume of smoke. "If you fail the test you'll be on the dole, won't you? Except you don't even qualify for that."

They stared at each other for a minute with no smiles or blinking. Then Beth said, "Just so that you don't get the wrong idea, Hugo. I'm waiting for Phil. He's the man you met the other day. My regular. I could have waited in the bath, but it's not so busy in here."

"Of course. Then I'm free to do other things and hope you're not offended."

"If I am, I'll leave."

Hugo put his notebook on his lap, wrote for few minutes then turned to his unfinished sketch.

"What are you doing?" she asked.

"I was writing some observations on art, things that we should all heed. If you're interested I'll elaborate."

"I pay attention to the things I like, mate. But go ahead. I'm sure this will be an impressive bit of philosophy."

Hugo put down the notebook and said in a quiet voice, "The art we create imposes order on the universe, but it also increases stress."

"Sounds frightfully interesting," Beth interrupted. "You must have had an abnormal childhood."

"Probably as normal as anyone's," Hugo replied and took a sip of his beer.

Beth let out a cloud of smoke. "Perhaps. But please go on. I may be rude, but I have a distinct curiosity to hear your opinions on art."

Hugo smiled, wrote a few more lines in the book, then said, "With the exception of art, I never learned a whole lot as a youngster. Consequently, I remained ignorant of some important aspects of the world. At sixteen years old, for example, instead of mastering a sport as you did, I was down to the beer parlor, in the men's section only, as opposed to the Ladies and Escorts. At that age I couldn't be expected to know about the ladies or the things they did in private with their escorts. But I was interested to find out."

"So you replaced the order of art with the pleasure of sex. Or was it the other way around?"

"Doesn't matter, because in a peculiar way, they're inseparable. Art, sex, the replacement of one for the other—all of this imposes a framework around the way we think. Tension, and the things we do to relieve the tension, define the boundaries and make them immutable. Stepping beyond is too painful to consider. If I were to compose a story about a desirable woman, for example, these limitations would determine the line and the resolution of its creation. A true story of love's gratification is a heartfelt glory. Writing about it, however, is a vicarious ecstasy. The paradox is an unbearably hard reality. The more vivid and telling the story I write, the more I'm tormented by the demons of my own creation—by a love that has no head or heart. As you can see, the fantasy of art is able to short-circuit the physical laws of real life in a disastrous way."

"I can see that fantasy has definitely short-circuited your life."

"It has. Recollections of things that actually happened impose no order in the world; and real history doesn't pretend to make things more bearable by its enumeration of fact. Like the totality of life, history is what it is. It gives us only an inkling of our successes and failures. Pure art, on the other hand, gives us the regret for what didn't happen but might in the future, if our inspiration is great enough. In both cases, we still have to cope with our disappointments."

Beth looked at him with a mixture of emotion. "I don't understand any of this," she said. "Except I catch a glimpse of deception. Deception is quite useful for you, isn't it?"

Hugo looked thoughtfully at her and the man standing next to her. It was the man he saw in the swimming pool. This time his clothes were even fancier, more tailored. He looked at Hugo with suspicion. Beth got up. As they walked away she looked back and with her finger gave him a wiggle of caution.

* * * *

"It's your test tomorrow, Hugo. A swim in the big bath will be fun." Moffat spoke through a mouthful of beans.

Hugo looked grim at the reminder. "Would they accept an oral exam?" he asked.

The Yorkshireman tilted his head to the side and smirked. "You've shown great valor in water to your knees. What's another eight or ten feet under your shoes?"

When Hugo walked into the large bath, Beth was on her way out. She had a towel around her torso; pool water dripped onto the floor. "Don't drown, Hugo," she said. "It's your job at stake, not to mention your life."

"You should be there. I need your assistance."

For a moment she slowed and the expression on her face softened. "I'll be watching," she said.

Tolly stood at the end of the large bath under the three-meter board with a stopwatch in his hand. Hugo stared up at the metal girders that spanned the building and held up the roof. He could also see them mirrored in the calm blue water. With a quick calculation, using the physics of reflection, he determined he was staring at a girder above the far end of the pool. That should be his minimum goal in life, the illusion of success. In reality the image marked the halfway point in his task of towing an inert body the length of the bath in the space of four minutes. As he considered the impossibility of it, he saw a reflection of a woman in a white swimsuit leaning against the handrails of the high board; then it disappeared in the chaos of moving water as Tom Mahoney jumped into the pool. The whistle blew.

Hugo dove in and grabbed him in the prescribed towing position. His first instinct was to apply his skills. But he had no skill and could only apply his strength. A quarter way along he was in trouble. Halfway up he was gulping drafts of pool water. Three-quarters the length of the pool and he was swimming underwater, breathing only when luck put his mouth in the air. Unavoidably, he sucked water into his lungs. He surfaced with a loud spluttering to clutch at Tom Mahoney's arms. The bath echoed with laughter and Tolly's loud voice. "Close to time, Mr. Haultain. Hurry up then."

He swallowed another mouthful of water. The pool was murky, the girders faded, but he continued to pull against the jeers and cheers and Moffat saying, "It'll be time at the Rose afore he's through. A little more effort, Hugo."

Then he sank and continued to sink with agonizing pain in his chest, grabbing at the formless water and confused about what to grab until he felt hands pull him towards the light. When he had surfaced and Toby Marshall had let go of his hair, Hugo looked level into the wet face of a woman, with her own hair swirling in the wash around her shoulders.

As soon as he could talk, he said, "Success. I'm still alive."

"You bloody well would have drowned if Toby hadn't pulled you out," Beth replied.

"I admit there was a lack of style at the end, a lack of your skill."

"You could never do it like me," she answered and pulled herself onto the pool edge. "But don't worry. It won't be me spreading the gossip." She walked away putting a towel around her waist.

Tolly came to the poolside and said, "Hugo, please come to my office when you've dried off."

That weekend Hugo and Tom Mahoney did the rounds. They went first to the Courtaulds Social Club then to the Palais. "I usually avoid this place," the Irishman said, "but tonight I feel like celebrating your success." He sipped from a glass of Guinness and took off his eyeglasses to clean them. Through the smoke and smell of spirits he said, "No gin for me tonight, just beer for the nourishment. I feel odd, crazy, like anything can happen: a beautiful bird, a bag of gold. It was a good thing you kept your job. And it's a better thing you didn't drown. You was red enough in the face. Toby was on the mark. I'd have saved you, but at first I didn't see where you'd sunk to. Christ, you sunk fast. You should have seen it…he had to dive right to the bottom and grab your hair. It was his sister that told him to do it, you know, to jump in a pull you out. They were all laughing like hell. I felt for certain Tolly would sack you. But he didn't, so let's go dance and listen to the music."

The next night Hugo detoured into the small room next to the Guildhouse television lounge. After dusting the top of the keyboard lid and piano bench he began a half-hour of fingering exercises. Thereafter he went twice a day to create his own music. On the weekend he stayed away from the Palais and the Rose, going instead to the piano room and closing the door so no one could hear. His fingers regained an easy dexterity and his playing improved. For the first time since leaving the piano at 836, he went slowly through his mother's sonata.

The following Tuesday he rode Nigel's bike to London. Avoiding any chance to meet Eileen he locked it up and walked to the British Museum. He went to the reading room and looked for books on Albert Schweitzer. That night he drank a few pints of bitter at the Apple Orchard, walked through Leicester Square then climbed the stairs to his usual room. Early in the morning he rode to Watford. There were no riders at the diner so he smoked patiently and drank cups of hot tea. At nine another bike swung in.

"Going for a ride?" Hugo asked. The man nodded towards the motorway. Hugo set the needle above one hundred miles per hour and held on. Without a pharing, the force of air on his chest threatened to tear his fingers off the handles. His forearms ached. A Rolls Royce shrieked with an air horn and passed him. At Northampton the valves overheated and the manifold pipes showed a bluish tinge. He tucked in behind a Jaguar and drafted for miles, shooting under the service bridge at Newport Pagnell with the white-pie faces at the window a momentary blur.

After his shift was over Thursday, he went into the small gym behind the locker room and mechanically did his workout, not thinking about the ride or anything but what his muscles were doing with the weight. He was wiping off his head when he saw Beth standing inside the door.

"Why are you doing this?" she asked.

Hugo finished drying himself and smiled. "Come in, Beth, since we haven't talked for a while. First of all I'd like to thank you. I owe my survival in the swimming test to the coaching you gave your brother, so he in turn could pull me out."

"You were certainly in trouble. I've heard some people around here say, 'Oh, Hugo Haultain could never be in trouble.' Personally I think you always appear to be that way. Your nasty attitude is trouble. Doing the ton-up, that's not trouble, it's childish and possibly suicidal."

"Ton-up?"

"You're a real tosser. Play ignorant and why not? But I talked to Nigel, who lives at the bike shop and he talked to a bloke who came off the M1 saying he's just had a ride with someone named Hugo."

She lit a cigarette, sat on a metal chair, and said, "You don't have feelings for much of anything, do you?"

Hugo shrugged. "You seem to judge people quickly and take an equally hasty interest in their welfare."

Beth smiled. "I take no interest whatsoever, chappie," she said. "But for some reason I find it a source of merriment to come in here and point out your shortcomings."

Hugo finished the last repetition of his set and wiped the sweat off his face. "Makes me nostalgic hearing that. Conrad was well into pointing out my failures."

"And who would 'Conrad' be?"

"My tutor. He pointed out the little mystery of how life contradicts death. It's the same paradox we see when contemplating the fact that eventually thermodynamics will overcome gravity. The conservation of energy notwithstanding, the result will be the death of the universe. As a rather lame echo of that point, I conceived a law I called the second law of dying."

"In human terms this would be?"

"Well, it's like this: The material world requires a constant infusion of energy to maintain its integrity. Likewise, the simple act of living day to day requires that we make a consistent effort to overcome the tendency towards disintegration. Given this tragic fact we can only imagine how rigorous the journey of death will be. To survive the trip, a person has to be in top shape when he dies. That's why I'm here working out—to get ready for death." Hugo set down the barbell.

Beth rose from the chair and walked over to him. She put her hand on his bare arm. "Death comes when you're sick or old."

"Not if you're hit by a bus."

"In that case you're in shape before, but not after. But it all helps I suppose."

"That's the paradox, isn't it? That's the part we don't understand—how the efforts we make while alive give strength to the soul."

"Do you believe in the soul?"

"Most of the time I believe in what makes sense. That's what Conrad tried to do, knock a little sense into my brain. But it was all a bit of joke, really."

"Do you believe in love?"

Beth stared at him waiting for his answer. She walked to the door and pulled out another cigarette, looked at the weights, and took it away from her mouth.

"Love," Hugo said. "That would be a topic for another day, Beth...love and desire."

"Where are you going for Christmas?" she asked. "Or does that also fall into the category of another day?"

"I'm going to play the organ at the Cathedral."

"Are you? That brings me to one more thing: Don't try to mock Phil like you do others, including me. His mates at the Jaguar Club tend towards taking things seriously."

"You must be proud to go with him."

"That's my business."

"I was going to ask you to have a drink with me," Hugo said. "I buy. You choose where. But it seems your dance card is filled to brimming. So I won't labor the point."

"Well, I guess that saves both of us a lot of trouble," she said, put the unlit cigarette in her mouth and pushed through the doors.

On an overcast morning three days later, Lucy called Hugo from the cafeteria saying, "Come here for a sec." There was no smile on her face. From the counter he could see Beth in the vestibule. Her fingers fidgeted with the strap of her purse.

"At two o'clock Sunday afternoon," she said, "I'll be at the Crow in the Oak."

"At two o'clock Sunday afternoon," Hugo replied, "I'll be drunk as a skunk at the Rose."

She looked ashamed, angry. "That's a pity because I was going to be alone." She pushed past him to the cafeteria door, causing all his breath to run out with a huge regret, and a remembrance of saying to someone that the real value in life was the willingness to say anything, anytime, to anybody as it pleased him.

Sunday's weather was mild. Hugo wore a thin shirt under his leather jacket. He rode to Nuneaton to pick up Tom Mahoney and waited for his friend to gather his things from the flat of a girl with black hair. When they got to the Crow in the Oak it was a few minutes past opening time. Hugo looked for Beth's blond head and sniffed, hoping that through the smoke and beer he might get a smell of her. But she was not detectable by any of his senses, so while the band played, he had two pints then went out and kicked stones over the pavement. Just as well she had not come, he thought. In a few months he would be gone and it made no sense to add further weight to the burdens of living. He walked around the corner of the building. The chrome fenders of the Bonneville gleamed as it lay in its stand; sitting on the bike was Beth Marshall.

Hugo paid close attention to the traffic, tried to ignore the arms that held him around the middle and the heat from her breasts. He took the ring road downtown to the Precinct. Wind shuffled paper and dust blew through the deserted malls and commons. Hugo held his scarf with both hands. They said nothing for five minutes. A dust devil sucked grit from the stones and flung it at them. He grabbed her hand and pulled her into a door opening. The whirlwind danced away.

"I won't be staying here for very much longer," he said.

"Why do you think I care?"

He turned away and looked at her reflection in a window. "Because you're here. Because you told me where to find you."

Beth walked around the large planter with shrubs that hardly seemed to be alive. She wore a tam, and Hugo was troubled by her general appearance, by the expression of sorrow on her beautiful face when she said, "When I wasn't training or studying I used to go out with mods, not with rockers. Mods dress fashionably. I was at the Margate riots for the show, not the politics. My mates would have taken you for an undesirable bloke. But I wouldn't have cared about that."

She turned away from him. "And I like the Stones and the Beatles. That's what I used to believe in back then—in being fashionable and in with the right people. There was a time in my life when I believed that I wasn't having enough fun."

Hugo strolled around the same planter, a great circle route across the top of the known world that had become a storm passage for him, a difficult journey towards truth. Paper and cigarette butts littered the pavement. Dust blew constantly with the moving air. He caught her at the end of the garden and said, "As a general statement of principle, what you believe in is not enough, Beth. What any of us believe in might be wrong because it is assuredly incomplete."

"Is it, Hugo? I'm twenty-four now—not so old really to believe that I'm helping people, and not so much into helping myself anymore. What should I do to complete that belief?"

Hugo examined her face and thought that as troubling statement of principle, Beth Marshall was not an item for a casual read and hope for a happy ending. What he saw was a brief phrase of description, an arrow pointing down a corridor lined with regrets. She stood ten feet away, next to stone bench that formed the periphery to the garden with her hips slanted at a relaxed angle. The wind ruffled strands of hair that flowed out beneath the tam.

"Before I can sleep at night, I have to write," he said. "It's a bit like taking a piss before you crawl in, to relieve the slight, nagging pain. Sometimes I get carried away and stay up most of the night. I get going on an idea or a face. Last night after reading about the problems in Africa I thought of this idea. It's about what we believe in and desperately pray to God to achieve."

Beth looked over the garden at him with no antagonism in her face. "As you said, you're leaving in a few months, off to view the world's problems firsthand, leaving the rest of us here in ignorance. So tell me about your idea, Hugo. What is it that we believe in, and pray for? Go on, attempt to jolt me out of my apathy, try to reduce my trivial appetites."

Hugo walked to where she was standing, took both her hands in his, and said, "Imagine two children close to death. One, a little girl, is surrounded by her family unto three generations: mother, father, sisters, aunts, cousins all praying fervently for God's intercession, as are the priests with their candles and incense, prepared to administer the extreme unction should the child fail and require passage to heaven.

"The second, a little boy, is sitting amid the wreckage of his mother's entrails, as we've seen in recent pictures from Africa—and the sharp machete about to fall and cut off the pathetic, forlorn cries of his fear and longing. Just as well that he should die now, we say, because given the hell on earth it would be better that he join the other small black angels who by now must be a majority in heaven. So he dies but not so the little girl. She has survived through the prayers of a multitude of friends, all registered servants of the Church and sufficiently pious, and numerous, to warrant divine intercession in the curing of the child's incurable disease.

"Would it be presumptuous of me to accuse the Almighty of showing favor to those of his creatures who can muster a contingent of faithful to volunteer prayers on their behalf? Would it be heretical of me to suggest that divine mercy apparently doesn't extend to abandoned, forlorn infants, who are doubly cursed: for being un-baptized so they not only die hideously but then have to fend for themselves in the infernal regions? Perhaps the population of angels in heaven is not so weighted after all with black babies, the poor or the forgotten. My point is, Beth, so long as you think long and hard about it, what you believe in may be incomplete, but it is never trivial."

Beth walked away, saying, "What else do you do besides thinking up morbid things?" Before he could answer she came back to him and stood so close that he could see the pattern on the buttons of her coat.

"I didn't mean that," she said.

"What didn't you mean?"

She put a finger on her lips then looked away. "I hear no one talking about such things," she replied. "I have too much fear. I tend to forget the things I can't understand."

"You don't forget. Your career depends upon some people living and some dying whether you understand why, or not. It will always be in your mind that the pattern of existence reaches beyond good or bad health."

Beth raised her hand as if to touch his face, then let it fall. "Do you ever have nice thoughts, do pleasant things?"

"I play the piano."

"What do you play?"

Hugo turned away, saying, "Just a little tinkling of the keys to ease the tension."

He rode her to Aldermans Green on the motorbike. The light had not quite gone from the western sky when they arrived. Beth got off saying, "Thank you. This hasn't been the happiest day of my life. You said things I find disturbing. But then you're a disturbing person. On the pleasant side I always wanted the excitement of riding on one of these big bikes."

On the way across the lawn to the cottage, Freddy Marshall stumbled onto the porch carrying his dog. "Beth!" he screamed. "Come in and make my tea, girl. Go on, lad. Get away with you."

"I'm so sorry," Beth said. "You better go. He hates bikes…does his best not to understand anything. I'm here only for an hour, my weekly visit. Go now, please."

The old man came further onto the porch, put the snarling terrier on the floor and shouted, "Be gone!"

Hugo backed through the hedge to the bike, kicked the pedal twice before it started. He twisted the throttle half open to sweep the Triumph through the curve and along past the hedge before the dog could get to him. But the animal was fast through a small gap and ran in front of the bike's wheel. As he swerved away, the throttle jerked three quarters open. The bike leaped ahead, pierced the hedge to the interior wire and catapulted sideways into the brush. Still upright with the motor roaring, it careened towards the high street with the throttle wide open. The sharp branches tore Hugo's foot from the peg and flayed the leather off his glove. At the end of the hedge the machine sloughed into the deep soil of the rose garden and fell over. Pin wheeling four times in eccentric arcs, it sheared every plant clean of growth before the motor stopped. Hugo sat in the dirt, listening to the front wheel spin and the pipes cool. Freddy Marshall stared out from the porch and lifted the dog into his arms.

"Look at my roses!" he screamed. "Don't go near him, Beth. Stay away, I tell you. He's a bloody menace, like the rest of his ilk. I'm callin' the coppers. Do you hear that, chappie? The police!"

Hugo sagged back into the earth and felt the gratifying humiliation of a buffoon. Beth stood next to her father in dismay. Her hands were still clutching her head. She mouthed the question, "Are you okay?" Hugo nodded and got to his feet. Before she could walk over to him, he picked up the bike and pushed it into the road. As he put his leg over the seat, he looked back and for a brief moment saw on her face an inexplicable mixture of grief and yearning.

When Hugo enquired if Mister Dring might be at his residence, the hospital receptionist concurred with a nod of her head. Hoping this might be true, he caught the bus that ran to Royal Leamington Spa and got off at Leek Wootten. Half way up Hill Wootten Road he saw "280" carved into a rock monument and turned into a wide drive. The porch light was already on. Knocking on the door, he hoped Dring would answer and save him explanations. But instead of the surgeon, a woman opened the door just wide enough to stand sideways in the opening. Her hair was a rich, red-brown, and slightly curled. From this observation Hugo determined she was the woman who had given him the ride into Coventry seven weeks earlier. She looked at him without familiarity and said, "Yes," in a formal tone.

"Is Mister Dring home?"

"No."

"Would you be expecting him home…in a reasonable period of time?"

She looked down at him. "And what would reasonable be?"

Despite the curtness, her appearance, voice, and manner suggested to him a connection greater than a short car ride.

"I suppose reasonable to me would be this: If I were to wait at the end of the drive for Mister Dring to return, would I die from the cold before he showed up?"

"I would expect so," she answered, "quite dead. Now if you'll excuse me."

A voice familiar to Hugo came from the back of the hallway.

"Who is it?"

"Nobody," replied the woman.

When he saw Beth come up behind Miranda, he bowed his head politely.

"You!" Beth said with surprise.

"You know this man?"

"Vaguely."

"Well I'll leave you to him. Don't keep the door open too long." The older woman disappeared into the hallway.

Beth crossed her arms against the chill. "You never stop trying, do you? Did you come here to harass Owen?"

"I see it as a challenge. Might I assume that the woman who answered the door was Mrs. Dring?"

"Assume away."

"I don't suppose it matters if Mister Dring isn't home. He'll be available at some point, I'm sure. Right now I should be aiming to catch the return bus and leave you to hob-nob with the boss's wife."

Beth narrowed her eyes. "I don't hob-nob with my own mother."

Hugo's brow rose slightly.

"Let me put a very fine point on this," she went on, "if you really want to talk to Owen, he's down at the pub having a drink with Phil and some of the lions of the town. I call them 'the lions' because if you go down there with your present attitude, I suggest you go armed as a gladiator."

Hugo held out his hand and she instinctively took it. "I suppose it would be cheeky to invite you down?"

"I don't ever go there when the lions are pacing the den even if the entertainment might be fun, which I am sure it will be if you insist. Good-bye." Beth turned. Before closing the door she added, "Don't go down, Hugo. I wouldn't like to see you humiliated."

The building containing the Leek Wootten public house was entirely engulfed in vegetation. In the near dark Hugo had difficulty seeing through the ivy and wisteria vines to where the faded sign attached to the stone. Inside, he was not surprised to see men wearing hacking jackets, cardigan sweaters, hunting caps. A cloud of pipe smoke mingled with the pinch of cigars and cigarettes. The publican had a bright red face and appeared content. The dartboard was busy. Men played checkers and some talked in loud voices. At first Hugo couldn't see Mister Dring or Phil Granby. He toured slowly through the rooms. Glancing into the smoking lounge, he saw them at a long table with three other men. One had the ruddy complexion of a drinker; another's face was marked with premature lines. The man in the middle looked slim, soldierly, a twin of George Blenkinthorpe.

Leopoldville, January 10, 1966.

On a day when the corridors of Lufungula howled with men bound for the bloody end that would expunge their criminality, Hugo watched the flow of bodies past the view port without seeing any sign of Martin Birks. Hours later when Mintou came into his cell, he enquired again.

"He is alive, monsieur, don't worry. I will arrange for your reunion within a month. Antoine is prepared."

"Of course you know that when I leave here, Birks comes with me."

"Perhaps he does. Perhaps by then he will be dead from disease. Many are sick in the north wing."

"What of the doctor?"

"He comes once a week."

"I've never seen him."

"If you get sick, you will see him."

"Or he will see me—to sign the death certificate."

Mintou laughed. "Certificate? We don't need the doctor for that. Even a child knows an old nigger that can't be saved. But for you, who knows?" He laughed again.

Hugo said, "Read me something, Mintou, from the book you stole. Let me know you're worth more than a casual laugh."

The sergeant read two or three sentences in French; but it was a conglomeration of phrases and solitary words spoken in a loud voice three, four, five times each to get the syllables in correct order.

"I could say you've made no progress on this," said Hugo. "Perhaps I should make greater demands. But I won't. Actually, you've done quite well and practice will make you better."

"I'm worn out with practice, monsieur. I find places away from the men to read and scribble on paper with your pencil. But I'm alone too much."

"Education is like that, Sergeant. But a warning here. The process of thinking and knowing things will turn you into something resembling the lonely snake in the forest. And you know that everyone avoids the magical snake because he has a far-reaching and mysterious ju-ju, can change into a well-dressed man spouting truths and prognostications, by which I mean he can foresee disaster and forestall the stupidity that causes it. If you continue and succeed, you will be feared by your own family."

"Is the ju-ju doctor like that?" Mintou tapped on the cover of the book with his finger on Albert's face. "Do all the villagers fear him?"

"You must decide that for yourself, my friend. But I'll say this: as we grope in the dark of our ignorance looking for a way out, we risk having vicious and greedy men take advantage of us. Such men built the city outside these walls and in the process, many an old nigger perished in slavery. Do you want me to say more on this and scare you into greater effort?"

Mintou squatted in his usual corner. Hugo threw him the payment of a cigarette and went on. "For a long time I was wary of Albert, the ju-ju savior of black and white men alike, and on each meeting I put his pronouncements before the court of my own judgment. In the comfort of a quiet room in a cheery English public house, on the occasion I am about to describe, I sat beside a wood fire that lent warmth to the men of reputation beside me, men who should have given me the final word about truth. On the dark walls of the room hung pictures of hounds and horses, which was an honest picture of life half a century ago. Near a long table hung the picture of a different scene and a greater truth. I put my face close to the lower edge of it to look for a subscript. A voice hoarse and sweet with whiskey said in my ear, 'In case the print is too tiny for you, Hugo, it says, "Napoleon Bonaparte, Emperor of France aboard HMS Persepheron on his way to exile in Elba." We see here the dictator of Europe standing near the railing as he watches the French coast recede. What is your opinion? Is that a mixture of defiance and regret on his face as unmistakable as the cocksure smugness on the combined visage of the naval officers watching him? He looks a bit like Von Raynor, don't you think?'

"I went back and looked at the print a second time before answering. 'I would guess from your own smug certainty that in a former home you had this print tacked on the wall.'

'It's a rare work. I would never have hung it in the tropics to be blighted with mildew. But I've never forgotten the lesson.'

'Lesson?'

'How easily we fall into the easy virtue of tyranny.'

'You're a democrat?'

'I'm a realist, if you must put a title to it. Democracy is not opposed to leadership, but every small freedom requires the protection of law, and laws are concocted and interpreted by men of flawed character. Law itself changes, even as the laws of the church, presented to us as religious truth, vary from age to age. In my case I reflect constantly on the laws of the Almighty and how we might make them apropos in a violent, degraded world.'

"I sat on the bench facing outwards, with him and the others in view. 'The table behind you is populated with such men,' I said. 'Like bitter tea they are all steeped in good laws. As lions of the town and leaders of the nation they drink their scotch and tithe to the Church of England. But do they benefit me? If not I'll have to point that out to them.'

Albert crouched stiffly and sat at the table beneath Napoleon. I put my satchel on the next chair, removed one of the spiral scribblers and began listening to the conversation. Dring glanced towards me and frowned.

'Pay attention, Owen,' said Reggie Everton and went back to his opinion of how things were worse in Africa since the great powers had abandoned the continent. The man with the puffy face agreed. Then they all talked at once, announcing foregone conclusions based on inadequate history. Following grunted agreements and shaking of heads, one man said, 'In the middle of this cesspool you've got Schweitzer, a bright little spark in the darkness. What do you make of him?'

I noticed that the ju-ju doctor sat impassively at this comment as if too many times he'd heard his name spoken with less intent by a weaver bird squawking in the trees, a man who took insults and compliments wearily and seldom with any impulse to reply. Braced by a curiously carved stick, he got stiffly to his feet. I walked towards the others saying, 'Mister Dring, what a surprise.' And with a nod to the old man leaving through the front door I sat next to the surgeon and began to express my doubts. And doubts I had, Mintou, too numerous for me to list and none of them helped along by Albert's intervention. Now if you'll excuse me I'm tired and we must still do your lesson."

Not waiting for a reply to his comments, Hugo ordered his student to recite words and phrases. After an hour's stumbling across a thousand syllables, the soldier went silent. His master lit a parting cigarette and tossed it to him. They smoked without talking until Antoine brought in a bowl of rice. Sometime later the jailer's radio tolled the night curfew with broken, stuttering voices from the station on Fernando Po. The tunes had a melody familiar to Hugo, like carols sung by children on Christmas Eve. He moved painfully on the leather case and tried to invent for his amusement, music more tuneful than a radio, images of candles other than his own, altars greater than his leather case, all with organ pipes behind and generous faces smoothing out the wrinkles of his despair.

Christmas Eve, Coventry, Warwickshire, 1964

The baths were closed Christmas Eve afternoon. Hugo had agreed to meet Tom Mahoney at the Jaguar, but first he wished to toast the café lady with a drink. The lights were half out when she poured an ounce of scotch into his tea.

"Your cheeks are redder than your hair, Lucy."

"What's that supposed to mean—that I'm drunk? I'm not, you know. Just a bit melancholy." She wiped her nose and added, "Anyway, you should be minding your own affairs, like what's with you and your friend?"

Hugo frowned. "What friend do you mean?"

"Don't play the stupid git. You and Beth Marshall."

"There's nothing doing with me and my friend. So let's have a small drink. The day's not done yet, and on Christmas Eve you should be happy when you go home to your family."

Lucy looked into the street and her mouth fell. Her face was a hand's breath from his. With a paper napkin he wiped away the tears that ran down her cheeks. "Things are never what they seem, Hugo, but let me tell you how things can be, how things could go for you if you don't take a proper interest. I've three children. I'm married to a good man...a good father to all of them, but young Eric's the apple of his eye. He's a bright cheerful lad and my Bob dotes on him. Eric's different, out of the ordinary with so much affection for his father. So why should something as uplifting as that tear at me? One Christmas Eve, when my Bob was away—he had to spend a deal of time away a few years back—anyway, this one night I went partying. I was lonely, young, and met a charming lad, wonderfully kind. I got carried away. I could never break Bob's heart and tell him that Eric is not his. They all look like me anyway...red hair and all. Every year on this night I have terrible guilt. I'm sorry."

Hugo handed her another napkin. She dabbed her eyes with it and continued. "You don't have any reason for guilt, Hugo. But you have other things that tear at you. Beth will be at the Rose tonight with Phil, and not much of a smile on her face either."

Hugo got up and went to the door. Lucy stood at the counter with her eyes burning. He walked back and put his arms around her and she sobbed with her long hair twirled around his face. "Go home to Bob and your kids, Lucy. They all love you to pieces."

She looked at him with a tearful smile of thanks. "If you're not doing anything for Christmas dinner, come to our place. Gordon Moffat comes every year. We'd love to have you as well. In fact, it's Beth who always drives old Gordon."

"I was going to have dinner at the Guildhouse, but I'll do that. Tell Gordon to give me a call in the morning, make sure I'm out of bed in time."

He kissed her on the mouth. As he walked out, she said, "You should know it was Beth who intervened with Tolly, convinced him you were worth keeping."

He turned to face her with hands in his pockets. "This is of no value to me."

"And why? Are you scared of something? She was here an hour ago and asked after you. You'll find her at Aldermans Green visiting her father. We shouldn't all be fools and tied to our regrets."

Hugo looked into his mind, tried to sort through his regrets and anticipate what decisions might lead to an increase of regret, what to a decrease, with some being unavoidable. He had already taken the decision to place Beth in a gallery of remembered portraits. His departure was imminent and a mental image of her was portable. He said a quick good-bye to Lucy and went outside to the courtyard where he intended to get on Nigel's bike and ride to the Jaguar Club. Tom Mahoney would be waiting for him there, already ordering

Christmas drinks for them both. When he wheeled onto Foleshill Road, however, he turned left instead of right.

On his march across Freddy Marshall's lawn, Hugo glanced at the ruined rose garden and smiled. Despite his accidental pruning, the plants would survive he was sure, and in the spring produce luxuriant flowers, some the color of blood. He turned to face the cottage with its decrepit, mossy façade, as derelict in appearance as houses in the Cedar Galleries. But he knew that it would endure for centuries still, because English builders were inclined to use stone instead of wood. Behind the house, the Green itself spread eastwards as it had done for a span of time greater than the history of towns or houses. Hugo imagined old geezer Freddy tramping towards the gray sky, feeling old, but not as old as the forest or the stones. Just nothing useful left to do but let his dog run free to bark at the ravens, and no one to love except the one animal and his only daughter, who visited once a week. Those facts made Freddy a man not much different than his own father. So where was Conrad? he thought. Dead, maybe. He felt an urge to confront him with questions, because Muir always had quick and precise answers for everything. And at that moment he would ask him, "Conrad, what am I doing in Aldermans Green? I can see nothing happening here." Hugo posed the question, and since he already knew the answer, started back towards the car park. The hedge was in his way or he would have found himself already at the bike, content to ride directly to the Jaguar Club. When he turned aside at the hedge, looking for a way through it, he saw Beth standing on the porch. She walked over to him with arms wrapped around her body for warmth. "Why are you here?"

Hugo scratched his head. "You know, I just asked myself that question and I concluded that for some reason I had an inexplicable urge to point out your shortcomings. But I couldn't think of any, so I was leaving."

"I don't believe a word of that, Hugo. You had a good reason for being here, just like I had a reason for being alone at the Crow last week. So given the season, I'll try a little honesty. I'm not happy this has happened. I thought my life was running along as planned. Then you. But you won't stay. You have no plans to linger here, no connection to Coventry, even to England. When it's convenient you'll be off, which in a way suits me fine. I understand from Phil that in the pub last week you rudely embarrassed Owen in front of his friends."

Hugo could think of nothing sensible to counter the remark. He thought of saying that he would stay because of her but the words came out, "I could stay because of you, but that's a reason some people might characterize as being untrue."

Beth shivered and wrapped her arms more tightly. "Hugo, the only thing I hear from you are the deceits that come out of your closed mind, much like the tatty little book you carry around and doodle in to justify your reasons for thinking everyone is more foolish than you are. Maybe we are fools—but who are you to judge? The sad fact is that despite your cocky attitude you're bloody well afraid. Well I'm afraid, too. I grab at illusions and cling to my orderly life." Beth took a deep breath, shivered and looked away.

Hugo shuffled his feet. "There are no limits to my queries," he replied. "I'm merely a person seeing a map of the world and deciding where he was going and how he's going to get there. Often, I make mistakes."

His hands fell and he took her fingers up. "But I do owe you an apology. You are right to say that it takes fear to survive; and fear is an unkind, selfish thing."

He tightened his grip on her hands. "You see, Beth, I'm trying very hard to convince myself that I don't want anything here. To survive the next year, I have to believe I don't want you."

Her fingers rooted inwards. She hung on for a moment before releasing his hand. "You're right. Leave before you've gambled on something valuable. I have to go. After Phil gets back, we're going to a party at the Rose."

It had been dark for an hour when the Jaguar Club opened for business. There was no cover charge, only a premium price for the liquor. Hugo parked the Triumph at the farthest distance from the building. On the long walk he smoked the last of his cigarettes and got more from the machine. While Tom Mahoney bought two pints at the bar, Hugo examined the matte black tile of the ceiling with tiny lights shining downward like phony stars. Then he looked around to see who was or was not at the club.

"See the bloke at the end of bar standing next to Phil?" the Irishman said. "He's the toff with the bent nose and red tie…that's Johnny Prescott. He fought Henry Cooper last year for the heavyweight title, losing in a split decision. I was thinking that I should go over there and smack him. I'd ask for his autograph and while he was signing his egotistical fuckin' name, I'd lay him out with a right cross. That would make my point."

"The point being that you're an idiot?"

"You're right. I shouldn't do it—you should."

"What point do I have to make?"

"The point of satisfaction. You could put his toff head right into that pickle dish."

Hugo opened his fresh pack of cigarettes and put one in his mouth. "You're the boxer," he said.

"I'm a derelict, a shadow of the past. But never mind that. Prescott's still a piece of fluff in my opinion."

"He took Cooper the full fifteen."

"Pure luck. Now, any cunt could one punch him."

"So do it for the priest, or baby Jesus."

Hugo lit the cigarette and finished the last of his pint. Mahoney ordered a bottle of Manns and slurped with his mouth wide open. "I'll pay you," he said. "Me whole pay packet, destined anyway for the collection plate."

"Twelve quid for a broken neck?"

"Beth Marshall would be impressed. I know you're dying for a roll with her."

Hugo's ears buzzed with the noise. "I think it's time we wandered over to the Craven Arms, Tommy. At least the leather has a good smell.'

Mahoney leaned backwards in his chair. His voice rose. "You'd be missing an opportunity. Look at Prescott's face. His skin's a layer of scum on a custard. Hit him hard and he'd pop wide open."

The publican craned his neck and frowned.

"It's time," Hugo said, taking his friend's arm. "We're leaving."

The Irishman pulled back and pushed a chair over. Beer foam rolled over his shirt.

"Piss off, you spineless git!" he shouted. "Twelve quid ain't enough for me to take a round from Johnny P."

As Hugo stepped towards the door, noise in the Jaguar Club died away. A hand shot out of the crowd and grabbed him by the shirtfront.

"Is it you that's paying for a round with Johnny P.?" asked a large man with a swath of greasy hair swept up from his forehead.

"Not at all, sir," answered Hugo politely. "Just going home to mother."

The hand tightened and a button flew off Hugo's shirt. "Perhaps Mr. Prescott would like a visit with your mom as well, because I know who you are."

"In that case you're invited to come along. A mug of hot choc and a pleasant tuck-in might keep you out of harm's way."

Another button flew off the shirt and landed on the bar. Hugo relaxed and giggled nervously. The man eased the tightness of his grip. With a sweeping motion Hugo swung him around and using the bent arm, pinned the man's head to the bar. The boxer picked up the button. "Let's have a minute here, Mr. Haultain. Doyle and I just want a wee word about the situation."

Hugo let go of the bouncer, who pivoted around and straitened his jacket. Off to one side he could see Phil Granby smiling and tapping the ash off his cigar. Johnny Prescott spoke directly saying, "Who's George Chuvalo?"

"You have that large a gap in your boxing knowledge?" Hugo asked.

"Cheeky ponce," said Doyle and moved towards him.

"Did you see him fight Cooper?" continued Prescott. "And see the stuffing fall out of our Henry's glove when he hit your man?"

"That was Ali's glove and Cooper's head," answered Hugo appearing bored.

"You know your boxing, lad. Do you think the stuffing would fall out of Doyle's glove if he hit your mate over there? Go ask him. No you can't, because he's gone, scarpered and left you to face us for a sum worth less than a week's beer."

Hugo nodded his head at the bouncer. "You're right. A few quid hardly seems enough to take down a grumpy midget."

Johnny Prescott curled his lip into a smile and restrained his friend. "What a wit, eh Doyle?" He stopped smiling. "Now, there's the door. Out you go. If peace on earth is too much to hope for," he said, "at least we'd like a bit of it here in the club."

Hugo turned to the bar and took a last sip at his drink. A girl with long, straight hair nudged her breast into the boxer's arm and stared at him. He wrinkled his nose at her and went out onto the street to look for the Irishman, who was nowhere in the car park or on the street, so he strolled along to the bike smoking a cigarette and thinking about the varied and colorful history of boxing.

"Hey, ponce," a voice called. Men ran along the pavement. Before Hugo could move, an arm pulled him backwards off the seat. Four men pinned him on his back. Fists and feet rained blows on him. Strong hands put his arm against the curb then thick shoes hammered onto his left arm with a dozen crushing stomps. Heels clicked across the pavement. Pressed slacks and shiny shoes marched past his face. One pair remained and a face bent towards the ground.

"I know who you are and where you live, ponce. Be assured I'll be having another word with your later tonight."

With difficulty Hugo rolled over to speak but found he had no way to make his tongue work. Alone in an empty corner of the car park, he contemplated the concept of speech until the nausea increased his confusion. He looked up. The chrome of the bike's exhaust reflected the sullen glow of the streetlight. Light rain began to fall. He got to his knees, then to his feet. Struggling to put one foot ahead of the other, he went into the high street and began walking. The rain turned to a downpour. His left arm throbbed with the cold and each stride shot pains through his back and ribs. Squeezing water from his hair, he continued at a faster pace in the direction of Stokehill. Sometime later, with the volume of rain still increasing, he fell exhausted into his cold room and steadied himself against the chair, tried to raise his head up from its stooped position to examine cracks in the brick. A spiral notebook lay open to an empty page. He thought about events at the Jaguar and decided to sit down and record the idea that violent revenge offers the best satisfaction, as bad money drives out good, or chill air cancels the warmth radiating from the single heat pipe traversing his room. On his way to the desk, he noted the reflection in the window and knew that he appeared worse than when he had first arrived at in Coventry. "This is a hospital," he recalled Beth saying to him. "You're lucky someone hasn't dragged you to the RSPCA and fed you a bone." And she was right. He looked like an abandoned cur and should take a few minutes to change into the clothes he had bought, as a mark of respect for the people who would patch him up. He shivered with the cold, and with his right arm hung a spare blanket over the window rod to keep in the small quantity of warmth.

Behind him the door shoved wider, admitting caroling music and the charlady's turbaned head. "Jesus, Hugo! Better let me swab out your cakehole," she said. "Did you say a bad thing to someone at the local? And look at those clothes. You're not agreeing with much these days."

Hugo wiped off his lips. "Just a small cut, Gerry, and a bad bruise on my arm." She washed off his nose and around the corners of his mouth. "You get lost in the rain as well? S'truth. Can you manage taking off those wet clothes? You should have a warm bath to wash yourself. Yes well, if you need me..."

Hugo went straight to the lavatory carrying the first aid kit. He stripped down and showered in the lukewarm water. Without looking at his left arm, he began winding it with gauze, using a complete roll to mask the bleeding. He opened his satchel and took out the black bag, which held a syringe and a vial of morphine. In ten minutes the pain began to subside and he was able to lay out his new clothes. When he had completed his dress, the figure in the door-mirror was polished, with black trousers, a blue shirt, and tailored jacket. He was pleased that he had a military look, the replica of a fashion that officers at the Russian court might wear. It lacked medals and gilt on the epaulets, but it seemed fine enough to impress the royal women. He could have been Prince Eugene, or Napoleon—familiar as they both were with the pain of defeat. According to Muir, he should resign himself to pain, would always be sailing through life on the destitute wreck of his sickbed, with legs never touching the floor. He looked at his reflection in the window, and feeling satisfied that self-preservation did not interfere with pride, walked into the drizzle to seek aid. Following him came the grating sound of metal heels. At the high street, the #32 bus was waiting; but instead of taking him toward the hospital, it rolled in the direction of Foleshill.

Chapter XIII

Coventry Cathedral

A thin, swirling mist faded the Christmas lights on walls of the Rose to indistinct halos. With rehearsed dignity, Dr. Haultain stepped off the bus, leaned against the wall to catch his breath, then pushed open the door of the public house. Using his right hand to carry a glass, he shuffled across the heaving floor and sat in the far corner. Strident chatter and loud music swirled around his ears and confused him; thick smoke drifted in a slender column to the lights, whose red and green color reminded him it was Christmas. But he thought it was strange to have heard no charitable words from the gaffer who pulled his pint, or any from the patrons either—only harsh, demeaning voices. On every side he was blocked in by conspiracies of subterfuge and pettiness.

"Is this Christmas as men actually see it?' he asked Jimmy Smythe from the Guildhouse, who looked up from his pint glass with a drunken, half-dead face. When he saw Hugo beside him, the millwright sat straight up and didn't hesitate to croak out a novel prophecy—that Christ might be crucified a thousand times, but all would be in vain unless, at some point in history, He exacted a swift and merciless revenge.

"I'm a stupid man, Hugo, and not up for debate," Jimmy went on. "I would feel a great comfort if God was as barbaric as I am, and strike down evil where it stands." When Smythe's head sagged forward in a drunken stupor, Hugo slid to the end of bench, content to avoid talk of evil, watch the barmaid, and tap out a Christmas tune with the fingers on his right hand. A tall figure drifted through the crowd. The man saw him, sneered and waved a finger as a warning or a threat. A fragrance of roses and clean skin replaced the foul smoke.

"I want to ask for a dance," Beth said. "I've danced with everyone else. Wouldn't seem fair to miss you."

Hugo got to his feet slowly and took hold of the table for balance. "It would not be a good idea to dance," he said.

Her eyes squinted. "You look quite drunk, Hugo, pale, not yourself at all. Strange, because you haven't touched your first drink, and I've had five."

She looked at his left arm resting on the half-buttoned jacket, then put her fingers to his marked face. "I heard you've been scrapping at the Jaguar. Disagreeable as usual—but your new clothes look smashing. Did you pick these out yourself?"

"Toby did."

"Our Toby. What good taste in one so young. Except I find it strange you're wearing a glove on the hand inside your jacket."

She took his right hand away and placed her fingertips on his left arm. In a voice not much above a whisper, she said, "I don't believe the excuse about dancing. Look in my eyes. If you keep on ignoring what you see there, someday more than your arm will ache."

She took another sip then leaned closer. "Actually what I meant to say in my tipsy state, was—if I were to grip your arm tightly in a gesture of fondness, you would probably find it uncomfortable."

"I object only to the pain of inconvenience," he replied.

"I thought you were the smart bugger who's ashamed to admit pain of any sort. Did you hurt your arm as well in the scrap?"

"A few bruises."

"Well that's a small miracle considering what I heard."

"So, you believe in miracles?"

"No."

"Well let me say something about them anyway, a short episode that will only take a moment of your time. I had this friend once. He was a certifiable moron, and dumb, couldn't mutter a word. Finally, he learned to say 'sam ting,' like he was trying to say 'same thing,' or 'I know' as in 'I know what you are saying.' But to the world he was still a moron, because he acted like a moron and no one would believe me when I said he wasn't."

"Is this leading somewhere?"

"No, but keep listening. One day he went bird hunting with friends but was upset at the shooting. He had a feel for animals, you see. Used to tow around a tiny pet horse on wheels."

Beth giggled.

"It is funny, isn't it? Quite hilarious. But there's more."

Hugo related the story of Milton's rehabilitation. The young woman in the blue dress blinked at Hugo when he paused at the end. But he couldn't say what was in her eyes or thoughts, except perhaps she'd been touched by his story. Her fingers rested gently on his left arm.

"A touching fantasy, Hugo, at least the bit I could understand. Why did you tell it to me?"

"It has a medical flavor to it. Did you ever hear of anything like that in your training?"

"Never. I suspect from the sound of it, that you just pulled it out of your brain."

"Consider it a contribution to the season."

A large hand came between them. "I think you better move on, mate. You're out of your depth here."

"He's not bothering me, Doyle."

The bouncer put his face closer. "I would say he is, Beth, because the lad should've learnt a lesson earlier tonight. Eh, Mr. Haultain. I hear you can't swim and I know you can't scrap. I'm amazed you're not back at the Guildhouse licking your wounds."

A short man came through the crowd. Beth took one of the two drinks he was carrying. Doyle raised his own glass to her and said to the man, "I was just reminding present company of the mishap at the Jaguar, Mr. Bradley. Our friend here caused quite an embarrassment with Johnny Prescott, a little scene that was bad for business. We dealt with it then. But I'm thinking that to get things straightened away altogether I should have another talk with the lad."

"So let's step outside and have a wee word then," said Hugo.

The short man frowned and shook his head. "You look a little beat up already, lad. You should have the nurse here dress you up."

"She already stands for him in the manner of charity work, Mr. Bradley. Kept him his bleedin' job, I hear. I thought it was amusing."

As Doyle led Beth away, Hugo felt his senses collapse and regretted stopping at the Rose. But he reminded himself that it was only a small detour from his journey to the hospital. He waited for a few minutes, stepped cautiously through the crowd, and pushed out the door into the night air. At the bottom of the stairs a shoulder smacked into him. To his left he saw Doyle grinning. The door opened. Phil and Beth walked out with the short man.

"Doyle, you said you were getting the car."

"Just a word here first."

Doyle lunged forwards.

"For Christ's sake, Phil, stop him!" Beth shouted.

Hugo turned to face them at the moment the bouncer struck his ribs with a fast kick. The impact swung him around. As he straightened up, his senses cleared and his anger fell away. In front of him stood one of a sorry dozen unschooled street urchins disputing marbles beneath the yellow lights of countless neighborhoods including his own. With little taste left for the fight, Hugo blocked the clumsy punch and jabbed his fist twice into the big man, who buckled, fell, sprawled onto the ground with blood pouring from his nose and lip.

Beth frowned. "You know, you almost had me fooled with the tucking of your arm into the jacket," she said. "You really didn't want to dance with me, did you?" She turned away and walked with Phil towards the car park.

Mr. Bradley came up to him and nodded his approval. "Very efficient," he said, "almost professional." Then they were out of sight in the rush of traffic and fog.

Behind the north wall of the Rose, the air was less choked by the fog. Hugo leaned his right hand against the brick and stared at the product of his vomiting. He heard Phil's car drive away and groped towards the entrance, using the wall of the building like a railing. At the transit stop Jimmy Smythe herded him onto the bus. Hugo protested, "I have to get to the hospital, Jimmy."

"No lad," he said. "We're going to services, you and I. That's the medicine we need." He handed Hugo a cigarette.

Across the road from the Craven Arms, the new Cathedral shone with a dim light. The old one smelled damp and rank. Together, they seemed a great distance from Hugo and getting further. But his Guildhouse friend guided him across the road and into a back pew. Hugo hummed a few lines from the hymnal but found he couldn't focus on the prayer book. His arm throbbed with an unbearable ache, which caused him to imagine what healing miracles might occur under Appleton's assertion that divine good taste might confer holiness to certain places and privileged people. But the line of townsfolk filing in appeared unaltered by the ceremony. Hugo could only assume that the mass of parishioners knew as well as he did that God did not bless buildings anymore than he blessed the contents thereof or the people therein. In other words there was no salvation for him here or elsewhere, only vague suggestions of goodwill, insipid shadows of generosity, and reluctant hints of where such values might exist. The organ sounded a run of opening chords. Hugo tried to sing the offering as loud as Jimmy, but gave up, concluding that it must be an infinite distance separating him from the Man who made the blind to see and cripples walk. He could only hope that in the real passage of time, his arm would heal unaided by privileged localities or divine intervention.

The church was almost full when a single man crept into the back pew. Mister Dring sat down wearily next to him and listened to the choir, his head lolling back and forth out of time with the music. Then he turned and said, "Merry Christmas."

The younger man held out his right hand and the surgeon took it.

"Is it 'Hugo', then?"

"Yes."

"Good. How long have they been at it?"

"A few minutes."

"Excellent. I was beginning to think I'd miss the service." With that he leaned into the pew and closed his eyes in meditation. When the music was finished, he got up to leave, paused, and said, "The other night I heard Phil say that you work at the bath. Do you know Beth Marshall?"

"Yes. I saw her this evening at the Rose."

"Very good. I'm sure you found her charming." Dring stared at him, "You don't look well," he said. "Appears you've got some blood on your jacket, there. If you've hurt yourself, you should get it seen to. The hospital surgery's open, you know. Even at Christmas there's someone on duty for those who need it."

Hugo knew that surgeon was correct. His vision was skewed, his head dizzy. He felt out of place. More accurately, the well-dressed parishioners of Coventry looked out of place. They had all melted into the blandness of the ceremony; their piety suffocated him. With sweat soaking his neck, he moved down the aisle towards the door in the hopes that cool air might refresh and reorient him to the direction of the hospital.

Lufungula Prison, January 21, 1966.

"Antoine!" Hugo yelled through the door. He was faint with hunger and sat back on his leather case. One more time he pulled himself weakly to the door-slit and called towards the jailer's room, tense with the possibility that the little man had abandoned him. For a day and a half he had seen no torturers, no Mintou, no Antoine with the food he required to live, and through living, choose carefully the facts and language of history both for his student and himself. He endured the night with his stomach in cramps and his mind obsessed with the imagined taste of rice and goat meat. In the morning, men of the interrogation service came for him. Throughout a day of significant torture, they were troubled by the sounds coming from his abdomen, being the only answers he would provide for their exquisitely crafted questions. Late in the afternoon, when they tossed him back into cell six, they were delighted that Sergeant Mintou waited inside, vowing to extract more than rude noises from him. When they had gone, Hugo said, "I need food, Mintou."

"Sorry, monsieur, but Antoine left for a few day's leave to his village. No one thought to replace him just for the benefit of your extravagant diet. Tell me my story, and then I'll feed you."

Hugo sat down with a breathy sigh. "You've certainly learned a few words, Sergeant, and mastered the art of how to annoy me. So learn this as well: if I don't get food, and soon, I'll be dead and you won't get from me the polish to shine up your speech. Your family won't understand anything you say and will assume you're a bigger idiot than when you left. Make a choice."

Sergeant Mintou shrugged. "You'll get food. I've already sent someone to the market to bring back rice. While we wait, I'll practice." He squatted in the corner and read from the book in an uninterrupted flow. Hugo heard only random noise until a soldier appeared looking guilty and saying he could find only fish heads and one plantain for the money. Hugo ate the fruit and picked the few pieces of edible flesh off the heads. With the last lick of his fingers he began talking.

"Christmas Eve, Mintou, and me attending church service, doing my spiritual duty to retain the power of a beneficial ju-ju. Not that you would understand what I was doing or what I'm telling you now. But listen anyway, as I've said many times in the past. When the priests and music had finished, I pushed outwards through carved doors of the Cathedral, and, revived by the cold, made my way beyond the circle of light to the threshold of the ruined church as a speedier route to my destination. The glass and wood and iron were gone from the blasted door, replaced by a baroque blackness that was by definition closed and bolted. I passed through this barrier effortlessly. I thought it must be a form of ju-ju as opposed to a miracle because it was apparent that God didn't live there anymore. Likewise, it was not troublesome to me that the lighting was no better behind the shattered walls. For years I had no bedside lamp to illuminate the books piled up by Conrad Muir for me to read. I managed to plow through them anyway. Navigation by dead reckoning became a habit; this time through the darkness of the ruins to wherever would best provide me with a crutch for the usual weaknesses of the body, if not the soul.

"But the thought of going anywhere increased the sense of fatigue, forcing me to sit down. From my position on the floor, I reached out for reassurance, but everyone of rank had departed along with God. All sense of myself—all my fancy ideas of life and death—had gone as well. My brain could generate no light, draw no horizon, build no mountains, create no ocean. Was I home? If so, the prints on my walls had faded completely into the plaster, the walls and windows erased.

"The sound of traffic on the high street drifted away. The thick curling of fog absorbed the feeble glow of electric light. My spine registered none of the damp cold of the stone. Existence became an annoying vacuum, with the world skewed and dissipating. Under my legs opened a clear path to the fire wardens burned in the bomb's blast. Desiccated gristle would be all that was left of ears and eyes and no one left but me to hear the strident prayers rising from the smokehouse abattoir next door, no one to see the brass figure of Lucifer tapping the infernal ash off his cigar, giving us the consolation of a bad smell. That is what I chose to think in my deprivation, Mintou, as I looked out on the space beyond my invisible feet.

"Time passed and I realized the smell was coming from the remains of my own cigarette. I snuffed it out and the air cleared. The tiny black box of life became permanently sterile. The music was finished; the impulse to create had faded, with no desire left to weep in self-pity, not even the stars to look at through the fog and nobody caring either way. Certainly the woman named Beth didn't care. She had already dismissed me as one who took a boasting pride in his thin layer of knowledge against the warnings of his father. Even to myself I had become a braggart, who should face up to being lost a mere fifty feet from the thoroughfare with traffic rolling by.

"Out of boredom rather than self-criticism, I called, 'Help!' No one answered so I added with a smirk, 'I will not go easily into that good night, I will walk proudly through the valley of the shadow of death,' then began to laugh as I saw the last light go out in the Cathedral. I lay still, breathed the fog and felt increasingly weaker. I called again with less energy. The Cathedral door opened and a light gleamed. Music flowed out to me, three giant chords, my God I thought, the chords to Grieg's monotonous *Concerto*. Then a man appeared. His glowing face revealed him as the church organist, known to you as the ju-ju doctor. He sat down heavily next to me with a glass in his hand.

'What are you really about, Mr. Recently Converted Parishioner?' he said. 'Incapacitated again. Well, I can tell you this much. You ain't stopping here. You think this sacred memorial is a doss-house?'

'I've been told that before,' I answered.

'That's right, the copper apprised you of that much. Then why back again? And again in a place that assumes a tragic meaning when it should be farce: a filthy shop, a wrecked ship, an infested tenement, a collapsed ruin.'

"Painfully, I shifted my position. 'A sacred memorial has tragedy attached, but also hope and dignity,' I said to him. 'You should wish to have such a glorious monument over your grave, and soon. The actuarial tables predict that Albert Schweitzer should be dead by now, having outlived his usefulness, another dead great man, benefactor of the sick and the poor notwithstanding.'

'It's been a good game, Hugo, a living. Better than stumbling blindly over an altar honored by heartbroken workers, if you can recall the image from former visits here. Struggling for a week they managed to erect a monument that soars unseen above you now, made from burnt timbers they found lying amongst the wreckage in the form of a cross. It would be a repentance if you got on your knees in front of it and humbled yourself in the presence of God.'

'God lives next door now and apparently is deaf to my pleas, without remorse for my condition.'

"The man sipped at the glass and let out a sigh. 'You should at least have a drink of this to ease your suffering. Good quality Cognac from across the way. It's a chronic shame I could never get a case of this down south.'

'Show me a way out,' I asked.

'Show yourself,' he replied. 'I won't be assisting a man who won't help himself. By that I mean use some reason. Do you remember my saying that faith doesn't mean a thing if you can't put it through the brain? Think on that, because no one else's faith or pain or remorse will be showing you a way out of here. Forget being the hero vaulting over stonewalls to escape. Heroes of action don't exist, only the great men of renunciation and suffering. With your self-inflicted suffering you've made a feeble start. To complete your journey requires that you think logically and for a long time on the benefits of renunciation. It's not a sin to be smart, you know.'

"I sat up stiffly. 'All joking aside, Albert, your view of the world is based on the feeling we should all have for the agony of living things.'

'My compassion extends best to living things who have the aura of humility, no matter how insignificant.'

'I renounce only my failures.'

'If you put that through your brain properly, it would include simply correcting them. I can see that it's more than the cold bringing you down. Here now, someone's coming. Better you're assured of their help.'

"I heard a vehicle drive up. Someone went into the Cathedral and soon after the lights went out. The Cathedral door closed with a bang. I yelled, 'Please help me!' Footsteps approached and with them a vague silhouette. A torchlight scoured the black floor in front of me. 'Here,' I called. The light faded, a car door closed and the sound of an engine faded. I tried to call out, but only a squeak dribbled from my mouth.

"The old ju-ju man said, 'That's pathetic. Your yelps wouldn't even disturb the dead under your feet. You're an unlucky sod, Hugo. Someone reports the door open and lights on. The Deacon comes back to see what's up and you couldn't even call him this way with your pitiful cries. Looks like they'll find you here in the morning, quite stiff, I'd imagine.'

'Oh no. It won't end like that, my vile friend.'

'If I should ever be as vile as you thought Muir was, that would be a compliment. He was my pupil and an attentive boy. I taught him something.'

'You taught him nothing.'

'Yes, it's a shame he felt obliged to run off and play father to a nincompoop like you.'

'Then shove off if you can't be of help.'

'If that's the extent of your repartee, I'll definitely be on my way.'

'I've exhausted debate, Albert. I'm exhausted generally, so just point me out of here, towards the high street and I'll be out of your hair.'

'I suppose I could,' he said. 'Not that you've been much of a host in your present position. But I'll only do it on the promise you not forget the job you're going to do for me.'

'What could I possibly do for you?'

'You have talents I could use.'

'I have no talents suitable to your situation."

"Have it your way,' said the old man and turned to walk away. He was my only help, Mintou. Without him I was lost, so I reached out and pleaded, 'You win. I promise to do one job for you. One.'

'At my place of business?'

'Do I have a choice?'

'No,' he replied.

'Then I agree, but under duress. Just get me out of here so I can clean up and get on with God's celebration.'

"Albert led me out of the Cathedral, to the high street, past the tobacconist's shop, and close to the transit queue with cars and horns and lights.

'The bus that stops here is your #38, Stokehill, so don't miss it,' he said, adding, 'Next time you attempt an exploration of religion, stay out the boozer. And let a practicing physician administer your drugs.'

Hugo settled back onto his leather case. In the twilight, he could discern Mintou's smiling face from the glow of teeth when he said, "That was a good story, monsieur. I'm getting fond of the ju-ju doctor and thankful he was able to save a few old niggers. I hope you'll live long enough to tell me what job you did for him."

"I will outlive you, Sergeant."

"If that is true, I have to ask…what would you do with the few extra minutes before soldiers cut you down with bullets or stones?"

Antoine called in the slit; and the sound of the returning jailer's voice set Hugo off on a tangent of lecturing and a description of his near starvation. He had not finished his tirade when the cover drew back across, the door shut and he could hear the two men walk towards the cellblock door. Alone in the darkness, he tried to balance Mintou's threat against the concept of good faith. That the sergeant might be influenced by the honor and trust in the book he was learning seemed his only defense against increasing hopelessness.

Eleven PM, Christmas Eve, 1964.

The man on the #38 Stokehill bus said, "Ye should clean ye'self up before going home, mate, or the old girl be on ye…and you without your supper."

"Haven't got an old girl," replied Hugo.

"Sorry about that," the man replied and smoked his cigarette in silence. Hugo swayed in his seat, thinking that it was a good thing that most people regret nothing in life so long as they get home in time for their tea. But tonight he had already missed his own tea, was supposed to be doing something else, journeying from an old church past a new one and so on towards…He had a vague memory of his intentions, but the old man lit another smoke, then whistled a Christmas song. Hugo's thoughts roamed to a tune Muir had often sung over the years and he began humming it loudly. The drunk looked over at him. "That's a good one, mate," he said. Hugo sang the words in a fast tempo and waved his right arm in a gesture of beating time.

At the next stop, a group of Guildhouse residents boarded fresh from their party at the Craven Arms. Edwin Dyer pointed and laughed at Hugo, saying, "Look boys, he's been scrapping again…on Christmas Eve too. Should be ashamed of yourself, lad."

Someone shouted that the injuries were yesterday's news so they all began singing carols in braying voices. Hugo joined in with a feeling of euphoria until the driver warned them to keep the peace. Then, watching the confusion of lights both inside and outside the bus, he recited to a sleeping Jimmy Smythe a story of romance and the dangers thereof, warning him that a man must always be careful to look over his shoulder to see who's doing what to whom. In four blocks, half the passengers were snoring. At the Guildhouse, Hugo woke his seatmate so he could get assistance through the unusually thick fog, a strong arm to carry him past the front door, and down the hall to #49 in the west wing.

Once in his room, he sat at the desk. The room was warmer because of the insulating blanket covering the window. He took off the jacket, thinking he should examine his arm and, if needed, shower it off before putting on a fresh dressing. He got the bandage unwound and arm covered with a towel before taking out his spiral notebook from the drawer. He felt tired, pathetic, fatigued with the doses of morphine, so he began to print, 'Something else to make me sleep. An old song I've just recalled.' Then with his eyes half closed and his face bent close to the sketch, he tried to determine if it resembled the woman he hoped it would be. He fell asleep.

Hugo had no idea it was exactly 2 am when he woke. He knew only that the noise of a hacking cough squeezed through the barely open door. For a moment he believed it was a hospital noise and raised his head from the desk. He was surprised to see in front of him the drawing of a woman. An artificial red seeped into her face and his surprise turned to anger. He spread out a clean sheet and tried to duplicate her face, but was unsure of the line of her nose. This diminished store of detail troubled him further. A short debate concluded that his failure in life resulted from a weakness of heart and not from any external, unimportant defects, like those in the portrait, which had a perfect resemblance to Beth after all.

The shock of remembering her was more than a petty agitation; it had the essence of the new blood that seeped from his arm. It was like a miracle to see the steady current wash across her portrait, floating him with it across Aldermans Green, further than the high street and beyond the town to a far point in history where he might never meet her again. This was a peculiar irony because, given the complexities of life, he should never have gone to the Jaguar or the Rose, should never have left his home, or his medical practice, or the sickroom either, with the world circumscribed by his bed, or left his mother to die of a broken heart. And he saw with the final blink of tired eyes that the woman sketched onto the page beneath him had her head raised, as if in disdain or disappointment, before she had walked back towards her father's cottage, with him wondering which one of them was leaving and what did it matter anyway.

As was her morning habit, Beth was up early. After the Christmas gift giving she drank a cup of coffee and was relieved that she had no hangover. Christmas was the day she liked best. She felt artificially buoyed by the notion of giving, caring, seeing God for what God was, is, and ever shall be. Her stepfather came into the kitchen.

"Are you going to drive Moffat to his Christmas dinner?"

"Can't get out of it. But I don't mind. He is so appreciative. There's always the usual, 'Oh I could get a cab or a bus, luv.' And I always say, 'Don't be daft, Gordon.'"

"How did last night go?"

"Everybody had fun, even Phil."

"Any excitement?"

"One scrap that turned a little mean."

"Anyone I know?"

"Doyle, Mr. Bradley's man."

"He's bouncing at the Rose now?"

"It was him who got bounced."

"Really. By whom?"

"Hugo Haultain, the one who insulted you down at the pub."
"Who told you that he insulted me?"
"Phil. He said that the man had been rude and offensive."
"He was outspoken."
Beth nodded. "Why? I mean what was his point?"
"He made the observation that chat in the pub reflects, in his own words, 'a dismal level of debate.'"
"So he came all the way out here to belittle you?"
The dog wandered into the kitchen. Dring lit his pipe. "So our Mr. Haultain scrapped with Doyle. It's sad what drink will do for a sense of courage."
Beth smoked her cigarette and stared out the window. "Hugo's a tough bugger. Two weeks ago he crashed his bike into Freddy's rose garden."
"Your dad was annoyed, I'm sure. Was he hurt?"
"In my opinion he doesn't feel much in the way of pain."
She shrugged her shoulders. Dring got up and poured himself more coffee. "Your friend was at the Cathedral last night for evening service. I sat in a pew with him at the back of the church. He seemed more than a little disoriented."
Beth got up and let the dog through the back door. "It's no wonder. Rumor went round that he insulted Johnny Prescott earlier at the Jag. Doyle's lads got him pretty good in the car park, with more than a few bruises. It must have been a big shock to his pride."
While they drank their coffee, Dring looked out the window at the dog running on the grass, then thumbed through the Christmas edition of the *Times*. Finally he said, "About that night in the pub. Phil was wrong. Your Mr. Haultain deflated some pompous arrogance with a list of grievances including, but not limited by, 'irrelevancies, inconsistencies, direct contradictions of facts, premises and conclusions; blatant errors in logic, numerous instances of hypocrisy, stereotyping and outright falsehood.'"
"Sounds awful."
"Not really. He said it with good humor and was polite. Unfortunately we weren't. The lads were quite rude to him, said some offensive things about his clothes and his work at the bath."
"How did he take that?"
"He didn't seem to notice or care either way."
Beth said nothing more about it, but had thoughts that disturbed her.

It was a perfect day with the shadows long through the beech trees and the hedgerows when Beth drove through Kenilworth and eventually to Stokehill. She found Gordon Moffat not ready, pipe spit dribbling down his chin.

"Did Lucy tell ye that Hugo's comin' with for Christmas dinner? No. Well, I'll be about five minutes. If you don't mind, go see if he's ready. Last night he had to be carried in by the lads. He should've sobered up by now."

"I don't want to go find him, Gordon. We're not on good terms. Could you go…at least see if he's all there."

"It's all right, luv. Go out that door to the commons and straight on to the west wing. He's probably up by now."

Beth did as he directed, walking through the common area and into the west wing. At #49 the door was ajar. She could hear music that seemed to run out through the gap. There was no reply to her knock. She thought he must still be sleeping and pushed the door wider. The window was shrouded with a heavy blanket. Even then, it was cold and she thought that the rare instance of winter sun would have done more to provide heat. She took a step in and her nose detected a sweet smell, a hospital odor she assumed was antiseptic for his cuts. With her eyes not yet dark adapted, she could barely make out Hugo's form, his head in the crook of his right arm, the left arm apparently stretched out and hidden by a small towel. She relaxed. The ancient, Middle-Eastern music coming from the small radio made her think of the dry mysterious land of the Christmas story, which in turn led her to the silly, improbable tale Hugo had told her of the fox's death and its effect on his afflicted friend. She smiled and let her eyes take in more of the dark room.

The bed appeared not to have been slept in. The tailored jacket lay on the blanket. She took another step inside, closer, silently so he wouldn't wake with a start. Her breath came out in a sigh and she smiled again. Coming up behind him, she would let her fingers wake him gently with a touch to his neck. But why would she do that? She didn't wish to care anything for him, wouldn't dare touch him. She moved the window blanket a half-inch and focused her eyes on the page of the scribbler and Hugo's face, which seemed white like bleached paper against the uniform crimson of the desktop and the towel covering his arm.

A moment of revelation spiked through her. She threw back the blanket to let in the full glare of the sunlight. What she saw made her nerves, her breath, her blinking eyelids stop. She knew then what she had smelled. And all the years of her training were just sufficient to keep her from falling to her knees. She stood directly behind him and looked down at his face, peaceful, as if asleep, like faces she'd seen in the morgue, but those faces had already been fished out of the coagulation of their own blood. His cheek was cold. Carefully her hand drew back the small towel that covered his arm. Splinters of bone jutted through the lacerated flesh, itself torn away in ragged chunks from the elbow to the hand, some of it still wrapped and the gauze so congealed in blood it looked part of the tissues. She could see where the damage to the brachial artery had resulted in a slow dripping of blood, like a leaky faucet until almost all of the large desktop was filled to overflowing. One drop, perhaps the last drop of his blood had actually hardened before dripping off, like a drop of water turned to ice. His face was lifeless. The hand holding the pen appeared already to be stiffening.

    She raised her head back, took a long breath and forced her fingers to feel the side of his neck. Then she calmed her own breathing, stilled the vibrations of her body, hoping to detect any sign of movement. Tears of relief welled to her eyes. She tore a strip from the soaked gauze, wound it tightly around his biceps and slid him to the blanket on the floor. After covering him, she grabbed a coin from her purse and ran down the hall to the pay phone.

    "Owen? Thank heavens you're there. Listen, please. Phone emergency services—have an ambulance sent round to the Guildhouse at Stokehill, #49 in the west wing. Make sure they have the usual equipment for a major loss of blood. And stat, Owen, for God's sake."

"Old Moffat?"

"No, it's Hugo. Christ, he's near bled to death. Be at the hospital. Meet me there—please."

"I'll be there."

Beth started to cry. "This is on my head, Owen."

"Don't be daft. Good-bye."

    She returned to the room and knelt with her legs underneath her and whispered, "How can you leave me like this, with all my regrets piled up in a moment." With her eyes closed and seeping tears, she tried to shroud her feelings. The sun was warm on them both and she listened to the ebb and flow of the mystic strings, consciously keeping the flow of blood going through him by the energy in her fingers. It seemed they would both die there together, such a long time passed before the breathless attendants arrived at the open door. When they had carried him out, she hesitated. Gordon Moffat stood in the door.

"Don't come in, Gordon."

    But he was already half way in and seeing the extent of the damage. "Its all right, luv, I saw much of this in the war, the blood draining away in the dirt. It's all right. If you'd like, I'll go the hospital with you."

    "No. Take a cab to Lucy's, or the bus and enjoy your Christmas. There's nothing you could do."

    Moffat smiled and put his hand on her shoulder. "He'll be all right, luv," he said, "right as rain." Then he shuffled down the hall, leaving her alone in the room. The music played uninterrupted, as it must have played in time to the slow dripping towards death. Funeral music, she thought and looked again at the desk. The pen lay across the page of the spiral scribbler. She removed it to expose the last lines written on the page. They were large, as if he had had trouble seeing. The page underneath was a sketch she recognized as herself. In near panic she ran from the heated room and down the passage, forgetting where she had parked her car.

Of his stay in the hospital Hugo chose to remember only a few things: that Gordon Moffat had convinced the Guildhall board to waive the cleaning costs and that likewise, Beth had agreed to waive the moral costs of saving him on the basis that Hugo had no personal assets to secure ten pounds worth of debt, material or otherwise. And to formalize the agreement she allowed him to feed her grapes from a small hospital dish. He also recalled a visit from a man on New Year's Eve, when he could see wet snow covering the hospital grounds outside his window. Mr. Bradley from the Jaguar Club had come to issue an apology on behalf of Doyle and his friends. It was an unofficial statement since Hugo had informed the investigating constable that it was no crime to fall over in a car park or to have consumed enough beer to impair memory of the event.

The rest of Mr. Bradley's conversation was with Beth, who was in the room, she said, only in the capacity of duty nurse. From this Hugo learned that in one week she was traveling to the Canary Islands for a holiday with Phil. After the visitor had left, Hugo drifted to sleep and was never aware that before leaving the ward, Beth had leaned over and kissed him twice on the mouth. Then hours later, going into the car park and feeling the snow going over her boots, she made the decision to end her association with him. She tried to smile and imagine white unpopulated beaches. But the only image seeping into her mind was a waterless ocean of sand that stretched to the horizon; and that night she dreamt of wandering across bone white dunes leaving solitary footprints that went this way and that to no particular place on earth.

When Hugo returned to the Stokehill Guildhouse, his room was newly cleaned, even the top and sides of the desk. Only one item appeared unusual. His spiral notebook hung by a string lengthwise through the rings. A dozen pages were separated by clothes pegs. A note lay on the desktop:

> This is the best I could do. The blood will never come out but I was told to wash it in detergent to remove the excess. I was just thinking, can there be an excess of blood?
> Beth.

The book had long since dried. The paper was curled and wavy. The words were legible, so he sat down and began copying. Later that day he walked into Mr. Tolly's office. "I'm not going to be much use like this. And not wanting you to agonize over my fate, I'll be on my way."

Tolly smiled. "You're oh so right, Hugo. A bath attendant who can't swim is close to the line that demarcates uselessness. A one-armed man who can't swim crosses well over that line. However, it has been pointed out to me, and not by Miss Marshall I might add, that since your installation in the small bath there has been a general increase in order and a lessening of mayhem and vandalism. My natural skepticism tells me not to believe such exaggeration. But for the few weeks left, you may be of some benefit to this place."

Hugo was about to decline when young Nigel came into the office with a pleading look on his face. Tolly added, "And Nigel had nothing to do with my decision," then went back to writing in his ledger. After the boy had taken him into the courtyard to show him the new fuel tank on his Triumph, Hugo took the #44 bus downtown and went into the Cathedral to hear the organist practice. Then he then walked the four miles to Stokehill, sat at his desk and calculated the effort he must put into restoring full use to his left arm. Every night he spent two hours practicing the piano and an hour at the gym. As soon as the arm could tolerate movement, he began jogging along the roads of Stokehill.

It was already February when Beth returned from the Canary Islands. She felt refreshed, filled with sunlight, keen to resume her life. More than that, she was resolved to make proper plans for her wedding because she had accepted Phil Granby's proposal of marriage. After settling into her flat she went to the bath. It was early evening and the small pool was packed. Nigel was on duty.

"Hugo's day shift now," he said.

She shrugged her shoulders and told him it was of no bother. For the next hour she wandered around telling the ladies of the bath about her trip and showing them the engagement ring she wore. For the next week she resumed her instruction and not once went into the small bath or near the cafeteria. One Friday she sat on the bench with her stopwatch. Gordon Moffat saw her and struggled up the stairs. He had just returned from a holiday in Newcastle.

"Our Beth. Welcome home."

"Welcome home, yourself."

For fifteen minutes she recited a postcard description of the Canary Islands and finished with her personal news. He looked at the ring.

"A beauty, luv. A real sparkler. You and Phil finally going to settle. It's all over the bath. A spring wedding?"

"Haven't really set a date. Probably in the spring. It's so busy now. And the summer? You know how hectic that is."

They sat for five minutes watching the swimmers. Then he leaned over and winked at her. "I was wondering, dear, the back is playing the devil with me from the train ride, and riding the bike in this rain doesn't help. So could you..."

Beth smiled at him and asked, "Gordon, can I offer you a ride home?"

She drove him to the Guildhouse, let him out at the south entrance but didn't drive away. As the windshield wipers swept back and forth, she stared towards the light in Hugo's window. She should call Phil to explain her absence, but was afraid to go in. If Hugo happened to be there when she phoned, she would ask politely about his arm. After using the coin box, she wandered towards the front door, then hurried back to the phone. There was no blood on the handset. She ran to his room. When she knocked, no answer came. She told herself that he was not in, not bleeding to death. She opened the door. The spiral notebook was on the bleak and scrubbed desk. The cleaning lady in the hall said, "If you're looking for Hugo, luv, each evenin' the past fortnight, he's been away doing something or other."

As she passed the dining hall, she glanced through the window. Working men drank tea and ate buns. Hugo was not amongst them or the few men loitering in the common area. She could hear music from a piano. The same chords repeated like a record skipping, but it had a random order, as if someone were practicing. What do you play? she had asked him, and he answered, a little of this, some of that—remarks that were irrelevant to her. She passed the music room, stopped, pushed open the door a few inches, thinking all the while about the nature of her sanity, wondering why it was that she would forever be opening doors to see if he was alive.

A gooseneck lamp shone on the piano keys. The profile of Hugo's face caught a portion of the glow from the white keys. His head was upright, his eyes turned down. He was playing chords, with his fingers moving along the keyboard as if playing the piano was a thing he had done since childhood. He stopped and massaged his left arm in a tired and perplexed manner. As she went to take a step into the room, he began playing the lullaby of his mother. Beth stood rigidly. With the soothing warmth of sun ebbing away she leaned against the wall. On her closed eyes flashed a view of Tenerife from the balcony of the hotel, with clouds floating across the intervening sea. She could picture an immensity of desert. As the moon sailed above it, vibrations of the night world rose in her throat like music pushed through dry and perfect air. Dry and perfect like her own skin and the scrolled ring offset by the tanned fingers of her hand, not white and scarred like Hugo's. When he had finished playing she walked closer to the piano.

"You should go down to Leek Wootten and play for Owen," she said.

Startled, he straightened with a jerk.

"Personally, I like the Beatles and the Stones, but Owen likes this music. He has the piece you just played on a record, done by a professional."

Hugo turned and smiled at her. "Welcome back."

"I won't say it's good to be back."

"Probably not."

"I'm getting married."

"I heard. Congratulations."

"Thank you. Phil proposed in Tenerife. It took him a long time to make me happy."

Hugo looked back at the sheet music. "And you will be happy, Beth," he said. "Phil is a good man. And I hear marriage can be rewarding for some people."

"Am I 'some people, Hugo?'" Without waiting for an answer, she walked over to the piano and put her finger on one key. She stroked it firmly and then listened to the note fade. "Actually, I'm glad I came here. You know, the one thing I really missed in Tenerife was hearing your opinions about the world, especially about my happiness. But it doesn't matter now because I won't be seeing you much anymore. In a way, you've been a distraction to me. And soon the distraction will be leaving."

She stroked the key again, then let the vibrations collapse into the air. Hugo smiled and said, "My friend, the former moron, did that—pressed the same key.... while he was still crazy. Afterwards, he played that note every chance he got. I concluded that he was absorbing the energy and one day he'd use it against his illness...like the high note a soprano would use to break a wineglass."

"Are you suggesting that I played that note because I'm crazy. Tell me, Hugo, is the wish to marry and be happy a mental illness?"

"No, Beth. You're infinitely more sane than me—and happy. I'm the one who suffers from uncertainty, and a longing for things just out of my view."

She shook her head and answered, "It's funny how you learn new things when you travel, about exotic places and yourself, about things just out of view. When you come home you see things in other people you didn't know were there. You do play the piano. I admit I was wrong. You played better just now than the music on Owen's recordings. You appear to have such a wealth of knowledge, so many talents, but they all seem to be spoiled because you resent the fact that so much of the world is outside your view. Well let me tell you, Hugo, that most of the world is outside everybody's view."

Beth turned to leave. When she reached the door, Gordon Moffat was standing in her way. "He plays beautiful music, eh luv? We're all grateful for that. It takes away the grime of this place. Did you hear about Beth and Phil, Hugo? Such good news. Take a look at the ring. She won't want for a thing with Phil. Not like going with a couple of doss-house blokes like us."

Gordon shuffled over to Hugo, who had come to the doorway. "Arm okay, then?" he asked.

"Right as rain," answered Hugo, and with that the old man shuffled off for his evening tea.

Hugo reached for Beth's hand.

"You don't have to be polite."

"I want to look."

He lifted her hand and examined the ring. "This is a very nice ring," he said. "I mean that sincerely. The design is unusual, original."

"What would you know?"

"I have prejudices, but I appreciate nice things."

He put his hand gently behind her back and moved her towards the piano, saying, "Could I have a closer look?"

"Be my guest."

He spent a moment with her hand in his, looking at her ring under the light of the gooseneck. He half smiled and said that if he had a jeweler's glass he could tell her all about the ring, its strength of design or flaws in the jewels if any—because he once had a jeweler friend who taught him many things and once made him a ring as a gift.

"The one I saw when you first came in?" she asked. "Why don't you wear it now?"

"It's in my satchel. I've lost weight and it falls off."

"May I take a look?"

"We were discussing your ring, not mine."

"Give it to me."

Hugo reached into his satchel. Beth put the ring under the light. "It's very beautiful. I can see lettering on the inside." Her eyes moved downwards; and when she had given the ring back to Hugo, she fingered her own. "I should go now. I never intended to come in."

She went to the door and turned. He took a step towards her, then went as close as he dared to see the reaction in her eyes when he said, "Given the thought that went into your ring, the person who gave it to you must care very much."

Beth went to turn away, but stopped and held his gaze. Her eyes filled with tears. "Thank you," she said with a hint of regret in her voice. "Phil does care. He complained only once about the price."

Chapter XIV

Beatles and the Stones

Lufungula, February 4, 1966.

"No harm," Hugo answered Mintou after listening to the soldier's excuses. "You'll get medicines for me regardless of who stocks them. It's part of our deal, Sergeant."

"It wasn't. I look after nobody but you."

"You look after me, you look after them. I've concluded that there's a world of good ju-ju to be had from saving a few old niggers, whether it's you or me who saves them."

Mintou looked away before getting to his feet. "They're going to die anyway. You prolong their agony."

He went to open the door and Hugo said to his receding back, "You know, Sergeant, we are alike you and I, both vicious and dishonest when it suits our purpose. That's why we get on. It's been a lifelong habit for me to make a deal and then renege on it. I see the same practical streak in you."

The soldier went back to squat in the corner and lit a cigarette. "You made deals with the ju-ju man to save yourself," he said. "How soon did he have to wait for disappointment?"

"Albert knew me from a child, Mintou. I imagine his expectations were low. Yet all along the trails of past and present time he's kept up the pressure. Each time we met was an opportunity for him to preach, as I said before, like the man who once upon at time came up the hallway of a place that was nearly as bleak as this. Surprised, I was obliged to say, 'Going for some tea, Albert?'

The ju-ju man answered, 'You've played your music tonight, Hugo. I appreciate that, but when are you to attend to my request?'

I stepped aside to let him pass. 'Soon,' I replied and apologized for the delay, telling him that I needed two good arms for the effort.

'Excuses,' he said then walked off leaving me to go through the Guildhouse dispensing what advice I could to gaunt, hopeless men who smoked corrosive cigarettes. Later, we all drank tea from large mugs and I considered giving the men an uplifting sermon as Albert might have done, which would address memories of the war and the dear faces of women and dead soldiers seen on dressers, because you should know, Mintou, that the men of Stokehill had been torn apart by war. When the cooks closed down the tea urn, I went back to my own room to put away my utensils before sleeping. I woke in the middle of the night and remained awake. The heat pipe groaned every few minutes. Down the hall, Albert's door was open.

'I was waiting,' he said.

'In Freiberg, when you were a young boy, you lay in your own sickbed until boredom and stiff limbs forced you into the air,' I said. 'Was there a gas lamp outside your window, under which you would see your friends playing?'

'Darkness.'

'Perhaps you developed the habit of smoking cigarettes like the rest of us and the dawn came quicker.'

'The dawn came early for me and stayed all my life.'

'*Let your light so shine before men.* Muir read me that famous verse from the Gospel of Matthew. But I see you not so much as a shining light but a mirror reflecting God. You are a second sun, Albert, illuminating a land already beset with too much heat but no warmth.'

'Aren't you poetic—and such a waste. Because the only thing I require from you is muscle, labor, the power in your arms and legs, all things you're not squeamish about. We wait patiently for you, Hugo.'

'With a promise from you of no tedious medical work. That was the deal.'

'Bring only your brutish back. I will supply the pick and shovel. You know my address. Don't let the heroes of the regiment mislead you.'

I rolled on the cot and pulled the gray blanket over me. Long before dawn I went to the dining hall and had tea with the shift women who began cooking at 4 am."

Sergeant Mintou smoked. The glowing end of the cigarette reflected into the cell from the dark of his eyes. "Why did you say, 'no tedious medical work', monsieur?"

"Because I was going to Albert's hospital and didn't want him to be mislead about my abilities."

"What would he be expecting from you other than the labor of an animal, as he said?"

"An inherited immunity from pain, Mintou, and a way of deceiving myself into accomplishing practical things. In the right circumstances, these characteristics can be useful. As a soldier, you know what I mean. You're accustomed to using cruelty, even against yourself."

Foleshill, Coventry, February 19, 1965.

While Beth was at the nurse's station, the receptionist delivered an envelope to her. In it were two sheets. One was a note that read, *I came to Coventry to see Owen Dring. Could you please give him the attached note? Thank you. Hugo.*

She shuffled the bottom sheet to the top. In uppercase letters was written, *Albert Schweitzer.* Below this was a series of names. At the bottom was the phrase, *SS Kyle Mission, now on the banks of the James River, Virginia.* That night she delivered the sheet to Leek Wootten. The next day Hugo was circling the bath at a quick march when Miss Sutton waddled out in her pleated tartan and handed him an envelope. The return address had the name, "O. G. Dring MD FRCS" attached. The note inside requested that he come to dinner on Saturday evening, a fortnight hence.

Afternoon. With one eye on the pool and the other on the page, Hugo wrote a passage in his spiral scribbler:

> Truth hangs in museums and warrants ten million at an auction. Art is a priceless arrow pointing towards the frontier of reality. But not every detail is worth the money. Some passages of Beethoven's Ninth are mediocre. But who decides the best of art: God—or us? Because good taste is fluid: art one minute and not the next.
> This explains why a gallery has high ceilings…thought and feeling must be able to expand in the silence. No words. Nothing spoken. No demands of the flesh or the mind, then on to our luncheon, to whirlygigs and entertainments. We appreciate a ten-dollar night at the play with the world as our companion—four billion patrons, and God showing up for the intermission. To say God intervenes, is to say He maintains the world as it is.

From the faint smell of perfume, Hugo became aware that someone had been standing behind him. He turned his head and saw Beth. She continued to read what he had been writing.

"Haven't seen you in a while," he said.

"Isn't it wonderful," she replied. "No dirty remarks, no digs in the soft parts. How is your arm?"

"Better. Some movements are difficult."

"It will improve."

He smiled at her. "Thanks for asking."

"I'm going for a quick tea. Want one?"

Jane Sutton agreed to take Hugo's place. They went into the cafeteria and Beth brought two cups to a table that overlooked the street and the small fish and chip shop across Foleshill Road.

"Still writing?" Beth asked. "No, don't answer. Sometimes your arresting observations are incomprehensible and I wouldn't want to contradict you with my comments."

"You were reading…"

"Just to see if there was anything insulting about me." Beth played with her ring. She took sips of her tea at regular intervals and they talked little. After a brief bout of awkward staring, she said, "I was reading. And as usual I'm disturbed by your thoughts. Now, I'm going to look for Toby. I might see you again before you leave Coventry but probably not." She started away but turned round and came close to his knee.

"You should be I wearing your ring, Hugo. Rings are a visible reminder of our direction in life."

Hugo watched the door close behind her. He considered the phrase, "might see you again," suggesting a small chance, like finding him sleeping in his room before the last of his blood leaked out—good luck but not a miracle. He sipped the last of his tea before replacing the supervisor at the side of the pool.

It was Saturday afternoon and every patch of water squirmed with children making noise and splashing in the shallows, dripping shapes above and distorted wriggling shadows below. It was Hugo's habit after a break to take note of the shapes below. His eye caught a blur in one corner of the pool. He counted ten seconds. The shape didn't move. He looked to see if any one else were watching, then looked back. No movement. He hesitated with a bitter memory of lost children; but Tolly was paying him to save lives and it demanded only the inconvenience of having the plaster on his arm dissolve to mush. He pushed through the door, jumped in, and pulled out the body of a small boy. When he had him to the surface he could see that the color around his lips was tinged with blue. He recognized the boy's puffy cheeks. A girl screamed. Parents gathered. After Hugo had the boy resting on the pool deck he gestured to Jane through the glass. She ran off to the phone.

Thick foam oozed from the child's mouth. Inside was a brown pulp that he dug out with his fingers. Then he flipped the boy over and pressed the small amount of water from his lungs. Jane ran over. Her shaking hands had difficulty opening the case containing the resuscitator. Hugo pulled it out, clamped the mask over the boy's face, and helped the supervisor turn the knobs on the airpark. A sobbing woman knelt at the head of the child and called his name, "Kelly, Kelly! Oh my Kelly."

Hugo adjusted the flow and placed his ear on the chest. The boy coughed and spluttered. A sigh of relief went from the mother and was repeated through the crowd.

"Good work," said the supervisor and got off her knees trying to look triumphant and official at the same time. Yet Hugo was not satisfied. Something about the episode was incomplete. He heard another phrase in his memory, about Kelly and graham crackers. "C'mon Kelly, Willy, eat your crackers. The bath closes soon. You won't get a chance for a second dip," and saw in his mind's eye the twins stuffing mealy wafers into their mouths.

He stood up and looked for Willy in the crowd, then shoved his way down the pool deck. In the far corner he saw the same inert blur. The crowd blocked his way, so he dove in and pulled himself along the bottom. With a sweep of his right arm he lifted the boy out, laid him on the deck, and tried to dig the mush from his mouth. A whispering panic spread though the crowd, but no sound came from the boy. His body was already cold and turning blue. A push on the chest brought only a regurgitation of water and more meal that further clogged his throat. The crowd had moved around them and the supervisor puffed along.

"Make way," she shouted and the crowd fell back. The same keening mother knelt at the boy's side stroking his leg.

"The emergency is on its way," someone said.

Hugo took the resuscitator from Jane, opened the large medical kit, and took out an instrument for clearing the boy's airway. Each scoop was replaced with more coming from inside. The mother was at the point of hysteria.

"Please, luv, we're doing our best," Jane sobbed, her hands shaking and with it the boy's head. She looked despairingly at Hugo and said, "We're losing him."

The mother moaned. Her thin scream of despair went to the core and froze him. He couldn't form a thought and was aware of nothing besides the mealy vomit lying by the boy's head, stinking like fermented ale. The closeness of the crowd and the heaviness of the chlorine intensified his dizzy confusion. A paralyzing fear cut off his breath. His left arm ached and his good right arm went down to support himself on the tiles. He had the urge to seek the farthest point on earth. He forced himself to put his right hand on the chest of the dying child and look at the haggard, grieving face of the mother, her eyes streaming with tears. A voice rang in his head, a matter-of-fact voice saying—I have a job for you, Hugo, with prestige attached, and the reply that said—no jobs, no more work. Then he straightened up and whispered to himself words that made the most sense: No more death.

The noise and smell of the crowd receded. Fresh air replaced the cloying stench of chlorine and vomit. In the kit was a scalpel still in its sheath, some soft tubing, a bottle of alcohol and some cotton swabs.

"What are you doing?" Jane cried.

"Opening an airway," said Hugo.

"No, no! You're not trained to do that."

Hugo didn't answer or pay any attention to the fact that she was going to pieces, with her hands shaking and her face white with fear. He looked at the boy's blue lips, the solid mass of hardening sludge around his teeth. With a swab of cotton batten soaked in alcohol he wiped the boy's throat just below the larynx. There was an abrupt wailing from the crowd. Someone cried, "Where in the name of God is the ambulance? Someone find a doctor."

Hugo looked at the supervisor's flushed, vibrating mouth. "You'll be all right, Jane. Tilt his head back, between your hands, absolutely still."

"Oh, Christ, I can't do this. You're going to kill him."

Hugo waited for the boy's head to stop shaking with the same erratic movements of Jane's hands.

"Perhaps someone else," she said, her voice trembling with fear.

Hugo set the scalpel next to the boy's pasty white throat. To the side of his field of view he saw a movement in the crowd. The hands on the boy's head slipped away. Another set took hold, with the left hand shining with the brilliance of a diamond ring. He looked into the eyes of Beth Marshall, who said in a calm voice, "Let me help you." Then holding her hands firmly, precisely on the boy's temples, said, "I'm ready."

Hugo cut. When he was finished, before blood from the wound could seep out, Beth had cotton around the opening, and with her deft fingers opened the incision and nodded at Hugo. He gently pressed the boys chest and with the crowd gasping, a flood of pool water and liquid sludge poured out. Then Hugo kept one hand on the chest, not allowing it to expand and pushed a tube through the opening. Once it was in, Beth held the end while Hugo maintained pressure on the rib cage. With four inches in the boy's airway, she stopped, cut the tube, leaving a long section outside. Hugo had the adhesive ready in small segments so the nurse could seal off around the tube and secure it. She then listened to the boy's chest and said, 'I'll provide the air.'

The nurse blew gently, regularly into the tube. With a constant rhythm, Hugo gently pressed on the boy's chest. The crowd stood silently, with only the occasional sniffling. Gradually, over the course of five minutes, color returned to the boy's face. Hugo stopped and put his ear to the chest. He nodded at Beth. A slight smile came to her lips. She continued to blow into the tube until the boy began to breath on his own; then she looked at Hugo and placed her hand on his injured left arm, which rested on the boy's chest. The medics arrived and prepared both boys for transport to the hospital. The crowd milled around, tensions eased. Children leaped back into the pool. Jane strode down the pool deck making incoherent announcements. Hugo looked for Beth in the milling crowd. He could see her nowhere, so he slipped into the courtyard, lit a cigarette and aimed himself towards the ring road on a clear afternoon. In an hour he was drinking a third glass of scotch at the Craven Arms Hotel.

*   *   *   *

The day had a look of spring but the air was not warm. Kings Cross Station was damp but the sunlight coursing through it gave the platform the feel of summer. Hugo took the Piccadilly line to Russell Square and found a room at the Marchmont Hotel. After lunch he walked past the British Museum and down New Oxford Street to find Suman Brothers Maps. At a tourist shop close by he obtained French and Spanish railway schedules. He took these to the British Museum reading room and spread them over a table.

By noon, the furniture, people, and art on the wall became distinctly bright. By three, the colors had washed out. Perimeters merged. Noses, hands, and moving lips hovered indistinctly around the rows of tables. The earth and the day slid by under the fluorescence of the sun and left no trace or arc on the carpet. At five Hugo folded up the maps, put the books back on the shelves and the schedules into his satchel. He looked many times for Albert. Before dinner he went to the Russell Square Hotel and left a note at the counter. At seven came a knock at the door and when he opened it, Eileen stood there.

"What's up with the arm?" she asked.

"A little scrap that's all."

"Brilliant. Not a good fighter, then."

"Not good at all. I'll have to be more polite in the future."

They went to the Apple Orchard, ate, and drank pints of bitter. They talked of the last few months: of Hugo's work as a bath attendant and of Eileen's drab life and her dreams of getting home to Ireland, which would mean more dreams of leaving for a better life and so round and round it went. From the foot of the fire escape Hugo watched her walk up the flights of metal stairs with the same feeling he had before, of his wish to see her free. She had wanted to go to his room and stay the night. But Hugo made excuses for his arm and kissed her cheek to say good-bye. Later, as he walked the blocks through traffic and over squares of brick, he had a sense of bodies dragging behind him, breasts and crotches and thighs—a moral drag of women's bodies stretching down the block, with never a thought for the June day when marriage strips away conscience as would happen to Beth and Phil. He lay on his sagging bed staring at the grimy window that fronted the empty, brick-strewn lot and thanked God that he would not be near the British Isles when that cataclysm occurred—that he would have the buffer of an entire continent between him and the anticipation of her ecstatic blue eyes.

Following a Sunday afternoon at Hyde Park Gate, he took the train back to Rugby. On the way, he considered the arguments of a speaker who attempted to give the crowd a lesson on West African history, on the slave trade, and the modern trade of making slaves of everyone. When he arrived back in Coventry and stepped onto the station platform, he had a surge of mistaken joy that Beth was waiting for him, with her hand outstretched, together with her anxious face and troubled, yearning eyes—unlike the dozens of women he had seen lounging in bed, unconcerned that he struggled to understand the value of pleasure as opposed to pain.

But the station was empty. The few passengers alighted and walked from his sight. He was left listening to the rainwater tinkle in the downspouts and wondering why his arm suddenly took to aching and remembering some unknown person asking if more than his arm ever ached. When he arrived at the Guildhouse, without changing his dripping clothes, he went into the piano room and played the sonata of his childhood lullabies. As he heard the last chord resonate to silence, he knew he had never played it so well.

Miranda Dring drove from Coventry with the air of a person moving from a hovel into the light of Hampton Court.

"I don't know what to make of some things today, Hugo. I suppose that's just a matter of my age and not the age we live in. Do you think there's a profound change taking place, this preoccupation with style of life? The Beatles and the Stones. Not long ago, people were more concerned with the style of their after-lives. The Church of England is fading."

The man in the back said, "Religion is blackmail, Miranda...that's a superficial view, of course."

"Would you like a mint, Reggie?"

"Most kind. Now as I was saying, that the style of one's after-life should be determined by threats or promises doesn't seem right to me. You know what I mean, the punishment we receive, or the reward, for believing or not. And who is to say if you believe or not. One can imagine a fearsome hell and no way to avoid it. Men have no choice but to ease themselves from beneath the weight of their sins by crying 'uncle' to God. At least the Catholic Church organizes this mass groveling in a humane way."

Hugo slouched into his seat watching the rural Midlands flash by, old stone buildings and men like Wing Commander Reggie Everton emerging from the public houses at half-day closure with pallid jowls. He imagined what it must have been like to be Adam or Christ or both, being forced to hear men give their opinions.

"Come to, chappie, it's time," said the Wing Commander. Hugo opened his eyes in time to see him whistling his way up the driveway of Owen and Miranda Dring's home. Carlyle, the Weinereimer, pulled Hugo up the pavement by his pant leg while Miranda Dring walked ahead.

"I see Owen isn't home yet. I hope he isn't held up with some unexpected surgery."

Hugo replied, "A small question: Is your daughter's hair the same color as yours?"

Miranda turned around and looked at him with surprise. "That might have been a difficult question to answer with any degree of honesty," she said, touching her hair. "This could very well not be my own color, you see. I could have had it dyed like my daughter's, and then I might have been inclined to tell you a lie. But this is entirely as is, both the color and the curl. So the simple answer is yes."

Before going in the door she consulted the dog by pressing her nose against his. "Carlyle likes my hair the way it is and wishes that Beth liked hers that way, too. Please come into our house."

In the drawing room Hugo found a leather chair to sit in. His glass was full of scotch.

"Yes, yes," said the Wing Commander, blowing deep blasts of smoke through the hairs in his nose. "No, no I wouldn't wish to be traveling in Africa at the present. I've read the papers. There's turmoil in a dozen spots, civil war in the Sudan and the worst of it in the Congo. Abysmal carnage. I know a man at the club who was at school with Mike Hoare." He slumped forward in his chair until his tightening collar turned his face scarlet. He tapped the Times on the armrest. "I'm acquainted with trouble, Hugo, but joking aside, the savagery is outrageous on both sides. But there's an element of imagination here. Africa itself adds a primitive power to it with elements of the jungle, ju-ju magic, terror."

Hugo sat facing the leaded bay windows and watched the precise nuances of his companion's expression. At fifty-two, Wing Commander Everton's face was only moderately deformed by the boardroom gin he consumed. In his right hand he carried a cigar and a glass. He drank after every fourth sentence. As time passed, he faded with the light until he became as indistinct as the drawings on the wall. After he had eaten some cheese to go with the port, he left. Hugo saw him off. When he could no longer hear him humming his way down Hill Wootten Road, he went back to his leather chair and looked around. A portrait of a stout man hung prominently on the wall. Next to the blotter on Dring's desk was a glass case shrouding a service revolver, much the same as Hugo had seen on Blenkinthorpe's end table. Beside the glass case was a framed picture of a soldier with the date 1946 scratched in the bottom corner.

Major Dring returned and Miranda sat them at the dinner table. They ate quietly and concerned themselves with local issues, of Hugo's arm and the episode of the twins at the Foleshill Bath. After the meal, Miranda poured the sherry from a decanter on the sideboard. Hugo had one drink and excused himself. He returned with his satchel, removed from it the photo of the *Kyle Mission* and the cluster of posed soldiers, then pushed them over the table in front of Dring.

The surgeon leaned back in his chair to smoke his pipe. He glanced at the print then pulled himself upright. "This gets a few questions revolving in my head, Hugo. But perhaps we should start with you."

Carlyle rose with a loud baying and ran down the hallway.

"That would be Beth and Phil," Miranda said. A moment later Beth appeared.

"Phil has to visit his mother," she said and looked at Hugo with surprise.

"You didn't tell me you were having company."

"Do we need your approval, dear? Of course you know…"

"Yes I know…" She turned and disappeared into another part of the house.

"My apologies, Hugo. Something's put her into her usual state of alarm."

Hugo took a sip of sherry, then told the story of his tenuous connection to Korrolus, his visit to the embalmed ship, the meeting with Blenkinthorpe and the voyage on the *Yildun*. In all cases he abbreviated his descriptions and the stories told to him. He ended with an account of Billy's retreat to the Channel Islands. When he finished, he stretched his aching arm to one side and saw Beth with a half empty glass in her hand. Without taking her eyes off him, she came to the table and lifted the photos from her stepfather.

Dring sipped his sherry in silence. He took the photos back from his stepdaughter. Finally he asked, "Why are you pursuing this?"

Hugo looked at the polished woodwork, the furniture constructed with craftsmanship from oak and rosewood. He rubbed his arm. Beth watched him closely while he spoke. "As a form of instruction. In some capacity my father participated in the war. He knew Allan Korrolus and had some other connection to the story of the *Kyle Mission*. I'm at loose ends myself and seek some distraction, perhaps a broadening of my horizons. I heard of the war only through stories and photographs. But when it came to the story of my father and his friends I was forced to consider the fundamental paradoxes of war and peace, of soldiers killing one minute and showing mercy the next. If you don't mind, I'll start to answer your question by expanding on that..."

"By all means," Dring said.

Hugo took a drink then hung his head forward. He paused to breathe before beginning. "One night, as I lay on my bunk in Von Raynor's ship, I put a simple framework around it. If you have an insane hatred raging inside you for an enemy, you desire to see his face as you kill him—for the compensating pleasure of watching him suffer and die. But with his death you risk losing, at least temporarily, the animosity that overrides your conscience. An excess of conscience is not a good thing for a solider to have. Therefore, it's best to shoot from a distance when the enemy has no face to either inflame or quell your hostility. Better still, bomb him from ten thousand feet. Up there, hate is not required as a motivating force and you see no evidence of the humanity burnt and shredded by your bombs, only a statistical outcome free from direct morality or guilt.

"Compare that to its opposite. From a mile up you drop food that will keep people from starvation. Your reward wouldn't be altogether different from the experience of the airmen who just let go with a load of bombs—that is, no direct consequence either way, except what you allow your imagination to tell you. But if you bring a man back from death with your own hands, and see the look of gratitude on his face as he is being helped out of the grave and not being put in, you can understand why the direct application of goodness is a desired experience. A maniac like Hitler may delude himself that he is God. But the surgeon in the field, like you were, actually is."

Dring nodded his head, was silent for a time, then answered, "Very good, but does this answer my question?"

"As a preamble only. At first I had no motivation to pursue anything. Korrolus was an accident, Blenkinthorpe a curiosity. Von Raynor was like a paid vacation at sea. And you, Major Dring, well, I guess you're like a chase down the rabbit hole—if I can be so crass. In all instances my purpose was to confront and eliminate the contradictions."

The surgeon lit his pipe. "Of course for me North Africa was no fairy tale and Rommel not the Mad Hatter. About the contradictions you mention, I can't really comment. You see, I don't talk or think much about the war, Hugo. It was an experience beyond comprehension, unless your were there."

"George Blenkinthorpe said as much. I sensed that his tale of Algiers was misleading, perhaps dishonest, and not just to spare my squeamishness. I asked him once to reveal his moral choices as they related to certain episodes. He never answered directly, but over time I sensed that he came to appreciate the dilemma."

"There's much George would like to forget and would lie about," Dring replied. "Personally, I talk only a little of it because as a surgeon stuck in a tent, I was never sure of the facts. Anyway, the violence of it puts Miranda off."

"As well it should, Owen. It should put you off too—like keeping that gun in plain view."

Dring smiled and continued without looking at his wife. "I'm not so put off as to forget those people you mention. They were all characters. I remember Birks the most. He was a tough career soldier, abrasive and proud. Strangely he had an interest in music. In North Africa, circumstances placed him in a position to befriend a man who taught piano. It was a man I also knew quite well because for two years he had been our concertmaster at the old Coventry Cathedral. His name was Conrad Muir, who you just mentioned was Von Raynor's brother. Muir had been a pupil of Albert Schweitzer, before Schweitzer went permanently to Lambaréné. The choir loved him. I aspired to be a singer and learned much from him. There are times, however, when I think my real interest in the choir was the presence in it of woman who sang lead soprano. Corrine was her name. For a time I was mad about her, but didn't stand a chance. She had eyes for Conrad, who was a dashing, energetic figure, with jet black hair, then only in his middle forties."

Dring stopped for a moment, stared at Hugo then resumed his story. "Anyway, Conrad and Corrine courted. They were the perfect couple. I always thought they'd marry. But something happened long before the outbreak of war. In 1935, for no apparent reason, Corrine went to Manchester and then disappeared completely. I was never sure of the circumstances. Birks and I were in the same regiment and went off to fight with the BEF. Fortunately we both came away from Dunkirk without a scratch." He reached behind him and took a framed picture from the sideboard. "Miranda will forgive me for saying this because it happened long before we met and I was still an impressionable young man. But at the time, it was a huge disappointment for me not to win Corrine. She was a striking woman, quite tall with an elegant, operatic voice."

He passed the picture to Beth and then it went around to Hugo. He looked at it for a long time. When he raised his eyes up, Beth was staring at him.

"Anyway, in nineteen-forty the Luftwaffe reduced the Cathedral to dust. This must have broken Conrad's heart. I knew, of course, that during the war, long before the bombs fell, he had gone to North Africa and eventually suffered serious injuries. It was one of those inexplicable coincidences of war that they brought him to me to patch up. That he survived was always a curiosity. I don't know what became of him. I brought this photo along from the organist's stall at the Cathedral where it hung along with many others since the new church was completed. Quite a resemblance, don't you think?"

"Resemblance to whom?" asked his wife.

Dring didn't smile. He put down his glass and leaned closer to Hugo. "On the surface of it, you came to Coventry to find me; quite a trivial reason to travel here. There was another reason wasn't there?"

Beth fidgeted in her chair and looked again at Hugo.

"What do you mean, Owen?" asked Miranda. "He's clearly stated his reason for coming. You're being rather presumptuous, aren't you? Please excuse my rude husband, Hugo."

Dring let his head fall for a moment. "Not presumptuous at all, Miranda. I'm just stating the obvious. And if I'm not, what is it that makes me want to leap to conclusions?"

"Explain yourself, Owen," said his wife with a frown.

"Well, there's the name."

"What name, dear?"

"I beg you for your patience, Miranda. All will be clear in a moment. It was an interesting story you just told us, Hugo. But it would not have materialized as such without a compelling reason to take an interest in puzzling bit of history that doesn't add up to a good yarn. Now, what else do I know? I know that you frequent the Cathedral—and not for religious observances. You come during the week to listen to the organ. You approached Henry Smith, the organist, and actually played yourself, quite well, he said, and took an interest in the history of the building, the choir, the photos on the walls, one of which you are looking at right now. Your interest in the organ is not surprising since you play the piano with virtuosity, Beth tells me—and by your own admission you were taught by your mother. One piece of music surfaced several times in your narrative, Beethoven's *Moonlight Sonata*, played by Allan Korrolus and featured prominently in Von Raynor's experience at the Mission to Seaman in Algiers, as played by Martin Birks, who taught it to Korrolus and, I suspect, was music that you heard as a child. Now, doesn't that go round in circles?

"You're quite right, Owen," blurted Miranda.

"But let me emphasize that it's not the circle of music and names that leads us along," Dring went on. "It's just one name—as it is one song." Owen Dring turned to Hugo and said, "Could it be that the woman in the photo, Corrine Haultain, is your mother?"

Miranda straightened in her chair. Beth remained still.

"She was," Hugo answered.

"She's gone?"

"Seventeen years ago. She was only thirty-four when she died; I was twelve."

"I'm sorry to hear that. Had she married?"

"Not to my knowledge."

"If you don't mind my asking, if you were only twelve when she went, what became of you?"

"Owen, these are questions of a highly personal nature."

Hugo smiled at her and said, "It's all right, Miranda. These things are no longer personal."

"My wife has a point," said Dring.

Hugo sipped his drink and looked at Beth, who continued to stare at him. Then with a quiet voice he began. "For as long as I can remember, my mother was assisted in her duties by my tutor, who had a suite in the house and made his living as a teacher. From the time of her death until I left home, he carried on with difficult chore of raising a sickly, invalid boy. His name is Conrad Muir. As you mentioned, he is Juri Von Raynor's brother—and also my father."

Dring raised his eyebrows slightly and sat stiffly back in his seat. He drank from his glass and took another puff at his pipe. When Hugo looked at Beth, she had leaned forward and was fingering a spoon. Twice she tapped it gently on his new cast. Her eyes never moved from his. Hugo shrugged his shoulders as if he could say nothing else. There was silence until Miranda said, "Hugo, can I get you some tea or coffee, perhaps?"

"Coffee, thanks."

As she left the room, Owen leaned forward again and said, "This is more than I expected, Hugo. I never for a moment considered that Conrad was still alive. Can I ask where he is now?"

"I don't know. Last fall he left, saying he was going home. I never knew what he meant by that." Hugo paused and looked again at the picture of his mother, who was young, just a teenager. "Conrad was always generous with me. He leaned towards constraint and discipline but underneath he was a kind man.

Later on it became my habit to refer to him in a derogatory manner because I resented my illness. It must have been a hellish life for Corrine. But I see now that she never would have coped without Muir."

"I don't know what else to ask, Hugo."

"You've pried enough," said Beth.

Miranda came into the room with a carafe. Beth set out the cups. Owen Dring finished his pipe and stirred his coffee. "To the other side of the equation, Hugo. I don't know why you are traveling along in wonderland or what conclusion you hope to bring about in your life. Your father's affairs in North Africa, insofar as the others figure in them, are not for bragging about. I know where Crasson and Wallace Fraser are. But Crasson is a greedy, ruthless man who gets his way. Wallace Fraser, who resides in Lagos I believe, still entertains the crowd with tall tales."

"And Martin Birks?"

Dring straightened himself in his chair. "Let me tell you something about Martin Birks: You'd never know it to look at him, but he was a genius, a fine soldier, a combination of art and muscle, opposites only as there are two sides to a coin. In some respects he was fearless—and that's not always an asset. He described himself once as being ebullient. Ebullient! Now that's an uncommon way for a man to describe himself. So in answer to your question, the last I heard he had visited Lambaréné and then got into trading. I hope he is still in one piece and not marred, like most men, by the disfigurements of the tropics."

Hugo looked into the placid surface of the liquid in his cup, saying, "The answer to your question, Mister Dring. I have no intention of going further than I'm pushed."

"Pushed by whom?"

"By the voice of my conscience—as we all are."

Dring nodded and replaced the photos in the envelope. Then he got to his feet and walked to the end of the table next to his wife. "Crasson had more to do with Conrad Muir in this affair than anyone else. I'm going to keep these photos for a little while. But you'll get them back before you leave."

When Hugo rose from the table, Beth was still watching him. Her face was milky and innocent in the scant light of the dining room, giving him the urge to get away, take the morning train to London, and set out for France with no more wasted time.

On the drive back to Stokehill, the countryside was covered in a thin mist that hovered around the great oaks mustered in fields and stone breaks. Hugo watched them speed past and imagined the history they had seen, so much more and varied than the few years he had witnessed of fading generations whose images he could barely hold in his mind's eye. He saw himself and Beth walking over the green to the east of Kenilworth Castle and reckoned he was seeing the remnant of a forgotten dream.

Owen Dring soared along the narrow lanes humming a tune. He passed through Stoneleigh with the music still vibrating in his throat. Otherwise, he remained silent until they were on the ring road and ahead the Guildhouse protruding from the mist like a barrow. The inhabitants drifted mutely on their way in and out of the building. Hugo thanked his host, who waved and turned onto the Coventry road without a response.

Chapter XV

From Aldermans Green

"Things," Hugo thought as he took a shower. Things on his mind, that's all there were, a few insignificant items. He shivered and felt the chill of cold water stiffen his legs. Then he dressed and went out. Behind the Guildhouse was a small wooded copse where a walk had always brought him the reassurance of a relaxed swinging of arms and legs, a military march to stiffen the rest of his body. The sun had beaten the night mist to a thin vapor. Although he knew exactly where he was going, the trail always seemed to take him towards his nose, with seldom a concern that the trees hemmed him in one way and then the next. He came to a track leading towards the distant stacks of the GE works. He followed it until it came around to the Coventry road. The Guildman's Square had a two-hour opening on Sunday afternoons. He drank two pints before returning to his room. A note lay on the metal desk:

> Next weekend I'm going down to Bristol to see a classmate of mine. Last chance before (!!!). Phil hates her, well doesn't actually hate her. They just don't get on and I dislike traveling alone. Would you consider coming with me? Just for company.
> Beth

That night Hugo ate his dinner wrapped in suspicion. At the bath days later, he said to her, "Phil would be upset if I went anywhere with you."

As a matter of course Beth looked past the children playing in the pool with a look of concern, then answered, "Phil's not a jealous man. And if he was, I'd say he'd better get used to it. Anyway, I wasn't lying when I said I hate to travel alone."

"Being alone is an easy thing to like."

"Being alone is an easy way out," she replied and went through the door to her swimming instruction.

They set off late on an early March morning and drove through Warwick, stopped at Stratford for a walk along the Avon River, then continued down the valley to Bristol. Using the map Hugo had bought, they navigated the city following the vague directions Beth supplied. After an hour she said, "We seem to be lost, and I'm tired. Can we stop?"

They went into a pub close to the museum docks. Beth sat for some minutes looking at the interior of the building. She made comments about the prints on the walls, the tile floor, and talked in a casual manner—as if she was pleased at their failure. Hugo played with the coaster. "You seem to be lost in other ways," he said.

"I am." She took his left hand and stroked Solly's ring with the tips of her fingers. "This is a beautiful piece of jewelry. I love the intricate patterns and the engraving. One day I should see it under a magnifying glass."

Hugo sipped his pint, watched her take the ring off his finger, and had an inexplicable regret for putting it on for the trip.

"I think you're stalling," he said. "Shall we resume with the problem of finding your friend's place? Do you have her telephone number?"

She slipped the ring back in his finger. "We're lost, Hugo, not because I can't find her place. We're lost because there is no 'her.'"

Hugo cocked his head to one side trying to frame his comments with a logic where he knew none applied.

"If there is no 'her,' I understand now why we're lost—and why you're even more lost."

"Do you?"

Hugo moved the coaster in circles. "Let me state the obvious. I'm about to leave England and instead of being home packing my bags I'm spending a weekend with a woman who's about to marry another man. Could you please tell me why we are here alone in Bristol looking for the address of a non-person?"

"Yes."

"Yes what?"

"Yes, we are alone in these circumstances because that's what I wanted—for the moment."

"And you always get what you want."

"Not always."

"What is it that you want, for the moment?"

"A chance to spend time with you and know you, away from the influences. Everything, everybody I see moves me one way and another. Because you're the most transient thing in my life, I see you as my point of reference. Topsy-turvy? Beth in the looking glass—with her point of reference soon to disappear."

They booked into a hotel in the center of the old city and got separate rooms. That night they went to dinner at the hotel and talked for hours about history, art and the continents strung south of Britain across the Channel. Beth wore an elegant dress that flowed over her body, with diamond earrings that matched the ring on her finger. She had sympathetic questions concerning his struggle to exist and grow outside his boyhood home on the side of the mountain. In turn Beth glossed over her upbringing, except to say that Freddy Marshal, for all his surliness, was a loving father who treated her well and had paid a full sum for her years of training. As they talked, Hugo watched the light from the candle dance on her lips and in her eyes. When the flame burned below the holder, he took her hand and they went up to their respective rooms.

Feeling wide-awake, he paced for a few minutes then emptied his satchel on the writing desk. For two hours he wrote of things he had observed in himself and his companion. At a point late in the night, he felt sufficiently tired and went to bed. Following a brief dream in which he drowned, he woke and stared at the glow of the casement. From a space below floated the noise of slow traffic and the busy docks. He clenched and unclenched his fists, then threw off the covers.

From the other side of the wall a few feet away, the presence of Beth Marshall bore on him. He could walk the short space in a stride. She would hesitate only for a moment before asking him in. It was a thing he could imagine, step by step—but not quite. He could see his hand running along the cloth to loose the buttons and open her top, but he had no picture in his mind of her breasts or face, the clothes falling to the floor, of her moving to the bed and lying with her legs straight and slightly parted. He could describe it. But no images formed. His yearning included no impulse to see her naked. For the first time in his life he desired a woman to be in his bed so he could sleep close by her. He would be content to touch only where sleeping bodies might touch accidentally, waking in the night to breathing and warmth, with no thought given to other pleasures.

A knock came at the door. Hugo opened his eyes to the daylight. The clock said 7:45. He put on his robe and opened the door. Beth was fully dressed.

"I usually get up early. I've never been able to sleep in. There's always too many things on my mind."

"Please come in."

She came into the room and looked around. "I ordered room service, tea and buns for breakfast. I put your room number on it."

Hugo went to the bathroom to shower. Beth walked towards the window but stopped next to the writing desk. She glanced down at the things spread over it: four spiral scribblers, passport, a bundle of letters with a sheet on top on which was hand-written a poem by W.B. Yeats. Hugo came out to find his razor.

"Who is the stolen child?" she asked.

Hugo shrugged.

"Could be anyone."

He went back into the bathroom.

"I'm sorry to be so nosey."

Hugo didn't answer.

"Stolen from whom, by whom?"

Hugo came to the door with his face lathered. "The Irish believe children are in danger of being stolen by the fairies. It is grieving parents who say, 'We know all we can of weeping.'"

When, fifteen minutes later, Hugo came out of the bathroom buttoning his shirt, Beth silently gathered up the papers spread over the desk. As she secured them with an elastic band, the busboy brought in their breakfast tray.

After a tour of the city they drove the eighteen miles to Weston-super-Mare and walked the beach, past ships sliding along the far horizon with the wind blowing across the wet sand. At the north end blocked by a headland of rock, Beth said, "Thank you for letting me read those letters from Albert Schweitzer to your father. Tell me what they mean to you."

"They're a curiosity."

"How curious are you?"

"Not very."

"Why? They seem to an important part of your father's history. Isn't that why you're here—to find out more, as Owen suggested?"

"Not really. I have other considerations."

"What other considerations?"

"I have questions about my life."

"Exactly what is your life, Hugo? I'd like to know; because I have come to believe over the last few months that you've been telling me a colossal lie."

Hugo walked ahead on the sand then turned around and took both her hands. "You have many questions."

"I'm sorry. If you like I'll stop asking them."

"It's me who should apologize," he said. "At least you've asked questions about me—but I've shown no interest in your life."

"That's not surprising. My affairs are pretty well cut and dried. I don't have 'other considerations.'"

She walked towards the birds wading in the surf, then stopped to face him. "That's not true either. I suppose you've been my other consideration. But we know which journey we are both to take and I think yours is a ticket to a pitiful aggregate of heaven and hell, which is to say I think you're lost."

They went for some distance further along the beach. The wind increased. Spots of blue showed between the scudding clouds. Hugo stopped and looked out to sea, then placed his hand on her temple to slowly brush back her curls. "Your mother says your hair is the same color as hers."

"It is." She closed her eyes and took hold of his right hand. For a few moments, she held it tightly to the side of her head. "I think we better be getting back," she said and released his hand, after brushing it across her mouth.

It was late afternoon when they found their way out of Bristol back along the highway they had come down. Before it was fully dark they ran into the dense fog of early evening. North of Stratford they could no longer see a hundred feet. The world crept in so tight the glow from the headlamps created an aura of opaque brilliance around the car.

"I don't even know if we're on the road," she said. "I'm afraid to turn one way or the other."

Hugo got out and felt his way to the left until he stumbled on a slope of ground that appeared to vanish into a ditch. He guided Beth a few more feet off the traveled portion of the road.

"I don't know where we are. But here is here, and no further until this lifts."

"The petrol is low," she said and shut off the ignition and headlights. The darkness was complete.

"I have two blankets in the boot."

Hugo retrieved them and Beth apologized. "They smell of dog."

"Dog is better than cold."

They got into the rear seat and lay down. "I want to know that your hands are warm so put them here," she said and Hugo could feel, even through the numb flesh of his left hand, the bare skin of her back.

As the evening wore on into night he was unaware of the passage of time or any desire he might have to speed the intervals between her slow movements, but from time to time she would lie clutching him tightly with her lips moving over his neck. He could feel her breath, and at many points her legs and breasts through the thick layers of clothing. He became fearful that sleep would intervene and cut him off.

That morning she dropped him at Stokehill. He thanked her for taking him along to see the non-person and having the chance to learn how it is to navigate in the fog even when the conveyance is stationary. Because, as they arrived, Beth said to him, "Fog is a thing that forces us to choose our way carefully."

He watched her car disappear into the Coventry road and knew that when night came, he might have difficulty finding his way down the corridor to the piano room.

A quarter-hour before the evening meal Gordon Moffat shuffled into Hugo's room. "Going tomorrow?" he said.

"Nine-fifteen train."

The old man paced in circles, then sat on the cot. He smoothed over the blankets with his bony hands before speaking. "You weren't much of a swimmer. Could have drowned yourself, almost did in the test."

Hugo nodded. "That mishap got me thinking that death by drowning would be almost painless. You just slip away after some gurgling and a brief moment of panic."

"Like the twins might have and all? You weren't a swimmer as I said, but you did some good here."

Moffat got to his feet stiffly with his arm supporting his sore back. He took a step forward to shake hands then went out and down to the evening meal. Hugo joined him in the cafeteria and said his good-byes to the tradesmen he would not see in the morning. He packed his things in the leather case, then sat at the rusting metal desk, staring at the emptiness of the wall now missing its row of books and without a trace of the blood that he was never aware of anyway. Inside the satchel was just enough money to see him to Algiers. He knew the daily living would be scant. Besides the attraction of Maurice Crasson's bad reputation, he couldn't say what other reason he had for going there. Language was no impediment for him to make his way generally, possibly work for cash. There was a small chance he would move south into the Sahara and continue the miles to Lambaréné. He had no official documentation to go anywhere because visas required more money than he could part with. He took his last shower beneath the instructions for continuing good health, and, after drying off, was resolved to proceed only on the basis of weekly, daily, hourly impulse.

For the first time since the trip to Bristol, he dressed in his good clothes and took the bus downtown. He walked past the new Coventry Cathedral. It was locked and dark. The ruins of the old church were hidden behind a curtain of evening mist, so he took the #44 to Foleshill. He had made no arrangements to meet anyone and had managed to sneak out of the bath before the staff could see him go and embarrass him with good-byes, or perhaps no good-byes as the case may be. He had not seen Beth since their arrival home from the night in the fog. He passed by the bath on the other side of the street and could see the brightly lit café, the windows to the office, the skylights above the big pool and through them the girders reflecting down into the water and showing anyone standing at the far end the distance they had to go before sinking to the bottom.

A car passed. Inside were people who frequented the Rose. His throat was drier than he thought it should be in the dank air, so he had the idea of his own send off—just one pint, a last throw at the dart board and walked down the pavement, west towards the Courtaulds works and the small, sweet-smelling building opposite. He pushed open the door with his good hand. No one he knew was there. The gaffer pulled him a pint without saying much. The table by the jukebox was empty, so he sat down and wondered what he would play, the Beatles or the Stones. He thought that if Doyle were to come in, he would say, "Here mate, we go back a way. You remember the nastiness at the Jaguar, the scrap by the north wall right here. Let me buy you a pint before we step outside for a word."

He took the ring from his satchel, placed it on the table, and had a sudden appreciation for the hidden mystery of Leviticus, the script buried by its small dimensions in the way tiny things were unseen before Leeuwenhoek stacked pieces of ground glass in the proper order to bring them into view. On his death he would be comforted that the words would be buried with him so as not to burden others with the weight of an impossible morality. He spun it round and put it back in the satchel. A man he knew came into the room and said, "Fancy a game?"

With indifference he threw two rounds of darts, winning and then losing. When he turned to get his newly cleaned jacket, he saw that it was being held up by Beth, with the arms open so he could put it on easily. He had not seen her come in and was overwhelmed with regret for neglecting the many opportunities he had had to tell her how lovely she was, like the princess who radiated the divine right royal women possessed, to be perfect in body as well as soul so the men who went to war might be encouraged to return. "Are we going somewhere?" he asked.

"No. We were never going anywhere, Hugo."

"Then, are we leaving here?"

"Yes."

He turned and put his hands back so she could slip the jacket over his cast. "May I ask where?"

"I don't know. But before we go, in case I forget, please take this." She handed Hugo a package. "It's the photos and some other things Owen included. Don't open it now. You'll have time on the train tomorrow."

They left the Rose and circled back onto Foleshill Road. As they walked she let her fingers slide into his until she was holding his hand tightly. "You look smashing in your new clothes."

"And you as well," he replied, "because it always looks to me like your clothes are new."

She looked up at him but didn't smile. They passed an alley and a couple kissing behind a storage rack. "I had a mate once," she said, "who was very good at screwing in the alley, standing up fully clothed, except the knickers and would hardly miss a pint in the round. Never mussed her hair or her clothes. For some reason I was envious of that skill."

"Why? With practice anyone can screw standing up."

She looked at him and this time her lips parted with a smile. "I was envious because I've never been able to feel pleasure as casually as that. But I understand that casual pleasure—and the pain of it—is a thing you've had practice at."

"I've hurt people, but I was never proud of it," he replied.

They walked past the baths and the little fish shop opposite and after a few more blocks, Hugo forget where it was they were. The night fog thickened.

"It's very chilly," she said and walked closer to him, almost leaning into his shoulder. After minutes of silence Hugo replied, "It's chilly now, but tomorrow is the equinox, March 21. A final misery before the time of hope."

She frowned. "Hope?"

"I divide the four seasons on the basis of how we perceive the sun. The time of decreasing light, increasing darkness, of decreasing darkness and increasing light. Summer, fall, winter, spring. Tomorrow is the best day—the start of spring, the first day of increasing light."

She gripped tighter on his hand and they walked down a maze of cold and narrow streets as if they were searching for a way home. Near the Leicester road they came to a dimly lit café and turned in. Hugo sat at the only table. After Beth brought back two teas, they sat silently while customers slouched in, ordered their take-away, and left. Beth never looked once at him until, with her hand wrapped around her tea mug, she said, "This is not a time of increasing light for us, Hugo. Tonight is the end."

"For two people who were never going anywhere, was there a beginning?"

Beth looked again through the window that dripped with condensation, rendering the traffic, the street, the passersby distorted and indistinct.

"I didn't lie. We were never going anywhere," she answered. "But futility can't deny that something happened, at least for me…from the beginning, when you first took me to task over Owen's title. At the time I thought it was unpleasantness and it would go away when you did. But it didn't go away. And when you came back the unpleasantness increased until it reached the worst, Christmas Day, with you sleeping, and my shock to find you were not sleeping but trying to leave me, trying to sneak away like a thief. I knew then I had confused something unpleasant with whatever it is at the opposite. And I admit that I said to what I thought was your corpse, 'Don't leave me like this, with the regrets of a lifetime piled up.' What do you make of that?"

Hugo leaned back in his chair, and for a moment turned away from the intense sadness in her face. "You're a nurse," he answered." You would have many regrets if you let someone die. But even that doesn't matter because dead or not, I am leaving. In a way, we're both leaving. I'm moving on because I feel compelled to, and you're settling in to a lifetime with the man who can supply your needs. There can't be regrets on this, or it wouldn't happen that way."

"You're good with words, Hugo, too smart by half. Because we are letting it happen. I crave a pleasant life, a nice home, nice kids, nice dog. And you crave some unknown thing you can never have. But you were right—perhaps both of us will always live on the edge of another craving with the thing we crave just out of view."

Hugo looked through the beads of water spread across the window glass. He touched his cast and moved it from side to side so that he could feel his arm underneath. She watched him and said, "Remember when I asked you if there was ever a time when more than your arm ached?"

Hugo smiled slightly, sympathetically and said, "It's better not to keep count of such things."

They left the café and took the bus to Aldermans Green Road. In ten slow minutes they had walked past the Crow in the Oak, past the rose gardens, and as the fog swirled across the meadows they stepped inside the cottage, which Freddy Marshall had abandoned for his weekly snooker down at Courtaulds Club.

"We have until ten," Beth said and put on the kettle.

They had another cup of tea out of respect for the cold night, and when she had put her cup on the counter Beth came and stood in front of him. Hugo looked at her sweater, how it folded under her breasts and flared onto her hips. He reached out with his good arm to pull her around until she was sitting on his lap, on a peeling wooden chair under a small kitchen light with the sound of the water still revolving in the kettle. He looked up at the clock and said, "Is it an hour we have left?"

"A bit less now," she answered and lay her head on his shoulder, put her arms around him, and remained that way unmoving until the water had stopped moving, sounds decreased through the old house, both their bodies had quieted and all Hugo could hear was her breathing like he had heard and become accustomed to in the fog that trapped their car in the night. He feared that he would never hear human breath again without feeling her presence. Decades on—thirty, fifty, seventy years, if he should live that long, and in the all the breathings of humankind he might hear, none would be the breath of this woman.

She straightened up and when she looked towards him he could see that her eyes were red. Her lips moved as if she was going to speak, but instead she lay her head back down, her arms going tighter around his back. He felt the tightness in her chest and put his left arm around her back, trying to keep the sharp cast from pressing in too hard. They sat motionless together in the chair as the time clicked over, the blood flowed inexorably round and he had committed to his nearly infallible memory the beat of her heart, the pressure of her breast against his chest, the smells that changed delicately from her sweater to her bare skin. He came to know intimately and forever the smell of her neck, of her hair and the subtleties of texture between the curls lying on her shoulder and the flesh of her cheek.

Until audible, increasing sounds came from outside, which caused him to focus his eyes and think of the world. Water trickled down the kitchen window, slow at first then harder, and soon the window frame rattled as the wind hit it. Beth looked up at the clock over the sink. It was time.

"I would like to send you something," he said. "Not a postcard. Maybe something unusual, unexpected."

"Please, no. No stories. No pictures. Nothing of your life." She went to the counter and reached into a bag taking out a single red rose. "I couldn't think of what to give you. We've been together for so short a time, like a flower blooming, a rose, a red rose for a rover. Because I'm afraid that you will never come back here. Why would you come? For me? Just another girl and soon a married woman and nothing else to hold you to a place like this."

Tears welled in her eyes. "Oh Hugo, why? I don't understand."

He let her hand draw him up from the old chair and they walked to the door. Without hesitating she opened it to a blast of cold wind that swept in with a spray of rainwater.

"You have to go now or I will die standing right here."

They embraced quickly and ferociously. Hugo could feel the tension go out of her in sobs and when she looked at him the tears went down her cheeks faster than the rain. She took Hugo's face between her hands and said, "If you have something for me, bring it yourself. It's the only thing I'll believe."

She reached up with her mouth and kissed him and kissed him again and again, with her wet lips moving on his and her breath sweet with tears. She stood back and put her fingers to the sides of her head.

"Good-bye," she said. And he looked at her face, her beautiful eyes swollen with the crying and wished he could say to her, "I love you more than life itself," but instead he receded into his mind, safe inside the convalescent room, sheltered by the glare of the window without the discomfort of weather or human contact—but emptied of will, void, a specter unable to intervene for good or love. And the image of her face drenched with the rain receded with him thinking, "Oh God, she is leaving me," knowing it was he who was receding, drifting over the lawn, along the hedge, fading past the rose garden and down the high street in the ghostly shape of absolute solitude, with only the smell of the rose in his hand to keep him rooted to the earth.

Beth watched him go over the lawn, and when he had passed through the gap in the hedge and reached the road, she put out her hand towards him. When he had disappeared and the rain continued to fall through the air onto Aldermans Green, through her bitter tears and her voice breaking, she whispered, "Don't come back, Hugo. Please. Don't ever come back." She stood shivering, empty; until some time later she heard her father's mutterings from the drive and tried to dry off her face.

Hugo sat in a compartment on the London Express and looked at his watch. They were nearly at Kings Cross Station and he had not moved. The leather case was by his knee and he was aware of the musty smell of the seats, the curtains, and the countryside fleeing behind him, the sucking air and staccato click of the rails when they passed a train heading north. He reached into his satchel and brought out the package Beth had given him. Inside was the folder containing the photos, and with it a note of concern from Owen Dring. There was another envelope with his name written in Beth's hand. It contained a bank draft for a hundred pounds and a note that said: *I knew you were short of money. When you eat, think of me.* He tried to smile but turned his face to the window instead so his expression would not disturb the other occupants of the compartment.

At the Marchmont Hotel he laid on the sagging bed and tried to focus on his vague task—how he might glean useful data from the one million volumes sitting on the shelves down the road at the British Museum. This was not a waste of time, if he could discount the fact that he required no more data. He simply had to leave, head south, cease his procrastination, not be turned around in his tracks like a boy in the story, who was always lost in the forest and him ending at the place he had begun—heading for the London Bridge station of British Rail and finding himself at Kings Cross instead.

"Where to?" asked the woman behind the wire cage at London Bridge. Hugo thought for a passing moment he should go by way of Canterbury to see Billy, but Billy was not there. He had gone south himself. No one he knew seemed to be here or there. Some were in the past and forever unavailable. Others he hadn't met so he found himself saying in a confident voice, "Dover, please."

As the train flew through rural Kent he tried to create useful information concerning the lives of Billy and Violet, how they might be getting along, perhaps married. He saw farmland in the process of greening up to springtime blossoms and invented for this fictitious couple the holding of garden parties, the administration of weddings after the style of their own. Billy, Hugo knew, would still be regretting his missed opportunity at the marriage of cousin Milton and Middle March, the artiste. But Billy would come to terms with this quirk of fate by realizing he would not live long enough to preside at his cousin's funeral. Poor Billy. It was Hugo's opinion that along with the gift of a sound mind, Milton had also attained immortality. In the line of well-wishers in front of the Bazaar that evening an eon ago, the hapless, former moron was now the tree of life around which the others gathered for shelter.

Hugo felt otherwise, not sufficiently in the world to cast a comforting shade, was more like Prince Eugene who, when *War and Peace* went back on the piano bench, dissolved into the index of characters, became the subject of a remembered sentence or two words in a paragraph, at best the face of a momentary recollection no greater from Solly's haggard face when he slipped the ring on Hugo's finger. His chest went tight. There was solace in jewelry after all. He opened his satchel to read the words of Leviticus on his ring, to feel a connection to Muir's old friend and therefore to himself. He reached in and let his fingers scour the small pocket but touched nothing. The pocket of the satchel was empty. He tore it open and emptied the contents of the case onto the compartment seat. People glanced at him. He went through each item, laid them all out to ensure they were not guilty of hiding a treasure. But the ring was gone. He felt angry, ashamed for his carelessness. With the man sighing behind him, Hugo replaced the papers, his passport, his personal items, then sat down. The man sighed again as the unpleasantness ceased.

At Dover he boarded a vessel to cross the English Channel. He bought a tea and sat in a chair overlooking the deck. He could have gone aft to watch the receding white cliffs. But he didn't for the reason that he had seen them once already. In the fading light of an autumn afternoon he had stood on the deck next to Violet Lewellyn to hear Richard Appleton delineate the hundred fifty million year geology of the chalk. With the light going red to the west, Violet had departed to exercise her spiritual affairs, leaving Hugo alone at the railing to consider his ties to the civilization beyond the cliffs. To that point, he had paced his experiences through short groupings of time—weeks, months, a few years only—the time necessary for him to grow beneath the branches of the rain forest together with the children playing in trees that sprouted hardly a lifetime ago. In the increasing dark of the last evening on board the *Yildun*, the weight of reality forced him to consider periods of much longer duration, of centuries and millennia. These were a requirement of historical perspective and formed the chapters of uncountable books.

As the channel ferry steamed towards the French coast, he thought of things he hadn't counted, of the risk of setting himself within the context of a long history, of putting his feet on English soil and digging a little into it to find his permanent place. Having no courage to look behind, he began to regret that he had dug his fingers in as deep as he had. The bare small of her back and sweet breath on his neck were now outside of any calculation of time he could make. Like Solly's lost ring, they had become a heritage he could never escape.

As the coast of the continent grew larger on the horizon, Hugo turned for comfort to his memories of Conrad's library and the uncountable items he had extracted from the volumes contained within it, some catalogued from literature, oft-quoted passages and works of erudition, famous, brilliant and old. He focused his eyes on the word "England" stenciled on the lifeboat hanging in its divots. He tried to associate this word with Muir, who had often stared through the sickroom window with the evidence of springtime deceiving his conceits. Hugo had many times heard his father recite in a sorrowful voice, "Oh to be in England now that April's there", before gliding backwards through the study door, himself little more than a parsed, metrical verse dug from a volume of schoolboy poetry. Hugo looked past his reflection in the ship's window and knew that in a week's time April would come to the land. To his delight and sorrow he knew also that the warmth of increasing light would make roses bloom in the garden at Aldermans Green.

Chapter XVI

Books are Heavy Freight

"*Par autostop*," said the boy to Hugo. "That's what they call it in France, my friend."

Hugo smiled at him. Cheap travel was a skill he admired, but he loathed the actual cost. Already they had stood outside Calais for many cold, inhospitable hours. No cars had stopped. That evening they walked back to the ferry terminal for dinner and a secure place to sleep. At six the next morning he woke surrounded by the filth littering a corner of the quay.

"The gendarmes never check down here so as to allow the foreign scum to accumulate in one spot," said the boy from Liverpool. "We're like dust."

He took a cigarette and offered one to Hugo. The boy huddled in his blanket tight against the wall. He looked into the gray sky. "And the rain falls like lead in the winter."

"It's spring," said Hugo.

His companion seemed not to care. With nervous regularity he tapped the cigarette ash onto his pants. When it was fully light they packed their gear and entered the terminal. The boy ducked onto a bench to avoid being noticed. He lit another cigarette. "Listen to that, eh mate. The rum de dum, splatter, slop, swish. The buggers don't half know how to mop a floor."

With his own eyes barely open, Hugo watched the men work methodically down the acres of tile floor with the mops sweeping one way and the other. The boy asked, "Why do Frenchmen wear dark blue? We Brits wear exciting colors. But the travailleur always wears the same blue."

"You're a smart little bugger, Roddy. '*Travailleur*'. Where did you get hold of a word like that?"

"I've been in France on many occasions, mate, for the football mainly. Come to support the lads and scrap a little. I know a word or two."

Hugo thought the boy probably knew three or four words to sustain his mischief. Then he thought no more, except to hope that the floor would dry in time for him to get into the café for a croissant and a coffee.

On the second morning, a truck driver took them through Abbeville and halfway to Chartes. In the afternoon they stalled again. Hugo considered the delay. He concluded that highway traffic failed to stop for the same reason country folk withdrew in their presence. They were both unshaven, their clothes were worn through in some spots, and the boy had a machete jutting from his pack. Often people came to the door to follow them suspiciously with their eyes until they were out of sight. At the places they bought food, people asked where they were going; when Hugo told them his destination, they said disapprovingly that Africa must be far away, too hot and very dangerous. Yet it didn't seem to matter why he was going; the green grocer or vendor of horsemeat seemed to secretly like the idea of his going somewhere, as if travel were a salvation and not a curse.

Near to the village of Dreux, they camped in a grove of trees. After eating, Hugo sketched the boy's face using the light of a wood fire. As the embers went from white to red to blue, he wrote next in his spiral notebook the idea that travel, like salvation, was a curse because it involved a series of unpredictable episodes with no fixed links except the road. As a ritual, he took to reading maps, then with his eyes closed tried to foresee future aggravations, which he hoped would compensate for the snail's pace of change. The small fire smoked, then died; the pall obscured the trees. He pulled the blanket up to his armpits. The boy clapped his hands to warm them and handed over the wine bottle.

"The *gnosh* you just cooked was almost as good as my dinners at home," he said.

"That's because I made it for your growth, Roddy," Hugo answered. "Food for your brain—or did it all go to your legs?"

"A few more glasses of this and my legs will be like pistons. But then I'd just as soon not walk anymore."

As daylight waned, the wet wood continued to smoke. Soon, only the smell was obvious. They slept. Next morning the first car that trundled along the narrow road gave them a lift the fifty remaining kilometers to Chartes.

In a bistro fronting a narrow street, Roddy drank his beer in the company of other foreigners and declaimed in a loud voice the gist of his successful day. "I dislike these people, you see. They're runty, they talk funny, wear ugly clothes, ride donkeys, drink piss, and couldn't give a shite if two proper people are left on the side of the shivering rue. Then Monsieur Gumby comes along, eh Hugo? Like three sacks in a coat. He talks many languages, some at the same time. He drives a Citroen Deux Cheval, small, but gets us here. He also likes to drink wine and he feeds us."

The patrons of the bar cheered him on with more beer and a pat on the head. "When fat Gumby speak," he continued in a louder voice, "it come out his nose in bursts, as if the force of squeezing his fat self in the little car puts pressure on his balls, eh mate, like the time he said 'pneu,' like we hear the Michelin man say; and 'pneu' when the tire man in Beauvais told Gumby that his 'pneu' was flat and his fat self not even in the car weighing it down. *Je me regret, Messieurs*, but I thought that anyone could have said 'pneu' without going fucking red in the face."

Hugo lifted his glass to the boy lighting his thirteenth Galoise and remembered only that the fat man, Gumby, had blown a stream of smoke out the tiny valves in his nose, called "*bonne chance*" back to them and sped off past the cathedral. As he listened to the talk of the tavern, Hugo looked out the window, past the traffic to see the soaring towers of the Cathedral, which glowed copper-red in the oblique sunlight.

At dinner, Roddy was drunk and opposed to delay. He spoke increasingly of the warmth of Spain and the Costa del Sol. But Hugo required a place to wash the sweat away from under the plaster, so they rented a room in a squalid *pension*. They agreed that he would pay two-thirds. As soon as they were in the room, the boy went wild with table wine and puked in the bidet.

"I have to use that basin to dress my arm," Hugo complained.

"I'm going out," the boy said, after he cleaned up the mess.

Hugo warned, "Come back with a woman and you'll sleep in the bath."

For the next hour Hugo swabbed the inside parts of the cast he could reach and regretted not having an instrument. In the middle of the night, Roddy came back with a red scuff on his cheek and a skinny whore. Hugo pulled him out of the bed, handed him his pack, and said in a kindly voice, "See ya." The boy went back into the street after Hugo had given the girl ten francs.

In the morning Hugo left his things in the care of the concierge before hiking the steep, intricate streets in order to approach the Cathedral de Notre Dame from an angle that suited his purpose—coming up from the side gave him a view of the nave pinched between ancient houses, with a green patch of grass below a flying buttress. Lying on this verge was Roddy, with the young whore walking away counting ten more francs. Hugo avoided him by taking the route into the open ground at the side of the structure. In a moment, the boy had smothered the area with the stench of stale garlic and cheap wine. "What's up, then?" he asked.

"This large spire is what's up, lad, way up, known as the south tower, completed in the year 1243 and I can't recall which book I read that in."

"Should I care?"

"Not in the least. By all means remain yourself. It makes you a more pleasant companion. Still, I'll try to increase your self-image by giving you a portable lesson. Auguste Rodin, the man who carved *The Thinker*, once called this structure the acropolis of France,' situated as it is on a hill dominating the town—a hill on which has stood some sort of religious building for seventeen centuries."

"This is all shite of course. I mean, who is blessed with such a memory?"

"Me, Roddy. Some shite is true and worth remembering," Hugo answered. "To help us in that task are small packets of bound paper filled with words, much like the Bible. And in one such collection, un *Histoire de France*, you can read a description of the crowning, in this very Cathedral, of Henry the Fourth as first Bourbon King of France, a military leader of note and writer of the Edict of Nantes, giving so-called Protestants rights instead of persecution and death."

The boy appeared irritated, so Hugo continued his instruction. Starting and ending at the South tower they walked him around the perimeter, with the doctor talking and smoking his companion's cigarettes.

"You see, lad, I'm keen for you to observe, first-hand, the wonder of medieval stained glass from outside before we go in to see them as they were intended, a form of painting using the light of day. Chartes is advertised in the travel brochures as a museum for this type of art. I made note of that fact at the age of ten. But not to worry, because many people are sixty by the time they understand any of it. Most likely, that will be your age when a light comes on in your head to illuminate, like these windows here, the dark, blind spaces. Now take care, Roddy! When we enter the Cathedral by the door just ahead, you do it with the stealth a doubter might show as he enters a space constructed of certainties."

The boy crept warily across the stones behind Hugo. Inside, burning candles soured the aromatic air. Only the tiny flames moved. It was silent and gloomy until a cloud moved away. Then for a full minute the vast interior glowed with a fiery brilliance as the spring sunlight passed through the rainbow of glass.

"Count them, Roddy—one hundred and seventy-six such windows crafted by guildsmen in the Romanesque style, and in that direction over there, the lancet windows depicting the Tree of Jesse, ancestors of Christ, panels that have survived the obscenities of modern society as well as a great fire in medieval 1194."

For an hour Hugo let the varying intensity of color shine in the boy's eyes and in his own faithless eyes, much like the sun penetrating the sickroom with sparkling rain-forest greens and the blues of the mountains. They left the Cathedral at three in the afternoon with Hugo not bothering to make reference to his companion of the intricate maze on the tile floor that covered the ashes of the Huguenots burnt for heresy or foolishness. The boy went immediately into a nearby pastry shop, saying he was hungry after the lesson, and came out with whipped cream on his face. He wiped it off with a shirtsleeve, then carried on to a bakery in the next street.

"Come with, Hugo," he called from a distance.

"You see, here's a different type of shop...and there's four more just like it, down to the end of the block."

When he returned, Hugo watched him chew through the white sugar with the crumbs falling into the gutter and tiny birds flying down. When his mouth was empty he said, "You've been to Coventry I hear. Did you go into the new Cathedral?"

"And the bombed one."

"You like churches?" the boy grunted then put his hands together. "Me too. Here is the church and here's the steeple; open it up and see all the people." He sat down with a child's grin. Hugo poured wine into an enamel cup and sat on the curb next to the boy without offering him any. Rain showers fell lightly from a passing cloud. Roddy stood up and jingled the change left in his pocket and took it out in a handful. "All that's left is old *centimes*. It would waste a meal packing it to Paris."

"Consider it money for the collection plate," said Hugo.

The boy looked up and down the street, then flung the handful into the air. The coins rained down like tiny bells ringing on the cobblestones. For a few seconds the passersby ignored them. A child picked one up, followed by his brother, and more children. The mother bent to steady her child and picked up a coin herself. An old man crossed the street and stooped to retrieve another. Thirty people picked at the money like small birds eating crumbs.

The boy smirked and said, "An offering to the peasants of France."

Two women jeered and the crowd moved off. The elderly man straightened with the pain of stiff joints wrinkling his face. He walked over and stood close to them. His face was red and he spoke contemptuously to the boy in a loud voice.

"Times have changed," Hugo answered. "What do you say, Pierre? The masons would not have cut stone for so little."

"They worked for the love of the guild," the old man replied, then shuffled away on his cane, glancing up twice to see the portion of Cathedral roof that gleamed from the wet. At the edge of town, Hugo sat on the grass and drank the last of the wine. Then he went alone along the gravel path with his heavy case and satchel.

Leopoldville, February 14, 1965.

The chief interrogator ordered his lieutenant to have a medical person examine the prisoner. The honest, pig-like sounds coming from him were in direct contrast to the perfidious answers they expected. They also feared that illness might lead to his premature death, which in turn would prevent the successful climax of their work. It made no sense to execute someone who was already dead. A ju-ju man was called to make a cursory inspection of the prisoner on the porch of the cottage. During the procedure, watched by the regular contingent of guards, Hugo volunteered no information on his condition, but instead asked the man what day of the week it was.

"Thursday, monsieur, February 14, if you care to know."

He told this to Mintou that afternoon, not bothering to tell his student the nature of the diagnoses or the trivial significance of the date. Instead, he sat on his leather case and explained that the lessening quality of his food was the simple reason for his digestive problems. Mintou squatted in his corner, expecting the weekly story.

After a period of silence he said, "What is the moral lesson for today, monsieur? Is it women, is it lies, or all together the sins of man which the ju-ju doctor has described for you, like the scenery of things you saw in your travels."

Hugo nodded and cleared his throat. "The lessons for today, Sergeant, are two: the first of these is the cult of romance, about which you know nothing. Secondly, since you've attained a level of thought where you can determine right from wrong, I'll include the gist of your opinions as part of your weekly test. So pay attention or you'll get left behind. In fact, getting left behind is the theme of the following episode."

Mintou held out his hand with the customary gift to his teacher of a cigarette. When he had taken two inhalations of his own, he squatted back onto his haunches to listen.

"After eating a plate of *pomme frites* at a railway lunch counter," Hugo began, "I dragged my case into the car designated on my ticket. I was curious about its apparent lack of comfort: hard wooden benches and no luggage racks. The lights were few and insufficient to see the print of a newspaper. I watched three men board the coach and slide into the hard seats. Noticing they didn't complain, I sat down with them and waited. In a few minutes the train eased out of the station with a noise that reminded me of the other small trains that have passed through my life, all of which left an unhappy memory. In a few miles I ceased to frown at the spartan nature of my journey. I was on my way to the warmth of the south, and rid of nuisances. By morning I would be in Toulouse, with more comfort than traveling with a child or begging rides in a fat man's Deux Cheval.

"Twenty minutes later the train rolled into a station that appeared to have the same facilities I'd seen at Orleans. Across the platform stood a shiny row of coaches crowded with passengers, some waving through open windows and clutching the hands of well-wishers. The men got off. Five others got on. Light from the fluorescent fixtures was sufficient for me to see my watch, which indicated ten minutes to eleven. I lay down and closed my eyes. When the train pulled away I felt secure in the gentle swaying of the coach and nodded off. A brief period elapsed before the train stopped again. I heard the second group of five men leave and more get on. I pulled my coat around me and used the satchel as a pillow. It was cold, uncomfortable, but soon I slept.

"During the night, with a regularity of stops, I woke many times to marvel at the bland similarity of French railway architecture and the thoroughness of planning. Travel across the countryside appeared to be timed in uniform segments. Through the night, I was rocked reassuringly by these miraculous stops and starts of the train, until daylight showed through the window. I sat up and rubbed my eyes. The coach was empty except the man sitting opposite, who must have got on somewhere in the French countryside, possibly at Limoges, being one more point on the railway that resembled all the others. The man had his arms across his chest and his chin lay on them as if he were dozing. I looked at him, then at my watch to confirm the time of day.

'Good morning, Albert,' I said.

"There was no reaction. I stretched and felt wide-awake, alert. 'We should be in Toulouse soon. Seven am arrival, although this train isn't making the speed I expected. Life is deceiving, but I suppose sleep fools us all.'

"The man opened his eyes and straightened himself. 'You seem to be fooled easily, my fellow traveler. You make a habit of letting clumsy observations lead to wrong choices.'

'Toulouse is a good choice—the south of France, close to the Pyrenees, Spain, sunshine, an early spring."

'But you're nowhere near the south of France, Bunky. If you take a good look we're just coming into the Gare du Paris Sud for about the nineteenth time tonight. Did you really think every station in France looked the same, and were all spread out with a yard stick?'

"My jaw might have fallen, but I recovered. 'What are you suggesting, Albert?'

'I'm suggesting again what I've suggested all along—that you are rather thick between the ears. But I tell you what. When you cross into Africa, you'll learn about standardizations more serious than railway schedules. You'll witness a regular spacing of disease, starvation, and death.'

"The train rumbled into a station that I confirmed had the same pillars, light fixtures and platform I'd seen all night, but the sign denoting the Gare du Paris Sud was just out of my view. I grinned foolishly at Albert and said, 'So what you're saying is that I've spent the night shuttling between Orleans and the mainline. This is an oddity I could enter into a book without fear of contradiction.'

'It's your attitude that's the oddity here, Hugo—and the quest you're on. Riding a train to nowhere is an embarrassment to be broadcast only by the Man of La Mancha, or someone nearly as crazy.'

'Like him, I slept where I could and was comfortable,' I protested.

'On a hard bench? Why not the Ritz? We can now add this to the old ship, the reeking back alley, the crumbling ruin. I'm getting tired of setting you straight.'

'I don't recall you setting me straight.'

'You're an ass, Haultain, content to hack away murderously with the blunt edge of stupidity, then on to an afternoon of bracing up those who are overwhelmed by misfortune. You're a pitiful contradiction.'

'But never the bleeding heart.'

"Schweitzer scoffed and wiped back his white hair; then bending at the waist to add emphasis to his whiny voice, said, 'Heart, you say. How's this, then? The question she asked was, "Has more than your arm ever ached?" The answer he gave was, "I don't keep count of such things." Such heartfelt, cloying self-pity—the quintessential bleeding heart, and Cupid's arrow right through it. Sets my knees a-quivering.'

'I'm here and she's there, living the life she likes,' I answered.

'Is she? You don't know about that for sure, do you. You never took a close interest in her affairs, in what she liked or didn't like. Too much into yourself.'

'There's nothing useful to be achieved by picking on me. We could have a chat about your neglected opportunities. You once wrote that Bach couldn't save his epoch, he could only save himself. Is this what you're doing, Albert, saving yourself by harassing the world? Because you can't save me or the world, mired as it is in the violence and greed of human beings unchanged in ten thousand years.'

'Your assessment is superficial. Bach saved himself because he focused on his music. That much is on the record; which is to say that he never looked to the results of his art, to any expectation of profit or reward or furtherance even of brutal humanity. Pay heed. You've looked to nothing—neither to your healing, or to the other side of your heart's desire.'

"A conductor climbed into the shuttle. 'Tickets please,' he called.

"I turned to pick up my satchel and without thinking replied, 'Get his first, I have to find mine.' I began shuffling through the debris at the bottom of my pocket.

'And to whom would you be referring, monsieur?' said the conductor indicating the empty bench across the aisle.

'I'm sorry,' I answered, 'Was I referring to someone?'

"After showing the man my ticket I went to the station café for a roll and some butter."

Mintou chuckled then laughed with a hoarse, grating stutter. "You went back and forth all night, getting nowhere?"

"Don't interrupt, Mintou," Hugo said with an edge to his voice, "or laugh at the misfortune of others, like I've done too often. You're better than me. You're a hero of your country's army and shouldn't have a gram of humor to waste on your enemies. And don't slow me down with criticisms, because once on the right track, I'll speak of my journey in accelerating words that I hope one day you'll understand. So here it is: All that day the express train of the SNCF glided smoothly and at great speed through the farmland, past the hill country of Limoges, and further to the south. By the afternoon I was touring the streets of Toulouse, ablaze with its colored umbrellas shielding boulevard patrons from the hot sun of springtime. I sat amongst them, sipping my cup of espresso, until I decided to go on through the town, as there was enough day left to hitch a ride to Carcassone.

"At the perimeter of that historic place I turned up a narrow lane off the main highway. Between the high walls guarding the Cité, the medieval towers, and ramparts of the fortress glowed in the angled sunlight of early evening. As I wandered past the walls of the keep, Albert came up to walk with me. He was eating a piece of fresh bread and chewing with obvious satisfaction. Between mouthfuls he said, 'I recall mention of the bleeding heart just now, Hugo. If I squint at this masonry just so, I can visualize the heart blood of the Albigenses running down the walls from their skewered bodies. Such ghastly things happened later with the Inquisition in its cruel attempts to eradicate heresy, to beat down the doctrine that equated the Church with Satan and the human body with evil.'

'I'm hungry myself,' was all I could think to say and had Albert show me where he had bought the bread. After eating I said, 'I've just had a thought about who supplied me this meal. What do you think she had in her mind with the words, "When you eat, think of me?" This phrase, Conrad suggested, was the embodying sentiment of his favorite book. Was it the redemption of love mentioned in both places?'

'Christ was also mocked on the cross,' answered Schweitzer. 'Love is depreciated everywhere but, like water, finds its own level. Here is a case in point. Quite near to this town, in the bitter fall of 1917, my dear wife and I were interned at a place in the Pyrenees named Garaison. This designation is a variation of the Provencal word, "Guerison," which means "healing." I will not invoke ironies here. We did what we could to justify a prison of that name, though for the duration of a hard winter there was pain and unavoidable death. In early spring, we were moved to St. Remy. The day room in that temporary prison felt familiar to me in a peculiar way: the bare walls, iron stove, and flue pipe seemed more than a remembrance of night dreams or fantasies. It came to me later, that this was the room depicted in Van Gogh's famous painting. More than a few times during my own pacing up and down it, I felt the chilly Mistral blowing through the chinks in the wall. Years before me, the painter in question must have felt the cold going to another depth, as if the brutal wind itself were sweeping his visions along the stone floor and into his unappreciated art.'

"The old man began looking for a place where we could sleep. He found a copse close to the wall of the fortress, which gave protection from the weather. Further on I found a similar shelter. When I woke in the middle of the night, I felt the presence of no one near me. I lay back down, put the stones of the wall against my backbone, and tried unsuccessfully to sleep. After a time, a woman in a blue velvet dress came to sit behind me on the grass, drawing her knees up to her chest with a shiver of cold. I slept soundly then, and woke prior to the dull red of dawn, knowing she had stayed, was close by in the last hours of darkness, quietly breathing as a comfort to me. I sat up. The irregularities of the stonewall pressed into me like the points of her breasts. With my own shallow breathing, I inhaled the fragrance of her hair from the flowers along the verge. But she was just out of my view, which is to say she remained in the past. I looked at my satchel and was thankful I had no picture of her, aware that paths diverge in ever-widening arcs."

The cell was close to being a uniform dark. The aromatic smoke of cook fires next to the prison scoured away the smell of urine. Hugo couldn't tell if Mintou was awake or even inside, but guessed that he was, since the grating metal door hadn't interrupted his narrative.

A voice said, "Would you like another cigarette, monsieur."
He lit two and passed one to Hugo. The tips glowed in the dark.
"Is this woman a ghost, a spirit preying on you, poisoning your mind?"
"What is your opinion of it, Mintou? You're supposed to give me an assessment of things as part of your lesson. But what do you know about women—a man who hasn't even had one wife yet, while Antoine has many."
"I'm of less age than you, monsieur. And to hear your story, you've had no more than me, no wives, just tales you've invented to account for a worthless ju-ju. That is my opinion."

Spain, early spring, 1965

By noon the day following Hugo's departure from Carcassone, he was boarding a small coach in Narbonne, since the motorway over the Pyrenees forbade the poor from begging rides. South of the mountains he passed through the territory of Northern Catalan. The bus stopped for a time in an unremarkable village. He went into a store to buy bread and heard familiar music played by children on a small phonograph.

"Los Beatles y Los Stones," a girl with dark eyes said proudly and pointed to the record on the flimsy turntable. He camped the night in a grove of pine trees adjacent to farmland, with the Mediterranean a series of blue strips between the trees of a windbreak, occasionally obscured by the fire he used to cook the eggs and onions he'd bought from the girl.

In Barcelona he remembered that Señora Manguel suggesting he seek directions from members of La Guardia Civil, crowned with their polished black hats. To Hugo they appeared robotic and foolish. Yet it was pointless to debate politics or justice, because General Franco insisted that his men see only to hurrying tourists through the sights of the country with the aim of keeping civil society free from influences. Instead, he learned from them the best and cheapest restaurants and the location of a comfortable *pensione*.

His room had a window with a view of a long, narrow courtyard walled vertically to six stories by balconies and windows. Each opening was lined with the faces of children; each railing bowed outwards with the bulk of Spanish mothers hanging their washing. Panels of clothing decorated the space like the flags of a dozen galleons. In the evening he ate fish and vegetables with working people, then sat in a square close by for the narrow view of the sea that separated the continents. After the next dawn, he took a train south.

Early on the morning of his last day in Gibraltar, Hugo climbed the stairs fastened to the east face of the huge rock. The view from the top gave him a wider, more complete view of the sea and beyond to the blue-gray of the Barbary Coast. The coffee he drank on the downtown street was a gift from the Spanish shopkeeper who fed him breakfast and told of tunnels bored into the rock for hiding generations of armed men, about the resident apes, the Moorish music playing in fruitful gardens, and the unknown future. At ten, he went to the docks and boarded the ferry to cross the straits to Tangier, and by so doing, put an end to the dillydallying or at least make an alteration to his map of the world that would, after a long wait, include Africa.

Lufungula, Feb 22, 1966.

Hugo had not eaten his breakfast when he was led towards the prison door together with four prisoners in leg irons. Antoine came up to him with a worried look and promised wine that night. "A double luxury, Hugo, you'll see. Today you'll live to get drunk. You will not die." But his voice did not sound optimistic. Taking Hugo's arm he said, "Bless you my friend. Those are condemned men," and began clearing his desk, being sure to put his orange radio in a drawer as he usually did when expecting trouble.

As the soldiers led Hugo onto the parade ground, four birds flew in a tight circle and landed on a blooming jacaranda tree beside the entrance to the prison. Their plumage radiated a fluorescence of green and red in the bright morning sun.

"It is the sign of death," Antoine called to him. A guard ordered Hugo to watch as the shackled prisoners climbed into the back of a jeep. One of them pleaded for mercy and a soldier split open his head with the butt of his rifle. The man beside Hugo laughed, slapped his face comically and pushed him into the black Fiat.

That afternoon a thin Hugo Haultain, his flesh pocked with numerous old sores and a few fresh wounds, went onto the veranda of the ministry, slapped his own face in a gesture of forgetfulness, and said to the guards, "I should have realized that death is coming for me today."

"And why would that be?" asked the senior man.

"Because the Commandant suggested that even in my own country, to cross a bridge without the necessary papers is treason. And I have no record of those papers." They all nodded agreement with the seriousness of the charge. Looking guilty, Hugo said, "I have no proof of permission or official papers to cross any of the bridges of my life."

The soldiers became more solemn than before. One ran his finger across the throat with a quick slice, then smiled. They all laughed and said in a happy chorus, "You're dead, Hugo."

The prisoner laughed with them until his stomach was tight with the effort and also with the cramps of his poor diet. Then he dabbed at the fresh cuts and festering sores with a piece of wrapper he had in his pants. In the other pocket he had a small bag of peanuts given to him by Antoine. He started with the soldier at one end of the porch, giving him a few, then reaching for his hand and shaking it. He did the same down the line until the entire guard had been paid properly and his pockets were empty. Later, the black Fiat of the Commandant, driven by the same man in stained trousers and filled with its customary two soldiers, made tunnels through the smoke and dust that swirled into the gaps of the thoroughfare. For an hour they drove randomly through the streets and alleys, stopping at semi-official buildings, sometimes at whorehouses that gave the impression they had been shoved bodily to the edge of the city. Each time they stopped, Hugo looked to see if this was the death house with the executioner sitting on the porch, smoking, relaxed, wiping his sweaty face with a rag. Until late in the afternoon they drove past the Memling Hotel and in five minutes were entering the gates of the Lufungula Police Barracks Prison. The birds had gone.

The driver who swung the Fiat into the compound shook his head at Antoine, who waited at the door of the jail with his arms hanging limply at his side. Hugo closed his eyes, and stuck on the inside of his eyelids, as if by magic, was a reminder from Conrad saying that he should not fear death; that whosoever believeth in good, as opposed to evil, would not die, regardless the intensity of pain. Hugo had decided at age eleven that all death was premature. As instructed, humans had a duty to rage against the death of the senses, which was really the death of pleasure. Whatever the gravity of this situation or its many possible conclusions, he was not a bone to be chewed by the God of Conrad's book, the Lucifer of recent discovery, or Mintou either— whether he was directing the events or not.

Hugo opened his eyes and said loudly, "Don't throw in the towel just yet."

The startled driver, turning his head to look said, "What towel, monsieur?"

Then the two in the front seat left the vehicle. After opening Hugo's door, they started to laugh hysterically, gestured towards him, and wiped their sleeves like phony towels across sweaty foreheads. Hugo laughed with them, all the while counting loudly, "One, two, three," and, to their amazement, shut and locked the car doors. Alone in the back seat of the Fiat, he lit a cigarette and puffed so furiously the smoke hid him.

The commandant walked to the car. "Open the door," he said to a hint of a face showing through the blue cloud.

"I should see a lawyer, Major. I should see President Tsombe himself." Hugo smiled with all his teeth showing and disappeared behind another emission of thick smoke.

"He is here," said the chief.

"Who? Where? I see nobody but you."

"Stop smoking and you will see that he is right around the corner."

"You're lying," Hugo answered with another false smile.

Soldiers began to pound their fists on the car and pull at the door handles. One raised the butt of his rifle to break the window. They were slapped away by the chief. "Do not harm my car," he shouted in a shrill voice and pleaded with Hugo. "I've called your ambassador. He will be here in five minutes. We'll wait for him inside."

"We'll wait right here," Hugo replied and kept puffing on his cigarette. He opened the window a crack and tried to fan out the smoke. A soldier stuck his fingers in through the opening and Hugo wound the glass up. Screaming in agony, the man gyrated against the car door. This caused the commandant to beg. He ordered; then he raged with fury. When a group of soldiers tried to turn the Fiat over with the conscript's fingers still stuck in the window, the chief appeared to go mad and began beating the hood of the car with his fists. Hugo taunted him with a waving hand. After finishing his cigarette, he rolled down the window and the man fell back waving his crushed fingers in the air. The troops around him screamed for revenge. Several soldiers carrying rifles ran from the living quarters on the second floor of the barracks, their feet thudding in unison down the metal steps.

Hugo lit another cigarette and let it dangle from his mouth as he massaged his left arm. It made him feel more optimistic to be continuing his rehabilitation, encouraged by a sense of the ordinary. He could see on the edge of the crowd one small arm with Sergeant Mintou's stick at the end of it. In a moment, it sank from sight.

For a last time, the Commandant stuck his nose to the glass and said, "Your Ambassador is here. He is coming through the crowd with a lawyer, with the President, monsieur." He grinned insanely and pointed at one of his own men. The soldier stood to attention at the privilege of being referred to as someone higher than himself. Then with a grimace of remorse, the commanding officer of the Leopoldville Garrison began smacking at the windows of his own car, then faded piece by piece, an arm, shoulder, his chest and face disappearing, as he was gradually subsumed into the throng pressing around him.

Dozens of boots and rifle butts struck at the Fiat. The windows smashed inwards and hands opened the doors. When the mob saw the prisoner sitting unprotected, they went berserk and smashed every piece of the vehicle. But none attacked. Two men tried to pull him, but fell back when he resisted. Hugo surrounded himself with the smoke of another cigarette and considered his strategy. He had no hope of defeating a hundred men, but some unaccountable fear was keeping most of them at bay. With that hope, he attacked suddenly from the open door, catching the men off balance. The collision staggered the first group. The swirling slip chain on his wrist drove the second tier backward into the men behind. He snatched a rifle from the ground and swinging it by the barrel, dodged his way to a troop carrier parked between him and the jail door. An officer came up from the rear screaming, "Shoot him!"

A dozen soldiers took aim. Hugo had a sudden urge to pray for some future connection to the world. With the steel carrier to his back and seeing his connections wither toward inevitable death, he felt free to assess the morbid fearfulness spreading across the parade ground. Men stalked towards him with rifles that didn't fire because his immediate death did not appear to be the cause of their concern. The first rank of attackers had already dropped their weapons. Wary faces circled past him, like spirit hunters coalescing around an ancient evil. Hugo sensed that he had ceased being a human being killed easily with a bullet—had become instead a ju-ju snake to be dealt a tough blow, a moral blow on behalf of the community. A few soldiers removed their boots and danced barefoot with grim, intent faces. A dozen more tore off their shirts; others stripped off their pants and all clothing. Many of the shirts were wound up as slings to propel stones towards him, the first bouncing off the truck with a musical ring. And then dozens more arced through the air—wondrous, colorful missiles, like jewels from Solly's case or the red painted rocks displayed by the Arab girl who had helped him in Morocco.

One hit his chest. Another struck his leg and one more his rehabilitated arm. Scores of rocks drummed onto the steel plates of the troop carrier. Then more rocks rained down than he could avoid; the dents, chips and cracks wore him to his knees, then to his hands and knees, finally to his belly to crawl backward in the choking dust. On the prison side of the truck the air was clear. He could see Antoine by the prison door. The jailer looked to be struggling with a prisoner, a young man Hugo recognized. He narrowed his eyes so he could comprehend that the youth in shackles, squirming in panic and fear, was the sick child from Antoine's village. He had got himself free as if from the grasp of his playmates, and with his heavy fetters making a strange music, began sprinting towards Hugo, coming to his aid perhaps—or seeking aid himself. The boy stumbled, fell, and crabbed his way through the dirt with his anguished face contorted with crying. Then the soldier chasing him raised his rifle and shot him four times and the child lay still only the length of his arm from the truck. Hugo saw the black holes pop open, the first rush of blood over the twitching torso. Then Antoine chased the soldier away and fell on his knees beside the dying body of his nephew. Hugo pulled himself along to the boy and touched his head saying, "I'm sorry, Antoine. This is my fault."

"Oh no," the jailer replied. "He is now beyond harm, and you are safe as well. They were going to shoot you, Hugo, had you gone inside. But now you have a stronger ju-ju and some real magic. They dare not kill you. No rifles. No death like my sister's boy here. The rocks are only to frighten you. And now they have no choice but to lock you in a strong cage, because the soul of this dead boy is bound to yours." Antoine spoke with no regret. Hugo put his head back down in the dirt and recalled a day in the deer garden when Albert had told him, 'Death occurs when your focus falls below the least of your expectations.'

"Expectations, Albert? What can I expect from this mess," he asked, with the stream of blood from the boy's wounds pooling around his face.

"What did you expect?" Sergeant Mintou asked as he lifted his prisoner up and put him on his feet, slightly off balance, leaning on the fender of the carrier with the filth of sweat and a mask of blood in his eyes. Mintou was pushing and shaking him rudely, then his right arm came round in a fury. The pistol butt slammed into Hugo's cheek and he went down, and down further until he found himself with no expectations at all, kneeling as if in prayer on the floor of his cell with the door still open. From the grate high up on the wall drifted the chaotic sound of sirens and mob-choir singing. Behind the cinder blocks of the building he could hear sporadic gunfire and Antoine wailing to dog-barking officers who screamed orders that no one seemed to comprehend or obey. Then came relative silence and the cry of a street vendor.

He lay down feeling no pain, just a little nausea and a heartsick turmoil; but this passed as well with the pair of hands he imagined passing in front of his eyes. Not his red, bent, warrior hands but those that were neat, white, and professional. He crawled to the door and croaked, "Thank you," down the passage. "And thank you again," he added. "It's been a waste but I'm only concerned about the state of my friend here." He looked to the latrine and the body of a condemned men, a man who had smiled often at him because Hugo had patched his many wounds and therefore considered him a friend (if smiles and a look of despair meant friendship)—this man lay face up in the latrine having bled to death in the filthy hole. Hugo stared at the mutilated corpse and wondered why he didn't hear a polite, civilized expression of outrage from the lions of the town, followed by a sickening yelp, the holding of an obese hand over a retching mouth, and a leaving quickly by the back door. He had nothing left to complain about and no power to leave, so he crawled over to the man and cradled what was left of his face in his own pulpy hands.

"Hope extinguished before life itself, my friend. Too soon. But for you, hope gone first and now peace. Rest ye, merry gentlemen."

He lay still holding the man until Antoine came in from the guardhouse to put him back in cell six. The sounds returned to normal. A gray light entered from the grate, with a pinch of cook smoke to mask the smell. Hugo put his satchel under his head, and in the hours of night struggled to escape the throbbing drone of memory.

Chapter XVII

Orphanage

North Africa, May 1965.

For seven days Hugo had stared at the coastline of Morocco swelling along the horizon with the color of starfish. On Tuesday, the second of May, he stood at the railing of the British ferry as it steamed closer to land. The hills and peaks to the south now made sense to him. Loose shapes tightened into settlements, then grew together as distinct pasture, houses and roads. The two girls standing next to him became nervous and pointed to features on the shore. "We are going to serve at an orphanage in Taroudannt," said the one to his right.

"It's such a long way from Leeds," said the worried one on his left. The first girl, Charlotte, added, "What Sara means is that we are quite unprepared."

Hugo nodded politely and smoked his cigarette. "Conrad beat it into me to always be prepared, always on your guard. He would often say, 'Never allow yourself to be overawed when events are grand or calamitous.'"

"'Be prepared.' That's a familiar motto. Was Conrad your Scout Master?" asked Charlotte.

The doctor shook his head. His face became lined with seriousness. "I could describe him as my regimental Sergeant Major, I suppose. Anyway, he was a tough man to the last gasp."

"You're an army man?" Charlotte asked with a look of admiration.

"An army of one," Hugo answered. The young women frowned with confusion. Charlotte laughed. "It's all nonsense, Sara. He's taking the mickey."

Hugo smiled, saying, "Life itself is nonsense, don't you think. We all need to laugh more." He then took both women down the deck so they could get a better view of the harbor. When their driver guided the Land Rover up the ramp and into Tangier, the women watched without speaking, taking note of the donkeys, robed men and everywhere music that scaled up and down in minor keys.

"It's quite medieval," said Charlotte. Sara nodded agreement, then pointed excitedly at the bazaar, at the flow of color with its warm, baking smell on an afternoon that was cloudless and hot. They stopped at an outdoor café to drink a farewell coffee to Hugo whose plan, he said, was to go east on the road, first to Oran, then to Algiers.

"We want to go west of Tangier and beyond as fast as possible," said Charlotte.

"To Marrakech," added Sara, "and over the High Atlas."

"You read maps?" asked Hugo.

"Oh yes. We're well prepared for that part of the journey. We'll be at our destination by tomorrow evening." She looked at the ground. Charlotte leaned on the table, wiped her brow, and said, "It's the brutality, the mutilation we're unprepared for."

The driver seemed agitated at the remark, so they drank up. Hugo gave them each a hug and watched their vehicle pull away through the narrow street. Then he walked by way of a stone road beyond the main buildings of town, all the way using his right hand to massage his left arm. From the heights, he could see the ferry making its way towards Gibraltar. The coast of Europe receded from him as well, and he heard a voice in his head say, "You won't escape," and wondered whether this pronouncement related to past or future issues. The road back to town took him through a place in his head where the limbs of children were bent double and babies lacked both their eyes.

The cluttered rooms of the Moroccan foreign office were stuffy and hot. "You'll have to go to Casablanca for the Algerian visa," said the man whose suit coat was a size too large. Hugo argued. The clerk declined to look at him, so he went back to sitting in the cool of the shadowed street to drink more coffee. For two hours he wrote and sketched in his spiral notebook with a fleeting vision in his head of the English women speeding along the road, halfway already to the capital. But that was not his doing. He felt no impatience, was at home in the idle Berber life, and settled by the possibility of leasing a room next to the residence of the famous and admired William Burroughs. The proximity would allow him to ask straight-out the question he had posed to himself when he was twelve, "What is your opinion of altruism, Bill, of doing good in an evil, slimy world ruled by the malformed beasts you so aptly described in your best-selling novel?"

He would not expect an answer to his query, but perhaps an invitation to "fuck off" as he thought Korrolus might have done if he had been less cultured. At three o'clock on a May afternoon, however, there was no presence of culture or evil or good with the exception of himself drinking the last drops of coffee. But there was one unexpected object. Down the steep slope of the street leading to his table barked a vehicle with steam rising from the hood. It stopped at the curb. He took his case in hand and walked to the intersection.

"Not prepared?"

"Seems not," said Sara, pacing in front of the Land Rover. Charlotte mopped her forehead; the driver raised the hood. Hugo set his case down and peered into the engine compartment. Water poured from a dozen holes in the radiator. The proprietor of a repair shop removed the burst unit and declared it beyond repair. "You will have to replace it, monsieur. But I don't have a good one."

The mechanic phoned, he went out, he came back, he went out again—all to no effect. The women brewed tea and waited. The sun went down and the heat fell away. Night grew pleasant.

"Better consider the hotel in the next street," said Hugo and resumed talking to the proprietor in his office. He outlined his plan, and the Arab laughed. "We can do that?" he asked. Hugo nodded and started for the door. The man made another phone call and prepared to follow.

"Where are you going?" asked one of the girls.

"To solve your problem. As payment you can take me to Casablanca."

"That would be all right," they said and left to find a room for the night. The driver disappeared into the backroom of the shop.

The moon had gone when Hugo and the mechanic ran down the road. The Arab had a radiator tucked under his arm with water still dripping from the attached hoses. Hugo helped him install it, then slept on the floor of the office for two hours until dawn. At eight the women came back and the mechanic made out the bill. The charge was only for labor and a few clamps. As they drove away, Charlotte said, "How come it was so cheap?"

"Was it a used radiator?" asked Sara.

Hugo nodded.

"It must have been very cheap indeed."

"As a matter of fact it was," said Hugo. "There's a style of business in North Africa that lacks the annoying formalities of payment."

"Did you steal a radiator?" asked Sara in loud voice, her eyebrows raised.

"Not just any radiator. There should always be some discrimination. Take note of the vehicle we just passed."

The young women looked closely at the rear of the vehicle speeding in the other direction. "You stole a police radiator?" asked Charlotte in a louder voice.

Hugo was making himself a crude bed on top of the luggage in the back and failed to answer. When he was tucked in, he said, "Please let me out on your way through Casablanca," then closed his eyes and went to sleep.

On and off during the days' drive, he was aware of the heat. Only once did he wake and wander into the scrub to piss, then drank water from the canvas bag. When he woke again it was dark. The only noise was the snoring of the driver, who had his head propped on the steering wheel. Charlotte lay across the back seat. A pillow cushioned Sara's head. Through the windshield he could see a massive silhouette obscuring the mural of stars. He wriggled himself across the luggage and unlatched the vehicle's back gate. The air outside was chilly and he sensed they were at a considerable elevation. His watch said five thirty. This would put them well beyond Marrakech and twice that distance past Casablanca. He walked a hundred feet from the truck to let curiosity displace his anger. The road still appeared to climb, indicating that ahead of them was the summit of the Tiz-n-Test Pass and the multiple summits of the High Atlas. Below him, through a cleft in the ridge, he could see the dark fringe of the Sahara. Along the ridges of the massif came the first glimmerings of dawn. With the light increasing around him, he waited in a soft depression for the others to wake.

When they arrived at the orphanage in Taroudannt, Charlotte said, "I'm sorry I let you down, Hugo. But we didn't feel safe traveling without you. If you come back this way, please visit us."

Lufungula, Congo-Leopoldville.

The day following the rebellion, the cell door opened and Sergeant Mintou entered with a man carrying a medical kit. He introduced himself as a doctor with the Danish Mission and proceeded to treat Hugo's wounds.

"There, a few dozen stitches," said the man. "I would prefer they allowed you to be transported to the clinic, Mr. Haultain. You would get better care and some x-rays for your head. But I'm told that's not possible."

"Thank you, Doctor, but before you go I have one request."

When the Dane had gone, next to Hugo's leather case was a Red Cross medical kit he had bought with the money hidden in his case.

"You'll need all this stuff to keep yourself patched up," said a smiling Mintou, "and the others Antoine brings, all his relatives, you understand, and not just any old niggers. If you carry on like this, you'll soon be as famous as the saints mentioned by the priests. Lufungula will become a place of healing." He laughed. "But don't ask for my help. I'm not good with blood or the moaning of those who are about to die. I'm a student now. I must spend my time learning from books and trying to understand why the ju-ju doctor took such an interest in helping you through life. You must tell me more, even if I am still ignorant."

He lit a cigarette and squatted in the corner. After Hugo had dug through the medical kit to gauge its contents, he sat on his leather case and talked; with the talk came a cessation of the pains that shot from his head to his knees. Mintou smoked and listened to the story.

"Late in the afternoon of the day we crossed the High Atlas," Hugo began, "the driver stopped a few minutes to allow me to buy supplies, then took me to a place on the coast just beyond the boundary of Agadir where a few goats grazed on the headland. I set my things in a grove of small trees, then took a book from the satchel, some pencils from a small case, and began to wander over the grassy dunes looking for something interesting to record. Below me the surf flowed back and forth on the beach. I sat down and panned my field glasses slowly along the unbroken horizon. There was nothing to see except the strolling old man who avoided the white foam spilling up the sand. He made straight for the spot where I sat."

"This would be the ju-ju doctor?" said Mintou, smiling.

"It was, Sergeant. I can see that you're as pleased with your new sense of observation as the doctor was with his criticisms. When he had sat down next to me in the sand, he said, 'Nothing to see. That's what you're probably thinking, eh, Hugo?'

'Aren't you always the smart old bugger,' I answered him.

'Indeed I am,' he said. 'And smart enough to assure you that there was lots to see in the year 1911, with the German warship *Panther* anchored off this point and the gunnery crew placing a few rounds on the dunes for practice. Some goats died. The shell craters soon filled with blowing sand. No damage done; just a warm-up for the war-to-end-all-wars. In that same year I completed my book on St. Paul and took my medical examinations.'

"I got to my feet and lit a cigarette. Albert followed me onto the beach. 'I passed in sight of this coast on March 27, 1913, on board the steamer, *Europe*,' he said. 'It was four-thirty in the morning so I missed looking in to see the goatherds, who would have been nervous. I was thirty-eight years of age and going to a hellhole of a place filled with disease and the least salubrious climate on the planet. We slaved for a year to build that first hospital. Then the war came, and as I mentioned before, my wife and I were interned by the French as enemies.'

'Did that give you a nice warm feeling about civilization?' I asked him and he answered without hesitation, 'We are redeemed by the small acts of individuals even against the collective sins of society.' He tossed a few small pebbles onto the beach. 'A few months later, we were allowed to continue our work. In 1917, however, with the war at its most horrific, we were shipped to Europe on board a filthy steamer called the *Afrique*. Now, what do you make of that.'

'Well, let me see,' I answered. 'You came out from Europe on the steamship *Europe* and back from Africa on a boat called the *Africa*.'

"Albert smiled as if I had used my own special ju-ju to solve a cosmic riddle. 'We both have the same wonderful consistency based on small things, which can be significant. This particular trivia suggests that we cannot escape our history. Africa had been four and a half years of abandoned labor for me. I would not return from Europe for another seven.'

'A wondrous and most ancient history, Doctor,' I replied. 'But it's now May 1965 and there are no ships in the bay. I feel no malignance surrounding me except the anger I have towards myself.'

"Albert tossed more pebbles down the dunes and complained that he was hungry. Dry wind blew from the land towards the sea, twirling his white hair into his eyes. When I made dinner for us, the constant rush of air fanned the flames of the cheap gas stove I'd bought in town. Small bursts of fire shot randomly from leaks in the seams near the burner head. I turned the flow down and the food cooked in an hour. That evening I swam in the sea while Albert watched, but the surf was flaked with a thick sludge that made me struggle through it like an animal. When I lay on the beach still dripping with water, the sand flies crawled onto me, so I decided to make my way into the town leaving Albert to sit and throw stones.

"At the only café that was open I sucked at the sickly sweet residue of a cola. When I mentioned this, the hotelier said, 'We Arabs like it that way. But mainly we drink mint tea with sugar. That's what we like for the thirst—for the heat, you understand.'

"And I did understand. On the Mediterranean coast just the mere sight of water made things cooler. South of the High Atlas, existence had become a labor for me. The residents were well-adapted, but still made comments. I engaged a man sitting at the hotel bar and asked his opinion.

'I can answer your query because I have had the good sense to study life at the Sorbonne,' he replied. 'Long ago human initiative in Africa evaporated with the water. The desiccation of the Sahara, caused by ignorance, has resulted in a culture of stagnation. High temperatures make men stupid, you see. From ignorance to stupidity.'

"He took the cigarette I offered, then continued in French, with a nasal monotone and the occasional Arab growl. 'South of the mountain spine, which segregates the green coast from the desert, the blessed sun in the sky cooks all things to inert uselessness. In the deepest Sahara, where I have been only once, the sun generates no life. What life wanders there, it destroys. Heat distorts the landscape and degrades perspective. It shrivels the human brain to hollowness, with just enough mass for the wind to roll it out over the horizon like tumbleweed. Genius whiffed away. In the Sahara, heat supersedes gravity. It is the dark Angel and the will of Allah.'

'Amen," I said, bowed respectfully to the man, and went down the dusty street by myself. The next morning I sat on the coarse sand and thought that I should be getting to Algiers. I left the campsite and walked for miles through the baking streets looking for the government office. Following an earthquake that killed thousands of people five years earlier, the townspeople rebuilt with no intention of duplicating the ancient styles. The numbing blandness of the buildings confused the fixed location of landmarks, allowing strangers the joy of blaming one more thing on the heat.

'The passport office is down by the market,' said a shopkeeper, 'just look for the flag.'

"The guard slouching in front of the prefecture was dirty and also inert, like a scrap of cardboard that might blow away with the next gust. I explained to him what I wanted, but he just grunted and shook his head. I repeated the information, 'I wish to go into Algeria.'

"The man stood impassively. I leaned over and said in his ear, 'Where is your commanding officer? Which door? I have important business.'

"This time he shrugged and looked away. I understood the man's position by looking at his hands, rough like a goatherd conscripted to stand in the sun, because abuse meant nothing to him. I lit two cigarettes, gave one to him, then slipped two packages of cigarettes with it. The guard blew the smoke out with a long sigh and stood listlessly out of the way.

'I wouldn't go to Algeria, monsieur. Not good. But the man who can help you is in the second door.' He smiled and took another puff.

"The commandant of the Agadir precinct was not obliging. He sat in his bare dusty office. There was no glass in the windows and the walls were rough with unfinished plaster. He took my cigarettes, lit one, and shook his head. 'You can't pass by way of Tiznit on the coast road,' he explained. 'The frontier for three hundred kilometers is in dispute with Algeria. There are constant skirmishes. Anyway, the French test their H-bombs to the east of the frontier, at Tindouf and the entire area is closed by Legionnaires for the summer.'

"I was confused at this meaningless aside. 'You misunderstand,' I said.

'Let me make it clear, my friend. Even if your documents were in order, they wouldn't amount to much down there. If they didn't get shredded by bullets or confiscated by the French, they would be vaporized in a poof of the big bomb.' He laughed and spun his arms out vigorously to imitate an explosion. He then stamped my passport with such force that the ink sprayed over the desktop. 'Everyone gets into trouble down there, *mon amis*, even the goat herders.' He winked and nodded towards the soldier slumping outside.

I paced with no frustration but only to keep my knees supple. 'I don't want to go to Mauritania, Chief,' I protested, 'but to Algeria. The thing is, without a visa I need to know what the border situation is.'

'Well, why didn't you say so? And what the hell are you doing here in Agadir? You're going the wrong way. Travelers here only want to go down the coast road or back to smoke in the bazaars of Marrakech. If you wish to sneak into Algeria, you have to cross at Figuig. But that is four, five hundred kilometers to the east. But I warn you, the frontier is mined and has an electric fence all along it as well. Only smugglers know a way through. They always know a way around things. That's the beauty of it.'

"He stood up as a sign of dismissal and put my cigarettes in his pocket. When I went back into the glare of the bright sun, the guard saluted and asked, 'What'd he say?'

I grinned at the man and answered, 'He says that it's a good thing that life's such an easy victory.'

"On the way back to the ocean, I bought tomatoes and eggs. Albert was resting in the grass and to my aching eyes appeared gaunt and aged. I cooked our meal hoping to revive my friend with some nourishment, then packed my things. Before leaving the beach I opened a spiral notebook. There were two volumes now, almost a stack a big as a small book. I shuffled them and arranged their order. All the pages were numbered. But the more ideas I put in them, written in words I could read back to myself, the more my ignorance bothered me. Somehow I was not applying the axioms contained in the immense and useless knowledge Muir believed he had stuffed into my head. Important things were evading me. Before the light faded completely I panned my glasses along the horizon.

The ju-ju doctor sat up when he saw me do this. He had the look of mischief in his eyes. 'If light bent more than Mr. Einstein believes,' he said, 'you could look directly into a certain hotel room in Tenerife and this would put you in mind of the marriage proposal and their romantic walk along the ocean sand. It's much warmer there than the chill of Weston-super-Mare and a night in bleak fog, with no more flesh to enjoy than her bare back. But don't concern yourself with that self-torture, Hugo—just imagine Richard Appleton polishing his Mercedes, with his wife rocking in her chair and praying that she have enough ju-ju to finesse her husband with a four no trump. In other words, concern yourself with small things. Stay away from the momentous force of love. It will be a sure bet for you—and a less of a risk for God.'

"I drank the last of my tea and replied, 'You've become the garrulous old man, Albert, who has forgotten the youthful habit of restraint. I understand that you were reprimanded for cutting your sermons short at St. Nicholas Church in Strasbourg. You defended yourself by saying that you were only a poor curate, who stopped speaking when he had nothing more to say.'

"Albert winked at me and lay back in the comfortable sand. 'And it's well known among the Bedouin that camels sometimes die of thirst."

Sergeant Mintou lit two more cigarettes and threw one across the cell floor. He was frowning and looked confused. "I don't understand about the camels…"

"It's another figure of speech, Léon, as I explained before, a way of describing one thing in terms of another."

"Yes. I see what you are saying, monsieur. You and the ju-ju doctor seldom run out of words. That's the secret, isn't it? You can say that words are like water in the desert. When you run out, you die."

Hugo nodded and closed his eyes. Dizziness came and went with his pain. The sergeant pried open the door. Before leaving he said, "I understand now that the important thing in life is the words we choose. Some have a better taste, like spring water as opposed to the mud of the Congo. That's why it's most important that you have learned to call me Léon."

With the closing of the door, darkness spread across the cell. Hugo struggled to light the candle and take the spiral notebook from his case. He tried to make a few notes, to write the word "Léon" and set it in the context of next day or next week. But his mind ran raced ahead with the provocations of unknown people and alternate futures. He saw on the blocks of his cell a dozen flickering landscapes joined by the bare bones of multiple plots. And in all of them, his own name was missing.

Southern Morocco, Summer 1965.

After lunch the next day, Hugo hitched a ride with a *chammioneur* who told him to ride on the hood-mounted spare tire. The man drove swiftly, recklessly along the winding road. They passed no settlements or any signs of village life. The gnarled trees were dotted sparsely over withered, brown grass. They soon caught up to a lorry carrying a thousand ripe melons. A half-naked boy rode on top of the fruit. He yelled something, waved his arms, and threw a melon back towards them.

"Throw another one...and another! Throw them all you little bastard!" screamed the driver. When Hugo had caught two large ones, he cut them up, threw one to the driver, and ate the other. An hour later they zigzagged through the narrow streets of Taroudannt and followed the fruit truck into a walled compound. Hugo sat in a small room on the mezzanine and sniffed the scent of orange blossoms coming from the orchard. Sara and Charlotte stood by the door.

"Sometimes children are born with defects—blindness, crooked limbs," said the British administrator. "They are killed by being dashed against rocks or abandoned to die of thirst. Sara, would you pour the tea before we dry out ourselves. You'll have to excuse her, Mr. Haultain. As you know, she's just arrived from England and is overwhelmed. It happens often to our neophytes—being overawed by calamitous situations. As I was saying, the little ones have some hope of survival here in the orphanage. This one was a few days old when we found him naked on the road to the Tiz-n-Test Pass. Blind infants are doubly cursed."

The woman patted the head of the scrawny boy on her lap. Sara poured the tea, smiling bravely as she held back her tears. Hugo carried the blind child across the roof to the edge of the parapet. Below him citrus groves filled the inner courts. The low, intense sun carried their shadows through the orange-flavored air, past the clusters of palm trees, and etched them onto the burnished hills. No clouds deformed the perfection of blue sky above the town. He stroked the eyeless head on his shoulder and considered this boy's present refuge compared to the sickroom of his own childhood. Hugo had had richly colored magazines illustrating the progress of world culture to impress on him the glorious despair of his solitude. The child in his arms would never see or hear of such things. He was secure in his ignorance. In his infinite wisdom, God would ensure equity between them by a consistent policy of alleviating no one's pain. Hugo rocked the child back and forth. He tried not to heed the boy's empty eye-sockets, which wept a continual stream of muddy fluids he was obliged to wipe out with his bandanna.

Sara came to stand at his side. "Who could abandon him?" she said with her lip trembling. Hugo hesitated for a moment and replied, "Who indeed? It's certainly not the will of God. The Almighty has no difficulty feeding a mouth attached to a body that can't fend for itself. Allah is not offended by weakness."

The next morning Hugo left Charlotte and Sara in tears. "You will cope with your own sorrow, to be sure," he said shaking their hands. "When it's too much to bear, start singing or write a letter to your future husband telling him of your passion."

"We don't have future husbands."

"There's no choice then. How fortunate you are." With that as an epilogue, Hugo carried his things through the arched gate and down the road towards Er-Rachidia.

In the late afternoon a bus bounced up the piste hidden in a cloud of dust that had been visible for twenty minutes. He climbed on board, requested a drink, then fell asleep. Quiet and stillness woke him. The other passengers were sitting next to the side of the bus. A few of them argued and pointed to a flat tire. The bus driver sorted through the luggage tank and grumbled in a bellicose voice to his swamper that he could find no jack. Hugo suggested they put jerricans under the bumper and dig a hole under the wheel. Men cheered. When the wheel turned freely the man searched through the canvas tool bag but found no wheel wrench. Voices murmured in response to the announcement that they were stranded after all.

Evening drifted towards darkness. In the twilight, the desert ran rough and fading to the south. On the left, the High Atlas rose obliquely with its summits reflecting the alpenglow. The heat radiated skywards. Hugo watched the colors fade and the earth's contours grow thick. Seeing his fellow passengers at prayer made him mindful of his errors and the need for better planning. He spread the Michelin Carte #953 on the sand. But before he could examine it thoroughly, the light was gone and the piste became a line marked by campfires. Night air washed swiftly from the High Atlas, spreading coolness through the valleys and making his hair dance. The shapes of night became indistinct, the sand and rock slightly silvered by the luster of multiple stars.

The driver spread his tea makings on a blanket, then lit the stove. Bursts of flame shot from the seams, causing him to jump off the piste. He turned the flow down a little and fifteen minutes later, the water boiled. He offered Hugo a cup; they all drank the tea in silence, until sometime past midnight lights crawled towards them across the earth. A half hour later, the driver of a large truck brought out a wheel wrench and insisted he have the privilege of replacing the tire. Hugo gave him a package of cigarettes. That night the bus coasted through Ouarzazate in moonless silence and at dawn stopped a few hundred yards beyond Er-Rachidia. Hugo got out and began to walk a trail towards the village, which was terraced steeply up the edge of a dry riverbed.

Waiting for nothing he sat on a thin metal chair set on the earthen floor of the village café. The front of the room was an open archway through which he could look down the steep, angled street, past the descending warren of doorways blackened by shadow. A morning breeze blew gusts of cooler air up from the valley. He drank thick, black coffee and watched the start of the village day, a thinly nurtured life in a poor village, squatting under the mountains, life that expanded concentrically with the rising heat of day. One by one the desert men slipped from the building to do whatever they did for a living. A few old men remained. Sharp, strident music blared from cheap speakers hung with wire on the adobe walls. Hugo sipped the bitter drink and swayed his head side to side in sympathy with the voice that sang of suffering and want.

In the late afternoon he climbed to the top of the last street, higher still onto the barren foothills and sat on a rock. To the south, a flank of the Anti-Atlas sloped down eastwards and he could see beyond it the flatness of the land, the desert proper going away from him towards the tropics. He slept under the stars that night and very early the next morning boarded a bus for the one hundred kilometer ride to Figuig. On board he found a Welshman afflicted with diarrhea. He sat behind Hugo and after a few kilometers, croaked in a loud voice, "I'm burning up with thirst. I need some tea."

The driver ignored him until it was time to stop for the break at Boudnib. The man, whose name was Roy, staggered around the back of the hut and unsteady on his feet knelt shakily to ready his stove. Twice he ran off a discreet distance and lowered his pants.

"I'll take care of the tea," said Hugo. "You take care of yourself." As Hugo busied himself with the kettle and the stove, the Welshman spread a line of puddles across the brown rock then staggered back. The water in the kettle boiled. Before Hugo could remove it, a screaming pillar of steam shot into the air and the stove blew violently apart. They all leaped back. A sheet of flame consumed the branches of a small bush. Roy guzzled water from his canteen and stared at the blaze. After a few comments, the driver announced that the bus was leaving. Roy announced in reply that he would be leaving for heaven soon, climbed into his seat, and collapsed. At Figuig he was delirious and incontinent. Hugo went with the other passengers to the frontier post to have their documents checked. Inside the building, the rude and deformed adjutant harassed the driver.

"There should be one more. Where is he?"

"He's very sick," said the driver. "He can't leave the bus."

"He's right," moaned Roy. "I can't stop here. I'm dying. Drying up like a gourd. I need medical attention."

Not satisfied, the officer ordered the soldiers to do their duty. With no concern for the sick man's complaint, they dragged him from the vehicle. Twice they threw him down so he could defecate in the town square. When they sat him on the veranda, he crawled into the corner and put Hugo's stove and tea gear by the wall, then he collapsed in pitiful whimpering. Hugo sat next to him and reluctantly scrounged in his satchel to give the sick man a tablet from a brown bottle. "This will get you to Oujda."

Roy trembled and swallowed it. With shaking hands, he continued to set up the stove beneath the nose of the adjutant. The chief came onto the veranda and waved his hand in contempt at the sick man. Distastefully tapping his toe against a skinny leg, he said to Hugo, "You will have to go to Oujda with the others, monsieur, and take this thing with you. No one can cross here. The frontier is in dispute. There is no way through."

"No way?"

The chief shook his head. "No way."

Hugo consulted the Michelin Carte #953 and showed it to the officer. "Who owns what? Moroccans? Algerians? It all belongs to Allah. You are all Muslims."

The chief smiled. "The Prophet says Morocco owns it and Allah says you will not get across here." He yelled further orders to his adjutant, who squirmed his thin body back through the door with an insolent smirk.

"Amen," wheezed Roy and looked up from his stove. "Morons, Hugo. Let them roast in their goat fucking hell."

He poured water in the kettle and put a match to the gas jet. When the open flame touched the gas, the second stove exploded. Roy staggered backwards. The shock went directly to his bowels. He stepped back from the wreckage of the stove and dropped his shorts, but as he bent, the fire singed his buttocks. He stood up with a jerk and a yelp, trying to avoid the progression of flames that spread up the wooden sides of the building. Hugo retreated off the porch on the heels of the commandant. Black smoke rose to the tops of the palms. The soldiers panicked and ran to the other side of the square where the chief rallied them. They all stood in a line and watched the building burn, with the naked Welshman framed by the inferno, screaming for revenge. Hugo went around to the back door, and with the aid of the bus driver, retrieved their documents. Then he took Roy by the collar of his shirt and shoved him into the bus, which was idling, ready for departure. It drove away through a screen of black smoke with Hugo waving encouragement to the sick man's miserable face pressed to the glass.

On the far side of the smoke he bumped into the malformed adjutant. "Quickly, monsieur. If you want to go across, give me one hundred dinars and I will see you get across tomorrow morning, first light."

Hugo examined the man's eyes for a sign of honesty, then supplied him with the exact amount.

"Go now to the café at the top of the next street," said the soldier. "Wait. A girl will come, who is a guide and a smuggler."

At the café Hugo ordered plain food and a carafe of coffee. In an hour all men except him had left the building to escape the heat of midday. Only the occasional goat wandered through the baking streets. Hot wind poured madly through doors and windows. Hugo waited. Throughout the day a few women labored up the steep thoroughfare. He waved at them with the mannerism of a twitch, but not one veil went lower than the tip of a nose, no raised eyebrows or smiles acknowledged his presence. He continued this scrutiny, until hours later, the old men returned. The wind eased. The patrons drank coffee and tapped their fingers to the music.

"More coffee, monsieur?"

"Enough," Hugo replied to his host. Wearied by the watch, he got to his feet. As he adjusted his straw hat, from a distant doorway emerged a tall woman with bare arms and bangles on her wrists. She drifted like a dervish along the distorted hill road, striding past dark thresholds, but lingered momentarily when she passed him. Her necklace showed dozens of colored beads, which she slid gently up and down a silver string. Reflections in her black marble eyes suggested to Hugo that he reconsider the benefits of sight. He stepped through the arched door into the road, which was deserted.

"I've been expecting you," he said, "hoping that I can proceed on this journey without fear of delay."

She made no move to answer. Hugo judged that the black stone of her eyes was set in the most perfect face in Er-Rachidia, perhaps all of North Africa; and to establish that fact he gently removed her veil to expose a mouth with white teeth surrounded by full dark lips. The girl put a finger to them in the gesture of silence. Hugo looked around, up and down the street. An old woman shuffled across the path and the girl covered her face with the veil. She reached into her bag and put a colored stone into Hugo's hand and ran away.

He turned the pebble in his fingers for examination. It was red and of no unusual shape. With the stone pressed in his hand, he wandered through the hot passageways. He pretended not to look for her, but turned at every movement of a dog or the scraping of sand thrown up by the wind. After an hour's search he entered an alley, to the stall of a merchant who had little else to sell besides used phonograph records, house wares, and old books. At the back of the shop were a dozen stoves set out on the floor for display. He bought a replacement from among the best made and another vial of India ink. After he paid the shopkeeper, he wandered back towards the books, hesitating by a burlap curtain to examine a display of red polished rocks. He picked up the brightest and compared it to his own. Then he moved his arm to throw open the curtain flap. His hand shook and sweat rolled off the tip of his nose.

"Something else, monsieur?"

"*Non, merci.* I've got everything I came for," he replied and left the shop. After walking a distance down the winding alley, he pulled his hat lower against the setting sun and considered how life contracts to single surprising elements, in this case, the distinct smell of the girl behind the curtain, less than an arm's length away. He walked further through the dust. The glare from the adobe walls blinded him and for a moment he felt he had lost his way. He leaned against a pillar feeling dizzy, mad from the heat, anxious that the fragrance of roses seemed to come from all directions.

As the light went at dusk, Hugo walked down the road that led to the border. It showed little evidence of traffic and was littered with refuse, some blown in, some dumped by human hands. In the final gloom he could see the frontier itself, the quarantine area with grotesque shapes of abandoned machinery and armor. Finding a secure patch of ground in a thicket of bush, he lay out his blanket. During the passing evening, thoughts went through his head about the need for clear boundaries. He would have written a few words on the struggle, to see under whose light the safe roads would be built so that he could judge who would triumph in the game. But he feared that even one lit match might reveal him. His sleep that night was dreamless, but he awoke startled, with his right hand rising in an arc to strike. At the sight of dark eyes he drew back and stared into the face of the Berber girl. She sat down against the trunk of a tree and remained motionless.

"As soon as it is light enough for us to see," she whispered, "we will go.... and go fast. We have only a few minutes to be across, through the fence. The guards are punctual. But at night they don't watch." As they waited for the light to be sufficient, she asked, "Why do you go this way? Why not just go to Oujda?"

Hugo slowly let out his breath. He went to light a cigarette, then stopped. "Since I was a boy, I had my heart set on seeing Beni Ounif."

The girl laughed. "Then you should see it," she said. "and get your visa."

Hugo readied his things. When she rose he followed. The track wound pointlessly through the debris. Without hesitating the girl veered through unexpected detours into areas where the going was slower. Other times, she ran over flat ground with no impediments. With the stench of rot and gunpowder in his nose, he stepped only where she had stepped, past the hulks of burned-out trucks and shattered tanks, avoiding cars shredded by cannon fire. They moved cleanly through the entire mass of steel and garbage to a narrow gap in the high metal fence, went through, past more debris on the other side, and into thick bushes. The girl collapsed into the dirt and lay shaded by the leaves.

When she had recovered, she said, "I'm going to a settlement north of Beni Ounif where my brother lives. Tomorrow morning I come back with other things, perhaps more people."

Hugo watched her face as she talked and estimated her age as fifteen. He reached into his satchel and took out some money and handed it to her. "I wish it could be more, but I don't have much."

She looked at the bills and smiled. "If it could be more, it would be more, I'm sure."

Hugo took her hand and said, "One more thing, my friend." He reached into his satchel, took out his knife, and handed it to her. He ran a line up his plaster cast with his finger. "Put it on the inside, sharp edge out, and cut this off."

She did so and when it was off said, "Why didn't you remove it yourself?"

Hugo examined his thin white limb. "Because now, whenever I look at my arm, when I watch it heal and strengthen into normal use, I will always be reminded of you, who helped me."

Her head nodded as she took the plaster, put it in the bag, and said, "Goodbye, and may Allah bless you."

In a moment she was out of sight in the thin stalks and coarse leaves of the grove. "And may you never lose your way across the frontiers of life and suffer consequences," he called after her in a whisper, then picked his own way through the undergrowth, and finding a road, walked along it until he saw the Poste Douane, a small shack on the edge of Beni Ounif, Algeria.

Dried spittle crusted Hugo's lips from his waterless journey across the frontier. His face and hair were filthy. He pleaded with mock distress to the sentry, who took him directly to the Chef de Surete, where he stood stiffly to attention and offered an explanation for the incomplete state of his papers—he had been driven out of Morocco by a violent official and had no opportunity to secure a visa.

"*Merde*," said the official.

Hugo smiled faintly. "No, that was the Welshman. He had very bad *merde, tres malade.*"

"And your lies aren't shit as well?"

"No. Life is a struggle, even for foreigners. We say what is necessary. That's how men go from crisis to crisis and stay married."

The officer nodded with his mouth open and his eyes going side to side. He walked to the window and stared at the open patch of sand then grunted. "How did you get across? The girl?"

Hugo didn't answer. The official sat down at his desk and took out a large book and pen. "It will cost you five pounds sterling for a thirty-day visa. That's the most I can give you."

"Five pounds is a lot of money," Hugo said.

"It is. But I do what is necessary to avoid the crisis you talked of. Not all of this money goes to public accounts. Some of it goes directly to feed hungry mouths."

"I don't object," said the traveler.

"Anyway, if you ever go south, you should know that the requirement of a visa for the Republic of Mali, obtainable I'm told only in Paris, will cost you forty pounds sterling. They make you pay down there, *mon amis.*"

Hugo put his passport in his satchel, walked to the door and said, "I hope never to go."

Chapter XVIII

Seamen's Mission

Hugo left Beni Ounif at 3:30 pm on Wednesday, May 19. He waited an hour for the first ride, a truck of the Ministre des Affaires Sociales. One Arab sat silently as he drove; the others made small talk. Hugo related the episode concerning his Welsh friend. The men laughed, talked, and smoked the two hundred kilometers to Ain Sefra, arriving after the desert twilight had died to darkness. They led Hugo to a café buried on the side of the main street. They ate chips and liver, drank coffees, and talked some more. Then in the dim starlight, Hugo walked three kilometers north to a place where cool air pooled in hollows of the Saharien Mountains. He placed his blanket ten meters from the road. The temperature fell lower. He shuffled through the books and papers and regretted not being able to find any warm clothing in his musty leather case, nothing to keep the cold away except what he could imagine. Around him the air was sterile, with no odor of vegetation.

    At six in the morning with the sun reheating the earth, he flagged a ride with a small lorry loaded with goats. In a few hours they arrived in Mecheria, which lay scattered on the hillside like an arrangement of bones. He chose not to enter its streets, but waited in the excited wind of the valley, content to eat food from a tin can. The landscape changed at Saida. Green foliage spread over the hills, and flowers glowed in the fields. He had some food and watched three men fight over something he could not comprehend. At Mascara a young Algerian driving an antique truck mistook his direction and took him to Oran. Empty, misused land melded with the concrete foundations of the city described in books as the center of a new era, the new domain, the new future of Ahmed Ben Bella, the President of Algeria's future. Hugo bought bread and ate a meal squatting with the dogs and beggars who gathered at the smell of food.

    The driver of a large Berliot picked him up the next day. By mid-afternoon the road carved upwards through forested hills. The rig labored up the grade to the summit of the Atlas and at the top, plunged fifty kilometers into Algiers. When they broke through the arc of high ridges joining land to sea, the young swamper pointed proudly. Spread across the western limb, the city curved like a visor of white houses dimpled with green cascading trees, lush squares, streets, and parks tumbling down amid ships floating on a blue ocean. For a moment Hugo felt the yearning of Juliana, who would have wept at the sight of her home.

For an hour he sat at a bus exchange and watched the ebb and flow of faces in the afternoon sun. He hiked up the L'avenue des Etats-Unis towards the summit and on the way asked directions from the sentries guarding the Presidential palace. They were surly and reluctant. Hugo offered them five cigarettes each. One of them gestured up the street. The attendant at the iron gates of the British Embassy pointed to the sign, which said that it was closed. He waited for the afternoon opening and made some enquiries.

At the waterfront he sat on a stone bench to watch the sun fall. In a few minutes the painted ships collapsed to indistinct points of light. He found a courtyard hours later, jumped the fence where it joined stairs to the railway, and laid out his blanket to sleep. Scurrying rats feet woke him a dozen times during the night. Sunlight, flies, and traffic made morning sleep impossible. In the northeast corner of Port Said Square he sat at a sidewalk café. At the next table a man with a plaid coat nodded politely. He was still talking when Hugo set off to find the address written on a piece of paper by the official at the embassy.

The building's directory did not list Crasson's name. Next to the correct suite number was printed "Von Raynor." He went next to the offices of Crasson et Fils in the dock district. A clear-faced young woman said, "Monsieur Crasson is retired. He will be either at home or his other place."

"Pardon, did you say his summer place?"

"Yes, summer place," she said.

He noticed on her wrist a gold bracelet set with jewels. "That is a very nice piece," he said.

"Thank you."

"I know something about jewelry. Could I have a look?"

She moved to take it off her wrist, but hesitated. Hugo told her to leave it on and took her hand. The woman frowned and leaned over. Hugo described for her the interesting arrangement of gems set with white gold suggesting her boyfriend must think highly of her.

"Or is it your fiancé?" he said, moving to the door. She looked suspicious and smiled at him with a curled lip. Hugo came away from the office knowing she had lied, that she had clearly said, "his other place."

At the family home a serving man said, "Other place, monsieur? He has no other place."

"How about summer house, a seaside villa, perhaps?"

"A summer house? Maybe you're referring to the Hotel Palma in Tripoli, where Monsieur Crasson often goes, but mainly in the fall. In summer, people here usually go into the High Atlas to get above the heat. Crasson has no such residence up there."

Neither did Hugo have a place to escape the heat—and the sun was hot. It was cooler on the promenade. For an hour he sat there, alone with his thoughts. The *Ville D'Oran* from Marseille docked, and crowds of people came and went from the edge of the rainless water. The port of Algiers, he knew, was rainless for the hot season. But the proximity to ships, docks and the sea would in other months have suggested to him the imaginary vessel of his youth that towed behind it the priceless freight of his early dreams. Hugo had a moment of regret for Solly's lost ring and the many other treasures he had recently turned his back on.

For dinner, he walked back to the café on the corner of Port Said square. He was surprised to see the man in the plaid coat sitting at the table where he had talked to him the day before. "You should have a better place to sleep, Hugo, at least better than the boat landing," he said. "Try the Mission to Seamen on Rue Santeria. You might find a bed there."

A man named Sloan was at the bar of the Mission, and introduced Hugo to the others. "Can't offer you a bed tonight, mate," he said in a north London voice. He pulled the draft lever with a thin arm, which looked like the leather strap on Hugo's case. "This afternoon we had to refuse three British ship-jumpers, That's what they were, eh Dora?—scarpers, young blokes leaving their ship in Bougie because they were homesick for egg and chips in West Ham. The Embassy's obliged to see to their welfare. I'm going off shopping for the buggers now. Want to come with?" He set out some pints, then continued, "About the bed…I don't think we can. What say Dora, probably not, eh?"

The director's wife stepped up. Her fatty bosom shook and stretched the buttons of her stained blouse. "Come tomorrow night, Hugo," she said in a kind voice. "Yeah, we'll do it tomorrow, lad."

Hugo went with Sloan to buy fruits and vegetables. After returning, he played darts with a Spaniard named Abdul, then wrote and sketched for three hours. That night he sat near the door and read through a book, published in 1958, outlining trans-African highways. While Dora cooked dinner, he ignored the sweet smell of grease and read, "The road from Mamfe through Kumba in the French Cameroon is tortuous but well maintained."

The next morning he borrowed a scooter from Sloan, who used it only for a periodic ride along the promenade. Struggling up the steep road, the small conveyance spewed a steady column of smoke. Hugo found a knoll at the top with a good view of the car park. Over the course of the day he left only to buy coffee. In the afternoon, a Mercedes parked next to the door. A man about sixty years old and the girl from Crasson et Fils went into the building. Hugo ran from the knoll, through the front door, and noted that the lift indicator had stopped at the eleventh floor. At dark, he rode back to the Mission.

On Monday no one came. On Tuesday, thirty minutes past the dinner hour, the man he thought was Crasson came out of the building. Hugo followed him down the steep roads, coasting the scooter through the twilight. They came into the main part of the city with the small machine zipping along in traffic behind the black car until it stopped at a restaurant. At the seven the next night he followed the man to the same place. On the following evening, Hugo dressed in his one good set of clothes and went to the restaurant. At seven fifteen the suspected Morrice Crasson entered with a squat, thick man whose eyes had the dull ache of a servant. Hugo asked the bartender to deliver a complimentary drink to his table. When it arrived, Hugo also went to the table carrying his own cocktail, glancing once at the bodyguard, who remained by the door.

"Monsieur Crasson, I believe. My name is Hugo Haultain. May I…"

Crasson nodded, looked briefly at him, then returned his eyes to the magazine in his hand. Hugo sat down; the square man moved closer. Crasson took a package of cigarettes off the table and took one out. When Hugo offered him the flame of his Zippo, the hand of the squat man moved onto his shoulder. The hand withdrew at a slight nod of Crasson's head. He leaned forward a few inches to put his cigarette into the flame. "*Merci*, and thank you also for the drink," he said.

Hugo reached into his pocket and took out the package. Before he could remove a cigarette, Morrice Crasson offered one of his. The square man stepped back. "*Merci*," Hugo repeated, lit his cigarette, then continued. "Monsieur Crasson, like many men, I have an appreciation for quality. This includes women, especially those who wear fine jewelry. Just the other day I noticed an attractive young woman with an expensive bracelet. At heart I'm a jeweler and know quality gems and good design. But this particular one, with a cluster of diamonds offset by alternating opals and sapphires was unusual. The settings were done in white gold with an elaborate filigree. I said to this woman, whom I didn't know, that her suitor must think very highly of her."

Hugo took a sip of his drink. The square man came around to his side. "The purpose of mentioning the young woman with the bracelet is this: I know another lady of notable good looks, quite young, just twenty-six. I'm of the opinion that she would be of interest to you."

"What gives you that opinion, monsieur?" Crasson's eyes remained fixed on his magazine.

"Because, when she was a bit younger, she was well-known to you."

"Do you have a name?"

"Yes I do. But the thing is: What am I doing talking away here like a fool, when I could be showing you her picture—not the best picture, mind you, with her just lying there."

Hugo went to reach into his satchel and the serving man stood closer. He opened it wide so the man could see into it, then pulled out the brown manila envelope.

"I don't want to look at dirty pictures here, monsieur."

"Not dirty, perhaps a bit rusty."

Crasson's eyes narrowed. Hugo set the envelope in front of him and the old man took out the photo. He looked slightly puzzled and fumbled for his glasses. "Is this a joke?" The squat man move so close that Hugo could feel his hip.

"A line of old rusty ships?"

"Read the name."

Crasson picked up the photo and held it close to his eyes. He started to smile then turned it over. "The *Kyle Mission*! Where did this come from?"

"I took the original picture. What you have there is an un-retouched, enlarged duplicate."

"*Tabernac*," muttered Crasson, sat further back in his seat, and had to relight his cigarette. "What did you say your name was?"

"Hugo Haultain."

"Of course, Mr. Haultain. You're a young man. May I ask what your connection is to this wreck?"

"I spent a summer with Allan Korrolus. It was a whim of his that I locate the remains of this ship. After that, by chance I met a man called George Blenkinthorpe, after him Captain Von Raynor, and a few months back, Major Owen Dring, all of them long retired from service."

Crasson gave half a smile and sat contemplating the photo. The bodyguard moved to the bar. "It must be more than whim for you to journey abroad meeting old men once connected with a dead ship. Or is this history of an academic nature?"

"One thing led to another."

Crasson raised his eyebrow. "All the way to North Africa?"

"Boredom, monsieur. Curiosity. Compulsion. Nothing better to do."

"Playing the tourist?"

Hugo nodded his head.

"As long as you are convinced. May I ask where are you staying?"

"The Mission to Seamen."

"The cot in the back room? I've spent nights there in past years. I daresay it hasn't changed. How is Sloan?"

"He's well, and Dora."

"Is the piano still there?"

"I play it from time to time," answered Hugo and took a sip of his drink. Crasson did the same before asking, "Are you free to have dinner with me tomorrow evening?"

"Certainly. I never turn down free food."

Crasson rose from the seat and smoothed his suit jacket. "Sometimes the traveler has to sleep where he can and take the food that's offered. I understand perfectly." Hugo nodded.

Crasson smiled. "So that brings me to my own curiosity. When you play the piano, do you by chance play Beethoven's *Moonlight Sonata*?"

"As dinner music only—a payment for board and lodging."

"And why not? And play anything else you like," the old man answered.

"I will. My tutor, a man named Conrad Muir, taught me many fine tunes."

Crasson raised his eyebrow and cocked his head in a questioning manner.

"Yes, many fine tunes, Monsieur Crasson. He remembered all the tunes he learned. Generally speaking Conrad was the kind of man who wouldn't forget the slightest detail of his life, most of which he related to me, being his only son. I've always thought that to be a worthwhile asset over a long life."

Crasson's smile faded. He turned to go, then held up his hand to slow the serving man. "Interesting connection. But one last question for tonight. The bracelet you mentioned, the one with the diamonds and opals...?"

Hugo took a drag on his cigarette and frowned. "I'm sorry, did I mention a bracelet?"

Crasson nodded and looked pleased. "Tomorrow night at six-thirty, here," he said, then went to the door.

Hugo walked along the promenade to the Seaman's Mission. When the patrons had left and Dora began cleaning up, he sat at the piano. But he had unusual difficulty reaching the keyboard, as if it was too high for his hands and he would require a boost, some greater effect than books piled on the bench. He was overcome by the sense that he would never be quite high enough to play it again.

The next morning he went to a boulevard café on Port Said Square. From his satchel he took out a copy of Schweitzer's *Aus Meinen Leben en Denken* that the shopkeeper in Gibraltar had given him. Flies droned around his head. He read the book for an hour, then scanned a few random pages of the local paper followed by articles in *Paris Match* dedicated to the triumph of bushmen, who staggered from the jungles barely able to move under the weight of mortars and machine guns. He scanned reports of disturbances in the Sudan, the partition of Angola, the succession of Katanga province from the Congo. The editorial spoke with disdain of fascists in the south of the continent who ruled, they said, with an iron fist.

Hugo folded the paper and decided such things were entertainment, but also relevant to his future needs. He sat in the bright and peaceful North African sun, obliged to acknowledge the hint of duplicity around him. People argued in the cafés with superficial restraint. Few smiled, but most seemed resigned to the coming change. Morrice Crasson would fit well, would be amongst the most vicious. The benefits of winning were many. Hugo imagined him in bed with the office girl, precisely at the moment of her ecstasy with her long legs spread wide on the sheets, and her jewels displayed coyly as an auxiliary delight.

As the sun dipped behind the western crescent of Algiers and the Mediterranean shone with a transparent shower of gold, Hugo's ponderings gave him a profound spike of optimism. He walked back to the Mission and dressed. Over dinner with Crasson, he related the contradictory details of his meetings with Korrolus, Blenkinthorpe, Von Raynor and Dring. Crasson seemed pleased, or at least satisfied. They were drinking brandy when Crasson suggested he stay at the flat disguised with Von Raynor's name, "the other place" as Hugo had called it.

The inner neighborhood, Leopoldville. March 7, 1966.

Past two months into the new year...Antoine slid back the port and said, "Master, I ask you to be merciful—you have some medicines now."

"What do you want, Antoine?"

"There is a man injured."

"Another one of your relatives? I already have too many people to see. Take him to hospital."

"You know that only the dead go to the hospital."

"What's wrong with him?"

"He is like the others you've treated, and the many still waiting—quite beset with infections. I can't stand the smell."

That night the jailer smuggled into Hugo's cell a man who kept saying, "*Merci, merci....*" The candlelight exposed, amongst a host of lesions, a large, infected wound on his leg. Hugo cleaned out the wound, stuffed it with gauze soaked in hydrogen peroxide, then wrapped it. Later he said to Antoine, "He must come once a day. The wound is too old for me to stitch together. But one thing...get Sergeant Mintou to bring more medicine, antiseptics, and bandages. He can steal them from the barracks commissary. Tell him the medicine is for me...to keep me alive. He would like that."

Over the course of two weeks, Hugo cleaned and bound the man's wound. When the man limped unsteadily into the cell weeks later, and ran his calloused fingers over the healing wound, he cried silently so as not to arouse the guards. With all aspects of his creased face, he gave Hugo a look of gratitude—but it was the one long finger pointing at his healing leg that brought the doctor to a point where he felt an enduring sympathy for him. After the final inspection, he let the prisoner limp from the cell using the leper Basile's carved walking stick. That night, with a fresh candle Antoine had supplied, he read a small portion of the book received as a gift from Korrolus and for the first time glimpsed something of the author's intentions. The following day he drew a sketch of his patient, with his finger pointing to the healing scar and his withered face in a clear light. But the man in the sketch who administered the aid was not a likeness of himself.

As time went and Hugo used his evenings and early mornings for dispensing what he could for other prisoners, he found his supply of medicines severely depleted. Mintou could find nothing to re-supply him from the commissary. "The soldiers sell everything they steal," he said.

A day later he came into Hugo's cell accompanied by an aide. "I can't help you any more, monsieur. Because of my new skills, I've been promoted to the rank of captain. As well, I have been ordered back to Luozi for a few weeks, maybe for good."

Hugo leaned back on his case and stared at the newly minted officer of the Congolese Army. "Congratulations on your progress, Léon. But I want the whole truth from you. Tell me now if you aren't coming back here. I will have to make other plans concerning your lessons, perhaps other plans generally."

"I have the book and all my instruction. I know how to study, monsieur. And, don't worry, I will find my way back here to pass your test. Hopefully, you will survive to pass mine."

The captain offered his hand, and Hugo took it. As he watched the young man slam the door shut, he sensed other means of survival forming in his brain, because he knew Mintou, if he returned at all, would not return in any mood to jeopardize his advancing career. On his next meeting with the jailer, Hugo told him, "Buy all the medicine and bandages you can find—from the black market if needed."

"I will do that, Doctor," said Antoine.

"Don't call me that," Hugo complained. "Others might get the wrong impression. I would be pestered more than I am now."

"You are already pestered to the limit, monsieur. You are getting the reputation as a man with limitless ju-ju."

With limitless energy, Antoine contributed to Hugo's medical ju-ju by purchasing gauze, antiseptics, and tape instead of wine or sweets from the local markets. When he was off-duty he ranged through the neighborhoods with one of his wives to find rare antibiotics. He bought things wherever he could find them, which included, as he said one day, "The Petit Pont Café and the Memling Hotel, both full of mercenaries here to screw the beautiful whores. And one other thing…if you should ever happen to meet my favorite wife, don't mention that I notice such things."

With Antoine receiving a cash bonus to strengthen his sense of duty, the contents of the medical kit expanded. Hugo also trained the jailer to differentiate between a chronically sick man and one who was temporarily under the weather. He would bring the sick or injured down the corridor on the pretense of escorting them to the latrine and instead secret them into cell six. Hugo would examine them to decide if he could help in a way that would see them back in their own cells before the guards in the north wing could react.

Soon the unofficial clinic expanded to include soldiers from the barracks. Hugo worried that the newly installed commandant would hear of the practice and shut him down as a threat. Weeks passed with no interference until one evening a soldier snuck in his wife for an examination of her troublesome pregnancy. For the next week, a series of guards paced outside in the corridor to make sure that, after using the latrine, all prisoners went directly to their cells and that no staff came into the cell wing. For a week Hugo sat alone and read. In the dark of the evenings and nights he recalled elements of the past. All the while he feared that if his duties did not resume, the past would catch up to the present, squeezing all future time into the static space of his cell. And if that happened, Captain Mintou would not get to write his test. But this state of affairs didn't last long. His next patient was the commandant himself, who came after eight days, saying he was too busy to go to the hospital and had a sore back. In the line forming behind him was the soldier with the pregnant wife.

Algiers, June 17, 1965

Crasson showed his guest the details of the suite, then made tea in the kitchen. Hugo walked around it for a second time and still felt he had not seen enough. The main room had a view of the harbor, a small window looking east and one west. On the walls were paintings of the desert and the sea. In the room that served as Crasson's office hung posters underscored with political messages. The largest was an official portrait of President Ahmed Ben Bella and next to it a smaller photo of Colonel Boumedienne. On the bedroom walls hung a photo collage of relatives. Scattered about were postcards of South America, a sombrero, and other less flamboyant hats. When Crasson poured the tea, he seemed preoccupied and looked around furtively, at the kitchen portrait and papers lying on the table. Hugo had the feeling his host was involved. In what, he wasn't prepared to say.

The old man took out his briefcase and the photo of the *Kyle Mission*. "Around Christmas, nineteen forty-two, a few days after Admiral Darlan was assassinated by a disgruntled traitor, I was called to off-load a ship bearing the name *SS Kyle Mission*, recently arrived in convoy from America. Strangely, the ship was commanded by a British naval officer, introduced to me as Allan Korrolus. He had a recent leg wound and after medical attention was ordered to convalesce aboard the freighter. We proceeded to plan the disposition of all the cargo. Besides the huge quantity of ordnance, this included a shipment of goods destined for trans-shipment on a coastal boat for Libreville. I knew for a fact that this boat had been sunk. Consequently, we planned to store the goods in one of my warehouses and wait for instruction. A short time later a man came into my office with receipts indicating ownership and explained to me what he intended. He rented one of my lorries, loaded it to the full and, going against my good advice, met his fate. Or that is what I thought. For your sake, monsieur, I'm glad I was wrong.

"For three years the rest of the goods consigned to Libreville sat in my warehouse. I had opportunity many times to turn a quick profit by selling them. But I resisted. I don't want to talk of morals here. I was convinced that they were black-market contraband, and even after the war, selling would have been easy. I was justified to recoup costs, and there was always a great need for things. One day in 1946, a man with a Swiss passport came to my door, a Captain Juri Von Raynor, and said to me, 'I think you knew my brother, Conrad Muir.'

"I said I knew him, had met him during the war. I told this captain what I knew of your father's adventure in North Africa and that he could have his brother's goods. All he had to do was pay me three years' demeurrage. We sat down together for a drink and he told me a tale I thought far-fetched. Since I was facing a man who made a reputation by sending ships to the bottom without conscience, I found it hard to digest that he had, for some quirk of his character, voluntarily refrained from sinking the *Kyle Mission*. Korrolus had told me otherwise. Of course he refused to pay me the storage costs, so I directed him to the Mission anyway, feeling he would be comfortable. There he met Blenkinthorpe and Korrolus. George and I had small business going, but Korrolus was still adrift after his discharge. In the next few days Von Raynor outlined a mad plan to distribute his brother's goods at a profit. Of course we considered him a bit deranged. And the hatred, the rawness of war never fades, never gets less. Not one of us would ever have had the stomach for getting involved with a bossy, arrogant kraut. Nevertheless there was guilt. We all had a memory of sacrifice. In the end, Birks went to equatorial Africa. Wallace Fraser got as far as Nigeria, with no intention of going further. And of Major Dring, you have brought me up to date."

"What became of the goods?"

"I bought them from Von Raynor at a discount, less my costs, but that was only prudent business." Crasson paced the floor, went out of the kitchen to the front window then returned before saying, "I'm going now. The linen has been changed, in case you're concerned."

Hugo nodded and declined to say to his host that although clean bedding was essential to good health, he wouldn't have objected to any fragrance the bracelet girl might have left on the sheets.

Crasson stood by the door. "I'll be back tomorrow," he said. "We can go for lunch at a favorite place of mine near the waterfront."

When he had gone, Hugo locked the door and went into the bedroom. He suspected the girl had made the bed because Morrice Crasson was no more a tidy man than he was truthful. With no real sense of security, he ripped off his clothes, laundered them in the bath, and hung them to dry. Then he washed himself, being careful to clean his left arm of the powdered trace of the plaster. Lastly. he sat on a cedar chest carved with the image of a dog and stared at the sweep of Mediterranean. After the glittering harbor lights became a blur to his eyes, he went to bed and slept for ten hours. He was already up when Crasson let himself in the next day.

"We will walk," he said, and they went off immediately on the route that would take them to the promenade on Port Said Square. Hugo noted that the serving man was not with them. On the way down the hill, Crasson seemed preoccupied. His chin sat on his chest and he looked up every minute to survey the street ahead. At the Boulevard Des Etats-Unis, he walked faster and Hugo had to jog to catch up. When they came to the gate leading to the

Presidential palace, the Frenchman slowed to a casual stroll and led them to the other side of the street. The sentries waved and Crasson faced the other way. When they had turned the first corner he resumed his brisk pace.

At the Café Des Deux Hommes they sat with a group of men who talked Arabic. Hugo drank coffee and looked out the window. Families walked the promenade and watched the ferry from Marseilles dock and unload. The atmosphere seemed frivolous enough, but Hugo thought it only superficial. His earlier assessment was correct. No one smiled; the crowd was anxious. People pointed as if they were poised to flee or strike out. Crasson had the waiter put more coffee and plates of food on the table. When they had finished eating, Hugo asked questions. He was sure Crasson might talk generally about the situation in Africa.

"I know a little," he answered. "But here is a revelation: the Belgian Congo five years ago. Imagine scores of blacks sitting on the railroad tracks west of Leopoldville. They wait for 'freedom' to roll towards them. But no one needs abstractions to be free, just the ability to make a living. The imperialists perverted things—and freedom became slavery. The Congo was the worst. Tens of thousands were slaughtered. But now comes independence. What's that? What's this word, 'independence'? Soon enough they realized that the freedom to wander around and do your business means nothing if hired criminals can take the food from your mouth, and your wife as well. Independence replaced Belgian overlords with local thugs, licensed to plunder and kill." Crasson lit a cigarette and continued, "So sorry for the people, eh, who at first welcomed the chance to see what 'freedom' looked like. You must admit, it must have been pretty damn big to be hauled around on a train." He chuckled. "Africa is not an easy place to travel, *mon amis*, with just a thin membrane of European civility stretched taut over a dead carcass. If you carry on from here, best to consider it a bizarre and dirty thing, like a good weekend in London: lots of fun but try to avoid catching a disease that might kill you."

Crasson resumed talking to his friends. Hugo looked to the figures scurrying along the promenade. People moved into the shadows. Inside was no less a feeling of aborted hopes. It was midday, but the windows and small candles barely lit the room. In some corners, the lack of details seemed a menace. Crasson appeared heaved with unusual anger as he offered comments Hugo couldn't hear. In the afternoon they went back to the flat along a different route. They had hardly arrived when his host said, "I go off again, my friend, but I'll be back in an hour."

He shook Hugo's hand firmly and for several seconds. He had the look of a man not quite ready to confess. Hugo bought food from a market two blocks away. When Crasson let himself in, he was stirring a pan of vegetables. They ate and spoke in half sentences of trivial things, then of Hugo's journey and African politics. Crasson smoked afterwards.

"Come with me for a minute," he said. They went down the lift and along an alley to a parked Land Rover. Fixed to the driver's door was the logo of Crasson et Fils. The old man handed Hugo a set of keys and a folder of papers. "The fuel tank is full. The vehicle is registered to the company, but this *carte de passage* shows you as the official driver—in case you are stopped."

Hugo fingered the keys and looked into the Rover. Crasson opened the rear gate and pointed inside. Hugo could see two cases of cigarettes.

"I import these. Take them. Bribery and corruption is not the exception."

Hugo strolled around the vehicle rubbing his itchy chin. Finally he said, "I appreciate your generosity, Morrice. But two questions. Am I going somewhere?"

Crasson didn't answer.

"And if I went, monsieur," Hugo asked, "why would I be stopped?"

The old man shrugged his shoulders and began to trudge back towards the block of flats. When they were at the door, he said, "Things in Africa never go as expected, my friend. Like those I mentioned, we do what we must to survive."

Crasson drove away in his Mercedes. Before he went to bed, Hugo packed all his things into the leather case and set it by the door. He put his few clothes on top of the cedar chest. Methodically, he went through every inch of the flat until he had turned up the equivalent of fifty pounds sterling hidden away in the backs of drawers and pockets of little-used suits. The last thing he did was to move the Land Rover three blocks away to a patch of dirt behind a fruit store. That night he had dreams of a queer, yellow vegetation that grew like a forest on the desert. The plants seemed already dead, decomposing, burnt by a steady drizzle of urine. He was crawling towards this malignancy when he heard Crasson's voice.

"Get your things! You have to get out quickly!" He handed Hugo a piece of folded paper. "I have time only for the salient points, my friend. There has been a coup by Boumedienne. Ben Bella is under arrest. There was a tip-off, and elements at the palace attempted a counter coup. They suspect that I was involved. I need time, a few days and Boumedienne's personal intervention."

Hugo took out a cigarette, but did not light it.

"You are my decoy," Crasson went on in a low, emphatic voice. "An accomplice, a foreign element they require to verify their suspicions. Of course it is untrue, but it will deflect their anger away long enough to get a reprieve. A week, maybe, and in the meantime, we will both have to endure."

"A week?"

"Not longer. This particular cadre has limited reach outside Algiers. Of course if they find you, they might shoot you out of fear or frustration. But if you follow my instructions you will be safe." He smiled; his expression was strained. "You're thinking that you can just walk away, *non*? But you can't. I have been watched—and you with me. Therefore you have no choice in the matter. This note will get you help in Constantine: petrol and carnets. Leave Algiers via the commercial route. After you have the assistance, cross into Tunisia at Souk Ahras. Lose yourself in the traffic and then in Tunis. Don't dally because in a few hours or sooner they will follow you. In the meantime, this will help you on your way."

He handed over an envelope Hugo could see was filled with American currency. Crasson turned, got a few things from his office, and went to the door. He picked up Hugo's case.

"I'll leave it by the door to the car park…in the left corner." He went out before Hugo could stop him.

After the elevator door closed with a bang, he dressed then took a look from the window. The sea lay calm in the morning light. Traffic moved through the streets. Some minutes later he heard the elevator door open then the noise of a scuffle. Voices in the corridor rose to a screaming. There was loud bang on the walls and more fearful screams. One voice was Crasson's, who was pleading something in Arabic. Hugo opened the cedar chest, climbed in and pulled the blankets on top of him. There was just enough room on the side to reach up and close the lid. The voices grew louder, then a loud smash like wood splintering and people bursting through the door. Boots resounded in the suite. He heard Crasson cry out in pain. Footsteps walked around the bedroom. The closet door opened and shut. Noises pierced the trunk lid: the slapping of human flesh, steel smashing through walls, a rifle bolt sliding in the breech.

The lid to the chest opened. Hugo held his breath as light showed through the piles of bedding. It became brighter as blankets were tossed aside. More cries shook the room; the chest lid slammed shut above him. The commotion faded to a murmur, then died away behind the closing outer door. He could hear other shouts and protests as if more searches were underway in the flats on either side. When no noise had come in through the wood for fifteen minutes, he opened the trunk and looked around to examine the flat. The place was a heap of broken furniture, lamps, books, and pictures torn from the walls and thrown on the floor. Large holes punctured the walls. Blood smeared the kitchen tiles and boots had tracked red patches throughout the other rooms. He got a large tumbler and put it to the door, then to the other two walls facing the corridor. No sounds. Outside on the street he could see no hint of disturbance. Cars went by; people walked. Further down, on one section of the Boulevard des Etats-Unis, he could see nothing. The road was abandoned. No people, no traffic. He watched for half an hour. Nothing passed this one section. He shook his head. An excitement rose into his throat. With his satchel over his shoulder he opened the door.

The hall was empty. He walked as quietly as he could down the eleven flights of stairs to the lobby. The closer he got to the lower floors, the louder became the echo of his boots. A listener would know he was coming. From the final landing he could see the front door. Two soldiers paced the hall. Hugo felt an easy sense of habit move into his feet and hands. He felt no fear and said to himself that it was shameful that a man would not feel fear when confronting armed men and the possibility of his own death. It would be more natural to have his legs quaking, heart pounding, his mind out of control as happened the night he fled wet and empty handed from Aldermans Green.

He tiptoed down the hall and opened the door. One soldier had gone into the car park to convene with frowning men. The other stood by the door, his gun ready with the barrel going around in whatever direction he looked. The leather case stood in the corner, shadowed from view; Hugo chuckled when considering the young soldier with a healthy shake in his muscles as he guarded Hugo's weather-beaten, inoffensive possessions. He walked up to the second floor and pressed the elevator button on the lift that went to the car park. When the door opened at the main floor, he was smoking a cigarette and drew back from the gun with mock horror.

"*Bonjour*," he said. "If you'll excuse me, that's my case in the corner. I'm going to Marseille this afternoon on the Ville d'Oran."

He gestured to the harbor as he retrieved his case. The soldier took his rifle up into Hugo's face and placed himself in front of the door.

"Oops," Hugo said. "Have to go and get some things I forgot," and lunged through the stair door and started up the steps. He was almost at the first floor landing when he could hear the soldier starting up the first flight yelling for him to stop. He went to the second door, opened it. and shut it again with a bang. Then he walked to the third floor landing and waited. At the second landing, the soldier stopped by the closed door and looked in through the safety glass. He opened it and went into the hallway.

Hugo listened. The door closed, then silence. He tiptoed down to the landing. He could hear the soldier running towards the door. It flew open, and at that instant Hugo swung his case with both hands. The weight of it knocked the gun to the floor and the youth backwards into the corridor, where he fell stunned and moaning in a heap. Hugo dashed down the stairs kicking at the gun, which clattered down the concrete in front of him. When he reached the ground floor, he ran out the main door, away from a group of men lounging at the spot where the Rover had been. He struggled down an alley, walked across a road and then, slowed by the heavy drag of his case, limped the three hundred meters to the back of the fruit shop.

He put the case in the Land Rover and turned onto the Boulevard des Etats-Unis. Instead of taking the commercial route, he sped directly towards the Presidential Palace. The entrance was blocked with tanks. A fleet of armored troop carriers cruised past him and began stopping traffic. Dozens of armed men held their positions. No one took any notice of his vehicle. He turned into a side street, and in an hour of slow cruising through bland, inoffensive neighborhoods, slipped unnoticed out of Algiers. With a last look in the mirror to the sea below the crest of the city, he merged with the flow of highway traffic. At that point, guided by his suspicions, he chose not to go east towards Constantine and the Tunisian border as instructed, but west. In two hours he was at Tiaret, in three hours avoiding a checkpoint at Blida by way of the backstreets. No other obstructions appeared. By ten that night he was south of Saida. He bought food in the town and camped for the night a half-kilometer from the road.

The next day, a gray sky appeared above Mecharia, with a veil of mist sweeping towards him. A brief rain spread across the dry land, and for five minutes he was soaked by heavy drops of water. The passengers riding in the truck parked next to him held their faces up, as if to receive the rare moisture as a blessing. The valley floor filled up with the runoff to form a series of shallow lakes. Before darkness settled, Hugo could see on both sides of the road, the brief, infrequent bloom of flowers that a few times a year colored the otherwise barren land. By afternoon of the following day, he was past Beni Ounif and close to Bechar. For the entire distance he had seen no evidence that he was being followed or, for that matter, was of special interest to anyone.

BOOK THREE

Chapter XIX

Tanezrouft

To Hugo's normal sense of temperature, the duration of the day's drive had seemed abnormally hot. As he approached Columb-Bechar from the northeast, he saw a few palms growing from a line of dunes. For the relief of shade, he drove straight towards them, stretched on the sand with his shirt off, and let the light breeze evaporate the stream of moisture soaking his skin. When he felt refreshed, he took papers from his satchel and began the process of planning for future events. Twice he had to wipe his head to keep the drops of sweat from fouling the ink of Crasson's note, which simply said he should contact the superintendent of Ponts et Chauseés in Constantine, a man named Fillion. With a few thoughts to that piece of evidence, he lay back down and slept. Near sundown, the flies woke him. To ease his cramped legs, he walked up the steep slope of a dune that arched above the level of the trees.

From the top, he could see the town below and the perimeter of adjacent land. The shoulder of high hills showed to the north and to the south and west, the level stretches of the great desert. But the air had cooled somewhat, and the sight of the green palms against the browns of the land was a refreshing sight. A moment of optimism displaced his anxieties. He had just sat down when the call to prayers rose up from the mosque that stood at the foot of the dune. With a steady cadence, the Mullah's voice filled the town and rolled across the hills. Hugo lay back in the sand and listened. He tried to put himself into the heart of a Muslim, but drew back. At one time, Muir instructed that the song of ritual was emblematic of all religious law. It was a sign of sacred intent, bringing believers closer to God. Hugo came to another view. In their heart of hearts and desire for salvation, individuals would believe what they would. But ritual in any form, he concluded, was essentially an instrument of church power, designed to bully the soul-weary into keeping their tired feet marching towards an ever-receding vision of paradise. Its ultimate intent was to ensure the immortality of the faith. The chanting stopped. The wind carrying the voice died to an insignificant whisper, and he was left to consider the fading vision of paradise as displayed to him by the map he had spread over the sand. Examining it, he had the feeling that a great distance had passed since Tangier. But it was a small amount relative to the span of emptiness that appeared to grind onwards in front of him—a journey not to be shortened an inch or a mile by rituals of any kind.

The office of Monsieur Amos Trudell, French citizen, who had commanded the office of the *Ponts et Chauseés* in Bechar district for twenty years, sat in a compound of sand. Hugo introduced himself as a former employee of Morrice Crasson, then drank the tea offered by his host. He gave an abridged summary of events. Trudell said, "I met Pierre Fillion a few times in Algiers before the rebellion. I can't say to whom he would owe allegiance. Down here, we don't care one way or the other, although I remember Fillion as an unprincipled meddler. He does well for himself because coups and war dominate the news in Africa today. As you know, President Ben Bella is out and Colonel Boumedienne is the de facto government of Algeria." He shrugged his shoulders. "One thing is possible here, my friend, and one certain. The first is your good judgment in anticipating the fact that by now you might have been in Monsieur Fillion's car heading back to Algiers for an unpleasant time. The other, that you should not be staying long in this town with a vehicle owned by Crasson et Fils. The army is in control, Houari Boumedienne is head of the army, and one never knows how equitable alliances are. Personally, knowing the lay of the land, I would say that Crasson hung you out to dry."

He drank some tea. The office stifled in the still air. To keep the dust out, Trudell had shut the windows. "And another certainty I didn't mention is this," he went on. "I strongly suggest you outfit with a larger fuel tank for the crossing."

"Crossing of what?"

"The Sahara of course."

Hugo nodded and felt an immediate surge of uneasiness. After a few moments he said, "Where would I buy a fuel tank?"

"Buy? There is no buying in this place. You must take."

"Take from where?"

"The Army motor pool across the street. In the hot afternoon, the guards are like doped sheep. And don't worry about what I think. I have allegiance only to France."

For two afternoons, Hugo watched and saw the truth to what Trudell had said. On the third day, he made one trip into the compound to unstrap a tank from its mounts and carry it out the main gate, waving at the sentries who stared at him in dumb silence. He mounted four new sand tires, bought jerricans for water, more fuel, and canned food. The last day before departure, he walked into the office of the ministry and asked how much he owed for the supplies purchased from the depot.

"Crasson pays. I will charge them as returns. After all, he is your employer." Trudell stuck out his hand and they shook. "One last thing. The Trans-Saharan routes are now a shambles. When you get to Poste Reggane, under no circumstances go south from there. This time of year the temperatures will kill you. And be aware, you're entirely on your own. Your credentials don't matter—but cigarettes, money, liquor, it all helps."

Hugo waved at him from the open window and passed out of the town limits. At the distance of one kilometer, the pavement ended and the Land Rover bumped along the rough piste. After an hour of surveillance ahead and behind, he pulled off the track to see if any vehicles followed. After a few minutes, it was apparent that the land was empty. Hot wind blew through the windows. He stared out at the desolation that stretched in all directions around him. In his mind floated an image of Algiers from the vicinity of Crasson's flat. The harbor was jeweled with boats, the sweep of the hill speckled in bright greens. It was a cool and pleasant except for a worker sweating at the labor of cleaning the tree-lined boulevard and taking little notice of Morrice Crasson's decomposing remains. Indifference is a thing easily felt in hot weather. Dead things dry up quickly and blow away; the smell is intense but doesn't last long, like the interest the authorities might have in a fictitious plotter, a man whose connection to the world grows less substantial in the desert heat. Hugo smiled and restarted the motor.

Going southwards from Bechar, passing few settlements or travelers, he noted how the whining, pleading, and rage of human voices had been displaced by increasing volumes of windy, mesmeric silence. In the solitude of the unpopulated land he found that conversation with himself decreased as well. When he did talk, it was of abstract, disconnected things with each item spaced over hours of time: a line of poetry from a volume on a particular shelf in his library, the girl Middle March playing one note on her violin, Beth's glistening body as it moved through the water of the pool. He thought impatiently of the growing heat and how it evaporated the moisture instantly from the flesh of his most provocative thoughts.

At Abadia, the junction to an eight hundred kilometer trail leading southwest to the nuclear test site at Tindouf, he waited in a small hut as a convoy of French Army vehicles passed hidden in the sandstorm that choked his lungs. His eyes stared straight ahead as the grit settled in them; he found himself for no reason saying to a waiting Bedouin, who stared back without comprehension—"A man I once knew said, 'I love the sea, but a day in the country is a bloody long time." When he got back to driving he said nothing to himself for the hour's journey to a junction where a road went east to Beni Abbes. A wooden hut stood at the side of the track. Hugo took out his stove, brewed some tea, and for the whole time couldn't think of what sensible things he might have said to the man in the circumstances.

It was past noon of the following day when he came to the oasis town of Adrar and stumbled on a party of five Germans. Their vehicle was undergoing repairs, so they used the Land Rover to go further into the oasis to purchase vegetables from a Spanish grower. The center of the garden was filled with an open cistern that supplied irrigation water. After they had bought produce, one of the men jumped in and others followed. Hugo swam and the intense cold of the water shot pains through his left arm. The owner discovered them in the mid-afternoon heat and yelled repeatedly for them to leave. When they were cooled, the six men climbed from the pool and drove back to the town. As the bullying heat of the sun subsided, an army vehicle forced Hugo off the road. A soldier put him in a cell for an hour.

"Cigarette" Hugo said to the chief who led him into a small room.

The man took the offered smoke. They talked. The chief said he was just doing his job of keeping the residents happy, especially the grower, who was an employer and the largest contributor to the economy.

"I'm leaving soon," Hugo said, taking twenty dollars from his pocket. "Give this to the Spaniard for his trouble. And for you the same, with the bonus of cigarettes."

"You're leaving soon?"

"Stamp my passport and I'll be out tomorrow."

"With the Germans?"

"They're on their own."

"*Merde.* Take them with you."

"When their vehicle is fixed, then you can get rid of them."

The chief shook his head and reluctantly stamped Hugo's passport. "Well at least you're free, monsieur. According to your papers, you've officially departed Algeria. However, since you are driving one of Crasson's vehicles, you can never really get away, can you?" He handed over the seized documents and took the cigarettes and money.

Hugo found a place for the vehicle, then hiked past the edge of the palms towards the unbroken horizon of sand to watch the climax of sunset. When the sun had set, the low hills of the Taidemait turned black and their contours traced abruptly on the sky. For an hour, thin horsetails of high cirrus clouds continued to reflect a multitude of pastel shades. With night and dimensionless stars for company, Hugo remained outside the oasis long after dark. In the solitude he concocted an elaborate logic to account for all the parallel paths that might lead him to richer destinations, where beauty was not a gratuitous complication of human affairs. At his resting spot beneath tall date palms, however, he made only one alteration to his real situation. Using paint purchased in Bechar, and the light of his torch, he blotted out the name of Crasson et Fils from the door. Then, at the first hint of dawn, he put Adrar to his north and himself beyond any reach of logic or comparisons. The rough track became the world. It was like being at sea, where the only considerations were navigation and keeping afloat.

The pounding of the wheels became more than uncomfortable the following day. The piste was a continuous washboard, with no option to drive on the boulder-littered ground where it bordered the Erg Chech. At midmorning Hugo came up to a small mound rising from the edge of the track, a hut built square of mud bricks but rounded to igloo shape by wind and particle erosion. The bottom half was buried by drifting sand. Within its shelter he spread the map and spanned the distances using a compass. The oasis of Poste Reggane was still two hours south. He traced with his finger the road east from it that would take him to Ain Salah and south again into the cooler elevations of the Hoggar Mountains, and the settlement of Tamanrasset.

He put the map back in his satchel and the satchel back into the locked box under the passenger seat. Before re-entering the hut he looked around. The horizon flashed and quivered with animations of structure and color: lakes, dark hills, iridescent trees and convoys of twitching phantasms—all products of the gross inequities of super-heated air. In reality he knew there was no water, no hills or trees, and that the human tenants of the earth were thinning to a few tribes clustered on remote dots of green, with life itself withered to meanness by the glassy furnace.

After eating the last of the fresh fruit bought from the Spanish grower, he remained in the hut. He knew that engine damage might result from the heat. All progress over the land would now occur in the cool hours of darkness, with the days used for sheltering from the sun. He tied a bandanna over his face to filter the sand that raced two feet above the desert floor. After sculpting a comfortable bed, he stretched out. There was little to see through the openings of the hut, so he closed his eyes and listened to the endless, rustling sand. As the sun sank a little from overhead, then further, still he opened his eyes and saw that according to his arbitrary watch, it was past three o'clock. He wrung the sweat from his bandanna and crawled out. The motor started and he was able to drive cautiously on the rough edge of the track.

After two hours of estimated time, he sensed the approach of a boundary, a demarcation of the earth. Quite abruptly, the piste fell away down an escarpment marking the southern fringe of the Taidemait Plateau. By a series of switchbacks the track descended towards the small patch of olive green marking the oasis of Poste Reggane. Half way down he stopped the vehicle and with his field glasses made a sweeping arc over the land. The settlement below appeared to him like a wharf-less, life-less port huddled on the coast of another dimension, itself a water-less ocean spreading flat beyond the limits of the known world, which was not forever because that illusion was spoiled by the settling dust of sandstorms. He remembered Trudell saying that no life of any sort existed to the south of this oasis. So once down the steep grade and into the settlement, he looked for the supplies he would need to avoid going there. He sought out the fuel dump, which was closed. He bartered for vegetables raised in neatly tended gardens and watered from aquifers eight hundred meters below the desert floor. In a small market he asked a thin man what it was like on the other side. "Occasionally, I go to Tamanrasset. Straight across you say? Only once in winter. Never in these hot months. The Tuareg can do it, but not me."

Hugo parked in a grove of trees and walked in the direction of the army barracks. He lit a cigarette and sat in a palm grove out of direct sight of the buildings. Parked in front were two Land Rovers. In an hour, six men came and went. A resident walked by and Hugo asked him where he could obtain potable water. The man led him to a manual pump, then sniffed at the cigarette smoke. When Hugo gave him one from a fresh pack and lit it for him, the man grinned. Hugo threw him the pack. The man bowed low and said something that he repeated many times, backing away to a discreet distance. Hugo filled his jerrican and bottle.

He went back to the fuel dump, which consisted of a hand-operated pump with a glass counter. No price was given. Down the street two men moved from the shade of one grove of palms to the next. A short distance on was a trader's shop with a battered van parked outside. Inside the shop, an Arab talked to a man who appeared European. Hugo lit a cigarette and offered the pack to the two men. They took one each. The European said, "*Merci*," and the Arab brewed more coffee. "*Café* monsieur?" he asked.

"Please. I also need some gas. Who runs the pump?"

"I do," said the Arab.

"How much?"

"Three hundred dinars a liter, about three-fifty American."

Hugo nodded. "How is it with the new government down here?"

"Nothing yet," said the other man.

"Could I get some petrol now?"

"No. I don't have any," the Arab explained. "But it should be here tomorrow, first thing. They run a small tanker down every two weeks from Bechar. Where are you headed?"

"Ain Salah, then Tamanrasset."

"Why there?"

"Eventually, I have to get to Lagos."

"Why?"

Hugo shrugged.

"By yourself?" the man persisted.

"Yes."

"Looks like one of Crasson's vehicles."

"I bought it from a man in Bechar."

The European said, "I heard Crasson was dead. When you're a merchant you walk the fine line. You can't sit the fence forever."

"No idea about that," said Hugo. He gave the pack of cigarettes to the Arab. "In the morning, eh?" He went to walk out and the European followed him.

"That vehicle—you should park it where I'm staying. I just came up from Tamanrasset on my way back to Algiers. You'll make it through the Hoggar, but this time of year, it's hot everywhere—in more ways than the weather. So watch your back."

In a walled grove of palms owned by an oasis gardener was a roofless courtyard adjacent to the main shelter. "This is my hotel room," said the Frenchman. "Don't have to worry if it rains. No rain. Put the vehicle over there so it can't be seen from the piste."

That night he and Robert Couch lay on the sand beneath the sight of endless stars and listened to the sounds of the grower's children drumming on metal barrels, on the sides of a derelict van, on any item that would reverberate. All the while they chanted circular, repeating variations on the same theme, which played like a counterpoint to the stories told by the two men, who smoked and drank Pernod.

In the morning they ate bread, sliced tomato, and couscous. The trader walked over and said he expected the tanker soon. Couch said "soon" could mean in the afternoon, this day or the next—or maybe in a week. After a small meal at one o'clock in the afternoon, Hugo ambled to the end of the short track that led to the fringe of the oasis. When he returned, he said to his host, "Have you been straight across?"

"Twice, but never since independence. You don't go that way in summer. Never. Let me tell you something about it. For three thousand kilometers to the west is barren rock and sand, not much water or anything else but a few salt mines at Taroudenne...all the way to the Atlantic. As you just saw, to the south is no better—a large, waterless stretch of territory indicated on the map as the Tanezrouft Desert, which means 'land of thirst' in the language of the Tuareg."

He lit a cigarette and drank more tea. Even in the shelter of the palm groves, the hot wind blew his hair this way and that. "Once you leave Poste Reggane," he continued, "the nearest well is Bordji Perez, about seven hundred kilometers. The first petrol is almost twice that distance, at Gao on the Niger. Every man who has gone the Tanezrouft route knows what I'm talking about, when he gets to Bourem and is happy to be breathing."

He stopped to drink his mint tea and smoke. With his eyes closed, he continued. "The desert Arab is different, you see. I have no quarrel with that. The modern world neglects him. All we want is a willingness not to impede our progress with stupid behavior. But it is our behavior that is stupid. The French supplied the model of superiority and built the route; but an independent Algeria abandoned it to the medieval Tuareg and the unbearable heat. Understand, now there is no road."

Couch stopped talking and poured tea into Hugo's cup. After a few minutes he resumed. "As I said, the route is now in ruin. Most of the five kilometer marker barrels are gone, all the way-stops looted—Poste Weygand and Bidon Cinq. In the old days you went in convoy. You had water and fuel, could shelter in the Quonset huts. The markers, what are they? When you were driving the piste, before the one behind disappeared, you could see the one ahead. You could navigate that way on the winter daylight. Leave here now, you're on the stars only and require a good compass. In places the sand obliterates the piste. If you are alone and your vehicle breaks down, you are dead. You must be good or lucky with your navigation to hit one point on the map. And should that happen, what is it that you face at Bordji Perez? From what others have said, the fortress is manned by maniacs, outcasts from the army who, far from giving you water, may as well slit your throat for a cigarette."

He talked with the occasional whistle for emphasis, but otherwise Hugo noticed no anxiety in his manner, as if for all his exaggeration, he was comfortable with the land.

"But you know, to the Tuareg, all of this is nothing. From time immemorial they have crossed this route with their caravans and continue to this day. They made the piste."

He rose slowly in the hot wind and walked to the pump. He put water on a rag and wrapped it around his head.

"For fifteen years I've done business in North Africa. I regret the capitulation of the Empire. The first Frenchmen in the Sahara were adventurers, but with them came the blight of politics. Regardless, they all withered in the sun.

General Lapperine, conqueror of the Tuareg, died a few miles south of Poste Reggane trying to be the first man to fly across the Sahara. In the Ahaggar Mountains to the east, Pere Foucauld, the Jesuit, was trapped and slaughtered in his Borj by cowards. And Heinrich Barth, the artist, he tramped from one side of the Sahara to the other as if he were strolling on a Sunday, although it took him five years. But these men are gone. A few caravans cross in the winter, and in summer only diamond smugglers use the route to flee north from Sierra Leone. Put on your hat and I'll show you something."

Couch put two canteens of water in Hugo's satchel and they passed the fringes of the palms. When they were free of shelter, Hugo felt the sand scour the skin from his legs. So he put on his pants and came back to the waiting Frenchman.

On the eastern fringe of the Erg Chech, a patch of flat gravel the size of France, the surface was pebbly and hard. Except for the pressure of heat, walking was easy. Whenever Hugo turned to see how far they had come, he could only see the rise of land marked by green around Poste Reggane. The ascending air soon obscured the color behind a shimmering veil. The world around them was flat and yellow like an ocean of baked earth. Over it, the hot winds blew ceaselessly. Floating on this sea appeared an object that billowed like a sail in the confused atmosphere. Hugo had first been aware of it from a distance of three hundred meters, but much closer it solidified into a wooden monument bolted firmly to an iron post. The abrasive air had rounded the edges of the hardwood.

"Look closely at this," said the Couch. He pointed his finger at markings, which resembled a foreign script. When Hugo stood closer, he could make out words scratched into the bleached surface:

Danger du Morte.
Do not leave the piste beyond this point

If any other words had existed besides these, they had been erased by the force of windblown sand. After staring at it for a minute, the Frenchman gestured with his arm to the right of the piste, where the fiery air cracked and rippled along the edge of the sky-dome. Then he looked at Hugo with idiotic delight. "This is wisdom, *non*? This contributes to our undertakings? Why not? Whoever wrote this was a master of the obvious."

Hugo read the message again and squatted on the hard ground. He stared west into the gale with his eyes drawn to slits so the lashes could filter the particles of sand. He couldn't keep himself from laughing. And he thought of all the things that were obvious in his life—his friendship with the moron, drinking at The Rose, and waiting vainly for a woman he knew to walk in from the rain. He took a drink from a canteen, passed it to Couch, and spread the Michelin Carte #953 on the desert floor. To keep it from blowing away, he put rocks on the corners and around the edge. They both squatted on their haunches like lizards, with the wind ripping at loose clothing. A drop of tepid water landed on the paper and evaporated instantly. The explicit details on the sheet were incongruous with the emptiness. Hugo drew a straight line across the map until it crossed a red diagonal line marking the frontier between Algeria and Mali. Then he carefully folded the sheet and went back to the signpost. After examining some marks along its lower edge, he turned his head sideways, knelt down, and squinted at bright scratch marks on the metal pillar. Then he called to Couch. "Come and read this."

He pointed to the etchings on the iron. The man squatted down and put his face close to the post. A foot above the concrete base, visible only in the shadow of a hand, were more words:

> Sail out on an ocean of heat.
> The sands sing a silent retreat.
> Leave bones for the future and brains for the past.
> Drink your health in a hurry 'cause liquid won't last.
> How much drink to cross here,
> Is it one jerrican?
> Nope—FOUR, ALMOST
> Is there peace and goodwill
> In the cradle of man?
> Nope—WAR, ALMOST

After he had finished reading, Couch pulled his knife as if to cross out the name written there. But he straightened up instead and put the knife back into its sheath. Making no more remarks about the verse, he motioned northwards towards the oasis. As they walked back, he said, "This was no whistling in the dark. No bullshit melodrama. Survival was always planned, the quantity of water, the condition of your transport, the skill of your navigation. It was like preparation for war. The words are right—danger of death. So you go east to Ain Salah and south by way of the high ground."

They arrived at the fringe of the palm in time to see the tanker pumping off the gasoline into an underground reservoir. Before they could get to it, an army vehicle arrived. The *chammioneur* stopped pumping, took a dispatch case from the passenger door, and handed it to the officer, who looked over to Hugo with a frown and nodded to the Frenchman. When they were back at the courtyard he said,

"You have your papers in order, monsieur?"

"Always."

Hugo went to the Land Rover, waited fifteen minutes then drove to the fuel dump with Couch. The tanker was gone. He had the trader fill the tanks to overflow and paid him cash. "Just to let you know, there is a vehicle blocking the piste to Ain Salah. There are eight soldiers, with a mounted machine gun."

Hugo took a deep breath.

"I've got another jerrican," said the trader. He went into the dump and came out with an old container and filled it to the brim. Hugo gave him a thousand-dinar note.

"You might make Bordji Perez," said the trader.

"No. I'm going east to Ain Salah."

"You know, monsieur, the *chammioneur* always reads the dispatches. Then he tells me. The commander's orders are to hold you here. It relates to Monsieur Crasson."

"I can evade the vehicle blocking the road."

"Are you going to dodge them as well?" He pointed towards the escarpment of the Taidemait. Four moving clouds rose into the air. Two came straight towards the oasis. The other two cut across the triangle towards the road to Ain Salah.

"Maybe Crasson hung you out to dry," Couch added.

Hugo shook his head, "I've been told that once already. My reply would be the same—Crasson did what's in his nature to do."

Hugo took out a carton of cigarettes and divided it between Couch and the trader, who said, "You won't have to go far today because those guys coming, they wouldn't go into the Tanezrouft, today or next year. Go easy on the water. You might make it across. *Bonne chance.*"

Couch wandered back towards the palm grove. Hugo turned the vehicle around and as he drove past the fringe of palms at the edge, the Frenchman waved. In a few minutes he was at the signpost. The sign leered up swiftly. Speeding past it, he glanced once more at the faded death's head and asked himself what the term "war" might mean to someone retreating from the inhabited world.

For an hour, while he followed the rutted marks across the flat desert top, he considered a number of permutations to the word, "war." By that time the engine temperature had climbed to the boiling point, all such thought was irrelevant. He turned west. In a few minutes he stopped, watched his dust cloud blow away and waited. Nothing appeared. He got out and wandered in a full circle around the vehicle, looking in all directions at the barren immensity, hearing only the wind as it ground sand particles into the metal of the fenders.

After parking the Land Rover north-south, he erected a shelter on the east side. This alignment protected him from the flow of wind and already benefited from the increasing shade as the sun descended towards the west. He weighted the loose sides of the canvas tarp with jerricans, making an opening on the north edge, then sat with his back to the vehicle. In an hour, he stopped writing. The intense heat wore down his will to think and his thirst seemed perpetually to run ahead of his ability to swallow.

Late in the afternoon the winds abated, the abrasive sands fell lower to the ground until there was only a fluttering of the canvas. He lit the burner, brewed mint tea and ate two pieces of bacon. Then he counted the jerricans of water for a third time, there being only two, containing five gallons less than the minimum amount required for him to safely traverse the core of the Tanezrouft. Impatient because of this, he got underway. At the intersection of the piste, he could see in the low angle of light, the scratch of wheels, camel hoofs, and other imprints of former passages that were now indispensable markers. To his right, the sun hovered bright and orange, then sank like a ship at sea. Slowly, the fire on the land evaporated into the night.

After navigating for a short time across hard ground, he saw periodic flashes of light. They came on towards him over the course of an hour, increasing in frequency until the apparent beam became a pair of headlights. A black sedan slowed, then stopped next to him. Two men got out. One was an Arab carrying a gun. The other announced his name as Charles Veudreux. The Arab fetched a water bag, a stove, and made tea. They sat motionless on the sand in front of the car and drank. After accepting one of Hugo's cigarettes, Veudreux said, "We're always well-prepared, but each time I come this way in summer, I vow it's the last." He stopped to drink and stretch his back, then continued, "So, if I may ask, what are you doing out here?"

"My papers aren't in order," said Hugo, "and there's an army patrol in Poste Reggane, if that's of interest."

"Apparently only for you, my friend. For me, it'll just cost more. So this is what I'll do to assist. I pay them less than they want—and tell them much less than that. Not that they would come out here, but information is relayed to the frontier. It would be better for you if the soldiers there know nothing. Other than this, be aware that you've traded a minor nuisance back there for a huge risk out here. If you survive the desert, and Bordji Perez, there are other problems for you."

Veudreux switched on the headlights. The passport he showed Hugo was filled with ornate and official looking stamps bearing the names of strange countries including Sierra Leone. He pointed also to marks on the pages, which indicated checkpoints on the long road leading from south edge of the desert.

"This is my point. The selling of these *carnets* is a source of money to soldiers who man the barriers in Mali and elsewhere. How else do they make a living? They get paid nothing at all to feed their families."

He sat back down. The land had become still and the only sound was their talk and the contractions of cooling metal. "So. You have no documents, and no caravans to cross with until late September. Army or no, I suggest you turn back. Go around Poste Reggane. Dump this vehicle in Adrar and they won't examine your papers too closely after that. Go to Algiers for the summer where a few dollars will buy you a job. And there are French women of course."

Hugo made no reply. Veudreux got up and opened the car door. When the Peugeot was rolling he said, "At all costs avoid the fort at Bordji Perez. A kilometer south is a Tuareg camp where you can re-supply." Hugo took the stove out and boiled some more water. For the next half hour he watched the red lights of the Peugeot shrink to an indistinct point on the horizon then blend with the stars. It was like the disappearance of life. He started the Land Rover, ran one wheel up on the ridge of soft sand at the edge of the track and accelerated to speed.

For the duration of the night he drove south under a cosmic half shell of stars. At many points, the piste branched into parallel tracks made by vehicles whose drivers sought routes free of ruts and washboard. Where sand and flat rock obliterated evidence of the path, he took a periodic fix on the pole star and determined a point of light 180 degrees south, compensating for the earth's rotation by veering slightly to the left a few degrees an hour. At irregular intervals, his lights illuminated the navigation barrels, a few still standing upright and visible from a distance. Abandoned vehicles permanently marked the piste, their only decay being the hands of men who detached what they could in descending order of value, until a few score of cars, trucks, and buses had become irreducible shells of metal.

Later in the night, when he was becoming fatigued, the headlights shone over Poste Weygand, a skeleton of Quonset huts, a half-dismantled radio mast, dented storage tanks partly submerged by shallow dunes. Everything transportable was gone or buried. Hugo turned off the motor. After a quick survey of the abandoned post, he stretched out on the sand to stare at the diamond stars with hardly a molecule of vapor or even the floating moon to obscure their perfect, unblinking brilliance. He felt like an insect trapped under a jeweled dome with the earth a crease of blackness around the edge. An hour on from the Poste, the rim of the east became less dark, then more light spinning out, like water flowing along the horizon. Color followed and higher up the reds and yellows cut into the black sky. Shades of blue spread westwards, and with the coming rim of sun, the heat settled like death. Two kilometers past the eroded corpse of a camel, he set up his shelter.

Sleep came quickly. At some time in the high heat of midday, waking was more than an ear cocked to the sound of snapping cloth. His tongue was swollen and a suffocating dust masked his face. The wind blew at gale force and he feared it would rip the eyelets from the tarp. He groped for the canteen. It was hot, as if he had just taken it off the burner. His stomach retched on the first swallow. The quantity of dust caked behind his eyelids made it difficult to see his watch, which said twelve-thirty, two hours before the zenith of heat. Everywhere he looked, particles were borne aloft by the speed of the winds that scoured all features rising an inch above the ground. In vast areas of the Erg Occidentale to the northeast, dunes would form and move in geometrically perfect crescents. What Hugo saw on the Tanezrouft was only surface detritus, but it was sufficient to slice the hair from skin and, in time, flesh from bones. Evaporation had increased to a level where an exposed, naked body would expire in minutes.

The hot wind accelerated. Twice he had to re-secure his shelter. When the gale reached peak velocity, he feared it might wheel him along the earth. So he lowered himself to the ground, stooped in the posture of a figurine. He curled further into the shade, drank another cupful, and invented, for comfort, an opposing fate—a forest of trees dripping with sleet and ice water melting along the branches of his memory. Encouraged by this vision, he expanded the pattern of opposites to embrace death as well as life. Dead memories, like dead bodies provide the nutrients for new thought and the hope of new life. This obvious conclusion should have brought him some joy of relief. Yet when he opened his eyes, he was struck instead with a shriveling sense of fear. The empty waste of the desert that stretched in all directions around him, like the swollen landscape of his brain, contained no nutrients for anything. His right hand swung down to pull the thermometer from beneath the vehicle. It indicated 141 degrees Fahrenheit.

He slid back down onto the blanket and passed the remaining hours imagining the comfortable elevations of the Hoggar and the higher, cooler peaks of his mountain home rising from the incomparable ocean, which seemed less in magnitude than the half-boiled water rolling across his tongue. Until, by small gradations, the wind lessened its fury, the sand rose only inches off the ground, and the terrible heat diminished. Soon the shadows of late afternoon slanted across the stovetop. He was able to brew tea and eat small bites of sausage, which caught like metal in his throat.

When he had finished and went to start the vehicle, the motor clicked over but there was no noise or fumes. Hugo had a moment of panic, then dropped the tailgate and pulled out his tools. While there was light he tested the electrical circuits and examined the engine for fuel leaks. It went dark. He brewed more tea then repeated his procedures with assistance from the rancid yellow of his torch. An hour later, the pale moon swung up from the horizon. He went through another futile round of repair. All the while, his body craved water, but he refused to drink. He contemplated instead the inevitable drinking of water from the radiator, and then perhaps his own urine. Or he could quit the rebellion altogether, do what he had done inadvertently on Christmas eve—slice open a vessel and painlessly fade away like the soldiers Moffat had seen die, with the ground blotting up the blood with no more of a mess than a red spot for the sand to scour. Bedouin from the first caravan of winter would happily scavenge his possessions. A Tuareg headman would take the responsibility for his corpse by picking the pockets and politely kicking a few pebbles over his embalmed remains. The moment his brain ceased to transmit he would know nothing of this. Nor would Beth, trying on her wedding dress at the third and final fitting, before walking into the Precinct and feeling grateful for the light of a full moon to help find her car.

Yet the moon was not full, and the dull light misled her to a dead-end of confusion at the bottom of the car park, with neither her vehicle nor any comfort in sight. Hugo, on the other hand, was relieved to detect a thin tangent missing from the moon's right limb, suggesting it was one calendar day short of complete lunacy. The night sand beneath his feet, therefore, was not a verifiable delusion, only nine-tenths so and also no shock to his brain that the vehicle parked on the desert floor had shrunk to the size of a toy, small enough to push along with his hand like Milton's tiny horse. Other shapes dotting the flat plain became bloated. Small rocks grew into boulders, boulders grew to the size of furniture; a line of rocks to the east became the rump of the Hoggar Mountains. It was a curious trick of the mind's perspective, with new angles and shading for his eyes, but nothing worth a moment's dread. Calmly, he looked at the profile of a man crouching on a baked rock resembling a kitchen chair, with his elbows on the tomato red table, sipping his early morning coffee from Billy's horse's head mug. The man didn't hesitate to begin his chatter once he knew that his fellow traveler had noticed.

"Are you forgetting your place in time—both the date and the day," he said.

"I can think of neither out here, Albert," Hugo answered. "What does it matter?"

The man laughed in derision. "The moon in June, with the croon and the swoon as the popular song goes. And tomorrow is the day, the twenty-first day of June, the first day of summer and many happy things. Did you forget? It's also her wedding day, the first day of decreasing light—and you out of luck. From my excellent understanding of the classics, it's the feast of cupid and solstice sport and, believe me, she won't be taking her pleasure casually. She will be consummating legitimate love stretched on a bed of roses picked fresh from the same garden you nearly destroyed with your adolescent tricks. And she will be happy, delirious in her erotic situation. Instead of the one grape you fed her in the hospital recovering from your well-deserved wounds, she will be eating bunches fed to her as she lies on silk sheets covered by little else than the fragrant air. And she won't be thinking a wit about you—you who deserted her in her time of need, scarpered, buggered off, chickened out."

"She had no time of need," Hugo replied. "And I left with a month's notice. What more did she want?"

"Oh, very business like, very efficient. What more did she want? She would have liked the truth. She might have considered altering her plans in life had you the spine to tell her your deepest feelings. She at least wanted a departure that was merciful for you both. And now she will get it. Because by all odds you will be dead in a few hours, stretched out in the sand with your tongue swollen in your mouth and choking you, thrashing around like the camel you saw earlier. Let me refresh you medical knowledge. Without water and salts your heart will stop…"

"That's enough!"

"Oh no. I'm not through yet. Let me say that if she hadn't come traipsing into your room last Christmas Day you could have had the easiest possible expiration, if a bit premature. Oh my. Did I say that? Me, the celebrated healer, with no medicine for you, not a drop. It wouldn't be good for Beth to see this, to even know of it."

"You can go now, my friend. If I die, can you be far behind? Look to your own soul."

"Me? My soul already reaps the harvest of duty—miserable job as it was—healing the primitives and going without."

"I'm gratified to hear that after all your good works, you're not an imitation of Christ, who was perfect."

"Oh, I'm aware of my imperfections, Hugo. I try to have perpetual love but like all men, I fall far sort. I'll have an awkward moment and the urge to snap, to demean just short of an unpleasant rage. Notwithstanding, those who note my passing will readily forgive these shortcomings. They will celebrate a reverence for life, not a fascination with useless death. Your intransigence assures that your demise will be like the passing of a discarded goat, and out here, not even a maggot present to celebrate with a good meal."

"I'm making an effort to get to your place of business, Albert, to do the work you've requested. But need I bother? Perhaps I should have limited myself to the study of your erudite works, all explained to me in exquisite detail by Conrad Muir."

"This would be the despised old Muir whose care you never appreciated; he, who illustrated the frailty of human nature, and its strengths? I gave him his first lesson in Bach's fugues, you know, on the organ of St. Nicholas Church in Strasbourg. He was a good pupil, a fast learner, although he was also one to take risks. You were certainly his cross to bear, which he bore admirably. He wanted to serve me further but your mother refused, saying he had to serve you."

"As well he should. He was responsible for me."

"What would you know of responsibilities or genuine direction, mired as you are in the same distorted sense of progress as present civilization?"

Hugo rested his eyes for a moment, rubbed them before saying, "It's very kind of you to think so highly of me," he said. "Consider me a fellow optimist, one who thinks he is efficient enough to survive the next few hours, if not days."

"I don't think highly of you at all. You've proven nothing so far. You are as degenerate as society. I recall from a piece I wrote long ago that our degeneration, when it is traced back to its origin, consists in the fact that true optimism has vanished unperceived from our midst. We are not a race weakened and exhausted by luxury as you would think, whose task it is to rouse ourselves to a greater productivity. On the contrary, we are hindered in our spiritual conflict by the very efficiency we have attained. Our notion of life has been degraded by it. The higher powers of creation are exhausted because the optimism from which they ought to draw their life energy has been sapped by the pessimism of our failures. Because false efficiency can never achieve prosperity any more than your sorry tricks can bring the glory of Beth Marshall's perfect face to shine on you."

The light of a new day began to color the landscape. The sun's heat pushed the chill air backwards. Hugo tried to rise and walk, but failed. "I promise to laugh more," he said. "I will seek joy wherever it is, Albert, right here if needs be. I will never again think of myself."

The effort of speaking made him sweat, tired him, so he leaned back into the cool of the tire, unwilling to think of anything but the woman whose presence he felt close by in the rise and fall of his own breathing. Then he stopped breathing altogether. His senses swam with an exquisite deprivation. Past him walked the figure of a woman. As Albert predicted, her solemn face was flawless in every detail—with the exception of one tear that ran down her cheek. The dawn's rising wind pushed the thin summer dress against the curves of her body. The increasing heat seemed a comfort to her. She quickened her pace, and the fearful red of the morning sky made her hair shine. Reaching out three fingers, she receded down the piste, having been unable or unwilling to touch him. Hugo resumed his breathing and lost himself in the deep of his memories, hearing only the rustle of moving sand. An hour later he opened his eyes. The line of rocks to the east was small, unable to seat a mouse.

When the light was sufficient for him to observe details, he unbolted the carburetor and took it apart. On a casting close to the air intake ran a hairline fracture through which excessive air might flow to the mixture. He lit his burner, melted some solder, and dripped it into the crack. He smoothed it with a small file and emery cloth. By the time he had bolted the assembly onto the manifold, the sun was well above the horizon. He started the vehicle and could make only a few kilometers along the piste before fuel vaporized in the line and stopped him for another day. The jerricans held little more than half the water he would need to keep alive. He felt for his knife and shut himself into the Rover to keep the wind's evaporation to a minimum.

When he had closed the door and felt the temperature leap up, he asked Albert, a man of known scientific ability, a question pertaining to the balance of evaporation and body temperature. Without freely moving air, would the gross heat inside the vehicle bake him alive? The answer, he reasoned, would come after the fact, and if 'yes' would be unknown to him. He lay still, determined not to think, to worry, or do anything that would augment inner heat. His watch hung on the knob of the glove box. Whenever he opened his eyes, he noted time's progress on ever-decreasing scales, using Zeno's paradox to prove that a watched pot could never boil. Every ten minutes precisely, he took a measured sip of water. He fell into an unthinking, unmoving state. He dreamed. Visions came and went with voices and music. An ache in his head grew worse. Pressure built from within. His eyeballs seemed poised to fall out. He had to move his tongue constantly to keep from choking. Nausea lessened his desire for water, but he kept drinking the required mouthful as measured by the clock.

Then at one point in the unknowable process of living, he recalled the watch hands indicating six o'clock. It would be past time and the heat subsiding. Using a great effort of will, he pulled the latch. With a rush, the air exhausted, the cooling desert wind replaced it, and made him shiver. He sat up and was dizzy. His abdomen contorted with pain. The ache in his head was terrific and interfered with his feet so that he could nothing but stagger to the shaded eastern side. The sun was approaching the horizon and the white of the sky had turned to azure blue. He assayed his water supply and determined he had done better than expected.

In a few minutes he was able to brew tea and sit for a moment to watch the colors settling over the land, over the settling air itself and the invisible mountains to the east. He might have wept for the beauty if moisture weren't an issue, or played a dirge, a requiem, perhaps a lullaby on the piano resting in the dusty bedroom down the hall from the tomato red table. Instead he beat time on the side of the fender and moved his feet as if dancing, thinking how ridiculous this deliberate wasting of time rather than one turning of the engine crank to know if he were to live or harden into a fossil. With a light step he continued dancing to the front of the Land Rover, bent down, and turned the starter handle with a violent twist of his right arm. The motor caught. He drove off with deliberate speed, and soon assessed that it ran better and easier than when he first left Algiers.

Within an hour he had passed the remains of Bidon Cinq, a smaller refuge than Poste Weygand, with only two huts picked clean and half-filled with sand. He stayed only a few minutes and sped south, pushed by the weight of accumulating hazards. Many areas of the piste now lay buried, and he churned through with all four wheels spitting sand rather than wasting effort and time on laying mats. Occasional dizziness caused him to lose focus, but the map, the odometer and his sense of dead reckoning told him where he might be, where he had to be.

At three am he was surprised to see on the map that he was only a few kilometers short of Bordji Perez and hours of darkness yet to reach the well. The short distance was most likely incorrect. Yet he sensed he was in the vicinity. For some time the land had been rising in elevation, becoming less flat. The moonlight exposed parallel ridges and a hill far off. But it was more treacherous for this variety. Hollows contained sand traps. The ridges hid vertical drops of three meters. Within an hour, the light would show vaguely in the east—and he hoped it would reflect the walls of the red fortress.

As he thought this, without a groan or a shudder, the engine stopped and the tires slid a few feet on the hard ground. With the last fuel in his lighter, he checked the motor. There were no wires hanging down and no fittings loose to the touch. When the motor cranked over, there was no sucking of air only the smell of leaking gasoline. He sat for a moment and considered the facts. In the daylight, he could rip down the carburetor and repair it. Or if his navigation was correct, he could walk. Failure on either count meant the full force of the sun would catch him. He drained the radiator into the empty water bags and took the satchel containing his papers, writings, and personal items. Slinging these and the water bags over his shoulders, he set out southward on foot with the last canteen of water held in his good hand.

After walking rapidly for an hour, he stopped and drank three mouthfuls. There was little sense in hoarding for a time that would never come. Whether his heart stopped at nine-forty or ten-fifteen was immaterial. It might stop at twelve noon promptly from the poisons in the coolant water. For now, it was sufficient to know that daylight and a sense of heat continued to increase. With a growing sense of panic, he quickened his pace, sometimes on easy flat ground, other times to his ankles in soft sand. Twice, he checked himself for trotting. The dunes and outcroppings of rock glowed faintly in the pastels of early dawn. He came to the top of a rise and took his bearings against the one dominating feature, a large hill or rock a few kilometers distant. He walked another hour. From the next ridge he could see over the shortened distance that the object was not part of the landscape but was actually the fort at Bordji Perez, its red walls faintly reflecting the stem of sunrise.

Driven by his thirst and the empty, hollow sound of the canteen, he continued his journey towards it before veering west as recommended by the smuggler. His feet struggled through the heavy sand. The sun rose higher and the heat increased. He put his fingers into the bag of coolant water, tasted the bitterness, the particles of rust on his tongue. His head felt light. A few hundred meters from the fort he could see the perimeter, ringed with barbed wired. From the high wall, a flat voice came down at him, then blew past in the rising wind. He tried to walk faster. More voices cried out and a wooden door facing to the west swung open. Soldiers ran through it to a gap in the wire. One yelled for him to stop. Hugo stooped to drop the bags containing the contaminated fluid. The sun was full, enough heat to get the sweat running down his face.

"Water please," he said to the men gathering in front of him. The soldiers said nothing in return. One trooper took out his canteen, but pulled it back when he heard a screaming from the door of the fort. A short man with a carelessly wound headdress strutted over the ground waving a pistol in the air. He came closer, pushing his way through the soldiers, yelling a continuous scream of excited, slobbering commands. "Who the hell are you?" he shouted.

"A traveler."

"From where?"

"North. The Tanezrouft."

"What, walking?"

"My vehicle is broken down."

"Papers?"

Hugo passed over the folder that held the carnet for the vehicle. The commandant looked at them and then said, "I want all your papers."

"They're in the vehicle."

"Then I want the vehicle. Go get it."

"It's broken down, doesn't run."

The man looked at Hugo with a strange bitter look that creased his brow. "I don't care about that. I want the vehicle."

"I say again, the vehicle doesn't work."

"Smart ass," the chief said, then yelled to the one soldier who carried a weapon, "Shoot him."

The man raised his rifle. Then he put it down and turned the other way.

"I said shoot him!" the commandant yelled again.

"Why would he listen to you?" Hugo said without raising his voice.

"Shoot him!" screamed the man with his face red, temples rippled with veins and his feet stamping the ground. The soldier with the rifle walked further away.

"Pay attention, Chief. If you kill me, you don't get anything. In fact, if I don't get water, you're out of luck."

A look of extreme disappointment went over the man's face. He turned and marched back to the fort, all the way screaming, "No water! No water!"

The soldier with the sympathetic look walked over to Hugo. "The small hut at the top of the ridge...go sit there and the Tuareg will come. Go now," he said threatening with the rifle barrel.

Hugo went back to the opening in the wire and began to trudge up the five hundred meter incline. Halfway, he stopped to rest and turned to look down at the parade ground. It was empty. The battlements of the fort showed no sentries walking in the glare of the sun. He sucked out the last few drops from the canteen. Inside the hut, he put his back to a wall. The light slanted through a door on the east side. His tongue swelled. His head ached. He poured radiator water into his canteen, tasted it, and spat it out. An hour later, he put some in his mouth and swallowed it. Time passed and with it came more heat and increasing nausea. The light in the doorway withdrew, until the shadow came to rest on the precise line of the threshold. The sun stood directly overhead and the building cast no exterior shadow. Hugo crawled to the door and looked out.

In a wadi some three hundred meters distant sprawled the tents of the Tuareg encampment. To one side of the nearest tent stood a single man clothed in a white robe. A black headdress masked his head and face. As he moved, sunlight reflected from the jeweled beads around his neck and the silver inlays on his rifle stock. When Hugo looked a second time, he was gone. He crawled back inside. Moments later, the light decreased. A woman with black eyes and full lips stood in the entrance. She wore silver bracelets on her wrists and a colored robe made of cotton. A brown scarf covered a portion of the black hair that reached to her waist. Into the hut she carried a brass kettle and burner, silver cups and spoons. Putting them at the wall opposite, she stood in the corner and waited. In a quarter hour three men entered and sat cross-legged in front of the utensils. One lit the burner, another poured water from a goatskin into the kettle. When it had boiled, he made mint tea. The woman carried a cup to Hugo.

"*Merci*," he said, drank it down then said, "*Aussi*," with his cup raised. One of the men felt his head and gestured to the woman. For the next hour she shuttled back and forth with the tea, a small cup every five minutes. After the hour they left, leaving behind the goatskin of water. Later in the afternoon, the woman came with a blanket, some dried goat meat, and a deep bowl filled with broth. Hours after the sun had set, he lay on the blanket and slept.

On waking, the first thing he saw was a pair of feet wearing sandals. A small man with blond hair squatted next to him. "Good morning," he said. "My name is Dieter Brun. Who are you?"

"A traveler."

Brun reached into a bag and handed him a chunk of bread. "Breakfast," he said, and while Hugo ate, boiled water for tea. When the drink was poured he said, "There's a Land Rover about six kilometers north, about four hundred meters off the piste. Looks like one of Crasson's with the markings painted over."

"You're know a lot," Hugo said.

"Not so much, comrade. The Tuareg are always aware of what comes into their territory. And they also know that the army looks for just such a vehicle, which passed through Poste Reggane a few days ago."

"I know nothing about that," said Hugo.

"The problem is," continued Brun, "the tyrant wants the Rover. Did you, by any chance, give him your papers?"

"Only a copy of the *carnet*. The rest are hidden."

"Excellent. One night soon the Tuareg headman will organize a party to retrieve your vehicle."

"And the army?"

"They have little equipment and no vehicles. The commandant sells everything he gets his hands on, no matter whose property. Understand that Bordji Perez is a prison camp. Of the men who are conscripted into the army and cause trouble—the dangerous ones they shoot, the ones who have potential they rehabilitate, the scum who are nothing come here. They give them a few rifles, with the hope that they will shoot themselves. In the meantime, they are the eyes and ears of the frontier."

"And the Tuareg?"

"The headman says that for a few francs he would clean out the fort in an hour. But if he did that, the army would send more. He lives in fear they will send better, and better would be more trouble for him. But we'll get the Rover and see what happens. In the meantime you stay here. I lived for two weeks in this hut until they became used to me and I got permission to live amongst them. They're hospitable, but suspicious. What did you say your name was?"

Hugo told him, then passed a cigarette to Brun, took one himself and used matches to light them.

"You see, Herr Haultain, I have the same problem," Brun continued. "Except my vehicle is thirty kilometers north of Poste Weygand. I expect by now it's picked clean and the remains will sit there until the world dies."

Brun left, and for two days Hugo lived in the hut. The Tuareg woman brought food, water, and he was able to make tea on the burner. There was always an armed man present for his protection. As the sun set on the third day, Hugo heard the squealing of camels. The party of ten men took a wide arc around the fort. While Brun and Hugo walked, the Bedouin rode easily in their saddles towards the spot where Hugo hoped the vehicle would be, with Brun reminding him that he needn't recall the location, because the Tuareg knew exactly where it was. Later, in the starry glow of night, with the moon just rising, Hugo saw the Land Rover as a black mark against a charcoal horizon. He put two ropes through the hooks in the bumper, extended them to the four waiting camels, and they began the long tow back. The next day, with the sun providing sufficient light, Brun took off the carburetor. Within half an hour he had popped out a small drop of solder blocking an air jet. He put it back together, refilled the radiator, and the motor started with two cranks of the handle. That night, by orders of the headman, they drove it to the west gate of the fort, took out the keys, and left.

The next morning, an unarmed soldier approached the hut with a message that the commandant wished a meeting. At the time preset by the headman, the army chief swaggered out of the fort and sat down on top of the vehicle's hood. He put both hands together as a visor to shade his eyes from the intense light of the setting sun. With their rifles slung carelessly, a dozen soldiers stood to one side of him and squinted as the tribesmen approached from the west. Hugo and Brun stopped a few feet from the Land Rover. Behind them walked six unarmed Tuareg and the headman cradling a rifle in his arms. The soldiers shuffled nervously. One of them looked back towards the fort. Thirty men were lined along the top battlement with rifle barrels pointing out.

"What do you want?" Hugo said to the chief.

"I want this vehicle, troublemaker. Then you can go free." He put a packet of paper on the fender.

"I think you're a liar," Hugo answered.

The little man's eyes bulged. His neck went red. "I have the vehicle now. Just give me the keys."

"I think you should hand me the *carnet* first."

"You're being foolish, monsieur, I don't need your keys, I can get this thing going without keys."

"You need them because the vehicle has a lockout, and it's not likely you'll figure where it is, or how it operates."

The little man became more agitated. "Then give me the keys," he screamed. Uncontrolled rage spread over his face. He slid off the hood and took a step behind the Rover. He narrowed his eyes against the glare. "One last chance, give me the keys."

His soldiers tried to raise the barrels of their rifles with one arm, using the other to shade their eyes.

"*Au revoir*," said Hugo and waved his hand. The little man turned as if to walk back to the fort, took two steps, and swung around with his handgun drawn and arm coming up. Brun pulled Hugo aside. A single gunshot sounded in the air. The chief fell backwards with a hole in the space above his nose. Sporadic gunfire sounded from high up on the fort wall. The young Tuareg beside Hugo fell, clutching his side. Hugo took hold of him, and as he dragged the wounded man to the shelter of the Rover, a volley of gunfire loud as thunder deafened his ears. A pall of smoke rose from the ridge to the west. A few desperate cries went up from the battlements. A man pitched eight meters to the ground and bounced off the sand with a puff of dust. The soldiers standing behind the truck laid down their rifles. Some leaned casually against the vehicle. The headman lowered his rifle and nodded grimly to them, as if he had just killed a troublesome goat. He gestured for the others to wait, walked to where the chief lay face-up, and used his toe to lift the dead man's head from the sand, which blotted up the blood that dripped from the back of his skull. Satisfied, he waved for his men to stand down, then came over to watch Hugo bandage the wounded man.

"*C'est fini*," he said.

Brun stood up. "We're safe now. There won't be anymore action from the fort."

As Hugo walked onto the ridge, the sun's rim dropped below the desert floor. Free from the blinding light, he was able to count sixty men from the encampment strapping their smoking rifles around them like ornaments. Talk murmured through the group, then fell away like the evening wind. The man who had been Hugo's bodyguard waved at him.

"The Tuareg will be gone in two days," Brun said. "They were leaving anyway, to a place somewhere between Bourem and Timbuktu, closer to the Niger as the heat builds. They'll be back here for the fall caravans."

"And him?" Hugo pointed to the deceased commandant.

"The soldiers will bury him in the graveyard east of the fort and be happy to do it. He will be listed as a casualty of unknown bandits. Second in command, or whoever is the strongest, will assume the leadership. No official record will be made of what happened. People here will only argue with the heat unless someone breaks a taboo. Getting rid of a stupid tyrant is not taboo." As they watched four men carry the wounded youth back to camp, Brun added, "People here are patient. They'll remember your help, as you will remember their's."

"What are you going to do now?" Hugo asked.

"Wait for fall, I suppose."

"Come with me."

"Without papers I wouldn't get far. And that would implicate you. They use any excuse to extract money. You might lose the Rover."

"The chief's gone. Ask for your papers back."

"One day a month ago he went mad and burned my passport. If I go with you it will be trouble."

"We'll do what we have to. If you want to get out of here without waiting three months, take my advice and come along. I have no visas. That leaves both of us with a shortfall. Can't be too much of a problem to evade the authorities in these wide open spaces."

"It's not all open, *bitte*. To the south are mountain passes, narrow valleys, the bogs of the Niger. You cannot evade detection forever."

"What's your point?" asked Hugo. Without answering, Brun went silently to gather up his belongings and put them in the truck. They shook hands with the Tuareg headman, then drove down the piste through evening twilight. Hugo could see standing by the last tent the girl who had been the bearer of the teacup, his constant companion the first days he was in the hut. She raised up her hand. Hugo waved back and said, "We'll drive until we get to the frontier at Tessalit, and then sleep. I want to cross into Mali before it gets too light."

They rounded a bend and the image of the girl receded in the side mirror. Soon, she disappeared. Brun said, "I guess my point is this, comrade—how willing are you to kill for your progress in life?"

Chapter XX

Frontiers

The piste now rolled over and between outcroppings of the Adrar des Iforhas Mountains. When Hugo tired of driving, they slept. At the first indication of dawn, they resumed the journey, talking as they went of random episodes, events that brought them together at this point. At the top of the first high ridge he could see, stretching away to the south, a wide valley twenty kilometers long set erratically with baobab trees. Before it was fully light, he stopped again and walked to a promontory of rock. With his binoculars he could make out the hut that marked the frontier between Algeria and Mali. There was no indication of people, only a wooden barrier across the track. Since temperatures were moderate, they continued to drive in daylight but were wary of contact. They had taken a wide berth around several settlements when Brun pointed to dust on the road ahead. Hugo parked in a thicket of low bush. At the last moment he jumped out and hailed a loaded truck. The driver described the checkpoints, the most significant being at Bourem, manned by soldiers who would demand money regardless of the state of their papers. He also cautioned against making contact with the Tuareg on the Gao road. Hugo bartered for local currency and food, then moved off. The first day they covered four hundred kilometers, leaving two hundred and seventy to the fortress at Bourem. In the afternoon of the following day they descended gently, with the piste becoming less rough. Palm trees replaced the stunted bushes.

 This increasing greenery and the expectation of running water gave Hugo the feeling that he was reentering a familiar world. It was with more gratitude than fear, therefore, that he came round a sharp bend and saw, three hundred meters ahead, a fortified pillbox to the side of a gate blocking the road. Soldiers slumped in the afternoon heat, one with his arm draped over a heavy machine gun. They returned to the desert wilderness and aimed southeast in the direction of Gao road. At the peak of one high dune, Hugo could see in the southwest the low walls of Fort Bourem and behind that the sun glinting from the Niger River. An hour later, the light faded and they went forward cautiously in the dark using only starlight to see the shapes of gullies and dunes.

The terrain leveled and they were able to speed faster across the valley floor. Then fires sprung up and they were in the midst of tents with Tuareg scattering from their path and a tribesman pointing a rifle in the window. A man appeared and Brun handed him a package. In an hour they had filled themselves with goat meat and dates. Scouts guided them to the road and they drove onto it without lights. Hours later, Hugo veered into the thick bush near the river so they could sleep in peace. As the light blazed along the horizon, he stripped off his clothes and waded slowly out. When the muddy Niger was to his waist, he soaped himself down, then squatted to let the water flow over and into his skin.

At the first indications of Gao they went off the road and parked. Each took a different direction into town and found his own way. At two in the afternoon they met at the vehicle and made their plan. At three o'clock, while Brun drove into the fuel dump, Hugo walked into the army barracks and demanded to see the commander. "I wish to file a complaint," he said then related a fictitious story of how he came to be there.

"We don't sell visas," the officer replied. "The government sells them in Paris."

Hugo took a smoke and offered one to his host. He lit them both with matches.

"Are you saying that I have to go back to Paris to get a visa?"

"No. I'm saying that I would like to see your passport."

"Why don't we just bargain a little?"

"No bargains," said the chief and called out. A soldier came into the room with his rifle raised. Hugo moved just far enough to his left to look out the window. He could see past the corner of the building to the attendant filling the jerricans. Off to the side, Brun argued with the soldiers, who made threatening gestures and pointed towards the barracks.

"I think I'm leaving now," Hugo said, and as the commandant ordered the guard forward, ducked through the door. The soldier who stood outside moved into his way. With the elbow of his right hand, Hugo knocked him off the porch and into a rubble pile. Screaming with pain and blood running down his face, the man tried to aim his rifle. Hugo ran past him, snatched the weapon out of the man's grasp, then turned the side of the building and sprinted into the adjacent forest. As he went through the trees that lead to the river, horns and sirens sounded. Armed men ran from hut doors and the soldiers at the fuel dump scurried towards the barracks. With one glance, he could see Brun driving the Land Rover back down the road leading northwest to Bourem.

Coursing southeast through the undergrowth, Hugo let his legs settle into a long lope. In five minutes the town had fallen away. The loud noises also diminished. Far off, he could hear engines racing, further on nothing but the sound of flowing water. He was alone on a dirt track that vanished in the fringe of river mud. He threw the rifle far out into the current, then increased his pace across the hard surface of a dry swamp. In an hour he had distanced himself from Gao by ten kilometers, stopping only once to fill his canteen. Three hours on, he turned north up a dry flood channel, crossed the empty road, and set out for a rise of land to the north. Thirst and hunger slowed his pace. At darkness he ate some cold sausage from his satchel and lay down to sleep. Late the next morning he climbed to the summit of a hogsback. All day he kept to the highest points of the ridge and at regular intervals scanned the terrain below with his field glasses. Before the sun had set, he climbed down a cleft in the rock and there hidden by leaf cuttings was the Land Rover. Next to it was a skeptical Brun trying to make tea from Hugo's rations.

The next day, they went further in the rocky hills and kept there, negotiating steep slopes with a hand winch and cable. Well past the Niger frontier and close to Niamey, they joined the traffic on a road built high on the north slope. To the south, stretched panoramas of the Niger valley cut by sweeping curves of the river. Dotted along its banks were villages set amongst groves of broad-leafed trees. Above the valley, grasslands ran to the horizon. Loping over it Hugo could see giraffes spooked by their passing.

With the first hint of poles carrying electrical wire, came the first paved road Hugo had seen since Bechar. On this welcome surface, they cruised the core of the city and noted the embassies, commerce, bars, and restaurants. Hugo followed a girl on a scooter, whose yellow hair fluttered from the rim of her helmet. She went into the north area of town, where the houses were ringed with drab walls. Swaths of green and bright color overflowed these boundaries and swept down hills to the river. The young woman stopped in a drive no different from the others. Hugo said politely, "We need a place to stay, away from prying eyes, you understand."

"There's a hotel in the city center, not far from the embassy district," she answered.

"Actually, I was hoping for something like a cheap hostel."

"No hostels," she replied.

A man appeared wearing torn pants and an Arab headdress. Hugo held out his hand and introduced them both.

"You could stay here," the man said as he examined the vehicle. "But this looks like one of Crasson's."

Hugo raised his eyebrow.

"You've been here for a while," the man said with a tone of confidence.

The remark confused Hugo. "Why would you assume that?" he asked.

"In summer, most people who come over the Hoggar find it difficult, almost impossible to end up this far west."

"We came over the Tanezrouft," said Hugo. The man squinted with suspicion. He allowed them to stay anyway, and that night went with them to a bar in the center of town. In the morning Brun presented himself at the German legation and announced at dinner that he would stay in Niamey. Hugo went the next morning to the Sûreté National to obtain a letter of clearance. The chief of security, a large man with a weary face, lectured him from memorized government text, then gave him a visa to exit Niger. "At the frontier with Dahomey, where the road at Gaya passes over the river," he said, "a man there will feed you. He is the husband of my wife's sister."

From the meal Hugo had at Gaya to the port city of Cotounu on the Gulf of Guinea, was a distance of seven hundred kilometers. On its way, the track passed through belts of thickening vegetation and humid air. Many times he passed lines of bearers transporting forty kilogram bunches of green bananas on their heads. On the second day of this trip, he stopped to smoke and watch one of the young women. Her enormous burden was balanced on a head supported by a thin neck and a thinner body. Her breasts swayed evenly side to side with the movement of hips, legs and bare feet. He could tell little difference, take away the fruit, between this almost-naked girl walking along the dirt track and a model he had seen in a magazine striding down a carpeted runway. They were worlds apart, but one sorry fact highlighted their solidarity: The first women survived, and the second prospered, for the reason that they both had no choice but provide the headman with a good lay. At the frontier marking the entrance to Nigeria, an agent charged him a levy of thirty pounds as a surety and guaranteed he would get the money back when he left the country. Hugo knew that the return of his money was unlikely. He reluctantly paid the cash, knowing he may as well have given it to the banana girl as compensation for the brutish reality of her life. Then he resumed his journey to the sea.

The metropolis of Lagos had already entered the wet season. With rain dripping into his eyes and the torrent almost to his ankles, Hugo inspected the main thoroughfares, the shanties, and markets overarched by billboards exhorting citizens to rid themselves of malaria. How blessed it was this time of the year, he thought, when the guaranteed monsoons—while increasing the likelihood of disease—at least rid the city of all the garbage that would float. Where such things were rid to, Hugo could not ponder. But he hoped, for the health of the next generation, it was far away in the very deepest part of the sea. That afternoon the attendant at a safe compound for vehicles said that the ferry to Apapa would take him close to the Seaman's Mission.

The Mission had no rooms available, only showers. When dark came, he drank a dozen beers with the sailors, entertaining them with stories told through the mouth of a fat man he referred to as Billy. When the bartender called time at eleven, he staggered into the chapel. The sparse light from a match outlined rows of wooden pews. Further in was an altar covered with layers of thin cloth—thin, but thick enough to provide him some hope of comfort. He removed his clothes, and in the stuffy air of the tropical night lay face upwards in silence.

The improvised bed was not comfortable. His body squirmed on the hard surface until he found one position that allowed him to relax. Dizzy from the drink, his brain could only manage a stilted reprise of its library of remembered sounds. He smiled to hear seagulls mewing in his ears and the hard rain making a river of the ditches. Void of any fear, he listened to the deep Atlantic roar and the wind screaming in the wires—or more in keeping with recent time— the screams of men he had removed violently from his path. The agony of their pain gathered into a chorus he thought appropriate for a Christian place— apropos as well that he hum with them, singing, tapping his fingers on the altar wood, marching tired legs onwards, with the cross of Jesus in front and spirits raised to a high pitch by the pipes, drums, and boot-heels of the Royal Navy at Westminster. He smiled to imagine scarred hands holding swords high, in salute to the war dead and Korrolus as well limping along in the ranks, arm only half-raised, not appearing particularly proud he had escaped death by Von Raynor's act of indecision, if indecision it was.

Finding only a trace of his own guilt or pride or mercy, Hugo dismissed the choir of complaint and gave a last consideration to his task of locating Wallace Fraser, the next member of the regiment he hoped to meet. In the meantime, lying naked, comfortable in his own sweat, he continued to drum his fingers on the wood thinking it really didn't matter what hymn he sang or whose carcass lay on which altar, because all souls would become one with the risen God— or perhaps not. For if all beings ascend to the level of God, then why had he forsaken himself? He strained to hear an answer. But the sounds coming from in or out of his head made no noise in the airless, overheated chamber. The place had its own murmurings like the mouth close to his ear that made the air stir like a cloth bellows.

"Good question, mate!" announced a tiny breathing voice in the front pew.

"But you've forsaken yourself nevertheless…with reason or no reason. And by so doing, you threaten to make my life a misery beyond what I've endured these past fifty years."

Hugo turned his head towards the dark pews. In the faint glow coming from under the door he could see Albert sitting with his legs crossed, arm stretched comfortably along the backrest.

"I thought you'd finally left me to live or die in peace."

"In peace? Now there's a bit of dodge ball. I've been watching you slowly dig your way along the last little while, like you knew what you were doing. And here I find you in another place of worship, this time having the great good sense to displace the false god from the altar you think belongs to you."

"It belongs to the proprietor of this building and the Church of England, all directed by men who know how to extort profit from a good habit."

"Perhaps you could explain for me the significance of symbols, of transmutations, of belief…and habit," replied the old man. "You profess to know the music of Beethoven, the inner voice of Tolstoy, the art of Rubens. So why the charade of calming your immortal soul with innocent beauty when you conspire to succeed by force?"

"I have never judged myself innocent," Hugo replied. "Taking your advice, I don't dwell on the results of my actions."

"Certainly not on your wickedness. But then most of us seldom do. Thereby men and women are not moved to show mercy, which sits adjacent to humility. But I tell you what. The man you knocked over in Gao—he could very well lose his eye. And the scant medical attention he receives now in the attempt to save his sight is nothing of the kind you received to save your arm, not to mention your life."

"I had no choice in the matter."

"You are drunk and disingenuous. Do no harm! What of that? Words I heard you say that night in the alley to calm a troubled conscience."

"History!"

"It is the oath you swore and should honor throughout your life, irrespective of the path you follow."

"Maybe when I get to your place of business, I might roll up my sleeves. As for oaths, that part is done and past."

"Nevertheless, I'm counting on your contribution to my efforts, Doctor. And one more thing, what of Beth Marshall? Is she done and past as well?"

"I would say so."

"Your callousness doesn't absolve you of her suffering, which she is now attempting to resolve by attending to your family."

Hugo struggled to sit up, moved a little too far, and fell to the hard stones, hitting first with his bare knees and elbows. Crying with pain and disbelief, he started yelling. "You're a wily old codger, Albert. What are you saying here?

There's no family left for her to attend to. Ibecks has succeeded Muxlow as the village idiot. Conrad Muir has put himself in the abyss of his own past."

He got to his feet and massaged his knees. "Albert, are you still here?" he whispered. Down the aisle nothing showed but the small line of light under the door. It carried no message, no shadow of anything from past or present. The only sound that came into his head was the humming on the bus, the old man chanting, "Better clean ye'self up or the missus be on ye…" and him replying that he had no missus, only a woman who ruled his thoughts as if she were the mother of God. Sitting down, he felt a tightness in his chest and sought to appease this discomfort by imagining the soldier in Gao and what miracles he might do to help him. He saw the man lying on his side, hand pressed to his eye, and blood pouring through his fingers. His moans mingled with the general choir of weeping in Hugo's head. He shut it off. Darkness congealed around him, thickening into the shape of a dusty, unfurnished room arrived at by an insufficiency of planning and willful neglect. Hours later, waking stiffly on the wooden pew nearest the entrance, he had only a moment to pull on his pants before the door opened and the light came on.

"Just gathering my thoughts, Padre," he said and left the Mission.

The place given by Morrice Crasson as the address of Wallace Fraser was closed, the door locked, and no note attached as to a time of opening. So he drove to the British High Commission. The receptionist could give him no advice as to a cheap place to stay, but advised him that the east coast of Victoria Island might be suitable. Close to the water he stopped at a small store and bought some canned goods. While he was bartering with the clerk, a man disoriented by drink approached and said, "Don't go to the beach, buddy. They'll have you for breakfast. At the north end is a ju-ju village lived in by cannibals. Set up shop there and your shrunken head will be on sale next week in the Onitsha market."

Hugo camped in the man's garden and for entertainment watched the Housa nightman search the grounds for black and green mambas, whose eight-foot long carcasses he hung over the fence railings in hopes their relatives would be warned off. The next day the alcoholic owner introduced him to his Nigerian colleagues who told him that despite advances in science and their own skeptical natures, they had hard evidence of magical events. One man showed him a wooden box containing a black feather and several white ones. He announced that the black feather was under the spell of the shape-changer in the swamp, who went in a man and came out a snake. "The ju-ju is good because the white feathers are the progeny of the black," he said. "They're an omen of a peaceful life for me and my family."

On his way a second time to meet Wallace Fraser, Hugo parked the Land Rover on the street front and made his way through beggars who had no hope of peace from magic or any other means. Pleading for money or food, they rolled after him on carts supporting legless torsos, or crawled on limbs bent and gnarled; some had misshapen, pocked faces or curved spines and all had cracked, sloughing skin burdened with sores and grotesque outcroppings of disease. Hugo gave each a half-crown. He was glad to be in the door, running up the stairs with the directions in his hand from Crasson, although he knew that the trader never intended that he arrive there. Down the hall was a door tagged with the name of an import company written in Polish and English. Hugo was relieved to see that the girl at the desk was at peace—free of scurvy, malaria, starvation, disfigurement, and all blemishes. She had a perfect London accent and smiled when he walked in.

"Wallace Fraser is out presently. He's a hard man to meet unless you're wanting to do business. Are you here to do business, Mr. Haultain?"

"I'm here to make Mr. Fraser rich."

Her smile grew wider. On the desk Hugo placed the envelope with the photo of the *Kyle Mission* and a brief note introducing him as a relative of Allan Korrolus and thereby an acquaintance of Blenkinthorpe, Dring, and Morrice Crasson. She took a suspicious look at it. When she snatched out to grab it, Hugo drew it back. The young woman held the offending hand and smiled to compose herself.

"Trust me, sir. He will get it. Does it contain any money? No. Just joking."

She took the picture from the envelope and she was still puzzling over it when Hugo left.

The next day he returned to the British High Commission to retrieve information. When he gave his name, the receptionist told him to wait. She returned from an inner office with a look of mock gravity, then winked coyly and said the High Commissioner wished to see him. Hugo nodded and set his shoulders straight before walking down the corridor. The face of the man at the desk was sour, fatigued. His eyelids were puffy and drooped. "Sit down, Mr. Haultain," he said.

As the High Commissioner began talking, Hugo noticed that from the window he could see the vicinity of Victoria Island and the swamps behind, from which he was aware emerged at certain times of the year erotically charged snake-men. He felt his feet go cold at the suggestion of shape-changers or juju men.

The man at the desk droned on. "I also have here a communiqué from Niamey, which suggest a string of offences that includes illegal entry, evading arrest, destruction of property...I say, I'm talking to you, chappie," the man said. Hugo turned away from the window.

"There is also a suggestion coming from the adjacent country of Mali that you may have been party to assaults there."

"I lacked a visa for Niger."

"And Mali?"

"The same. All of the rest is gossip—or exaggeration."

"Whatever the truth is, Mr. Haultain, if I hear of any mischief from here on in I won't be slow to act."

The High Commissioner put aside Hugo's file and took out another one as a sign the hearing was over. As he rose to leave, Hugo said, "I understand, Excellency, that the British legation in Lagos is hosting a gala on Saturday night next and that people of note are invited. Would that include..."

"Not you, Mr. Haultain, by no means the likes of you."

On his way out he stopped by the receptionist's desk. "Do you have a guest list for the official reception?"

She smiled and nodded. "Yes I do. But you can't see it."

He leaned over close to her face. "Just have a look and see if a Mr. Wallace Fraser is on it."

"Why should I do that?"

"No reason. I'm an old friend of his family, who has given him up for dead. But it doesn't matter. We'll just have to let them suffer."

Unbelieving and with great patience, she peered over the top of her glasses. "The list reads, 'Wallace Fraser, escorting a Miss Hazel Twist.'" When he left, Hugo also had in his hand an invitation card with his name on it.

"A party for us," muttered the man next to Hugo in the receiving line. "The headmen of the nations, an international cartel of freeloaders, all committed to peace in Africa so they can eat their fancy sandwiches and drink free champagne."

They moved on down the line; the man was joined by a woman with dark eyes, her hair pulled back tightly from her face and the excess curled up at the back. She winked at Hugo. At regular intervals she touched his arm. Her escort slicked back his hair and wiped the palms of his hands on his suit jacket. In a few minutes of chat they took their place in front of the High Commissioner, who said meaningless, ingratiating things. The couple moved on and the smile faded from the host's face. A small map of veins glowed red in his cheeks. He shook the intruder's hand and was about to protest when his wife reached out also for the guest's hand and smiled graciously, asking to be told who he was.

The doctor grinned and the woman shook harder and touched his arm with such intimacy that the High Commissioner turned away. Once through the line, Hugo moved off to the refreshment table looking for someone who might be Wallace Fraser and his companion, Hazel Twist, but amongst the wandering crowd could see no clue to their identities. Still watching and making mental notes, he ate a few rolled sandwiches and a mango desert. He was inching towards the bar when the High Commissioner, accompanied by two aides, cut him off.

"Mr. Haultain." The diplomat spoke in a quiet, stern voice. "Recently I recall we had a little pow-wow. At that time I warned you against incursions into my territory. Now that you've wormed your way in here, we can discuss this." He brandished a manila folder and took a letter out of it. "These are official complaints from the government of Niger detailing other offences. Official and duly noted complaints, you understand. And let's not forget Mali, gossip or not. May I ask how many other countries you have had your joy ride through? I suspect even worse—that it's your intention to make more unpleasant work for the diplomatic service."

Hugo felt an uplifting tingle in his hands and feet, the lightness of a boxer like Johnny Prescott, primed and wiped clean by his trainer. With his left hand he smoothed out his pants and shuffled his feet. The Commissioner resumed talking. "Because, my man, I won't sit idly by, as I said before. I can confiscate your passport, forcibly repatriate you, and have you charged with mischief...as well as giving you a large bill for the costs."

Hugo finished eating the pastry that was in his right hand and wiped his fingers on a napkin. Then he cleared his throat, and in a voice touched with anger, said, "If you've finished, sir, with all due respect I might be tempted to say you're out of line with your false accusations. And in regards your attitude...were I to take some dainty trifle from this table, say that nice cake over there topped with mango slices and whipped cream, quite a bit of hard work for your pastry chef, I might add...were I to be bothered by you the least bit more, I might be tempted to push it into your pompous mug with a delicate touch so that it dripped down your shirt front. It would be a reminder of the cushy situation you have here at taxpayer's expense."

Hugo finished the last of this sentence as the aides carried him to the nearest door, out into the morbidly humid air, and threw him onto the pavement of the car park with such force he wrenched his left arm trying to break the fall. Still on his hands and knees, he leaned on the pavement for a few minutes, fighting back the dizziness of pain. He was not far from the Land Rover and crawled over to it. Reaching to the handle, he noticed two pairs of legs standing to one side.

The curving, muscular calves belonged to a woman in her mid-twenties. She was wearing a wide-brimmed hat over her dark eyes and a ruler straight nose. She had a look of grave concern, no passion in her eyes, and reached out her hand as if offering to help him up. But she withdrew it politely when she saw the bleeding abrasion. The man said, "That was a foolish thing to have done at the table, my friend, but entertaining to say the least. I love a good scene."

When Hugo tried struggling to his feet, a large hand reached down to pull him upright. The woman said, "This is Wallace Fraser."

Hugo shook the offered hand and said, "When I last looked at the guest list, Wallace Fraser was paired with Hazel Twist. Nice to meet you, Miss Twist."

With an exaggerated sense of delicacy, Hazel shook hands. "Glad to meet you, Mr....?"

She looked at her companion for a cue. The man shrugged his shoulders. Hugo smiled and introduced himself. Fraser pulled out a silver case and passed it around then lit the three cigarettes with a gold lighter.

"Well that's good," Hugo said. "All of us smoking away here like lost relatives. As to my place, I left a package at your office a few days ago describing the family tree."

Fraser's face lightened. "I recognized the photos, but not the connection."

"The connection will come later," Hugo said and looked around him like he was expecting more trouble. They each took a nervous drag on their smokes, then Fraser said, "We're on our way to a club downtown. I think you should join us instead of waiting here for the police to put you on the street. Apparently, we each have something to say."

It was steaming hot inside the Roxdale Lounge. Hugo had four quick cocktails and thought how delighted Albert would have been to attend with him. Here was happy music: a trumpet, saxophone, piano, and drums, combined in the West African high-life tradition. Dutiful men played the instruments. Much like Albert, they were musicians and émigrés, not necessarily to the jungle but, Bourbon Street, Greenwich Village, Soho, and Rive-Gauche, to fancy up the venues and ruin their health.

Wallace Fraser finished his fifth drink together with his sixth preposterous story. As he talked, his gray hair showed white in the stage beacons, his creamy face unaffected by the tedious stream of hyperbole. He seemed a man who would accept any finish to his life's unhealthy strut so long as it promised another drink and a good screw, being the two best of a bowl-full of tropical pleasures. He was drawn tightly as were the others into the circle of gathered tables as if to repel the curfew, because at four am the maitre d' would expel them from the dignity of culture into the woe of the beggar's gauntlet. Hugo counted twenty-two heads and could see from their agonized smiles that they cherished any postponement to an equatorial dawn. Wallace Fraser drank the last of his Tom Collins and addressed their hopes.

"I want to end tonight with the most exciting story I could tell, albeit my contribution to it, my character so to speak is minor. But I'll let you be the judge."

The waiter came with another tray full of drinks and a line of hands passed them along. Fraser gratefully took one and lit a cigarette. His forehead shone with uneven streaks of perspiration. He was saying, "This story concerns myself, of course and a few others. The time was January 22, 1942, on the road to Oran as it crossed the west ridge above Algiers. I was part of a group charged with exterminating local Vichy resistance to the Allied invasion. As day wore on we had stopped to rest at the eastern end of a section of the road and were feeling apprehensive, on edge. An hour before, a Royal Marine and some Yanks had been killed in an ambush. We could now and then hear other fire, not a pitched battle, but guerilla skirmishes.

"I was no hero and it didn't help my morale to know that our group was commanded by Lieutenant Martin Birks, a veteran of Dunkirk. He was a tough character, particularly outrageous in the risks he was prepared to take. I kept my eye out for him, I did, and followed George Blenkinthorpe everywhere we went. George was a sapper, a cold fish and always had his own eye out for mines and traps. We had just got back on the move when a gunner named Hutchinson caught up to us and said there were four more dead from mortar fire in the next street. It was beginning to sound like pitched battle was close. Worse, we feared another ambush.

"Then Hutchison, a man big enough to carry his 20-millimeter Browning with the ease of a sidearm, spotted a large lorry pounding up the road, dust streaming behind. The vehicle had no markings, so we had no idea if it was us or them, so to speak. We moved closer to the road. Hutchison set up his gun, ready to put a burst into the cab, which must have terrified the lorry driver because he braked suddenly. As it skidded to a stop, we came under attack from a small building opposite. We dove for cover as machine gun fire raked across the bodywork of truck.

"I remember the driver giving off with a vile stream of invective in assorted languages including English, German, with a few words of Latin too, according to Birks. He was screaming in fright about surrendering, pissing himself as he cowered behind the wheel. Hutchinson returned fire with his big gun. It was a deafening racket, with the clanking of spent shells on the hard ground and the reek of powder. A bursting mortar shell hit close to the back of the lorry nearly knocking it off the road. Hutchison was killed instantly, his head blown off by shrapnel.

"But we persevered. I crept through beneath the lorry and kept up a steady fire on the building. George and Martin managed to get in the cab and shove aside the driver. George took the wheel and Birks grabbed the Browning, threw it on top of the boxed goods in the rear, and began to fire through the shredded canvas. More shells burst close to the lorry, but Birks kept at it. I was in myself, by that time, to continue firing with my sten, while George maneuvered his way through the maze of huts and buildings at breakneck speed towards the direction the lorry had come. In short order, we came into the safe territory of Algiers. We ground to a stop, the lorry reduced to flapping fenders and two good tires. The patrol surrounding us were at first suspicious, until we fell out and collapsed on the ground, all except the original driver slumped in the passenger seat in rather poor shape. It was something of a miracle he was alive at all.

"A Captain Owen Dring commanded the medical tent. The place was short-staffed so Dring saw personally to his friend Birks, who had a minor wound in his side, then was called to attend to the driver, who they had set on the ground next to me. He was still conscious and upset, but apparently not at the fact we had just rescued him from certain death. When Dring came to examine him, the wounded man introduced himself quite formally, then repeated what he had said to me, in effect that his lorry contained contraband bound for Oran. In his delirium, he confessed to six more loads to haul in ten days or, as he said, "People will die." Dring leaned over him, called the man by his name and told him that he was nearly dead himself and wouldn't be taking any more lorry trips for the moment. A few minutes more he was wheeled out, and that was the last I saw of him.

"The lorry was still at camp when Birks, sufficiently recovered from his wounds, returned it to the warehouse in Algiers to relieve the man of awkward questions the military police might have asked him regarding the nature of his business. It was there that we met Crasson and Korrolus and confirmed by the papers found amongst the man's things, that the contents were indeed as the Swiss man described, contraband goods destined for the black market. The manifest itself was stamped with the name 'Crasson et Fils, Algiers.' Crasson had heard Korrolus' story of survival aboard the *Kyle Mission*, shown in this photograph that Mr. Haultain has brought along for our entertainment. After hearing of our trying time, and thinking it adventurous, Crasson took our picture, with all of us smiling and agreeing to benefit jointly from distribution of this windfall. After all, we had risked our lives in securing it. In turn we had helped save a man's life and kept him out of the brig for his misdemeanors."

Wallace Fraser lent over to give Hazel Twist a nudge on the cheek. She moved slightly at the touch and looked towards Hugo. "At any rate," Fraser summed up, "we all moved to other theatres of war. Dring went to Italy and gained the battlefield rank of major. I went back to England and briefly fought in France. Birks' injuries, sustained at the Kasserine Pass in February, forty-three, gave him a VC for his gallantry but forced him out of action. George found himself in Algiers for a time. Later he married one of the young nurses from the hospital as I am going to marry Hazel, should she consent to living with an old man who still has metal lodged in his hip."

Miss Twist moved her legs and pursed her lips at Hugo, whose head spun round with the liquor and the lateness of time. He turned to watch the trumpet's bell flash in the stage lights. The wavering notes, muffled and rich with the mute, accompanied the toast Fraser was giving to his friends. When the glasses were raised, Hugo asked, "Did you remember by chance the name of the profiteer who drove the truck full of contraband—the man you rescued?"

"Oh yes. One of the strange quirks of mind is to remember items of trivia. I recall that his name was Conrad Muir. Yes. I would never forget his name because apparently he was the brother of Von Raynor, the U-boat commander Korrolus alleged to have evaded. I thought it strange that full brothers would have different names. No, this is not a fantasy, Hazel, but the unlikely truth."

Wallace Fraser collapsed in his seat to the audible claps of the audience. The elements of his story went round in Hugo's head, snared here and there on random points of connection, perhaps not all random with some being unavoidable. The host soon became incoherent with the drinks that kept arriving via a waiter who always seemed fresh and invigorated. Hugo knew that he was fresh because he had read somewhere that men born to West Africa required the hot, vaporous atmosphere to make their blood circulate. On the contrary, Hugo felt out of his element, dried, thick, and stale like Fraser's story, a poor tale, a discredit to Muir, who was not so old and vile as he wanted his son to believe.

That night in Fraser's house, Hugo listened to noises through the wall. He conceived them to be an attempt by the host to pin Hazel Twist to the bed, but determined later they were the geckoes making their way up and down the walls. There was also the internal noise of his own misery that he was powerless to disassociate, in a dream that came later in the night, from the cries of a woman with her hand outstretched to him.

Chapter XXI

Lambaréné

The route east from Benin City sliced through villages lined with farm animals and human aces dulled by malaria. Rain and traffic made the surface of the road rutted and greasy. Part way across a narrow wooden trestle, Hugo braked suddenly and reversed to the west side. Speeding down the one-lane road on the opposite bank was a loaded truck. Three Yurobas in the dark cab were visible to him only by their smiling white teeth. As the truck rushed past him off the end of the bridge, Hugo suspected the maniacal set of their mouths indicated some cruelty ahead. The reason for their panic showed a kilometer further on. On a sharp corner close by a village lay the overturned wreck of a bus. The engine still creaked with the dissipating heat. Eighteen bodies intermingled with the sheared and bent metal. Human gore mixed freely with the dismembered parts of goats and chickens. Those alive still spewed blood.

One man picked his way through the carnage with his head clenched between shaking hands. Standing on the roadside the other villagers chanted ju-ju prayers for the living and curses for the thieves, who had stolen things they could carry off readily, leaving their bloody footprints on the pavement. After extinguishing a fire burning in the engine compartment, Hugo helped the lone villager tend the wounds of the six people still alive. Then, starting with the children, he began covering up the dead, chanting as he went the language used in Conrad's favorite book—suffer them to come unto me. Yes Lord, he thought, of course they seek refuge because all children suffer in this land. And of course they suffer more because they are heathens or animists who live and die with the aid of tokens, fetishes, human flesh, skulls, and magic potions, all items for sale in the Onitsha market, some taken from other wrecks. Before he resumed his journey almost all the victims had perished, the last being a legless boy who, despite Hugo's attempts to stop his bleeding, died with his small hand clutching the collar of his crushed dog. Content with the almost uniform conclusion, the villager announced to the waiting crowd that the two survivors had simply responded to the miracle of the traveler's special ju-ju.

With this poignant memory guiding his driving hands and feeding his anxieties, Hugo found himself that evening at the Asaba ferry, waiting in a long line of trucks and cars on the west bank of the Niger River. He had a clear view of the lights of Onitsha on the opposite bank two kilometers distant, with its inventory of heads and perhaps other human parts including fingers and toes for charms, offered for sale at retail prices. All around him was a languishing merriment and through the air the sounds of high-life music played on portable radios set besides burning fires. He tried to lather up enough soap to get the blood off his hands, which the ladies in the queue assumed was from the butchering of a chicken, yet were prudent to look away on the off-chance it was not only African blood, but human as well.

The next morning Hugo was on the second ferry across the river and once on the Onitsha side, drove through the market stopping only to buy a battered flute he could see from the road, not delving down alleys and passages where he could have bought other sacraments. At Enugu he stayed with an English family recommended by Wallace Fraser. The man said they would leave Nigeria soon because in some circles rumor implied that competing forces were threatening civil war. In the eastern district the roads ran through increasingly thick jungle covering steeper terrain. After a hundred miles he reached the frontier at M'fum, where he expected blank stares at his receipt for the thirty pounds he had paid for surety. But the clerk examined the document, stamped it as being paid, and dealt three bank notes from a metal box.

The bridge exiting the country had little traffic, so Hugo stopped in midspan and stared into the cataract of an unnamed tributary of the Cross River. He put his hands on the wood of the rail and thought how alike this water was to streams flowing from the main ranges of his home, created from the perpetual showers predicted by the voice on the radio, with each shower, puddle, and pool more diffuse the further it journeyed from the source and having greater connection to the land. Some became cluttered with debris or otherwise fouled by local circumstance. He remembered the chlorine-tainted pool in Coventry with the water churned to froth by those seeking the pleasures of life and not too much death. His hands grasped the pitted wood of the rail as they had gone round the limbs of the drowning boys, pulling them out of their graves as other hands had pulled him up from the pit of his own failures. On the green fringes of his mind he saw a woman's hand slip into view. But he was less certain now of her assistance. In the jungle were no means of purifying the instruments of healing and also no means to purge disappointment, as should be the rule everywhere.

On the Cameroon side of the bridge his disappointments lessened. From Ekok the road climbed and with the moderate rise in elevation, temperatures fell. Further on people waved. When he stopped at the first village to purchase fruit, the shopkeeper spoke good English and thanked him with a smile. The road kept climbing and more people waved. With each mile and the narrow road switching back and forth through more vertical terrain, the people seemed less burdened, more content. He arrived in Mamfe an hour before dark, but was told that the road running down to Kumba allowed one-way traffic on alternating days.

"It's steep, narrow, and treacherous," said the smiling man at the government post. "You will have to wait out tomorrow, then leave on the following morning."

Hugo set up his camp in one of the buildings fronting the road. Once the sun had gone, he set his mind to the lush, happy sounds of talking drums, stringed instruments, a flute and the beating of hands on wooden tabletops. The next morning he parked the Rover near the front of the line and gave a teenage boy a crown to watch it. He put the sharpened blade of his machete next to the boy's throat. "Anything missing when I come back and I have the juju to make you bleed and never stop, you understand?"

The boy grimaced and said, "Yes, master."

Hugo went a few paces. "On the other hand, M'usa, if nothing is gone, you get a second crown."

The boy smiled with all his white teeth and waved his arm at Hugo, who adjusted his satchel and put in his fingers to feel for the bag of food, a bottle of tea, and the flute. He walked away from the village along a narrow track lined with tall trees overcome with monkey chatter and birdcalls. To the northeast was a mountaintop faced with volcanic rock. A ravine littered with cones of talus split its western slope. By noon he had picked his way along the narrow trail, negotiated the steep pitches of the peak and was sitting in the open. The brilliance of midday cast a white pall across the hills. Seeking shelter from the sun he squeezed into a hollow depression, consumed his rations and tea, then passed the hours filling his spiral notebook. When the heat subsided he began his practice of the flute, determined to master simple scales before reaching Lambaréné. When next he shifted his focus to the outside, long shadows accented the valleys and deepened the texture of the forest. He pulled himself back onto the crown for a last look, which showed him in all directions only a wisp of smoke here and there to mark villages and human activity.

At the bottom of the scree he plunged into the undergrowth. The growing dark increased his wariness of predatory animals, all of them hungry, curious, threatened, as he was but him with no dark-adapted eyes to gauge sounds that might be all out of proportion to size or risk. He guessed the direction of the road and made for it by cutting a path through the tangle of bush. Unseen things removed themselves with a flutter of branches. He kept cutting, walking, and sweating until, as the darkness became complete, he tripped and fell face down onto the mud of the track.

When he returned to Mamfe, the convoys northbound from Kumba had already arrived with noise and campfires. The drivers talked amongst themselves, telling their stories for the amusement of those who would venture out in the morning. A few watched Hugo closely. It was a strange thing, they said, for anyone to be out at after dark with no light or gun. M'usa showed him the untouched Rover. Hugo had him check the number of boxes and jerricans then gave the boy the other crown and a sixpence as well. He bowed low several times and went off laughing into the night. Hugo sat on the edge of the group and watched the fire. That night it poured rain with monsoon ferocity.

The road down to Kumba was muddy and pocked with sharp volcanic rock. Beyond and through Doula was level and easy going to Yaounde in the interior. After lunch the British Charge d'Affaires offered Hugo a case of cheap scotch and a detailed map. Later, at a shop that sold espresso, he examined the sheet. The road into Gabon had sections marked "Dry season only" or indicated little more than a trail, a cut-line through the bush, with multiple river crossings by un-stated means. He pushed south early the next morning, and for two days drove steadily on a rutted, hole-filled track, floating many times on rafts across deep waterways.

Ten kilometers south from the crossing of the Abanga River the road improved, becoming wider and less rutted. The map indicated that he was fewer than thirty kilometers from the Schweitzer hospital, which stood on the north bank of the Oogue River. The time approached sunset and the rapid onset of night, so he stopped to make a small fire. At this latitude the dry season persisted and dead wood burnt easily. After eating he removed one book from his satchel and shuffled the pages. The text appeared foreign, the words unreliable. Dissatisfied, he stretched on the ground near the shut case and let his fears wander. As close as he was to a dot on the map, the mark he had aimed for in life was as remote as the starless black above him. Interesting places, important people seemed a wearying distance across sterile ground. He lay awake for hours inventing fruitless, mediocre resolutions. Thoughts of a general uproar or a string of premeditated lie seemed a more profitable activity, but only if he could muster his remaining strength. He turned his head away from the road and shut out the sound. The idea of the jungle around him, and its uniform, featureless space, allowed him to sleep.

Morning was not the cause of his waking. The dawn light was insufficient to penetrate his eyelids, but he could hear the crackle of burning wood, feel the perfumed smoke tickling the hairs in his nose. Then the fire blazed up and sparks showered his blanket. In the half-light, birds cawed and monkeys howled. The man sitting on the stump close to the fire remained silent. Hugo lit his first cigarette. For five minutes the man cooked the breakfast bacon in a dented pan. When it was finished, he threw it on a plate and said, "I always cook for visitors."

"The thing is," Hugo replied, "did you make fresh coffee?"

The old man turned to him and tossed a small dry branch into the fire, which blazed up. "You bet, and I made it just for you. Preferably, I'd drink a tumbler of scotch. But I'm out of the habit. In fact, I haven't enjoyed a good swig down here in years."

"These are strange times, then," said Hugo. "I've said all along that you should be seeing more to yourself. I have eleven bottles of scotch but I'll be using these as future payment for services rendered. So you'll have to make do with the coffee, which is quite good in my opinion."

The man snorted. "Your liquor isn't a payment for anything. It's a bribe. But I'm not surprised you would color things with the glow of your own superiority. Your opinion is as ill-formed in this as everything else. Let's talk about this so-called coffee. 'Quite good,' you say. A cup of bitter tasting chicory and you think you're in heaven. You may have lapses of common sense, but we can't accuse you of being hard to please."

"My opinions have shown me many things thus far and I expect to see more."

The old man stirred the fire with a green stick. "With your stunted vision, your dismissal of the good things that wander into your life, I wonder just what it is you expect to see."

"I'll see what I came for: Albert Schweitzer as he presents himself to the world, in his special place of business, a lifetime of toil creating the focus of African medicine."

The old man took a drink of his coffee and made a sour face. "Well, you won't see much if that's what you're expecting, because you're already well past the center of medicine. West Africa alone has variations of disease numbering in the hundreds, and the afflicted well into the tens of millions."

Hugo nodded. "This is indeed good news," he said. "Because I'm not really interested in medical issues, only in making good my promise to you in the hopes that I'll be blessed with an exciting experience."

"You'll have an experience, I can offer you that. Starting with a small hospital built over the course of fifty years, burdened by the stress of the tropics and two world wars. You'll see the buildings, the staff, and the villagers carrying their sick. The facility a short way down the road is indeed a shrine to blessings. And it will bless even you because its purpose is to relieve small burdens, to increase joy through the cessation of specific pains, the restoration of individual health. In so doing we have no time to indulge the frivolous. As with all of us, you will participate in a way that is suitable to your talents even though you have come to believe that hard work like digging the ground is beneath you."

Hugo sipped his chicory-laced coffee and the old man threw more sticks into the fire. "I've never dug in the ground, even to amuse myself," he said. "It was deficiency of my childhood. There was no sandbox in the sickroom."

"What a certainty of recollection—that you've never put your hands into the real earth. Not like Conrad Muir, to whom you owe your rich upbringing, who bravely served both God and me. Confronting the bombs and bullets he made no difference between himself and strangers, to whom he owed nothing. You, on the other hand, have dug your way into people's lives like a stinking little worm, like one of the obscene parasites we see in the tropics that get beneath the skin and create misery. In other words, you've had a nice play in Freddy Marshall's rose garden."

"Not with malice. Never with the intent to hurt."

"But you did hurt her, and others, because you are without any idea of ethics. Let me tell you something. Let me sermonize because I am a Christian preacher as well as a physician and feel at ease in the pulpit. I say to you—what is the status of this basic ethical attitude, about which I have been thinking in the loneliness of the jungle for fifty years since I first confessed it before ever seeing Africa? And in Africa, I came to see the sad truth. Somewhere I wrote that we cannot escape the fact that the Christian ethic has never become a power in the world."

"I recall that passage, Albert—read it the day I met Allan Korrolus."

"Did you? How gratifying. There is hope for the person who reads and learns from it, and hopefully also for mankind that presently behaves as if the teaching of Jesus did not exist—as if Christian behavior had no ethics at all. Whatever heights your conceits puff you up to, Hugo, in the final analysis, all knowledge of ethics amounts to an awareness of life, a reverence for life in its infinite and yet ever-fresh manifestations. How amazing are the newborn of all species. How mysterious this living and dying! How fantastic that in all existences, something comes into being, passes away again, comes into being once more and so forth from eternity to eternity! How can it be? We can do all things and we can do nothing. For in all our wisdom we cannot create life. What we create is death. The tiny beetle that lies dead in your path, that you have crushed carelessly under your boot—it was a living creature, struggling for existence like yourself, rejoicing in the sun like you, knowing fear and pain like you. And now it is no more than decaying matter, which is what you will be sooner or later. Reverence for the infinity of life means the removal of alienation, restoration of empathy, compassion, and sympathy. It is human reason that acts here. Do you comprehend that, my wayward fellow traveler? It is reason alone that discovers the bridge between love for God and love for all creatures, however dissimilar to our own. The Lord sayeth—thou shalt not kill, injure, or maim—even an ignorant soldier who is in your way. Remember that you can thoughtlessly kill yourself as well. When you destroy your own soul, you take down other souls, the love that others have for you. Don't do it. Contribute what you can, like you contributed freely to ease the labor of your fake uncle."

A small bird hopped close, then flew back to the trees. Hugo lit a cigarette, remained silent, and stared at the wall of greenery. When he next had a thought, the fire was burnt to ashes. He put the flute to his mouth and blew three rising notes from distant memory, then in a few minutes was packed and gone.

It was an hour of slow travel on the rutted earth of the track before he drove into the hospital village, passing groups of natives camped by the road and behind buildings, through the smoke of their cooking fires and past goats grazing where grass flourished in the shade. A woman in a white uniform walked in front of the slowly moving vehicle. She had a disjointed, haggard face, a large nose but eyes that appeared intelligent and discerning. She smiled at him.

"Is there somewhere close by where I can camp?" he asked.

She came closer to examine the Land Rover. "Where did you come from?"

"North."

"How far north?"

"London."

"I see. I would have said that was impossible. But then it seems I would have been wrong."

"It's quite easy if you follow directions."

"I would think not. Now, for the camping. I suppose anywhere out of the way would be all right. But you should see Madam Ali as soon as you can. She is the administrator and authorizes most things."

"And Albert Schweitzer?"

"What about him?"

"Nothing. But I thought I would offer...."

"Most of what we need here is medical help. There is always a great need for nurses."

Hugo pursed his lips and nodded agreement. "And doctors?"

"Madame Ali is meticulously organized. She recruits physicians well in advance, from Europe and America. Dr. Schweitzer's prestige helps in that regard."

"I see. Well then, perhaps some other job?"

"Perhaps," she said. "I believe they need laborers..."

"Just joking," interrupted Hugo. "A moron wouldn't labor in this heat."

"Quite right. Anyway, if you want to contribute, as a tradesman or something, you'll have to talk to Madame Ali. In the meantime, about the hospital...the building in front of us is Dr. Schweitzer's personal quarters. Across the road is the dining hall. Concerning meals. There is one rule here: Everyone who comes is fed. Just ask the staff what time dinner is."

"Eating would be welcome."

She stared a moment at Hugo's face then added, "And while I'm at it, beyond the dining hall is staff quarters and to the west are the hospital buildings. On the far side, some distance from the hospital, is the leper colony. To the east, just beyond us is the physical plant. And that's about it for the quick tour."

"Thank you," said Hugo. The nurse walked on towards staff quarters, but after a few paces came back and said, "You've come a long way."

Hugo nodded.

"I'm sorry to say that if you've come with the hopes of meeting Dr. Schweitzer, you'll be disappointed. He doesn't receive visitors anymore. There are too many people who want to meet him just to say they shook his hand...for a point of bragging or pride. Does that make sense?"

"Certainly," said Hugo. "He's probably shaken too many hands."

She smiled and said, "Yes."

"One last question. Have you ever heard of a man named Martin Birks?"

"The name is familiar. But many people pass through."

"He's a trader, I've heard."

"Perhaps the name is familiar. Ask Jurgen, the maintenance man."

"Thanks."

The nurse went off into a trail marked by the sign "Plantation." Hugo placed the vehicle in a grove a few hundred meters from the main group of buildings and walked down to the river. It was not as large as the Niger but the trees on the south bank showed as a uniform line of green. The water was darkened with silt, the banks muddy. There was a small dock strung into the current and a dozen pirogues were tied to the rough planking. Upstream, he could see terraced gardens of vegetables rising from the edge of the river. He used the rest of the day to make notes and diagrams in his spiral notebook concerning the geography of the two hundred and twenty acres of the site, the locations of the seventy buildings, and recorded as best he could the essentials of the conversations he had with numerous people. He watched the weaver birds building their nests, monkeys playing in and on the buildings close to trees, the parrots and the miniature antelopes penned beneath the doctor's house.

The dinner bell rang at five. Hugo went into the hall and sat next to a physician he had questioned earlier. After introducing the new visitor to his wife, the man said something to the effect that Schweitzer may not come because he didn't always attend. Hugo considered that for a sip or two of his juice, then thought he should inform his seatmate that, of course, Albert would attend. The great doctor might be akin to a piece of data in a textbook and now an old man; he was also a mouthpiece for theology, a musician, winner of international awards, philanthropist, thinker, a healer of bodies and minister of the gospel. But, above all, he was a fellow traveler and knew that his companion had arrived.

With this thought buoying his hopes, he finished his juice and discussed issues of charity with the Spanish doctor. When at last the face of his friend appeared at the door, Hugo could do no more than stare at him in dismay. At ninety years old, worn by decades of relentless dedication, Albert Schweitzer was a thin, frail man. His luminescent white hair flowed out from beneath his helmet and he came into the dining hall slowly on the arm of a nurse. He sat with difficulty and said grace in a weak voice. After dinner, as was the custom to honor and please him, Bach's *Toccata and Fugue* went out into the twilight air from a decrepit transcription disk recorded by the doctor himself fifty-three years earlier at the Cathedral in Strasbourg. To Hugo it seemed like a funeral dirge.

That night he lay on his blanket and was unable to think of much else but the image of the old man, the spent years, the wards full of sickness Albert had faced and he had witnessed today—and inside one ward, a small girl lying on the sheet, her body a half-inflated balloon with crinkled skin puckered like plastic where the needles went into her arm. She had died in the late afternoon before he could sit down to his first meal, and no one was to blame for her demise but fate. The next morning he spoke with the same doctor, who directed him to the physical plant where he would find the only useful work on Madame Ali's list.

"This is my pride and joy," said Jurgen Leibrand, the hospital engineer, pointing to the new Deutz dynamo, which he explained they had received six months previously. "It generates a steady 240 volts, when—and if—we get it going. It will provide the power for the new operating theatre at the far side of the hospital grounds."

"You are waiting for it to be built?" enquired Hugo.

"It was built a year ago. The new equipment has arrived and been installed. Birks helped with that. But it's useless without power."

"So what's the problem, no wire?"

Liebrand pointed to a large reel of shielded cable standing in the corner of the shed. "The problem is that we can't run the cable overhead because it would be worn away by the teeth of monkeys, the beaks of the parrots, the weaver birds, chewing insects, and then rust. It has to be buried."

"So bury it."

"Not so easy. We have no machinery. There is no option but to dig a trench by hand. Understand that the ground here is baked hard—a rough sort of clay with the texture of bedrock. The distance from here to the theater building is two hundred and thirty meters and the cable needs to go a meter in the ground. The natives couldn't conceive a minute of such work. Understand that the temperature here, night and day, is over a hundred degrees Fahrenheit and the humidity, one hundred percent. In those conditions, using a pickaxe and shovel would exhaust a man before he had made a small hole in the ground."

Chapter XXII

Dr. Schweitzer's Trench

The morning after Hugo's conversation with Jurgen Liebrand, the staff of the Schweitzer hospital, if they were observant on their way to other tasks, would have seen a single man, stripped to the waist, swinging a pick at the hard ground next to the shed containing the Deutz diesel set. He had a bandana wrapped around his head and over it a stained felt hat. His left forearm was reinforced with a crude canvas bandage. He stopped often to drink from a bottle of warm water and when it was empty, would go to the well, thirty meters up the hill. Progress that first day amounted to a one-meter hole in the ground, and few people noticed. On her way to dinner that night, Madame Ali, who kept a close watch over all details of the hospital, noticed a hazard that someone might fall into and made a mental note to ask Liebrand at dinner what was going on.

Hugo lay that night in his blanket feeling dizzy. It was the same scrambling of thought and rising pressure in his head he had suffered on the Tanezrouft. He tried to drink as much as he could, but felt nauseous when he had more than a half-cup. At breakfast he sprinkled his porridge with salt. The dizziness remained. But two hours after he began his labor, a young African girl named Callie stood over the trench with a tray that contained a pitcher of cold liquid and a glass.

"Madame says you must drink, and drink often," she said, and Hugo could not recall anyone saying words with such melody.

"Then I will," he answered and took a sip. The drink tasted sweet with a slight flavor of salts. That day his digging brought him out from beneath the shade of the palms into the muted glare of the sun. This forced him to wear one of his fading shirts with holes in it, but that was soon replaced by a clean white one brought by one of the nurses, who also brought a proper bandage for his arm. By lunch, a crowd of Galoas had gathered and remained large as new onlookers replaced those who drifted away. The staff began to detour in their usual routes. They would nod and say, "*bon jour*" or "hello" or just smile.

When he went into dinner an African worker said, "If you wish to shower, Madame says you can use the staff facility."

That night he slept in the rear of the Land Rover without the itch of salt and dirt on his flesh and woke without the headache or dizziness. He walked to the trench carrying his pick and shovel, slowly turning his left wrist and arm to ease the stiffness before wrapping it. On the third day at his labor he focused himself on two discontinuous tasks. The first was his small advances over the terrain when he was using the pick. The second was the excavation of the trench with his shovel. During the second phase, advancement was zero but the overall shape of the trench changed in unpredictable ways, with a half shovel over the top and the next one full and the trench larger by that amount. This minutia of observation and the encouragement of the crowd kept his mind off the constant thirst and the aching fatigue that crept early into his left arm. He stopped every ten minutes to gratefully drink the lemonade supplied by Callie. They became a team, and whenever he looked she seemed to be there, with fresh juice and pieces of fruit. As he put his tools away that afternoon, a staff member came to him. "I have instructions to take you to your quarters," she said and led Hugo down the road marked "Plantation" to a small cottage divided into two rooms. The south one was his and into it he moved the satchel and the leather case with his books and flute.

Over the three weeks Hugo required to dig the trench, he kept his labor at a level the watchers would have thought impossible under the conditions. But they were unaware that the digger was not influenced by the weather. He heard things in the wind and from the course of his memory that told him what pace to keep. He constructed harmonies of work from the sounds of the pick hitting the clay or the shovel scrapping the bottom of the hole. The mute face of the trench yielded clues to the necessary force of the swinging pick. The noise from the village and the hospital fed data to him. Everyone and everything became a factor in the constantly repeating equation. Occasionally he was confronted with the bone white face of a visitor jetted recently from New York, whose floatplane from Libreville landed on the Oogue and washed aside the pirogues. The next day he was entertained again by the little plane climbing above the jungle, returning to civilization with the indignant matron after she is expelled by Madam Ali for doing nothing but interfere.

Yet the core impetus for Hugo's effort was the glimpses he had of the afflicted: the men wormy with bilharzia, the children whose bellies were distended by kwashiorkor, the grotesquely deformed and the comatose bush people borne into the village on crude stretchers. He could feel the anxiety of the healers, impatient for his progress; sensed the urgency of the surgeons who amputated, cut, stitched, sliced away tumors in antiquated conditions then walked to the edge of the trench and gave him another nod. And all day were nurses who ploughed through the crowds and applauded the two meters he had dug since they last looked. After a week he began to receive invitations to select and private gatherings. But nowhere, except at dinner, did he see Albert Schweitzer.

"Don't be offended, Mr. Haultain," said Madame Rhena, Schweitzer's daughter, who sat on a low bunk with the gas lamp shining on her face. "He no longer has the strength to make small talk, to meet new people, because he is compelled by habit to engage the newcomer, to hear their tales, to tell the story of his own ideas to the world." She then related description of her visits to Lambaréné, of being captive in an equatorial outpost. "I was only a girl when my father brought me here…"

Hugo sat back and heard her voice blend with the shadowy shapes that moved on the walls, walls that did not diminish the night howls of monkeys and the singing of birds. He saw her lips move with the elegance of a hand playing the organ. She spoke of the evolution of the village and the function of the hospital through five decades of turbulent history. In the gloom beneath the bunk sat her own daughter combing invisible hair and smiling to hear the goat kids squealing in the yard. The candles in the surgeon's hut burned at various rates and random intensities. Some were robust. Some faint. Hugo drank his cup of wine and thought only that the life of Albert's daughter had formed into a strange, malleable shape; that her witness to the doctor's many years, stacked end over end, would give her a perspective wider and deeper than his own depleted view. He never spoke once because he felt he had nothing to contribute.

At the trench marking of one hundred fifty meters, the native girl Callie put the noon juice on the ground so that Hugo could see that the glass cast no shadow. She did this to indicate that with three more cycles of picking and shoveling, they would break for lunch. But when he straightened up he saw standing next to the glass a pair of shoes, with the shadow of the famous doctor buried under his feet. His white shirt had the top button undone and the sleeves rolled to his elbows. The strength of face shadowed by the pith helmet gave him the impression that at any moment Albert would hop into the ditch and drive the pick into the trench face right up to the handle.

Hugo bowed his head as a matter of respect. In his mind he could imagine Madam Ali saying, "What you see here, Herr Doctor, is the very essence of madness—this digging, digging and more digging. But, God bless him, he is making our trench, although his motivation at the moment is bland and inoffensive; that is to say Mr. Haultain is trying to prove to himself that he can for once in his life go from point A to point B without veering off course. The heat of life has a way of disorienting men."

"He will not lose his way," Albert replied. "It would take a moron to get lost digging a simple trench."

Schweitzer leaned forward with his large hand extended. Hugo expected it to feel like brittle chicken bones; yet when they shook, the fingers exerted a fundamental pressure. With no words coming into his brain he leaned on the shovel and remained as silent as the crowd, who were delighted at the suspense, because they had not seen the doctor outside for weeks, let alone in the heat of midday to shake a laborer's hand. Schweitzer leaned close over the trench, so close and at such an angle that Hugo readied his hand in case he should have to catch him.

"Albert?" he said as a warning to his friend that he was still subject to certain laws.

"Yes," said Schweitzer in a strained whisper, almost into Hugo's ear. "Yes, I know. You think that my knees are going to buckle and you can just lay me out and not trouble the undertaker. But let me interrupt, Hugo. Know it or not, through this entire journey, I've been obliged to direct you every pick and shovel of your way. I wouldn't do anything now to impede your progress. This is the most work you've done at a stretch since Muir sat you down to commence your medical studies. So you just carry on. And don't worry, I'll be hearing of the final shovel full and the cheers given by all and sundry to your glory. Hugo the savior! God bless Hugo, the mortal who said he had never dug in the earth and now the digger of the most important ditch on the planet!"

The doctor gestured to the crowd. He raised his voice, saying, "My friends. I want you to meet the one man who didn't run away at the sight of a shovel. He volunteered and is proud of it. We all volunteer sooner or later and some of us receive prizes for it. But understand, even with the expectation of glory, self-sacrifice is always the last part of us to rise from the mud."

The crowd cheered and clapped. The indigenes, Galoa and Pahouin alike, smiled broadly and nodded their heads with approval. But as Schweitzer released the digger's hand to stand straight Hugo replied in a loud voice, "I'm doing this to pay off my debt to you, Albert. Let there be no talk of volunteering."

Madame Ali frowned and looked confused. She took the doctor's arm. Again Schweitzer lent over the pit and turned his head to the nurse.

"I think the boy's had a bit too much sun, Madame. Persuade him to take the afternoon off." Then he leaned further into the trench and said in a faint voice, "Now, you do as the nurse instructs and sit in the shade for the rest of the day."

Then with disdain, he swept his hand towards Hugo as if he were dismissing a vaudeville dandy. The villagers cheered one last time. The nurses and doctors clapped as the old man stepped uncertainly towards his own quarters held up by the strength of Madame Ali and Mistress Callie, who had taken his other arm. Hugo took his drink, made three cycles of picking and shoveling, then went in to lunch. As he ate, Madame Ali came up to him and told him that if he returned to the trench that day he would lose his privileges and be banished from the hospital.

A week later, under a granite sky, Hugo inspected the few meters of ground yet to be dug and calculated that he was less than two days from completion. He put down his tools. Indistinct shadows told him it was early evening. Darkness would come as usual, the light gone with the speed of a candle snuffed by a cone. Dinner was already over so he sat against the wall of the new building drinking the beer Callie had smuggled from the kitchen. He massaged his left arm only out of habit because whatever his treatments, it had not stopped aching for twenty days. A startled monkey leaped from a vine onto the roof. It scolded and threw wood at him. Hugo remained sitting with his shoulders leaning into the building. From time to time he threw sticks back at the monkey and contemplated sitting there all night exchanging such pleasantries. He was a citizen of the village now, a known face. The inhabitants would not be troubled to see him disappear when dark came, assured that he would reappear in the dawn light to resume his work. But instead of lingering, he went to his quarters when the bottle was empty. Callie arrived at the door an hour later with a platter of food. Hugo took the tray and might have said to her, thank you, Callie. I hope you have the best of all possible lives because men should fall on their knees to honor your words, "You must drink and drink often."

In fact he mumbled, "Thank you Callie," and watched mutely as she lowered her head in deference and stepped back into the night. After eating the plate of rice, he opened his spiral notebook to write something about acts of kindness. Yet his hand would not move. He set his nibbed pen down and ran his eyes over selected paragraphs. In everything he examined, the text appeared more awkward than ever. The words edged nervously along the page, bullied and degraded by the imprints of nails, fingers, hands, and bare feet scuffing the paper with the inevitable filth of living. The annotated record of life thus far, events as unique as the mysteries he had seen pacing over the young girl's face had shriveled to the reluctant debris spilling from his notebooks. He could think of no language that would surpass the law of diminishing returns. Like Callie, the woman from Aldermans Green had long ago stepped back into the darkness. What did she look like? What had she been wearing the last time they touched? Hugo lifted his chin off his chest because there was a rapping at the door.

"Come in."

An old villager he had not seen before stood at the door. "Sorry, Master, but Doctor want to see you."

Hugo went to his satchel and took out a brown manila envelope and followed along the plantation road, although he couldn't be sure he was going anywhere with the old man, whose eyes were clouded with cataracts. Schweitzer was sitting in a wicker chair. Netting fell over the windows. The desk and other chairs were piled with the books and papers documenting a lifetime. A few sheets of manuscript hung by string behind him. None of it smelled old. There was no evidence of camphor or mildew or blight as he expected. The room gave a sense of being vaguely new or ageless or possessing a repeatable shape, as stories are scaled down without alteration or made huge like heaven, days that grow to be centuries apart. The old Pahouin floated from the room like a piece of muslin.

Schweitzer was writing in a journal. Hugo remained silent and watched him at his place: bowed, reverent, lost in a half-century of inner life, in the Bible, the Qua'ran the Upanishads, the revolutionary fugues of Bach spread across the notation sheets under his arm, all beneath the black equatorial sky, where the monkeys sifting through the trees, the forgotten lepers in their colony had often wept to hear this one soul resonating loudly for them. In their own tranquility, the antelope foraged beneath the floorboards of the suite.

"The deer have come back nicely in these few months," Hugo said. "I understand they were all destroyed last March, because of disease."

"It was rabies. Only the dogs, cats and monkeys were killed," the doctor replied.

"But don't concern yourself too much. 'We all have to die' is the trite remark, is it not, that brushes aside our fear." The old patriarch took out a cloth. "You see how I have to wipe away the fluid that runs from my eyes. You did that for a blind orphan in Morocco a few miles ago. And I thought then how confused men are, driven by the needs of the moment, the cruelties they can't avoid. Here, give me your hand."

Hugo helped him to his feet and reached for the cane. They walked together into the night. "I don't do this often anymore, Hugo. Not once in six months. Tonight will be the exception."

The doctor leaned on Hugo's arm, and in the dark, interrupted only here and there by the light of cooking fires, they shuffled past the hospital towards the leper colony. They entered through a gate and came to a man sitting on a stoop. He had bandages wrapped around his face and interrupted his whittling of a stick to bow deeply. Schweitzer sat next to him and leaned against the hut wall. Hugo offered the leper a cigarette, took one himself, and lit both.

Schweitzer talked. "I've created this village, this hospital, as my life's work. It draws the Galoas from the hills and the Pahouin people from the far jungle, often entire families with one or more of them sick, infirm, eaten by parasites, or starving. It's a magnet also for helpers, healers, the curious, status seekers, those starved for any salvation. I am surrounded by bodies, spirits, souls in sickness and health. Just think, Hugo, some things aren't palatable and smell putrid from the outset. Others have the taste and touch of the sublime. I have trouble joining my senses with my brain—rationalizing disease with ethics and beauty. The outline of what I see and feel, I sometimes draw into a pattern of words."

The leper kept whittling. From time to time he stopped and smoked the cigarette. Albert leaned more solidly against the wall and continued, "The Nobel committee donated the money to finish all these huts you see here. How generous of them, how considerate of Alfred Nobel, God rest his soul."

"He sold dynamite for that honor," Hugo replied, "was the inventor of the bombs that destroyed the Cathedral at Coventry and countless other buildings."

"Don't get too smug in your assessment. There's many a crook on the path of causality and blame. We can never be completely sure of who did what to whom, or with what intent."

Hugo puffed on his smoke. "That's good. Because in my opinion too much conscience, too much thought of responsibility can ruin an otherwise perfect tale."

The old man breathed deeply and set his hands firmly on his knees. "I noticed that you carry around books. I wonder if they tell a perfect tale?"

"The ones written by me?"

"The books that fill your case, not the sorry little scribblers you fill with nonsense. What would you have to say that might be original?" Schweitzer turned to the leper. "What do you think, Basile? Could he have written anything worthwhile?"

"Why do you ask him?" said Hugo. "He can't have an opinion because he doesn't even know who I am."

"I do have an opinion," answered the Pahouin. "Because it's all over the village who you are, monsieur. You're a ditch digger, a slave, the man who would kill himself to impress the great doctor and get to shake his hand when others donate money, fly halfway round the world, and are sent home empty-handed."

"Attaboy," said Schweitzer. "Let him know the truth about his pretensions, his good works, which are as meaningless as his pretty face."

"But let us hear his own answer to your question, master, about the worth of his writing."

Hugo sat smoking and said nothing in reply.

"He wouldn't answer, Basile, because he is afraid of the healthful, revitalizing effects of the truth as it relates to his affairs. So I'll answer for him. Hugo knows this woman in England, you see. I've heard her make some comment or other at inauspicious moments to taunt him, or so he thinks. But never mind. It was on the day of his leaving, the moment she wept that he walked over the boundary and into the next influence. He called it 'getting on with life' when he was really balancing on the edge, neither here nor there, procrastinating about the direction in life he was supposed to be getting on with. For at that moment he believed that he could have the best of both worlds. It was like the eternity at the edge of death, with the desperate hand just out of reach—the rich, fruitful hand extended for him in vain, like those devastating fingers of God drawn by Da Vinci."

"I struggled to get here, Basile," interrupted Hugo, "overland, more like a creeping ant or a roaming jackal, to complete my task. I deserve some recognition."

"What does he mean, master?"

Schweitzer reached out his hand to Basile and the leper took the doctor's fingers. "He's talking about getting over his adolescence and dealing with defeat. Like taking a real good kick in the teeth and trying to smile at the same time. He's justifying a fruitless chase, a false odyssey—Don Quixote with none of the romance, full to the brim with red-hot words. That's what he's talking about."

"He's good with his talk, master, don't you think? You and him are the same. Both can talk. But does he have something other than this to offer? Maybe I can help. What could I give him?"

"Another walking stick, Basile."

"Another one already?"

"For him, not me."

"Yes, of course. I have one already made. It is a little different, Doctor, a little better."

The old leper reached into the dark behind him for another stick. Schweitzer took hold of it. "It's very light. It almost floats away from me."

"It's for someone who is in great need of assistance, master,"

"So why didn't you make one like this for me?" Albert said peevishly. "I'm the invalid, the old man. He's as strong on his legs as a mule, a John Henry of a man with a pick in each hand to dig the trench. Why does he need uplifting?"

The old Pahouin kept smoking as if he had not heard the doctor's complaints. Eventually he said, "It's made from a special kind of wood. We have some groves on the upper Oogue near Medemgogoha. He will be able to lean on it for a long way. You are going to heaven soon and don't need a special cane." Schweitzer brushed back his hair and turned his pained face away. Basile giggled and winked at Hugo. "Okay. I was only fooling. I made it for you, Doctor. You in turn can give your old cane to him—but only if he can make use of it."

Hugo lit another cigarette for the leper and watched it glow. "I don't need a cane, Basile. Give it to someone who is sick or old."

The leper smoked and let the smoke drift from between his white teeth. Schweitzer was already on his feet trying out his new cane. "Thank you, Basile," he said and began walking up the trail. Halfway to his lodgings he said, "I apologize for being rude, Hugo; I didn't mean to discuss what my needs are. I must be fading already, worried about my direction. Because what I've done in my life has never been about me. It is important you understand that. But so close to the grave, I feel I've a right to complain, especially to you, who understands—or should I say crudely, you who doesn't care a tinker's damn about my condition. So let's talk about you once we are back in my palace. I will just float along here with my new cane. Thank you again, Basile."

The doctor strode down the path with Hugo sprinting to catch up. When they arrived at his quarters. Schweitzer said, "I have a great yearning for work right now. When you have finished the trench and are preparing to go, we can talk in earnest. That would be best."

"I was not planning to leave."

"Were you not? How do you know that? Remember that some things you can't plan or risk losing your way." He turned and went in through the door and Hugo heard him talking to the antelope fawns penned under his room.

A few days later when Hugo visited the leper colony and Basile asked, "Did the Doctor give you his old cane?" Hugo replied, "He did."

"Did you keep it?"

Hugo nodded at the leper. "I kept it, Basile, because today I feel old."

At the last shovel full of dirt that Hugo tossed from the completed trench, the surgeons, the staff, the entire village toasted the honor of his work. The next day he helped Jurgen Leibrand lay the cable and backfill the trench, a labor that attracted many hands because shoving in loose dirt is an easier story than taking it out. During the following week Hugo tried to resume his writing. In the intervals he rested and practiced his flute. He had a standing request with Madame Ali to have five minutes with the doctor, but no word came. Everyday he paddled a pirogue up the river, feeling comfortable enough with the water to find a way through the back eddies of the rapids so he might continue to the next village. One night came a knock at the door. It was Madame Rhena. "Father wants to see you. Can you come now?"

Again he followed down the plantation road to the doctor's quarters. Albert Schweitzer sat at his desk with his daughter next to him. Madame Ali sat to one side, petting an antelope fawn.

"Congratulations, Mr. Haultain," she said. "You have done us a great service. Its effects will flow to all who benefit from the improved facilities." She looked with concern at the old man, who was laboring for breath, then continued, "The Doctor has some strength tonight so we would like to hear a little more of your story…how you came here and why."

Hugo said, "Very simply. I came on public transport from London to Algiers, then overland with a vehicle of my own." He placed the manila envelope on the desk in front of Schweitzer. "The contents of this may explain, at least partly, why I'm here."

The old man fumbled with the flap but eventually pulled out the photo, the letters from himself to Conrad Muir, and the photo taken in Algiers. He held up the picture of the *Kyle Mission* to the light, squinted, then turned it over. "What is your connection to these men?" he asked in a weak voice.

Hugo told his story with extreme brevity, making no effort to retain the flavor he once thought it had. When he had finished speaking, Schweitzer swallowed some tea then began to talk as if he were addressing his remarks not to Hugo but to the others and beyond to a wider world.

"We thought we were prepared for the war, placed extra orders, but not all arrived. The steamship *Brazza* was sunk off Cape Finesterre with the last of the drugs and surgical supplies. The hospital was out of business, the sick sent home, the staff dismissed. Only a few remained to do the work, Doctor Goldschmidt and Anna Wildikaa, God bless them and the rest who stayed to endure the fighting that took place here, the forces of Vichy finally losing out to the free French and us caught in the middle. As the shelves emptied, new supplies came sporadically. Conrad Muir and others of the Society found new sources. When my wife was able to make her way here through Angola in the summer of forty-one, Muir was moved by her accounts of our desperate situation. He worked tirelessly, although I understand his personal situation was heartbreaking, having to leave a son and the boy's mother to travel abroad on their own. In December of forty-two when Vichy surrendered to the Allies, he traveled to Algiers. The usual circumstances of war had stalled supplies bound for us. Muir was attempting to reship these when he was caught in partisan fighting. I never heard anything else from him or about him until August of forty-six. At that time we were trying to cope with the demands falling on us after hostilities ended. Out of nowhere appeared a truck driven by a man named Birks. It was a small vehicle and overloaded with a few supplies and fresh medicines. It was then that I learned the existence of this ship and your father's ordeal."

Callie appeared at the door with a tray with fresh tea and buns. She looked at Hugo with a brief smile, put down the tray, and left. Schweitzer held the photograph of the ship in his hands. "I understand you have met with all those in this picture except one, Martin Birks, the hardened soldier and winner of the Victoria Cross, who was rendered sufficiently insane by war to journey six thousand miles to deliver a few bandages and bottles of medicine to strangers."

The doctor sipped his tea and ate one mouthful of bun. A number of times he had to wipe his eyes. "Birks has been here many times over the years to fix things. The last was a few months ago before he left suddenly to go back to Congo-Brazzaville," said Madame Ali.

As Schweitzer listened to his nurse, he turned pale and his breathing became more labored. Madame Rhena looked again at the photo of the *Kyle Mission*, then pushed it towards her father. With a large nib pen, the doctor signed below the individual letters Allan Korrolus had stenciled over the photo.

"Now the sharpness of my memory is gone," he said. "Perhaps Madame Ali has more?"

"Look for Martin Birks at his trading post in Mindouli," she said. "If he is not there, as we have heard, return immediately to us. With the war on, anything else is madness."

She put both her hands on Schweitzer's shoulders to steady him. Hugo refrained from offering his hand, choosing instead to bow and walk away.

Two days later he cleaned out his small room, checking twice to verify that the only thing he left behind was a bag containing a bottle of scotch marked with the name of the Spanish doctor and his one set of good clothes for Basile. After loading fresh food and water, he said his good-byes to the staff, to Madam Ali, and to Rhena. As the vehicle rolled down the track, Basile and Callie stood by the roadside waving. Beyond Lambaréné and into the dense forest that led to the frontier, Hugo recalled his last moments above the antelope pen. When he had reached the door and turned, the netting over the bed obscured Schweitzer, with half his face looking up from his desk, only half a smile saying, "Get on then with it, lad. There's work to do. We will both survive."

Hugo gripped the wheel and prepared himself for the worst. Because, in the vault of his memory, he saw also the morning Albert had risen from his bedside, stretched his legs thankfully after a decade of ceaseless vigil to voluntarily and permanently depart the sickroom. From then on he had become what he foretold, no longer an ally but a fellow traveler concerned only with laying out the map of moral choices. And it would remain this way. Of the living and constrained Albert Schweitzer, Hugo knew he had seen his last.

Chapter XXIII

Deal Léon an Ace

Coventry. April 14, 1965.

Three weeks after Hugo's departure, Owen Dring walked down the aisle of the new Cathedral. He had been trying to arrange interviews for Smith's replacement but was now late for his afternoon surgeries. Stopping halfway down the aisle he thought he had forgotten some daily chore, here with the flowers or the prayer books. A solitary man sitting next to the aisle appeared to be the only parishioner. Dring hadn't seen him, so when the man moved forward, it startled him.

"Sorry," the old man said. "I didn't mean to give you a fright."

"Hmm. No bother. Just lost in thought." Dring smiled politely. The man looked familiar, but in his position, everyone becomes an acquaintance. He strolled on, getting back into revamping his schedule.

"Owen Dring?"

Dring stopped and turned, a little annoyed at the delay. The man's face, his eyes especially, were formed into a mixture of sadness and apprehension. He said, "My name is Conrad Muir."

Dring stepped towards him and took hold of the edge of the pew.

"I've come to apply for the position of organist you have advertised in the *Church Times*," Muir said. "It said that I should contact you."

Dring put out his hand and the two men shook. "I'm very sorry I didn't recognize you, Mr. Muir. It's been at least twenty-five years since Algiers, and longer since the Cathedral choir."

"I remember the old church well, sir, and the people. A privilege it was. But if you'll pardon me, I recall almost nothing from Algiers."

Dring agitated. "If you'll excuse me also, here's my card. I should be finished with my surgeries about six tonight. Please come around to the hospital and we'll drive down to Leek Wootten for dinner. I would like you to meet Miranda, my wife."

Muir examined the card and nodded his head. He looked puzzled by the invitation. "That would be nice, Mister Dring."

"Excuse my presumption. I'm assuming you'll be free. Where are you staying?"

"I have a room at the Craven Arms."

"Very good. Six o'clock then. And let's hope I'm not delayed." He held out his hand. "I am truly delighted to see you again, Mr. Muir."

Conrad Muir turned to watch the surgeon walk out. He was troubled by the fact that he had no recollection of meeting Owen Dring and expected no one in Coventry to have remembered him, far less be so delighted with the memory they would invite him to dinner.

At the Coventry and Warwickshire Hospital, Beth sat with her legs crossed and a cup of tea on her lap. She talked to the head sister and turned to see a man walk by the door and then reappear. He was tall with thick gray hair. Although elderly, he had a determination in his movements. His shoulders were slightly stooped but had unusual breadth. For a moment Beth thought she knew him, possibly as a former patient.

"Can I direct you?" said the head sister.

"I'm looking for Mister Dring's office."

"I see. Do you have an appointment?"

The man smiled. He had a business card in his hand and glanced down at it. "In a manner of speaking, yes," he said. "I believe he is expecting me. He told me to call round at six."

"Of course," said the head sister.

"I'll go and see if he is in his office. Who shall I say is enquiring?"

"Conrad Muir."

Beth felt a sting of nerves. She stopped sipping her tea, stared at the man for a moment, then said, "Please sit down, Mr. Muir."

"Thank you," he replied and sat opposite. Beth continued with her assessment. The man in front of her had all his teeth, which were in good condition, and he didn't smell. His clothes were tailored, pressed, coordinated, and his shoes shined. This could not be the old tutor, the disreputable Herr Muir of Hugo's description and therefore not Hugo's father. Perhaps it was a coincidence of name and of place. Not sure that she should be on her best behavior, she took out a package of cigarettes and offered one to Muir.

"Thank you, no," he said. "I used to smoke, but it's been many years now."

"Are you living in Coventry or just visiting?"

"Just visiting—for the moment. How about you, Miss?"

"Beth Marshall," she held out her hand and Muir took it. "I was born here." She lit her cigarette, "I hope you don't mind?"

"Not at all, feel free."

She took another couple of puffs, blowing the smoke sideways. "I'm Owen Dring's stepdaughter," she said.

"Are you? Yes, well it's been a long time. I came a few times to the original Cathedral, before the war, as a visiting choirmaster," said Muir. "Apparently, I met Owen at that time, but I must admit I don't recall the occasion. Presently I'm applying for the job as organist."

Dring appeared suddenly at the door without the head sister. Muir leaned forward to get to his feet. "No, no, just sit down, Conrad...may I call you Conrad?"

"By all means."

"Good. Have you introduced yourselves?"

"Yes we have," said Beth.

"Let me go through the details of history," said Dring.

"He's done that already, Owen. Says he doesn't know you from Adam. And I don't blame him. The man's here for a job, not a reunion."

"Of course, Beth. Nevertheless, Conrad is a distinguished musician and choirmaster, whether he remembers me or not. And I also remember him for many things from the war. Now, if we are all satisfied with the introductions shall we go down to Leek Wootten for dinner? You and Phil are invited, of course."

"We have a prior date. But I will come along afterwards."

"Yes, yes," said Dring.

Muir got up. "It was nice to have met you, Beth. May I call you that?"

"Certainly."

"Good. Then I'll see you again, I'm sure, if not tonight."

After they walked out, Beth was left with thoughts about Hugo, his whereabouts, his view of the world that made her feel even less sure of her own direction. At dinner that night Conrad talked of his career as a teacher in the New World and provided few details of his personal life. He never once mentioned Corrine Haultain or, like his hosts, made any reference to Hugo.

With the influence of Owen Dring, Conrad Muir received the position he had applied for. After a few weeks Beth went into the Cathedral to hear him play. When he had finished, she went into the organist's stall and said, "You probably play the piano as well."

"I do," he answered.

"Do you know Beethoven's *Moonlight Sonata*?"

Muir hesitated and looked at her. "I know it, yes," he said.

"Could you play it for me? Just the slow movement. A friend of mine plays it. But he's gone now and I would like to hear it again. There's a piano in the choir room."

As they walked down the corridor he asked, "Do you like music, then?"

"I prefer the Beatles and the Stones. I know very little about classical music, but the *Moonlight Sonata* has become familiar to me."

Conrad sat at the upright piano and played the slow movement. Beth closed her eyes and listened closely to the music as Hugo had explained it to her. When Muir had finished, he said, "In my time I've done a little tutoring, in music, literature, the arts generally. It's heartening that you take an interest."

His eyes drifted out the window to the birds moving through a mulberry bush. "Strangely enough, this was a piece I never taught anyone."

Beth came often to the Cathedral and listened to Conrad practice. He stuck mainly to church repertoire, the hymns and music for the liturgy. One day they were having tea in the Cathedral lounge and Beth said, "I'll confess to you, Mr. Muir, I don't usually spend much time here. Owen does, of course, because he's a churchman at heart. But I like to hear you play. So that's why I'm here."

"And you didn't like to hear Smith play?"

"He must have been okay, I suppose, for him to be in that position. But to be quite honest, I never heard him play because I seldom came into the church."

"Then why have you come to listen to me?"

She didn't answer. After a time she said, "Mr. Muir, would you play at my wedding?"

"I'd be delighted to, but only if you promise to call me Conrad."

"I will, but only if you play me one more piece on the piano."

They went into the choir room, where Muir sat down and adjusted the bench. "Now what was it? Perhaps I don't even know it."

"Grieg's *A Minor Concerto*, just the first minute or so, the first ten bars."

Conrad looked at her, frowned, then turned to look at the keys. His attention was away. He hung his head as if he had forgotten her request, then he put his hands to the keyboard and played the opening chords. Beth closed her eyes. After a minute, he stopped.

"Was that enough?"

"Yes. Thank you."

He got up from the bench and shuffled back to his tea. She followed him, and in the hallway said in a gentle, sympathetic tone, "Did the boy, who was your usual student, learn this piece as well as the *Moonlight*?"

Conrad turned and said, "I don't understand what you're asking."

"The young boy you tutored, whose mother was fixated on a particular piece of music that you came to dislike. You taught him this piece instead?"

Muir put his hand to his mouth and looked confused.

Beth continued, "From what I understand you did more than tutor him in music. Because he was an invalid, didn't you teach him about history, art, mathematics, religion, and just about everything else?"

Muir put up his hand as if to direct her to stop. He looked at her, but seemed unable to speak. His eyes narrowed.

"I'm referring to Hugo Haultain, your son," she said.

The old man looked away and let his breath out before sitting on a bench. "How do you know about Hugo?"

"He was here, for about four months. In fact he left on the twenty-first of March, on the spring equinox, he insisted on telling me."

"I see," said Muir and leaned back with his hands together. "You obviously know something of him. Is he coming back?"

"Not likely," she said and went closer to the old man.

"Do you know where he went?" Muir asked.

"To Africa. He mentioned once that he had a job to do for your friend, Albert Schweitzer."

Over the summer Beth saw Conrad Muir only on the times he visited and they would take Carlyle for a walk. He kept his queries to her life as a nurse and an athlete. He talked sparingly of Hugo and offered no details. The subject seemed to tire him. On his visits they would content themselves with sitting wherever it was dry, and she would throw sticks for the dog and the words would flow easily between them or not, but the bond increased and they always felt comfortable together. She came to know him well and came to the conclusion that his health was poor.

One day near the middle of September, Beth excused herself from the large bath and went for a cup of tea in the café. She saw an old copy of the *London Times* and pulled it onto her table. She lit a cigarette and slowly scanned the articles. One headline caught her eye. It was from Reuters, datelined Paris, and read, *Albert Schweitzer dead at ninety in Lambaréné*. She quickly read it, picking out the highlights of his life. She fingered the rings on her left hand, extinguished her cigarette, and said good-bye to Phil. She left her own car behind and instead took the #33 bus to the Precinct. It had been a long time since she had been in the Craven Arms. She enquired at the desk, then walked to the second floor and knocked at door #18.

"Beth, this is a surprise," said Conrad Muir. "Come in. Come in."

She didn't move, but looked down at her feet and then at him. "Conrad, I want you to teach me to play the piano."

He hesitated and put his hand to his chin. "Of course. But please come in." Beth didn't move.

"I will teach you to play," he said in a kindly manner. "But I can't begin the process if you continue standing there."

She smiled sheepishly and walked into the room. "This is a nice suite, Conrad."

"Thank you. I've always felt at home here. I used to live in this hotel before, you know. That was when you could look out that window onto the south wall of the old Cathedral."

Beth watched him walk to the window and peer out, only for a brief glance, then turn back to her.

"I don't think I've ever had opportunity to see these rooms," she said, "the place has always just been here."

"Yes, well. Can I get you a cup of tea? There's a small hot plate in the room."

When he had put the tea in front of her he discreetly pushed the ashtray closer. "Thank you," she said. "But I've just quit smoking. Had my last one a half hour ago."

"That's significant."

She sipped her tea, pretending to look at the details of the décor, then said, "Albert Schweitzer is dead. He died a week ago, but I just read it today in the *Times*."

"That's also significant," said Conrad sadly. "I read it also. A great loss on many counts." They were silent for a time but, as always, the silence was easy and welcome. Finally he said, "Is there a connection between Schweitzer's death, the cigarettes, the piano lessons?"

"I could try to be witty and say that I'm substituting a bad habit for a good one."

"And Schweitzer? Does he have a connection to your choice of the piano?"

"I could never play the organ as he did. It's rather too big for me."

"Why play at all?"

"Why would anyone choose to learn an instrument?"

"But you're not anyone. You are you. What prompted this sudden interest?"

"I could pay you, Conrad."

"That would be a gesture of respect, even a mark of commitment. But I have money. My wants are few and lessening. Still, you seem to be avoiding my questions."

Beth frowned but remained silent.

Muir took a sip of his tea and continued. "I don't teach anymore, but when I was a tutor, I became accustomed to success. If I were to commit to teaching you the piano, I would like to think that my next pupil had more than a frivolous, passing fancy in learning to create music."

Beth looked at him and set her cup down. "I'm a nurse, a good one, because I learned from Owen Dring, who is a skillful surgeon. I'm good at analyzing things and mastering manual tasks. Could I put these traits to good use as a musician—even as a beginner?"

"It's a long process, Beth. You would have to learn quickly with me as your teacher. Could we count on you maintaining an acute interest just to please an impatient, old teacher?"

"I'll be frank, Conrad, and give you my opinion as a nurse. You're trying to tell me that your health is failing, to the point that your doctor has given you a certain time to live and that time is short. Consequently, you can make better use of your energy than trying to teach a beginner how to play scales—knowing she might quit anyway and you would end your life on a note of minor failure."

Muir looked at her and smiled slightly. "You knew Hugo quite well, didn't you?"

"We argued some."

"I expect you mean by that, the formal sense of the word 'argue.'"

"No. We bickered like cat and dog and were nasty to each other, but usually after some debate. The bickering was just to have fun after the seriousness. But being at each other's throats was probably the most satisfactory thing about our brief time together."

"I dare say it was," Muir said, then got slowly to his feet and went to the window. After a moment of watching the traffic run past the Cathedral, he said, "So that's that. I will use my remaining life in the joy of teaching you how to play the piano."

In May of the following year, Owen Dring stopped outside the door to the Foleshill Baths as Phil Granby walked out. "Good to see you, Owen. Coming for a swim?"

"You know I don't swim," replied the surgeon. "I just want a word with Beth."

"She's gone in to start lessons. I'm going for a quick drink and then will pick her up in a couple of hours. In fact she may still be in the cafeteria."

Dring found her sitting alone in the corner. She jumped up when he came in. "What, did somebody I know die?" she said.

He sat down and Lucy put a cup of tea on the table. "Actually we've had a successful day."

"Then why the visit? It's not every day, or month, you come here."

"Could you come round to the house this evening?"

"That's it. You've gone out of your way to request my presence at home. Does Mother have yet another chore for me? Does Carlyle need walking?"

Owen sipped his tea patiently. "You'll be there, say about eight or so...?"

Beth nodded her head. "I'll phone Phil and put him off till later."

When Beth went into the house on Hill Wootten Road, Owen called for her to come into the study. On his desk was a crudely wrapped parcel. It bore the markings of the Foreign Service, the Embassy of Great Britain, Democratic Republic of Congo-Leopoldville. A note written by embassy staff stated that it had been delivered by Captain Léon Mintou, ANC. Beth read the markings on the top, the name of her stepfather, and knew whose writing it was.

Dring said, "I thought you would want to see this," and then opened the ripped and scuffed package. The loose top sheet was an illustration of an African man with his lined face and expressive eyes looking half way to the floor. The long fingers of his right hand were stretched out as if requesting something, while those of his left felt the edge of a long wound running down his leg. The background to the sketch was a wall with high up on it a single grate. Attending to the native was an old man with thick white hair and a bushy moustache. The manila envelope underneath contained fifty-three more drawings. On Dring's desk was a photograph of the *Kyle Mission* with the edges curled and ripped. Beth stared a long time at the signature of Albert Schweitzer, then examined the attached note, which read:

Easter, Lufungula Police Barracks Prison, 1965. I have heard officially that Schweitzer has been dead for many months. Birks, however, is still alive and by next week we will know the best.

Beth left her stepfather to examine each sketch. Putting on her coat and muffler she went into the early spring chill with Carlyle baying to be let off his leash. When she reached the high point of land that showed the great sweep of farmland running towards Kenilworth Castle, she sat and wept.

A week later Dring read in a corner of the London Times:

Rebellion At Leopoldville Prison Put Down With Force.

He set the newspaper aside in his study next to the drawings and did not mention seeing the article to anyone.

When Conrad Muir was committed to the Coventry and Warwickshire Hospital, Beth arranged to take lessons on the chapel piano. He had been there a week when she wheeled him in and sat on the bench. After finishing her piece, she nervously fiddled with the hem of her skirt. She had the feeling that Conrad had just died because she could hear no sounds, no breathing, no chafing from the leather webbing of his chair. When she turned, he was slouched down, the dressing gown pulled around his shoulders. There was the mark running down his cheek into the stubble of his beard, which might have been from a tear.

"Thank you," he said. "Technically, this piece is not difficult. But there are considerations of subtlety." He wiped his brow and eyes with a cloth and took a sip of water. "It's almost a cliché now to mention that Beethoven was going deaf when he wrote it, was deaf when he created the Ninth Symphony, forcing the sounds to echo in his imagination instead of his ears. That was courage. So I now have to face some things myself. My love, Hugo's mother, has been gone for years. Just now, when I listened with eyes closed, I had a feebleness of heart that deluded me into thinking that she plays it one last time. How beautifully, with a crazy mournful yearning, you play it—with hope, with passion for the future. Corrine's playing had no such hope. Of course she wasn't playing it for me. In essence she was playing it for no one. For a dead fantasy, maybe, for a hopeless dream of what life should have been."

Beth wheeled him back to the ward and put him to bed. When she left an hour later, she didn't go to the car park but began walking the streets, remembering that a year had passed since Hugo cut open the throat of the little boy choking on the crackers. She felt the rings on her left hand and let the tips of her finger go across the diamonds, remembering the fact that nerve endings can feel sensation to microscopic size. On the shining gold band beside her engagement ring she could feel no sensation from defects or dirt or any impediments to its luster. When she had walked herself to exhaustion and was at the hospital door, she ran in and went directly to Conrad's room. She put her hand on his and stayed there on a hard chair trying to stay awake as the hours ticked by—until she was sore from sitting in the coma of near-sleep and realized that Conrad's skin was cold. Her fingers, which recently could detect no flaw in the gold, pressed against his neck with the expectation of feeling nothing. She covered his arms and his face, reported to the nursing station, then left the building. It was four in the morning.

Only a few vehicles remained in the car park. She felt bereft of everything, not even cars or people for company or the customary rain falling down. The sky was clear with stars spread across it. She looked up and wondered what truth was, if not in the simplicity of the night sky. But she knew also that part of her distress was that she had not eaten in hours and warm food would be the best cure for her emptiness. More than this, she felt the need to be patient and let time go by. Then someone she knew might open a door and say, "Come inside, Beth, I have a miracle here that will satisfy you."

At Conrad's funeral she sat in the back with Owen and Miranda. At some point in the service, she found herself praying in gratitude for the soul of the man who had taught her to play the piano. Music, she had read, was ineffable, perhaps God's reply to prayer. She pulled back from that idea by recalling the images Hugo had described of the one child who lacked prayers and the other who had a thousand given on her behalf, and how the outcome of lives and souls might thereby be affected. She hoped dearly that he was right, that supreme love was not contingent, that there could be no deal making with God. Prayer could only be prayer if it was simply a bowing of the head, like a hymn sung in a manner expressing shame or remorse.

Lufungula Police Barracks Prison, April 27, 1966.

With Captain Mintou absent for some weeks, Hugo felt a greater burden of loneliness. Although he could not discard a sense of mistrust, on the surface he conceded a shallow affection for the man. The young soldier had become part of his routine, which was itself the most substantial event in each day's curriculum. Without it he drifted. During the hours of daylight, sitting alone in his cell became as laborious as the digging of a long trench. Only the night offered him the void into which he could project his variegated thoughts. On one particular night, when there were no flickering cook fires to tarnish the purity of his visions, he observed a thin sliver of light falling across the floor. This was followed by human noise, but no substance greater than a shadow. Distressed, he sat upright for a moment, saw nothing, then fell into a shallow, uneasy sleep, with the biting insects keeping him half awake. Later, with a glimmering of dawn fooling his eyes, he woke sufficiently to hear a sound much like the slow breath of a baby after feeding from the breast, or a person already dead and no longer concerned with nourishment of any kind.

"Is that you, Albert?" he said.

"Sort of."

"Are you all right? It's been many months now."

"Oh, I'm all right, Hugo, at least better than you…with the hope of heaven, and soon."

"You're a bit ahead of yourself there," Hugo replied. "What I mean to say is: Of the billions inhabiting this earth, you of all people, deserve some reward. With your honest reverence for life, you've earned heaven, and then some. But we're never sure, are we? Doesn't the New Testament say that our good works are as filthy rags? Am I right in concluding that Paul said that, and you're the expert on St Paul? A lifetime serving mankind might count for nothing in the end."

"Quite right. It's not for us to decide."

The invisible figure squirmed around in the grit of the floor. "This place needs a good disinfecting, my friend. I had trouble finding a clean spot to sit down. It must be more than an inconvenience to live here."

"Isn't that the truth? I should be calling the maid."

"Do that. The filth of this place must add to your suffering."

"Oh, I'm not suffering any more. I've endured some abuse in here, but that part is over. The torturers could see that it was for no good reason. Agony can lead in unexpected directions. In my case, pain led them nowhere because they knew I would never take the easy way out."

"You took the easiest and most direct route out of Beth's life."

"You don't give up, do you, Albert? She is dead history."

The indistinct figure a few feet from Hugo's legs shifted like a small rustling wind. "Not dead at all. Quite alive and ruling your heart, as she will do for a lifetime of regret. Anyway, fate will soon put that misery in its place. As for myself? As soon as I'm done dealing with you, I'm confident in receiving the peace promised by the Savior." Albert smiled in the dawn light and ran bent fingers through his hair. "But I tell you what, Hugo. Over the last few months you've shown a minor interest in tending to the urgent needs of those around you. I plan to linger for a day or two yet. Watching your history play out will be my final act for humanity. After that I refuse to be involved with this place on the reason that I'm told heaven provides overwhelming amusements."

Hugo turned over and touched the rough cinder brick at his head. "I appreciate your concern, Albert. The habit of service is hard to break. But with me you needn't bother any longer. I'll manage. I've learned something of the lesson. I've even considered returning to Lambaréné—not to interfere, just to putter around and be more useful than I was the first time around."

With that comment he lay still and listened to the sounds from the street filtering through the grate. He could hear nothing from inside, feel no air going in and out of mouths other than his own. Albert had passed on many months ago, he was sure—in the early morning of September 4, as he had duly noted, then described to Léon Mintou. In his dream that night, all doors to the world had been closed. Beyond the black of unconscious, he had seen every line on Madame Ali's brow as she touched, then folded lovingly, the doctor's withered hands—stared at the dear face before her tears came. He saw and felt in his bones the dawning light of memory create a red glow on the roofs of the leper colony and on the face of Basile, outside his hut, continuing his nightlong task of whittling and polishing in order to finish the figure of Christ he would place on the coffin.

On May 10th, without warning, Hugo was raised from the pit of his mourning when Antoine opened the cell, then led him down the corridor, through the open gate and into the north wing. In the dim light he pointed to a door open two inches. Hugo shoved through into the cell, knowing he would have only a few minutes to talk without risk of detection. Martin Birks led him into the corner farthest from the door and both men squatted facing the wall.
"The least amount of chatter," he said.
Hugo pressed his fingers on the old soldier's arm to indicate he understood. In a few words he informed Birks that his wife and children were in good health and waited for his return. Then he removed the folder from his satchel, placed it on the concrete floor, and opened it. With a flick of his lighter, the photo of the *Kyle Mission* and the portrait of the soldiers glowed brightly in the near-black of the cell. Hugo let Birks look at them for a few seconds, turned one sheet over to show him Schweitzer's name and signature underneath. Then he extinguished the lighter and said, "My father is Conrad Muir. Allan Korrolus sent me to take the photo."
In two minutes Hugo told Birks the core of what he had been told by the others. Without hesitation, Birks replied in a whisper, "A few small adjustments, and you will have to trust my honesty on this. Von Raynor, your uncle, was correct but so was Korrolus. The German fired first on the *Kyle Mission* because Captain Korrolus, by his own admission, was drunk. As a permanent reminder of his misconduct he was branded with the wound to his leg. But then it was Von Raynor who hesitated, in fact became the despised bleeding heart. He was sitting on the fence wondering whether to sink the ship or not when two destroyer escorts pounced on his sub and drove him off.
"Thus, the goods for Schweitzer arrived at Algiers. So did your father. Sensing Crasson's duplicity and greed, he took the chance of transporting the shipment to Oran rather than taking the Frenchman's offer of reshipment from Algiers. Some of Fraser's story is true except this: We had already come under attack when Muir wandered by chance down the road and could quite easily have slipped by on an alternate route, leaving us to our fate. Instead, he chose to help. Hutchison was blown to pieces in front of him and I was partly disabled. George dared not move from behind a truck wheel and Fraser was frozen with fear, pinned down behind some debris.
"It was Muir, who, I recall, kept up the fire from the dead man's gun. When no enemy appeared to exist, all being dead or gone, George took to the wheel of the truck and we sped back to Algiers. Later when I asked Dring how the

civilian was doing, he said, 'what civilian?' Muir had not been in the vehicle when we arrived. Fraser said he had been hit during the fighting, was left for dead on the ground. I was dubious. Some days later a patrol found Conrad hiding, half-dead from thirst and a number of wounds. Dring worked hard to save him, not because Muir was an acquaintance, but because Owen apparently never tires of patching people up.

"After the war I was in Algiers by chance with Korrolus when we met Von Raynor at the Mission to Seamen, with him attempting to trace the whereabouts of his brother. Much later, I learned that Muir had joined his family overseas. I also learned the scope of this intrigue. With the exception of Dring, all the others profited from the black market sale of the goods bound for Lambaréné, led in that regard by Crasson. Years later I heard from Schweitzer where Muir was and wrote him. It was on his return correspondence I got the impression that after searching your father out, Korrolus had done his best to smooth his conscience with a few visits and a contribution to charity."

"What became of your friend, Louis Morrow, the man you came here to help?"

"That's a bit of joke, isn't it?" Birks replied. "He bought his way out of here with a few dollars a week before they jumped on me."

When Birks stopped talking and the resulting quiet assured them that no one had heard their voices, Hugo got to his feet saying in a whisper, "To end our holiday in this place, there's a drama unfolding to the advantage of us both."

"A holiday—or a death of boredom?" Birks asked.

Hugo gripped Birks' hand tightly. "Be ready for a sign," he said and closed the door behind him. As he reached forward to slide the bolt, strong fingers closed on his neck. The dark figure of Antoine pulled him back, then went noiselessly to the cell door, locked it, then led the way down the corridor past the stinking latrines.

In a place that had no winter and therefore no spring, flowering bougainvillea at the entrance to the prison had always seemed to Captain Mintou less a beauty and more like a discoloration of the cinder block. But not this time. On his arrival in the guardroom, he had Antoine take him to the door of cell six, where he marched in and squatted in the corner. Noticing that the place lacked all contrast, he conveyed to Hugo his observation that bright things seemed more beautiful if displayed against a dark surface—against a bleak time or a context of impending death.

"Welcome home," said Hugo.

"This isn't home."

"It is to me. And from your comments, you were unhappy to be away."

Mintou grunted disapproval. "It suits you—but not me. Even with the flowers it's an ugly place. You are getting ugly as well, monsieur. But I suppose you don't look any worse than when I left. You've survived, which is good. In a few more days I will pass my test. Are you confident in me?"

"You will write books and be famous."

"But will I be able to understand my books?"

"Just write them, Mintou." Hugo turned his pad to show a finished drawing of the captain leading his marching regiment.

Léon Mintou smiled and nodded his head in a gesture of satisfaction. "A reminder for me, monsieur, of who I am now. But we don't have forever. I must do my exam soon."

On the following Monday night, although the days of the week hardly occurred to him, Hugo had Captain Mintou come to his cell and write things from memory or as he dictated them. Next, he had his student sit beside him on the case and read passages from the selected book. When the test was finished, he told the soldier to come later for his results. The next morning when Mintou returned, Hugo took from his case a package he had wrapped in cardboard and bound with twine.

"Read what I have printed here, Léon."

Hugo pointed to the exterior script blocked out with the dark capitals. Knowing little English, the former Sergeant struggled with the words, "Please deliver to Major Owen Dring, MD, FRCS, DSO, Coventry and Warwickshire Hospital."

"Very good. I want you to bring me back a piece of paper signed by an official of the embassy with their stamp on it and your signature as well. When you return with these things accomplished, I will give you the results of your test."

Captain Mintou complained about the setback but went anyway. The next afternoon, he scraped open the cell door and handed Hugo an envelope with the letterhead of the British Embassy. Hugo handed him back a sheet of paper with remarks concerning the exam.

The soldier smiled. "I did well?"

"I don't flatter people with useless compliments, Mintou. You began your career with an impossible burden of ignorance. I was not convinced you would ever be able to walk properly and smoke a cigarette at the same time. But you're a driven man, a dangerous person, a bad character who would throw his own people into the furnace for his ambition. On the other hand, you're now capable of recording the results of pouring oil on fire instead of water. The choice for justice is yours. Now, which way do we go from here?"

"Tomorrow night, have your things packed."

Hugo nodded and Mintou asked, "You warned your friend?"

He nodded again towards the man backing out the door, then sat to stare at the wall. Through the grate issued sounds of a stringed instrument, a child's screams, and talk going around the cooking fires. Talk also went around his head of balances and equations. Before the next morning's dawning of his final day in cell six, he had a great need to identify the essence of what Léon Mintou meant to him; of how he must deal with a newly enhanced, refurbished officer in a nondescript, piecemeal army who might in the final accounting turn out to be one of two things: the equivalent of a bad smell or the person the ju-ju doctor described. He lit his second cigarette of the day and blew the smoke into the steaming air. The rush comforted him, although it did nothing to quell his general anxiety. Only a certain number of facts would contribute to his survival. As unlikely as they were, the facts pertaining to Captain Mintou had the most bearing. And of the many small things Mintou believed in, only three applied: first, that Antoine's murdered nephew lived fresh and cunning in Hugo's heart; second, that the man who journeyed with him as a fellow traveler, the ju-ju doctor who saved old niggers, was a favorite of the God that ruled the world; the third and most important thing strewn along the path of Mintou's new awareness was the sign Hugo had left for him to stumble over in the book he had studied; and this related directly to the greater lesson of honor and good faith.

The next evening, after packing his satchel and case, Hugo lay with this fragile hope on the concrete floor, listening for any indication that the captain was initiating his plan. Time wore on with more hours of solitude. He smoked the last of his cigarettes and squirmed to ease the pain in his back. He tried to visualize future history, a page with snapshots of picnics in the woods or a neatly written account of survival. Nothing came to him. The sounds behind the grate receded into faint music and behind it a barely audible rasping, like metal sliding over stone. Across the blackness of the floor fell a lengthening sliver of dim light. Someone was opening his door, millimeter by half-millimeter. He could now hear other sounds coming from the direction of the north wing—loud voices, a radio and the laughter of women. In a few minutes, the door had opened a half-meter.

Hugo could smell the nervous sweat and heard a voice saying, "Antoine is getting the guards drunk, including those in the north wing." Mintou slinked in from the door. "Two others are in the north wing unlocking Birks' cell," he added. "After we get outside, they will unlock all the doors they have time for. As soon as we hear quiet in the west wing, we will know the guards have gone."

"What about Antoine?" asked Hugo.

"He will be blamed for this. They will shoot him."

"Not if he goes with us."

As they crept out of the dark cell, Hugo stopped. He was troubled that he had forgotten something. A brief flick of the lighter caused his doubt to shrink away, but not his sadness. The flash of light had illuminated the dismal cage from which the next prisoner would have no hope of escaping. To offset this despair, Hugo took a small memento from his satchel, kissed it, then threw it past the closing door and into the farthest corner of the cell.

As he did this, the sounds in the guardroom drifted outside. Cautiously Mintou went through into Antoine's room then opened the door to the parade ground, urging Hugo to follow through it and not make too much noise dragging his case, which looked heavy as an anchor. They crept along in the darkness close to the wall of the prison. Hugo watched the captain, half expecting a wave of his hand, a loud shout to betray his double-dealing.

"Stay by the gate," Mintou ordered then marched back to the guardhouse door and went in. Hugo held his breath. From down the rows of vehicles in the motor pool came giggling, laughter, protests, and the smashing of bottles. Within a minute two figures appeared and hurried down the wall. One was a man whose features Hugo could not make out in the darkness, but hoped was Martin Birks. The second was a barefoot black man. He moved like a feather being wafted by the night breeze, or perhaps held upright by the walking cane Hugo recognized in his hand. Two more men came out of the guardroom door and ran along the wall, then a flood of men, and Mintou was calling with a loud whisper, "Go out the barracks gate. Go now—quickly!"

As he said this, a guard screamed and came to the door of the north wing. Hugo could hear more loud voices and many running feet. When they had gone only a few hundred meters, the siren sounded and vehicles pulled onto the street. Gunfire sounded sporadically from the compound. Once beyond the walls of the prison, they ran along an alley littered with debris. In minutes Hugo fell behind. His legs were weary from lack of use and crumbling under the weight of the case. Birks came up beside him trying to assist with legs as weak as Hugo's. Both men stumbled and gasped for breath.

A soldier dashed between houses. Using the light from a nearby cooking fire, he knelt and fired at them. Birks fell from view. Captain Mintou ran from the same direction. He waved his stick at the trooper with a curious motion. The man stopped and saluted. Hugo collapsed next to his case with a sigh. The captain marched over to him and stood with his feet together, hands clasped firmly behind him in a posture of superiority, as if at last he was in command of his world. Hugo thought it rewarding to be confirmed in his assessment of Mintou's character, but had a moment of disappointment. Léon

Mintou did not resemble a newly literate, disciplined officer in command of anything; instead, he seemed distant and detached, at loose ends—like a man shrinking to invisibility. The trooper crept closer with his rifle pointed at Hugo's head, looking to the officer for a command. Seeing none, he hopped backwards and took a closer aim. His left eye blinked nervously. Sweat rolled onto the breech. Too late he sensed something from behind as a Birks' tattooed arm came around his neck with a knife sliding towards his throat.

Mintou stepped forward. "No!" is all he said. Then "no" again and twice more the same word pronounced in gentle voice before turning Birks' arm and the knife to one side. He took the rifle away from the soldier and motioned with his swagger stick for him to stand off. The man backed away until he was clear, and when he had vanished in the shadows of the alley, Captain Mintou threw the rifle aside, took Hugo's heavy case then went ahead of them as if he had seen little, done less and was carrying nothing.

As they walked on, more army vehicles flashed by on the road. Hugo secured his satchel firmly to his side and twice hid with the others behind mounds of garbage. And always someone yelled for them to get away because all who lived in the vicinity of Lufungula knew the unpleasant aftermath of rebellion. After traversing a series of streets, they saw a dark outline of a vehicle blocking their way. Men jumped out, hands helped the two prisoners into the back, and pushed them under the wooden benches. Hugo found himself covered with a blanket and right in front of his face, the nose of a young woman speechless with fright. The motor started and the vehicle bounced onto the thoroughfare, then swung wildly from street to alley to street with shots fired from the back.

Then the commotion died. The vehicle picked up speed and rough road smoothed to pavement. Hugo drifted to sleep, then was aware that the vehicle had stopped. When he opened his eyes, he could see light. They went forwards again slowly and he could hear the sounds of the ferry engine, could feel the bumping down onto the north side and the short drive into the army base at Luozi, which was good because he was at that point prepared to urinate through the floorboards.

The captain took this into account and waited a few minutes before ordering everyone to assemble on the porch for muster. Hugo looked down the line to see the huge, shoeless figure of Martin Birks standing next to Antoine the jailer, together with his favorite wife. Lined up with the other soldiers of the brigade was the man who had opened Birks' cell and all the other doors of the prison, the man who had threatened to shoot him at the outset. The only outsider was a man with a withered face and a thin body clothed in rags—the prisoner with the long white scar on his leg. Hugo was glad to see that he was supported by a carved cane, formerly the property of A. Schweitzer, recently deceased.

They stayed only a few hours in Luozi. A soldier woke Hugo and Birks to issue Captain Mintou's request that they meet with him. "The Army will come to know our part in this episode," he said. "But they can only identify me, Antoine and the two others who were inside the jail. For our immediate safety, the ferry will not cross again today."

"Come north," said Birks. "I can buy you papers for Congo-Brazzaville and fit you into the business, at least long enough for you to settle."

They drove up the north route that afternoon, with Hugo and Birks sitting in back with the others. Towards evening they were at the frontier village and met by the chief, his wives, and twenty children. The captain said good-bye to the men who were remaining, but failed to wave or watch as the truck sped back down the track towards the basin of the Congo River, marking its retreat with a plume of dust. In a few minutes Birks had negotiated an entry price with the young soldiers who played with their rifles around the frontier post. With the guards behind them, the six men and one woman walked around the final bend where they could see the trader's shop surrounded with concrete walls and wire gates. Hugo was barely able to drag his leather case along and was assisted by Captain Mintou. Both men respectfully hung back—so that when the first sight of the group stirred the children to screams of delight, and from the door a minute later ran a woman weeping with joy, it was Martin Birks who was out front and falling to his knees to wrap his arms around the waist of his wife and put his face silently into her apron.

The clean white canopy floating above Hugo had a soothing pattern. He lay for hours in his bed without moving, staring into the intricacies of the fabric until drowsiness closed his eyes again. For the first day, only one or other of the children disturbed him by bringing food. The second day Captain Mintou came three times to sit with him and read slowly from a book. Birks came in also that day with coffee and they talked for hours about Lambaréné and Hugo's decision to eventually return there. Then he got out of bed and dressed in clean clothes to join the other guests and Birks' family in the shade room at the back of the main house. Hugo sat down at the piano in the corner, and with no warming of his fingers, played the slow movement of Beethoven's *Sonata*.

"Charmaine, I used to have a bottle of wine in the cellar," said Birks when the music was finished. "Is it still there?"

She nodded, fetched the bottle, and poured a little into plastic tumblers. Then the group sat or stood as Birks said, "I don't know exactly what it is we're toasting here—our present good fortune or old memories, or perhaps new memories. But I do want to toast Captain Mintou for his bravery and Doctor Haultain for his part."

His voice broke slightly as he held up his glass. The others held up theirs, although some had no idea of the ritual and were just waiting patiently to drink. Antoine in particular seemed confused and afterwards took Hugo aside. "I'm pleased that Monsieur Birks also gives you the title, 'Doctor,' which you earned by your labor at the prison. It is only right that we be named for the thing we do."

Over the next week, while Hugo recovered his strength, Birks offered to drive him to Kabinda, from where the trader had secured Hugo's passage on a fish packer to Angola. From there it would be easy for the doctor to arrange air travel to Europe. The day before he left, Captain Mintou came into Hugo's room accompanied by the man with the scar on his leg. His face was less withered and he smiled.

"His name is Joshua," said the former captain. "He is a musician who plays stringed instruments and wants to serenade you. It's the only thing he can offer as gratitude."

Hugo went with them into the piano room. Joshua sat on a low bench. His limbs stuck out at odd angles like sticks. When he began to strum and pick the strings, Hugo could hear in the music, see in the man's eyes a peculiar tranquility that beat back his overwhelming pain, as no fragment of his body appeared free of humiliation. He played for a long time, with one theme running seamlessly into the next, and he did so with a peaceful face and his legs crossed. When the music was done, the man smiled, and told Hugo with his eyes to understand that he would give more, if he had more to give. Hugo took the long, elegant fingers into his hand and held them firmly.

The next day he went around the compound shaking the hands of everyone there, last of all, the captain's. Hugo held it for more than a moment, then said, "There was a moment when I was going to shoot you with your own gun, Léon. But I had a sudden dream in my head that you were a friend. What a reckless thing to think. And of course I expected you would shoot me instead for such stupidity. I expected it right up to the time we walked in here, but then I knew we had crossed into another place."

Mintou nodded and smiled. "I was never going to shoot you, Doctor…if I may be allowed to call you that. If only you had known. You see, deep inside, I'm a coward. When I was a boy I couldn't bring myself to wring the neck of a chicken, much to my father's disgust. It was his idea that I become a soldier so that he could talk of me to his friends without cringing in shame. At first I was afraid of you, monsieur. More than once I wished the guards had wrung your neck in prison. Each meeting forced me to think that if I was more like you, I might become an officer and able to do a soldier's work properly."

"You'll have trouble in the world, Léon, but less so now," Hugo replied. "Perhaps you're the person the ju-ju man described, who respects life. As regards you and me—you're the better. All along, you've known in your heart what it is we lose through killing."

*   *   *   *

To pass time, Hugo walked along the sea wall that fronted the port city of Luanda, Angola. Beside him was a man named Scutter, a dissolute Rhodesian late from his mercenary adventures in the eastern Congo. Hugo sat on a stone bench to let an African boy shine the old boots Birks had given him because his own shoes had worn through.

"No one ever shined my shoes," Scutter said to his companion, who appeared not to care one way or another. Flies swarmed over the boy's face until gusts of sea wind blew them away. Hugo touched his soft, wooly hair.

"Those flies are attracted to me like I am attracted to you, master," the boy said. "They perform for me and I perform for you. It is my duty, as it is theirs."

"Cheeky little kaffir," said the Rhodesian.

The boy looked at him with great forbearance because he didn't understand why anyone would bother to say such things. He remained silent at his work until the mercenary got up and walked slowly down the esplanade. When he was out of range, Hugo said, "You can talk now, friend. Tell me the strange things that you know, and I don't."

The boy smiled and squinted at the receding figure. Finally he said, "If I do my duty, I turn into one of five snakes and crawl off to my home, which is near the square by the hotel. Want to know something else, master?—I'm told by my uncle that the sand of the Kalahari is dry and fine, miles below the course of airplanes that carry people like you, with the dunes appearing to have the texture of fine cloth. And each dune is like the last, as each grain of sand is the same. I never get enough to eat unless I am a snake and drink milk three days. And it takes three sheddings of my skin to crawl to Port Anthony and ride the train to Windhoek where my father lives; but my greatest desire when I am a snake is to die and become your shoes. Then I walk off with you and be at the foot of your bed when you are with the ladies. But most likely I will be in the square tonight and do what I have to do. Perhaps I will be unlucky and fall into the fountain and drown because I can't swim."

"What's he saying?" asked Scutter, who had walked back to see if the boot polishing was finished. Hugo let the Rhodesian light another of his cigarettes.

"He's talking about revolution."

"Wouldn't matter what he says. Kaffirs talk only nonsense and tend to kill the thing they fear."

They had a beer in the town, went to the hotel and in the evening witnessed the first skirmish of a dispute between tribes, over money, over power, over settling differences relating to age-old fear. Hugo watched all he could stomach of the killing before going to bed and in the morning to the airport.

The Super Constellation lifted easily from the runway. As it banked to the right, he recalled that with its three vertical rudders, this peculiar aircraft was designed by a rich man who had little use for fancy clothes, had his lunch delivered in a brown bag, and could also have lived joyfully from an old leather case and a satchel. Hugo was content to abbreviate this connection and focus instead on the coast of Africa sliding below him. He could see the Congo River spilling silt into the Atlantic and the hypnotic texture of the endless jungle upstream with no hint of villages like Luozi or great capitals like Leopoldville.

The hours went with the monotonous green passing two miles down. He calculated that the irregular path of a waterway that suddenly appeared might be the Oogue River. Next to it, where the towering clouds swept into the horizon, buried close to the deer garden perhaps, would be the remains of Albert Schweitzer—and with him deceased and the fate of the hospital unknown, the leper Basile, still whittling his magic walking sticks would wait sadly for the good intent of ordinary physicians to drain away into the irreconcilable forest.

Twilight faded. Hugo settled his eyes onto the sequential firings of the inside starboard motor. With nightfall came turbulent, nauseating storms. He finished three beers and had an urge to borrow a cigarette. The deep vibrations of the engine increased his haze of perception. With unfocused eyes he saw the colors running from the exhaust ports down across the trailing edge of the wing, bleeding energy into the atmosphere and looking exactly like the jellied ribbon that yesterday had oozed from the hole in the shoeshine boy's head. He fell asleep.

In his dream, the string of blood formed into a snake that undulated along the surface of the fountain water next to the polished stone, quite dignified in its going over the marble edge, squirming its weary way over the boots of soldiers to avoid the hot shell casings tinkling onto the pavement. With a jaunty air it by-passed the screams of pain and hatred, slithering on its thankful underbelly along the seawall and over time the pleasant journey to Port Anthony so as eventually to be in Windhoek and the home of the boy's father.

Hugo woke sweating and tried to arouse himself from the confusion. For some reason he looked at his boots, then reached for his cigarettes, forgetting that he had quit smoking. The previous afternoon he had declined the offer from Scutter, "Cigarette, Hugo? It'll get you through this nauseating mess and the cheap beer."

They were sitting on the third floor hotel balcony enjoying the spectacle of mobs screaming, chanting in the square, trying to see who was on whose side and the progress made by machine guns and the occasional popping of small arms fire. To the astonished priest who sat next to him, the mercenary said, "I told my friend Sandra over there, she should not be sticking her head too far out if she valued it."

"I'm sure she can hear bullets hitting the hotel, Nelson," said the priest. "She'll take care."

"As well she should. You've got to admit, Padre, that it would be a waste to let sweet Sandra get her rosy ass shot off."

The priest looked at him with disgust.

"No wait," Scutter said. "What I meant to confess to you, Father, was that the boy who polished my friend's boots, well you can never predict these things can you? You can see for yourself, the poor little kaffir's floating dead over there in the fountain, and no priest of his own color to give him the last rites."

Hugo let this voice carry him towards another fitful sleep. The airliner drifted out over the Sahara, past Niamey and the last glimpse of light, before there was no light at all or anything below in the Tanezrouft, being the hot season and perhaps not even smugglers on the move across its surface. They touched down briefly in Malta and the old lady in a front seat said that it was a blessing to be so close to heaven after all her years in Africa.

During an unexpected stopover in Lichtenstein, Hugo sat behind a café eating cheese from a tray. The trellis surrounding the courtyard was full of flowers. Taking his wine glass with him, he walked past a display of roses, which glowed deep red in the late morning sun. When he sat back down with a full glass, some words came to him:

"A glass of wine in Lichtenstein, a red rose for a rover."

He tried to remember where he had last heard that phrase, or perhaps two phrases, each heard at different times and him not sure either where or when. But he had no doubts concerning the exact time of his departure from Lufungula or the corner of the dismal cell where he had deliberately kissed, then deposited as a blessing the dried rose petal taken from Aldermans Green.

Chapter XXIV

Lost Jewel

In London, Hugo went immediately to Poste Restante. The clerk handed him two letters: one from Milton Muxlow, the other recently arrived from Coventry. He took a room at the hotel in Russell Square. Lying on his usual bed, with gratitude and optimism he first read the news from Milton. The typed and unsigned letter from Coventry merely said,

> *To Hugo Haultain, should he ever return. Your father, Conrad Muir, died on April 23, 1966 at the Coventry and Warwickshire Hospital. After a memorial service he was interred in the Kenilworth Municipal Cemetery.*

Hugo sat up and wished he had a cigarette. He went to stare at the bricks in the empty lot and consider the concept that Conrad Muir, his father, had now become one of the unrecoverable war dead. There was no longer any hope of shared books, or music, or debate, all the various activities from his years of convalescence that were now beyond recovering, replacing, restoring to good health. In fact, Hugo was now aware that there had been no sharing at all once he had became old enough to value solitude. In the breakfast room the next morning, a resident said, "Have a smoke mate? No? You used to smoke when we last saw you in."

Hugo nodded, tried to eat his toast, and think of all the things he used to share, all the things he didn't, and how he seldom gave a thought to the difference. The air reeked of a mixture of smoke and cold bacon rinds, all things not worth sharing, so he left. At the Apple Orchard he drank a half-pint of mild. The British Museum was open. He paid admission and walked for hours through exhibits of the ancient world. He took the tube cross-town to Hyde Park and listened to the same man talk of imperialism in Africa. That night he lay in the sagging bed behind the grimy window and thought of what he would face tomorrow and why he was going. Perhaps someone had found Solly's ring. He hoped everyone he knew was in good health and that his parcel from Leopoldville had found its way into useful hands. He would visit the cemetery and put a flower on Conrad's grave. The letter from Coventry implied that someone there had seen him, most likely at the Cathedral where he would have gone to meditate on the mother of his son. Who would have gone to his memorial? Lastly, he thought it sad that his parents were not buried together on the slope of the rainforest mountain so they could at least enjoy eternity together to make up for the years when they were both alive.

He went outside and walked briskly down Great Oxford Street. The movement of air allowed him to ponder the moment with some relief. He had lived well over a year now in expectation of tomorrow's events knowing all the while it was foolish. At best he would politely admire her baby, offspring being a possibility in that period of time. He would pat the little lad on the head and suggest someone teach him Grieg's *A Minor Concerto* with the encouragement that he not whine too loudly about the lost opportunity of playing with his friends, or perhaps her friends. Because gender is never assured in breeding and even the determination of fatherhood is a fact not accepted by all. The next morning he got up a reasonable hour, showered in the semi-cold water, and took the tube to Kings Cross.

Entering the station he wondered to himself why he was lugging his leather case around when his satchel would well enough carry everything he needed. He had no need for the books now, he thought—perhaps he never needed them. His clothes were less and worse than when he first arrived in England. But there was no self-pity in this contemplation; it was merely a statement of fact. He went onto the platform and was struck with a thin, inaudible connection to the millions of rivets, massive baroque girders and the frequent oddities of British Rail, setting cheap wax toilet paper next to the priceless oak door, close to—but really a world away from Coventry, with no rhyme nor reason for returning.

From the compartment window he watched the summer hills and valleys come and go with emerald fields streaked with the brown of ploughed fallow. The stations and the miles were marked by the sucking rush of passing trains and the staccato click of the rails. A suffocating heat had burnt away the mildew of the old coach. He closed his eyes with drowsy fatigue. The trucks rocking across the switches woke him.

"Rugby," said the conductor.

In a minute he had transferred to the silver diesel and went his way the last few miles into Coventry Station. A few people left the train and vanished through the doors to waiting transport. He recalled the day he had arrived from

London hoping Beth would come to meet him, just the part of her she could spare, as if she could split her interests willy-nilly amongst a handful of competing interests. He rested his heavy case in the waiting room expecting nothing this time.

"Tea, mate? Perhaps an ice?" said the attendant. "Weather's a bit hot. But I'm not complaining."

"Thanks. I'll just rest here and wait for the bus."

When he had finished his tea he took his case to the wicket. "Is there a locker?"

"In that room over there. A shilling will get you a day."

"Could I just leave it behind the counter? No? One thing more, what time is the next train back to Rugby?"

"Fifteen hundred hours. Three pm to you."

Hugo got off the ring-road bus at Freddy Marshall's cottage. As he walked by it, a gust of wind shook the hedge fronting the flowerbeds. A penny for the guy, he thought, a penny for dreams we have of cherished gardens. There was not a tire mark left in it and the bushes were covered in blooms of red and yellow roses. The car park was empty, but behind it the green itself spread away to the edge of the sky with only the tops of the trees and a roof here and there coming up into the blue. He walked down the high street past the Crow in the Oak; and resisting the temptation to go in for a pint, took the bus to Stokehill.

At the Guildhall he walked through the common area unnoticed. He glanced into the west wing, put his case by the music room door, and tiptoed in. The light went on at a twist of his fingers. The top of the piano was layered with dust and hadn't been used since last he played, whatever it was he played the night he returned soaking wet from Aldermans Green. This time he closed the lid so as not to make a noise, then went to the office. No one had seen or returned a ring. The woman looked suspicious and checked the small receipt he carried before retrieving the few things he had stored.

The receptionist at the Coventry and Warwickshire Hospital said, "I remember you. But I'm sorry, Beth isn't here. I believe she was at the bath this afternoon for two o'clock lessons."

"Actually, I was hoping to see Mister Dring."

"Well you are in luck. Mister Dring's in his office, I believe."

Hugo stood at Dring's door and watched the surgeon writing. When he glanced up, the pen fell out of his hand. "This is more than a surprise. Come in, sit down."

Hugo sat on a chair.

"To be quite honest, I had concerns about you. Does Beth know you're back?"

"No."

"I see. Well you should know that I received your package."

Hugo nodded and squirmed in his chair.

"I heard that Albert died," said the surgeon.

"A few weeks after I left Lambaréné."

"And Birks?"

"He's well and married to a Vietnamese woman. Runs a trading post in Mindouli, Congo-Brazzaville."

Dring smiled, then scrutinized his face. "Have you been well?" he asked.

"I've had some setbacks."

"Yes, of course," replied Dring. "And the arm?"

"Right as rain. I have you to thank for that."

"Nonsense. Anyway I assume you've received the letter about Conrad."

"I did," Hugo replied. "Quite a surprise, but in keeping with the varying histories of him."

Dring picked up his pen. "Perhaps. At any rate, I can tell you where to find Beth. She could tell you more."

"That's not a good idea."

"Don't be daft. Why are you here in the first place?"

Hugo felt a twinge of remorse and confusion. "I left some things at the Guildhouse," he answered, then looked at his watch. "So I'd best be getting on."

"Getting on with what?"

"I had plans to do things here in England then travel elsewhere. But along the way I've put a few things on the tab and should try to clear off the debt. In fact, I'm going back to Africa in the hopes that the debt's not too large."

Dring nodded and frowned at the same time. Hugo stood up and said, "I'm returning on the three o'clock train to London."

He stretched out his hand for Dring, who took it and said, "She's at the Bath this afternoon and then assisting me at four. She would be disappointed if you didn't say hello."

Hugo stood opposite the Foleshill Bath, knowing he should have gone there first. But there were crowds in the bath with no consideration given to privacy or an intimate meeting of eyes, if not fingers. He had wanted to exhaust all options, catch her unawares, perhaps going to her car when no one was around. Yet this was fine, he thought, because seeing her from a distance would be sufficient to satisfy his curiosity and cause them no distress. The carrying of his heavy case had tired him, so he went into the little fish shop across the road to rest while he waited. After thirty minutes of sipping his tea and drawing on the napkin, he was prepared to go across and inquire. Perhaps she would be instructing in the large pool. This view might give him a little more of her history, so he could add her to the growing list of other, more complete histories. As he got to his feet, Phil Granby walked out of the bath with Beth. They talked for a minute; he kissed her on the cheek and walked in the direction of the Rose.

When he had gone, Beth hesitated on the stairs. The summer dress she wore went over her breasts and hips like rainwater. Her hair was long and no longer blond. She shaded her face from the sun and looked at the street as if she sensed he was there and was trying to search him out. But of course he was invisible, a nonentity, a smudge inside the window that could be anybody, was nobody, because she was not seeking anything with her gaze but a sense of summer air and the relief of distance. She turned back into the building. The sun slipped behind a cloud.

Hugo sat back down and stirred the half empty-cup of tea, which swirled then stopped. Those were the facts, the things he had just seen, so predictable a child could tell it. No difficulty in that and no hope that it would be otherwise. By the time he had finished his tea, the sun had emerged. He went back onto the street and stood in the warmth with his hands in his pockets. There was no logic to his going into the bath now. His presence inside would be an impertinence, an embarrassment. He would go back to London then on to Lambaréné as he had intended, being satisfied that he had confirmed the color of her hair.

But instead of going down Foleshill Road, he stood on the pavement. He thought of how far, at least measured in miles, he had come to see the summer dress, the slow turning of her body, and the rich hair falling away behind. He thought of taking one more look, just a few minutes watching her at the pool to see how she appeared away from the sun. As a car went by he hesitated then went to step into the road a second time. But another car brushed him back, then another one, followed by yet one more and lastly a row of automobiles that stretched all the way to Leicester and beyond—suggesting there would always be something to cut him off. It was a lesson in boundaries he knew Conrad had had little success in teaching him. Looking at the spot where she had stood, Hugo wondered if novelties had relieved her of the boredom, if she had wilted in a desert of pleasantries as he predicted, with only her stepfather to provide a brief shower of hope. He looked down at his case and noticed as if for the first time, the gouges in the leather and the gross discolorations on its sides. He wondered if general blindness had flawed his conclusions, that Beth was happy and would remain so all the days of her life.

He went up Foleshill Road, this time with a glance towards the spot in the sky where the clouds were gathered strangely out of time and place with the blue of heaven behind. It seemed a safe refuge for him, up high, out of harm's way, and alone. He walked faster towards it until he was running and was soon out of breath. His left arm ached to his shoulder from carrying the heavy case. At the next bus stop, the #33 was waiting to take him back to the station.

After telling Phil to meet Mr. Bradley at the Rose, Beth returned to the large bath. She gave instructions to her swimmers to do a dozen warm-up laps, then went into the cafeteria to relax. The sun streamed in through the front window and glinted off the three diamonds of the ring on her left hand and the other two set in a gold band next to it. From habit she stared at them until Lucy walked over. She was frowning and looking through the window, pointing in alarm. "Oh my, my," she said. Beth looked at her as if a significant event were occurring, a thing about to fall on her head.

"What's set you off?"

"Is that Hugo Haultain standing on the curb?"

Beth swung around. Hugo had his hands hanging by his side and appeared to be looking right at her but she realized all he could see was the reflection of the city in the glass. He looked much older, leaner with his face visibly scarred. His clothes were almost as bad as the ones he wore when he first walked into the hospital over a year before. Around his shoulders was the worn and dirty satchel. The old leather case was at his knee. He went to cross the street towards her and a car brushed him back, then another, and two more. Her hand went to her mouth and she swallowed, breathless and frightened. She turned away to look at the children's pool. The screams and cries of delight faded and she could hear only the sounds from her memory of the anguished mother as she watched her dying boy—and the deliberate manner Hugo used to prepare the tools he required as if he knew exactly what he was going to do and would accept the consequences of failure, because there would be no failure. How obsessed she became in her desire to know how that was possible. As the sounds of the bath returned to her ears she added to her anxious thoughts the only kiss they had shared and how at night when it rained she could feel his mouth, could hear her own voice saying, "Hugo, don't ever come back."

"Beth, he's leaving!" cried Lucy.

She pushed back her chair and in a few seconds was running for the door, down the stairs, and onto Foleshill Road. Empty. She ran to the corner. Nothing. She got into her car and drove to the Guildhouse.

"Yes, he was here earlier, luv. He'd left some things when he left last year, you know. Asked if anyone had found a ring. He took a few books away. Said he was going for the train, asked what time the buses left Foleshill."

She paced the vestibule, trying to think of what to do next. She took a coin from her purse and found the pay phone. A voice said, "Next train to Rugby is leaving in ten minutes."

Hugo sat in the station's tearoom. He poured the cup full and put in a small amount of sugar. "Been busy, guv?" he asked the vendor.

"Not much, the usual, a few visitors and the regulars."

Hugo nodded.

"You didn't stay long."

"Not long," he replied, then took out his pen. He pulled a napkin from the dispenser and wrote on it. "A glass of wine…"

It was nice that the sun was more or less out. The heat calmed him, made him think that he should have said hello to Nigel, to Toby, to Tom Mahoney if he was still alive. But there was no part of the story to rewrite and keep whatever was precious from fading like the clichéd rose. He scribbled some more words that allowed him to finally break into pieces. Pain must be allowed a presence, he thought, because misery is a necessary condition for life, a simple compass that never failed. The train rushed into the station. He glanced up at the shiny sides and felt better. Trains were simple. There should be a reverence for uncomplicated things, for intimate conversation and a shared life. With his right hand he picked up his leather case and walked towards the open train door.

Beth drove into the carpark. Through the station windows she could see the bright side of the train. The lot was full. She sped twice around and parked in the passenger zone. The whistle sounded. She pulled open the heavy wooden door and ran through the waiting room. Silver flashed by her eyes. She reached the edge of the platform to see the end of the last coach slide by and recede down the line under a plume of black smoke.

"Oh, God, come back."

She let her hand fall to her sides and felt no more anger or frustration or hate for missed opportunity. She looked at the sky and the unusual clouds tinged at the edges with mother of pearl. The warmth on her face resisted the despair beneath as the last glimpse of the train blinked between the trees of the forest. She called after it, "Go on, then!" and turned to go back to her idling car. A man with a leather case stood next to a table under the eve. He seemed confused by the look of anger on her face and was trying to smile as if to mask his distress.

Beth took hold of a chair for support, saying. "Did you hear what I just said?"

"No," the man answered.

"I said to the train, and what I thought was the last of you—I said, 'Go on, then!' It's the kind of thing you would say to someone you were glad to be rid of, someone to whom you had once said, 'Don't ever come back,' but he did—and then left again like a thief and a liar, much to my joy."

She leaned on the table as if to catch her breath. "Because that's what you've been, Hugo, a thief and a liar. You stole from me my happy life, my content life and you lied, to mock and belittle me."

Beth swallowed and put her hand to her breast to calm her breathing. Her voice calmed too, but was edged with bitter tears when she said, "I found an envelope recently, Hugo, just a month ago, a rerouted letter that came unexpectedly into my hands because I have been receiving lately all the post addressed to your father. This piece was from your usual place of business and addressed to you, Doctor Hugo Haultain, if you are the person of that name, or are they in error there? Is it true that you're not a mad drifter sitting at the edge of kiddy's pool thinking it was just fine to let the world and me go on being ignorant, pretending that I would just see who it was you were as if by magic. Is this your 'other consideration'?" She sat heavily on one of the chairs. "I'm sorry. I need to sit down."

"Are you all right?"

"Just the heat."

"Let me get you a cold drink."

When he returned, she was staring at her hands, which were placed on the table. Hugo covered her left hand with his, then lifted it up to stare at the rings, especially the wedding band with its two large stones.

"They're a perfect match, don't you think, Hugo, the rings, the diamonds? I am very happy, very proud to wear them," she said.

He could see that her eyes had a profound sympathy, were so lacking in mockery that he shook his head and sighed. "Before I leave," he said, "I want you to know this. It was my deliberate intention to lie, to steal, and cheat, to make myself as objectionable as I could. Because I didn't want to interfere with anyone's peace, and by doing that, interfere with my own. I could have simply said, 'These are my skills, this is what I am, but don't wish to do it anymore.' I didn't want to be involved is the simple answer, because everything until now has been dead history."

"Dead history? You come with me. I'll show you what dead history is…and then we'll see if you're sorry."

They got into Beth's car and in a few minutes were past the ring road and onto the highway. In silence Hugo watched the passing farmland, houses and cars and wondered what he must have been thinking when he decided to come back. But he was certain now of one more fact of history. At Kenilworth she turned off the road and parked alongside a copse of colored bushes. Hidden in the growth, small birds sang.

They walked ten feet apart across the first segment of grass before coming to the thicket. Beth went closer to him and walking with an easy gait took his hand and led him through the forest He recalled the night she had done that when they left the Rose and could feel no difference in the touch of her skin, the tightness of her fingers on his. When they came to another expanse of lawn, he realized that they were in a cemetery, most likely the resting place of his father. After strolling up and down a few rows of horizontal gravestones, she stopped in front of a slab of polished granite. Carved on it were the words:

> *Conrad Muir, August 9, 1893–April 23, 1966.*
> *Oh what would the world be, once bereft*
> *Of wet and of wildness? Let them be left,*
> *O let them be left, wildness and wet;*
> *Long live the weeds and the wilderness yet.*
> *G.M. Hopkins*

Hugo looked at it then back at Beth. She put her arm around his waist and for a moment leaned her head into his shoulder. Then she said, "Only a month after you left, Conrad arrived at the Cathedral and said he was applying for the job as organist advertised in the *Church Times*. He played for Owen and the other officials and got the job. On every occasion after that he played the organ until he became too sick to attend services. By that time we all knew who he was, your father, although he told us nothing about what you did. I nursed him the last few weeks at the hospital. He never said this to me, but I got the feeling that he lived in the hope that you would find your way back here before he died."

Hugo kneeled down next to the grave. With his head bowed, he traced over the inscription with his fingers. "Before I left home a few years ago," he said, "Conrad and I came to a partial accommodation, which was good because generally we didn't get along. But I always thought I'd see him again."

He got to his feet and walked back to her.

"We became quite close," Beth said with tears in her eyes. "He told me about your mother, what a beautiful person she was, about his friendship with Albert Schweitzer, and how he had hoped that somehow you would come to appreciate the world and yourself—a hope I didn't understand until recently."

She turned and walked onto the hill above the grave. Hugo watched her go, with her summer dress blowing in the wind and her hair, which had the rich color of her mother's. On the other side she stopped to look over the tops of the oak and beech trees and beyond to the towers of Kenilworth Castle. When he had caught up, she said, "He was peaceful at the end, Hugo. I told him that I loved him because he had been very good to me, and not for the father he was, which I don't know, do I…because I only know about the sorry time that you and I have had."

She lifted up her purse which was slung loosely around her shoulder with the strap coursing down between her breasts. Hugo put a finger up to her one eye and wiped the moisture onto her temple.

"I gave him little to be proud of, Beth. Wherever I go from here I'll have to come back with a rose for his grave to honor him, and by that I mean to honor you as well for the care you gave him." He turned away and began walking down the hill towards the car. To clear his eyes he looked at the one strange cloud that drifted to the east, hardly changing its shape against the flawless blue, a blue had seen arched over dry lands that were watered deliberately from below and not from the capricious sky. When she had caught up, he said, "All my life I have had the company in my head of someone I imagined was a ridiculous, common old man. At Lambaréné, Albert Schweitzer was frail, but not common or ridiculous at all. No one was allowed to see him. I did one small job for the hospital and while doing this, he came to the site briefly to say, 'I want to thank you for this work,' and walked away on the arm of Madame Ali to cheers of the crowd. But he didn't go far before turning and saying, 'You should dig a little deeper. The trench is still too shallow. It's a bit like you, Hugo, like the man who lacks the depth required to be of real service."

Hugo gave a last look up the hill in the direction of Conrad's grave then took Beth's hand and began the walk back to the car. When they were on the ring road, she asked, "What are you going to do now?"

"The next train leaves in two hours. If you don't mind, please drop me by the Precinct. I'll wander around there and then walk to the station."

When that car was parked in front of the Craven Arms, she gripped the steering wheel and looked at him. "Perhaps you could take the eight o'clock train instead of the five-thirty," she said. "I have some things that you should take with you, letters from Conrad mostly and a few personal items he wanted you to have. Come round to the hospital when I've finished, then I could drive you to the station."

Hugo was silent, as if he hadn't heard her. Finally he said, "The eight o'clock train is soon enough." From his pocket he removed a piece of paper torn out of a spiral notebook. "The plane back from Africa stopped in Lichtenstein. We had lunch in the garden of a hotel and I thought of you."

"Why were you thinking of me?"

"Because your note said, 'When you eat, think of me.' So I often did think of you. In the rose garden when it occurred to me that I might see you again, I recalled a phrase I heard many years ago and you repeated the night I left—as if you could have known what was in my mind. So I made something out of it."

He handed her the sheet of paper and said, "You can read it later."

"Why not now?"

Hugo took a deep breath and tried to smooth back his hair, as a gesture of sorrow. "Because it ends where it began—in futility," he answered. "I think that was the word we used at a time when it mattered."

She put the paper in her purse. "If it ends in futility why did you bother writing it down and giving it to me?"

Hugo looked towards the ruins of the bombed Cathedral, then back at her. "I want you to know something of what I feel…how much I appreciate those things you gave me that you couldn't have known were precious. So you better go now or you'll be late for the surgery. If you don't mind, I won't come to the hospital later. That would be the best for both of us. Perhaps you could do me the favor of sending Conrad's things to London."

Hugo got out and stood on the curb next to his case, straight and tall with the appearance of formality he assumed when things were serious. Beth leaned toward him and asked, "Why did you come back to Foleshill?" There was no hostility or whim in her voice.

He glanced again at the Cathedral. "It was pointed out to me by someone in that building across the way that I haven't been forthcoming in our time together. So perhaps I should end this with the truth. When I left Mindouli I told Martin Birks that had an idea of where I was going to end up. On the flight to England it came clear to me that I would end up going back to Lambaréné." He looked at his shoes then took his hand from his pocket. "I told him that I had to return to England first, to find a thing of value which I'd lost and wanted to take back with me, a gold ring. But on the journey I came to know what that meant."

He hesitated for a moment and shuffled his feet. "I won't say that I am in love with you, Beth, which implies that love is something that goes in and out of fashion. So what does that leave unsaid? I suppose it would lead me say that I have loved you from the beginning and no matter how hard I've tried over the past year I couldn't rid myself of that feeling. A love for you will always be with me."

He took a breath and looked at her. "And the thing of great value that I lost here wasn't the ring. It was you. I apologize for saying this because it's not a thing that simplifies your life, I'm sure. Perhaps if I had been able to say this before I left, it would have made a difference."

She looked at him. Her lip trembled as she came back around the side of the car and stepped up to the curb. "At the hospital are the papers of Conrad's that I mentioned," she said. "But there's also two gifts—small items whose importance I should explain."

Hugo didn't smile or nod, but watched her as if he were seeing her face for the first time. Beth glanced at the clock tower and said, "I have to go or I'll be late. The surgery is over at seven. Promise me that you'll come to the hospital. It will just take a minute."

Hugo smiled. "You go, because you can't be late. I'll come of course."

As she ran to the car door, Hugo caught the expression in her eyes of a promise she wished she could keep, and became regretful for his own. The car pulled away. He watched it merge with the traffic as if seeing it for the last time. He picked up his case and turned to go in the opposite direction. Because of this he failed to see that in the next block, Beth's car pulled to the curb, because a clear and safe vision of the road ahead was washed away by the extent of her weeping.

Chapter XXV

One Penny Gift

Hugo went to a snack kiosk in the Precinct. In the summer heat it was almost empty. The shops were closing. He sat on the stone arbor to drink his tea then opened his case to remove some papers. On each was written words and sentences describing a character whose history resembled his own. Curious to find more evidence of the past he began taking books out. Near the bottom was *War and Peace*, the thick preponderance of *Gray's Anatomy*, *Sayonara*, *All Quiet on the Western Front*, *Robinson Crusoe* and lastly the thin volume by the doctor. There were many others, but all counted these few represented the small library that had raised him high enough to reach the piano keys, and higher still to deal with life. He spread them over the stones next to the stack of spiral notebooks, which numbered eleven, exactly the number he had bought from the wholesaler less the book he had given to Captain Mintou. They were all full, each page numbered and on the top of each the total of words and a running count of all the words he had ever written. On the right side of the case he set the remaining books by Albert Schweitzer. He found and read his favorite passage, then glanced at the bookmark, which was the note from Beth.

    As the sun drifted behind a building, he began the process of connection using his fingers to represent events, the living being on his good right hand, the dead on his weak left, knowing that some events like the wasting of muscle slip into oblivion. One book in his case was the illustration. He searched through the pile on the flat stones and found a compilation by the Argentine, Borges. A quick search found a story whose theme hinged on the death of a Saxon tramp who had the privilege of being the last person in Britain to have seen the pagan sacraments. There must have been as well a last set of eyes to see the living Christ, he thought. Hugo recalled an oak outside his window with branches shaped like a raven's wing and silhouetted against the yellow street lamp with children playing in the shelter of that benevolence and no longer his enemies. In time this tree would be reduced to firewood, and when the last of his generation died, all evidence of its beauty would default to God.

He looked at the crude drawing he had done of Conrad and realized it was the only likeness of him that he possessed, because he could remember seeing no photos of his father. He tried to think of the last time he had seen him, his final glimpse, walking away or sitting quietly at the table. He remembered the coffee they had shared in the old house in the Cedar Galleries, with across the square the ruins of the Bazaar seeming to be an offense to Conrad's sense of order. The snow was lower on the peaks of the mountains that day. Conrad suggested it was a time for him to escape the draftiness of winter. Hugo wondered now if the old man knew it would be a final parting.

"I've given instructions to Solly to make something for you. Something of gold," he had said.

"Why?"

"A good luck charm."

"You don't believe in luck—or charms."

"Not so, Hugo. Inevitability carries us in a certain direction, but the details swirl by randomly. On occasion things work to our advantage and we think of it as luck. But you are quite right. We can't charm ourselves, or fate."

"What is this piece of jewelry?"

"Solly will decide. I've only given him some words to inscribe on it."

Conrad looked across the square at the crumbling sheds, then continued, "You think your heritage is obscure, but it's not. Anyway, let's have another coffee and then you can tell me if you've made any headway in solving your dilemma."

With this remark the conversation ended. When the coffees were finished and Hugo's smoke was stuffed out in the ashtray, they left the house. Instead of dropping around the day of his leaving, Conrad phoned to make the parting short.

"Take care of yourself, son," were the last words Hugo heard his father speak. Perhaps as time passed, his mind would yield more details of the preceding years. Hugo knew that as he dwelled on things, time's pressure squeezed them into conscious memory. For the moment, he could only get to his feet and stare down at the finger where Solly's ring should be and wish he could remember the last time he'd seen it. Circling around the stone planter he noticed that the oval-shaped cloud with the fringe of gemstone had not moved in hours or was simply a cloud similar to the first, produced by a force in the atmosphere more stable than human affairs.

Rummaging further through his case to find the flute, he played a few notes and then laid it on the stone next to the disposable books and the fading spiral scribblers. He smiled with the realization that his case was empty. At the bottom were no personal items of decoration, no eyeglasses or aftershave or medicine—and no spare clothes. As he went through the final process of connection, he was left searching the stains on the cloth liner for clues, any mark or rip that might provide him with an epigram on the illustration of a point made in another volume which in turn might be a reference to something else, and so on. Because a slim thread of connection and little else was all he could distill from his life. He picked up the flute and played the first few bars of the *Moonlight* as he done for Birks at Lufungula.

Passersby glanced towards him. One woman had a coin in her hand and looked for the hat to toss it into, then instead, tossed it into the open case. People stopped to read a title, or perhaps two. A man came up and asked if he was selling books. One woman offered to buy one, in fact said she had been looking for just such an edition of *Sayonara*, unavailable in England. Hugo looked at her in amazement.

"You want to buy it?"

"Yes."

"You can have it. Here." He thrust it at her. "Everyone should have a copy, Madame."

The threat of receiving it for nothing caused her to step away. The man next to the woman shuffled sideways to a safe distance. Hugo picked up other books and started to make the rounds of the gathering crowd.

"And you, sir, fancy a used edition of *War and Peace*? Does anyone want a cheap book? And you, my man…here's a splendid translation of *All Quiet on the Western Front*. Relive the Great War, from the opposing view, of course, but no further cost to the reader. Take them, my friends. They're too heavy to pack around. My arm is breaking from the weight."

The crowd backed away from him. People made comments and a constable appeared. "A little bit of Covent Garden, then?"

"No, sir."

"There are laws against hawking wares without a license. I shouldn't imagine you've a license?"

"These aren't wares. They're books and I'm giving them away."

"Free stuff…that's always a good come on, isn't it?" The constable picked one up and opened it. "A bit moldy, this."

"You get that in the tropics. It's the humidity."

"Junk, then?"

Hugo looked at the mess laid out on the pavement—mildewed, dog-eared books with stains on the covers and pages, and the other papers with tears at the edges. Even the few sketches he had made recently were soiled and torn.

The entire library set out for an estimate resembled something dumped out of garbage can. He looked at the constable with a familiar sense of emptiness and said, "It's had some use. But junk more or less, you're right. That's why I was trying to give it away."

"Better you throw them in the bin over there and not leave it for others to mop up," said the constable. "And better do it soon and clear out."

He pointed at the flute. "Now there's a good profession, mate. Go busking down at Piccadilly. No law against that."

Hugo waved at the officer as he backed away. The crowd dispersed. He gathered up an armload of books and threw them back into the case. A girl appeared at a shop doorway and her light summer dress made him pause for a moment. For an instant he thought it was Beth, who may have had good reason for taking off her winter coat and gloves and scarf. But of course it wasn't winter and it wasn't Beth, but a young girl walking past him, smiling before going through an archway to the west. For some reason she stopped, perhaps remembering an item at the store, and stood paralyzed for the moment by a petty indecision.

The backlight of the setting sun masked the few features he could see. Shadows intervened and twisted her smile of carefree youth to an expression of regret, made sharp and cruel by the rising wind. It was to Hugo the bitter weather of a time long past that drove the rain into her thin dress and bare arms. Into this freezing downpour she put her hand, as if to suggest she had lost something, or let some treasure slip away. In the same fashion, Hugo had let a simple memory torture him in many hopeless, shameful corners of solitude, realizing that when he died, this occurrence would cease to have meaning for anyone.

The girl vanished from the archway. He went to the opening and found the breeze blowing through it was warm and happy, suggesting that he should put his own memory in its proper place. In a few hours, time present would bless him with the privilege of recomposing the artifacts of his mind. He would ensure that Beth's face and hair were framed properly in a warm light, her smile content, her manner secure as befitting the portrait of the woman he loved, respectful of the last person to have seen his father alive.

After gathering his things in the case, Hugo walked aimlessly through the corridors of streets. Music played in his head. He hummed a tune but couldn't remember the title. It was something intimate, flowery, unlike the masculine associations of sweat, beer, cigar smoke drifting from the Craven Arms. He stopped to look up at the stupendous figure of Michael with his foot on Lucifer's head, then continued down the footpath with the curious tune accompanying him to the Cathedral door and reminding him that he was listening to a requiem. He was surprised to find the door open and for a moment forgot why he had come back.

"Albert, are you there? Tell me, what did I forget to take with me?"

He shut the door behind him and, out of habit, felt for the light switch. But there was no requirement for illumination. The amphitheatre glowed brightly, hung as it was on one side with a mirror and on the other with the portrait of a young woman with ultramarine eyes and wine red cheeks. She wore a summer dress. On her face was an expression of inconsolable grief that he concluded was revision or fraud. Whatever the case, he had the urge to whisper a final good-bye to her and with it a good-bye to them all. He hurried down the corridor to the organist's box. The picture of Corrine still hung on the wall beside the assembled choirs and past musicians. He opened his satchel and took from it the crude sketch of Conrad Muir, and finding a tack in the desk drawer, pinned it next to the framed photo of his mother. Then he returned to the main space, sat in pew at the back, and let his eyes run around the walls, surprised to find no mirror, no girl in her floral dress.

How easily eyes are deceived, he thought, and looked to see instead the stained glass impressions of Mary and Child, not him with Corrine, merely the living God and his earthly mother. Below the child he saw a white head, someone not standing but leaning, just like he had done with his strong hand extended into the trench—Thank you, Hugo, for this gift to the hospital, to the people of the Ooguwe region, because they would not have had their operations done in a modern fashion if it wasn't for your ability to dig the hard earth and shovel it out of the way.

Here in the Cathedral, however, the doctor seemed insubstantial, gaunt, and thin so that nowhere did his body obscure Hugo's view. The old man leaned over to steady himself on the pew back.

"You don't look well, Albert," Hugo said.

Schweitzer frowned in a petulant way. "Of course I don't look well. I'm dead! Have been dead for almost a year now."

"Yes. That fits well with the fact that all along you've been a bothersome quirk in my imagination, a volunteer in my delusions, like a leek sprouting in the deer garden."

"Well, thank you very much. Leeks were always good in the soup."

"And now you're dead, which is good because the dead can't be expected to occupy much space…except in the encyclopedia. Is that how it goes?"

"I have no presence at all, Hugo. It was a good game while it lasted. An occupation."

"So the ghost of the great man presides in this church as an inconvenience to the living?"

"I'm here for no purpose beyond a little peace. I wrote some things that were true. I like to contemplate just how true they were. And besides, I have your question to answer. Or don't you recall your whining when you opened the door, 'Albert, are you there? Tell me, what did I forget?' I've seldom heard things more pathetic than what's come out of your mouth in recent times."

He sat for some minutes with his head bowed towards the altar, or that's the way it appeared to Hugo, who had trouble seeing him at all. The silence grew. Hugo fidgeted with the hymnal, then looked up one of his favorites, about the all-loving nature of God, implying the devious course of human affection.

"How about that, Albert?" His voice startled him and he wished there had been loud organ pipes playing to mask the chatter of triflers.

"How about what?" the old man said without turning his head.

"Imagine having to learn not to love."

"Why would you do something like that? Doesn't make any sense to me."

"It's futile. She said so herself. Today is June twenty-first, her first wedding anniversary—and tomorrow is the first day of decreasing light."

"Decreasing light. What does that mean? You really are a silly twit."

"Why am I silly?"

Schweitzer turned stiffly and put his arm along the back of the pew for support. He crooked his head around so that he was staring; all Hugo could see were the gray-blue eyes. "You still have a few moments left before you run away," he said. "Just like the first time you went. As I recall you didn't stop loving her then, even after you'd gotten on the train, the boat and into Africa. On the desert, when I was giving you a dig in the soft parts about her wedding night, I could see the heartbreak in your hard eyes. What was your response? Getting right back into the violence of the world...being obnoxious and troublesome because that's a good way to push out your failures. I don't need to tell you what you forgot. You said it correctly to her just now. But I'll tell you what you did forget—that's she's quite right in giving you the send off."

"I don't blame her. She's doing the right thing, the only thing in the circumstances."

"Of course she is. But don't worry, I suspect she'll give you a memento of herself to take away, something personal you can love instead, like people give pets or jewelry. But a word of warning here, Hugo: See to it that you reciprocate. She's earned a little respect with her efforts to see your father properly taken care of while you were off doing mischief."

"I owe her more than respect. That's the problem."

"The problem is, you've made a mockery of it, turning your life into a sordid little story. That's not what Muir was trying to do for you. But it's done. So go play me a tune as a last departing—but not that wretched *Moonlight*. You've played that to death. Beethoven wrote a nice little *bagatelle*, you know, with the same poignancy to it and well within your limited talents. Now, however, I request Bach, a fugue like the one you heard at Lambaréné, that would make the deer lie down and the people stand up."

Without looking left or right Hugo walked down the center aisle and into the organist's box. He played the piece Schweitzer requested, and as the music surged into the huge space of the Cathedral, he was filled with a heartfelt sympathy for life that he thought might give Albert courage to start upwards on his journey, sympathy Hugo could never show outwardly to the world lest he be accused of weakness. He played with such passion that when it was finished his left arm ached and he was unashamed that his heart ached as well. As the last chord died on the arches above, he slouched over the keyboard, and with no resistance left in his pride and no one to watch, he let the tears pour down his stubbled cheeks and soak his shirt. If spread over the course of his life, it was a meager flood—tears for Conrad and Corrine, the shoeshine boy, Antoine's murdered nephew, the lepers and sick of the village, the moron, the fox, the children playing under the yellow street light and finally the loss of his love—so few and thinly spread there were no tears left for himself.

He felt a hand on his shoulder. Without looking he brought his fingers around on top and felt thin bones, the gaunt tension over the knuckles and the bulge of vessels through which the blood had ceased to flow. He turned his head and caught sight of the hand. It was not disfigured by death but youthful, strong, with a brown tinge of sun to the skin. Hugo turned to stand up. The hand pressed him down.

"No. You just sit and rest. Contemplate as well the words Muir left you. We can't understand what goes on in life, but we know all we can of weeping. So it's time now for you to accept the gift Beth has to give you, have the courage to say good-bye to her properly—and for the last time. You must now look to a place of healing and see what the world might yield."

The hand went from his shoulder, the door closed, and Hugo could hear him going down the corridor. As the footsteps receded, their noise grew in volume and dimension so as to shake the building; then they ceased with a sigh, as if the presence of Albert Schweitzer had grown so large that he could step through the evaporating roof of the building, then move delicately over the bronzed forms of the Archangel and Lucifer so as not to crush the head of the devil. Hugo went from the organist's box and stood next to the altar. All the pews were empty. Transformed by the color in the glass, the incoming light made the air around him sparkle. He left by a side door and on his way past the main entrance, checked to see that the doors were locked securely.

At the Precinct he caught the #38 bus that would take him to the Coventry and Warwickshire Hospital by seven o'clock. It had just turned onto the ring road when there was an explosive sound and the vehicle spluttered to a stop. The conductor consulted with the driver, then announced, "Appears the motor has given up, folks. As there's no mechanic on duty tonight, I'm afraid you people will have to walk or find other transport."

A buzz of discontent circled through the passengers. A large man approached the conductor and complained loudly to no effect. A man staggering with drink replaced him and threatened to punch the driver. The first man shoved the drunk.

"Here. It's not his fault."

"Fuck off."

"You're a sorry excuse..."

The men shoved each other and the other passengers moved quickly off the bus or to the front. One woman moaned, "It's the heat."

Hugo stepped between the two. When the smaller man swung his arm in a punch, he found himself sitting back in his seat and Hugo's face close to his. "You should be helping the situation here, Jimmy."

"Bollocks."

"Still a stroppy little bugger, eh. Been down at the boozer?"

The man's eyes grew wide and he struggled to get up. "And you're a cheeky sod and all. Let's be stepping outside for a wee word then."

Hugo pressed his hand harder on the man's shoulder and put his mouth closer to his ear. "Now, what kind of help is that? I mean, these people are pleasant folk like you, who want nothing more than to make it home in time for their tea. Instead of getting in the way, as I said before, you should use your skills as a millwright and help me repair this vehicle."

The look on the man's face changed from antagonism to fear. He raised himself carefully off the seat. "Piss off," he said, edging past the conductor and onto the road. Hugo fetched the driver and his tool kit. When they reached the rear of the bus, Hugo was not surprised to see Jimmy Smythe kneeling on the pavement, his hand over his mouth in an attitude of perplexity. The door to the engine compartment was already open.

He nodded and said, "Fuckin' hell, Hugo. You should've said something. If I knew it was you, I would never have turned like that. A long time ago Gordon Moffat was spreading it around the Guildhouse that you were dead. Said he'd read it in the *Times*."

"No harm done, Jimmy. A rumor's as good as a laugh."

Hugo looked into the engine compartment. "What's your opinion?"

The millwright groped with both hands on top of the motor. "A clamp on the turbo feed come undone, that's all. I might need your help to get it back in there. Here, lets have a look." He adjusted a large pipe and removed a loose piece of metal. He handed it to Hugo, then said, "It's good to see you, mate. I always knew Moffat was a lyin' sod."

When Beth completed the surgery she looked at the mess in the theater and felt a moment's pride for her ability to focus and execute her duties even when the turmoil inside had caused her to spill the afternoon tea. After cleaning the instruments she went to wash up. As she slipped on her rings, she noticed that her hands were shaking. In the office, she glanced briefly in the mirror, sat down, and waited. Hugo was already five minutes late. At seven thirty she looked at the things she had put on her desk and felt empty inside, regretful, so alone that she couldn't bring herself to cry. She began to pace around the room, agitated, thinking of Conrad's insistence that she look again at things she had dismissed as irrelevant or insignificant.

Her hand snatched up the purse she had owned for years, pulled a piece of paper from it, and read the crudely printed words:

A glass of wine in Lichtenstein,
A red rose for a rover.
A drop of blood to join the flood
And get me down to Dover.

When she had finished, she got up from her chair and went back to the mirror. Then she returned to the paper on the desk and wondered if the words meant good-bye. They did not say good-bye. She looked again at the face in the glass and felt proud of the strength it showed to do what was necessary.

At that moment, Hugo was cutting across the hospital car park on a route that took him past Beth's car. He thought of the day he had first arrived and the walk they had taken out of the building and the dismissive tone to her voice. It was her right to dismiss him then. He should do the same now and relieve them both of further burdens. But he had promised to come and was already late. Inside the vestibule, the only movement was his reflection in the window. Down the main corridor, he could see no one. When he came to an intersecting branch, he looked to his right and stopped. Beth stood beside the office door in her white uniform. With the exception of her hair, she was as she appeared the first time he had seen her. He turned away. When he looked back she was watching him with the same expression of curiosity and alarm. She held out her hand to him.

"I'm sorry I'm late," he said holding out his own hands, which were covered with grime. "The bus broke down. The driver needed some help with the repairs. The conductor was thankful enough to offer me a free ride to London tonight—if I can get down to the terminal by nine." He glanced up at the clock. "But I guess I'm getting ahead of myself. We have a little time left."

Beth took him to a washroom near the office where he removed the grease. Then she went over to the desk and removed two boxes. Inside one were stacks of papers and letters, which he took and put into his satchel. The other box contained personal items belonging to his father. Hugo kept some and left the rest for disposal. Lastly, she handed him a small, wrapped jewelry box. "One of the gifts I told you about, from an admirer."

He opened it and removed a medallion made of gold hung on a gold chain. He examined it closely. Before he could remark, Beth said, "The diamonds are real—as certified by a jeweler. The gold is eighteen carat, which is reasonable considering the value of the gems."

Hugo shook his head. "Thank you. But why would you…?"

"Don't thank me—it's not from me," she interrupted.

"Then who?"

"Here's a story you can write in one of your notebooks," she said in a quiet voice. "A few days after you left, I was a little dazed, you see, wandering around the bath trying to give instructions. A well-dressed woman came down the hall. I hardly recognized her, but not so the twins, who were also in their best clothes. One of them came up to me, young Willy, with only a small scar on his throat, and handed me a box. 'This is for you, mom, for helping us,' he said. His brother Kelly came over and said that he couldn't find the man involved, so wanted me to keep the other box. I thanked them both and their mother, Mrs. Royston, and said that I would keep it safe, because you never know when people drop in unexpectedly."

Beth put the medallion into his hands, then glanced at the clock on the wall. "I better go and change. I'll be leaving soon myself and you'll need a ride."

Hugo watched her go down the hall past the chapel with its piano. He sat on a wooden chair in the empty corridor. He looked at the medallion and wondered what the mother might have given Beth that would be fair trade for the return of her son. There was a time in his life he was certain of the answer and could talk his way past more than that. Now he was skeptical about any valuation of life, or of happiness. He raised his head to see, on the opposite wall, the framed sketch of the prisoner, Joshua, with the pestilent wound on his leg and a likeness of Albert Schweitzer tending to the injury.

In the distance he could hear hospital noises. Up and down the hall echoed the paging of doctors, buzzers going intermittently and the sound of hurrying feet, all things he had once felt comfortable with. From down the same corridor he heard piano music muffled by the intervening noise, unrecognizable to the resting patient or the busy nurse accustomed to hearing the groans of the afflicted. And Albert's dislike notwithstanding, the notes of Beethoven's *Sonata* floating down the corridor were still as glorious to him as the moon rising on the Tanezrouft, as glorious as love itself—but also as sorrowful.

From the satchel he removed the photo of the *Kyle Mission* and the torn image of soldiers. Looking at them, he felt the last of his anger fade away to nothing. The music faded with it or perhaps diminished in volume as if a nurse had turned the radio dial so as not to be diverted from her duties. He put the photo back and leaned forward with his elbows on his legs, thinking about the men, the music, the past and his dead friend, the doctor on the wall, whose eyes on the paper receded to dots of charcoal. When he looked up, he was staring into a blue cotton blouse.

"Sorry I took so long," Beth said.

"Not long at all," he replied. "There was familiar piano music to pass the time—played on the radio, I suppose."

"I heard it too. But it sounded like real music, like you were playing it."

Hugo smiled slightly and said, "For all my practice I could never play it that well, Beth...never with any meaning." He held the medal up, looked at it and said, "But I seem to have gotten into the habit of neglecting things that have meaning."

Beth's mouth hinted at a smile. "You don't notice the important things because you talk too much," she said.

Hugo grasped his fingers tightly around the medallion and looked up at her. "I do. In fact there's been too many words between us, and most of them were mine. So a few last words before I go, a question concerning the gift a grateful mom would offer for the life of her child. You never showed me what they gave you."

Beth took the gold band off her ring finger, held it up to him, then put it in her other hand. "In your confusion you missed this—the ring with two diamonds just like yours, a matched pair for the twins."

She reached down and took off the engagement ring. "This is also a beautiful piece of jewelry. I designed it myself, you know. That's the reason I still wear it. It stands alone quite well even without a wedding band. I kept it, bought it back actually, after I called things off because I thought in my own confusion that one day it would be better matched to the ring given you by your father's friend, Solly."

Beth put her purse in his lap. Hugo looked down at it but could only say, "I don't understand."

"The ring you lost, never to be found, or I expect that's what you thought when you looked for it—even today at the Guildhouse. You see, no harm done. No one could ever have found it because I put it here in my purse after I had taken it from your satchel the night we were last together at the Rose. Please forgive me for being as big a thief as you are."

She reached down for Solly's masterpiece. The ring shone brightly, and even in the dull light of the corridor Hugo could see the inscriptions on its inner surface. Her left hand pressed into his chest as if she were leaning on him for support. With the right hand, she took Solly's ring, the gold band from the twins, and lastly her own engagement ring and put them all into his right hand, together with the medallion. A tear rolled down her face.

"Take these with you when you go, Hugo, please. But the greatest thing you would regret not taking with you, is me."

With a mixture of joy and uncertainty, he let his head fall silently forward to rest on the space beneath her breasts. When he raised it a moment later to look at her, she brought her mouth across his cheek and kissed him. In the curve and movement of her lips he could sense a permanent, overwhelming hunger. With his left arm trembling, he reached up and twisted her around so she was sitting in his lap. Her head went down on his shoulder, warm mouth against the skin of his neck. They remained that way, unmoving on the old chair, until the sounds decreased through the hospital, both their bodies had quieted and Hugo was aware only of her slow, gentle breathing, the texture of her hair, the warmth and fragrance of her skin.

Disbelieving, he glanced up at the clock on the wall and asked. "Is it an hour we have left?"

Beth brushed her lips across his cheek, kissed him again softly, and answered, "A bit longer now."

978-0-595-36333-9
0-595-36333-4

Printed in the United States
38289LVS00003B/5